2234

VICTORY FROM PEACE

KENNETH TAM

2234

VICTORY FROM PEACE

MARTIAN WAR - OMNIBUS 4

KENNETH TAM

Published in Canada by Iceberg Publishing, Waterloo

Library and Archives Canada Cataloguing in Publication

Tam, Kenneth, 1984-
    2234 : victory from peace / Kenneth Tam.

(Martian War ; omnibus 4)
Contents: The Mars convention -- The Egesta
    crisis -- The pax terra -- The articles of empire.
ISBN 978-1-926817-44-6

    I. Title. II. Series : Martian War ; omnibus 5.

PS8589.A7676T84 2012   C813'.6   C2012-904155-6

Iceberg Publishing
55 Northfield Drive East, Suite 171
Waterloo ON N2K 3T6
contact@icebergpublishing.com
www.icebergpublishing.com

Cover Image: Wesley Prewer
Cover Design: Kenneth Tam

INSCRIPTIONS

THE MARS CONVENTION

"I know nothing of the business of ruling."

- Tsar Nicholas II

THE EGESTA CRISIS

"Peacekeeping is not a soldier's job, but only a soldier can do it."

- Professor Charles C. Moskos

THE PAX TERRA

"In the present crisis, government is not the solution
to our problem; government is the problem."

- Ronald Reagan

THE ARTICLES OF EMPIRE

"Accept the things to which fate binds you,
and love the people with whom fate brings you together..."

- Marcus Aurelius

THE
MARS
CONVENTION

THE AUTOBIOGRAPHICAL REMINISCENCES OF ADMIRAL THE LORD KEN BARRON FOR 2234

THE MARTIAN WAR - 13

KENNETH TAM

FROM THE AUTHOR

In 1905, the world looked on in shock as the Empire of Japan dramatically crushed the Navy of Russia during the Russo-Japanese war. On land in Korea, the Japanese were similarly successful with their campaigns; Tsarist Russia was defeated by an Asian nation. In a time of rabid racism, that was quite a blow.

Though the Japanese declared war, and attacked slightly before the declaration reached the Russian Government — a pattern the United States would see again in 1941, many still believe that Russia prompted this conflict by intentionally threatening Japan's interests in Korea, and thus compelling a response. Why would the Russians want to start a fight with the Japanese?

There is a theory that famously suggests that the Russians were seeking a 'short, victorious war' to boost their government's popularity. Think about it: you go to war with a supposedly weaker adversary, stomp all over that foe, and then all of your people feel better about themselves, and their government.

Well, if that's really why the Russians triggered the fight, then the 1904-05 war had to be a rude surprise.

The defeat was such a shock, in fact, that it brought about a Russian Revolution.

No, not the famous one — not Lenin and his Bolsheviks. It would take a defeat at the hands of the Germans to bring that about. But a popular uprising took hold in Russia in 1905, as the people expressed their disgust with their rulers. Only the loyalty of the Russian Army kept Tsar Nicholas II in power... until 1917, when things finally spiraled out of control.

This is one of history's great cautionary tales. Government leaders initiating hostilities for public relations purposes? At least we don't see that sort of thing happening any more. The very notion would be *ridiculous*...

Yeah, I know, go ahead and do your own joke... And, of course, draw whatever connections you like to our friends in the Martian Imperium.

Meantime, I'm going to thank some people.

As always, numerous characters in this book are based on real-world friends of mine, so I extend my gratitude to all of those people. I hope your characters do you proud!

My good friend Peter Caron continues to be a sounding board and a wise advisor for this series. We'd all be in a lot of trouble without his counsel, believe me, so many thanks again to him! Wes Prewer's artwork simply gets better and better, and that's no easy accomplishment, considering the high standard he always sets. His input to the story has also been hugely important, so I must thank him yet again.

And finally, as ever, my thanks to my parents, because Jacqui and Peter continue to be my partners in Iceberg Publishing, and the best family I could ever ask for.

Atlas, cheers.

– Kenneth Tam

FOREWORD

First, for longtime readers, I should acknowledge that yes, this is indeed a new format for the books of our series. Starting with volume thirteen, the first of the year 2234, we've changed sizes on you. It's better for the environment, the publishers say. I think that also means it's better for their bottom line, but I'm cynical...

I can also tell you that the first three years of reminiscences are now available in yearly omnibuses... omnibi... compilations! That, I think, is also a money-grab, but even I have to admit it's a convenient one.

Anyway, sorry if changing the format has wrecked your neat bookshelf arrangements. I know mine are ruined. But rest assured, my annoying storytelling remains unchanged. What a relief.

Let's begin.

I have a question for you: if you decisively win a war the other side started, how should you go about negotiating the peace?

There are a few obvious options. One is to invite the defeated leaders to come to your home planet, to see the splendor of your government and society, and to be completely embarrassed by the strength of your civilization. This one isn't too popular in history... off the top of my head, I honestly can't think of a time it was done.

But I like it. I like the idea of immersing the other side in everything they were trying to destroy... but I'm mean-spirited.

Another option is to pick a neutral site somewhere, and negotiate there. That way both sides feel safe, and neither seems to have an advantage.

I'm sure there are plenty of examples of that method, but only one seems pertinent right now: after the Russo-Japanese War in 1905, the two sides negotiated their peace treaty at Portsmouth, New Hampshire. This, in retrospect, was wise.

The third option is one chosen often, I think because conquering armies do like to show off a lot of the time. Defense Command had no interest in pursuing this path, but it wasn't our choice... we're not an army. No, the only *army* the Empire had or has belongs to the Emperor.

So guess what he wanted to do...

Did you guess: 'Take the highest ranking leaders in the Earth Empire to Mars for negotiations, allowing the incompetent Imperium to play host to the most important peace conference since the advent of normalized space travel'? If you did, congratulations, you win a brand new washer-dryer!

I'm sorry, I know that's over the top, but the whole thing still just seems so daft to me. It's not like we had a *polite* war. It's not like we didn't know what sort of propaganda they'd been spewing about us the whole damned time. The people of Mars were convinced that Special Branchers were evil secret policemen who would kill you at the drop of a hat, and that our spacers would rape and pillage like pirates.

So putting a large chunk of our fleet into Martian orbit, and having our negotiations in the Martian Capital dome, was a good idea?

My editors are probably pretty mad at me for basically spoiling the whole plot of this book right here at the start, but I'm sorry, this is *stupid*.

No, not just stupid, *stoopid*.

It is, however, what the Emperor wanted, and because of the traditions of the Empire, we were in no position to stop him getting his way. The Prime Minister and the Foreign Minister could have demanded to have separate official negotiations take place on Earth, or at Ceres, or somewhere else… but if the Emperor went to Mars and started speaking (supposedly on behalf of the Empire), our elected leaders had to follow.

Otherwise the mess he could create — the unchecked promises he could make — would likely start another war.

So we were going to Mars at the start of 2234, and boy, were we ever excited.

The only good news for us — and by us I mean the veterans of the Belt Squadron and Jupiter Force, along with some fine ships we'd joined up with after the Fleet Clash — was that we weren't part of the Emperor's delegation. We left that joy (misery) to a good friend of ours…

But I should stop getting ahead of myself.

This book is about the beginnings of the diplomatic mission to Mars, and the start of what history has come to know as the Mars Convention. Let's make some peace.

CHAPTER ONE

DIPLOMATS EN ROUTE

I've tried three times to start this chapter, and each time I've failed. It's a pacing thing, I think. The first time, I tried to start the story too early, before we left for Mars. The second time, I tried to jump in too late, when we were on our way. Both times, something felt lacking, and forced. So I'm hoping the third time is the charm.

I'm also going to try something different, to improve the odds. As was so popular last book, I'm starting this one with a certain former adversary of ours.

It's the last time, I promise, but it's really interesting…

Or I think so, anyway.

Bort McWebsbert was standing on the landing pad outside the Parliament Buildings, waiting while the Minister of Foreign Affairs, Craig B. Macdonald, finished making arrangements with his staff for the trip up to *Wolf*.

Macdonald was going to be traveling to Mars aboard our fair frigate, and as the senior captured officer in our custody (and frankly, the only one from the other side any of our people wanted to deal with), Bort was going to come along, to help smooth over the initial meetings that would precede the Mars Convention.

This, I should tell you, was early January of 2234. That's significant for a couple of reasons. First, it reveals that we are indeed in a new year for our series of reminiscences (in case you were worried!), and second, it tells you something about the weather on Capital Island.

Namely, that there was a slight blizzard blowing. The wind was gusting up to 110 kph, which probably sounds like a lot, but isn't unusual for a Capital Island winter. Snow was coming down, heavy and very wet because it was only a few degrees below freezing, and it was mostly drifting sideways.

All of this meant that it was hitting Bort up side the head, so to speak. And our poor Asteroid-born counterpart simply had no experience in dealing with such a trauma. If you're from Venus or the Belt, you may never have experienced snow either. In point of fact, many of the people who live on Earth never get the proper North Atlantic blizzard experience.

It's generally a Canadian thing. A Capital Island thing in particular.

Anyway, Bort was freezing, wet, and trying not to let his discomfort show while Craig Macdonald, a Scotsman not entirely unaccustomed to this sort of weather, made sure his staff had everything they needed out of his ministerial offices, and then ushered them aboard.

Now, my editors were surprised that Macdonald was doing the ushering himself — surely a minister wouldn't stand out in a blizzard for logistical purposes!

Well, frankly, they're right. Many ministers would get aboard the pinnace and wait for their staffs to sort everything out, but Macdonald was one of the few politicos who

Daragh Ryan didn't hate, remember. He was one of those 'lead from the front' types, and also partially bloody insane.

And not wanting to appear in any way less weather-worthy than a politico, Bort wasn't going to board the pinnace before Macdonald did. Not *long* before, anyway.

His teeth were chattering, though, and he seriously wondered how the hell humans managed to survive in environments where they couldn't program this sort of thing out of the weather.

Sure, space is much colder than a blizzard, but somehow the blizzard felt worse. Chilled him to the bone. Space could do that, but he'd be dead before he felt it. Capital Island wasn't so merciful...

Hm. That's a very twisted point of view, which I'm going to now conveniently leave behind. Because Craig Macdonald finally headed for the ramp of the pinnace.

"Ready, Admiral McWebsbert?" the Foreign Minister asked — yelled, really — as he pulled his collar higher up around his face.

"Yes sir!" Bort bellowed back.

Macdonald waved up the ramp, and Bort gave in. Leading the way, he entered the pinnace and immediately took a relieved breath. The air in the government small craft was carefully processed and filtered, just the way he liked it.

Brushing off his Defense Command-provided jacket with his hand, he headed for a window seat, then pulled off the coat and stowed it overhead. Sitting, he presented an unusual sight for the staffers and the Minister as they boarded behind him: a red-clad Martian Admiral was on their flight.

Yes, Bort was back in uniform. Hostilities were over, and this was a diplomatic mission, so it seemed appropriate.

There's a funny story about that, though. The uniform Bort had been wearing when he was captured was pretty much trashed (and slightly radioactive). We cleaned it and tried to restore it, but it was beyond saving, so the one he now wore was actually off the costume rack from a war movie. Not kidding. The only place we could get a Martian Admiral's uniform in time for Bort's departure was from a motion picture set. Apparently our theft set the production of *Red Menace* back three days.

Wearing a costume that was supposed to be his uniform was apparently somewhat unsettling to Admiral McWebsbert — it felt right in some ways, and totally wrong in others. At least the costume had fully-functioning microfilament bags for decompression... not all movie costumes are fully functional, but parts of *Red Menace* were going to be filmed in space, so they'd sprung for all the fixins.

Lucky Bort.

As the pinnace loaded up and the hatch shut, Macdonald dropped into a seat across the aisle from the Asteroid Admiral, then buckled his seatbelt and let out a huff, "Looking forward to the trip home, Admiral McWebsbert?"

Bort looked at the Foreign Minister, then had to bite back a retort.

Macdonald, like many politicos, was astute enough to see that something was left unsaid, so he prompted, "What'd I say?"

"Home," Bort's tone was more gruff than usual.

Macdonald had been dealing with Bort enough over recent weeks to have a pretty good rapport with the Admiral, so it only took a few seconds for him to recognize his error, "Right. Back to Mars, then?"

Snorting a laugh, Bort shook his head and looked out the window, "Whether I'm looking forward to it or not, we're going, sir."

Macdonald grinned at the resignation, "That's exactly what I said to the PM. Minus the 'sir' part."

Letting the conversation taper off from there, Macdonald settled back in his seat, and a few moments later the pinnace's engines roared and the craft launched itself into the blizzard-ridden skies.

Half an hour later, Karen and I arrived in *Wolf's* landing bay two observation deck. As I've said, our fine ship was going to transport Macdonald and Bort and the rest of the advance team to Mars, and I tell ya, we were incredibly excited.

I really should lay off the sarcasm…

"This'll be a great trip. I'm so excited I want to fall over," Karen said dryly, folding her arms as we peered through the glass out onto the deck.

I didn't say anything for a second, trying to figure out if there was a way I could make a joke about her quip. Nothing came to mind, "I can't work with that."

Karen glanced at me, "What?"

"You want to fall over? I can't come up with anything to go with that."

"Nothing?"

I shook my head, "Let's be honest, it's not the greatest setup for repartee you've ever put out. There's not even a double-entendre there. How are we supposed to generate smoldering tension if there isn't a double-entendre?"

Karen pursed her lips and puffed out her cheeks thoughtfully, then nodded, "Good point."

She then took a few seconds to come up with something a little more playful. But like me, she was running dry on clever turns of phrase with double-entendres.

"I'm fresh out," she said at last, then frowned and shook her head. "God, we're stuck in such a pedestrian groove."

She was right, and this wasn't a new development for us. What we were complaining about here was our seeming inability to reacquire some of our cheeky humor from before the war… and hell, even from during the war. We were both feeling so drained at the start of 2234. Hostilities were over, and we wanted to get back to our cavalier, house-collapsing ways… but everything felt flat.

This was a problem. And it was going to arguably lead to even bigger problems.

Bottom line: we were both trying too hard to be clever and witty in each other's presence… to bounce back from the fatigue of the war… and we were failing. Spectacularly.

"Should we stop trying?" I asked after a pause, and Karen glanced at me again and shook her head.

"We're just exhausted. Once we get back into the swing of things, it'll come."

She didn't sound completely convinced, and I wasn't either.

But it wasn't worth worrying about; we were still together… back together, in fact… and we had the opportunity to restore our old ways. That was a good thing.

Sort of.

Sorry, I keep thinking ahead. I've over-analyzed far too many aspects of 2234 in the years since, so it's slightly habitual. For now, the diplomatic pinnace was coming in.

There was no ceremony as the black craft slipped into our bay, and then set its feet down on our deck. The space doors closed behind it, the bay repressurized, and Karen and I headed out there at an easy pace to meet our esteemed passengers.

By the time we reached the small craft, the ramp was already coming down. We waited briefly for it to settle on the deck, then looked up at the hatch and waited for someone to come through.

Sure enough, Craig B. Macdonald led the way, carrying his briefcase in one hand and a box of files under the opposite arm. It looked precarious.

As he came down the ramp, Karen and I looked at each other with frowns, but we didn't get a chance to fail at repartee, because he called out a greeting to us.

"Aha, Admiral, Commodore, hello. Thanks for ferrying the politically-inclined of us to Mars!"

He said that with some difficulty as he balanced everything he was carrying, and then he didn't stop at the foot of the ramp to say anything more — he hurried past us toward the hatch. That was, well, unexpected. Elected officials carrying their own files just seemed uncanny.

"Are all your leaders as uncommon as that man?"

Karen and I both recognized Bort's voice, so we looked back to the pinnace just in time to see him descend, carrying only his kit. None of the staff had wanted to give a Martian any boxes of files to carry — we liked Bort, but it still seemed like a bad idea to give him a box full of sensitive ministry files, just in case.

Unnecessary precaution, of course, but seemed prudent at the time.

Because one of Bort's hands was free, he extended it to Karen, then to me. We greeted him with smiles that weren't forced — we hadn't seen this man in months, but we'd parted on good terms, and we knew that since he'd arrived on Earth, he'd been very cooperative with Foreign Affairs in getting the convention arranged.

We weren't friends yet, though — I suppose friendships with enemies take more than a few pleasant conversations to solidify.

"Welcome back aboard, Bort," Karen's greeting was warm, and our Asteroid counterpart nodded.

"Glad it's under different circumstances," he said.

"Damned right," I agreed, and then I nodded in the direction Macdonald had gone. Whether he'd been aboard a *Predator*-class frigate before, or just had an uncanny sense of direction, I have no idea, but the Foreign Minister was heading for the lounge, and a flight deck technician was kindly holding the hatch open for him.

"We better catch up with him."

Karen and Bort nodded, and so we did — while the poor ministry staff started unloading the many materials they'd brought with them to facilitate the planning of a peace conference. I never asked what was in all the boxes… probably better that I don't know.

Anyway, that's enough for this chapter. I think third time may indeed have been the charm, so let's move on to something else.

How about... our good friend Charlie Peters!

CHAPTER TWO

DISGRUNTLED PATIENT

My friend Charlie Peters had been doing his very best to be a good patient. He and Lia were both still in the hospital on *Venus One*. Lia was in slightly worse shape than Charlie — she needed more skin and flesh repairs, due to the multitude of small wounds she'd suffered. Charlie had had a smaller number of bigger things swapped out, so he had some new organs and joints… you know, the usual.

Yeah, I'll just continue trying to make that sound casual…

Seriously, though, Charlie had been through his share of operations, and though he needed a cane now, he could hobble along pretty well on his own, provided he didn't overdo it. He was still very weak from the months of inactivity, and the amount of energy that was going into the healing process.

What all of this added up to was a Major (soon to be Lieutenant Colonel) Peters who wasn't feeling great, but who'd been basically confined to a hospital room for four months.

Even Charlie's superhuman determination to be a non-cliché good patient couldn't hold out that long. He needed something to fill the daytime hours… some sort of activity that could let him feel like he was contributing again.

Or he was going to go crazy.

Lia saw this clearly enough — she was in the bed beside his, after all. And since she was a bit less mobile, she didn't have anything to do other than nag him about it.

"You should go for a walk. Flirt with some nurses or something," she suggested one day — interestingly, the same day we'd welcomed Craig Macdonald aboard *Wolf*.

Charlie was sitting in bed, reading a book about the centuries-dead concept of 'fluxed' faster-than-light travel, something scientists were beginning to look at again for the first time since its dismissal as a viable technology back in the twenty-first century. As she made that suggestion, he lowered the book and narrowed his eyes suspiciously, "Say that again?"

"Go flirt with the nurses," Lia said directly. She'd been staring at the muted vid screen in the wall, which was showing another stellar episode of the Geraldine Coilier Show, but now she looked at him and flashed a smile. "If you charm them, you might be able to get double ice cream."

"Double ice cream?" he feigned ignorance with that question — he knew what evil his Lady had in mind.

"More for me," she clarified, knowing he already understood what she meant.

"Aha," he said. "Well, if it's in the service of your Ladyship…"

He managed a wry grin as he slid out of bed and grabbed his cane. He was past the gown phase of treatment, by the way — he was in standard-issue patient pants and shirt.

Now, there's no denying this was a flimsy reason to leave the room. Lia knew it was ridiculous, and Charlie did too, and they both knew the other knew. She just wanted to give him the chance to get out without having him feel guilty for leaving.

Emerging into the corridor, Charlie actually took a relieved breath, then was confronted by a choice: left or right.

He turned left.

If he hadn't, the fate of the Empire might have been different.

No, I'm not overdramatizing that.

He passed a doctor arguing with a temp called Donna as he went that way, but didn't quite catch what they were going on about. After a few minutes of slow walking — taking it easy on his new knee — he found himself in the patient cafeteria.

This was a dreary sort of place — not because of the décor, which was clean and bright, but because of the generally down mood of everyone in it. Many wounded officers and enlisted from Defense Command and the Imperial Army, often short of limbs or internal organs and facing a long period of recovery.

Compared to a lot of these people, Charlie was damned lucky, and he knew it.

"Morning Major Peters... sleep well?"

Evaline was one of the nurses in Charlie's wing, and she appeared beside him as his eyes scanned the cafeteria. Glancing at her, Charlie smiled politely in reply, "The usual."

"Lady Hawke slept well too, then," she winked at him.

People don't wink at Charlie. That's just not done. But Evaline winked, and there wasn't really anything Charlie could do about it, except make sure he looked embarrassed. He and Lia had started pushing the rumor of their relationship after they'd been in that room together for a couple of months, using it as a plausible excuse for what they knew was coming next — Charlie going back to *Hawke One* with her.

So having nurses tease him about it was a sign that their efforts were proving successful... and it was highly awkward and uncomfortable.

Well, as a Special Brancher, Charlie could handle discomfort.

Evaline left him be, and he trudged over to the sandwich counter. He'd been eating solid foods for five weeks, though all he could stomach because of the drugs were the sandwiches provided here. He pulled one out from under the glass and then retrieved a bottle of water before easing his way over to a table.

So far this was all pretty run-of-the-mill — a day in the boring life of a hospitalized wounded soldier.

What happened next was the fate-changer.

From the corridor opposite the one Charlie had come down, a hobbling Imperial Army soldier appeared. This man was missing a hand and was wearing an artificial foot, probably victim of an improvised bomb somewhere in the Mercury dome. But he wasn't alone; four of his buddies, all in Imp uniforms, were with him.

It looked pretty typical: soldiers coming to visit a wounded comrade, to buck up his spirits. Charlie had no love for the Imperial Army (obviously), but this struck him as a good thing for them to do.

He sat down gingerly and started eating his sandwich, and yet again, it tasted like nothing. Apparently, thanks to all the drugs he was on, his sense of taste was simply gone. It was actually the last thing he'd get back when he left the hospital... but that's irrelevant now.

The sandwich was better than nothing, so he ate slowly, resolutely trying to taste it.

Meanwhile, the Imps sat down one table over, completely oblivious to him. Nothing unusual there.

Then they started joking and telling stories. Again, pretty typical — started out with some gossip from their unit, the 44th Lancers (I have no damned idea why they were called Lancers — that's an old cavalry unit name, when horsemen were actually carrying lances). After that, though, they quieted down a little, and started chuckling about things that were decidedly less innocent.

I'm not going to repeat what Charlie overheard. There's no need to. I'll give you some ideas, though. How many times could a woman be raped before she went insane? Was it easier to bayonet a man when he was tied up or when he was running? Who screams more when their daughters are stolen by soldiers, mothers of fathers?

Not kidding. Wish to God I was kidding.

They were just *talking* about these things, in a public cafeteria in a Defense Command hospital.

And Charlie was sitting four meters away, using his recently-restored hearing to listen in.

He didn't stop eating his sandwich. He didn't do anything to suggest that he was paying attention. He did chew a lot slower, but that aside, he just listened.

They didn't mention any locations that he immediately recognized, but they told stories about what one of them called 'the good old days'. Charlie wasn't sure what that meant, but he knew the guy who'd been wounded had participated, because he was correcting some details, and joking with the others about their inadequacies in performing certain war crimes.

All of this while sitting in a public cafeteria — admittedly not a full one.

The soldiers of the Imperial Army weren't too bright.

And Charlie let them go on. He was pretty sure he overheard reference to several instances of three different war crimes — rapes, looting and murder — and he filed away as many details as his medicated (but still very sharp) mind would allow.

Some of the soldiers of the 44th Lancers were having far more 'fun' on Mercury than was, in fact, legal.

Let alone *right*.

Charlie simply sat there and chewed his sandwich. It took nearly an hour for the soldiers to make their apologies and lead their friend out of the cafeteria, so they could go back to whatever horrors they were doing in their district on Mercury.

As soon as they left, Charlie stood and began trudging back to his room. On the way, he mentally replayed pieces of what he'd heard, taking advantage of listening skills that had once been used against pirates in bars in the Belt, and which now were urgently needed.

When he got back through the door into his room, Lia greeted him with a friendly barb, "Where's my iced cream?"

Then she saw the expression on his face. Anyone else, except maybe me, would have thought it neutral and normal, but she knew instantly that something was wrong.

So he told her what he'd overheard, and she was similarly unimpressed.

"Going to report that to the Brigadier, or Aunt Witch?" she asked quietly, deadly serious.

Charlie paused in thought for a moment, then nodded. He went back to his bed, grabbed the comm remote, and dialed Marlene Stoll's office.

There were questions to be asked.

CHAPTER THREE

THE IMPERIAL CHARIOT

In Defense Command, we do one of two things when an officer proves to be very good at his or her job: we either reward that officer, or punish him or her.

So what fate for our old friend Christian 'Mik' Mikaelsen? If you'll recall back to *The Mercury Assault*, he did a hell of a job fighting a pair of monitors. The duel had cost him his ship — the aged *Cyclops* was being paid off for scrap, having fought its last gallant fight.

But it had been a victory, and one we made sure to talk up, because we figured Mik deserved to be recognized for it. As a result, he'd been in the press a little bit — one story among many, so not as much individual attention as he deserved, but still some. He'd been granted leave. He'd been nominated for the Lutherian Cross, and the Felix-Wolfe Corporation had offered him a sponsorship contract.

A good few months at home.

Unfortunately, the good news didn't last. John Fiora and Daragh Ryan, admittedly with the help of Greg Noyce and even myself, did something rather unpleasant after all the hooplah died down.

Mik was given command of *Ark Royal*.

Now, I'm not being stupidly cute here. This isn't a bait-and-switch with sarcasm... you know: 'Oh we did something bad... haha, actually, we did something good. Had you going, didn't we?'

No, it wasn't like that.

If you'll recall, *Ark Royal* was a supercarrier — very similar in appearance to *Bonaventure*, but loaded with planes instead of mags and lasers. So already, to any good battleship officer, this ship was a step down.

But if that was the only downside, it would have been a walk in the proverbial park. The *Ark* was still a massive and modern vessel, and flawed design or no, Mik would make something of the ship.

That wasn't all, though... because the *Ark* was also Luther Gregory III's personal vessel. If he ever left Earth, he had to travel aboard that ship — hence the name *Ark Royal*.

So, being kindly folks, John and the rest of us had decided to give our friend Mik one of the least enviable jobs in the cosmos: he had to babysit the biggest diva in human history, on the most ridiculous quasi-diplomatic visit in human history.

You're welcome, my friend.

Now, if you know Mik, you'll know that he's a very politically astute fellow. These days his fingerprints are all over the Belt Party, and though he's officially retired from public life, he's still one of the most trusted go-to people in Belt politics. He's a natural leader — it's inevitable.

Back in 2234, he was obviously the same man, but he hadn't yet made his political mark. It may be safe to say that the events of 2234 actually helped push him into government, but he wasn't there yet. Like most DC officers, he was somewhat wary of ambitious politicos in general, and he was even more cautious about our Emperor.

Which made preparing *Ark Royal* for a cruise to Mars terribly fun.

"The engines work, mostly," Georgina Yamagawa had been the Chief Engineer aboard *Cyclops*, and with her old ship gone, she'd been transferred to *Ark Royal*, along with most of Mik's old crew. Now she was wiping grease from her hands with a rag, and sounding about as disgruntled as usual.

Mik was in the massive engineering compartment of *Ark Royal*, looking for an update about his ship's readiness, and that was Yamagawa's assessment. Things were mostly working.

"Well that's something, anyway," he replied stroking his goatee. "Think the yard work will hold up?"

I should provide more background here. Remember all the way back to *The Almost Coup*, when George Parks-Dawes had been killed on *Ark Royal's* bridge during the Battle Over Earth? The supercarrier had gone in for repairs after that fight, but because it was a carrier it had been thrust to the bottom of the pile.

The yards had been given priorities: first, they had to finish the *Bonaventure*-class battleships, then repair the damage to other battleships after Glorious February, then finish the four battleships of the *Hokkaido*-class.

No one actually started working on *Ark Royal* until the middle of 2233. The ship's crew had been stripped and assigned to newly-commissioned ships, and the massive wreck of the carrier had simply been left alone to stay frozen until the yards could do something about it.

By the time Mik got aboard, not long after the Fleet Clash, a lot of work had been done, much of it by civilian contractors, so he had some serious concerns that the ship wouldn't be up to military spec.

He wasn't expecting to need to take the *Ark* into a gunfight, since hostilities were over, but he still didn't want his critical systems to fall apart halfway to Mars, with the Emperor aboard.

So now he was taking a last tour of the repaired *Ark Royal* before the ship broke dock for an abbreviated shakedown cruise. Mik wasn't coming with *Wolf* and the squadron carrying Craig Macdonald, but he was still departing in a couple of weeks, and that wasn't much time to test every system aboard a carrier.

"It'll fly, I think," Yamagawa said a bit brusquely. "Or I'll hit it with something heavy until it works."

Mik smiled at that prospect, "You miss *Cyclops*."

He said it cheerfully, but there was no way he could speak of his venerable old ship without an undercurrent of regret. His loyalty to that battlewagon had been strong.

Yamagawa's had been too, "Yeah. This thing is too shiny and impersonal... the way the Emperor wants it to be. Once it's dirtier and lived-in... that'll help."

It was honest feedback, and Mik appreciated it. He nodded too — as he told me later, this ship gave him an unsettled sort of feeling. It reminded him of a model home

— you know, one of those houses builders do up to try and convince buyers to hire them to build houses? Those are always very, very fancy, with all the trimmings, the most stylish furniture and the posh features... but you get the feeling that no one has ever lived in them. That they're all for show. That they have no soul.

Ark Royal was like that. It was a ship that Dave Caldecott had championed, and despite having been a part of the Battle Over Earth, it felt like it had no real history.

So it was up to Mik to make some history with it.

We'll see more of that later. For now, Mik left the engineering compartment and went to locate his new ship's XO, the veteran Finn Yaalon, and its Captain, Yolanda Burke, who you might recall from *The Almost Coup*... she was *Ark Royal's* XO (and the only survivor from the ship's previous senior staff).

"So if we do anything wrong... he's liable to claim that Defense Command is trying to interfere with the peace process?"

Commander Finn Yaalon spoke of the Emperor with distaste, and Mik stroked his goatee and nodded at his longtime officer's words. The two were sitting with Captain Burke in the day cabin off the *Ark's* bridge, reflecting on the nature of the mission before them. Some of the sensitivities surrounding the situation had been relayed to Mik in an earlier message from John, so he was going over them with his people.

It didn't make for fun conversation.

"I think you may be assuming too much, Commander," Yolanda Burke wasn't quite on the same page with Mik and his XO about this — she'd been linked to the Caldecott Circle back before the war. That faction of DC officers had sided with Luther Gregory III, as you might recall from *The Almost Coup*, and now some of her former loyalties seemed to emerge with her words.

Mik glanced at her, and Finn Yaalon's eyebrows went up.

"Perhaps," Mik commented first, before Finn said anything too abrupt, "but we have to be conscious of the fact that there was almost a coup before this war started. I think it's fair to say none of us want those tensions to be revived. So we need to make sure it's a smooth trip to Mars... and a safe trip back."

Mik liked Yolanda Burke — they'd worked together on *Ark Royal's* repairs since his return from Venus. But he didn't know for certain where her final loyalties lay, so he was being careful, and he needed his *Cyclops* veterans to be similarly cautious.

There'd inevitably be plenty of politics to deal with on this trip, and he was looking forward to none of it...

"We'll make sure, sir," Finn Yaalon said crisply, and Burke nodded too.

"The Emperor will see Defense Command at its finest," she concurred.

That promise didn't comfort Mik completely, but he nodded, then came to his feet, "Enough talking about this. Finn, want to walk me through the new fire control systems?"

"Yessir," the Commander rose, and then both men nodded to Burke before leaving her day cabin.

As they emerged onto the massive bridge of the supercarrier, Finn lowered his voice and leaned closer to Mik, "Sir, you think the Emperor is going to be up to no good?"

I should say that Mik wasn't as wrapped up in the Emperor-hating as I was, so he wasn't completely ready to condemn the man off-hand. Finn Yaalon had heard other stories from the rumor mill, though, and he'd become edgier since the loss of *Cyclops*. For both those reasons, Mik decided to remain the voice of calm with his loyal subordinate.

"Anything is possible. I won't know until we're on our way... maybe not even until we're on our way back. But I want you to talk to all the *Cyclops* veterans aboard. Make sure they stay disciplined, and follow our lead. I know there are rumors about the Emperor, Finn, but we must be professional. Unless he gives us a *real* reason not to be. Okay?"

Ark Royal's XO nodded slowly at his Commodore's words, and then added, "We'll do what we have to do, sir."

They went on to examine the fire control systems, but when Mik finally got some time to himself later in the day, he could only sigh and shake his head. He felt like he was falling into the midst of a political quagmire, with an untested ship and a mixed crew.

And boy, was he ever right.

Like I said before, you're welcome, my friend...

CHAPTER FOUR

MOONLIGHTING

When Charlie talked to Marlene about what he'd overheard in the cafeteria, she'd immediately passed him off to an agent from Defense Command Intelligence. This was somewhat unusual — not the fact that the Vice Admiral commanding at Venus was delegating this job, but that DCI was handling it.

Here comes some exposition... it's important stuff, so hang in there.

Policing the activities of soldiers in a war zone is the business of Defense Command Security Forces Shore Patrol — sometimes shortened to SFSP, or often just SP — and the Imperial Army Military Police — the MPs. Defense Command Intelligence had no authority over military personnel, so putting a spook in charge of dealing with abuses on Mercury struck our intrepid Major as odd.

But he knew there were numerous reasons why DCI could be called in — first and foremost, the ranks of both the Shore Patrol and the Military Police had probably been emptied, their personnel filling gaps in front-line combat units. There had been plenty of casualties in recent months, and every ground force was feeling the pinch...

Though it was also possible that Marlene felt she couldn't trust the Shore Patrol or the Military Police to handle this matter. She might believe they were involved...

Charlie wasn't going to jump to any conclusions. Instead, he did what Charlie always tends to do: he approached his re-direction to DCI with an open mind.

Well, mostly open. He waited until Lia had left the room for a physio appointment before placing the call — past experience had taught him it was always best to keep unrelated people out of interactions with DCI. Otherwise they might get dragged into situations they really didn't need to suffer through.

DCI had a way of overcomplicating things. Though to be fair, the last time Charlie had crossed paths (or swords) with them had been part of the Battle of Deep Black, when he'd had a hell of a time in a bare-knuckles fistfight with one of their rather elite superagents.

Mel Fox (now Mel Samuels — wife of our intrepid Marshal Samuels) had been in character as one of Grant Merger's pirate Captains, and Charlie had been in character as the guy trying to capture her. Well, he hadn't realized it was a 'character' — we thought she was a savage pirate, and he moved in to grab her.

I'd tell you who won, but I don't want to spoil the fun for all those people who endlessly argue over who would win in a fight — Special Branch or a DCI superagent. Also, both Mel and Charlie could kill me with a moderate humidity level, so I best remain neutral...

Which is a tangential way of me saying that Charlie and DCI didn't exactly have a cuddly history. He didn't want Lia to be mixed up in any call with them.

Sitting on the end of his bed in his hospital room, Charlie keyed his comm and sent a realtime ping to the contact Marlene had provided — the investigator who'd been put on the case. Charlie was expecting a typical DCI agent… you know, an improbably young, generally attractive, disarming and not at all dangerous-seeming girl.

Instead, Andrew Alexander appeared on the room's screen: "Defense Command Intelligence call centre, Andrew speaking. How may I help you?"

Charlie immediately thought what anyone would think — wrong number.

First of all, call centre? And then Andrew (Drew, he goes by) didn't look like much of a superagent: he was male, which simply didn't fit the stereotype. However, he didn't appear at all vicious, which invariably meant he was a really dangerous superagent, because no one suspected him until he started killing…

But let's not get carried away. For now, Charlie opened his mouth to make an apology about contacting the wrong person, but Drew cut him off with a laugh, "Sorry, Major, you've got the right guy. I was just messing with you."

Great way to start a relationship, wouldn't you say?

"You know who I am?" Charlie winced as soon as that question left his mouth — he didn't want a DCI agent to see him outwardly surprised about anything.

Drew laughed, "You know I know who you are. Come on, I'm a spook. If I didn't know things I'm not supposed to know, I'd actually be running a call centre."

There seemed to be genuine good humor in those words, so Charlie pretended to loosen up a bit. Still didn't trust this guy, though.

"Good point. Did Admiral Stoll give you the heads up, or did you just psychically know I was going to call?"

Drew Alexander grinned and shrugged, "Not at liberty to say."

"Great," Charlie grumbled.

Laughing again, Drew shook his head, "Oh fine, she called. And I just sent a car over for you, and filed a fake doctor's order with the nurses station on your floor to have you escorted down to it. Figured you could sneak out, but that's probably harder to do until you lose the cane."

Charlie blinked, and Drew laughed again.

"Come on, I'm DCI. Of course I'm going to show off the first time I'm on the line with a legendary Brancher."

The next thing Charlie grumbled was less polite, and wasn't picked up by the comm microphones. Just as well.

"Don't worry, they'll think you're going out for some test or something. Lia won't suspect you're stepping out on her or anything."

Mention of Lia was like a little bolt of lightning, and Charlie stopped tolerating the tone: "Watch it."

Drew held up a hand of apology, "Sorry, I know. The rumors have been circling pretty well, it's impossible to miss them."

Charlie scowled, and that just seemed to egg the DCI agent on, "Come on, I'm giving you a compliment. The way this is going, no one's going to have any idea how long you've really been seeing her…"

Stare of death and chaos from Charlie.

Drew's smile faded and he tugged at his collar in a pantomime gesture to demonstrate he got the message, "And, of course, I'm sure you could probably kill me with your cane when you get here. So I'll stop talking. See you shortly."

The link cut, leaving Charlie on the end of his bed, slightly fuming at the energetic spook.

"Know-it-all damned spies with their damned stupid know-it-all-ness..." he muttered, then got to his feet and headed for the door. He had a car to meet, and a spy to whack with his cane.

The ride from the hospital to the DCI headquarters took literally thirty-two seconds — it was two doors down, in a building that seemed perfectly nondescript. Charlie was directed by the driver to go in and take the elevator to the third floor, which he did. Emerging from the lift, he found the whole floor was a single great open office, and only one person was there.

Drew Alexander was shorter than Charlie had expected. He looked taller when he was sitting, but he had short legs and when he stood he was damned near a foot shorter than Charlie. He still seemed non-threatening when he approached Charlie with a grin, and our intrepid Major gave him an unimpressed glare in reply.

"Welcome to our field office," Drew extended his hand.

Charlie took it out of courtesy, and that's when he got a clearer read of agent Alexander. Something about the man's handshake was dangerous... he was outwardly unassuming, but his grip had a quality that suggested he'd done some messy jobs in past.

"They always send the short guy to kill the hard targets," Drew seemed to read Charlie's mind, and he said that with his seemingly ever-present smile. "They can't see me coming unless they look down."

Charlie wasn't sure if it was a joke... but since Drew was a spook, he decided to assume it was serious.

Didn't matter: for all the professional rivalry between Special Branch and DCI operators, they were on the same side, and neither man was inclined to put a bragging contest in the way of this investigation.

Drew gestured Charlie towards a desk on the far side of the large, open office, then led the way there. As our Major settled into a chair, the spook began, "Now, the reason the Admiral sent you to me is pretty straightforward... I've been collecting quite a few reports on this sort of war crimes talk for the past month and a half. We've been getting fragments of it for longer than that, but when SP and MP failed to track down any of the incidents, Admiral Stoll got a bit suspicious and handed it to DCI."

Charlie's expression through this whole chapter has basically been a scowl, and now that scowl intensified. He didn't like the idea that Defense Command's internal policing mechanisms might be corrupted — he certainly didn't deny that it was possible, he just hoped it wasn't the case.

"Obviously the Admiral trusts you, and it's no secret as to why. So when you called in, she suggested I chat with you about this... see if you can detect a pattern I've missed," Drew went on.

That sounded sensible. If there were more reports of the sorts of things Charlie had heard, then whatever he could do to get to the bottom of them would be well worth it...

"So what do you say? Partners? You can moonlight as a detective while you finish recovering," Drew offered that suggestion as he sat back in his chair.

Charlie thought about it briefly, then nodded. It would be much better than convalescing in the damned hospital… even if he had to work with this Drew Alexander guy.

"I'm in," was his answer.

Andrew Alexander couldn't resist shooting back: "I knew you'd say that."

Charlie went for his cane, but ultimately no one was harmed.

CHAPTER FIVE

DIPLOMATIC CONVOY

"Be with you in just a minute, Admiral…"

Craig B. Macdonald was reading two things at once, or at least he appeared to be. A cloud of ministerial staffers seemed to follow him around, and each one had a pad with something important on it — something Macdonald had to approve, or know, or see…

I just stood still and watched the parade as he paced back and forth inside the briefing room he'd taken over, and dealt with it all. When people have asked me why I never pursued a political career after the war, I usually point to events like this one. Watching a man whose entire life was basically at the beck-and-call of the government, I decided that was not how I wanted to spend my retirement.

No jokes about how the Navy did the same thing.

It's different, really.

Sort of. Shut up. It *is*.

No, I was all set to spend my time after the Navy settled down with a family, not worrying about government, politics, war or peace…

I'm not going to discuss how that turned out, because we'd be getting way ahead of ourselves. And I might get hopelessly distracted by what happened in 2235.

Craig Macdonald finally finished looking at what his staff needed him to see, and they temporarily scattered. Like Starlights peeling away from a target after a strike… they'd expended their ordnance, so now they were going back to rearm, and soon they'd return to hit him again.

In the meantime, the Foreign Minister smiled, then let out an overdramatic sigh and grinned, "This is a *great* job. You can have it if you want."

I was still trying to be on best behavior with the Foreign Minister, so I didn't actually reply with 'hell no'. Instead, I grinned and folded my arms, "I think I'll pass on that, sir."

"What if I club you over the head and make it to an escape pod. Then you'll have to do it," he countered, and I shrugged.

"I've got the best two squadrons of Starlights in the fleet. They'll find you and drag you back here."

Macdonald shook his head and laughed, "Well shit. I suppose I'm stuck with this crap."

I could see why Daragh actually liked this guy. The Scotsman lacked the used-car-salesman quality that so many politicos seemed to radiate. I never doubted that he was a political animal — he knew how to deal with people, and he knew how to work issues to his advantage. But I never got the sense that his only aim was self-aggrandizement. Indeed, I think he was actually doing his job on behalf of the people of the Empire… staggering, I know.

Anyway, we weren't just meeting to complain about workloads; Macdonald needed to talk about what we were going to do when we reached Mars.

"I sent the protocol package for the approach… it look alright to you?"

I nodded, half-surprised that I was being asked if I liked a protocol package that came out of Foreign Affairs. We hadn't dealt with any diplomatic protocol since before the war (not counting the farce we made of it in *The Hawke Mission*), but whenever we did, typically a Foreign Affairs agent called us, told us to do exactly what they said, and we grumbled and agreed.

To be fair, usually the person who called with the protocols had no power in setting them… so maybe standing in the room with the guy who had absolute power to create protocol was an advantage.

Anyway, back to the narrative: "Looked fine to us. Won't lie, Foreign Minister, it'll be awfully odd cruising into orbit and not shooting at anything."

Macdonald chuckled, "Well, if things go bad in the leadup meetings, you might have more shooting than you know what to do with. I know some things about the Navy, but not as much as I pretend to. The ships with us… good in case trouble starts?"

The fact that a politico — the head negotiator for the moment — was confirming that our military option was in place was somehow comforting to me. I know that's messed up, but I found his practicality reassuring.

My answer was a nod, "This squadron is the best you could ask for."

At this point, if we were in a movie, the stilted exposition dialogue would begin, with me telling Macdonald what ships were in the squadron, and where they'd come to us from. Macdonald knew all that already — he knew the names of the ships and where they'd fought… he was asking about my assessment of their abilities in case the Martians decided to reconvene the war when he landed and laid down the law.

But since I've failed to outline our squadron for the mission so far in the book, I'm now going to provide you with some cumbersome exposition paragraphs. You know the type. At least the information is not in the form of awkward dialogue.

Ours was a seven-ship group, including many of the veterans who had survived Mercury and the Clash: *Wolf, Nova Scotia, Guangxi, Friendly, Nanton, Corner Brook,* and *Adelaide.*

Of course, with *Nova Scotia* came Wes Pellew, who was sort of the deputy commander for the mission. Karen and I expected to be caught up in diplomatic stuff when we got to the red planet, so Wes would be making sure everything stayed civil in orbit while we pretended to be pleasant with the Martians.

Sela Kinder still had command of *Guangxi*, and her continued success with that mostly-reservist-crewed ship demonstrated to just about everyone in the DCN that she could rightly be named alongside the Belt Squadron elite. Damned glad she took that deal to run *Semaphore* back in 2232, in return for a later frigate command.

Matt Baxter was obviously still aboard *Friendly*, and my old corvette and *Wolf* were the only two veterans remaining from our old Belt Squadron. Other ships were still intact and would rejoin the squadron, but for now *Lion, Cheetah, Lady Grace* and the rest were all in the repair yards, and their people were still being patched up.

Nanton was under the command of Lisa Sims, the young officer who'd earned her promotion back in *The Gallant Few*, and it was a fine addition to our force. So was Wes'

Independent Squadron corvette *Corner Brook*, skippered by Grace Kuhn.

Finally, we had Bruce Arama and his reservists with us, because there's no question that *Adelaide* belonged in such elite company.

This, I think you'll agree, was a good force — though you'll notice we had no battleships. Those were coming later, with the Prime Minister and the Emperor. Our smaller squadron was going in first with Craig Macdonald to set the conditions for the Mars Convention. Once those preparations were done, the main fleet would show up.

In practical terms, this meant we couldn't fight the Martian home fleet if things went poorly — we were a fast squadron, and we'd have to run like the wind if difficulties arose. That was why the Foreign Minister was asking whether our military options were solid, and given those seven ships I just named, I think you'll agree they certainly were.

The Martian home fleet could outgun us... but they wouldn't be able to get their hands on us if they tried.

Anyway, back to dialogue. Macdonald was trying to sort out exactly how we'd play our cards when we arrived: "So, this is a diplomatic occasion. We shouldn't rattle the saber too much... but I don't believe we should pretend that we didn't win the war. You think your crews can handle a careful balance of confident showing-off without going over the top and infuriating the Martians?"

I smiled, "Rub it in, but not too much?"

Macdonald nodded, "That's a better way of saying what I just said."

"I think we can manage that, Foreign Minister," I answered, and Craig grinned.

"Good. And I order you to use my first name. No one else does, and I'm likely to forget it if that continues."

I liked this politico. I really did.

"Whatever you say, Foreign," was my oh-so-clever answer.

"Oh good, a crap comedian. We're kindred spirits..."

Macdonald and I started talking about the particulars of diplomatic protocol.

Chapter Six

The Asteroid Boy

Bort McWebsbert had toured *Wolf* once on his own after the Fleet Clash, but now that we were headed to Mars for peace negotiations, it seemed fitting that he get a better (and guided) look around. This was a job Karen took on while I was dealing with the Foreign Minister, and it was a learning experience for everyone involved.

"So this mag crew services the weapon, makes sure it's fit for fighting..." Karen was explaining as she led Bort through one of the mag compartments. The crew there was standing at attention, all of them reportedly feeling a bit awkward at having not only a DC flag officer, but a Martian, snooping around their space.

Not that they minded Karen — obviously, as a former skipper of *Wolf* and hero of the Empire, she was most welcome. And not that they had any special hatred for Bort, either, because despite him now wearing red, the rumor mill had started circulating stories that he was the 'alright' Martian — the only good one.

No, they just didn't like having any brass at all sniffing around their compartment, because while they kept their mags in excellent working order, they never bothered to scrub or polish enough for a flag inspection.

But it didn't matter, because neither Bort nor Karen were paying any attention to the clutter away from the weapons.

Bort had never seen the internals of a DC weapons system before, and as a man who'd been on the receiving end of our mag fire, it was a grim sight.

"Your fire control is... different," he said simply. He was thinking 'better' instead of 'different', but he couldn't bring himself to say it. On Martian ships, there was only one team dedicated to servicing all the EM turrets. On *Wolf*, we had multiple teams, and as we talked about last book, much better ergonomics.

For instance, Bort was able to stand upright (no crouching) in this mag bay on *Wolf's* port side. Aboard even *Olympus Mons*, he'd have had to crawl through ten meters of service shafts to get this close to a gun turret.

By now, though, Bort was getting pretty good at containing his shock. The lifestyle of the humans on Earth had forced him to improve his abilities in that area... we had such a different way of living.

It was something he honestly admired, as he'd always suspected he might, but it wasn't for him — not now, anyway. His duty remained to his fleet... even if they were probably going to execute him for 'losing the war'.

Karen finally led Bort out of the mag bay (much to the relief of the crew) and as they emerged into the corridor, the Asteroid-born Admiral shook his head slowly. He didn't actually say anything, but Karen noticed the gesture and prodded gently.

"Everything alright?"

Bort didn't look at her, but he tipped his head slightly to the left, "I've been among your people long enough that I shouldn't be surprised by any of this anymore."

Karen smiled gently, then shook her head, "I doubt I'd be doing as well if I were plunged into Martian society or the Martian fleet."

That was a fair point, and Bort glanced at her, "Perhaps. But that wouldn't just be your fault. Ours is a much different lifestyle than yours, and I think I prefer yours."

I do believe that was one of the most honest and open things Bort had yet said to us — he'd always been frank to a point, but he'd never let down his guard about his home to quite that extent.

"I'm sure we could arrange it that you make the move, if you want to," Karen offered gently, stepping a bit closer to him so she could lower her voice. "Once the treaty is done… hell, we could see if we can get it into the fine print of the treaty. You and your family, of course."

Bort's eyes fixed on Karen's, and for a second he wasn't sure how to read the intention behind those words. He told me later that he was awfully, awfully tempted by them — that he'd very much like to be a part of the world he'd spent the last few months immersed in, and the fleet that made his look like a dungeon.

But despite what the movies often imply, it's not so easy. The Asteroids were Bort's home, and he was one of those people who couldn't casually walk away from that connection, even if the alternative was genuinely and unapologetically superior.

He wished he could live the sort of life we had in the Empire. He really wanted something like that for himself. He wanted something like that for the family he hoped he'd have a chance to start.

But he was an Asteroid boy. Epsilon was his home, and even if he could take Casey Flynnboldak with him, he couldn't abandon where he came from.

I sympathize with this, because I have very similar feelings about Earth, and particularly Capital Island. There are times I can't stand the politics of this place, or when the lack of climate control can be an annoyance. But it's where I'm from, and who I am, and no matter how bad or good it is, it'll always be home.

So Bort appreciated Karen's offer, but now he shook his head, "I'm from Asteroid Epsilon, Commodore McMaster. That place is where I should die, if I'm given the choice. No matter how much you show me, I have to go back there."

Karen had been studying Bort's expression as he went through that thought process, and she told me shortly thereafter that she'd predicted much of what he was thinking. She was from eastern Canada herself; she understood what the connection was like, even if for her it was different.

She'd made her offer, and he hadn't taken it, and because of that she almost respected him more — and understood him better.

"That's fair enough," she said quietly. "Perhaps, then, you can work on changing your home… adopting the things you like about us. Share them with your people."

Funny, he was thinking the same thing.

But that was for later.

He nodded again, and then took a breath, "Possibly. Now, though, I want to eat, if that's fine with you?"

Karen nodded, "Of course. How about the Officer's Club on the rec deck?"

Bort blinked; the last time he'd been there, he'd been overwhelmed by the very fact that the bar existed, and that Shelby McLaws and Adrienne Thompson had been there. But perhaps now he'd be better equipped for a sit-down meal.

"Alright," he agreed, and they headed that way.

CHAPTER SEVEN

PIECING THINGS TOGETHER

The voyage to Mars was, as will not surprise you, largely uninteresting. The Foreign Minister got his staff ready, Bort assisted him, and Karen and I dutifully did our jobs as liaisons and pseudo-diplomats.

But beneath the surface, there was quite a lot going on aboard *Wolf*, and in the other ships in our squadron, so here's a long chapter of vignettes to show you where things stood in several different areas, after all the losses we suffered in 2233.

Rufus Chang was set to be promoted.

Our fierce Special Branch Major — the only active survivor of Mercury — was going to be a Lieutenant Colonel, as soon as the paperwork cleared... but that was reportedly going to be a while, because some of Dave Caldecott's old cronies were still (STILL) running the personnel departments, and they were using the ceasefire as an excuse to slow down approvals of promotion requests.

Daragh Ryan was working on this problem (with his shotgun) but it was slow going, because the removal of the 'wartime necessity' clause was decreasing his leverage with the bureaucracy. It was complicated (and it was bullshit) but it was happening. Just about every person who was due for a promotion would have to wait as long as a year to get it.

But that, I should say, didn't matter to Rufus. He was glad to be alive, and gravely saddened that of twenty-four shooters who'd gone into the Mercury Capital Dome from *Wolf*, he was the only one that remained. His rank wasn't going to alter either of those sentiments particularly.

What he was currently doing, though, would keep him plenty preoccupied: he had a new squad to get into shape.

Sort of.

Five officers. We were heading to *Mars* with the Foreign Minister to set up peace talks... and Defense Command could only spare us five new officers to fill out our Special Branch contingent. Four of them were rookies, right out of selection.

I wish I could blame Bureau of Personnel for this, but the reality was that we'd suffered so many losses on Mercury that our Special Branch and Security Force complements were in dire straits. Most of the ships in our squadron heading to Mars had no Special Branchers at all. This was a problem, obviously, that we'd investigate after the war, and which would lead to those discussions of the Defense Command Marine Corps.

We needed troops dedicated to dome assault — shooters with more combat training than SF, but who were less elite and more numerous than Special Branch. More on that much later, though.

For now, Rufus was working with the five new officers who had been assigned to *Wolf*: Captain Clarissa Hutchinson along with rookie Lieutenants Maggie Joyce, Selma

Koestecki, Bobby Franek, and Simon Keynes.

They were all in the Special Branch armory, having just finished a training session, and as they started racking their equipment, Rufus couldn't help but recall whose lockers were being re-occupied by new faces.

Clarissa Hutchinson was in Raza Weiss' space. Raza was recovering on Earth now, but it was expected he'd never be in the field again. Selma Koestecki had Terry Schroeder's old locker, and he was certainly dead. Simon Keynes had Ben Belete's old spot... it was hard not to dwell on those who'd gone before.

And evidently — and uncommonly — Rufus unconsciously allowed the recollection to become partly evident on his face.

"We'll do them as proud as we can, boss," Clarissa Hutchinson leaned in close to Rufus without him even realizing she was there, and her quiet assurance carried equal measures of confidence and regret.

He appreciated the tone, and he nodded very slightly before she went back to her work.

"Alright, shower up, let's go get some food," our Major with the mismatched eyes said, and the Branchers got cleaned up for a meal.

"Well, Gene, here we go."

Jim Hannigan was still our XO, and as we cruised towards Mars he was trying to sort out one of the other Mercury-caused personnel gaps aboard *Wolf*. Omar Cunningham, our now-former security chief, was still on the Martian outer capital, a key officer in the HQ there after a series of casualties had thrust him into the job.

Many of our SF were still on Mercury — all of our security officers, and about a third of our enlisted security personnel too. Defense Command hadn't been able to send us any replacements for these folks either, again because of the shortage in security personnel... and that meant we were running a skeleton crew for SF.

In fact, our senior person in security was the man Jim was talking to in *Wolf's* security office: Eugene Sengooba. Eugene was a Chief Petty Officer — one of the senior non-commissioned officers aboard our frigate... but that rank was likely going to be an impediment to him performing his duties when we got to Mars.

If we needed to throw our weight around in terms of security preparations, it would be difficult for a Chief Petty Officer to make things happen — other ships would have Lieutenants in his job, and while there was no question Eugene's experience would earn him the respect of his counterparts, his lower rank would overcomplicate the situation when we dealt with the Martians.

Ideally, then, we would promote Eugene to Lieutenant, and get him in position to be our security officer... but that wouldn't work, because if we got him commissioned, we'd have to start him at Ensign, then rapidly promote him. Strictly speaking, that sort of thing isn't done... and when Caldecott's people are being bastards in the Bureau of Personnel, it *certainly* isn't done.

We considered invoking the 'Hawke rule' — Ian Hawke tended to promote people to whatever rank he liked, and then browbeat the personnel department into making it happen — but given the sensitivities we were facing with the Emperor, we didn't want to play it that way either.

So after racking his brain, Jim Hannigan had dusted off the fleet manual, read it basically cover-to-cover, and brought us a solution.

Now Eugene looked at the box of rank pips that was sitting open on his desk with slightly wide eyes, "Sir?"

"We actually had to have those made in the machine shop, because we weren't carrying any," Jim smiled at Eugene's expression.

"Well, I didn't think the rank existed anymore."

"They were trying to get rid of it, but apparently they hadn't managed to do so before the war started," Jim shook his head. "So, Gene, congratulations!"

Eugene Sengooba came to his feet as Jim extended a hand to him across the desk, "Thank you sir."

"Well done, Master-At-Arms," Jim nodded, and they shook hands.

Eugene Sengooba was now our security chief, with a rank that our fleet had been in the process of abandoning and which certainly didn't outrank 'Lieutenant', but which was more consistent with his responsibilities. Promotion to Master-At-Arms made him a full Warrant Officer (as opposed to Ensign or Lieutenant — 'commissioned' officer ranks), which meant we could keep the bureau out of it. That sort of technicality is probably more detail than you need, but anyway, it was a special position that Eugene richly deserved, after his years of fine work on *Wolf*.

We were glad to have him running security for the coming year.

There was a good deal more socializing on the trip to Mars than we'd seen aboard *Wolf* since that long haul out to Jupiter. The crew wasn't getting lax, of course — Andrea wouldn't have allowed that — but as I think we began to see at the end of *The Fleet Clash*, everyone was feeling lighter and freer… there was no shooting ahead (that we could foresee) so the 800-pound gorilla had left the room.

Hm, not sure if that metaphor worked, but hopefully you get the idea. Our crew didn't have to worry about fighting.

That in mind, the Officer's Club was active on a fairly regular basis, with originals like Andy Jenson, our Chief Engineer, and Alicia Morgan, our doctor, even finding time to surface and relax. This had been a rare occurrence during the war, as there was always more to do.

But the composition of the crew had changed mightily since the last time *Wolf* had seen such easygoing times. Erica Martin had been our Helm and Navigation Officer back then. As I'm sure you'll recall, she was lost in the Clash. Matt Baxter had been our XO; now he was skippering *Friendly*. Kyle Stranks had been our Security Officer, and he'd been lost aboard *Idaho*, dying a quiet, heroic death that everyone seems to forget, but which warrants remembering.

So when the command staff came together one evening for beverages, and invited Karen and me to attend (briefly), it was a different group of men and women who we saw.

I recall when Karen and I turned up, the laughter had already begun. Andrea had taken the watch on the bridge that evening so the senior staff could socialize, and they were taking advantage. Andy and Alicia sat together, as the last two originals aside from

Jim Hannigan. Our elite XO was next to his bridge crew — Shelby McLaws, our new addition in 2232, and Felicia Khalid, our fine Sensors and Communications Officer who'd taken over after Kate Levec was wounded at Sinope.

Adrienne Thompson, our eternal Combat Group Commander and elite Starlight pilot, was sitting on Shelby's other side, and Eugene Sengooba had come to the table, wearing his Master-At-Arms pips for the first time, to much acclaim.

There was drink circulating, some alcoholic and some not, so Karen and I sat down for a couple of the latter variety and basically remained appreciative — but awkward — outsiders. We'd attended the gathering because we'd been asked, but as much as these were our crew — really *my* crew, from the *Friendly* days — we couldn't socialize completely. We were their commanders, and while we could share the good cheer and listen to some stories from the old days, we couldn't truly join in.

I have no idea why I'm including this vignette. I mean, it doesn't forward the plot particularly — it's a scene about Karen and I saying nothing, and just sitting and listening to *Wolf's* senior staff tell stories, and laugh, and drink a bit. I can't even remember the stories being told.

All I do recall is an immense feeling of pride, because while I wasn't their skipper, I felt very much that this was still my crew. That's not to undercut Andrea, just to say I felt like I owed them a great deal, and it did me good to see them well.

That they'd invited Karen and me, and that we'd agreed to make an appearance, was just as telling, because Admirals and Commodores don't often turn up at such gatherings — even to sit awkwardly aside as we did.

I hesitate to say we were all a family. With no offense to my dear colleagues, I wasn't as close to them as I was to my parents. But we were a team, a fine team that had come through a lot together. Some were new faces, some were originals, but we'd been through so much. And I was very, very proud to see Jim Hannigan as the leader of the bunch — the XO — after his years at Sensors and Communications. I was very pleased that, after all the fighting, Shelby McLaws was still a southern belle, with all the charm and professionalism we'd encountered in our first meeting with her. I was delighted to see that Felicia Khalid, who'd come into her job overwhelmed, turned out to be a truly first-class Sensors and Communications Officer. I was incredibly happy for Eugene Sengooba, because I felt he was being properly rewarded for his fine work. And I was comforted that Alicia and Andy were still the same old specialists — one a healer of engines, the other a fixer of people.

I sat mostly in silence (laughing when appropriate) and enjoyed the company of these people, and while there was that awkward distance between us due to rank, I did feel at home.

This was my crew. And in the coming year and a half, that would prove both an incredibly good… and perhaps incredibly terrible thing.

So that evening sticks out in my mind as a story worth telling, and yet I have no idea why. Nor am I really telling it, I'm just talking about it. It's important, somehow, but don't ask me to give you a good reason.

We were still a crew. A happy ship, with officers loyal to each other, and no matter what we faced in the months to come, there would be no driving a wedge between any of us.

+++

Except Andrea.

You couldn't drive a wedge between her and us — that's not what I mean. She just wasn't happy. And she did feel apart from all the rest of us, and not just in the way that a Captain usually feels isolated.

She was still alone, and trying to re-learn how not to be apart from everyone else because of the horrors she'd seen. I know you might be sick of this story — might be thinking 'can't she just get over it already?' She was thinking the very same. And maybe in a wonderful fictional world of joy and puppy dogs, she could have.

But no, the insidious thing about what she'd been through, and what she now suffered, was that it was imprinted on her, deeply and completely. It wasn't going away, and she was coming to terms with that.

Slowly.

She was trying to learn ways to cope with the things she'd seen. She hoped that she'd be able to reason with them, or that with repetition they'd lose their power. You know how you can get tired of a song, and it can lose the effect it once had on you? She was hoping for that, because if it happened then at least she wouldn't be rendered so grim every time she saw that boy get pushed into that airlock.

But that's not how it worked. Because every time she saw that scene in her mind's eye — as vividly as if it was for the first time — she felt the same way. The same wrenching way.

So it might be tiresome to read about, because it was certainly tiresome (what a weak word) for her to suffer through. But it was the reality of the situation. It had been only a couple of years, and all that time had been fighting. She hadn't come to terms with any of it... she'd only admitted it to a chosen few.

And that wasn't enough to relieve her of her burden.

It was getting to the point now where she didn't know what she was going to do about it. She wasn't worried about getting her crew killed anymore, at least, because of the ceasefire... but that was small comfort.

What was she going to do?

She didn't have an answer. Instead, while we socialized in the Officers Club, she paced her bridge, arms folded and her stare fixed 1,000 meters away. She could ask Wes — the elite Commodore Pellew was cruising within realtime communications range, and he'd made it clear before that she could talk to him...

Though she hadn't. Not since before the Fleet Clash, months prior.

Instead she remained contained within herself, frustratingly determined to cope alone.

It wasn't the right choice, and she knew that. But right or wrong, it's what she did.

So *Wolf* cruised on to Mars, with a happy crew, a damaged Captain, an Asteroid Admiral with no love for his superiors, a Foreign Minister, and a couple of flag officers who were trying to re-learn our old cavalier ways.

I don't think there's much point lingering any more on the trip itself... time to get down to the problems we found on the red planet.

CHAPTER EIGHT

MARS

It's a very uncomfortable feeling, watching Mars get bigger and bigger on your main screen. We were all on the bridge for the sight — me, Karen, Andrea, Craig B. Macdonald, and even Bort. And our Asteroid-born guest included, I think it's fair to say none of us were terribly buoyed by the sight of the red world.

"The Martian escort squadron is approaching on the port quarter," Felicia Khalid announced, and I nodded to her.

"When the call comes in, put it on the main screen."

"Aye."

We were about two hours out from the planet, and the Martians' home fleet was finally sending a line of destroyers and destroyer-escorts out to monitor our progress. As screen two flipped up a chart showing the icons of those five ships coming our way, my immediate instinct was to call for action stations. Sure, this had all been arranged through our embassies on Ceres. Sure, they were supposed to lead us into a standard orbit and put us in touch with the President's Office, so we could land our envoy. Sure, this was all supposed to go to plan.

But I sure as hell didn't trust the Martians. Should have been more open-minded, but I wasn't.

"Well, if they start shooting at us, we'll have them outnumbered," Wes Pellew was on Battlelink, along with all the other skippers from our squadron.

I glanced up at his screen with an uneasy smile, "They still have one of those *Tharsises* left, don't they?"

Wes chuckled, then shrugged, "True. Then we'd run away."

"Yes please," Craig Macdonald put in helpfully. "Not that I doubt the sincerity of my counterparts. I just don't trust them. No offense, Admiral McWebsbert."

Bort glanced from Macdonald to Wes (he was still shocked by the ease with which we could put all our COs up on our bridge screens), then answered, "None taken."

The Martian escorts turned and fell into line beside our squadron as we cruised on towards the red planet, and things remained silent for another twenty long minutes. It was just strange. It shouldn't have been — before the war, we'd been in plenty of situations where we cruised near Martian ships without shooting at them. Back in the pirate fighting days, we'd even teamed up with them once or twice.

But three years of trying to blow the hell out of them changed a person.

"Signal coming in from the planet," Felicia Khalid finally cut through the silence, and I glanced back at the Foreign Minister.

"So, if it's a politico, you talk… if it's an Admiral, I talk?"

We'd sorted that out a couple of days prior, but being a complete rookie at diplomacy, I wanted to confirm the distribution of labor one more time.

Macdonald answered with a nod, then tugged at his collar a little bit to make sure he looked his political best.

"On screen," I gave the order to Felicia, and she nodded and tapped one of her officers on the shoulder. A *WolfNet* loading screen popped up, and then took its time. Again, the Martian Vantage operating system was proving a bit pathetic, but I put thoughts of our superiority out of my mind. I needed to be on best behavior, because screwing up here could restart the war. Not worth it, even if I was confronted by the most insufferable twit I could ever imagine.

And chances were good that I would encounter just such an individual...

The screen cleared at last, and a man wearing a Martian suit appeared, "Welcome to Mars, delegation of Earth. I am known to be the State Minister of our government, Henrich Dewar."

He did actually say 'I am known to be'... no idea why he put it that way. But he was a politico, which meant (much to my relief) Craig Macdonald was up: "Good day to you, Minister. I'm Craig B. Macdonald, Foreign Minister of the Earth Empire. We've come in accordance with the arrangements made between our embassies on Ceres."

"Yes, of course I know you have," the Martian said quickly, and I wasn't sure if his words carried a hint of frustration... or something else. "Our ships will escort you into parking orbit over our Capital Dome, and you will remain on the course that is sent to you while in orbit. At six o'clock in the morning, Mars standard time, your party will be welcome to land."

He sounded like he was in a rush, and then the picture flickered. It only flickered once, so I assumed it was just poor Martian signaling equipment. Hell, that may be all it was.

"We'll sync our clocks with your transponder, and happily oblige," Macdonald replied with a nod. I glanced at him as he said it — he wasn't frowning, but I got the sense he was also finding something awkward about this exchange.

Was it just the Martian way of doing business?

"Very good, I will await your—"

"Is there anything else, Minister? Any other details that need to be revised before we land, or will the arrangements made three weeks ago between our Ceres embassies be sufficient?" Macdonald cut off the Martian's exit with that lengthy and rather explicitly-worded question, which nearly got a frown out of me.

The Scotsman seemed to be sensing something fishy, but lacking experience in government, I had no idea what he was getting at.

Henrich Dewar nodded in an awful hurry, "All as discussed. We will see you in the morning!"

Then the feed cut.

"Someone seems edgy," Karen's observation was dry, and Andrea and I both nodded in agreement.

"That because he lost the war?" Andrea raised the question, and Bort replied with a frown.

"Seemed like more than that..." he said distantly, then fell silent. He was still a member of the Martian military — whether he disliked their organization or government was irrelevant; he wouldn't easily voice his criticisms about them.

"There's definitely something wrong," Macdonald folded his arms and his brow creased. "Unless they're more desperate for peace than... well, frankly, they are. There's no way he should be satisfied with diplomatic arrangements made provisionally by a couple of ambassadors three weeks ago. He should have been posturing... telling us the time had changed, or the arrival point, or the agenda..."

Macdonald was thinking out loud, which was useful for the Naval officers present because none of us would have noticed the lack of jockeying that was supposed to be natural between diplomatic and governmental offices.

"What could be throwing him off so much that it's making him cooperative?" was my question, and Macdonald had to shrug.

"Damned if I know. But remember that military option we were talking about at the start of the trip?"

I nodded.

"Yeah. Just... be ready in case we need it."

I stiffened slightly, and glanced at Karen. She absently fiddled with the end of her ponytail, puffing out her cheeks to show her lack of eagerness.

On the Battlelink screen, Wes verbalized our thoughts: "Great, now the diplomat is telling us to get ready to shoot things. Anybody else getting a warm feeling about this mess?"

We all were.

It was going to be an interesting trip, to be sure.

Chapter Nine

Diplomats

"Do I look like a diplomat to you?"

Karen was tugging at the collar of her dress uniform, scowling at her reflection in the darkened black glass that fronted the wallscreen in my cabin. I was still fixing up the collar of my under-shirt, as a preface to donning the actual dress tunic... a process I wasn't looking forward to. Her question drew my eyes to her back, and as she saw the reflection of me looking, she turned round.

"I haven't worn this thing since... since I don't know when. I feel like a peacock."

The comparison made me grin, which made her scowl even more. She didn't like dress uniforms... many of us didn't... because they were relatively uncomfortable. But that wasn't the reason for her general unease: we were getting ready to take part in the diplomatic mission with the Foreign Minister. And that was going to be exciting.

Like dental surgery is exciting.

"You look like a diplomat with very pretty tail feathers," I offered my reply which, as you can see, was attempting to be clever.

Karen wiggled her posterior slightly at the comparison, "I can shake my tail feathers."

I have to admit, I stared... then I laughed and went back to my dress uniform tunic. It was longer than a standard uniform tunic, you see, and covered in decorations and ribbons and all manner of other ornate things that are completely pointless but look special to those who care.

I shouldn't belittle it... I just couldn't abide wearing it.

Still, requirements of the service and all that.

As I started pulling on my jacket, it immediately became clear that it was going to be tighter than the last time I'd worn it. Too much time doing weights in the gym had made my shoulders too big.

Yes. Go with that.

Seeing the difficulty I was having as the sleeves rode up around my wrists, Karen helpfully came in behind me and started tugging on the shoulders, trying to help.

"Yours still fits the way it's supposed to," I muttered as she turned me around.

"You need to lay off the shoulder press," she smiled as she tugged at the lapels. "You look like a peacock too now. Care to shake your tail feathers for me?"

I smiled, "I'll need to watch your example for a while longer before I can pull that off."

Chuckling, Karen pulled her ponytail up onto her left shoulder and played with it innocently, "Well you didn't actually say no."

"True," I turned back to my bed, where the last of my dress uniform equipment was spread on the unmade sheets. All that remained was the Belt and holster, with my sidearm strapped into it.

"Still think we should be carrying?" Karen's mag was already around her waist, and her right hand instinctively fell to its grip.

"Probably not, but whether we look like diplomats or peacocks…" I started to strap mine around my waist, and Karen finished the thought for me.

"You want to be able to shoot anything you need to shoot."

I closed the buckle and turned back to Karen with a nod, "Best-armed peacocks they'll have seen in a while."

"I should shake my tail feathers for them," she shrugged.

That made me frown, "I don't see how that'd help."

She shrugged, "Sorry, I just like saying it. It's funny…"

I groaned, and we left my cabin.

It was six o'clock Martian time, or in our parlance, 0600. But owing to different standard time zones, it was actually just a little before lunch on our day of departure, so no one was too rushed or tired as we all rendezvoused in landing bay one.

Craig Macdonald was, of course, coming with us for this trip, along with a personal assistant and two other staff. Bort was coming too, as were Rufus and his new officers — all of them in Special Branch dress uniforms instead of combat kit. Their job was strictly security, though that wouldn't be made any easier by the equipment limits imposed on them — no MAG-90s, no tac vests. Sidearms only.

But of course, being Special Branchers, they could kill you with an amoeba's backpack, so we weren't worried.

Eugene Sengooba and three SF were also coming down, officially to be helpers (fetch coffee, carry files, and so on)… but really there in case we needed extra help, since we didn't have a full Special Branch squad.

We also had two 'Naval liaisons' with us — officers who would keep in touch with the squadron overhead, even if Karen and I were in closed-door sessions with Macdonald and the Martians. We'd had a number of volunteers for the job, but we'd settled on Jim Hannigan and Shelby McLaws. They were both obviously quite experienced, so they could handle the sensitivities of this sort of mission.

All in all, then, it was a pretty complicated setup — four politicos, an Asteroid Admiral, ten security people of one sort or another, two Naval officers, and two would-be diplomats. Nineteen people total… twenty if you counted Chet Srisai, the Special Branch shuttle pilot who'd take us down to the Capital Dome.

As I was doing that math in my head (smoke pouring out of my ears), Karen and I were approached by Craig Macdonald, who wore a somewhat concerned expression on his face.

"Foreign Minister," Karen greeted him for us both, and he nodded to her.

"Good morning, Commodore McMaster my dear…" Yes, the charming Scotsman got away with 'my dear'ing Karen. He then looked at her waist, and mine, pointing at my sidearm, "I see that all of your officers are armed… not just the security people."

Aha. I winced a little, and waited for the inevitable next salvo of diplomat-speak about the need not to appear threatening.

Then Craig unleashed his fury: "Have any extras? I'd feel a bit better if I had something concealed in my jacket. My staff too."

Er. Not what I was expecting. The Foreign Minister was asking to go into a diplomatic meeting… packing heat?

"I. Uh."

Yes, my answer to Minister Macdonald was that coherent.

Karen was a bit quicker on the draw, though, and she nodded, then waved to Rufus Chang to join us. As the Major arrived beside us, she smiled at him, "Rufus… the Minister and his staff need concealable mags to carry. Have anything that fits the bill?"

Mags small enough to conceal in a suit weren't standard issue aboard ship, but if anyone had them, it'd be Rufus — remember how many friends he has in armories and R&D shops around the fleet?

Clearly surprised by the request, he nodded, and then set about finding one of his officers to go back to the armory, and to pick up a bunch of compact MAG-11s. Macdonald went away happy, and Karen and I waited until the officer, Maggie Joyce, returned with the weapons. Once the politicos were set, I glanced at Karen and shrugged, "All aboard?"

She nodded, "Sure."

Turning, she saw our newly-minted Master-At-Arms standing nearby, "Eugene, let's get everyone loaded up."

The Security Chief nodded, then waved his SF toward the craft, having them pass the word around as they did.

Rufus was at the foot of the ramp, looking severe as we approached.

"Thanks for the help. Missing your usual kit?" I asked him, and he nodded.

"I'm only carrying three things that explode. Do you know how few people I'd be able to bring down with so few bombs?"

I grimaced slightly — explosives sure hadn't been friendly to Charlie's squad on Mercury — but shrugged, "I remain confident in your destructive ability."

He nodded earnestly, then we passed him and headed up the ramp.

The pinnace filled quickly as officers and politicos alike came aboard and quickly found seats. It was a fairly unassuming affair, with Macdonald and his staff sitting towards the back in a cluster, the assistants filling him in on the last few details one more time — things he'd asked them to remind him of, and so on.

Bort sat in the aisle across from Karen and me, and as I glanced at him, he looked uneasy.

"You going to need us to run any interference for you?" I asked across the way, and at first he didn't realize I was addressing him. I still didn't feel like I could call him 'Bort', but I was getting to the point where 'Admiral' felt too formal… so I was trying not to have to make the decision.

"Hmm? Oh. Just call me Bort."

The fact that he answered the question I was pondering, instead of the one I'd asked, was somewhat weird, so I glanced at Karen and she shrugged.

"He'll be fine," was her comment. "He's pretty impressive, after all."

She looked away as she said that, so I frowned at the side of her head, "Excuse me?"

Looking back innocently, she shrugged, "Well, you know, he's technically a rank higher than you. And he's spent even more time working on the shoulder press than you have."

I'm pretty sure my jaw dropped, and that was the reaction she was looking for. She chuckled and looked away again, "Just saying."

"Well someone's flirty today," I prodded back, and she laughed again.

"Jealous?"

"No, I've never wanted to be flirty."

That one earned me a winning smile, and then we were interrupted by the engines of the pinnace humming to life.

"I suppose he's alright," I muttered, looking straight ahead. And then I smiled.

Karen whacked me in the side of the knee with the back of her hand, and the pinnace rocked up off its feet and settled into a hover while the flight doors opened.

Moments later, we were in space, heading down to Mars.

On the bridge of *Nova Scotia*, Wes Pellew was very, very suspicious of the whole situation. Standing with folded arms, he watched enhanced camera feeds as our shuttle slid out of *Wolf's* bay one, to be encircled by Adrienne Thompson's Starlights from Wolfstar squadron.

"Good luck..." he said very quietly, and then he started to pace his bridge deck as Chet Srisai began circling us down towards the Capital Dome.

"Well, they're off," Matt Baxter observed from *Friendly's* bridge — now that he was operating as squadron commander, Wes had Battlelink connections to each of the ships in orbit up on his screens. It'd stay that way pretty much the whole time we were there, at least until the *Bonnies* showed up, because this all just seemed too dangerous.

Damned Mars. Wes couldn't stand Mars. At least the northern part. But that's a different story, which he'll kick me for hinting at.

"Think this is going to go as smoothly as they say?" Bruce Arama asked dryly from *Adelaide*.

Andrea snorted a laugh from *Wolf's* command deck, "No."

A smile spread on the Kiwi Commander's face, and he folded his arms, "Well, at least I'll have a good story for the kids. If we don't all die here."

"Don't even joke," Sela Kinder pitched in from *Guangxi*.

"I wasn't," Bruce replied, and Wes huffed a sigh, then shook his head again.

"Damned Mars," he said.

Damned indeed. We had *no idea*.

CHAPTER TEN

MEANWHILE, BACK AT THE RANCH

"The Emperor's shuttles will be landing shortly, sir."

Mik Mikaelsen was also wearing his dress uniform, but for a completely different reason. And arguably, his reason was no less painful than ours. Welcoming the Emperor to *Ark Royal* was going to be so much fun he could explode.

The officers and enlisted men and women around him in the waiting lounge beside the Supercarrier's landing bay one would form a huge, finely-turned-out procession as soon as the space doors closed behind the three shuttles carrying the Emperor and his... whatever his minions were called. Courtiers? Assistants? Entourage? Whatever.

Of course, Luther Gregory III's personal guard was already coming aboard via other landing bays... a regiment of Imperial Army blockheads would be encamped on the ship for the duration of the mission to Mars, which was just plain delightful. Carrying a load of such sheer stupidity was a problem in itself, but now the Emperor would have 1,000 fighting men to draw on, should he have a problem with the Defense Command personnel aboard ship.

It seemed highly, highly unlikely that such a clash would come to pass, but Mik was still very conscious of the fact that he didn't have so much as a single Special Brancher at his disposal.

So it was going to be a very, *very* political cruise. And a slow one, too, because while they'd be setting out soon, they had to wait for a message from our squadron confirming that the arrangements for the Mars Convention were in place. Perhaps that would get taken care of in the week it took them to reach the red planet at proper cruising speed... but if it didn't, they'd slow down, or even come to a stop in space, waiting for the call to approach.

Great, a long flight with the Emperor...

Glancing at the officers around him, Mik took a centering breath, and waited for the Imperial eminence to get his ass aboard *Ark Royal*.

Prime Minister Douglas Pope descended from his pinnace with a briefcase in one hand, and the other outstretched to John Fiora. The First Lord was waiting on the deck of *Bonaventure's* number one flight bay, and he smiled at the PM's arrival.

"Good to have you aboard, sir."

"Glad to be here," Pope answered honestly. He reasonably expected this to be a quiet cruise for him — limited media access (John had taken only seventy reporters, including our old friend Jessica Qing, aboard for the trip), and no Question Period to worry about. Pope would be working while en route to Mars, but at least the demands on his time would be fewer... he'd be able to get more done.

And then he'd have to wrangle the Emperor and negotiate a fair and effective peace.

"My staff will see to your staff... I'll take you to your cabin," John gestured in the direction of the flight bay's exit hatch. The Prime Minister nodded, and the two fell into step side-by-side.

"Your officer receiving the Emperor?" Pope asked quietly as they went, and John nodded. He'd already briefed the PM on Mik, and why our friend had been subjected to this particular job. None were better for it than the Commodore from the Belt.

Now Pope nodded, "Good... good. I wish we could let him get lost. But it'll be such a mess as it is..."

They exited the flight bay as Pope said that, and John could only agree. It would undoubtedly make life easier at the bargaining table, and reduce the chance of catastrophic demands or concessions, if the Emperor didn't reach the convention due to something like 'engine troubles'... but things were wound too tight at home now. Any appearance of disunion and the next coup might not be so 'almost'.

"Parliament going to be alright without you?" John asked almost under his breath, and Pope sighed quite wearily.

"Probably."

I haven't done a good job outlining the political machinations that had been going on in government, I fear, so I better do that now. The ceasefire had seen the end of the truce that had existed in Parliament since the war had begun, and now the opposition parties — chiefly the regionally-based parties for Earth and for the Belt — were ratcheting up pressure to cut military spending, review the charges of corruption that had been circulating at the start of the war, and do a whole bunch of other things that I don't need to get into.

Pope's Empire Party did have a majority in the House of Commons, theoretically rendering it immune to such attacks... but the Empire Party had been welded together out of two deeply divided factions less than a decade prior, and Olivia Bennington, the deputy Prime Minister — now in charge, with Pope gone to Mars — was the leader of the losing faction. If the party fragmented at all, the government could fall, and a coalition government might come in.

That may all sound like random political hot air, but a coalition would likely cause a great deal of difficulty as the Empire transitioned out of a wartime economy into a peacetime one... a lot of half-finished ideas would probably end up surfacing, and get put into operation.

But that wasn't the real concern. If things went that way, it'd be unfortunate, but still constitutional. We mightn't like it, but we'd have to live with it.

The bigger problem would lie with the Emperor, because he was undoubtedly behind some of the trouble being stirred by the opposition parties. He'd have promised them his support, in return for a few revisions to legislation that was currently limiting his power. The opposition MPs wouldn't have been daft enough to promise him anything major... but as much of an ass as he was, Luther Gregory III was a snake of a politician. He probably had a back-door trick in mind, that would allow him to defy or overturn the elected assemblies, and restore the Imperial throne to the glorious heights it had enjoyed in the old Empire.

That was the real concern. We didn't know how he'd do it, but we figured the Emperor was pulling the strings.

And we were right.

So peace had to be negotiated, but in such a way that the Emperor had no leverage against Defense Command, or the Prime Minister. If anyone stepped out of line around him, he could use it as evidence of corruption, fracture the Empire party, bring down the government, and probably seize power for himself.

It was going to be a fun trip.

And by fun, I mean… well, you know what I mean.

Dammit.

So as John Fiora took the Prime Minister to his massive cabin deep in the neck of *Bonaventure*, they were thinking about the many ways this situation could go terribly wrong. There were plenty.

Mik's procession came to attention behind him, and he squared his shoulders and fixed his eyes front as the Emperor began to descend the ramp from his polished-white pinnace. Luther Gregory III looked out over the neatly-assembled Defense Command welcoming committee with an air so smug it dripped, but Mik ignored that.

As the man reached the deck, he stood in a strange sort of pose for a few seconds, then he drifted toward Mik in a somewhat awkward fashion.

"Your Majesty, welcome aboard *Ark Royal*," Mik's words were crisp.

Luther Gregory stood at an oblique angle to our elite Commodore, and considered him through narrowed eyes, "You are from the Belt, aren't you Christian?"

Mik's eyes remained front, though he found it difficult to contain his surprise at the attempt at familiarity.

"I am, your Majesty."

"And you were never one of the Fiora Ring, were you? You were separate from all that?"

Mik couldn't help but let his eyes drift sideways to the black man wearing white, "I was a Captain in the free belt, your Majesty."

Luther Gregory nodded, "Yes. My people tell me that, despite your wartime associations, your heart is in the right place. I look forward to our voyage together. I am sure there will be no problems with our trip, to shake my confidence."

A compliment Mik didn't want, and a threat he didn't need, all wrapped into one. Bastard.

"Allow me to show you to the Imperial cabin," Mik answered by ignoring both, and the Emperor seemed to approve of the cool side-step of the bait.

With that, Mik began leading Luther Gregory III deeper into *Ark Royal*.

CHAPTER ELEVEN

IRONY

I was about to start this chapter by saying 'landing on Mars was like landing on any other planet'. Thankfully, I realized how terrible an opening line that would be. Unfortunately, I still told you I thought of it, so now you may heckle my ineptitude.

Anyway, the place was... well... it was Mars.

We came down under Starlight and Interceptor escort, and the flight was really quite uneventful. Because the Capital Dome was large, they had a proper landing bay, so Chet Srisai floated us straight into it, landed, and then we waited for the doors to close behind us. As the Martian atmosphere was pumped out and the breathable air pumped in, we all got to our feet and peered out the windows of our craft.

The landing bay seemed about as posh as the Martians could manage — it was carefully painted, floor to ceiling, and polished to a brilliant shine. It had a stately feel... but there was something unsettling about it. Like it was trying *too* hard, if that makes sense.

Though keep in mind, given my clear and abiding love for the Martians, I doubt there's anywhere they could have landed us that I wouldn't have criticized in a similar fashion. I'm unreasonable.

As the air became correct, a company of Martian troopers hurried out onto the deck clad in their ceremonial uniforms, rifles at their shoulders. They clomped together in lock step, then wheeled, closed up their ranks and came to attention. It was cute, how they were trying to impress us.

Sorry.

Then a delegation of what appeared to be politicians stepped out in front of the troops, looking about as haughty as you'd expect. They were all dressed in similar, high-collared suits — purposely austere. As I've said before, it's a teutonic look that they seem to go for — very much like what Crusader knights might have designed, had they been time-travelled to our day and age. Not lavish or garish, I'll give them credit... but very starched, and very stilted.

The welcoming committee was ultimately impressive, if over-done. Seeing that it had finished turning out, Craig Macdonald took a deep breath, then stepped into the aisle, "Alright, everyone, we go down that ramp and are on best behavior. We have no reason to believe that they'll torture and kill us all as a faint reprisal for their losing the war, so let's none of us think about that."

Yes, those were actually his words, and then he laughed nervously and headed for the hatch. Eugene and the SF guards caught up to him there, since they would be leading the way down the ramp. As we got into order — Craig, Bort, me and Karen, Shelby and Jim, followed by Rufus and the squad — we took a collective deep breath. Then Eugene opened the hatch, and we stepped out into the artificial Martian air.

It tasted funny.

The next few minutes were awkward. Mostly, Karen and I just stood on the bottom of the ramp while Craig exchanged pleasantries with the Martian counterpart politico, who seemed about as agitated as Minister Dewar had been. It appeared as though he was in a hurry to get us out of the landing bay, and into the convoy to the President-for-Life's government compound.

I just figured he was anxious about having Defcoms on his planet. I was incorrect.

While they talked, some of the officers present from the Martian side glared at Bort. The optics really weren't good for our counterpart from the Asteroids — he'd lost the Imperium's most powerful squadron, he was a lowly Asteroid-boy Admiral, and now he was landing on Mars with us. They'd be keyed up to shoot him, that seemed pretty clear… but then that was an advantage to him being with us. Because they couldn't shoot him.

We hoped, anyway.

And, of course, there were stares at the women present. Three in the Special Branch squad, two of Eugene's guards, one of Craig's staffers, and Shelby and Karen. The finely-turned-out Martian troopers and the flight deck personnel were all getting an eyeful of Defense Command's unthinkable and hedonistic practice of including women in the military.

Our officers and enlisted women simply ignored the stares.

Eventually, we got moving. The company of troopers led the way out of the bay, and out onto the 'lawn' outside the building. This was interesting; the flight bay was essentially like a giant warehouse with one end jutting out the side of the dome. Inside, it was surrounded by a lawn and parking lot, much as a building on Earth would be — instead of being part of a larger military complex, as was the custom in the Belt, and basically everywhere else.

That wasn't the only difference, though: the dome above was transparent, and pretty massive too. The biggest domes on Venus are only fifteen kilometers across. This Martian dome had to be twice that size — a construction accomplishment, I'll admit.

So we could see out to the naturally red morning of this part of Mars, and that was impressive. But we didn't pay it much attention, because as soon as we got 'outside' onto the lawn, the reason for all the Martian politicos' edginess became very, very clear.

I think the polite word for what we were looking at is 'demonstration'. Or perhaps 'protest'.

The first word that came out of Karen's mouth was less charitable: "Riot?"

There were thousands — and I do mean *thousands* — of people in the street beyond the lawn and parking lot. A tall cage fence separated them from our field, and I had to assume there was an energy current running through the metal, because the mob was keeping a safe distance from it.

But there were plenty of people. And they were chanting, and yelling, and waving signs. I noticed at least one black sun flag on fire, and someone had gone to the trouble of putting a dummy in something that looked like it was supposed to be a DC uniform, and hanging it with a noose from a tall pole.

We weren't feeling the love.

The company of well-turned-out Martian troopers hurried across the lawn as we watched, spacing themselves at equal intervals behind the fence, rifles ready. They were in *crowd control* mode.

"What the hell…" was the question I uttered under my breath, and I came to a stop. As I stopped, Karen stopped, as did Shelby, Jim, Eugene and the guards. Rufus and his Branchers continued to follow Craig and the staffers, but soon they were all stopped too. We all drifted together to watch the spectacle, and our hosts tried to mollify us.

"I'm sorry, there's been some negative feeling towards the end of the war," one the Martian politicos, whose name I never got, tried to make apologies to Craig, and our Foreign Minister managed (barely) not to sound incredulous as he answered.

"And by that you mean there's rioting in the streets?"

The Martian politician paled, and then waved toward the ten-vehicle convoy we were bound for. It included four tanks, three armored personnel carriers, and three stretch hoverlimos, "You will be well escorted while these demonstrations are put down."

I didn't know how to react to that — so many things about what he'd said seemed wrong. First of all, public demonstrations seemed very unusual for the stereotypes we held about the Martians — wouldn't their oppressive government have suppressed them by now? Or were they having problems keeping control of their own population?

And they figured a ten-vehicle convoy was needed to keep us safe — over half of it armored? What the hell sort of firepower did the protesters have? Or were our Martian counterparts just being extra cautious?

I looked at Karen, and her expression revealed she was quite unimpressed, "Well, the day won't be boring."

"I'd say if they get a hold of us, our day won't last very long either," Shelby quipped smoothly, her fingers playing on the handle of her sidearm. "Adrienne keeps telling me I should spend more time practicing on the range with this thing."

I glanced at our Helm and Navigation Officer, "Just point and shoot, Shelby. If I can do it, you'll be a pro."

She smiled charitably, and then I glanced past her at Eugene and Rufus, who were standing side-by-side, "Gentlemen?"

They both looked at me, and then Rufus shrugged, "I can't blow them all up, but if it comes down to it, I'm sure we'll be able to give them a sufficiently potent reminder of their mortality to send them home."

Craig Macdonald overheard that, and his eyebrows went up, "I know who I'm taking with me into Question Period next time. We agreed, then… the convoy?"

I shrugged, then nodded. Karen did the same, and together we all headed towards the line of vehicles. A couple of platoons of Martian troopers in battle dress were with the vehicles, and as we approached they started pointing us to our respective transports.

We were sent to the APCs.

The limos remained empty.

"Well, it's comforting that they're using decoys to keep the snipers away from us," Jim observed distantly. "But it's rather disturbing that they feel the need to. And that everyone can see which vehicles we're actually getting in."

That was the sort of reaction we were all having. It didn't help that as we got closer to the column, we were also getting much closer to the fence perimeter — to the jeers and screams and taunts. They were saying some pretty incredible things. The one that sticks with me, and I swear to God I both heard it yelled and read it on a protest sign, is: 'I won't let you rape my baby!'

Hearing that started to put this situation into context for me. Remember all the propaganda we talked about in *The Fleet Clash* — the belief, seemingly common on Mercury, that we were a horde of ravenous monsters? Well, assume that impression was as strong, or even stronger, at home on Mars. After all the spin this government had done to justify the war, the people here truly believed we wanted to do every man, woman and child on Mars grievous harm. Hell, maybe we'd slave them out!

Now, put yourself in the place of an average Martian. Imagine that you genuinely, deeply, truly believe those things. And then imagine what you'd do if you found out your government was giving up the fight against us, and potentially was going to let evil Defcoms have their way with your home.

I think you could be forgiven for being out in the streets with a sign, ready to overthrow the government to protect your family.

So I do believe there's irony in this: the Martian government was desperate for peace, because they knew if they walked away from the table, we'd annihilate them. But now the very people they'd whipped up into a propaganda-fueled frenzy were telling them to keep fighting.

Whoops.

The first inkling of this revelation was trickling into my brain as Karen and I started towards the APC to which we'd been directed. It looked like a coarse, military machine... but it had hardened sides, which I preferred to a cushy limo at the moment.

And then something else happened.

Bort dashed past us, heading for the fence at a jog, defying calls from various guards for him to stop. For a moment I thought he was trying to make a break for it — perhaps they were going to 'disappear' him, and he wanted to try to get the relative safety of the mob?

Instinctively, Karen and I followed him, hands on sidearms. We didn't know if we'd need our mags to stop Bort, or stop troopers, or stop rioters... but we wanted them ready to draw.

Because we went, Eugene followed, with Shelby and Jim right behind him and his guards. And because we all went, Rufus and three of his officers followed as well — Captain Hutchinson and Lieutenant Joyce staying with Craig Macdonald.

Of course, seeing all these Defense Command personnel heading for the fence made the Martian troopers edgy, which under the circumstances was even worse. So basically, right there, we nearly restarted the war.

Because of Bort, which he's been embarrassed about ever since.

Fortunately, he slid to a stop right before hitting the fence, and when he stopped, Karen and I stopped, and then the whole chain of moving people behind us stopped in turn. Everyone waited, and beyond the stretch of fence we were facing, the crowd felt silent.

Seems that having the monsters of Defense Command facing them had an intimidating effect, at least initially. That was good, because as one of my editors just pointed out, had any of them been armed, the chain link fence wouldn't have provided us much protection. Odd that the thought didn't occur to us at the time... kind of a good point now that I think about it. Yikes.

One woman was completely ignoring us. She was much closer to the fence than anyone else, and by her dress — skirts to her boots, and a fine jacket and austere turtleneck, topped with a hat — I had to assume she was someone of a certain... class, I suppose is the word. She was staring at Bort, with an expression that...

"Oh dear, I think that might be his woman," Karen shook her head in mock disappointment. And then, in complete contravention to the incredibly serious situation, she added: "Really, what does she have that I don't?"

"A hat," I answered immediately.

It was the first time in a long time that we'd been able to joke so blatantly in the face of trouble, and I couldn't help but grin. Seemed we were getting some of the old cavalierness back. Maybe a bit too much...

But Karen certainly had it right: the elegant woman on the other side of the fence was Casey Flynnboldak, the dancer who Bort had not yet managed to marry, and who hadn't quite managed to marry Bort. He hadn't so much as mentioned her to me, but I guessed correctly that she was a dancer — it was something in her bearing that gave it away.

Not that any of that mattered, because the mob was starting to get its courage back. And they were staring at Casey — one from within their midst who evidently had a connection to the evil Earthlings. They marked her for interrogation... or whatever the hell a mob would do under these circumstances.

"What's going on here?" Craig Macdonald was suddenly walking past me, and then he stopped alongside Bort, looking at the elegant woman, ignoring the mob and the danger it implied. "I haven't had the pleasure."

My editors think that allowing the Foreign Minister to get this close to a riot was stupid. I hate it when my editors are right.

"This is Casey Flynnboldak," Bort said, his eyes not leaving hers. "We need to get her in here."

By now, a Martian officer and the Martian politicos were hurrying into the picture. Bort clearly outranked the company commander, so he marked the man and gave orders: "Deploy a platoon to bring that lady inside, immediately!"

The officer commanding the company stared at Bort open-mouthed, not sure if he should be taking orders from a man who'd come in on the DC shuttle after having lost the *Tharsis* Squadron. The Martian politicos puffed up to argue as well, but Bort stepped in close to the company commander first.

"Listen, Captain, you're going to follow orders from an *Admiral*, aren't you. Or I'll throw you over that fence to do the job by yourself."

Bort clearly out-massed the Captain, and the smaller Martian paled. Then one of the politicos stepped in closer, ready to unleash some harsh words. Craig Macdonald's hand landed on that man's shoulder, though, and our Foreign Minister smiled.

"I think the Admiral's request is reasonable. And I support it. So I'd suggest you retrieve Miss Flynnboldak, before I ask Major Chang to do it."

Talk about throwing your weight around. I think Craig Macdonald has a bit of a chivalrous streak (both his ex-wives might argue, but he'd been drinking far too much when he'd been with them), and he also wanted to take the opportunity to remind the Martians of who would control these talks.

They had to do whatever we said. And they had to be grateful when we didn't ask them for an arm and a leg.

This was a small thing, and the Martian politico seemed to realize that. He nodded to the Captain, who then ordered his troopers to switch off the electrification of the fence in front of Casey, and to prepare to repel rioters when they temporarily pulled out a section to let her in.

It actually went quite smoothly, I think because Rufus and three other Branchers, all wearing black, were standing at the fence, staring ominously at the crowd. Sure, they were wearing dress uniforms… but according to the propaganda, Special Branchers were some sort of evil wizards who could inflict death with their glares.

So the propaganda got it at least partially right…

Casey Flynnboldak came through the fence, and then she and Bort shared an embrace, right out there in front of everyone. I nudged Karen as they did, "I'm sure you can take her."

"I'll make do with what I've got," was her answer.

Oh we were getting back into fine form.

With an arm around Casey, then, Bort headed back towards the APCs, and we all followed in a huddle. He went into the one Karen and I had been pointed to, so we boarded and sat opposite the pair, with Jim, Shelby and Eugene coming in behind us. Then they buttoned up our transport, and the hover engines fired.

We were going for a joyride across the Capital Dome of Mars.

Yay.

CHAPTER TWELVE

STREETS

We weren't off the ground for more than ten seconds before the questions started. Casey Flynnboldak was sitting very tightly pressed up to Bort, with the wall being her only companion on the other side. I make this point because it looked to us like she'd picked a corner so she wouldn't have to sit next to a Defcom, and so she could put Bort between her and us.

She probably believed the propaganda too... which says a lot about her relationship with Bort, since she was willing to share an APC with us in spite of our latent monsterism.

Anyway, the questions started fast.

"How... what are you doing here?"

There was a texture to Bort's voice that we hadn't heard before — he was speaking as though he and Casey were alone in the back of the APC, which is something Karen or I might do in similar circumstances, so we certainly didn't hold it against him.

Casey shot slightly uncomfortable looks at everyone else in the APC, and Bort followed her eyes, "You can speak freely. They're... trustworthy."

That was a significant statement to make, and it seemed the gravity of it was lost on none present — Casey, Bort or the rest of us. It was the first time he'd come out and said what he thought of his Defense Command captors, and he had no reason to lie to Casey. We'd all have been flattered, but that really wouldn't have fit the situation.

With sufficient confirmation that the monstrous Defcoms around her were friendly ears, Casey started talking, "Everyone knew when you were landing. Everyone. I had to come and see for myself, and I'm very glad I did..."

I'm pretty sure my eyebrows went up. I know Bort's did, and Karen's certainly climbed as well. Bort was the first to ask for clarification, "They... who? Knew what?"

Casey realized she needed to back up and establish context (something, as you know, I often need to do): "Since the ceasefire, there's been a very strong undercurrent of public resistance. The government hasn't been able to control it... I think because some of the military is on side with it. Your entire itinerary for this visit has been out there for weeks. When you were to arrive... where... the possible routes to the government compound..."

Oh that was comforting to hear.

"Sorry," Karen cut in gently. "I'm Karen McMaster. So, you're saying they know everything about this visit... and the information that's been released to the public has proved correct so far?"

Casey nodded, and Karen sat back and looked at me. We were both pulling out our comms a second later, as were Jim and Shelby. There were plenty of people who needed to be warned about this little hiccup.

❖❖❖

As soon as Craig Macdonald got my message, he lowered his comm and looked straight across the aisle at the Martian politico who was sitting tensely, and beginning to sweat. The man immediately realized Craig's eyes were on him, and a look of genuine and unbridled panic took over his face for a few seconds before clearing.

"You have leaks in your military, and you have organized protesters who know exactly where we're going to be, and when, for this entire day?"

The Martian swallowed.

"And your people insisted that we don't change the arrival time, or anything else established at Ceres?"

Craig was asking the questions in a neutral tone, but being a good politician, he still seemed to sound very menacing. The Martian settled back in his seat and blinked rapidly, seemingly trying to figure out what to say.

Another of the Martian politicos seemed a little more ready to answer, "We kept some things the same, because if we changed major points the information would have leaked out again. But this column is made up of the President's personal guard. They're absolutely loyal. And we've changed the routes to the compound to decrease the chance of taking fire."

"Taking *fire?*" Craig's tone was no longer neutral.

The Martian nodded, then spoke as though the words tasted bad: "Yes, Minister. Taking *fire*. Some commands within the military may have been providing equipment to the rioters. They will be found and dealt with."

Craig didn't like that answer, "Oh, will they? How long have you been looking for them? Seems to me you have a big *fucking* problem keeping order in your own *capital*. Which begs the question why we should think any agreement we make with your President will hold water."

His tone was definitely not neutral anymore, and the Martians all fell silent as he raised his comm and called back to me.

"Well they changed the routes. That's comforting," Jim sounded about as happy as when he'd acknowledged the decoy vehicles. By now we were cruising through the streets of the Martian Capital Dome, staying low to the ground so we couldn't be shot down by shoulder lasers, or whatever kit the Martians had for bringing down armored vehicles from on high. Remember, a shot to the hoverpad and we'd be down like a fireball... staying low kept the APCs' heavily-armored sides between us and trouble.

And yet somehow I still wasn't comforted.

The additional background Casey was providing to Bort didn't help.

"I left the troupe after the ceasefire... I came here when the word got around that you'd be coming with the delegation," she explained, speaking quietly to Bort even though there was no way she couldn't be overheard in the small space. It felt somewhat strange listening in on their more private conversation, but under the circumstances it was necessary.

"Then a few weeks ago, the word started spreading on the streets about where you were going to land, and when, and even with who. They knew about the Empire politician, and the flag officers you'd be with. Not all the security... but still..." her voice trailed off, and she looked at us, still somewhat uncomfortable with our presence. "The movement is strong... they're terrified that the President-for-Life will strike a deal that slaves out the people, in return for him becoming a Lord in the Earth Empire."

Well, perhaps in spite of all the propaganda, President Godwin had problems with public opinion. Shocking.

"There are thousands of them... more. And as I say, there has to be some military support..."

Karen scratched her jaw at that, and then started drumming her fingers on the handle of her mag. We really were driving into a fun little situation. And with due respect to Rufus, we didn't have Charlie here to bail us out.

At least we were armed. And presumably, this column was loyal to the President, and would thus protect us... against a city ready to rise up?

"Commodore Pellew would like a word," Jim Hannigan lowered his comm. He'd been on with the squadron, filling them in on the situation, and evidently Wes wasn't liking what he was hearing.

I held up my own comm, and then patched in to Jim's frequency, "Hi Wes."

"I'm putting the squadron on standby alert, and rounding up every Brancher we have left to come get you out if necessary," his tone was sharp. He was in no mood for half-measures, which I quite appreciated.

"Thanks. It's a huge dome, so I doubt it'll be easy if it comes to that. And it might also mean war if you do. So kid gloves."

"Yep," was his simple answer. "I'll only open fire on the surface as a last resort."

It took me a second to realize he was kidding, and then I chuckled, "Yeah, I really hope it doesn't come to that."

"Indeed. Keep safe down there."

I shrugged, though he couldn't see it, "We'll do our best."

That was the end of the comm call, which was good timing, because as soon as we cut that link, the APC swerved hard, and then we heard a thud from outside.

The vehicle's intercom crackled, and a very calm and professional Martian-accented voice cut in, "Sorry sirs, one of the limos ahead of us was just shot down. We'll be accelerating to maximum speed."

I looked at Karen, and she looked at me, and the thought we seemed to share was 'what the hell did we just get ourselves into'?

What indeed...

CHAPTER THIRTEEN

CHARLIE, WE NEED YOU!

Karen and I had been making overt efforts to get back to the pre-war way of doing business, but one key ingredient was missing from that time in our lives: Charlie wasn't nearby, to rein us in. Don't get me wrong, Rufus was a properly elite Major, and more than capable of keeping us alive, but he wasn't the sort to stop us going off the handle.

More on that later. The point of this chapter isn't us, it's Charlie, because he was still working with Drew Alexander in the DCI office just down the street from the hospital.

And they were getting *nowhere*.

It had been more than a week, and by rights, Charlie figured he should have found something — some indication of the facilities where the blockheads were raping and murdering with seeming impunity. But none of the locations they were giving seemed to exist.

Though it pained him to admit, Charlie reckoned the bastards had come up with a very sophisticated method of renaming places... a code for locations, so that if they were ever overheard and people tried to investigate, this exact frustration would occur.

"We need a cipher of some sort," he sighed, sitting back in his chair in the office. He leaned back a little too far, then winced as a pain shot up his side.

"Come on, blockheads created this system. How hard can it be?" Drew Alexander prodded with a smile.

A cold stare from Charlie put a stop to that expression. Prolonged exposure hadn't helped him get used to the spook's mannerisms...

Two new reports had come in during the last week, and still nothing that gave them a reference point. They didn't even know what dome the blockheads were using for their 'sport'. Or if multiple domes were involved.

"Dammit," was all Charlie managed to mutter in reply.

He closed his eyes, and felt his brain start to swim. He'd been at it for three hours today — not that long by empirical standards, but he'd realized days prior that it was getting to the far end of his tolerance in his current physical state. Soon he'd need to break for rest.

"Getting sleepy?" Drew Alexander poked again, and this time the glare Charlie shot him shut him up completely.

Then he did something that Charlie found almost more maddening: he backed it down several notches, and said something intelligent.

"Well, maybe it's time for a new approach to try to crack this. We've been looking for a system that replaces the names of facilities, which might be based on a key location near their home base... that hasn't been working... so maybe we could try to look for references to comparative spatial coordinates, try to create a map and then overlay it with the Mercury domes. Want to give that a shot?"

One of the most annoying things about Drew Alexander was that he could switch from mashing buttons to making sense fairly seamlessly. He was suggesting that they go over all the reports again, and try different methods to unlock the blockhead code. It'd probably take a while, and a good deal of the work would have to be done by computer, so there'd be database searches to run, interpretation to do…

Stuff Charlie wasn't going to be clear-headed enough to work on now that he was hitting the three-hour wall.

"We'll start on that tomorrow," was his answer — as much approval as he was going to give the irritating spook.

Drew grinned, "I'll start inputting the variables so you'll have plenty to look at by the time you arrive."

Charlie nodded in grim satisfaction at the promise, and wondered whether the new approach would make much of a difference. Didn't matter; they had to try. Standing gingerly, our intrepid Major left the office.

Lia was sitting up in bed when Charlie returned to his room. She'd been reading through reports from the Protectorate, and prepping some messages to her advisors there, regarding the eventual announcement of her father's death, and her impending succession.

It wasn't light material, nor easy, but she was handling it very well indeed — better than any normal person could expect to. But then, as we know, Lia is by no means normal.

Charlie's arrival interrupted her work, and as she lowered the pad she was working on, she instantly read the tired, rather frustrated look on his face, "Still nothing?"

He shook his head and limped to his bed with the help of his cane, then eased back to perch on the side of it.

"Well, I suppose if it was straightforward, Shore Patrol would have been able to do it without you," she offered gently, and the comment — which could have been taken the wrong way — simply drew a nod from my friend.

A deep sigh came next, and he rubbed his forehead with his free hand, "Alexander's got some ideas for a new angle to follow starting tomorrow… different ways to try to crack the code. Hopefully that'll get us somewhere… but I feel like I'm missing something. Head's just not as clear as I need it to be."

A slight frown crossed Lia's brow, and she laid her pad on the tray beside her bed, "Well you were blown to pieces not long ago."

Charlie winced and shook his head, "No, that was the rest of the squad. I was just shredded."

Realizing her quip was a bit too close to home, Lia shook her head, "Sorry. But you're doing good work instead of just convalescing, and that counts for something."

She was right, and Charlie knew his fatigue was contributing to his frustration as much as anything else, so he took a deep breath and slid further back onto his bed. Lia started to pick up her pad again, shaking her head, "I'm going to need your help with the arrangements for the transition. I think I've got them straight… but I could use a second opinion."

Charlie blinked a few times, hoping it would clear his mind, but it didn't really. He was hearing names of places that sounded oddly familiar but not at all tracking through his thoughts, and it was still going nowhere.

"I'll need to wait until I can clear my head more," he said quietly, and Lia nodded.

"Yep, I know... oh, quick, come make out with me!"

That one got Charlie's eyes to open abruptly, and Lia was looking at him, one hand very subtly pointing towards the door. The nurses were outside, and would be looking in on them any moment now — they needed to continue planting the seeds about their relationship, for the rumor mill.

So he had to do his part towards that end.

As difficult jobs went, that one didn't qualify, so he slid off his mattress, crossed the gap to Lia's bed, and did as he was told. The strange names continued to float through his mind...

CHAPTER FOURTEEN

GAUNTLET

The APC didn't have windows, so there was no way for any of us to know what was going on outside its armored sides, except when the driver piped in over the intercom to provide an update.

It was not fun.

We hurtled through the Martian Capital Dome, and occasionally we heard the hums of lasers or mags firing outside, though the sounds were never contextualized for us. At sharp corners, we'd all sway into each other, and then wear slightly-too-relaxed expressions as we tried not to look as unsettled as we really were.

It wasn't even like we could take comfort in having Special Branchers at the wheel — at least with them, you'd know that you had the best people driving. But we didn't even know if the Martian drivers were regular troopers or Commandos...

Then our vehicle slammed to a halt. It was sudden stop, and we all slid towards the front of the vehicle, meaning Bort half-crushed Casey, and I squeezed Karen into the wall. It might have been comical, but none of us were in that sort of mood, and just as we started to right ourselves, our friendly driver patched in over the intercom again.

"We're down the main boulevard from the government compound, but there is quite a crowd here. This next part may get violent."

I can't describe how comforting those words were.

Looking down at Eugene, Jim, and Shelby, I drew my sidearm, "Just in case. Provided we don't all go down in a ball of flame."

"Remind me never to go on a road trip with you," Jim drew his own weapon, and I actually laughed.

Bort did too, and then he leaned across the aisle, "That looks like an arms box behind you, could you pull out a couple of pistols?"

I turned in my seat, saw there was a case built into the wall behind my head, and then cracked it open. Sure enough, four Martian EM pistols were inside, so I pulled out two and handed them over, while Karen shut the lid behind me.

As soon as Bort had them in hand, we lurched violently again, and the droning hum of the engine got powerfully loud.

"Here we go," Karen said quietly, and we all settled into our seated positions as best we could (which wasn't very well, because of the bench configuration).

The next five minutes were... well, odd. It was like sensory deprivation — like being in the middle of a huge fight with all your bridge screens dark, and no source of information about what's going on outside your hull. Karen later said it reminded her of her experience aboard *Lady Grace* during the Clash — after the ship had been totally disabled.

Everything we heard through the hull... from the hum of a weapon to the dull thud of what might have been an explosion… we tried to figure out what it meant, without looking too worried about it. It was agonizing for all of us. We had no control over anything, and no information about what the threats were.

Was there a mob here with weapons, or torches? Or was there no one here, and had some of the military turned against the government and come out to stop us? Were we looking at a civil war in the making, or was this all going to settle down?

What the hell were we doing here in the first place?

If it was maddening for us Naval-types, owing to our control-freakishness, then it was murder for Rufus Chang. It felt very wrong having someone else do his fighting for him, particularly when that someone was a Martian of questionable ability.

The curse of being a Special Brancher like our elite Major Chang is that you know all too well how vulnerable things really are. As soon as he'd seen our convoy, the first thing that had gone through his head — purely out of instinct — was a list of the top three ways he'd bring it down. Or top ten ways, perhaps… because there were plenty.

Not being able to watch for any of the threats that might lead to one of these ten modes of destruction was unpleasant, and it was worse for him because he could immediately identify just about all the sounds he heard — after all his time on Mercury, he was pretty familiar with the noises Martian ground weapons made.

He knew for certain that someone in the Martian military had left the armory unlocked, accidentally on purpose.

And apparently the mob knew how to use many of the toys.

Fortunately, they didn't know how to use them very well… so far.

Keeping his sidearm in hand, then, Rufus controlled his breathing, and waited to get out of the tin can that was ferrying him to this diplomatic meeting.

The third APC was alive with conversation, because Craig B. Macdonald wasn't enjoying his ride, and because he had Martian politicos to grill about the situation.

"So we're not actually talking about a civil war?" was his most pointed question, and the pale Martians shook their heads simultaneously.

"The balance of the Navy remains on our side, so there can't be a civil war… it's just unrest…" one of them replied, apparently thinking that distinction would be reassuring.

"Seems like a lot of unrest," Craig shot back. "They're *shooting* at us."

"They'll be brought to heel," the more militant-seeming politico said sharply, and Craig frowned for a couple of reasons — he didn't like the idea of people being 'brought to heel', and he also doubted the Martians could pull it off if they tried.

Perhaps they could, but sitting in the back of an APC that was apparently taking fire, his confidence in the Martian ability to maintain order was at a rather low ebb.

"Well, I won't allow my Prime Minister to attend any meetings unless this dome is secure. Unless you're looking to start another war… which, actually, I'm pretty sure your people have done enough to make happen, if we weren't in a reasonable mood."

That was political hardball from a Scotsman who knew how to play the game, and the Martian politicos again shrank slightly. They were bargaining from a position of weakness in the first place, and now their position was being eroded further by their own people.

To quote a famous politico who I won't name: they seriously needed to get their shit together.

There was no mistaking the sound of the tank crashing. Ours was the last APC in line, so when the rearguard tank went nose-first into the street, the grating metal sounds shot through us, generating the sort of shivers you hate to have racing up and down your spine.

Then our vehicle was buffeted — not too badly, but enough for us to figure we'd taken some sort of hit. We accelerated, and then we went up, and then we dropped hard onto the ground. No idea what we'd landed on, where or why, but we shared glances that basically said 'This'll end well.'

My exact words were actually somewhat different: "This will end poorly."

The rear hatch began to open without warning, and we were all instantly on our feet, mags ready in case we'd dropped into the middle of a riot. Our possible fates if that was the case struck me harshly all of a sudden — being killed by a mob, probably tortured and burned... that would not be the sort of end I'd been looking for when I got into this business.

To put it mildly.

But as the door lowered, we saw an empty green lawn, and a number of buildings beyond it — some near, some quite far away.

"We had to crash-land on one of the lawns of the government compound. We're behind the fence, and should be safe."

That report came late from our friendly Martian pilot — but at least he remembered to tell us. With the door open, the sounds of the mob outside became louder, only to be drowned out by the hum as the other APCs and the remaining tank landed near us. Seemed they were going to keep us all together... out in the middle of nowhere on some lawn of the government compound.

Shelby and Eugene edged up to the door with mags ready, then peeked out around the frame.

"We're about twenty meters from the fence..." our Helm and Navigation Officer observed with a frown. "There aren't many troopers guarding it."

"Must be energized," Bort frowned too. He had one arm around Casey, and one of his EM pistols in his free hand. The second Martian sidearm was dangling precariously from Casey's fingers — she clearly hadn't had occasion to use one before.

"Let's get out for now..." Karen stepped around me, her mag nestled comfortably into her right hand, where it had done much work in years past. She descended the ramp first, looking immediately towards the fence.

Her eyebrows shot up again at the sight, "That's... a big welcoming committee."

We all filed out of the vehicle behind her, and as I got a look at the street, I had to agree. It was a solid mass of people, with more protest signs, burning effigies, and chants and cries.

And obviously some of them had to be armed.

"We better get inside a building... some place with heavy doors," I said distantly, and with nods of agreement, we all turned towards the other APCs, which were now unloading onto the lawn.

The Martian drivers were forming up as an escort, which wasn't terribly comforting, but I was glad to see the Foreign Minister out safely, and Rufus and his officers ready to step in if things went even more pear shaped.

"That's the main building," one of the Martian politicos pointed to a structure far in the distance, perhaps a kilometer away. It looked impressive enough, but that was quite a walk...

"Can't we just re-board and hover up to it?" Craig put the question to the Martian before I could, and the man shook his head.

"Restricted air space beyond 300 meters. We'd be shot down by the sentry guns."

I'm not sure who in our party looked more disbelieving at that statement, but this time it was me with the first verbal reaction, "And you don't think you could get a pass for us, owing to the fact that we're the *peace envoy* from the *Empire*?"

It wasn't a good day for these Martian politicians' blood pressures, because the one I'd pointed that question at looked awfully uncomfortable as he shook his head, "Under the current situation, the guns have been hard-wired to full defense mode. In case someone in the military betrays the President-for-Life and tries to shut them down."

Again we were overcome by stunned silence.

Until Craig, whose diplomatic patience was long gone, asked again: "You're certain your government is in a position to negotiate peace on behalf of the people of this fucking rock?"

"Oh yes..."

"For fuck's sakes," Craig turned away from the Martians and strode up to Karen, Bort and me. "Wish we could just evacuate. But you understand we can't yet?"

I nodded. The Martians could be right — they could get control of this situation yet, and then we had to make sure we didn't do anything to jeopardize the peace. We had to be understanding and tolerant, because we couldn't risk making a mistake that would send us back into hostilities.

Technically, we were all expendable to that end... though I knew I'd draw the line at losing people to an angry mob. If that was the sacrifice demanded of us, I'd shoot back first, and I got the sense Craig would too.

For now, though, there was an electrified fence between us and the riot, so we'd just have a brisk walk to the central compound of a paranoid President-for-Life. And then negotiations.

We'd be chatting while Mars burned.

Fun.

With a grunt, Craig started walking towards the building, and that meant we all started to follow. Getting back to the ridiculous sentry guns being wired to 'KILL' mode, Karen asked an innocent question: "So what if the President needs to escape by air? Wouldn't the guns shoot his car down?"

One of the politicos looked back at us with a sour face, "Where would he go? There is no escape. This is the best-protected fortress on Mars."

He just had to say that out loud.

Because almost the very second he spoke, Rufus recognized the sound of a Martian explosive, the shockwave of which knocked us all flat on the grass. Being the elite Special Branch Major, though, he was first back to his feet, and the first to see the GIANT HOLE (apologies for the emphasis) the rioters had blown in the government compound's fence.

When I managed to roll over and look back that way, I swore and shook my head.

Karen pushed herself up into a crouch beside me, and looking at the gap in the barrier, she let out a breath, "Honestly?"

"Really," was my answer.

"What's the closest building?" Rufus demanded coolly, and one of the Martian troopers assigned as our escort pointed to a nearby structure. Looked fairly big, probably had heavy doors.

As the mob started pushing through the breach, and rapidly overwhelmed the unfortunate guards who were there to stop them, Rufus straightened up, "Let's go."

Go we would. The rioters were after us. Because — and this should be no surprise — the Martian government and society couldn't keep its shit together.

Lucky us.

Chapter Fifteen

Overhead

Wes was pacing around his bridge aboard *Nova Scotia*, waiting to hear from us. After we'd warned him about the mob out in the street, he'd ordered every enhanced camera in the squadron to start pointing down at Mars, and thanks to the transparent dome structure, he was indeed able to see the streets of the Capital.

It was just difficult to make sense of what he saw, because we had no reference maps. His Sensors and Communications Officer had managed to tie the coordinates being pinged out by our comms to a line of vehicles that could be seen by the cameras, but it was by no means the detailed sort of tracking he'd have preferred.

Still, he was able to watch that escort tank taking a dive, and he'd just about ordered an assault landing when it did. But none of our comm signatures went down with the craft, so he waited, and sure enough, our APCs landed on the extreme perimeter of the government compound, and we stepped out.

That was a relief for Commodore Pellew.

Then he saw the plume of the explosion against the fence, and shook his head before looking up at the skippers on Battlelink, "Stand by all volunteers for landing."

The landing force he'd arranged — fourteen Special Branchers from six different ships, along with seventy SF and volunteers from seven different ships — wouldn't have much chance of evacuating us given the size and the organization of the mobs... but it felt as though he had to try. This situation was so ridiculous that it verged on the surreal — how could the Martians, who we'd seen to have such an iron grip on their society, lose it all so completely when it mattered most?

Well, like I've said, their propaganda had been too good for too long... and that raised a question in Wes' mind: if the volunteer landing force went down, would they intimidate people, or provoke an even more violent reaction?

Could go either way.

Could go *both* ways.

There were few ways this could end well... and dammit, even if it *did* end well, the question we had to ask next was what this all meant for the coming convention. We had to be careful not to sabotage negotiations with the Martian government...

"Signal coming in... the Martian flagship, I think," *Nova Scotia's* Sensors and Communications Officer interrupted Wes' musing, and he looked up.

"Oh good," he said, then nodded to one of the bridge's blank screens.

A buffering screen popped up, and again it took time to load as our OS XX tried to work with their Vantage operating system. After that delay, a typical-seeming Martian Admiral appeared.

"I am Admiral Gustav Morencie."

That was all he said — no follow-up to the introduction of his name. Wes just stared at him for a moment, and when he realized the Martian wasn't going to add anything, he revealed that his patience was thinning.

"And you're filling one of my bridge screens why?"

Not the most diplomatic question, but under the circumstances, I think it was pretty fair.

The Martian looked ruffled, but he retained a rather disdainful calm, "I can assure you that loyal marine troopers will be dispatched to secure your officers."

Wes stared at the Admiral for a second, and then another second. Then he voiced the question that immediately came to mind: "What do you mean *will be*? Haven't they been sent out yet?"

Admiral Morencie seemed to look down his nose at our Commodore Pellew, which I don't need to tell you is highly rude, and not a terribly good idea. His answer was sour, "Communication is difficult at the moment, but the rabble will shortly be sorted."

"Sorted? The rabble that some of your people have evidently been supporting will soon be sorted?" Wes took a step towards the viewfinder, so he'd get a bit bigger on Morencie's screen. "Now, with all due respect, you're going to get this situation under control, or I'll personally call back to Earth and alert them to the fact that our diplomatic envoy has been attacked. When they get that news, they'll still come here, but the four *Bonaventure*-class battleships that wiped out your *Tharsis* Squadron won't be cruising in with bright running lights in parade formation. They'll blow what's left of your home fleet out of space. Get. This. *Sorted.*"

I think you can tell how Wes was feeling just now — he wasn't in a charitable state of mind.

And he was right, there were grounds to write off the peace talks because of this needless drama. But we wanted peace almost as much as the Martians did, so he knew this was a mostly-empty threat.

Admiral Morencie didn't know. He was probably upset at getting told off by a 'mere' Commodore, but instead of protesting, he recognized his weak position, sniffed, and killed the link.

Captain Roslind Young was on *Nova Scotia's* bridge, so as that happened she crossed to Wes' side and scratched her cheek gingerly, "You, um, let him have it."

"Yes I did," Wes nodded, folding his arms. "He damned well better do something about it too."

Rozy decided not to pursue the conversation, moving away instead.

"You did notice that his flagship is the last of the *Tharsises*, right?" Andrea Kiley put the question to Wes over Battlelink, and he looked up at her with a frown.

"I did. That significant?"

Andrea looked genuinely amused at Wes' seeming fearlessness before an enemy with almost-war-winning firepower at his disposal.

"I wouldn't worry, Captain Kiley," Bruce Arama inserted himself into the exchange. "We got away from three of them before the Forge. As long as you're willing to run, they can't catch you."

The Kiwi Commander was saying that with a bit more confidence than he actually felt, but he did have a valid point — he and his ship had escaped that first battle, when

Bort's squadron had surprised Shauna Cass. He knew better than the rest of us how to get away from the beasts.

And this time, too, there was only one — *Ascraeus Mons*.

Of course, no one should have been thinking about trading fire with the Martian, since we were trying to negotiate peace… but old habits die hard.

Wes remained grim, watching on the main screen as the tiny figures of the diplomatic envoy hurried across the lawn towards a large building. He could see the bolts of mag fire lancing from our group towards the fence as we went, and he hoped we'd all find shelter safely.

And that the Martians would do as they promised, and sort out this mess…

CHAPTER SIXTEEN

HOLE UP

"It's been a while since I've had to barricade a door with furniture," I said (perhaps groaned) as I straightened up. I'd just finished pushing a desk in front of the entrance to the building we'd entered, and Karen smiled as she passed behind me, heading for a nearby window.

"Just like old times," was her answer, and she was right.

We'd run from some pirate hit squads in the old days, and holed up in buildings a lot less solid-seeming than the one we now occupied. This Martian construct was made of the same salmon-colored concrete that seemed common in the Capital Dome, and its windows and doors did look as though they were built to withstand a riot.

Though since we knew the mob was armed, we weren't sure how well the place would handle punishment.

Clearly, the desk I'd just pushed up against the back door would make it immune to explosives…

"This is the Groundskeeping Central Command," the head Martian guard, whose name I never got, announced as he passed through the corridor behind us.

He was gone again as soon as he finished speaking — he and his shooters were checking each office within the building for windows, while Rufus was preparing the main entrance and lobby to receive.

Karen and I had volunteered to secure the back door, and now that we'd blocked it with the desk, and also locked it, we were confident we'd done all we could.

Well, not really, but there wasn't much else to do.

For a groundskeeping building, it had to be said that this one seemed rather elaborate. It appeared to be two stories, the bottom one filled with offices and the top one presumably the same. There was also a huge garage attached to one side, which Eugene and his three guards were seeing to.

Seemed we had a pretty fancy place to hole up.

But holing up in the face of this sort of mob was just not wise. There were thousands of them, and including our Martian protectors, there were fewer than forty of us. Not a good balance.

"So, we're in an outbuilding of the government compound," Karen came to a stop beside me, her mag still in hand. "Chances that there are secret tunnels running from here to the central building?"

"There must be," I agreed.

Politicos always liked to have escape tunnels… surely whoever had designed the oversized palace grounds would have had some installed.

Turning back towards the lobby, we headed up the corridor and arrived in time to see Rufus straightening up and dusting off his hands. He'd planted something between the inner and outer doors of the main entranceway, and as he turned back to us with a smile, I knew it had to be something that went boom.

"Just a really powerful magbang," he assured me as he stepped inside. Then he looked past me at Clarissa Hutchinson, "Any luck locking this place down?"

Wolf's new Special Branch Captain was working at what had been the security desk, with the Martian guard who usually manned the post standing aside with a miffed expression. He'd been the only person in the building when we burst in (no idea where the staff were — maybe they were rioting too) and he wasn't exactly taking the situation in stride.

Hutchinson was following instinct and a few directions from one of our convoy guards, and after a brief delay she nodded. Almost instantly, a 'thunk' sound resonated through the structure, and we presumed that it meant everything was locking down.

"We're at atmospheric breach alert... nothing will open without an alarm sounding, or the internal pressure door to that section closing. But we're still thin-skinned... this may only buy us time," the Captain came to her feet, then waved for the Martian to resume his station.

I don't think he liked getting direction from a woman, but we all ignored his unpleasant expression. The building was now locked down, but it still wasn't armored. One thing at a time...

Rufus turned to me, "Best we can do, until we find a way out of here."

"Good... see if you can convince one of the Martians to tell us where the secret tunnels to the main building are."

With a smile, Rufus started working on that problem.

Bort found an office with no window, then hurried inside with Casey. She was still holding precariously onto the pistol he'd pressed into her hands, but as soon as she had the chance she dropped it on the desk.

"I... what should we do?"

She wasn't used to situations like this. Karen and I could play cavalier, but Casey was a professional dancer. No artist of her variety, male or female, from the Empire or the Imperium, could be expected to know what to do when chased by a mob.

Bort wasn't fully prepared for it either, though he'd slipped easily into combat-commander mode, and was calm and collected.

"We'll wait for the President's Guards to close down that breach, then go to the central compound. After this... well, it may not be safe for us here. I think we may be able to stay with the delegation aboard *Wolf* for the time being..."

He still wasn't sure about that last part, but it was the best option he could think of. It was clear the military on the ground was either divided or losing control, and a mob that was happy enough to shoot at a legitimate Imperium convoy probably wouldn't have any problem drawing and quartering a man like Bort.

So sleeping in orbit could be wise for his health... and now for Casey's, since she'd been spotted with him.

"With these people?"

It took him a moment to register her question, and its meaning — like so many, including his late friend Art O'Thomson, Casey still thought fairly certainly that Defcoms were bad. Sure, the government might have exaggerated some of our horrific penchants… but by and large, there had to be enough truth in the claims to mean we were real monsters, right? We were an Empire, after all — those are never good, even when their founding Articles insist upon equal rights for all.

Actually, I think by Martian standards, that's one of the things that *made* us evil. But anyway…

Bort took both Casey's slim hands in his free one, "They're not what you think. I promise. These ones in particular."

Casey Flynnboldak looked distressed, but she nodded slowly, deciding for the moment to accept Bort's judgment. He clearly had spent more time with us and nothing seemed off about him. She'd expected months in Defense Command custody to have left deep marks on him. She'd been prepared for him to be bitter, wounded, and perhaps broken.

But he was the same. Over-earnest, rather unsophisticated, and very powerful in his sincerity. She'd missed him as much as he'd missed her… she just hoped the mob didn't tear them both to pieces before they got to spend proper time together.

"I should go out there… we'll need every shooter to secure this place until help arrives," Bort said distantly.

"Do you have to leave? I'm no good with that," Casey nodded to the weapon on the desk, and Bort looked at it, then at her, and then at the doorway.

"Just… hang on a second…" he headed to the door, then leaned out and looked to the left. Shelby McLaws was passing from one office to the next, so he called to her.

She stopped, then moved down the hall to stand facing the Asteroid Admiral, "Sir?"

"Lieutenant, would you be able to stay here, and assist Casey… in defense of this part of the building?"

Shelby took one look at the Martian dancer, and Bort's meaning was immediately clear. To quote our southern belle Helm and Navigation Officer: "Miss Flynnboldak was genteel and elegant, but fragile. Rather like a flower. Not trained for a combat situation."

"I'll take good care of her, sir. Please let Commander Hannigan, Commodore McMaster, or Admiral Barron know of my whereabouts."

Bort nodded his thanks, then locked eyes with Casey one more time before departing. She watched him go with a lump in her throat — she feared he'd get killed, though that in itself was a feeling she was used to suppressing. As much as she hated the stereotype of the Martian wife sitting at home, fearing for her warrior husband, Casey did worry about Bort.

But here was a Defense Command woman in her company, and damned if she'd show any weakness before Shelby McLaws. To her later shame, Casey believed that Shelby had likely earned her position by sleeping her way there, and charming every man around her.

Now, Shelby's a perfectly charming woman, but I very much doubt any man on *Wolf* had captured her interest. Nevertheless, there was awkward silence between the two for a time. And considering Shelby's general ease in dealing with people, that's saying something.

+++

There was a cramped boardroom within the groundskeeping building, and there we found Craig B. Macdonald and the Martian politicos. Craig's staffers were also present, though no DC or Martian guards were there when Karen and I arrived.

"Ah, good," Craig was standing on one side of the table, glaring down at the Martians who were seated opposite him. "We secured here?"

I glanced at Karen, and we both nodded.

"Best we can be. The mob hasn't come up with anything to break in with yet, but I'm sure they will soon. This isn't much of a bunker," I answered.

Karen picked up right after, "We were hoping one of these gentlemen could show us the secret passages to the compound."

Those words earned her open-mouthed stares, and Craig grinned at the reaction, "Don't worry, we won't tell anyone."

The politicos got flustered, except for that same Martian who'd been cool and short about the fate of the protesters when Craig had been asking about them back in the APC. He snorted and shook his head, "There are no tunnels to the *groundskeeping* building. We're outside the inner cordon."

He said that with enough conviction for Karen and I both to think he might actually mean it, though we'd still need more convincing.

"The inner cordon?" Karen moved closer to him, turning her mag slightly in her hand. I don't think she was intentionally trying to look menacing, the gesture just happened to come across that way.

"Yes, where the sentry guns would have shot us down. A radius of one kilometer from the central building. Everything inside that radius is strongly protected, and the tunnels are there. But out here, this is the killing field."

Killing field. In fortification terms, we might have called it a 'zone of fire', to be more polite... but I immediately started piecing together what this Martian was saying.

This government compound was a fortress, with the main building housing the President at the center. There was probably an inner ring of secure buildings, all of them linked by tunnels, and another ring of defenses — sentry guns, and bunkers — beyond that. We were outside all of those important areas, in a building that was part of the buffer zone — ultimately useless land separating the important stuff from the city beyond.

If there was ever an attack on the Capital Dome, and troops tried to storm the main building, this area (including the groundskeeping building) could be flattened, so there'd be no cover for advancing troops.

A killing field.

"So you landed all of us outside the protection of your inner perimeter?" I asked sharply, and the generally-defiant politico glared at me.

"Like I said, the inner perimeter is fully activated. Nothing flies over the base without getting shot down. *Nothing.*"

Craig shook his head and then reached inside his jacket, drawing his compact MAG-11 and looking it over, "Can someone show me how to make sure the cell is charged? I think I might need it."

The Martian politicos looked aghast that the Foreign Minister was armed (and perhaps fearful that he was going to shoot them, though that wasn't Craig's intention).

Karen went over to demonstrate the weapon to him and his staff, while I shook my head and slid my own mag into its holster on my hip.

"Some place you guys have here," I drew my comm and started calling *Nova Scotia*, so I could fill Wes in. "So what do you suggest now?"

"We wait for the Presidential Guard to clear the breach, then we'll be taken to the central building to make arrangements for the convention," the same Martian spoke again.

I smiled in the way you smile at someone you really want to smack, but can't, "Looking forward to it."

In case you missed it, I was being sarcastic. I wasn't looking forward to it at all.

Shocking.

CHAPTER SEVENTEEN

SIEGE

Because we'd locked down the building as if there was an atmospheric breach in the Capital Dome, everything about our salmon-colored concrete bunker was air tight. I mention this not because oxygen was a concern — the building had a big filtering plant for atmospheric emergencies, so we were okay for air. No, this was significant because it meant we could hear absolutely nothing from the mob that encircled the building outside.

That was weird again — in some ways worse than being cooped up in the back of the APCs. We couldn't hear *anything*. But we could watch.

"I think he's saying something unpleasant," Karen nodded at one of the ringleaders who was standing above the protesters to the south of us. He was either quite tall, or he was standing on a box... and he was definitely whipping the people around him into a furious state.

"That's their ringleader," one of the Martian politicos was at another window just across the lobby from us, and he shook his head. "The gall of the man, to bring his rabble here."

"Awfully big 'rabble,'" Jim Hannigan observed dryly, so none of the rest of us had to.

"Germaine Blovuspaco," the politco seemed to ignore Jim's retort... instead reverently saying those two words, which at first I didn't realize were supposed to form a name.

Craig Macdonald was standing further back in the lobby, looking at some messages on his comm, "That his name?"

The Martian nodded, and then it actually registered.

Germaine Blovuspaco.

I believe the appropriate thing for me to say now is 'do your own joke.'

If I actually stopped at that point, there in the lobby, to unravel the ridiculousness of everything that was happening, I would have just thrown my hands up in the air and yelled 'done'. What the hell were the Martians thinking?

Well, to be fair, it was hard to figure out exactly which Martians to blame for this. If I were in Germaine's shoes, maybe I'd have been equally ready to derail a peace process, believing that Defense Command was going to come in and slave me out.

So the blame was then to go to the Martian government, who richly deserved a good beating for having the gall to start this war in the first place... and for failing to keep control of the situation when our diplomatic mission arrived.

But could I blame the President-for-Life for not sweeping the streets of people? The only way he could have done it was by force, and then civilians would have been killed. Could I blame him for *not* killing his own people?

It all would have made my head hurt, had I stopped to think about it then. Fortunately, I was too caught up in the very real problems we were facing: there were thousands of people outside the walls of a groundskeeping building who wanted us either gone, or dead, or both. I had twenty people under my charge, including the Foreign Minister of the Empire, and even if I had enough firepower to sweep the mob aside, doing so might jeopardize the peace.

I had no bloody clue what to do, so I was very much hoping the Martians were going to come through with those promised troops, to make the decision for me.

"When should we expect the President's Guards to get here?" Karen approached the Martian politico who'd identified Germaine Blovuspaco, and his answer was harried.

"Soon. I'm sure they'll be here soon."

I just about started laughing. It was all so absurd. How the *hell* had they gotten this so wrong? How had these *bastards* been able to nearly beat us in a war?

Because during that war, the mob outside and the politicos inside had all been on the same team. Now that they were apart, they looked daft. Together, they'd been more of a challenge...

Bort McWebsbert came up alongside me with a frown, then gripped his jaw with his right hand while his pistol remained firmly in the grip of his left one.

"They should have been here by now," he said quietly enough that only I could hear him. I glanced at the big Asteroid Admiral, and as our stares met he shook his head once. "It's been half an hour. No way it takes that long... if the Guards are following orders."

Mutiny? Great. Just great.

I nodded in the direction of the corridor behind the lobby, and Bort and I left the windows to drift that way. As we got out of earshot of the Martian politicians, the Asteroid Admiral shook his head again, "Presidential Guard is supposed to be good. So either they're deployed somewhere else, or they're not accepting orders to break up the mob."

It was the first useful 'inside' assessment of the situation I'd gotten, and no surprise it was coming from Bort.

"Think the President is still in control?"

Bort sighed and shrugged, "Don't know. I can't imagine they'd go to all this trouble to bring us in if he wasn't. If radicals had control, they'd have turned us over to the mob at the landing bay. Maybe the guards are just refusing to open fire on civilian protestors."

My mouth thinned to a line, and I nodded. I actually couldn't blame the bastards, if that was their motivation. Perhaps the President's personal troops were telling him that they'd only open fire on Blovuspaco's rioters if they charged the inner perimeter... that would be different than coming out to collect a bunch of Defcom scum.

Complicated and ridiculous.

"So if that's the case, we're on our own?" I asked distantly, and Bort's eyebrows went up.

"Maybe. But if I know Godwin... well, the Grand Admiral Staff will still be loyal. They're always loyal. And they'll have marines aboard ship who would do the job. It'll just take time for them to get down here. I wouldn't be surprised if they're already on their way."

Loyal marines, to shoot up the crowd. Useful for us, and yet unthinkable.

"Jesus. I hate diplomacy," I muttered, then drew my comm and opened the link to *Nova Scotia*.

Wes came onto the line with no delay, "Everything still okay down there?"

"For now. Bort thinks the President's Guards might be refusing to break up the riot. Any sign that the Martian fleet is planning to send down reinforcements?"

There was a pause, then an answer, "Nothing conclusive on our scopes, but we'll call you if small craft start landing. Their Admiral... Morencie, I think... did say help would be sent."

Good news and bad news at the same time.

Bort's expression twisted at the mention of Morencie's name, and he explained the reaction: "There'll be troops coming. Morencie's married to Godwin's sister."

"Charming," was my answer.

For a few seconds, we all fell silent. Then I sighed, "Alright, we'll see if we can find a way out of here before the marines come down. But if not... we'll hold out."

Wes' reply couldn't have been more appropriate, "This is pretty bad."

"You're very right," I said, and then we cut the link.

Re-holstering my comm, I shook my head and then looked at Bort, "You think the politicos are right? No tunnels from here to the other buildings?"

The Asteroid-born Admiral frowned thoughtfully, then shook his head, "I don't know. I can take a couple of the escort troopers down to the basement and have a look, if you don't mind."

The tacked-on quasi-request for permission struck me as funny, and I did grin at it, "No need to request permission, they aren't my command. And don't you outrank me?"

Bort snorted a laugh, "Was wondering when you were going to figure that out, Rear Admiral."

"Yeah, just don't let it go to your head. Have a look and let me know."

Nodding, Bort headed back for the lobby. I started to do the same, but I caught sight of two women in an office out of the corner of my eye — Shelby and Casey. Our Helm and Navigation Officer was on her comm, replying to messages from Andrea about our location and the layout of the building. Casey was just staring at me... not maliciously, or curiously. It was a heavy stare, and I had no idea what it meant.

Didn't matter anyway.

Karen stepped up in front of me before I could move towards the lobby, and as she stopped she smiled in the way she smiles when she's not really smiling on the inside. Oof, bad sentence... what I mean is she was masking frustration with a pleasant expression.

"I think they've put together a battering ram. And they might even light it on fire."

I stared at Karen for a few seconds, and her oh-so-fake smile widened, narrowing her eyes, "Oh yes. We're officially in a goddamned castle siege with a bunch of Martians led by some guy named Germaine *Blovuspaco*. I'm not keeping very cool at the moment."

That last sentence wasn't meant to be funny, and I certainly didn't take it to be amusing. Karen was getting frustrated, perhaps angry, and you know how that sort of thing can end. Spike through the ears and such.

Our good humor of earlier in the day was turning very dark, very quickly. And why shouldn't it be? This first diplomatic envoy was turning into a gong show, and we didn't even know quite who to blame.

The thudding on the main lobby door started a moment later.

CHAPTER EIGHTEEN

MEANWHILE, A WEEK AWAY

John Fiora was sitting in the office adjacent to his cabin aboard *Bonaventure* when the message arrived. Our mighty flagship had just checked in with one of the communications ships between Earth and Mars, and a quick message from Wes Pellew had been waiting for him.

He was expecting — perhaps just hoping — for a routine check-in to say that all was well, but of course, it wasn't that.

"Good day, sir. Just wanted to report that we've had a snag here… seems the Martian people are rising up against their government because it's negotiating with hedonistic murdering Defcoms. We only found out about this when the mobs of protesters started attacking the Foreign Minister's convoy in the Martian Capital Dome. The entire landing party is isolated and holed up in a building on the Martian government compound. Martian marines will reportedly clear the situation soon… but it could remain complicated. Will update when I have more information."

As the image of Wes froze at the end of that report, John found that his mind was blank. He sat back in his chair with his eyebrows right up, and dropped the pad he'd been working on.

When thoughts did eventually start working their way through his brain, the first line he recalls was 'What the hell?'

After a few moments of shock, he reached across his desk to the comm button and called the bridge. Captain Lennox Williams had the watch, so the Sensors and Communications Officer put him on the line.

"What's the story, boss?" Lennox was upbeat — he had no reason not to be.

"Establish Battlelink with all group commanders, and inform the Prime Minister's staff that I'll be over to see him shortly."

That chilled Lennox's good spirits almost instantly, "Aye sir."

As the line cut, John got to his feet. There was rioting on Mars? The last time Defense Command had been anywhere near riots on Mars, the red planet ended up declaring its independence. How much would this complicate matters?

He had no idea, so he went to find the Prime Minister.

Mik had no interest in spending time with the Emperor, but it seemed necessary that he himself deliver the news that had been passed on from *Bonaventure*. If the Commodore commanding *Ark Royal* showed any reluctance about informing Luther Gregory III of the troubles on Mars, it might look like Defense Command was trying to hide something.

So once again, Mik was feeling oh-so-fortunate to be in this babysitting job.

"Your audience with the Emperor is granted," one of Luther Gregory's staff… retainers… whatever the Emperor's henchmen were called… waved Mik from the outer waiting room in *Ark Royal's* posh VIP quarters. Following the waved hand, the elite Commodore stepped through an open door into the inner waiting room, and then he was directed straight through another door into the outer receiving chamber.

Inside the brightly-polished room, Luther Gregory was sitting neatly on an ornate throne... well, ornate by shipboard standards. Aside from two guards, he was alone, suggesting to Mik that he'd come to the receiving room explicitly for this meeting.

"Good day, Highness," Mik nodded, only realizing after he spoke that he wasn't properly following protocol. The Emperor didn't seem to care.

"You have word of Mars?" the man asked distantly.

Mik nodded, "Indeed, your Eminence. The people are protesting the planned peace talks. The Martian government believes it can regain control of the situation, but our contingent, including the Foreign Minister, Admiral Barron, and Commodore McMaster, is currently being isolated in a building on their government compound."

Luther Gregory's eyebrows went up at that report, and then the corners of his mouth turned down slightly in disdain, "Your colleagues are so desperate for war that they're trying to disrupt our negotiations? It is well that I am going to Mars myself."

That... was one interpretation. Mik was honestly surprised by it — unsure whether he'd failed to be clear, or if the Emperor had misinterpreted, or if the man was blatantly and transparently lying to test Mik. Or if Luther Gregory III was just fucking clueless.

"Based on the information I have, our people knew nothing about the troubles until they were swept up in them, your Highness. They're not disrupting anything."

Pushing back did seem risky to Mik, but he wasn't about to bend before the Emperor either, just in case this was some sort of test.

Shaking his head, Luther Gregory smiled, "Perhaps. Perhaps you haven't been given the full story, Commodore Mikaelsen. Perhaps you're one of them. I still have hope for you, in any case. But it sounds as though the healing balm of the Emperor will be needed to rectify this situation."

Mik schooled his expression, and decided it was time to retreat. Quickly.

"That's all I have to report, your Majesty. If you'll pardon me?"

"Of course, Commodore," the Emperor nodded, and then Mik turned on his heel and walked out. That was also against protocol (showing the Emperor your back?!) but he wasn't thinking about stilted traditions. He wasn't sure what Luther Gregory's angle was yet.

But the man clearly had an angle.

John Fiora was standing on the bridge of *Bonaventure*, arms folded as he tried to figure out if he had the resources to deal with this sort of problem. Now, it occurs to me that I've failed to elaborate on exactly which ships were going with *Bonnie* and *Ark Royal* to Mars. It's pretty simple: all four *Bonaventure*-class Battleships (*Bonnie*, *Terra Nova*, *Bonavista* and *Hibernia*) along with *Ark Royal*, six frigates and six corvettes.

Commanding the escort group as a whole was Commodore Shannon Hunter, who you may recall from back in *The Gallant Few*. Once this squadron combined with ours at Mars, I was supposed to take over as second in command, superceding her... but now it seemed entirely possible that I'd be unavailable for the job.

Escorts weren't the problem, though — the diplomatic formation (or battle group, if need be) was powerful, but it didn't have enough SF or Special Branchers aboard to handle a situation like this. Indeed, the only concentrated ground force available right now was the regiment of blockheads on *Ark Royal*, and there were ever so many reasons why John couldn't rely on them.

He needed SF and Special Branchers, just in case...

"Get ready to record me," John looked down from his position on the stage at the front of *Bonnie's* bridge, catching the eye of Commander Jorge Allende, the flagship's longtime Sensors and Communications Officer.

Without missing a beat, Jorge tapped one of his many staff on the shoulder, and the bridge viewfinder locked onto our First Lord.

"Message for Daragh at Admiralty House. We need a battalion of SF and Special Branch... at least 500 shooters, preferably veterans from Mercury. Put them aboard a combat storeship and send them direct to Mars at full speed. We may have a situation there in need of special solutions. Fiora out."

It was a very simple message, and it might make no difference, but John figured he had to try. Some SF had come back from the Martian outer capital... they were mostly on leave, or getting ready for deployment back to their original ships (or new ones), but now John would combine them into an independent force. The needs of the fleet's ships were secondary to the requirements of peace.

If peace could be maintained.

The message was sent to Admiralty House, and then Second Lord Daragh Ryan got down to the business of trying to find enough combat-ready personnel to fill John's order. More on that later; for now, *Bonnie* and the diplomatic squadron pushed on towards Mars... still at least a week away.

CHAPTER NINETEEN

TALKING POINTS

When a mob of angry armed people is trying to ram down your not-terribly-strong door, what do you do? My first instinct (and all of our first instincts, I think) was 'shoot at them', but that seemed like it'd be unproductive. Instead, we went with a much more passive option: talk to them.

Of course, because we'd tripped the decompression alert, finding a way to actually be heard by them wasn't so easy — the building wasn't equipped with any sort of loudspeakers, and if we opened a window, the building computer and its stupid Vantage operating system would assume that we'd lost an atmospheric seal, and close off the entire section, trapping our speaker inside.

The only way out, we discovered after a quick conversation (I nearly wrote 'interrogation') of the building's security guard, was to go out through the rescue hatch in the roof. That meant going up the utility ladders and into a cramped airlock, then out onto the flat concrete top of the structure.

If they had snipers in buildings across the street from the government compound, we'd pretty much be sitting ducks up there, which was a fun prospect… so this was daft, but there weren't too many options. We were trapped, and if there was any chance a few rousing words would buy us time, the risk had to be taken.

"Who goes?" was Karen's question once we located the ladderway on the second floor, and I didn't have an answer. Who among us would be best at calming the fury of a mob who thought Defense Command was coming to enslave their world?

Probably not a hated Defcom.

Craig B. Macdonald had come up to the second floor with us, and he tilted his head thoughtfully, "I could go… but then they might kill me."

Karen nodded, "Yes, you're a part of the evil Imperial government, after all."

"Yes. Babies are my favorite meal," he agreed bitterly, invoking a little Jonathan Swift for anyone who was paying attention. Both Karen and I got the joke, though the Martians present looked awfully confused.

The point was that no Empire representative could go up there… at least not at first. That left us looking at the Martians who'd come to the second floor with us: the vocal Martian politico (for the record, I never got his name, which is why I keep calling him 'the politico'), the head of the platoon that had escorted us this far, and Bort.

"Well, they probably think Bort is a traitor to his people, corrupted by us decadent hedonist types," I observed, and then glanced at him with a shrug. "Sorry."

He answered with a shrug of his own, "Not your fault."

"So that means it's down to the two of you," Craig turned his gaze on the Martian platoon leader and the politico, and they both looked at each other with not-quite-terrified expressions.

I would have expected one of two reactions from the Martian politico in particular: cowardice or supreme hubris. I therefore figured he'd consider it too dangerous and send his underling, or he'd believe he was invulnerable because of his position, and then would storm out there and tell the mob what-for.

Honestly, I wasn't doing either Martian enough credit, which is not something I expected to ever admit to myself. But it was true enough.

"It's my duty," the politico said somberly, and distantly. Then he looked at the platoon leader. "Your men will need you. I'll need some protection, though."

"Two volunteers," the platoon leader nodded immediately, then pulled out his communicator and made the call.

A moment later, two Martian troopers clomped up the stairs from the ground floor, joining us in the corridor outside the utility room that contained the ladder to the roof. The platoon leader explained the situation to them, while the politico stared at the wall and kept his breathing under control. He was obviously worried, and I couldn't blame him. And he deserved credit: he was doing the hard job, fully aware that it might get him killed.

I want to say here again, one more time, how ridiculous this all seemed to us. That a member of the Martian government — the iron grip of the red banner — was facing a threat to his life from citizens who had been so thoroughly indoctrinated… well.

You get the idea.

"Good luck," Craig patted the man on his shoulder, and then the Martian and his guards went on their way.

We went to find a window.

I don't know exactly what was said by the Martian politico on the roof. The building being atmospherically-sealed, the sound didn't travel. He didn't turn on his communicator, either, so I don't believe any of the Martians stuck inside with us had any more idea than we did.

Instead, we all crowded around windows overlooking the side of the building with the main entrance — the side from which the 'revolutionary' Germaine Blovuspaco was preaching.

The crowd appeared to be chanting — many mouths were moving, and signs were waving to and fro, so it didn't seem that anyone was falling silent to hear the words of the politico. That said, we didn't know if he'd started talking yet, so we didn't jump to any conclusions. We just waited.

Which, I can assure you, was as much fun as… um… waiting with no idea what's going on when your life is in danger.

Hmm, I think that simile failed.

Unfortunately, so did our politico friend.

Our first clue was the zap of reddish energy that shot out of the crowd as we watched. There were too many people for us to pick out the shooter — even Rufus, watching from a window on the first floor, couldn't source it.

Then we all saw the body of the politico drop to the crowd below.

"Shit!" the Martian platoon leader was in the office on the second floor that Karen,

Bort, Craig and I had chosen as a viewing point, and as soon as he said that he hurried out, racing for the utility room. He was probably thinking of getting his troopers off the roof in one piece, but he was too late. There was *no* cover up there.

One plunged into the crowd not long after the politico, and the last one died on the roof.

As you might be able to tell, the situation was going from purely ridiculous to deadly dangerous as well as ridiculous. And any tolerance or desire for peaceful resolution was getting washed away.

"I know as the politician and supposed diplomat, I'm supposed to turn the other cheek and try and figure out how to talk our way out of this..." Craig B. Macdonald said as he watched the crowd strip the politico's body, "...but I'm strongly favoring the military option right now."

As he said that, he drew the mag sidearm we'd provided him, and then he glanced at Karen and me, "Let's try not to do anything that jeopardizes the peace. But let's not let them think they can walk over the Empire with a rioting mob."

"Suits me just fine," Karen said grimly.

"I've always been a bit of a jingo," I added.

We were ready to go down shooting, if it came to that.

Hopefully, it wouldn't...

CHAPTER TWENTY
HAIR PULLING

Wes Pellew wasn't impressed by the Martian handling of the situation. As he paced *Nova Scotia's* bridge, he kept looking at the clock, and wondering when Morencie was going to get marine troopers into landing shuttles and down into the Capital Dome. After an hour had passed without activity, he lost patience.

Turning to his Sensors and Communications Officer, he shook his head, "Nothing from *Ascraeus Mons?*"

The Lieutenant Commander shook her head, and Wes nodded slowly in reply, "Alright then. Get a message to them. I want to speak to Admiral Morencie."

He knew what he was asking wouldn't be as easy as just sending a message to a DC ship — the Martian flagship would probably have fairly tight controls over its comm traffic, particularly under the present circumstances.

But the message needed to get through. It was the least Wes felt like he could do.

"Think he's stalling?" Matt Baxter was still on Battlelink (as were the rest of the squadron skippers) and he had overheard Wes' order. Now the Commodore of the Independent Squadron looked up at the British corvette skipper.

"Possibly. We don't know the political dynamic here... Bort McWebsbert said the man is married to the President-for-Life's sister, but maybe they're not that close."

Matt nodded slowly, "Perhaps."

"It's also possible that it's just taking them time to load up a sufficiently large landing force, and plan their operation," Wes added, sounding resigned. He then folded his arms, "And I know in his position, I'd be frustrated if the guy in my position was breathing down my neck... er. You know what I mean. But he needs to be reminded we're watching."

Matt smiled at Wes' obvious — and I think quite proper — frustration, then nodded, "I tend to agree."

"If I suggested we threaten to restart the war if he takes too long, would everyone look at me strangely?" Andrea quipped, her expression blank.

Everyone did look at her funny, but because it was Battlelink, it looked like everyone was looking at everyone else funny. She laughed — probably very inappropriately — and then Wes noticed a loading display pop up on one of the other screens.

"Loading now. If I start getting too pushy, just make some noise," Wes took a step to the left to get a better look at the correct display. He kept his arms folded.

After a moment, the Martian Admiral appeared, and as Wes had predicted, the man seemed somewhat irritated at having been interrupted. Hopefully that meant he was busy with landing preparations... not that he was sitting on his hands and secretly hoping the mob would force the government's hand, and restart the war.

"*Commodore* Pellew," was the Admiral's greeting, and to Wes it sounded like he was trying to subtly pull rank.

Now, as far as I'm concerned, Wes had done more than enough by this time to be an Admiral himself, and he would be soon after the war, but for the moment he was still a Commodore. So theoretically, he was at a disadvantage to this Martian.

Yeah. Right.

"Admiral, I was hoping to see your marines landing by now," his greeting was flat and to the point, and Morencie's face twisted into a mild snarl.

"I'll bet you did. Planning a proper landing operation takes *time*, Commodore. We have to make sure we have enough assets in place, and deploy from the correct areas. This is a very complicated situation. I'd hoped you'd recognize that."

He was saying that Wes' demands (politely phrased though they might be) were unreasonable. Perhaps he was right. Perhaps, under other circumstances, I'd now go off on a rant about how the movies always show landings to be easy and straightforward, ignoring the preparation that's required to make them work.

There's validity to all of that.

But I'm not going to go on that rant, because I'm still stuck on the whole YOU AGREED TO PEACE TALKS BUT HAVE FAILED TO SECURE THE SUPPORT OF YOUR OWN PEOPLE, THUS PUTTING OUR DELEGATION AT RISK part of this ridiculous tale.

I'm sorry, it still gets to me now. It's like inviting someone over to dinner while badgers are in the living room eating your children. Yes, that's a needlessly gruesome analogy, but that's because this situation was needlessly gruesome.

The damned Martian government, self-righteous and self-important, had called us asking for peace after they *started* the war. They *asked us*. And then we show up and their people — the ones they supposedly protect and control — decide they don't like losing, so they're going to start rioting and try to kill us?

I take it personally. More personally because I was part of the delegation, but like Wes, I would have had no patience for it even if I hadn't been on the surface.

It's just... *stupid*.

But it was happening. We could pinch ourselves all we pleased. A guy called Germaine Blovuspaco was still trying to stop the peace talks, because he believed all the lies of his government.

I don't know, the whole thing just makes me angry. And while I can't fairly blame the people of Mars for being taken in by the lies, and wanting to defend their homes... and while I can't blame the government of Mars for not gunning down otherwise-innocent civilians in the street... I can be totally bloody annoyed at the complete stupidity of the society that created such a backwards sort of crisis.

Bunch of bush-league imbeciles.

My editors keep taking out the four-letter words I write into that sentence. But know that I'm thinking them. Lots of four-letter words.

Anyway, Wes was having similar thoughts (with less bitterness, but more immediacy) as Morencie glared at him. He shot the Admiral down with cool efficiency.

"I know it's complicated, Admiral. But when the host of a party lights his own house on fire, the guests aren't obligated to be understanding when he stops to tie his bootlaces before getting them out of the building."

I think he did that rather well. Morencie looked angry — like someone had hit him across the jaw with a number twelve wrench.

The Admiral glared, then backed off a little, "We'll be launching in twenty minutes."

"Good," was Wes' answer, and then with a nod, he had the feed shut down.

He stood silently then, before looking back up at the Battle-link screens.

Matt Baxter's eyebrow was up, "You think he has any idea what bootlaces are? I think their uniform shoes are loafers."

Wes blinked. Defense Command didn't use laces either, come to think of it.

"Well if he didn't before, he does now," Bruce Arama pitched in from his screen, and the skippers laughed edgily.

It was a mildly funny diversion, but diversions weren't ultimately what they were after. They wanted marines on the ground, because there was a battering ram coming at the door of the groundskeeping building, and our negotiators had been shot off the roof with malice.

Diplomacy, I tell ya, is just not easy.

CHAPTER TWENTY-ONE

ISOLATED OR OVERWHELMED?

Shelby McLaws was continuing to keep an eye on Casey Flynnboldak when the trouble began. They were still downstairs in an office with no outside windows, and Casey had decided to make an effort at small talk. She still wasn't convinced that Bort's relative confidence in us Defcoms was deserved, but Casey was by no means a close-minded individual. She was willing to be corrected, if the evidence compelled her to change her perspective.

"So Adrian commands your ship's Interceptor squadron?" she was asking, and Shelby nodded.

"She certainly does," was the answer, and as you might predict, at the 'she' part of that sentence, Casey couldn't keep the surprise off her face. A woman — Adrienne Thompson — was our fighter commander?

There was no chance for her to probe further, though, because there was a heavy crashing sound from outside. Shelby had been sitting on the edge of the desk in the office while Casey sat on the couch opposite it, so now our intrepid Helm and Navigation Officer slid forward onto her feet and headed for the door.

Another crash echoed through the building before she got there, and then the door to the office slammed shut, and a soft hissing sound filled the air.

Decompression alarms sounded.

Stopping right in front of the door, Shelby looked up and around the frame. The seals had definitely been engaged — the office they were in had been isolated from the atmosphere in the corridor beyond. The lobby must have been breached.

Breach was definitely one way to describe what had happened. A wheeled vehicle of some sort (I have no idea what it was for) had been augmented with a huge metal pole on its front, and had been driven into the front entrance. On the first go, it had broken through the outer door, and on the second ram it got all the way in.

Rufus was waiting for it, and with just his sidearm in hand, he forced the driver back away from the vehicle, then disabled it, mostly choking off the entrance.

Martian troopers then took over the defense of the entrance, shooting anyone who tried to climb over the felled battering ram to get inside.

Seemed like an effective defensive arrangement, but as Rufus turned away from the door, he caught sight of Captain Hutchinson and Jim Hannigan standing at the security control desk with the Martian guard who'd been on duty.

Approaching the collected officers, Major Chang holstered his sidearm with a frown, figuring out what must have been going on, "Decompression alert problems?"

Jim looked up, "Shelby and Admiral McWebsbert's friend were just locked into an office, and I'm guessing all the other offices down here, and the stairways to the second floor, are locked off too."

On cue, Jim's and Rufus' comms pinged simultaneously. Shelby was calling *Wolf's* XO to let him know she was stuck in the office, and Eugene Sengooba was calling the Special Branch Major from the attached garage, to let him know that he and the SF volunteers were now sealed in.

"We need to get this thing switched off," Clarissa Hutchinson said evenly, predicting the thoughts of both her veteran superiors.

Jim scratched his temple and looked down over the shoulder of the Martian guard (who now seemed rather resigned to the fact that he was getting orders from Defcoms), "Here's the problem, though. We switch off the decompression seal, all the locks on the windows and the doors around the building are going to disengage. Won't be hard for anyone to break in."

This was the problem with holing up in a building that had no military pretensions at all: the seals that engaged to keep our atmosphere safe made it tough to get into the building (without battering rams or other, slightly more modern military gear), but they also didn't have internal overrides. No one designing the building would likely have foreseen the decompression seal as a tool to use against rioters, so there was no way to separately control the internal doors unless the seal was restored.

Now, one editor has asked if this would hamper rescue efforts if the dome actually had been decompressed, and the answer to that is no. If the atmosphere inside the building was compromised, and rescuers in EVA suits came into the building and started opening individual office doors, anyone inside those offices would likely die before they could get into appropriate protective gear. The offices, I should mention, were still connected to the building's life support systems — there was no concern about running out of oxygen for Casey and Shelby. They were just trapped.

Anyway, all of this is to say that the only way Rufus and Jim could un-isolate themselves and the rest of us was to remove the seals that kept rioters from simply popping open windows and doors, and sauntering in to get us.

Was it better to be cut off from each other but mostly safe, or to be together with an angry mob storming through the place?

When we got to the bottom of the stairs, we found the emergency door there shut. Karen, Bort and I had come down to check out the situation, while Craig remained in an office upstairs, he and his staff with mags in hand and watching the surging mob below.

"Damned thing," I kicked the pressure door in a juvenile fashion, then looked back at Bort and Karen. "Must have broken through the lobby door…"

Karen nodded, drawing her comm and connecting with Rufus, "Situation?"

Our Chinese Major with the mismatched eyes let us know that everything was stable, but that we were cut off. This was pretty much just after he'd gotten off the line with Eugene, too, so he hadn't had a chance to come to a recommendation about the doors — open them or keep the building sealed.

Because Karen's comm was on speaker as he explained his situation, she, Bort and I all heard the particulars at the same time, and we exchanged glances.

"Give us a second, Rufus," Karen said, then muted her comm. "So, apart and secure, or together and vulnerable?"

Bort was worried about Casey, as was certainly his right, but his perspective on the situation was sound: "They'll eventually break through. We could keep the seals up until then… wait as long as we can before letting them in."

I remember being profoundly struck by that suggestion — not because of the suggestion itself, but because one of our former adversaries was reasoning through the problem the same way we were. Before now, we'd clearly seen that Bort was the best of the Martian Admirals… but being on the ground in the middle of a difficult situation, and making decisions with him in a natural and organic way… that was something that resonated.

Of course, there wasn't time to dwell on such observations.

"Works for me," was my answer, and Karen nodded, then noted a twitch in Bort's expression.

"Shelby's one of our very best. Casey's in good hands," she added, then unmuted her comm. "Rufus, make sure you can deactivate the seal easily, then stand by. Don't deactivate it until they're about to break through elsewhere… we want to lock them out as long as we can."

"Roger that, makes sense," was the Major's answer, and then the line cut and Karen re-holstered her comm.

"How long until we can expect the cavalry?" I asked Bort, and the Asteroid Admiral gripped his jaw and shook his head.

"If they were my marines, they'd be on the ground by now. They wouldn't have a pre-set plan, but I'd have sent down Jack Dwyerigan and he'd have established a foothold to get things started."

I didn't know who Jack Dwyerigan was, but obviously I'd find out after the war. For the moment, though, I nodded — Bort's perspective on a situation like this would have been different than Morencie's, and somehow that didn't surprise me in the slightest. He elaborated further.

"But Morencie is very cautious. He could be taking a damned long time to get things moving…" he shook his head. "Better that we're ready to wait a while. I can't see this thing lasting more than a few hours, but they don't *need* a few hours to get in here, if they're smart."

"Great, so it's down to whether rioters led by Germaine…"

"Blovuspaco," Karen filled in.

"…right, Germaine Blovuspaco, are smart enough to break into a civilian building on decompression alert," my words were dry. "Should we start a pool on how long?"

"No," Karen's answer was flat, and she started checking her mag power cell. "I'll start a pool on how many we shoot, though. I'm looking for double-digits today."

That's not something I expected Karen to say out loud — especially not with Bort here. That was the sort of thing she would have said a long time prior, before the war. When she was younger, angrier, and more inclined towards doing damage.

It was a surprise to hear that sort of anger resurfacing now, over rioters (as opposed to Pions or a crisis like Egesta), but I decided not to analyze it. Actually, if I'm honest, I think I may have taken it as permission to up my own anger level… if that makes sense.

You know how sometimes you can be frustrated by things, but trying not to let them get to you, and then someone else starts unloading about the problem, and you let yourself join in… even if you shouldn't? This was something like that.

Though I was confident we wouldn't get out of hand. They were only rioters, after all… they didn't deserve the full treatment, as some others might.

I don't know if Bort picked up on the slightly sinister overtones in Karen's words — he was relatively preoccupied with other matters — so we didn't say anything else, just started back up the stairs to rejoin Craig Macdonald at a window.

We had to wait for the cavalry to arrive… and unfortunately, that cavalry was Martian. Seemed like it could be quite a while.

Chapter Twenty-Two

Cavalry

"Sir," *Nova Scotia's* Sensors and Communications Officer halted Wes' pacing with her word, and then nodded towards the main screen. On it, the icons of a dozen Martian small craft appeared, escorted by a wave of Interceptors.

"Looks like the cavalry is setting off at last," Matt Baxter observed dryly from his screen, and Wes nodded.

Two hours late, the marines were finally dropping to do their jobs. Wes could only hope that these troopers were indeed loyal to the government, and that they wouldn't get down there and switch sides.

It was hard enough to trust the Martians when they were all working for their government towards peace... now Wes had faith in none of them.

"Wolfstar Squadron still ready to fly, Andrea?" he looked up to the screen showing *Wolf's* bridge, and our Irish skipper nodded.

"Adrienne kept her pilots in their planes."

Wes paused in thought for a moment, then spoke, "Alright, have them escort the Martians down. I doubt they'll like it, but I'm still inclined to look over their shoulders."

"Gladly," Andrea concurred, and then looked off screen.

"Volunteer landing force stand by as well... if it falls apart down there, we'll send in our own strike," Wes added, turning his eyes back to the enhanced visuals the cameras of the squadron were recording through the transparent Capital Dome.

Our position was very clearly surrounded by a sizable mob... but at least it didn't appear that the building had been compromised, and all the comm calls from Shelby and Jim were reporting no serious threat.

Perhaps everything would stay static, and then the marines would land, put the situation to rights, and the crisis would be settled.

Wes folded his arms. He'd believe that when he saw it.

Karen, Bort, Craig and I were still looking down on the mob through an office window when my comm chirped. I pulled it from the holster on my belt and keyed the connection active: "Please tell me you have good news."

"Does a dozen shuttles full of Martian marines count as good these days?" Wes answered with a question, and I grinned.

"Right now, yes."

"They're on their way down, and I have Wolfstar Squadron keeping an eye on them in case someone up here tries to get in the way. Should be on the ground in thirty minutes, based on current speed."

I nodded, "Good. The riot seems to have cooled off a bit for the moment, so hopefully it'll break up without too much drama..."

Karen looked directly at me as soon as I said that, and I frowned and lowered my comm, "What?"

"Don't say that out loud," she said sharply, and she wasn't entirely joking. Not worth tempting fate.

Bort was still looking out the window, and as if on cue he leaned forward, narrowing his eyes. Karen, Craig and I all noticed this, and tensed.

Then he leaned back, seemingly satisfied that whatever he was looking at wasn't dangerous. Karen gave me the 'see, don't tempt fate!' look, and I raised my comm again, "We'll be in touch soon, Wes."

"Nothing happened when you said that thing you just said, did it? Don't tempt fate like that..." he answered.

"I know, sorry. Over and out."

I re-holstered my comm, and Karen took a deep breath, folding her arms as we waited.

Things did seem to be cooling off, but this mob had still killed three people that we knew of, including a Martian political official, and the President's loyal guard seemed unwilling to do anything about it. Would the Martian Navy's finest be any more inclined to break up a crowd of civilian protestors?

Adrienne Thompson was leading Wolfstar Squadron with her typical skill, keeping her mind clear of personal concerns as she rode her plane down into Mars' atmosphere. She was an extremely experienced combat veteran, so putting fears for our diplomatic envoy out of her head wasn't *too* difficult for her.

Compensating for the wind shear as the Martian atmosphere thickened was also keeping her busy. She hadn't done much work in a proper atmosphere for many years, and she'd certainly never flown in Mars air before. The roar of the engines — usually muted in space — and the drag on her acceleration were very noticeable.

As Wolfstar Squadron held its formation, Adrienne noticed that the Martian Interceptors had peeled away. The craft weren't rated for atmospheric flight, meaning they couldn't escort the landing shuttles all the way down to the Capital Dome. Presumably, some atmospheric fighters would be coming up from the ground to offer close protection to the landing force...

"Keep your eyes open for friendly escorts from the ground," she spoke into her helmet headset.

Her pilots acknowledged over the comm, and watched as they dropped further into the atmosphere. No contacts were turning up on anyone's scanners, which seemed quite unusual, so Adrienne called up to *Wolf*. Felicia Khalid was at her station, and took the call.

"Commander, what can we do for you?"

Adrienne's head was on a swivel, looking left and right as she scanned the widening Martian landscape beneath her fuselage, "I'm not seeing any atmospheric defense craft coming up to escort us. You have anything on sensors?"

Wolf's detection gear was unquestionably more robust than a Starlight's, so Felicia quickly checked with her operators, then replied, "Negative, Commander. Airspace is clear."

Andrea then cut in on the exchange, "I'll check with Wes, see if there's anything from the Martians on that."

The call was muted while Andrea passed the question on to Wes, and Wes' Sensors and Communications Officer tried to get Morencie on the line again. This was the problem with fighters like Martian Interceptors; they were space-capable only. Our 'atmospace' capable Starlights were patently superior.

And they'd need to be.

Adrienne's ear crackled — one of Wolfstar's veteran pilots calling in: "Ma'am... I think I've got a vapor trail on my three o'clock... sensors are picking up a missile of some sort..."

Adrienne's plane detected the weapon in that instant, and her screens flashed red in confirmation of the warning. She was speaking immediately, "*Wolf*, this is Wolfstar 801, declaring incoming hostile fire. Missile bound for the landing ships."

With that, she hauled on the stick and her Starlight banked hard to starboard, then dove towards the threat.

Morencie appeared on *Nova Scotia's* screens almost in the same instant, still looking flustered. Wes wasn't going to help the situation any.

"Someone is shooting at your landing ships. Where's their escort?"

As greetings go, that one didn't seem too warm, and Morencie clearly needed a few seconds to digest it before responding. Then a warning call from somewhere on his bridge drew his attention away from the screen and he moved out of shot.

Wes was unimpressed. Looking back at the Battlelink screens, he found Andrea's face, "Tell Adrienne to destroy any incoming missiles. If hostile craft appear, wait for our okay before engaging..."

He was tying the hands of our Starlight pilots with those orders — they couldn't shoot at a seemingly hostile plane without authorization, but at least they could shoot down its missiles...

Adrienne got that authorization through her helmet just as she and her wingman, Lieutenant Hannah Lim, were bearing down on the warhead. It was some sort of atmosphere-only missile that looked military, but which actually wasn't moving too fast; the sensors were getting a good track on it.

And it seemed to have come up from the surface, not from another aircraft. Hopefully that meant there wouldn't be any dogfights to worry about.

"*Wolf* from Wolfstar 801, looks like a surface-launched missile. We're engaging."

"Roger that," Felicia replied in her ear.

Adrienne led from the front — that was her style, and why her squadron trusted her implicitly. Keeping with that habit, she activated her targeting computer and locked onto the slow-flying missile, then lined up a mag shot.

It was fairly undramatic after that: the missile ceased to exist in a storm of golden energy.

So that sorted the problem... surely...

+++

Wes was staring at a blank screen over to *Ascraeus Mons*. Morencie was away from his bridge's rotating column of command screens, undoubtedly trying to find out what the hell was going on. Maybe if the Martians knew how to design their bridges properly, he could have been getting that information without losing the ability to have face-to-face communication.

After attempting to be patient for a couple of moments, Commodore Pellew decided to throw another cat amongst the pigeons.

"Our planes just shot down the missile. It was fired from the ground. Do you have an escort coming, or should we strafe the target ourselves?"

He wasn't actually planning to give Adrienne clearance to strafe anything, but he suspected that broadcasting those words over the speakers of Morencie's bridge would get the man back in front of his viewfinder.

As usual, Wes was right.

Slightly wild-eyed, Morencie reappeared, "Our atmospheric escort has been... delayed..."

Which Wes took to mean 'never left the ground because they don't fully support the idea of using marines to break up a demonstration of civilians who don't want to be raped and murdered by Defense Command'. And again, we learned later, Wes was right.

"Well good thing we put Wolfstar Squadron on the job, isn't it?" he asked dryly, and Morencie said nothing. "I won't be giving my Starlights permission to open fire on any targets, airborne or ground, unless you give me clearance. I'm not restarting this war. But you better keep an eye on your sensors and be quick to give me latitude if someone unauthorized is coming up. Because if we lose a plane, that *will* restart the war."

It was a bit of a bluff, but Wes' continual brow-beating of this Martian Admiral was having the desired effect. His answer was a nod, and then he looked away from the screen, but stayed present.

Nothing was going to be easy today.

CHAPTER TWENTY-THREE

BREACHES

Eugene Sengooba and his guards were staying fairly close to the now-sealed doorway that connected the garage full of groundskeeping vehicles to the main lobby, where Rufus, Jim, and most of the shooters were. In order to keep an eye on the entire cavernous garage — which was essentially the size of a small warehouse — they'd all climbed up onto the back of a rather large vehicle, and it was there that they were perched when one of the massive outer doors began to buckle.

"They're starting to breach the garage," Eugene warned us through his comm.

Almost in the same instant, on the other side of the building, an energy weapon of some sort — either a shoulder laser or an EM cannon — punched a fist-sized hole in one of the office windows. The door to that office was already sealed shut, which would buy some time once the rioters pried their way in, but the breaches were beginning.

Rufus remained in the lobby, a grenade in one hand and his sidearm in the other, taking stock of the situation. The office breach was bad because if the rioters got through the door there — and that wouldn't be too hard — they'd cut off access to the stairwells (they'd be in the corridor between the lobby and the stairs). The garage breach was bad because Eugene and the SF wouldn't be able to hold out for long in that place.

The seals needed to come off soon.

Pocketing his grenade, Rufus pulled out his comm and called me, "I think it's time to lift the seal."

I was still upstairs with Karen, Bort and Craig, and as I heard that message I exchanged glances with all concerned.

"Fort up on the second floor, and hold the stairwell?" Karen suggested.

"Sounds like a plan," Bort gave a nod.

With that decided, we turned our eyes back to the Foreign Minister, who still held his MAG-11 tightly in hand. He shrugged at our implied question about what to do, "I'll defer to your judgment on this one."

That was enough consensus for us, so I gave Rufus the go-ahead, "Alright, pull the plug. We'll meet you at the back stairs."

A moment later, soft hisses filled the building as seals were released on every door and window.

I should have said this before, but I suppose it wasn't as pertinent then as it is now: fourteen Martian troopers remained from the platoon that had been with the vehicles. I don't honestly know how many they'd started with, but some had gone down with the destroyed limo, others with the tank we lost, and then two had died on the roof.

Fourteen remained, and they were all in the lobby with Rufus, his five Branchers, Jim, and the Martian security guard who'd been on duty. Once the seals released, they were joined by Eugene and his three SF, as well as Shelby and Casey. A total of twenty-eight people on the ground floor, all armed. Craig's staff were in an office on the second floor, and when Karen and I went down the stairs, the Foreign Minister would join them.

As the seals came down, the noise from outside abruptly became audible, and we discovered — much to our surprise, I assure you — that the crowd wasn't exactly singing songs at us. Well, some of their chants had a musical quality, but it wasn't exactly family listening.

They didn't immediately realize that the locks were off, though, so Rufus sought to exploit their inattention by moving quickly.

Pointing to Jim and Eugene, he nodded his head in the direction of the corridor that led to the stairway. That corridor ran to the back of the building, and entrance to the stairs was just a few meters from the back door, which was now unlocked. It seemed like a good idea to get a fire team down there right away to secure our avenue of retreat.

Recognizing the instructions, Jim drew his mag and silently led the way. His strides were quick and purposeful, but he wasn't running. Eugene and the guards fell in behind him.

The building wasn't very big, but that walk looked absurdly long to him as he got into the corridor. He took it steadily, and then as he came to the office Shelby and Casey had been stuck in, he knocked softly on the door.

"Shelby, it's Jim."

Our Helm and Navigation Officer had kept the door shut, knowing there could be numerous breaches as soon as the seals were released, but now that she knew there were no immediate incursions, she opened up.

Her mag was drawn, and Casey Flynnboldak was holding onto the weapon Bort had given her.

"Upstairs?" Shelby confirmed in a whisper, which probably wasn't necessary but felt appropriate.

Jim nodded, and then moved past the doorway. Shelby followed, then Casey, and finally Eugene and the guards.

They continued to move steadily down the corridor, staying to one side, mags up.

Not too much further. The interminably long walk was only taking seconds, but heart rates were way up, and beats felt like sledgehammers. How soon would the rioters realize they had their chance?

Jim caught sight of Karen and me, waiting in the doorway to the stairwell, keeping our eyes on the back door and prepared for trouble. We were only a dozen meters apart — soon he'd reach us and we'd have a strong team in place to keep the rioters away from the stairs.

Then the back door opened, and Jim wondered if he should have been moving faster.

At this point, I was fully back into the headspace of the old days. I hadn't been on many landing parties during the war — after Kate Levec was shot during the operation at Io, I pretty much kept out of them, except on Pion Rock when it had been absolutely necessary.

Now, though, I was starting to feel the familiar sensations — the pounding heartbeat, the upright hair on the back of the neck, the slowing down of time. These were things that I'd become much too familiar with during the cavalier days of the Belt Squadron, when Karen and I would storm pirate houses and get into trouble in pirate bars...

But along with those familiar feelings were some new ones, because if I'm honest, in my younger days — even as a Captain before the war — I'd believed a bit too much in my own invulnerability. The war had made me far more aware of my own mortality, which in turn made me less sympathetic to those trying to do me harm.

It wasn't a game anymore. It never should have been, but now it *really* wasn't.

When that door opened I turned and raised my mag. I was close enough for the shot to be really easy, so when the first rioter stuck his head through in surprise, I sent a mag bolt into his face. Back he went, convulsing and knocking down the men behind him.

"Move!" Karen ordered instantly, swinging out of the stairwell doorway behind me and dropping to one knee in the corridor.

The back entrance stayed open, and rioters tried to push through — a yelling and screaming mass of people who seemed to think I'd killed their friend. They obviously didn't understand the mag settings we used for crowd control.

Neither Karen nor I waited for anyone to force their way through the door, though: we started shooting like it was going out of style.

Systematically, we blasted anyone who came near the entrance, until a convulsing mass of bodies was piled up there as a barricade. As this happened, Shelby grabbed Casey gently by the arm and led her into the stairwell, followed by Jim. Eugene and his guards remained in the corridor with us, the newly-minted Master-At-Arms stopping beside me.

"We'll secure this point, sir. You should–"

At this moment, one of the armed rioters decided to shoot at the entrance with a shoulder laser, so the wall to the left of the door frame blew apart in a shower of debris.

I was fortunate to have been mostly sheltered by the stairwell door frame, but everyone in the corridor was battered with chunks of salmon-colored concrete.

Karen got her arm in front of her face almost instantly, but a supersonic chip still gouged her scalp just below the hairline, in almost the same spot Josie (the Pion leader) had cut the previous year. One of the SF got a serious chunk in the forehead, and went down like a ton of bricks. She was quickly carried upstairs by another SF, who'd been lightly wounded.

As the dust literally began to settle, I pulled out my comm, "Get out of there, Rufus!"

Our Major had heard the explosion, and he appeared at the lobby end of the corridor with a half dozen of the Martian troopers from our escort. He directed them to reinforce our position, then turned back to the main entrance. I didn't realize it then, but the rioters were forcing their way in from that side as well, and it was all our Branchers could do to keep the mob back from dislodged windows on several sides.

But we had help coming... the six Martian troopers Rufus had dispatched were hurrying up the hall...

Then rioters burst out of one of the offices halfway up the corridor — the window in there must have been pried open — and got between those Martian troopers and us at the stairwell.

My response to this was as you might expect: "Shit."

I started shooting, and the first two fell quite quickly, with the Martians hastily shooting down the rest. Once that immediate threat was apparently contained, the leader of the half-platoon of red troopers then directed two of his men to watch the breached office, and hurried in our direction with the last four.

But then rioters started coming out of other offices too.

This situation wasn't close to being contained.

"Rufus, no time for a fighting retreat, get out," I called into my comm, and our elite Major appeared at the other end of the corridor again, where a rioter unwisely tried to deck him. That rioter ended up with one leg pointing the wrong way, and then Rufus waved his Branchers and the remaining Martians to join him in a brutal retreat.

They'd have to force the hallway. We'd have to hold the stairs long enough for them to get out.

Bort was at the top of the stairs when Shelby and Casey got there. As soon as Shelby saw him, she led Casey his way, and then very politely shed her charge.

"Sir, if you wouldn't mind," our southern belle nodded to the Asteroid Admiral and then, with a smile, maneuvered Miss Flynnboldak into his company. As soon as Casey was safely there, Shelby turned back to the stairs and began making quick defensive plans with Jim.

Leading Casey away from the stairway, Bort headed for the office where Craig and his staff were now holed up — one without any outside windows. As they entered, a couple of the more panicked staffers started raising their weapons, but they stopped long before thinking of pulling their triggers.

"I should be out there with them," Bort said quickly, giving Casey a square, earnest look. Her reply was not the sort we often see in Defense Command, but was one that seemed appropriate to the situation and to the culture from which both Casey and Bort hailed.

Big kiss. Craig Macdonald assures me it deserved violins. Instead it was backed by the sounds of mag fire, mob chants and screaming, but it was nevertheless quite dramatic.

Then she said: "Come back to me."

Now, this is a line I'd normally say could only happen in movies, but you know, I'm not going to make fun. I know for a fact that Casey meant what she was saying, and I know for damned sure Bort intended not to disappoint her.

"I will," he said, and then swept out of the room.

Craig and one of the women on his staff then helped Casey find some cover behind the desk they'd tipped over.

Our Foreign Minister was sitting in an office, armed and ready to make his last stand.

He tells me he was seriously rethinking some career choices just then, and who could blame him.

My first mag power cell was nearly dry, despite the fact that I was using relatively low output settings as I shot the Martian rioters. Karen's objective of getting into the double digits for the number of rioters shot was proving eminently doable, too.

The situation in the corridor was positive mayhem.

Even though the back door had been blasted to double its width, Eugene and his remaining shooter were able to keep people back from it. Attempts by the rioter with the shoulder laser to widen the breach were unsuccessful, too, as the sides of the building were ultimately still reinforced concrete — much stronger as the shots got further away from the original door frame. That helped.

The number of rioters streaming out of offices and into the corridor between us and the lobby was a problem, though. Rufus and the Branchers easily out-matched any angry civilian, but the Martian troopers weren't so elite.

Meanwhile, neither Karen nor I were in terribly sympathetic moods, as I've suggested.

She looked positively scary, because the cut to her scalp left a lot of blood running down her face, and she was dividing her efforts between mag fire and throwing punches.

Remember, she could kill a Pion leader with her bare hands (and a spike). Angry rioters weren't doing at all well.

Then one rather large fellow tackled her. He had to weigh twice what she did, so the laws of physics gave him a momentary victory as she landed hard on her back and slid over the smooth floor, right into entrance of the stairwell. He then tried to get a knee on her chest, so he could beat her face to a paste with his big fists.

I turned to intervene, but another rioter came for me, getting inside my guard. It'd been a long while since I'd had to go hand-to-hand with anyone, and the guy who picked me was spry. He drove a fist into my stomach, but he'd thrown the punch without much strength behind it. The key with hitting someone is to transfer the energy from your legs up through your torso and out through your fist.

After I side-stepped, that's how I got enough power behind my punch to break his nose. He then staggered, fell, and went mouth-first into the door frame of the office behind him. I didn't get to see for certain, but I imagine he was spitting out teeth afterward.

Didn't matter — I needed to intervene with Karen's attacker, because if I was right... I was right.

What some of the wiser pirates had learned in the old days was that fighting Karen was, generally, a stupid idea. She'd mellowed over the years, and during the war, she'd really done a fine job of locking up the old anger that still simmered deep down (Pion incident excepted), but the conditions today were just too ridiculous. And this guy had wanted to mash her skull.

So her self control, hard-learned over the years, was switched off by the time I looked back at her.

Both her knees were on the rioter's chest, and I guess he must have pulled a knife on her. Here's a tip: never pull a knife in a fight if you aren't absolutely confident you'll be able to keep control of it.

Now Karen was leaning over the man's face, the knife in her hand as she peered into his very, very wide eyes.

"Last creature that pulled a knife on me was a Pion," she was saying. Somehow, over the chaos, I remember hearing her soft words very clearly. "Actually, that was more like a spike. But I put it in one ear, and out the other..."

The man struggled, so Karen grabbed him by the scalp and bounced the back of his head off the floor.

"I regretted that, though. I realized I should have gone straight down… through the eye and out the back of her skull. Would have pinned her head to the floor…," she continued.

The man was in sheer terror for his life now. It didn't help that blood from Karen's scalp wound was dripping onto his face.

"So what I have to ask," she smiled, "is which eye is your favorite."

Now, at this point my editors are freaking out. What the hell is Karen doing? Well, we've seen Karen angry before… Pion Rock, and before that at Egesta. Doesn't happen often, and throughout the war, she'd always managed to keep it in check.

But remember, we'd been doing everything we could to get back to the old days — to the cavalier days of quips and adventure. And in pushing hard to get back there, we'd overshot the mark just a little. Angry Karen, like she'd been when I first met her at the Academy.

Before the Martian could choke out any sort of answer to Karen's question, I knelt beside her, and as she noticed me, she glanced my way.

I guess my expression said it all. She blinked, wiped the blood from her eyes with the back of her hand, and then tossed the knife.

"Don't tackle a lady," she looked back to the rioter with those cool words, and then she pounded what was left of his nose so that he wailed.

By this time, all the defenders who could were falling back into the stairwell, so Karen and I decided to start up the steps, mags ready to shoot any infiltrators.

Rufus and his Branchers were close behind, with those Martian troopers who remained standing. We took the steps a few at a time, and I ended up being the first to the top of the stairs, where Shelby and Jim had set up a makeshift barricade of desks on the landing. I hopped behind it, as did Eugene and his remaining guard. We then covered the rest of the retreat.

Only eleven of the Martian troopers got to the top of the stairs. What happened to the rest was undoubtedly quite unpleasant, and I do regret that they were left behind. But the chaos tapered off once everyone reached the second floor. Hotheaded rioters tried to rush the stairs, but were shot down easily. It'd take a while for them to organize a better attack, and we hoped that'd be time enough for the cavalry to arrive.

Hopefully we'd done our fighting for the day.

CHAPTER TWENTY-FOUR

OLD HABITS

Karen entered the office Craig and Casey had taken shelter in without realizing they were two of the people hiding behind the desk. She holstered her mag and started unzipping her tattered and soiled dress uniform tunic, then opened her shirt collar far enough to get cool air onto her neck. That done, she started feeling the side of her face.

The man she'd pulverized had managed to hit her with a solid punch, and he'd loosened a tooth or two. She was already starting to swell up.

Then she'd very nearly pinned his head to the floor with his own knife — not something she'd been planning on doing when she woke up that morning.

The adrenalin was beginning to ebb, and uncomfortable feelings were surfacing. But for the moment, at least, the blood on her face was the worst thing she had to deal with.

"Damned scalp," she muttered to herself, then drew her mag and swung out of the room.

Apparently, Casey Flynnboldak was open-mouthed with shock by the time Karen stepped out, and Craig glanced at her, "Problem, Miss?"

Casey said nothing, but I think it's safe to say she'd never seen anything quite like that before — obviously, pugilism wasn't a common pastime for Martian women.

When I found Karen emerging from that office, she stared at me for a moment, and opened her mouth to say something. No words came out, and I recognized why.

"Let's get you cleaned up," I offered. "Before you lose too much blood."

With the instincts that make Special Branchers so elite, Rufus' new medic, Selma Koestecki, happened by at that moment, wearing an entirely neutral expression.

"Need a seal for those cuts, ma'am?" the Lieutenant asked.

It didn't seem likely that the Brancher — or anyone else from our defending party — had seen exactly what Karen had been doing at the base of the stairs, but as seals were applied to wounds, I couldn't help but feel a little bit self-conscious for her.

I shouldn't have felt that, obviously. It had been a brawl, and we'd fought for our lives... no shame in that. I certainly didn't have a problem with anyone knowing how much damage I'd done to one of the Martian rioters...

But in a nostalgic moment, I felt worried for Karen.

That probably doesn't make much sense. Without me explaining the circumstances under which we'd met... without me talking about the very old days, when she'd been a much less kindly sort of goddess... I can't really explain the depth of my worry.

Jim walked by, then Shelby. Neither seemed to pay us much attention, but I wondered if they were purposefully ignoring us. What would they think of Karen, if they quite recognized her state of mind? But then, they'd seen her fight hard before. Never like this, but they might not know her well enough to see the difference. Few could. Charlie, but he wasn't here. Maybe Matt Baxter, but he wasn't here either.

It was irrelevant, though. Karen was fine, she hadn't killed anyone. And under the circumstances, even if she had... it was a bit like Pion Rock, after all. Fighting was necessary...

But everything had been much more brutal on Pion Rock. Her response to Josie had been equitable. Less so here.

"Hey."

I blinked, realizing that my eyes had been travelling away from Karen so much that I hadn't seen Koestecki leave. A handful of wet napkins had been provided, I don't know from where, and Karen was now wiping her face as she spoke.

"Help me, please," she said quietly after a few attempts, and I took the napkins from her, and started trying to scrub the dried blood from her cheeks with gentle-but-firm strokes.

She closed her eyes, and I could tell she was focusing on her breathing.

"Shouldn't have done that, right?" she asked very softly after a moment, and I didn't speak.

What happened next was answer enough. The napkins were in my left hand, and my right hand was on her cheek, holding her head as I tried to clear off the blood. Without consciously meaning to, I slid that hand down from her cheek to the left side of her neck, and my thumb ended up under her chin, against her throat.

Her eyes opened immediately, and my gaze locked onto hers.

That was an answer.

"Need to stop trying to reach back for the old days," she whispered as she recognized the feeling against her throat, and then pressed closer against my hand.

She was right. There was nothing I could say in response, so I let my hand slide away from her neck, and then studied the pink streaks that were left on her cheeks, "You'll need a shower to get the rest off."

She nodded, blinked twice, and then reached back and pulled her blood-matted ponytail up onto her left shoulder, and into its usual place — right up against the side of her neck where my hand had been.

Closing her eyes for another second, she took a breath. When her lids drew back again, Karen was back — the wartime Karen, the one who was firmly in control.

She didn't say anything else, just got to her feet and moved past me. She needed a few moments to clear her head, so I let her go.

As she did, I looked around, wondering again if anyone had seen us. Jim and Shelby were busy with Eugene, posting guards. Rufus and the Branchers were similarly getting into position. No one seemed to have noticed...

"You and she have a different relationship than I thought."

One Admiral had seen us. And unfortunately, or perhaps fortunately, he was a very astute one.

As Bort came up behind me, I glanced back over my shoulder, then dropped the wet, bloody napkins to the floor before wiping my hands off on my already-trashed dress tunic.

"A lot of history," I answered honestly.

The Asteroid man came to a stop beside me, and both of us watched as Karen reached a window at the far end of the hall, and looked out at the rioters who were still beyond the building. Plenty remained out there.

"No one else seems to have noticed," Bort continued, and I realized he could tell I was uneasy about that very possibility.

"They're all used to seeing her fight. Mightn't notice the…" I stopped. There was no reason to say this to anyone, let alone an enemy Admiral.

But dammit, Bort didn't actually *need* me to say it: "She was in a different headspace than usual?"

I paused, then I looked at him, "War wounds. They'll heal."

He looked back at me, and though it wasn't much of an answer, he nodded slowly.

There was no more time for conversation; my comm chirped, and Wes was on the other end of the line when I hit the button: "Their marines are entering the dome not too far from you. Shouldn't be too long, hopefully."

"Good to hear… they broke in so we've moved everybody up to the second floor. Lost some of our Martian escorts, but the delegation is still intact, except for some cuts and bruises."

There was a pause on the line as Wes digested my report, then he said, "Wolfstar Squadron is doing circles over the dome, in case you need them. I don't know what they could actually do to help… but they're there."

"Thanks," I said somewhat absently, then concluded the conversation. "Talk to you when the marines arrive."

The line died, and I looked up. All I could see was concrete ceiling, but somehow it was comforting to know that Adrienne and our veteran flyers were looking over us… even if there wasn't a damned thing they could do to help.

"What's up?" Karen had returned with silent ease, and now her relaxed expression was something of a relief.

A goddess. I mean that.

"Adrienne has Wolfstar Squadron right overhead. Won't do us a whole lot of good, but they're there," I answered.

Karen smiled, "Glad to hear it."

Hopefully we could get out of this mess soon. Because the day had gone from ridiculous to scary… and that latter part had little to do with the Martians themselves.

CHAPTER TWENTY-FIVE

RIOT BREAKERS

The marines who stormed onto the grounds of the government compound didn't seem terribly understanding. I didn't know then (and still don't know now) enough about the comparative character of different units in the Martian armed forces to be able to tell you much about the troopers who were part of this force... but based on what we saw from the windows, they were a hard-nosed and fiercely (unsympathetically) loyal bunch.

And loyal to the Navy, not to the President.

Interesting dynamic indeed. While the Presidential Guards watched from their defensive perimeter hundreds of meters closer to the central government buildings, the marines from Morencie's squadron hit the crowd hard.

They didn't wait to open fire; as soon as they were in range, we started seeing mag bolts crossing the field. It wasn't immediately clear whether those bolts were lethal or non-lethal, which gave us all a very uncomfortable feeling as we watched. I was going to say 'sick' feeling, because civilians would have been dying if the bolts were lethal, but I was a bit too numb to be ill.

Anyway, it was ultimately a moot point, since the marine troopers' EM guns were set to non-lethal. Though because Martian technology is truly less sophisticated than ours, I understand that the non-lethal settings did much more collateral damage than our mag stuns would.

No matter. The crowd started to react, turning on the incoming troops and hitting them with everything. The occasional weapons, including the shoulder laser that had blown open the back door frame, raked the marines as we watched them come on. Some died, which drew anger from many present.

But there were hundreds of marines, and they were very well armed. Their style lacked the precision of Special Branch, but they knew what they were doing, and the job wasn't difficult: keep shooting at the mob until it broke up.

A simple job that the President's Guards or any other coherent, properly-armed combat unit could have done hours before, sparing the lives that had been lost. If the government of Mars could get its act together.

At least it was being done now.

It took a surprisingly long time for the crowd to realize it was out-matched. Some of the more hotheaded types charged away from the groundskeeping building towards the centre of the government compound, and then we got to see exactly what the now-deceased Martian politico had meant when he warned us about the inner defense perimeter. Sentry guns popped up, and after a delay which I assumed came from the defense control bunker identifying them as non-friendly ground targets, they were burned to a cinder.

No non-lethal option for anyone attacking the government building. That was high treason.

But apparently, attempting to kill the Defense Command delegation *wasn't.*

I don't know where I fall on the morality of any of this. I was just very glad when the rioters at last fled away from our erstwhile fortress, and the Martian marine troopers set up a strong perimeter for us.

As we began hearing the boots of the troopers thudding on the floor below us, Bort McWebsbert rejoined Karen and me. Casey Flynnboldak had one arm around him, and seemed awfully self-conscious, particularly when she looked at Karen (who now appeared a bit more civilized, with her various cuts patched). Even without understanding the implications of what had happened, post-fight Karen was still a very shocking sight for the Martian dancer.

She remained silent, but Bort spoke, "Commodore McMaster, remember what you mentioned about protection?"

He was referring to something that had been said a week prior, and which had nothing to do with recent events, so it took Karen a moment to recall the conversation they'd had during Bort's tour of *Wolf* — the one that offered our protection. When that clicked, she nodded, "Changing your mind?"

The Asteroid Admiral shook his head, "I'm still returning to my home after this is over. But I think I may need some... help getting there. We both may."

Casey's arm tightened around him as he spoke, and Karen and I both got the message. Given what we were seeing — the spotty attention to duty by various Martian military units — Bort was concerned that bad feeling towards him and Casey might lead to violence.

What I'm saying there, if that was too subtle, is that Bort doubted his own armed forces would provide him or Casey any protection if people came to kill them as traitors.

"You're welcome to stay aboard *Wolf* until the situation calms down, at the very least," Karen said smoothly, and nodded to Bort and to Casey.

Casey did *not* look comfortable, but she nodded back. Bort looked slightly relieved, and did the same.

I said nothing during the exchange — there was no need. A couple of moments later, Martian troopers called up the stairwell that they were friendlies, and Rufus and his sharpshooting Branchers let them come up. We'd been rescued.

And now, after all of that, we had to start negotiating with the government of Mars, to make the arrangements for a peace summit which our Prime Minister and Emperor would attend.

I thought right then that the first subject we'd need to cover in our meetings would be a simple one: SECURITY, in capital letters.

Ridiculous goddamned start to this whole peace process.

CHAPTER TWENTY-SIX

DIPLOMACY

I wasn't sure how diplomatic Craig B. Macdonald was going to be when we finally got to the central government building, and started our talks. As expected, we had to walk up the lawn to get there, and it was unsettling to watch the Martian sentry guns as they followed us all the way. Given the day we'd had so far, we were in no way confident the people running those guns wouldn't open fire on us, and Rufus had explosives ready in case the weapons needed to be silenced.

Craig seemed to be very neutral as he walked. I can't describe his apparent attitude any other way — he was responsive, and clearly paying attention to everything... and yet he seemed to have no reaction to what was said, or what he witnessed. I wondered if he was shellshocked after the siege. He wasn't, he was just saving up some energy.

He'd soon expend it.

Entering the main government building was, for us, like entering a different world. The place was very richly appointed, with rugs and gold trim and any number of gaudy fixins that seemed entirely at odds with the concrete culture we'd come to expect from Mars.

What was even more surreal, though, was that fifty of the President's Guards were there waiting for us, in their finery, and as soon as our battered and bloodied delegation was led into the gleaming lobby, they snapped to attention.

So they'd been here the whole time, and hadn't come out to help us? Charming.

Karen, who was probably the most torn up of our Defense Command personnel, was near the front of our group, and she got quite a few stares. I did too, though at least my dress uniform was partially intact. Leading the way into the deeper corridors of the building was our Foreign Minister, with his staff in tow. At least no one dared to ask for our sidearms — there'd likely have been some heated discussions if such a request was made.

It took five minutes after we entered the building for our delegation to get to the grand chamber (a seriously overdone conference room) where our initial meeting was to take place. If we hadn't been interrupted by rioters, I expect I might have taken time to be disdainful of the ornateness of the place — it came across as a palace, which I suppose it probably was, and I didn't approve. I never liked Ian Hawke's tendency to make things gaudy, and I've never liked the style of decadent Emperors. I guess I'm a bit of a peasant.

Anyway, after we were led into the room, the Martian politicos and troopers who had been with us for the day were taken away, leaving just the twenty Imperial personnel (and Bort, who I somehow classify as one of us), plus Casey, who was staying very close to him. She'd never been into this building before either, so the richness of the place was an eyeful for her too.

Perhaps even more so than it was for us, considering the way this very government had decried Imperial decadence in its propaganda. What would Germaine Blovuspaco (who escaped the marines and disappeared, by the way) have thought if he'd seen this place? Would the people of Mars rise up against their government if they realized that the President-for-Life had gold inlay in every door frame?

Ah well, that was a question about which I did *not* care, because all I wanted was to get our business done, and to get the hell back to my ship.

Instead, though, we waited, alone in that massive, ornate meeting room, with its long table and posh artwork on every wall. Nearly half an hour passed before someone came in, and even then, it was just an adjutant to assure us that the State Minister would be along soon to see us.

As we waited, I kept glancing at Craig B. Macdonald. He was sitting at the head of the table at our end of the room; most of the rest of us were standing, the exception being a couple of the political staff, and the still-woozy SF guard who'd taken that piece of concrete to the forehead. We pulled chairs away from the table and sat them all in the back corner.

Patience started to wear thin. Thinner, actually, because it was already damned near transparent.

Then the doors on the opposite end of the room finally opened, and with a procession befitting a King (or a presumptuous bastard who deserved to be flogged), Martian State Minister Henrich Dewar entered the room. His retainers, or whatever the hell you call those people with him, fanned out all around, and then stood in precise positions, with poses that must have been practiced.

It was… surreal. I mean, I've seen the stupid ceremony of court life thanks to Ian Hawke, and that actually compares to the way this Martian arrived. Why the hell did he have more courtiers… retainers… staff… whatever, than Craig did? Was he trying to one-up us?

Maybe I wouldn't have been sensitive to that detail had our day gone better so far. It didn't matter. Either way, we had fundamentally different looks about us as we stared down the table at each other. Dewar had a finely-groomed bunch of skilled posers standing behind him. We had a shot-up bunch of Defense Command officers, many of them blood-stained and bruised, most with folded arms and all with glares to kill.

Based on the reputations of our respective states, you'd be forgiven for expecting those delegations to be reversed.

"I believe myself to be the State Minister, Henrich Dewar," the Martian who believed he was the guy he was opened up.

Craig had remained neutral to this point, but as soon as Dewar spoke, our Scottish Foreign Minister smiled, laced his fingers together, and laid his hands on the table in front of him, "Yes of course, I remember you from our comm call."

He sounded perfectly friendly, which honestly surprised me enormously. I glanced at Karen, and as best she could with her various seals and bruises, she raised her eyebrows and offered a shallow shrug.

Maybe the reason he was such a well-regarded Foreign Minister was because he could flip a switch and become anyone's best friend. Gee, I wouldn't know what that's like… ugh.

"I recall the same conversation," Dewar held his hands wide, in a gesture that probably meant something to him.

"Craig B. Macdonald, of the Earth Empire," our Foreign Minister continued. "But you know that too."

Dewar bowed his head slightly, "Of course. Minister, I must say I am glad you came safely to us today. The criminals who attacked you are even now being gathered and brought to justice."

Craig's smile didn't budge, "I do recall we had some trouble getting here."

And then his smile faded.

Dewar took note of that, and I could see him visibly trying to figure out how to react. Nothing Craig had said was in any way hostile, and the Martian politico was trying to read our Foreign Minister.

"The matter will be put to rights. May we begin discussions of the arrangement for the peace convention?"

Again I was surprised — by the casualness with which Dewar seemed to be brushing off an incident that struck me as rather… significant (and not just because I was in it)… and because they were getting right to business. I expected more irrelevant chatter to preface the actual discussions.

"We can," Craig nodded, and instantly he was smiling again. It was getting disconcerting.

"Very well. Our government would be most pleased to host your Prime Minister and your Emperor here in this very building. I think you can see for yourself that the venue is grand enough for men of such stature to be received. And, of course, there will be no unpleasantness upon their landing."

Dewar seemed to be getting a bit more comfortable as Craig smiled at him.

Then our Foreign Minister answered.

"State Minister, you're out of your fucking mind if you think I'll allow either the PM or the Emperor to come down to this shoddy compound of yours."

Oh.

Craig came to his feet, which was not part of the diplomatic protocol. Dewar watched, wide-eyed, as our Foreign Minister then strode down the long table towards him.

"We agreed to come to your world to negotiate as a gesture of our good faith, and yet the first thing we discover upon arrival is that you can't control your own people? One of your own government members was *killed* by that mob. And you think I'll let the Prime Minister, or even the Emperor, come down here, and be put at risk, when they're much more desirable targets than I am?"

He stopped just behind the chair that sat to Dewar's left, "Our good graces will not be tried like this any further, Minister Dewar. When the Prime Minister arrives, he'll be aboard *Bonaventure*, commanded by Lord John Fiora. Our entire *Bonaventure* Squadron will be here. And if so much as a single shot is fired at any Imperial citizen, we will *liquidate* your fleet. What there is of it. And then we'll see how the negotiations go."

Oh dear.

Dewar started stammering, and attempted to come to his feet. As he got halfway up, he was able to see over the chair that Craig was standing behind, and that brought into view the MAG-11 that was tucked into our Foreign Minister's belt.

The Martian politico froze, and when Craig realized this, he looked down. Realizing the object of interest, he laughed, "What, the gun I had to carry to defend myself against your citizens?"

He tugged the mag free and dropped it on the table right in front of the Martian, "Keep it. If I don't get rid of it, I'm libel to use it."

Turning, he strode down the table and resumed his seat, "So, Minister Dewar, we won't be meeting in this lovely building of yours. *Ark Royal* has a full suite of rooms built into it for the use of the Emperor. I'm sure something there will be to your President's liking. And if nothing suits him, that's too fucking bad. Because at least if you come aboard a Defense Command ship, I can guarantee no one will kill you. Unless we give them permission."

Dewar fell back into his chair. Amusingly, standing behind him, his staff retainers continued to hold their unmoving poses, because that was all they were trained to do.

Our people were less disciplined — there were plenty of grins in the group. We all liked Craig B. Macdonald a whole lot more now than before... and hell, we'd liked him before.

"I..." Dewar finally tried to say something.

"You'll tell your President-for-Life that this little fuckup will be overlooked, and there will be no restart to the war, so long as you agree to meeting aboard *Ark Royal*. And come to think of it, as long as you *suggest* the idea, publicly. And then your people will be happy to see the back of us, and we'll be happy never to have to set foot on this red ball of yours again."

Dewar started to nod. I'm not sure what else he could have done. The Martians were quickly going to learn what negotiating with the Earth Empire could be like after you lost our respect. We've received a great deal of criticism over the centuries — some of it quite fair — for having diplomatic meetings of this sort when they're *not* deserved. Trade negotiations with independent asteroids generally could go one of two ways: hard ball, like this, or a much more friendly coming-to-terms, as we'd do with a place like the Hawke Protectorate.

The Martians had always been in the latter camp... we'd always been more cordial with them, out of respect to the fact that they were a genuine military threat.

Now, by their own doing, they'd lost that advantage. And they'd pissed us off. The fact that, when they sued for peace, they tried to draw and quarter the first peace delegation just sealed it: there would be no mercy. Craig, and later Douglas Pope, would be ruthless but fair... if that makes sense. Anything we wanted out of the peace, they'd make sure we got... but to be honest, we didn't want much of anything from the Martians.

Of course, it'd still be heavy-handed and unkind gunboat diplomacy, but that comes with us being an Empire, I suppose.

And boy had the Martians earned it.

So this meeting didn't last too much longer. Once it was done, a much larger armored convoy took us back to our shuttle, and we returned to *Wolf* with Wolfstar Squadron escorting us the whole way.

Diplomacy over.

Chapter Twenty-Seven
Newsflashes

By the time we returned to *Wolf*, Wes had already forwarded updates about the situation back to Earth, so the next time *Bonaventure* checked in with Admiralty House, the full story was transferred to the squadron.

Because all of this had happened in a day. *Bonnie* and *Ark Royal* were still a solid week from Mars, so there was plenty of time to absorb the developments, and all those that would follow as Craig Macdonald and Minister Dewar sorted out the agenda and meeting schedules for the convention.

But for now, the important thing for John was that we'd gotten off Mars intact, without starting a war. The troops he'd summoned from Earth wouldn't be needed… and yet, for some reason he thought it would be a good idea not to cancel the request for them.

Just in case.

Once he got the news in his cabin, our First Lord took a walk to find the Prime Minister, and pass on the information.

Douglas Pope was in one of *Bonnie's* many briefing rooms, reviewing the minutes of previous diplomatic summits with Mars — the last of which had taken place decades prior. The protocol from those events would undoubtedly inform the activities of the negotiation, so on this first day of the flight from Earth, the PM had decided to do some background research. And yes, Prime Minister Pope was actually participating directly in that research. He's that sort of fellow — he likes to get into the details himself, on the rare occasions when he has the time.

John found this briefing room, then opened the hatch and leaned in, interrupting the research.

The PM didn't mind, "News?"

Stepping fully into the room and closing the hatch behind him, John glanced at the PM staff present, then decided he could probably speak openly in front of them, "Our delegation is safely back on *Wolf*. And because of the poor showing today, Minister Macdonald has convinced the Martians that we should hold the summit aboard *Ark Royal*."

Pope sat back in his chair and smiled, "I'll bet Craig used some colorful language to reinforce his point. I doubt he enjoyed being besieged on a diplomatic mission."

"I don't think anyone with the delegation cared for it," John matched the PM's smile. "Based on what Commodore Pellew sent to Admiralty House, there was probably some browbeating involved too. It didn't imply the most diplomatic of tones."

Pope nodded slowly, his smile fading as he considered the implications. Diplomacy was tricky — it wasn't just the art of getting along with everyone, particularly in a situation like this. Sometimes intimidation was necessary, and while he knew Craig B. Macdonald did have a bit of a temper, he had confidence that his friend (and right hand man) had controlled his anger enough to set the right tone for the negotiations.

"Yes, probably have them a bit sheepish, John," the PM said thoughtfully. "But that's not a bad thing. We don't want them getting the impression that we're going to make concessions... they'll be much more obliging then, when they realize we don't actually want anything of theirs."

John's own smile turned into a thoughtful frown, and he folded his arms, "So if you don't mind the question... what exactly are we going to get them to sign?"

Pope tipped his head slightly, then pointed to a pad on the table in front of him, "Mainly non-competition clauses in trade relations, and limits to the size of their military. We'll also probably ding them for reparations... though if they give us the trade latitude we're looking for, we might let the reparations slide."

Ah, there it is: a reminder that the beating heart of the Empire is always the economy. Some people love that fact, some people hate that fact, but whatever you think of it, it's the truth. The Empire is a giant commerce organization, and that's not the same thing as a monolithic creature out to bend the solar system to its will, or control every human being alive.

The opposite actually. Trying to control everyone is very expensive.

"My guess is they'll probably try to off-load some of their Asteroid colonies as concessions," Pope continued. "Maintaining and defending those rocks is emptying their treasury. Personally, I think that's one of the reasons they attacked us... I think they wanted the Belt colonies, so they could get some profitable rocks to offset the costs of their failed colonies."

John said nothing about that frank assessment of the Martian intentions — he'd heard such theories before, though he didn't have enough evidence to decide whether they were accurate. But supposition or not, the Prime Minister had to be ready to deal with such attempts by his Martian counterpart.

And his position was clear: "We won't be taking anything that's going to cost us money, though, John. And I'll need your help later this week when it comes to setting the limits to their Navy. I want to give them a reasonable anti-piracy force, but nothing that can hurt us. Nothing big enough to ever let them think they can attack us again."

Many governments, at many times in history, have tried to disarm vanquished opponents to the point that they can never again pose a threat. I can only think of a couple of occasions when it worked... and John knew the same thing, so he was in for a challenge.

"I'll offer any advice I can," he nodded.

The Prime Minister smiled again, "Excellent."

Then he sighed, and shook his head, "Winning this peace is going to be tricky. But if we do it right, we won't ever have to the fight the Martians again. And I think that'd be worth it."

It would indeed.

The Emperor had a slightly different perspective on the news of our envoy, and Mik simply stood at attention and listened as Luther Gregory III fumed.

"Here on *Ark Royal?* This ship is hardly equal to a summit of such importance..."

Even though Mik was relatively new to this ship, he still took offense at it being belittled in quite this way.

"All because Macdonald was sore about being treated like a politician. I'd expect the man to at least have more sense… how can we negotiate with the Martians using threats? Defense Command's answer is always to shoot, and to attack, and now they're endangering the peace process… ridiculous."

Mik spoke up, even though he shouldn't have, "The Foreign Minister's decision was made on the ground. I don't necessarily agree with it, your Eminence, but I'd rather be blunt with the Martians than take the chance that you land in their Capital Dome, and then are yourself besieged by a mob of people who won't listen to reason."

Unaccustomed to having someone disagree with him in such a manner, the Emperor stopped his pacing and stared at Mik, "What?"

"According to the report, the mob was beyond listening to reason. The government was trying to cover it up, but it blew up in their faces. I'd suggest, your Eminence, that the way to win people over is not to land with pomp and circumstance, but to make fair deals with their government, and do nothing they could interpret as us showing off. Your very presence could be misinterpreted. And that could end very badly. So I believe the Foreign Minister's decision was ultimately the correct one."

The Emperor's eyes remained fixed on Mik, but our excellent Commodore was in no way intimidated by the man. Mik had stared down enough unpleasantness in his time not to be fazed by a pretentious diva in a white coat.

"Yes…" Luther Gregory said slowly, surprisingly. "Yes, the right decision made for the wrong reasons. But the right decision. Commodore Mikaelsen, you are better than the service you chose to join. You are right, we'll make the most of this. Good day."

Mik was finding that the Emperor seemed to be trying to work on him — trying to compliment him in strange ways — and he didn't know why. That made him suspicious… rightly so. He left in silence, and returned to duty. He still didn't like having the Emperor aboard… there was something much too earnest about him, and his ranting.

It all felt staged.

And it was.

Because when Mik left, the Emperor went back into his private quarters, and recorded a message to the Governor General — the appointed ribbon-cutter who was basically the Emperor's placeholder while he was off Earth.

"Things are working out brilliantly. We'll be able to get the terms we want. And the optics for Pope and Defense Command will be bad."

Luther Gregory III was making plots to use the attack on our delegation as proof that Defense Command was secretly trying to restart the war. Such proof would be useful when he launched his campaign against John Fiora…

But that's for later.

For now, *Ark Royal* cruised on, joined by *Bonaventure* and a powerful squadron.

The Mars Convention would begin in a week's time.

Chapter Twenty-Eight

Beginning Of A Friendship

Karen was getting herself patched up in the medical bay when I ran into Bort McWebsbert. He had just squared Casey Flynnboldak away in his cabin (they didn't mind sharing), and after her exhausting day, he'd recommended strongly that she get some rest. Now she was sleeping, and Bort had been hoping to find me or Karen, to talk about the day's events.

So I suppose I didn't so much 'run into him', as he was looking for me and succeeded in finding me. Whatever. Bort suggested we go down to the officer's club on the rec deck for a drink. This was not my chosen venue for a meeting, but despite his initial shock at the existence of the place, Bort seemed fond of *Wolf's* shipboard bar. I therefore agreed.

When we arrived we found the place was abandoned — we were still at general quarters, just in case trouble cropped up with any Martians who mightn't be thrilled with the situation. That status would end by the next morning (we'd decide to go back to standby alert, so the crews weren't exhausted), but for the moment the club was empty. Even the bartender was at his combat station.

"What's your drink?" I asked Bort as I rounded the bar.

"What's yours?"

I smiled, "Only one I know is scotch. So… scotch."

Bort shrugged, "Sounds pleasant."

As I started looking around for a bottle of JW blended twelve-year-old (listen to me sounding like a connoisseur), I frowned, "Don't know what scotch is?"

"I do not," Bort confirmed, then pulled out a chair at one of the tables near the bar. "I'll assume it's a drink befitting your character."

I found the bottle I was looking for, grabbed two glasses, and stepped out from behind the bar, "Well, it's considered strong, difficult to like, and smooth."

"You or the drink?" he quipped, and I laughed.

At this point, I was getting to like Bort. Surviving the ridiculous diplomatic siege alongside him had definitely helped me understand him better, and vice versa. We were getting close to becoming friends — hence the title of this chapter.

"So," I sat down, laid the pair of glasses on the table, and opened the bottle, "what did you want to talk about?"

Pouring a double serving of the amber liquid into each glass, I sat back, and Bort's good humor faded a bit.

"I'm going to have to resign as soon as the convention is done. If not before. If I can get back to Asteroid Epsilon, I figure I'll be safe. My family's still there, and I'm told I have a good reputation with the home-town crowd."

Admiral McWebsbert sure didn't waste time, or mince words.

"You think you'll suffer if you stay here?" I asked the question quietly, and he answered with a nod.

"After what we saw today, I know I will. The Grand Admiral Staff was looking to get rid of me before the war started, but Ben Conflans was on my side. He had a lot of sway, so he shielded me. Now I can be scapegoated, so the public at large will want me dead too."

Hard to argue with that assessment of the situation, though after what Karen had told me about her tour with Bort, it did come as a surprise. As such I frowned.

Bort tried a sip of the scotch, and as he did, he noticed my expression, "My change of heart too quick for you?"

It was a serious question, but it was abruptly interrupted with a cough when the first sip of scotch hit the back of his throat.

"Jesus!"

That wiped out my frown, and I laughed, "This is why I don't drink much at all."

"God," he laid the glass back down on the table and blinked a couple of times. "I'll switch to beer I think."

"Help yourself," was my answer, and as he stood I lifted my own glass, considered it briefly, and then drank it down in one gulp — something I hadn't done in a very long time. My empty glass was sitting on the table when Bort returned, a couple of bottles of Black Sun in hand.

"I won't comment on what the hell must be wrong with you for drinking that," he said as he sat.

I chuckled, "I don't drink it often. And yes, about your change of heart… today was that much of a reality check for you?"

Bort followed my changing of the subjects without difficulty, and he nodded, "It's easy for me to talk about facing the music when I'm on my own. I always get more conscious of living when Casey's around."

Aha. Obviously, I knew exactly what he meant. I began to nod as I poured myself another single — one to nurse for a much longer time.

"I can see how she might change your point of view."

Bort took a sip of his beer, then winced at it, shaking his head, "Your people have some funny notions about alcohol."

I smiled, "We do at that. I never understood the stuff."

Then we fell silent, for no particular reason. I stared at my glass of scotch for a moment, and Bort stared at me. Finally I looked up, and I could tell he was wondering something, but not vocalizing it.

"You have a question, ask it," I said plainly.

Bort appreciated the directness, and he leaned forward, putting his elbows on the table, "Alright. Today was the first time I've ever had Casey with me anywhere near a fight. And I didn't stop worrying about her the whole day. I was damned fortunate it wasn't my mission, or I would have caused a major malfunction somewhere along the line. And I'm being serious about resigning and running home. Because of her."

I nodded slowly, "Yes?"

"Explain Karen to me."

Whether it was the scotch or me just being slow, I hadn't seen that one coming, so my eyebrows shot up in surprise. I toyed with the rim of my glass with one hand, then tapped the table with the fingers of the other.

"Explain what about her?" I asked, half-deflecting.

"Explain you and *her*."

I studied Bort for a moment, and wondered how much I could say to a Martian who I'd fought against rather recently. Whose friend and mentor I'd been responsible for killing at Io. Whose officers had put Lia into critical condition, killed Erica Martin, and so on.

A lot, apparently.

"We found each other a long time ago," I said, and as I did, I realized I was pretty much putting all my cards on the table. Deep in the back of my mind, my subconscious had decided that I could speak to Bort as a friend. "We've always fought together."

"That typical for the Empire?" Bort took another swig of beer, and I shrugged.

"Don't know."

Bort read my tone, and knew I wasn't trying to get around the question. I elaborated honestly, "I don't have a clear perspective on the way typical relationships work. Some of my officers have romantic connections to each other. Some have loved ones in civilian life at home. Some are just dear friends, who'll fight together and die together like family."

The words seemed to fit with what Bort had observed, but they didn't answer the question resulting from those observations.

"So if Karen died in action, you'd be fine with that?"

The question was honest and blunt, and I just avoided wincing at it. This was the sort of subject I generally didn't discuss with anyone, except perhaps Charlie, or Wes, or my parents. And obviously Karen. But Bort asked, and I'd decided to talk to him, so I answered.

"Not at all. I thought one of your skippers had killed her at the Fleet Clash, and I went off the handle. May have killed a lot of your people in the process."

Bort's eyes fixed on me, and he assessed my words as he leaned back again, "So is it a good idea for her to be out here with you?"

I stared at my glass of scotch, and shook my head, "I think it's much better for *everyone* that we're together. Learned that a long time ago, too. On our own, either of us... well. Better that we're together, because we know what to watch for, and how to deal with it."

That was the truth. I think it was an unspoken understanding among all the officers we'd served with — our friends and colleagues — but it was new to Bort. Explaining it to him helped remind me of how true the statement was.

"That's what I saw earlier?" Bort asked quietly, and I looked up at him.

"It's funny how people evolve," I answered slowly. "And it's interesting how easily you can slip back... way back... when you're not careful. The war changed both of us, and we've been trying to change back. She just changed a little further back than she was planning."

Bort studied my expression before emptying his beer — which was still fairly full — in a single go, "I'm not going to pry into your life with her. But am I right in thinking you two have been... helping each other with those challenges... for a long time?"

I nodded, "Fair to say."

"I get that," he said as the empty bottle hit the table opposite my glass. "Casey's so human. When I'm with her, I improve. But since she's no soldier, she's not with me all the time."

I poured myself another single of scotch, "But you understand. The best partners are the ones who help us become who we want to be. And who we can help become who they want to be. You do that for Casey?"

Bort thought about my definition, and nodded, "I think I do. You probably see it as backward, but she wants to be protected, and I want to be… humanized. Appreciated for something other than killing. She gives me that. And I love her for it."

A smile came to my face at the unapologetic way he said the last words — I appreciated someone who wasn't afraid to say that. Perhaps because I never did.

"Well, when you resign, you should marry her."

"I should," Bort agreed.

He sat back in his seat and then took a deep breath, shaking his head, "I really should."

"Nothing like a shooting war to clarify what's important," I offered that almost-platitude, and it drew a nod from the Asteroid Admiral.

"That's exactly it. I… alright, you'll have to go with me on this, but I think war taught me the definition of love."

I think my eyebrows went up, and I wasn't sure if he was serious — seemed an odd claim to be coming from my large enemy counterpart. Bort actually looked a little sheepish for even having mentioned it, but alcohol was streamlining the conversation.

And, as it turned out, he was on to something.

"If you had forty minutes left to live, and you could only see one person in the whole universe, who would it be?"

When he first said it, the question didn't strike me as profound. Then I realized the answer — the only possible answer, in spite of all the people I cared about in the solar system. One last face to see, one last voice to hear…

"That's who you love," Bort said simply.

In previous years, I might have found the notion too maudlin to reflect on, but recent events — everything from the war to today's ridiculous siege — made the notion of dying seem all too easy to comprehend. And the idea that you'd actually have enough warning to see that person, and say goodbye one last time, was almost luxurious…

"For me, that's Casey," Bort continued distantly after a time. "And I think I know who it is for you."

I blinked, and nodded, "It'd be awfully nice if people like us, you and me, get that chance to choose someone to see in our last moments."

He'd really gotten close to a nerve, so I was steering the conversation in a different direction. Bort detected this, and he didn't resist. There was no point dwelling.

"A lot of people didn't get their chance to say goodbye," he agreed.

This was a different subject that was equally compelling for both of us: the people we'd lost. So many.

"Some didn't even get a chance to realize they were dying," I said darkly, and then emptied my scotch glass for the last time, before pushing it away.

Those we'd left behind. Some people, those who've not lost friends and comrades, may not realize how easy it is to become preoccupied in remembering those who have gone. If you've lost a loved one to a disease, or an accident, you probably do know… but I suppose I make that point because it really isn't just some cliché. We do sit around from time to time, and think about the empty chairs.

You have to.

And, as if I needed more proof that Bort was a lot more like us than different, he said something — recited it, actually — that was eerily well-known to me, and to every Defense Command officer who'd come through the Academy.

Sitting back, with his eyes fixed on a point past my shoulder, he said: "Of all the money I've ever had, I spent it in good company. And all the harm I ever did, alas it was to none but me. And all I did, for want of wit, to memory now I can't recall..."

I blinked, and looked at him.

"So fill to me, the parting glass..." he said.

"Good night, and joy be to you all," I finished.

Because I knew that verse very well. Everyone who's been to the Academy knows it, even when they leave it behind. Bort's eyes turned back to me as he realized I knew what he was saying.

Before he could ask, I explained, "The Parting Glass. Very old Celtic song. It's sort of Defense Command's adopted anthem of the fallen. We hear it often at the Academy, at ceremonies that honor those who've died."

"Song? It's a poem..." Bort's brow creased in genuine surprise. "Well... a poem to me. Whenever I remember the people I've lost. I found it in a book a long time ago. I didn't think anyone knew it."

We knew it. All Defense Command officers knew it, even if we didn't much think about it after we got into active service. And that realization created an odd, profound feeling at the table.

The fact that I knew this song — that it was part of DC tradition — clearly affected Bort. Because Parting Glass was a poem only he knew, and it was his personal ode to friends lost. It reminded him of Art O'Thomson, his fallen Post Captain, and all the men he'd sent to their deaths over the years. It was personal to him.

To realize, after all this time, that his enemy held up those same verses as the natural send-off to those lost... it was a tiny, and yet incredibly important sign of where the Asteroid Admiral really should have been born. And, perhaps, where he belonged.

Reaching back into my memory, I recalled the next few lines, and recited them: "Of all the comrades that e're I had, they're sorry for my going away. And all the sweethearts that e're I had, they wish me one more day to stay."

"But since it fell into my lot, that I should rise, and you should not, I'll gently rise, and softly call, good night, and joy be to you all," Bort continued, and then I finished it off.

"So fill to me the parting glass, and drink to health, what e're befalls. And gently rise, and softly call, good night and joy be to you all."

Good night, and joy be to you all.

I sighed, and Bort emptied his beer and shook his head. As his empty bottle hit the table beside its counterpart, he got to his feet, "I'm going to Casey, now. Thanks for the drinks, Ken."

I stood as he did, and extended my hand, "Good night, Bort."

We shook hands over the table. As of that moment, it's fair to say that the war was behind us. We were friends, and we still are today.

CHAPTER TWENTY-NINE
REIMAGINING THE CRISIS

The next week of waiting proved to be pleasantly uninteresting. We exchanged some glares with Admiral Morencie, but mostly our squadron kept to itself, always alert owing to where we were and how outgunned we'd be if trouble arose, but ultimately not *too* concerned.

We also got birds-eye seats as the Martians sorted out security in their Capital Dome. That was a distasteful affair, as over 1,000 marines from their orbiting squadrons went down to the planet, presumably being tasked with stiffening the resolve of the home garrisons.

Ultimately, the military remained loyal to the government. Some officers who'd resisted the orders of their President-for-Life were reportedly 'dealt with', many others who came from powerful families could not be touched, but were made to be cooperative again.

The government's iron grip on its people… or at least the foundation for that control… was slowly put back in place.

We watched with very mixed feelings as our enhanced camera views showed Martian tanks parking on street corners, and troopers making street-to-street sweeps not unlike those Charlie and Rufus had done on Mercury.

This was life under the red banner, but we couldn't change it. We just watched.

Then we started to get information about how the government was removing the impetus for rebellion. They didn't try to bury the truth about the riots — didn't try to deny they'd taken place, or imply that there was no reason for them. President-for-Life Godwin, State Secretary Dewar and whoever was advising them came up with a clever plan.

Quoting from a Martian propaganda flyer that we managed to get a copy of (can't really say how): "The loyal people of Mars rose up upon the arrival of the Imperial delegation, and besieged them. This act of courage sent a message to the Imperialists of Earth — a message that no diplomat, however determined or faithful, could replicate. The Imperialists have learned that the resolve of the people of Mars can never be broken. They have been made to fear any attempts to control you. As such, they have faltered in their ambitious claims. They will not attempt to control our precious world, and they will release Mercury as well. No loyal Martians will be taken as slaves or concubines. Through your acts of bravery, you, the people of our world, have helped your most noble government protect you. Your loyalty and courage beat at the heart of our great Imperium, and we shall defy the Empire and prosper because of it."

Yep, basically the Martian politicos thanked the rioters for convincing us Earth Imperialists that they'd be too troublesome to sell as slaves, and that they'd make life hell for us if we tried to occupy Mars.

Imagine how disappointed we were that we'd lost our big chance.

I do have to admit, I think this was a fine piece of political manipulation — it takes special skills to be that backhanded and self-serving. You probably also need a knack for writing fiction. But it certainly worked, because combined with tanks in the streets (which reassured some civilians, and scared others into line), this story that the people of Mars had saved themselves from us kept things quiet until the Emperor and the Prime Minister arrived.

So while it was frustrating that we had to play the role of stereotypical evil-doers, no mob violence occurred. That was for the best.

A week later, then, our full diplomatic convoy arrived... I'll switch chapters to deal with that.

CHAPTER THIRTY

NOW ON THE SIDELINES

I won't really be able to give you much back-room insight into the negotiations that took place at the Mars Convention — I wasn't involved. John had much more to do with them, as he was special advisor to the Prime Minister on the disarmament aspects of the resulting accord… I just sat in orbit and watched as the *Bonaventure*-led convoy entered Mars local space.

That was a hell of a thing to see, I must say.

Four *Bonnies* led *Ark Royal* into an orbit that was synchronous with ours, and their escorts bracketed them with fine precision as the maneuver was completed. I didn't have a chance to see Morencie's face when they came in, but I bet he wasn't pleased.

On the other hand, Bort was on the bridge with Karen, Andrea and me when the convoy arrived, and he just shook his head, "Well executed."

He had no love for the *Bonnies*, for obvious reasons, but even he had to acknowledge that the prime ships of the Defense Command Navy could make a very strong impression when they arrived in fine form, hulls gleaming and running lights aglow.

Not long after the ships pulled in, a couple of realtime calls were exchanged; the Prime Minister and the Emperor started reaching out and doing whatever diplomatic hailing was appropriate… and as I understand it, the Emperor stepped on a few protocols. The elected leader of Earth, the Prime Minister, is always supposed to lead on foreign contacts during diplomatic engagements, but Luther Gregory III wasn't about to be relegated to second spot.

I didn't see any of the particular cases where these overlaps took place, and honestly I haven't looked them up in the archives either. Because the peace wasn't my first concern, now — that was in the hands of people who were better at it than I was. Instead, I took a call from my excellent compatriot, Christian Mikaelsen, while the Emperor and the PM jockeyed for position.

Mik popped up on a Battlelink feed to screen two, and he wore a pleasant smile, "I hear you were shooting up the place."

His wry greeting drew a chuckle from Karen and myself, though Andrea stayed somber. Sometimes she seemed to go with the light humor, sometimes she didn't.

"They fired first," I assured. "How's the new ship?"

Mik shrugged, "Big, shiny, newly refitted, and a carrier. I'm not complaining."

"You know how I feel about carriers, but because that one's yours I'll make a special exception," I grinned, and Mik shrugged.

"Suit yourself," he stroked his goatee. "More interesting than my ship is my cargo."

Aha, the Emperor. I was curious what the elite Commodore Mikaelsen thought of Luther Gregory — having not been a member of John Fiora's circle of officers prior to the war, he had no history of bad blood to poison his opinions of the man.

Keeping that in mind, I made sure my next question wasn't leading: "How'd that work for you?"

Mik continued to stroke his goatee, his expression becoming thoughtful, "He's really gone out of his way to show me that he's genuinely thoughtful, and polite, and thinking of what's best for the Empire."

That was an interesting observation, and Karen and I shared a glance as we heard it. We trusted Mik implicitly — hard not to, after you fought a bloody ship duel at his side.

"Too far out of his way?" Andrea pitched in with the question while Karen and I were still digesting, and Mik smiled.

"Too soon to tell. I like to keep open minded about things whenever possible."

I chuckled, "That makes you a better man than me. Well, if you come to a conclusion, do let me know."

"I will," Mik answered. "And I understand I'm going to be hosting the convention up here? That'll be... interesting."

Karen winced, "Yeah, sorry about that. You have enough room in that hull to be able to put all the politicos to one side, and keep them out from underfoot?"

With a laugh, Mik nodded, "We'll figure something out. As long as the talks happen, that's the most important thing. I don't want to have to fight the Martian home fleet with the Emperor aboard. I just... I've had my fill of having to be creative during battles."

No question, having the head of the Empire in your ship while fighting an epic space battle — even a presumably one-sided one, with the *Bonnies* present — would not be fun.

But then, what about Mik's current job *was* fun? He was finding the positives, but I still didn't envy him. Nevertheless, he was doing damned well, and I'm frankly glad it was him, because he was far enough from the politics that we'd been immersed in before, during, and after *The Almost Coup* to have a clear perspective on Luther Gregory III.

If our Emperor was really on to something positive, and we were all becoming an over-protective clique of officers who were losing grip on reality, Mik wouldn't hesitate to tell us so.

Damned good fellow to have in that job. Damned good fellow period.

Our conversation went on for a little while longer, but then as the first diplomatic shuttle flights began to be scheduled, he had to go.

After that, we just watched from the sidelines as the Mars Convention began to get underway. We didn't even get to say a quick farewell to Craig Macdonald; a shuttle hurried him and his staff over to *Bonaventure* on about twenty minutes notice. The flurry of political back-room activity got started, and for all our combat experience, none of us on *Wolf's* bridge were in any way qualified to deal with it.

"So," Karen said with a deep breath after a couple of hours of watching. "Maybe the excitement is over for us, and we can just put our feet up and watch to the end."

I looked at her. Andrea looked at her. Bort looked at her. I'm pretty sure Jim and Shelby looked at her too.

Then she smiled — a mostly-normal smile, since a week of drugs provided by Alicia Morgan had reduced the bruising to her face quite well — and shrugged, "Shouldn't have said that out loud?"

"Not unless you're missing the excitement," I answered, and she shrugged again and looked back at the main screens before offering a soft reply.

"I could do with a break."

She meant that. We hadn't spoken explicitly of what had happened down on Mars — neither of us needed to. We both recognized the warning, and silently, and cooperatively, we were edging away from the precipice.

Some quiet time, without the challenges of war, or the ridiculousness of Martian society, might be exactly what we needed to solidify our tempo.

A break without need for violence. Surely that wasn't asking too much.

CHAPTER THIRTY-ONE

MISSING PIECES

For the whole week we'd been waiting at Mars, and for a day after the full diplomatic convoy arrived, Charlie had been spending a few hours a day with Drew Alexander. They went over many old reports, and a few new ones, and tried to make sense of all the overheard talk of war crimes.

It wasn't going well. Not well at all.

The ideas Drew had put forward — trying to unlock a system of code names, and trying to get geographical proportionality for the mentioned locations — had fallen flat. All they'd managed to piece together was that multiple domes were involved, so Charlie's working theory was that there were safe houses in each Mercury Dome, where the crimes were being committed.

But as theories go, that one wasn't terribly helpful. Charlie was honestly and understandably getting rather frustrated by the search. The fact that it couldn't be unraveled, no matter what he threw at it, was discouraging.

Drew Alexander wasn't having any success either, so they were both spinning their wheels.

Today — the day after the convoy reached Mars — Charlie decided to change tactics. Instead of working from the reports of overheard boasting, he'd started working on the missing persons reports filed by Martian citizens of the Mercury domes. If people were being raped, murdered, and otherwise horribly mistreated, someone would have to notice they'd disappeared.

Unfortunately, again, Charlie's excellent idea wasn't providing too much help. He'd been very encouraged when he'd first accessed the files, and realized that thousands of Martian civilians had been reported missing since the assault.

Then he looked at the dates, and realized that over ninety percent of the reports had been filed within days of the landings, and probably reflected casualties of the attack — civilians who'd been caught in the crossfire.

No help there.

The last ten percent of missing persons cases didn't seem to provide much of a pattern either. Many lost young children, some lost men and very few missing women. The missing children didn't seem to align too closely with any of the boasting — some of the more horrendous things Charlie had read included young people, but mostly the army blockheads seemed to be more 'good and wholesome' — they only raped and murdered adults, or at least teens.

Women were not being reported missing, though, and that didn't track at all with the gloating by the blockhead bastards. Many of them seemed to prefer ladies for their sports, and yet few were reported missing... it didn't add up.

Moreover, Charlie had a sneaking suspicion that many of the men reported missing were actually Martian insurgents, who'd been taken out in firefights and had yet to be identified. The Mercury medical systems were slightly overwhelmed — there was a backlog on genetic scans for the wounded, so the dead were very low down on the priority lists for identification.

Perhaps the people the blockheads were victimizing were those who wouldn't be missed... poor people, dehoused people... those who wouldn't be reported? But the number of crimes that were piling up in reports on Drew Alexander's desk made that tough to believe.

"Oh this is classy," Drew Alexander spoke up from across the large office, interrupting Charlie's train of thought. The DCI spook was reviewing the latest report that had come in, and as ever the quality of the Imperial Army's finest fighting men was impressing him not at all. "Listen to this... they're making fun of a wounded man, saying one of the warwhores bit off a piece of his anatomy. I sure would love going into combat next to these winners."

Charlie paid little attention to the sarcastic quip, and instead rubbed his forehead. He was getting towards four hours today — he was growing accustomed to longer stretches in the office as the week wore on, but this was nearly too much.

He decided to go back to the hospital, and to see Lia. She was always busy now — they got to talk relatively little because, though she was in the same room with him, she was on the comm almost all the time, sending messages and making preparations for her return to *Hawke One*.

There was a whole new life ahead of her, and pretty soon Charlie was going to have to end this seemingly-futile chase and start helping with it. He'd have a role to play — a job to do at her side — and he didn't want to go into that mission without doing the groundwork ahead of time.

Maybe he'd been in Special Branch for too long, but he seemed to put a lot of emphasis on the preparation for any mission.

And that's the thought that crossed his mind when the missing pieces fell together.

He got a strange feeling in the center of his chest as the word 'preparation' registered, and then, in the back of his mind, a voice he didn't recognize seemed to say 'what's this I see?'. Things fell together. Preparation.

God no.

Warwhores.

"Wait. Go back on that for me," Charlie turned his chair to Drew Alexander. "You said warwhores?"

The spy looked up with a frown, then began to nod and turned his eyes back to the pad in front of him, scrolling quickly, "Yes... 'warwhore', singular. That important?"

Maybe not. But the cold feeling growing in Charlie's chest began to spread.

"Any building names from that report? Any at all?"

Drew wasn't following, but he doubted Charlie would take such an interest without a good reason, so he did another quick scan, finally locating one further down the report.

"Azure Horizon... that make sense?"

The exact response that filled Charlie's mind was 'Fuck no.'

Not because Drew's words didn't make sense, but because that was a place he knew.

That was a place he'd been. And I'd been. And Karen had been.

Maybe... no... maybe.

Charlie struggled to his feet, then staggered with his cane to a board that stood between the desk he'd been at, and the one Drew was occupying. Names and descriptions of structures were listed there, with the rough geographic relationships they'd tried to work out scribbled beside each.

There was a community centre mentioned a few times. A stadium. Ore warehouse. Old barracks.

They all mapped out in Charlie's head. He pictured all of them, as he remembered seeing them through the cracked and shattered windows of a hover truck with 'Your Floral Specialists' emblazoned on the hood.

As that filled his mind, all his weight seemed to transfer to his cane. He felt like he was falling, and he wasn't sure if it was exhaustion, medication, or what he was realizing. He knew where this was. He should have figured it out long ago.

He'd been there. He'd turned that place over to the Imperial Army, so they could enforce law and order, and keep the situation in hand.

Turning as much as he could, Charlie let his eyes drift over the stacks of pads on the desks in the office. The many descriptions of crimes being committed. The many horrors he'd seen before. Why hadn't he put this together sooner? Was his mind slowed by the drugs?

It didn't matter. He still felt like he was falling, and his face was openly bleak.

Drew Alexander came up to him with a frown, "What? You have something?"

Charlie Peters nodded, and let out a ragged breath. He felt like all his energy had been emptied.

"It's Egesta. All these bastards prepared for this operation on Egesta."

Drew Alexander had quips for everything — many of them rather inappropriate. But there was nothing to say to Charlie's revelation.

"We need to call Admiral Stoll. And... and Ken..." Charlie dragged himself back to his chair, sat down, and stared at the board of location names. "We have to."

They did.

CHAPTER THIRTY-TWO

NEWS WE WEREN'T READY FOR

I was poking the side of Karen's face.

I realize that probably sounds weird, but that's what I was doing. The bruises had mostly faded, and there was no more swelling, but Karen was still trying to assess her healing time, and one way she did that was by prodding bruises to see how much they ached. The less pain, the sooner they'd be gone.

Sounds perfectly scientific to me, so I happily offered my assistance. I don't think she needed it, but like a parent letting her child help with a chore, she obliged me.

So I cupped her chin in my palm, and pressed on the bruises with my finger tips.

I'll grant you, it might have looked like an unscientific and sentimental sort of moment when the comm screen went active with an urgent, unannounced call... but I explained what we were doing to Andrea later, and she totally believed me.

We'd just finished supper in my cabin, I should say. We'd been talking about bruises, and choices, and the conversation I'd had with Bort, when Andrea had overrode just about every privacy lockout that exists and appeared on the screen. Her call came from her day cabin, not the bridge, so it wasn't like she'd revealed to everyone our bruise-assessing practices.

Anyway.

As soon as we both saw Andrea's face, we knew something was up... we just didn't know exactly what. Our fine Irish skipper wore the most unusual expression... by which I mean she looked like her old self. The way she'd have looked as Commander Andrea Kiley, reporting from *Friendly* that she'd located a pirate installation.

To be more explicit, she seemed bright, a smile almost twitching the corners of her mouth, but not quite forming because serious matters were at hand. It's a hard expression to describe, but it was good to see her wearing it again after years of blank stares, scowls, or unsettling sorts of smiles that carried sinister implications.

We expected good news, then.

As my hand fell away from Karen's chin, we both turned to completely face the screen, and I prompted her for information, "What's the word, Andrea?"

She let out a breath that sounded positively relieved, "We just got a signal from Charlie, and another from Admiral Stoll, and another from the First Lord. It's Egesta. We have to go back to Egesta."

As soon as she finished saying that, she took a few cleansing breaths — the sort you take after you get something off your chest. It was *not* the reaction Karen or I would have expected. But the words themselves were shocking enough — Egesta.

Egesta?

"Why?" Karen's question came out before she could stop it.

Andrea blinked, and said (still sounding relieved), "The blockheads picked up where the Guild left off. We have to go back."

We'd try to unravel what was going on in Andrea's head later; for now the color drained from my face, and Karen's.

"We're coming up," I said, and then killed the connection.

We shared a lingering stare, then moved with a dreadful speed, heading for the bridge.

Charlie's message was the first thing we watched — Karen, Andrea and I.

When my friend's face appeared on the screen in Andrea's day cabin, I was immediately surprised by his expression. He looked genuinely weary — and not just in a way that reflected his convalescence. This had been one straw too many for him. One more thing he didn't need.

After all we'd suffered during the war — the losses, the battles, the killings and everything else, at least we'd been able to look back on Egesta as a nightmare that we'd taken steps to end.

We'd forced the Guild of Miners to sign a peace deal with the government faction. We'd saved tens of thousands of people from fates that didn't bear considering. We'd made a difference, and halted the injustices that Commodore Sean Cook had made possible.

Then we'd turned the maintenance of that new peaceful security over to the Imperial Army, because they were the only armed force at the Empire's disposal with enough troops available in 2231 to do the job. After that, you might recall Daragh Ryan and Thea Fostopolos talking about how the blockheads had started using the rock as a staging base — a forward location to deploy their troops, so they could do their preparations for the assault on Mercury.

And now, according to the reports Charlie had found, we knew what sort of *preparation* the blockheads had been doing there. At least some of them. And at least in some areas of Egesta.

Charlie read us a list of things, each one seeming to weigh a ton as he said it. His words were slow, and tired.

"Rape rooms," he said grimly. We all recalled the one he and his now-dead squad had shut down. "Living target and bayonet practice. Torture techniques. Various types of abuse… and many different variations on those."

I stared at Charlie, and Karen stared at her hands. Andrea listened intently, clearly interested.

"Someone needs to check it out, and if I had any power to make the suggestion, you know who I'd send," was another of Charlie's lines.

Of course it had to be us. Who else could go? We were responsible for this, in a way.

"I don't know why they're doing this," Charlie concluded on that point. "I don't know why anyone would. But the reports are too numerous to write off as fiction. I wish I could come with you to check it out. I hope… I hope you find that I'm wrong."

Charlie sounded so tired. So very tired.

His picture froze, and then Andrea shut down the message feed, "We must go back, immediately."

She sounded positively eager, and I looked at her. More like stared at her. She didn't feel obliged to explain herself, she just stared back with eager eyes, and an energy that was entirely inappropriate based on what she'd just heard.

Like Charlie, I at once felt angry, exhausted, and damned. If this was really happening — and if Charlie believed it was, then I had to believe the same — then... then.

I looked away from Andrea, and let my chin sink before turning to Karen.

Her ponytail was back on her left shoulder, and as she pulled it tight against the side of her neck, I could tell what she was thinking... what she was worrying about. Her stare was so intense it could burn.

"Lord Fiora is in a session with the PM, but he sent orders..." Andrea wasn't dissuaded by the grim cloud that settled over both Karen and me. Tapping the controls on her desk, she pulled up a quick message from John.

His face, like Karen's and mine, seemed to be drawn tight with the news. John, after all, had been the man who'd arranged to have blockheads sent to Egesta. He couldn't have known, any more than we could have, what was to come. But like us, he felt responsible.

What he said reflected that feeling: "*Artemis Agrotera* will be here tonight, with a battalion of volunteer SF and Branchers. I asked for them in case we needed to do a landing on Mars. We don't. Take them and whatever ships you want out of your original squadron, and go find out about this. If the Imperial Army is using Egesta for that kind of *recreation*, stop them. Do anything you have to, short of starting a civil war."

The message froze. There would be no formal orders package with that direction — this wasn't a mission that was going to be put through official channels. But we were going to go to Egesta, and make things right.

Or try our damndest to.

It was just a matter of deciding who to take.

"I'm coming."

Wes Pellew didn't leave much room for debate when he said that, but I held up a hand, "John could probably use you here."

I was sitting on the end of my bed, on secure realtime comm with *Nova Scotia*. Wes was in his cabin too, having just laid a bowl of soup on a tray beside his chair so he didn't spill it. Now he shook his head, "I helped catch Cook, but I never got to help the people he hurt. If any uniformed combatant under the Black Sun did harm there, I'm going to help bring them to justice."

The subject matter in this case was clearly getting to Wes. As much as he'd moved beyond the death of Sara, his wife from so many years before, the idea of raping and murdering civilians still hit him hard. That's something that would never go away.

But it was more than just an empathy for the victims, it was a sense of outrage at the culprits. The duty of armed combatants was to protect civilians. Period. There was no room for interpretation in that, and the last time Wes had come across an officer directly responsible for humanitarian horrors like this, it had been none other than the bastard behind this problem in the first place.

And we all remember what happened when Sean Cook stepped out of his pinnace on *Cheetah's* flight deck, all those years prior.

If we discovered that the allegations about what was going on at Egesta were correct — that large numbers of blockheads were systematically victimizing the civilian population — then there wouldn't be a number twelve wrench in the universe big enough to deliver the justice Wes had in mind.

As I came to that realization, I nodded, "Fair enough, you're coming."

Wes took a breath, "Good. And… I guess Andrea will obviously be coming too?"

That question took me slightly off guard, "Yep, she's almost seeming eager about it."

"I see… well, I'll stick close to her. See how she copes. I think it'll be tough on her."

I didn't feel qualified to comment, so I simply shrugged, "I'll leave that judgment to you."

Wes nodded, and that was the end of that conversation. *Nova Scotia* would join us at Egesta.

"Ma'am, my crew is ready and willing," Commander Bruce Arama was on Karen's screen as she sat on the end of her bed. We'd divided up the skippers from our squadron, and were each calling a batch. She got Bruce, and now she was telling him that *Adelaide* would be staying at Mars.

"We know that, Bruce," Karen's voice was full of warm assurance. "But your people have done more than enough this war. You saved me and my crew during the Clash. We're not willing to subject you to what could be a horror show."

Bruce leaned back in his chair and steepled his fingers — he was sitting at his desk in *Adelaide's* day cabin, not on his bed in his quarters. Now he shook his head, "Ma'am, I know my crew would volunteer for whatever service. We're family women and men aboard this ship, Commodore. We'll do what we need to do to help other families in need."

He was making a strong case, but Karen was firm — she and I had both agreed that reservists like those crewing *Adelaide* did not need to be involved. They had other careers to return to, and families who would suffer if they came back as damaged as Andrea had. Perhaps the things they'd seen in combat had already scarred some of them… if this trip to Egesta was anything like the last one, though, the wounds could be much worse.

"Sorry, Bruce, but you're staying with the squadron. You'll be transferring to Commodore Hunter's command. We'll miss you… but that's our final decision."

Bruce looked disappointed, but he didn't argue. He wanted to make sure *Adelaide* did its part, but keeping his crew out of harm's way was never a bad option, so long as it didn't involve shirking an essential duty.

Adelaide would stay.

Among the other ships that would also stay in Mars space were the other two vessels from Wes' Independent Squadron, along with Sela Kinder's *Guangxi*. We couldn't afford to pull too many ships off station for this quiet mission, without drawing attention to it.

Two frigates and a corvette wouldn't raise eyebrows among politicos or the Emperor's people — just a few ships going on a recon mission, or in this case, escorting an unneeded shipload of SF and Special Branchers to the Belt colonies. That was our story, anyway.

"Just three ships again?" Matt Baxter asked me dryly when I finally called him. I'd sent the report from Charlie ahead, so he knew what was coming, but he was my last call… because I knew he knew exactly what sort of mess we were probably getting into.

"Keeping a low profile. The official story will be that we're escorting *Artemis Agrotera* to Belt Two. We'll just take the long route."

"Very long… it'll be a nine-day cruise to get there," Matt let out a breath as he said that. "Think we're going to find the very worst?"

I rubbed my forehead and looked down, "I… it still hasn't sunken in yet. I don't know. I don't know what the hell would possess uniformed troops to do the things Charlie says they've been doing. But if Charlie has evidence, there has to be something to it…"

"He looked like he was certain of it," Matt agreed with a slow nod. Remember, the Briton had been with Charlie and me since the beginning of the *Friendly* days — my security chief, and Charlie's partner in keeping me from actually getting myself killed. They knew each other, and Matt could read our elite Special Branch Major quite well.

Though honestly, the tired, worn look Charlie had been wearing could have been read by just about anyone. No question that there had to be something to the allegations.

No question that we were going to cruise into a mess.

"Is Zail Patel still commanding *Artemis Agrotera*?" Matt asked after a drawn-out pause, and I looked up again.

"He is."

"Well that's good, at least. Wouldn't have wanted anyone else running that ship for this mission," Matt leaned back in his office chair (he was in *Friendly's* day cabin). That was a good point, too — Zail, who'd been with us at Io, was faultlessly reliable, an excellent officer. The sort we'd need at Egesta.

Dammit. Back to Egesta.

It was taking time to sink in, because it was such a shock to the system — we'd just been worrying about Martians, and peace negotiations, and politics. And now we found out that the humanitarian mess some of us had only just managed to get over… and some of us still hadn't gotten over… was coming back?

Sorry I keep repeating that general sentiment, but it kept circling in my mind. Every time I thought it, I tried to accept it, so it wouldn't be a fresh revelation next time through. But that didn't work. Because it was *Egesta*, and it was back to get me again. It'd take more than a couple of hours for me to escape the initial shock.

"Alright, as soon as *Artemis Agrotera* comes into realtime range, we'll let Zail know, and then we'll boost. No time to waste," I finally broke out of my musing, and Matt nodded.

Without another word, our signal was cut, and I flopped back on my bed and sighed, covering my face with both hands.

Dammit. Egesta. Dammit.

CHAPTER THIRTY-THREE

NEW REALITY

When Charlie trudged back into his hospital room, Lia was deeply embroiled in a backgrounder document that outlined the developments among the Hawke Lords since she'd been out of commission. All through the time she'd been commanding her squadron in combat, she'd managed to keep on top of what was going on at court, and how the Lords there were coping with her father's somewhat unusual 'reclusive nature'.

They *still* didn't know he was dead, you see. Talk about controlling the flow of information.

She was going to have an interesting time when she returned to the Protectorate; she'd have to win the confidence of all those Lords and Ladies, and that would take a combination of things. The fact that she'd performed very well in two massive battles would add to her credibility, but her charm and her incomparable abilities as a courtesan would be necessary too.

That meant knowing everything about everyone, so she was studying.

Because of her focus on this subject, she didn't initially look up when Charlie filled the door of their room. She was conscious of the fact that he was much later than usual, so she hoped that meant he'd made some progress, but she didn't immediately pick up on the grimness that clouded around him.

But after a few seconds, the atmosphere in the room had grown noticeably darker. Detecting this feeling, she frowned and lowered her pad, her eyes traveling up to the Major.

Her description of him was, and I quote, "fallen down and really hurt."

Charlie later described it as a 'room spinning, try not to wear your lunch' sort of feeling.

Between the two of them, they probably put it better than I ever could.

Realizing that something significant had happened, Lia laid the pad on the tray beside her bed and struggled to sit up. Injuries and immobilized parts of her physiology made that effort difficult, but she managed, and then she waited a few seconds to see if Charlie would say something as he perched on the side of his bed, facing her.

He seemed to be staring at nothing, so she decided to prod, "Found them?"

A nod was his initial answer, but he didn't appear to be paying much attention to her. Then he seemed to realize where he was. He shook his head slightly and let out a breath, all in such a way that left Lia genuinely concerned. She'd never seen Charlie quite so affected — not after his squad had been wiped out, not... ever.

"What was it? What was the last straw?"

She knew this had to be cumulative — no single problem could ever throw such a cloud over Charlie. It had to be something bad, that when combined with everything else, was just one tragedy too many.

As I've been saying a lot in recent books, Lia's damned smart. And she was absolutely right.

"The Imperial Army has been staging on Egesta since we left the place in '31," Charlie said quietly, gravely. "We just discovered that some of the people and locations they're talking about in their boasting sessions… are on Egesta."

Lia blinked. She knew what a profound, muted effect the events of *The Independent Squadron* had had on Charlie. He'd survived it, he'd dealt silently with any demons, and he'd moved on. She appreciated that strength of character. But one thing he'd said to her was that, in the end, Egesta was a place were we'd done as much as we could do, and that we'd made a difference.

Charlie had never been under the illusion that our intervention would make the asteroid colony right as rain. There was no reset button. But he'd thought that at least we'd put an end to the horror.

Now it seemed we'd stopped *one* horror, only to invite another one in.

"Why would they be taking those sorts of liberties?" Lia asked, referring to the blockheads.

A lopsided shrug was all Charlie could manage in answer, and his gaze started drifting off again as more thoughts filled his head. Lia looked away and allowed the same to happen to her. Why would blockheads attack civilians? Was it revenge, or sport… or just because they could?

Lia knew Earth history as well as I did, though often she pretended not to. She knew that many soldiers, at many times in our world's history, had done horrible things just because they could.

What of the Imperial Army? Were they that bad?

She pondered that briefly, until she discovered with some surprise that Charlie was beside her bed, and leaning towards her with some difficulty. He was clearly aiming for a kiss, and she wondered for a moment if there was a nurse at the door — a need for them to reinforce their courtship story.

But there was no one in sight. Charlie just kissed her, softly, and she kissed back. Then, as he straightened up, he ran his fingers over her hair, and stared at her. He didn't say anything — he didn't need to. She got the message instantly, because these two had that connection.

Charlie was glad to be here, with her, because he didn't want to have to deal with Egesta a second time. Because he'd fought countless battles, lost his whole team, and nearly lost his life. He'd done his bit for the Empire, and now was his time to find some peace.

He was here with Lia. He wasn't going back to Egesta. And I don't think anyone could blame him for being relieved about that.

If you try to blame him, remember he's a Special Brancher, which means he could kill you with color temperature. Though honestly, he wouldn't do that. For all the jokes I make about the many ways he could kill you, he never would.

So instead, remember he's my friend, and I'll kill you if you suggest he didn't deserve all the happiness he could get.

And believe me, I could kill you. And I would.

Charlie was free of the war and the killing, an honor and a privilege he'd earned the hard way. Now he sat in silence with Lia, and together they breathed deep the peaceful air.

That was as it should be. Even if little else was.

CHAPTER THIRTY-FOUR

NO PASSENGERS

Bort McWebsbert and Casey Flynnboldak were in the observation lounge off landing bay two when Karen and I found them. They were both packed, though that wasn't saying much — all of Casey's belongings were still down in the room she'd rented in the Capital Dome, and she wasn't likely to be going back for them. All she had were the clothes she'd worn that day, and a number of simple garments drawn from ship's stores.

The kit that Bort had carried from Earth was his only luggage — his movie-set uniforms and his other assorted gear all fit into a duffle that he had slung over his shoulder. Both of them were watching through the glass as a pinnace from *Bonaventure* put its feet down on the deck, and space-suited technicians made sure it was secure before closing the space doors.

Again, Bort took note of the differences between Defense Command and his fleet, but he was becoming very accustomed to our methods. And his feelings about them were different.

Anyway, when Karen and I stepped in, Casey looked back over her shoulder first, and her expression was only slightly more comfortable than it had been after our siege in the groundskeeping building. For her entire week aboard *Wolf*, she'd been mostly cloistered in Bort's cabin... she wasn't taking to us as easily as he had.

That was fair enough — culture shock can hit everyone differently, I figure — so Karen and I both just nodded to her politely.

Noticing Casey's movement, Bort turned to face us, keeping his arm around her as he did. The seemingly constant physical connection between the two intrigued me, but I didn't remark — another cultural difference. There were plenty.

"Sorry to have to send you off like this," I opened weakly, and Bort shook his head.

"Not to worry. Your cruise to the Belt wouldn't be the place for us."

The way he said 'cruise to the Belt' indicated to both Karen and I that he knew we were up to more than the cover story we'd given him. But he didn't ask for more information, and I didn't offer it — we were friends now, but we both understood the requirements of the service.

"We've passed along the information about your situation to John Fiora," Karen said next. "He's aware of the danger you're both facing, and he's going to make sure you can get cleanly away from here once the convention is done. Don't know exactly how that's going to work, but it'll be one of his priorities."

Bort nodded, though Casey seemed more skeptical, "Your First Lord gave his word on this?"

She didn't have the contextual background to know how connected we were to John Fiora, so she didn't realize that when John told us he'd do something, that meant he was giving his word.

This wasn't the time to try to explain all that to her, though, so Karen simply nodded, "It's certain."

Casey still didn't seem comfortable, but she replied anyway, "Thank you. Both of you."

We nodded in reply, and then an awkward silence descended on us for a moment.

"We really appreciate this," Bort finally said, and then glanced over his shoulder. "I think our shuttle is waiting."

I looked past him and confirmed with a nod; the space doors were shut and the deck crew were unbuttoning a couple of atmosphere-sensitive systems to make some adjustments before the doors opened again.

Time to depart.

"Well," I said, stepping forward and offering my hand to Bort, "good luck to you. I'm sure we'll be in touch again, once this mess is all finished. Maybe we can come visit you at Epsilon."

Bort took my hand with a smile, and nodded, "I don't know how popular that'd be, but I've never cared what's popular."

Then I gingerly shook Casey's hand — something she didn't seem entirely ready for, but a gesture I thought was important to make.

As Karen and Bort shook hands, though, Bort said something to her, "You two are a hell of a team. You make each other better. That's important."

Karen blinked in surprise at the words, and Casey glanced at Bort before shaking Karen's hand too. We didn't say anything else, and neither did they; leading the way, the Asteroid Admiral opened the hatch to the flight bay, then held it for Casey and shut it behind them both.

We watched from the lounge as they both boarded the pinnace that Lennox Williams had kindly sent over for them. Then we stayed there for nearly ten minutes, watching as the craft was buttoned up, the deck crew prepared for vacuum, the space doors opened, and the small craft flew away.

The whole time, we didn't say a thing, and then once the ship was gone, we left the lounge. Two hours later, *Wolf, Nova Scotia* and *Friendly* turned away from Mars, and cruised out to meet *Artemis Agrotera* at 185 kps. When we rendezvoused with Zail Patel's ship, we marked our course for Egesta and boosted that way. We weren't wasting any time at all.

Cruising again towards a nightmare.

CHAPTER THIRTY-FIVE

WAYFARERS

It wasn't until our nightly dinner two days after boosting for Egesta that Karen finally asked me something about what Bort said to her. His comment — that we made each other better — had been bouncing around inside her mind for all that time, but there'd been so many other things to think about... so many other things to dwell on... that she hadn't brought it up.

Until we were finishing supper, me in my chair and her lying on my bed in the same old style.

"Bort said we make each other better."

I was finishing off the last of the rice on my plate as she spoke, so I looked up and nodded, "He did say that."

I then shoveled the rice into my mouth and started chewing. Karen had just finished her food (her serving was smaller), and as she placed her knife and fork at the five o'clock position, she bobbed her head from side to side in thought.

Then she didn't actually say anything, so I finished my own food and put my tray on the floor, taking a swig of water from my bottle to wash the food down.

"You want to go somewhere with that?" I asked, and Karen shrugged as best she could in her lying-down position.

She then began staring at the backs of her hands, and particularly at the healing of her knuckles. They were mostly back to normal, same as the side of her face, so she was theoretically ready to scrap again.

"Last time I was on Egesta, I nearly strangled the Lieutenant Governor, didn't I?" she asked, reminding herself of that occasion. You'll probably remember it too — the Governor who'd been drinking and refusing to take any responsibility for letting the social preconditions get so out of hand that the Guild could get away with what it did. Karen had put her on a desk and left her no option but to negotiate.

"Doesn't 'strangle' imply using two hands? You were only using one," I frowned thoughtfully, and again Karen shrugged.

"Don't really know the definition. Choked her, though."

"You did," I agreed.

She fell silent again, and then she turned her left hand over and started massaging the scar on her palm with the tips of her fingers. She didn't say it, but she was remembering the spike that had gone through there on Pion Rock — and the place she'd put that spike when she'd torn it out of her own flesh.

And then she thought of what she'd said to the unfortunate rioter, and what she'd nearly done to him.

"I never plan on doing what I do... when I get like that..."

If I hadn't known what she was thinking about, I suppose that would have made no sense to me. But of course I knew. Of course I understood. Her hand traveled to the left side of her neck, and she absently ran her fingers over the skin there.

"We're just re-finding the balance," I replied, transparently trying to put her at ease. "It would be foolish to think the war's effects could be brushed off before the peace is even signed. We just have to stay watchful."

"And not pin a guy's head to the floor with a knife through the eye?" she finally looked at me.

I winced.

"It was a rough day."

"And I should have kept it together. I'm supposed to be unflappable, remember."

Her words were more uneasy than I'd heard in some time. I don't know if that'd be a surprise to you… that after all of the fighting we'd done, she'd get down on herself now, about this. But she did. Because Karen was worried that the effects of the war on her character would be like the effects of radiation on an exposed spacer. Lingering under the surface, eroding integrity, and causing later destruction.

She'd come so far in the many years we'd been partners in crime. So far since the night in the bar. And now, whether it was sensible or not, she had to wonder if she was losing that progress.

During the war, and on Egesta, she'd done some pretty brutal things. But they'd been fair responses, under the circumstances. With the rioter, she'd nearly gone beyond that limit of proportionality.

It worried her.

I suppose, if we think back to what she'd said after Pion Rock, it had worried her a bit then too. But now it worried her more.

"Back then, you wouldn't have worried about maybe crossing the line," I reminded gently, and she pulled her ponytail back onto her left shoulder, letting it sit along the side of her neck again. She'd been doing that a lot more lately — not the left shoulder thing, she did that often. But as she had back in the early days, she'd started pulling it right up against the side of her neck.

She'd once told me she did that as a reminder. I'd never questioned her about it, and in the cavalier years, she'd eventually stopped doing it.

But it was back now.

She sighed.

"I… sorry. I shouldn't be self-pitying."

Her apology struck me as ridiculous, and I said so: "You call it self-*pity*. I think it's reasonable concern for the wellbeing of anyone who crosses your path. And I think you're reading a bit too much into… recent events. But in itself, that's a good sign. It's a sign you don't want to turn back into the person you were."

At this point, one of my editors bled a lot of red ink onto one of the draft manuscript pages of this book, saying 'Stop being cryptic, who WAS she, supposedly?'

I may answer that at some point. Just not now. But Karen wasn't always unflappable. She and I came a long way together before these books started, and though it had never been so explicitly important as it was now, we'd both changed a fair amount.

As Bort put it, we made each other better.

Better people.

That, I should point out, is one of the reasons I tended to go all unprofessional when she was at risk. Whether that meant racing to her quarters when she was exposed to the then-unknown toxin on *Idaho*, risking poisoning myself just to be next to her, or going right off the handle during the Clash, when *Lady Grace* went dark.

Neither Karen nor I would have been on this ship, doing the jobs we were doing, if we hadn't been a team for so long. We wouldn't have been there if we'd met under different circumstances, or if we'd made different choices as cadets.

So it was the fear of losing it all that was getting to Karen.

But anyway, it was all irrelevant. That was the point I needed to make.

"Listen. You *didn't* do it. As long as we're together, we're fine," I tried to make those words sound like an inevitable conclusion, but instead they drew a sharp stare from Karen.

"Don't say that out loud."

I blinked in reply, "What?"

"War's over. But… don't say that. Don't say that we're together. In case… fates…"

She trailed off, but we kept staring at each other. She really was more shaken up than she'd let on for days. There was a lot of turmoil beneath the skin of the goddess.

So I made a stupid decision: I decided to tackle it head-on.

Standing up, I moved over to sit on the edge of the bed. My hand traveled up her back, then stopped on her left shoulder, and I gripped her firmly.

"We do have each other right now. After all the worrying we did about being apart last year, let's not waste time we *actually have together* worrying about what it'll be like if we're split again."

It was possibly the wisest thing I'd said in a long, long time. And the most ill-advised.

But Karen was, I think, needing to buy into it. Slowly, she nodded, and then she took a deep breath.

"So on Egesta… you check me, and I'll check you. Just until we're sure that I'm… that we're both back on form?" she said.

"Sounds like a plan to me," I agreed.

It would not be a good mission, but we were together and we were both alert. It was the best possible way to take on the task.

As *Wolf, Nova Scotia* and *Friendly* led *Artemis Agrotera* towards Egesta, we both consoled ourselves with that fact.

AFTERWORD

So there we are. The people of Mars had damned near derailed the peace process before it got started, but we managed to get things in line all the same. Frankly, no one wanted the war to go on, so that was a big helper in finding common ground (or, in this case, dictating what ground would serve as 'common' for the negotiations).

We'd learned quite a few things about Mars, about Bort McWebsbert, and about ourselves… and we watched the Emperor put himself in the position he wanted to be in.

All of that, though, felt rather secondary to what Charlie discovered. It wasn't really secondary — the fate of the Empire quite literally hung in the balance because the Emperor was throwing his weight around, but for us, the return of the Egesta situation… well.

We were going back there, and next book, you'll see exactly what we found. You'll get a picture of why today, Egesta remains one of the darkest moments in Imperial history — even when compared to the war itself.

I'm not really looking forward to writing it any more than I was looking forward to going there, but it's a hell of an important situation. So I'll see you next time, in *The Egesta Crisis*. Keep well until then!

THE
EGESTA
CRISIS

THE AUTOBIOGRAPHICAL REMINISCENCES OF
ADMIRAL THE LORD KEN BARRON FOR 2234

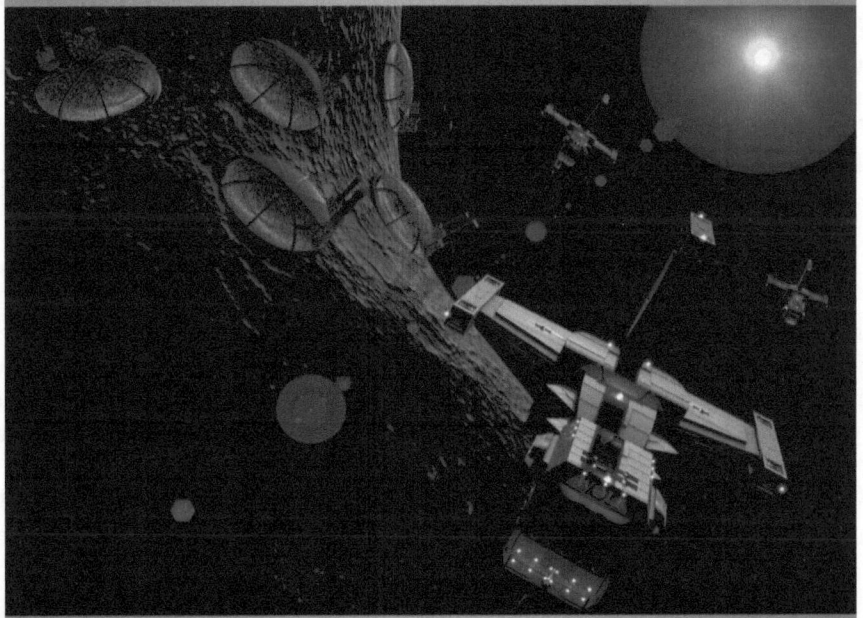

THE MARTIAN WAR - 14

KENNETH TAM

FROM THE AUTHOR

The Japanese Army captured the Chinese city of Nanjing in December of 1937, as part of the long conflict between those two countries that preceded the Second World War. What followed were six weeks of terror, witnessed by numerous Europeans who had been trapped in the city, and who were (because of their race and nationalities) exempt from the atrocities.

I am sad to say that the various things you'll read about in this book weren't invented by me... mostly, I based them on my research on Nanjing. The subject is still a hugely sensitive one for both China and Japan, because at time of writing, the historical truth of the event remains disputed.

Nevertheless, I think it happened.

And, I fear, it's a sign of the very worst that can come of a certain kind of soldiering. I think it's very fair to say that different armed forces, with different traditions, can react in very disparate ways when faced with a situation like Nanjing, or Egesta.

Defense Command, based unapologetically on the Canadian Forces, reacts differently than the Imperial Army, which is based much more on the stereotypes of bravado that a lot of people associate with the military.

I think it's important that we highlight and recognize the differences between the professional cultures of individual armed forces — that we don't paint them all with the same brush, or assume that because one army is trained to be ravenous and unforgiving, all of them must be that way. What happened at Nanjing, and what happens on Egesta, takes place because the soldiers involved are taught to operate in a certain way.

Having spoken to Canadian Forces Generals, Colonels, Majors, ship Commanders, Sergeants, Sappers and Private soldiers, I know that our modern personnel are trained much differently. We should take pride in that, and give them a great deal of credit for their genuine intelligence, perseverance, sacrifice, and their determination to do the right things.

Call me a militarist if you like... by book fourteen, I think you'd be within your rights to... but I think highly of many of these people, and I'd humbly suggest you do the same.

Now, as ever, thanks must be given. Many characters in this book are based on real-world friends of mine, so I extend my gratitude to all of those people. I'm obliged to them for their indulgence!

My good friend Peter Caron remains a fundamental contributor to this series, and must be thanked once again. Wes Prewer's continued input on the story, and his work on the covers, is simply excellent, and as ever, I thank him too.

To close, I must thank my parents, because Jacqui and Peter continue to be my partners in Iceberg Publishing, and the best family I could ever ask for.

Atlas, one more time.

– Kenneth Tam

FOREWORD

This book has caused me trouble.

I suppose, given the subject matter, that shouldn't be a great surprise. Egesta is not something I've enjoyed talking about... well... ever. And this particular chapter in the history of that damned rock was at least as bad as the one we went through in *The Independent Squadron*. Not many reasons to feel enthusiastic about writing it.

When I first sat down to draft this volume, then, I did so with steadfast determination: I was just going to put my head down and write it.

Halfway through, I ground to a halt. I couldn't stand it. I stopped writing for damned near six months.

When I finally went back and looked over what I'd done, I knew I couldn't continue the way I was going. If I was having that much trouble getting through the events, I could only imagine how impossible it'd be for someone reading it. Time to start over.

I don't like gimmicky approaches to telling stories. I don't like flashbacks, or stories told out of order, or any of the other things writers of fiction do when they need to mix up a formula. But this one time, I'm going to sacrifice my preferences. This book isn't going to be quite the catalogue of horror that, strictly speaking, it should be. Instead, we're going to have a different cadence than usual — long chapters, isolated points of view. It's the best I can manage under the circumstances.

I'm going to tell you what happened on Egesta. I'm going to take you there with me, Karen, Wes, Rufus, and everyone else... but I'm not going to try to do a chronological survey of the whole mess.

If you need the macabre details, they're in the DC archives.

All I'm going to include is what we ourselves saw, because that's bad enough.

I realize that this is perhaps a disservice to the people who died — because I'm feeling squeamish, I may not do full justice to what they suffered. But I figure — and perhaps this is just a rationalization — that it's better if you and I can actually absorb some of their story, instead of walking away from it altogether.

Like I said, maybe just a rationalization. But I'm tired of all the death I've had to write about as it is...

Before I start, though, I should remind you of what had happened on Egesta. *The Independent Squadron* covered the setup: Commodore Sean Cook and his Independent Squadron had stopped by the asteroid for some recreation time. The government had ignored their requests for liberties (as well the government should have), so Cook had paid the Guild of Miners, a supposed workers' union, for recreational rights.

Paid them with a stockpile of EP-5 rifles.

The injection of relatively modern weapons into the Guild had been disastrous, because Egesta had been, to put it mildly, an unstable society. The Guild had been robbing from the miners it represented (in the guise of union dues that just kept getting higher), and blaming the government for the trouble. The government, in turn, had tried to crack down on the Guild, making itself look entirely guilty. Tension resulted — civil war style tension.

But the government had absolute control, because it had employed Boscawen Mercenaries to maintain order. They were readily able to do that, until the Guild was armed by Cook.

Then it all went to hell. Because of an Independent Squadron officer.

So we old Belt Squadron ships had done something about it. Mark Gunney and Andrea Kiley, then commanders of *Honesty* and *Friendly*, had found the rock in turmoil, and intervened as best they could. They got three ships of survivors out of there, and Mark had come to Hawke Two and summoned us to help put an end to the crisis. Meanwhile, Andrea had stayed on the ground, and had been scarred for life by what she saw.

We ultimately hung Cook, the bastard. Wes Pellew then took over the Independent Squadron and liquidated its crews, redeeming the formation completely over the course of the war, but the original crisis was nevertheless Defense Command's fault.

Remember, school kids being herded out of airlocks?

Lia Hawke sent a force of her Guards to Egesta with us, and with their help we'd managed to stabilize the situation, and compel peace between the Guild and the government. We'd protected thousands of government-affiliated civilians from rape and murder, too.

But we'd used a very heavy club to bash the Guild into submission: we called in an armored brigade of Imperial Army blockheads, under Howard Pedro Azuma. All the Egesta civilians had feared the Emperor's infantry, which were known to be a very blunt instrument. They had thus complied with our demands for cooperation, to avoid reprisals.

Once the Imps arrived, we packed up and left — back to our war against the Martians, certain that we'd put a stop to the horrors of Egesta.

As it turned out, we'd just installed a new sort of terror. If you recall back to *The Mars Convention*, my friend Charlie Peters had discovered that the Imperial Army troops on Egesta had started turning the tables on the Guild fighters. While the army flooded Egesta with troops, all of them preparing for the Mercury assault, Guild-affiliated civilians had been raped, or used for live bayonet or target practice... just about anything the blockheads could think to do to them.

I don't know why they did this. Charlie doesn't know. None of us know. We've asked, they've replied, but nothing they've said honestly answers that question. Because for all the excuses I've heard made... I still don't *know*.

Sorry, I realize that may not make sense. It's just... doing what they did is to us like trying to breathe water. We understand it's possible (for a fish), but we're not physically equipped to do it.

You see, then as now, Defense Command had a certain *identity*. We protected civilians. It's right there in the name: we *defend*. If that meant we had to fight pirates in a prejudicial manner, we'd do it. If that meant knife fights with Martians, we'd do that too. If goddamned *aliens* showed up and tried to hurt Imperial citizens, we'd bash them over the head until they stopped, or until they used their death rays on us.

We wore uniforms. Civilians did not. That meant our first reaction always had to be protection.

But the traditions of the Imperial Army were different. Those men fought for the Emperor, and they were trained to be tough and brutal. I guess it wasn't easy for them to switch off.

Imagine how sympathetic I am to such an excuse.

Uniformed combatants who seek to abuse and torture and kill civilians violate a principle that I hold to be almost sacred. And that's what Azuma had done.

So I suppose it's time for us to find out exactly how that turned out for him.

Hint: not well.

Chapter One

Starting At The End

Karen had to leave the room.

Brigadier Howard Pedro Azuma was sitting at the other end of the table from me, and his expression remained *defiant*. Just once — *once* — I'd like to get a criminal bastard like him across the table from me, looking like he actually realized what he'd done was wrong. All the ones I've come across seem not to comprehend… they seem indignant that someone has stopped them from committing their crimes.

Worse, Azuma was actually needling us, and doing a good job of it too — Karen literally had to walk out of the interrogation room. She couldn't hold it together any longer, and as the door shut behind her, Azuma smiled in the most snide fashion.

"She's got a weak stomach," he said.

I wasn't sure how long it'd be before I had to follow. This man was a real, honest, monster.

"Be glad she left," I answered simply. "A noose will be easier on you than she'd be."

My words were rather matter-of-fact, and if Azuma had been at all sensible, he would have detected the menace in them, and backed off. But he didn't. He was still angry at what we'd done, and convinced we'd be the ones in the nooses after the dust settled.

"Big talk. You two… all of you. You cower behind the rules you create, refuse to let yourselves be who you should be. You think we could walk into a place like this, in the wake of all the shit you stopped, and let the Guild just be? They needed to be informed of who was boss here. We had to dominate them."

I just stared at the Brigadier.

"So we made their pretty ones our sport. And hotheads who were causing trouble or resisting became bayonet fodder. After two months, we had complete control of the situation. No one would dare challenge the new government."

I kept staring.

"They're not Imperial citizens. They're scum. You have to admit they don't deserve any better."

He clearly believed what he was saying. I don't know how anyone could so totally believe such things. But he did. He really, really did.

On the other hand, I fully believed the man deserved to die. And I was awfully tempted to just take care of that. I could have shot him, or dispatched him in other ways, right there in the interrogation room.

But I couldn't give into such a desire. Technically speaking, we could have made it legal. I was a flag officer, after all, so that theoretically meant I could have done some sort of court martial and sentenced him to a fittingly torturous end.

However, there were good reasons not to. Not moral ones, because morality and I have an on-and-off relationship, but — and I hated this as much as I hated him — political ones.

As if I didn't feel dirty enough when simply talking to Brigadier Azuma.

See, when we arrived at Egesta, and landed the battalion of troops we'd taken with us from Mars, and done all the things you'll read about in the coming chapters, we had known we'd have to be careful. We couldn't shoot criminals on sight, because if we did, the Emperor could dismiss any claims we made about the blockhead conduct on Egesta.

"They killed our troops with no fair trial, and no evidence," he would say.

And then God only knew what he could do.

We had to bring back the criminals — Azuma included — for trial. The more upstanding and decent among you readers are probably thinking that we should have brought them all back for trial on principle alone. You people are better than me, and I congratulate you for that. I needed more reasons.

Anyway, my failure to reply to Azuma's tirade about getting control of the planet eventually prompted him to speak again: "We are *soldiers*, Barron. You should accept that all fighting men have needs."

I blinked, and then I stared at him. Sometimes the blindness of fools can be truly confusing, but it wasn't confusion that I was feeling. You have to ask yourself, how can someone be so *wrong*? And how can someone that *wrong* get command of an entire armored brigade in the Imperial Army?

Well, I suppose the last two words of that paragraph do a lot of the explaining — it was, after all, the *Imperial Army*.

"You are *soldiers*, are you?" I leaned forward with those chilly words. "You sat here all war and did *nothing* while we were out there fighting and dying. And now you say to me you have *needs*? My officers, my spacers have *needs*. Needs that come after fighting for years against a real enemy. Oddly, though, none of those *needs* include raping and pillaging and murdering."

Azuma stared at me, then began to smirk again, "There it is. Out from under the veneer of civility, you let loose a little of your *real* anger."

"You think I'm a psychopath, I know," my answer came, somewhat surprisingly, with a smile. "I'm surprised that doesn't worry you more."

"You're a psychopath afraid to let yourself be a killer," Azuma shook his head. "You can't free yourself from the rules the way my boys could. My boys are *real* fighting men."

I've never fully grasped his argument — even today. I suppose he was using one of those half-mad 'war is hell' theories to justify his position. It's all madness, so the only way to do your job is to accept the insanity, and embrace the killing.

Funny, I came from an extremely effective combat squadron of veterans who hadn't adopted that approach.

"You know, Howard, what confuses me most about you is that you can continue to preach your bullshit, knowing that you've never actually been in combat, and that I've personally ordered the death of thousands of people. And killed plenty face-to-face, since the pirate-fighting days."

Those words, at least, brought a little bit of doubt to his eyes.

"You really haven't wondered, have you? You haven't even thought about what I could do to you. What I *would* do to you?"

Azuma's eyes narrowed, "No. You just keep denying the true nature of combat. The true nature of soldiering. You're no threat to me."

He was *still* arguing.

And, honestly, I was well past tolerating his bullshit.

Standing up, I started moving down the side of the interrogation table towards the seat he occupied. He was chained down, of course; I could do whatever I liked and there wasn't a whole lot he could do to resist.

"So if right now I stopped denying it, and rendered you blind and deaf, that would be real soldiering?" I asked coolly.

Azuma sneered again. Blockheads... really?

"Well, here's the thing. As much as I'd love to do both of those things, I think the nature of soldiering is to resist such urges," I stopped beside him, and leaned down. "I'll never pretend I'm *good* as a fighting man — not because I resist my baser urges, Brigadier Azuma, but because I find it tougher to resist them than do some of my peers. Consider yourself lucky that I don't make an exception for you. Because if I ever lose my reason for not turning out the way you want me to, a lot of people will die. And if you happen to live to see such a day, you'll never have to imagine what I'll do to you. I'll make you watch, for weeks. It will be my pleasure to do so."

That soliloquy of menace finally silenced Howard Pedro Azuma. I still don't understand his reasoning, or what he thought he'd accomplish by baiting me. Perhaps he selflessly hoped I'd kill him, and thus betray our case against his beloved Emperor...

Somehow I doubt the hedonist was that loyal.

But I didn't have the will to stay around and find out. As he fell silent, I turned for the door. Enough jousting with the monster, we were headed for a clash of a different sort...

Before we find out more about that clash, though, let's go back in time... back to Egesta...

CHAPTER TWO
GETTING THERE

A day before our convoy of *Wolf, Nova Scotia, Friendly* and *Artemis Agrotera* reached Egesta, Karen and I were both still coming to grips with what we expected to find. We'd spread pads out all over the bed in my cabin. They contained every report Charlie and the DCI agent Drew Alexander had put together for us — all the gloating that the Imperial Army soldiers in Venusian hospitals had done.

There was a lot, and all of it had an eerily familiar quality. Not a good thing at all.

"So best guess is they turned the tables on the Guild... giving the Guild a taste of their own medicine," Karen said darkly, drying her hair with a towel. She'd just taken a long, hot shower to try to freshen her mind, but nothing could wash away the sickly feeling she had.

I nodded, "Seems most likely."

That was as far as we got for a few minutes, and it wasn't a new thought for either of us. One of the first questions we'd had to ask ourselves upon reviewing these reports was exactly who the blockheads would be so happily raping and murdering. Our best theory was the whole process started when the Imps learned what the Guild had done to their own people, and decided turnabout was fair play.

"We know they're down to their original brigade again," Karen spoke, once more stating a fact that we already knew.

The armored brigade that had originally been sent to Egesta was still the garrison force on the rock — and because of the large number of troops sent to Mercury, we knew that it was unsupported. In fact, it had been stripped of many vehicles and some equipment, so Brigadier Howard Pedro Azuma, the monster in charge, barely had more than 1,100 men under his command, and a decreased complement of tanks (no one knew exactly how many, but we guessed as few as thirty).

That was a help, because it meant the 500-person Defense Command battalion we had aboard *Artemis Agrotera* would face less opposition when we moved in.

But neither Karen nor I found much comfort in the fact that stopping atrocities would be easier than otherwise might have been the case. As small favors go, that one is relatively microscopic.

Lowering myself to sit on the corner of the bed, I rubbed my eyes with the thumb and forefinger of my left hand.

"It won't get any easier until we get to the other side, I think," Karen's words had grown soft.

"You're certainly right about that," my reply was ponderous, and then I glanced back at Karen as she picked up another of the pads, shaking her head.

"We're going to have to go in carefully... locate these sites and get them secured before they can destroy evidence, or organize to stop us," she said. It was clear that the shower really had helped refresh her mind just a little. She sounded a bit better.

"I don't think it'll be a pretty operation. In any sense of the word."

Karen nodded at that, scrolling through the pad with the thumb of one hand while her other pulled the towel around the skin of her neck, wiping off drops of water that had begun trickling away from her hair.

"You and I could go straight for Azuma... cut the head off the snake. The rest of the landing party can disperse across the dome. People will need help, all at once if we can manage it. We should probably lead the way with volunteers... hold back the battalion until we know exactly where they need to concentrate. Because as soon as heavy units start landing, they'll know what's coming."

She was definitely thinking more clearly now, and I said so.

"The shower actually did clear your head," my smile was wry and tired, and her eyes lifted from the pad and found my gaze before she smiled too.

"Well if you need one, go ahead."

Managing to chuckle once, I sighed again — was that sort of day — and then nodded, "I may just take you up on that. In a minute..."

I paused, and then looked down at all the pads again.

"When we actually do start taking these bastard blockheads into custody, we're going to have to be careful. No shooting on sight... we'll need to put them on trial. Make examples in the press. If the Emperor is playing games with the fate of the Empire, and these are the shock troops he's going to use to enforce law and order on the streets of Earth cities, people need to know what they've done out here."

Another cold reality. No matter what we saw down on Egesta, we couldn't start reprisals against the Imperial Army — or, more specifically, we couldn't start drumhead trials followed by quick executions — because the Emperor wouldn't be held to account if we handled this internally.

Even if he didn't know about the goings-on at Egesta, these were his personal troops. They swore their oath to him, not the elected government, so this was his chain of command, and it'd stick to him. The bastard.

As long as we didn't get carried away, and give him an out. If we started making people disappear, he could say we manufactured evidence and were afraid to take it before a real court... that we'd started executing his troops in an effort to intimidate him.

So in the midst of all this, we had to be politically astute.

Thinking that, I definitely felt like I needed a shower. It might help clear my head... but we were still bound for Egesta. I wouldn't feel clean, no matter how much hot water I used up.

When we'd reached Pion Rock, we'd all had grim feelings. When we'd gone into the last battles against the Martians, we'd all harbored intense foreboding. But none of that honestly compared to whatever it was I felt when we pulled into orbit over Egesta.

Seeing the place come up on screen one on *Wolf's* bridge was physically uncomfortable, though I did my damndest not to show it. And it wasn't just me. Jim Hannigan, who hadn't been down there much last time, but knew what had gone on, looked grim. Shelby McLaws, who'd done several turns on the rock (she'd been Helm and Navigation Officer aboard *Friendly* back then) was looking unusually ruffled. Karen stood silent, like a tower of stone.

On the Battlelink screens that linked us to the other ships in our group, Matt Baxter wore one of his tightest expressions. He'd seen more than enough last time. And Wes Pellew, who hadn't been here before, but had allegedly broken Sean Cook's face with a number twelve wrench as first punishment for the original troubles, looked grave indeed.

Only one among us seemed like her old self, and that was, in itself, a complete atavism.

Because it was Andrea Kiley.

She seemed more at ease in her own skin at this moment than any time I'd seen her since before our last visit here — she was breathing easier, she was clearly more relaxed, she even seemed gentler.

And that just didn't make sense to me.

But more on that later.

Our arrival was unexpected, and unannounced. Because Egesta was in the middle of nowhere, we hadn't put a guard ship on it during the war. The Imps would see us pulling into orbit thanks to their control of the colony's detection grid, but they wouldn't have any idea why we were here, how long we were staying, or if any of us were even thinking of coming down.

Hopefully, we'd catch them by surprise... and whatever they were doing, we'd then be able to stop it.

"Anyone hailing us?" Karen didn't move as she asked the question of Felicia Khalid, and our Sensors and Communications Officer shook her head.

"We've been detected by active sensors, but no communications as yet."

"They're either very surprised, or they don't know what to say," Andrea observed in cool but comfortable tones.

It didn't matter — I knew we best not wait: "We're not going to give them any time to try to hide anything. We'll lead with a strong landing party from each ship, down to the cargo docks we went through last time. All volunteers for now."

Karen and I had explained this to our elite skippers already, but it felt like something we actually did have to say again. Andrea nodded, as did Matt Baxter and Wes. Then my eyes shifted to the screen bearing the fourth Captain with our group: Zail Patel, of the trusty combat storeship *Artemis Agrotera*.

Zail was carrying the scraped-together battalion of SF and Special Branchers — the muscle we'd have to use to get control of the situation on the rock below.

"Zail, can you get the battalion ready to land? We don't want to lead with them, but we need them ready to come down at the drop of a hat."

The Indian skipper, who'd been with us on the run out to Io, who'd helped save many of *Lion's* crew out there, and who'd then joined the Mercury assault force, was more than up to this. He nodded confidently, "As soon as you need Colonel Ronald's forces, they will be on the ground."

Colonel Ronald, by the way, was a lucky get for us: you may remember Garth Ronald was one of the senior Special Branch officers on Mercury during the landings and occupation. He'd gotten away from that planet and back to Earth just in time for Daragh to dragoon him into commanding this mixed battalion, which John had requested be put together in case of more rioting on Mars.

Garth knew Rufus very well, having used Rufus' and Charlie's squad to great effect before it was wiped out. He had both Majors' endorsements, and that gave me immense confidence in him, even though I'd never spoken to him before our preparatory comm calls on the way to Egesta.

So Zail Patel would make sure that *Artemis Agrotera* delivered Ronald and the battalion as soon as we knew where we needed them.

One step at a time.

A familiar, hollow numbness settled over me as I pulled on my tunic jacket. I had strapped my mag belt to my waist and made sure every power cell on it was fully charged. I'd put on my landing party boots. I'd holstered my comm.

But it was as I pulled on my jacket — the last thing to do before I could step out of my cabin — that the feeling really hit me. The numbness I'd had before, in that week on Egesta. My subconscious mind seemed to remember it very well, and knowing what we expected to find, it was preparing for the worst.

I stepped into the bathroom and checked myself in the mirror. How I looked didn't matter, so I'm not entirely sure why I bothered, but I suppose I wanted to see whether the empty feeling was evident on my face.

It was, at least to me.

I didn't dwell or stare; I left my cabin, and headed next door. As I reached out to Karen's hatch, it swung open on its own, and she started through, then stopped in surprise as she saw me standing there. Under other circumstances we would have smiled, but instead I just stepped back and gave her room to exit. Then we headed for the airlock which was hitched to the chute down to Egesta.

"Ground control was alerted when we made the final docking approach. But the bastards won't have had much time to get ready!"

That yell came down the hall behind us, and we both stopped walking and turned to see a smiling — indeed, smiling — Andrea Kiley jog to our side.

"If we get moving, we should be able to catch them," she said eagerly, then fell into step with us, her high cadence spurring us to move faster.

Neither Karen nor I had spoken much about the escalating changes we were seeing in Andrea — we'd been too preoccupied — but they were getting pretty obvious.

She was happy to be back here, and we couldn't comprehend why. But more on that later. For the moment, our focus was on getting down to the rock and stopping whatever was happening.

When we got to the airlock, the assembled volunteers were a study in contrasts, which further surprised me. Rufus and his Branchers were in a line near the front, all carrying their MAG-90s and looking as cool as you'd expect... though none of them had been here before. That's not to denigrate them, not at all... just... well, they hadn't been here before. Our recently-promoted Master-At-Arms, Eugene Sengooba *had* been here before — he'd watched Mark Gunney accidentally kill a woman in order to prevent the outbreak of a shooting war — and he now appeared tense, but obviously ready. He carried only a sidearm, like many of the volunteers, though many who felt comfortable enough hefted

MAG-90s as well.

Other officers were coming with us, too, like Shelby McLaws, who knew this place and wanted to go down again. Adrienne Thompson, the commander of our fighter group, was still haunted by images of the frozen bodies of the spaced children she'd seen doing overflights last time, and wanted to go into the dome now, to stop that ever happening again. There were many people with similar motives.

"Alright," I spoke up as we came to a stop before the group. "They only found out we were coming a few minutes ago… not enough time to get rid of the evidence even if they've figured out why we're here. Look everywhere, and when you find something, call the cavalry. We have a battalion on *Artemis Agrotera*, Mercury veterans ready to drop to clean up the mess. Don't take on the army all by yourselves. Remember the discipline it took when we were here last time? We need that again. And I can pretty much guarantee it won't be easy."

As I spoke, I scanned the faces of the officers and spacers clustered around the lock, and I knew they would deliver the same efforts now that they had before. It would be difficult, but they would be effective.

With that, I escaped my musing: "Let's go."

I looked at Karen, and for a very long second we held a stare that said as much as it had to. Then I stepped into the airlock and entered the chute. There was no question of anyone else leading this time, even Rufus. Karen followed, then Andrea, then Rufus' officers, Eugene and the rest.

All going down to Egesta again.

Now, let's split up the story.

CHAPTER THREE

WHAT WES AND ANDREA SAW

When Wes parked *Nova Scotia* over Egesta, he really didn't know what to expect. He'd obviously read our reports from last time, and much more importantly, he'd spoken to Andrea about her experiences on that mission. He was the only person to whom she'd confided those horrors, and he remained the only person she felt had the credentials to even begin to comprehend the feelings she had deep inside her.

That was because he'd experienced tragic loss. Years before, I should remind you, his wife Sara had been assaulted and brutally murdered by a gang of Belt Widows who'd followed her home after a hospital shift.

Wes had lost it after that. He'd been a pilot on my wing at the time, back aboard *Alberta* with Greg Noyce as our skipper. From one of the best flyers on our combat wing, he turned into a fanatic, and he started fighting do-not-resuscitate duels with any Belt Widows he could find.

We finally stopped that experience with a clash of our own, which I don't care to discuss again. All that we need to remember for now is that he'd seen enough, and suffered enough, that he had the credentials to talk to Andrea.

That was good, because he expected this mission would bring up a great many traumatic memories for our Irish skipper.

Andrea was foremost on his mind as he readied himself for the mission. Moving from his closet to his bed in his cabin aboard *Nova Scotia*, he couldn't keep her off his mind. He pulled on his jacket, strapped his mag to his hip, and grabbed his old pair of flight gloves from the bottom of a bin in his closet, then headed for the chute down to Egesta.

Volunteers from across *Nova Scotia*, some of them former Belt Squadron personnel who had been to this rock before, were waiting at the airlock when Wes arrived. These were his women and men, a crew he'd assembled carefully back in 2232, and which he believed was the best in the fleet — the way every CO believes his or her crew is the best.

Unlike most who make that boast, though, Wes had a real case. They were as good as *Wolf*'s crew. Of course, *Wolf*'s crew was better, because they were my people and it's my name on the cover of this book… but really, these *Nova Scotias* were better too.

Thanks to my editors for letting me get away with that one.

"There'll be a lot of emotion surging when we go down. No matter what, we need to stay focused. Discipline, today, and we'll help the people who need us," he announced to his volunteers.

They answered him with a chorus of "yes sir".

Then, Wes Pellew, Commodore of the new Independent Squadron, led the way down to Egesta.

When he reached the bottom of the chute, Wes found that we'd already arrived in the cargo facility that, now as before, served as our gateway into the Capital Dome. I was in the process of essentially taking the surrender of Major Steven Wang-Roth, one of the Imperial Army officers who'd resisted Azuma's orders, and had been confined to the cargo facility for his troubles.

Wes didn't join us as Karen and I interrogated the man. Instead, he spotted Andrea, and nodding for Rozy Young, his Flag Captain, to take over the cadre of *Nova Scotia* volunteers, he headed towards *Wolf*'s Captain.

She must have sensed he was coming; she turned to him before he was within a dozen meters, and her expression stopped him dead in place. He stared at her face, and almost had to do a double-take.

Her smile was warm, and genuine. Her eyes almost sparkled, and she looked happy, relieved even.

It was a look neither he nor any of us had seen in years… not since the eager but quiet Commander Andrea Kiley had taken over *Friendly*, and begun terrorizing pirates. And not what he'd expected to see from her now.

"According to the Major here, any Imps who resisted Azuma's orders to enjoy themselves were isolated at the cargo structures… means we shouldn't meet resistance at any landing point," she approached him as she helpfully explained what Karen and I were getting out of Wang-Roth.

Wes didn't process her words at first, and instead blinked a few times as she came to a stop in front of him. His eyes studied hers — and also their corners, and the lines around them. So often, the lines around the eyes told the true story of a person's state of mind.

Hers were relaxed. Absolutely at ease.

Before he could comment, Karen and I were moving towards him, Rufus just behind us. Matt Baxter joined us and we all came together around Andrea and Wes.

"We can start moving into town. If what he just said is true, they're not ready for us, so we can start sending teams into the domes, and then call Ronald's troops as soon as we know where we need them," I explained. "Karen and I will go to headquarters, and find Azuma."

Frowning, Wes looked from me to Karen and back, "Do you want me to come along?"

I glanced at Karen, and she shook her head, "We'll cover more ground if we split up. Probably better to have more officers in more places, in case we need to call the battalion down on multiple targets. And we'll be able to collect more evidence that way."

"Try to catch the bastards with their…" Matt Baxter stopped himself. Finishing the quip with 'pants down' in this context… just no.

I nodded, and then Andrea instantly warmed to the idea, "I'll take a team and head to the far side of the dome. I know some of the trouble areas…"

"I'll join you," Wes didn't even let her finish her sentence.

We could have objected — sending two of our senior officers off together probably wasn't the best distribution of resources. But I think we all feared that Andrea was going to find something terrible, and either take it out on the blockheads, or on herself.

Better to have Wes with her.

And to answer an editor's question: no, we couldn't order her back to *Wolf*. I mean, I technically could have, but imagine how that might have gone. She *desperately* wanted to be down here. What would it do to her state of mind if we denied her? I know, the risks of exposing her again might outweigh those of restraining her... but none of us felt like we had the moral authority to do anything of the sort.

Perhaps that makes us enablers. I won't deny it. Either way, she was with us. And Wes was with her.

It didn't take long for our cluster of officers to break up and get on with their individual missions. Being spread thin as we were, we moved out in a collection of threes and fours, planning to scout for hot spots and call in the cavalry (Ronald's professionals) if there was something we couldn't handle.

That meant Andrea and Wes were supposed to have at least one other person with them, but as it turned out, they left as a pair.

This was an interesting, arguably regrettable decision, that each of them came to for different reasons. On the one hand, Wes didn't want anyone crowding Andrea's personal space if she found herself in a difficult emotional position. On the other, Andrea didn't want or need help. She'd tolerate Wes, even appreciate his interest to some limited extent, but she didn't want anyone holding her back.

So they set off together, commandeering a vehicle from the car park outside the warehouse, overriding its computer, and then starting a casual drive through the Capital Dome.

Wes had never seen this place, so the eerie, almost-normal quality of it was a real surprise. Intellectually, he knew that's the way we'd found it last time, but it was different to see it in person — to try to reconcile the grim expectations he held with the not-too-ominous facades.

As the buildings floated by, he watched from the passenger seat. Andrea drove, as she had many times during her previous mission to this place, and he stole regular glances at her. She looked... at peace. At one point, she caught sight of something and smiled just a little, then went back to looking at ease.

It seemed to Wes to be the precursor to some sort of breakdown. He didn't understand it; for his part, he couldn't imagine returning to the scene of the crime, so to speak, and not having a strong negative reaction. It was coming. Just a matter of when it hit.

"Where are we headed?" he asked eventually, making sure the question sounded casual, not prodding.

"I want to show you the airlock," she answered.

The airlock.

Wes blinked, and looked at her directly, checking for signs of strain on her face. Nothing. *Nothing.*

"Are you... sure you want to go back there?" he asked, unable to keep a frown of confusion off his brow.

A single nod was her answer, before a deep breath and: "Absolutely."

It was said with genuine calm, and Wes still didn't understand. I wouldn't have, nor would Karen. None of us had done much reading up on the variety of ways people can deal with post traumatic stress. Some of the unbelievable ways.

Andrea was about to show us, though.

"I always thought this section of town had potential," Andrea remarked as they moved to the side of the dome where the fateful airlock could be found. "The Imps don't seem to have done much to clean it up."

Wes didn't actually know how to respond to that. Small talk seemed so entirely irrelevant...

"It's just up here."

Before the Independent Squadron's elite Commodore could really process those words, and the baffling tone that carried them, he felt the vehicle slowing, and then stopping. He looked out, straight through the windshield, and found that they were indeed facing an airlock. A large one, meant for emergency docking.

Instantly he imagined the scene that now haunted Andrea — the files of 'posh' school children, the offspring of the hated government class, being sent into that lock, and decompressed. Because it pleased the Guild to do so.

Wes felt a physical chill at that mental picture. His jaw set and his brow ached from the scowl he wore. This place was horrible.

Then he looked at Andrea, expecting her at last to be somber.

She was already climbing out of the car, so he hurriedly opened his door and stepped out too. She was ahead of him, so he followed, and by the time he came up alongside her, she'd stopped. Her eyes closed, and then she took a deep breath, as if trying to absorb the place through powerful lungfuls of air.

When she let out that breath and opened her eyes, complete relaxation had settled on her face. Liberation might actually be a better word. For the first time in years, she felt respite.

And believe me, that made as little sense to Wes, and to all of us, as it's probably making to you right now.

"You... alright?" Wes couldn't do anything but ask, and Andrea smiled and nodded.

"I am. Really, I am..." her eyes started to travel along the wall of the dome beside the lock, then to the inner doors, and then to the open ground around them, where the children had been made to line up and wait for their unspeakable fate.

"Andrea... it's okay not to be alright with being here..." Wes took a step closer to her, trying to help her break down the walls that he guessed had to be containing her anguish.

She shook her head, "I know that... you just..."

Stopping, she let her eyes close again, and then reopen. After that she turned to Wes, and explained, as best she could, her baffling response.

"I see this place... this *exact* place... every day. Every night. Every hour, unless there's a battle on. I see the children here. But I'm never *really* here when I see it. I'm on a ship, millions of kilometers away, fighting a war that I don't care about. When I should be *here*. When I should be making sure those children aren't at this lock. For the rest of my life, I'm always going to belong here. And now, here I am."

Wes stared at Andrea.

This was different than what he'd experienced after losing Sara — different by a mile. He'd known that his experience and Andrea's were only very loosely similar, but at this moment, as he realized our Irish skipper had been consumed by her trauma, it became clear he had a long way to go before he could even begin to understand her problems.

Let alone help her through them.

But being the damned fine officer and gentleman he is, Wes Pellew wasn't about to give up.

"So… being here means that what you see when you close your eyes… matches what you see when you open them? You're not in two places at once?"

Andrea took another deep breath, and then shrugged, "Sort of like that, yeah."

She turned her gaze back to the lock, "After being here for so long… I don't know, whatever happened in the war, it always felt like I *had* to come back here. Because in a way, this was the only thing that mattered. Only thing that still does…"

Considering the pain of the past two years, Wes found that assertion to be a little startling. But he wasn't going to judge.

"I think it's wrong, feeling this way," she continued. "I should be torn to pieces remembering what happened here. But I'm selfish… I'm relieved because being here makes *me* feel more human. And that's wrong. But… but it's how it feels."

A couple of possible responses to those words trickled into Wes' mind — perhaps he should tell her not to feel guilty for looking after herself, or that she couldn't change the past — but he got the feeling such platitudes would be flimsy. So he didn't say anything.

They just stood there, and stared at the lock, for what seemed like an eternity.

When they finally got back in the car, Andrea Kiley — our old, warm, friendly Commander — was driving.

It wasn't healthy. Andrea suggests I could compare it to an addict who'd been in a long period of withdrawal finally getting a new dose of a toxic drug. I'm not sure that's appropriate or fair.

Either way, she was still driving, and their tour of the Capital Dome went on.

Chaos started to creep into the streets when Colonel Ronald's troops began appearing in force. We really hadn't planned this operation properly — almost the opposite, really — because having two senior officers in a hijacked car while one of Special Branch's skiffs shouted down three blockhead tanks just two streets over… that was poor planning.

We're very lucky we didn't suffer for our cavalier approach… but then, I honestly don't think any of us had the necessary self-control to plan it properly. We all wanted to get in, make a difference and get out. As any proper professional officer may tell you, sentiments like that can be the most dangerous — get people killed, one way or another.

But at least Wes was making progress with Andrea. His eyes remained on the street beyond the passenger side window, but his mind was fully focused on *Wolf's* Captain, because for the first time in all the months he'd spent trying to coax words from her, Andrea was finally speaking openly and easily.

I won't repeat everything she was saying. She was telling a lot of horror stories that hadn't affected her as profoundly as the airlock incident had, and which don't bear repeating now. Wes was listening, and asking questions — he was engaging, and using this opportunity to find out more about what she'd seen here, and how she'd endured it.

Andrea Kiley was a hell of a strong woman.

And as Wes listened, he was increasingly… *impressed.* We'll go with that word.

But then he stopped listening, because a squad of blockheads was running towards them down the sidewalk ahead. Only one was armed with an energy rifle, while the three others were in various states of trying to get their clothes back on.

"Trouble," he said firmly, and needing no more prompting, Andrea swung the hovercar in front of the runners, and in a flash both she and Wes were on the sidewalk, mags up and yelling for the blockheads to get on the ground.

At this point, Wes tells me, Andrea had lulled him into some sort of complacency. He misread the situation, and looking back he blames himself completely for what came next.

I can't argue with him on that, but I certainly do sympathize. He handled it better than I would have.

"We're not resisting!" the previously-armed blockhead was lying on his belly, hands on the back of his head, the energy gun on the sidewalk beside him. Hurrying over to the bastard, Wes kicked that weapon out of reach, then addressed all four of the Imps.

"Where were you running from, exactly?"

By now, Wes realized that they had an audience — civilians were peeking out of houses and emerging onto front porches up and down the street. I should have said this earlier: they were in one of the modest housing suburbs on the edge of the dome, a sector which had been a fairly Guild-centric zone during the last mission here.

Undoubtedly, prime abusing ground for the blockheads, since anyone who could even be connected loosely to the Guild was considered fair game.

This is something I should pause to clarify: all those Guild fighters from *The Independent Squadron* were long dead.

All the people who'd cheered them on were similarly gone.

To sustain their wants, the blockheads were going after the rest of the population — any house which had once been registered by the Guild (over the course of forty years of Guild records) was fair game… which pretty much meant every house, since the Guild had been the only union on the rock. Even some families that had been victimized by Guild fighters were targeted again, because while the current generation might have been government class, the previous one could have had a unionized miner in it.

Basically, if a blockhead took a liking to your daughter or son, an excuse would be found.

So these people who started poking their heads out of their front doors weren't the same ones who, years prior, had threatened us, or raped and pillaged. To be sure, they let things happen, and some blame might be assigned to them for not standing up to the radical, dangerous element within their midst… but even if they were guilty, the blockhead version of justice was wrong.

"We… were…" the blockhead on the ground started to stammer, but Wes had had enough.

None of the witnesses on that street, and there were many, saw Wes kick the blockhead's face, so he therefore obviously did not do it. Teeth and a lot of blood from someone's broken nose did appear on the sidewalk. Coincidence.

"On your feet. Walk us back to wherever you were," the Independent Squadron's Commodore ordered after the blockhead stopped his inexplicable wailing.

"Or bite the curb and let me stomp on your head," Andrea added, just to make sure a disproportionate level of threat was there for motivation.

Wes was too busy to wonder if she was serious.

The blockheads — four regular, stupid Imperial soldiers — complied, and as they got to their feet with their hands on their heads, they led the way back down the street. Neither Wes nor Andrea had yet called for backup. They probably should have, but neither thought to.

It didn't take long to get to the house in question. A woman had lived in the modest little place on her own. Her name was Moira, and the nature of her relationship with this blockhead squad, and indeed, their entire company, had been... precarious. She suffered a great deal to make sure the blockheads didn't space her parents. That was one of the threats they'd use, when they decided they didn't just want to rape someone.

When the blockheads stopped in front of this house, Wes was already thinking tactically. They hadn't said what exactly had happened here, but if there was a victim inside, we could hope to get testimony.

That meant someone had to stay outside with the prisoners, and someone had to go in and look around.

Now, you might be thinking the division of duties here would be natural: don't leave Andrea with the prisoners. She'd come a long way, but she was still the skipper who nearly got past *Charlie Peters* to shoot prisoners in *The Dark Cruise*.

But Wes made a severe mistake. He completely misread the situation.

"Sit them down... I'll have a look," he said. Andrea paused for a moment at those orders, then nodded.

Waving her mag, she indicated that the four blockheads should seat themselves on the curb. They were all sheepish now, and obviously fearing the consequences. They had *no* idea.

Wes left them behind. He trusted Andrea's self control. Keeping his mag in hand, he turned up the path towards the house. The door had been rammed off its hinges. Reaching the front steps, he climbed them and stepped carefully through the doorframe, wary of some sort of ambush, unlikely though it seemed.

The trouble had already begun, but he didn't realize it just then.

His eyes had to adjust to the dim light inside. The place smelled surprising clean, and as his vision adapted, he could see it was a neat little home — clearly a place someone had taken pride in, as much as one could.

The trouble got worse, but he still didn't notice.

Moving further inside, he left all thought of Andrea behind as he carefully looked around. There were shoes, coats... ahead, at the end of the corridor, he could see the kitchen was off to one side, with a modest little family room opposite it. A standard design, not unlike those found in affordable housing throughout the Empire.

Big, big trouble now. And he was honestly oblivious.

Finally, his eyes settled on the woman who was dead on the floor. She was right in front of him, face down, naked and butchered. The blood was still pooling. She hadn't been dead long, but he was still too late.

Yes. Yes, this was trouble.

Wes Pellew slipped his mag into his holster, and then he stepped carefully towards the body of Sara. He crouched down, brushed her dark hair from the side of her neck, and checked for a pulse. There was none, but he had to check.

Maybe if he'd been back minutes sooner, instead of flying his goddamned missions all the time, he could have stopped them. Maybe if he'd listened to her, and gone into base admin, they could have had a house in a better part of town, and these bastards wouldn't have been able to follow her home from the hospital.

He crouched there and stared at her, still not realizing the trouble that was afoot. He was taking his time, and under the circumstances, he shouldn't have been.

Eventually, he stood up. He looked around him, around his wrecked house, and felt very cold. Turning away from her, he squinted at the light pouring in through the doorway. He could have sworn it was nighttime when he'd come in here, but no matter.

Purposefully, he walked back out of his house. He paused to try to close the door, but it fell off its hinges when he attempted to right it. No point. Descending the steps and moving down the path towards the sidewalk, he saw Andrea had her mag trained on the blockheads, and they were all sitting quietly, backs to him.

Around the street, people were standing on porches, curious to see what was happening.

The trouble should have been obvious. But Wes still didn't recognize it.

Coming around the blockheads, he stopped beside Andrea and drew his flight gloves from his pocket. Pulling on the left one, he looked to the men sitting on the curb, "Which one of you killed her? The one who was armed?"

That man, with the mysteriously broken face, shook his head urgently, "N-n-n-no sir..."

"It was Willie! Willie Ney!" another hissed quickly, and one man shrank at the mention of his name. Too much of a coward even to protest being sold out.

Satisfied that his left glove was fitting in the same old comfortable way, Wes switched to putting on the right one, "Good. Willie, get on your feet."

The blockhead shrank back further, but Andrea still had her mag on him, and that slowly compelled him to rise. But Andrea was frowning, and she glanced at Wes, "I've never seen you wear gloves before."

He didn't hear her, instead waving the Imp out from behind his friends, to stand on the street, "Get up. Come on."

His tone was gentle, though his prodding was insistent. The blockhead and his three comrades were all clearly confused by this reaction, though none of them quite knew what to expect. Actually, I'm sure that's not true: they were expecting to be executed in the street. Because obviously they didn't know Wes.

I mean, being a Commodore, he could have done a quick drumhead court martial. He could have found a way to legally execute these bastards. But no, there would be no execution.

His gloves were on, and I'm probably the only person who would have realized how profound that was. Wes had stopped wearing those gloves a long, long time ago. To this day, he doesn't know why he pulled them out of the bottom of his closet when he was preparing to come down to Egesta.

He'd kept them, in all the years since he'd last worn them, as a warning. A reminder of the day I'd shot him in his last duel.

"What are we doing, Wes? You... going to beat him?" Andrea asked, keeping her voice low.

He still didn't hear her. And it didn't matter. His words to the blockhead answered her question.

"Willie, I challenge you to a duel."

Perhaps not the most menacing line on paper. But I can imagine his tone, and his expression. They were the words of a man you have no doubt... no doubt *whatsoever*... will kill you. Someone for whom killing just isn't that difficult.

The blockhead tensed, then protested, "No!"

"Thank you for accepting my challenge," Wes didn't really hear the man.

"I'm unarmed!"

Wes was already turning and stepping into his shooting stance, drawing his mag and letting his hand fall to his side.

"Andrea, please give him your sidearm," he then said. "I call for a DNR duel. To the final death."

"*No! I said no!*"

You'd think a blockhead would be more willing to shoot it out with a Defcom Commodore. You'd think that the arrogance of a man who could stab a woman to death in her own house would not crumple before a Naval officer with a mag, especially when that officer was offering you an even chance.

But there are two factors that led to the collapse of those expectations: the blockheads were cowardly, raping, murderers... and Wes had the look of death. I've seen that look, from the other side of the street in a duel. It's cold, and I remember believing there was a better-than-even chance that it would be the last look I ever saw in life.

Not an inviting prospect. But a likely one.

"I won't do it!" the blockhead was starting to sob now. "Please! We had to shut her up! She'd have told people what we... what our company was forced to do."

Squealing little bitch was trying to pass the blame.

"Andrea, arm him so I can kill him," Wes said simply in reply.

Wes wouldn't shoot an unarmed adversary. Every Belt Widow had been given a chance to stop him. Every one of those fuckers who'd left Sara lying naked just inside the door of their house on Belt Two. The door off its hinges. The kitchen and the living room at the back of the place. All of it kept neat.

Now Wes was standing just outside his house, ready to avenge his wife.

Reality and memory were, as you can tell, all jumbled up.

Until Andrea Kiley's hand came to rest on the side of his face.

Our Irish skipper realized what had happened. In all his concern for her, Wes had assumed that he'd be fine with whatever he saw on Egesta. But people have triggers, and no matter how much time has passed, no matter how far you've come, sometimes those same triggers... they don't really go away.

Wes had just walked back into his nightmares, and unlike Andrea, he didn't find it a relief to be there.

"It's me," Andrea said softly, pulling Wes' face and his gaze towards her. "It's me, and you're not going to do this. You're past this, and you're not going back."

Staring at her, Wes didn't really understand the words. He wasn't himself.

"If you can't get away from Sara's death, then I never can get away from here. You have to get past this, show me how to get out."

Wes tells me there were two people in the known universe who, in that moment, could have stopped him. Andrea was one of them.

There wasn't some moment of clarity. There was no instant where Wes thought 'my God, what am I doing?' None of that. He just stared into Andrea's eyes, part of his unscrambled brain reminding him that this woman did indeed know something about what he was doing. That she had the credentials in pain to give him orders.

So he slid his mag back into its holster.

"Willie, get your ass back on the curb," Andrea's tone left no room for interpretation. The blockhead did exactly that.

"Thank you... thank you ma'am..."

"Fuck you. Be silent," still no room for interpretation.

"Go back to the car... drive back to the locks. Get up to *Nova Scotia*. I'll call for help and get these bastards sorted..." Andrea said softly with a genuine tenderness in her tone.

She tells me that this moment, more than everything Wes had ever said to her, connected her to him the most. Because she saw firsthand that his anger at Sara's death was *deep*, like hers. And seeing him almost lose it — almost stop being the gentleman who'd pledged to help her — made her realize quite how much she'd miss him if he stopped being who he was...

I don't know if that makes sense to you, but it sure makes sense to me.

So she, who was relieved to be at home here on Egesta, would deal with the situation. It was time for Wes to go.

And listening to her, he did exactly as he was told. He pulled off his gloves, and walked back to the hovercar. He left Andrea towering over the blockhead bastards, who had truly begun to realize they'd dodged a bullet.

This, I think it's fair to say, was a very bad day for Commodore Wes Pellew.

Worse was still to come, but that's for later.

Let's leave Andrea and her prisoners for now, and see what happened when Rufus Chang got into action.

CHAPTER FOUR

WHAT RUFUS SAW

After the ridiculous drama we went through in *The Mars Convention*, Rufus Chang knew his new team pretty well. The comfort level he'd enjoyed with his old squad still wasn't there — that would take years to develop — but he was confident that the five shooters who'd joined his Special Branch unit were equal to the job they faced on Egesta.

None of them knew exactly what that job would be, of course — none of them had been on the rock before. Charlie had been with us last time... and with no offense meant to Rufus, I did regret that my best friend wasn't with us now. He'd seen it all here before... he already knew what it would be like...

But Charlie was recovering from the damage wrought by the many sacrifices he'd already made, mental and physical. He'd more than earned his right to sit this one out, so he was with Lia, in hospital, getting better so he could start a new chapter in his life.

That meant the job of rearranging any blockheads who were particularly troublesome would fall to Rufus. Lucky them.

Keep in mind, Rufus and Charlie have very different styles. Both of them could kill you with any number of highly unlikely tools, but I've always thought Rufus' approach to be more... direct. He likes explosives. He was one of the first Special Branch officers in history to have a grenade launcher fitted to his MAG-90. He carried a Japanese-style tanto instead of a fighting knife. This is not really a guy you want to run into when you've done something wrong.

Now that's not to take anything at all away from my friend Charlie. Recall last time we were on Egesta how quickly and efficiently he informed some Guild fighters of their misdeeds, usually by putting them in traction. But that sort of immediate reaction to a situation had a different look and feel when Charlie did it.

Sorry, I know that explanation probably doesn't help too much.

Suffice to say, none of the blockheads would be counting their lucky stars that Rufus had stepped into Charlie's old role for this mission.

And that statement should be my cue to get us into some narrative. Because the Azure Horizon Community Centre, formerly the headquarters for the Guild 'Elders', and the site of the atrocities that had tipped Charlie off to this entire situation, was Rufus' target.

He and his Branchers came down with the rest of us, landing in the warehouse and supervising the disarmament of the guards there. That was straightforward. Then he'd concurred with our decision to break up into teams, to scout ahead so that Colonel Ronald's battalion would know what targets to focus on when they got to ground.

He immediately decided to go to Azure Horizon. He'd read Charlie's reports about what was probably going on there, and it simply seemed impossible for him to go elsewhere. The place held unfinished business for Charlie, and because Rufus and Charlie had become great friends and comrades, and were both Branchers, that meant it held unfinished business for our Chinese Major as well.

So Rufus, like Andrea and Wes, commandeered a car from the parking lot. Unlike Wes, though, he had a tougher journey ahead of him: Azure Horizon wasn't in the Capital Dome, and the blockheads we captured, particularly Major Wang-Roth, explained that tanks were sitting at the entrances to all of the inter-dome tunnels, backing up the checkpoints that controlled traffic flow.

Getting through wouldn't be easy, and once he got to Azure Horizon, the work would be difficult too — they'd have to secure the centre and wait for reinforcement, but there was no telling how long it would take Colonel Ronald to put SF into the domes beyond the Capital.

Challenging, then, but by no means beyond the abilities of Rufus Chang.

Only one officer would accompany him for this, since the rest were needed to look after me and Karen... but two was enough. So it was Lieutenant Simon Keynes in the passenger seat as Rufus drove their hovercar towards the tunnel to Egesta's Dome Five.

The checkpoint was the first obstacle. It was still early in our landing — the blockheads hadn't been warned that we were coming to arrest them, so when Rufus edged his hovercar up to a quiet intersection opposite the tunnel entrance, the Imps sitting there with their tank were none too alert.

"Hard and heavy, or sly, boss?" Keynes asked quietly as the two studied the situation.

It was a good question — a tank was a formidable challenge, of course, but this being Rufus, he knew exactly how he could blow the thing up before any of the blockheads would even realize what was happening.

Still, would that make sense? Probably not. Once Ronald's troops were on the ground, we could afford to start going force-on-force. For now, though, tipping off the Imperial Army to the fact that consequences were coming might endanger the other small teams that were scouting in the Capital Dome.

"You have a strong stomach, right Simon?" Rufus asked the somewhat cryptic question, and the young Lieutenant looked at the Major and then nodded.

"I don't like seafood, but other than that."

"You leave someone behind when you shipped out?" was the Major's next question, and Keynes shook his head.

"Last girl left me just after I got out of the Academy. Been solo since then," he answered, not entirely sure what point there was to the question.

Then he got it: "Alright, boss. I'll play the wide-eyed kid."

Rufus took a breath, then nodded, "Sorry."

"No problem. I look young enough."

That was true. Keynes looked like a kid, and to the testosterone-fueled blockheads, that might be enough of an excuse.

Either way, Rufus wouldn't enjoy this next part. Not one bit...

Easing the car forward, our elite Major made his way to the checkpoint. The guards caught sight of him just as he began to decelerate and roll down the window. A senior-looking blockhead came up to meet him; as soon as he recognized the uniform of a Special Brancher, his face hardened.

"Orders?" was the gruff question, and as it was asked, the five other men at the checkpoint all perked up. One of them smacked the armored hull of the guard tank a few times, alerting the crew inside to pay attention.

"Don't have any," Rufus answered plainly. "Just landed on leave."

The army man at the window had the stripes of a Sergeant, and now he scowled at the two officers inside the car, "Well maybe people didn't tell you that this colony is under martial law. Sir."

Rufus leaned towards the window slightly, then patted the MAG-90 in his lap, "That's why we're armed. We hear there's still trouble around?"

The Sergeant narrowed his eyes, then shook his head, "Not much anymore."

"Strong checkpoint if there isn't trouble," Rufus smiled, and the Sergeant got irritated.

"Listen, you ain't coming through here without orders."

The men at the checkpoint became even more alert with that statement — their energy guns started swinging into more aggressive positions. But obviously, Rufus didn't become at all vexed by the show of bravado.

"Well, Sergeant, if I can't get to Dome Five, where am I going to find the recreation I'm after?"

I have a difficult time hearing that question in Rufus' voice. You know how you sometimes can't imagine someone saying something? Yeah. But Rufus was doing his best.

The Sergeant was very suspicious now, "And what sort of recreation is that, sir?"

Rufus leaned closer to his window, and smiled with great difficulty, "A buddy of mine got taken out by an explosion on Mercury. He went to hospital on Venus, and there he heard some men from one of your regiments, the 44th Lancers, talking about the best spots on Egesta. Said Dome Five, the Azure Horizon community center, was *the* place. Now I'd like to check this place out, but I'm patient. But my brand new Lieutenant here has something to prove. You understand?"

Rufus nodded towards Keynes, who was very purposefully shifting uncomfortably in his seat.

"First cruise, it's tradition to christen the new boys," Rufus added. I honestly don't know how he managed to say it, and he's not sure either.

But the overtones were the sort that this Sergeant fully understood. He leaned back from the window, "Who in the 44th Lancers said this was where to go?"

Rufus frowned, "I don't know, but my friend told me that was the unit."

Of course, Rufus had just pulled that regiment out of one of Charlie's reports.

Would it be enough?

Yes. Because as far as the blockheads were concerned, repressed, barely-controllable lust was one thing all fighting men had in common. I happen to disagree, but it was part of the military culture of the Imperial Army.

"It ain't free," the Sergeant said finally, and Rufus grinned.

"I pay you, or at the door?"

"Since you don't have orders, you pay both. And probably at the checkpoint on the other side of the tunnel too. And we don't take no IOUs."

Rufus nodded, and then shifted in his seat so he could pull out his wallet. Not a piece of combat equipment he routinely relied on, but it'd be important today.

"There a bank machine around here?" he asked.

He was directed to a nearby terminal, where he took out a lot of cash, and Keynes did the same. The Navy would repay them both for their spending.

They entered the long tunnel to Dome Five.

It cost Rufus and Keynes a small fortune to get past the checkpoint on the other end, but the money spent also got them directions straight to the Azure Horizon community center. And the Sergeant at the second checkpoint had also suggested that Keynes would enjoy either a girl called Heather, or a boy called Andy, depending on his preferences.

If you feel the need to induce vomiting, do your own joke about customer service.

Anyway, Rufus and Keynes pulled up to the Azure Horizon facility in their car, and switched off the hoverpad.

"Think we can get away with MAG-90s going in, boss?" Keynes asked the prudent question, and Rufus was already contemplating the answer.

Having their weapons with them would increase their options, but it'd make talking their way through the door much more difficult — why the hell would Special Branchers need that sort of firepower to get down to business?

"Let's try it. Use the old 'never parted from your weapon' excuse. They might buy it," Rufus said thoughtfully. It was worth the attempt, and if they had to hand in their mags at the door, they'd figure something out once inside.

Both men were Branchers, after all. They were themselves weapons.

Climbing out of the car, Rufus took a breath and made sure his wallet was in hand. He let his MAG-90 dangle from its harness, and following his lead, Keynes did the same. There was another checkpoint at the front door of the community center, and there were two tanks in the parking lot, though both appeared to be powered down. The half-dozen guards present didn't pay the approaching Branchers much attention until they got close. Eventually one nodded in their direction, compelling the rest of the blockheads to look the same way.

Then they were all on their feet, acting tough and making sure to hold their energy guns in the most menacing way possible. It wasn't very tactical; their posture was intended mainly to intimidate.

But as soon as Rufus held up a roll of currency bills, they all started to relax.

"Good day, gentlemen."

The Sergeant commanding the checkpoint was the most suspicious of the bunch, so he approached with weapon in hand, then grunted: "Closed."

Rufus looked back at the parking lot, and it was indeed quite empty, aside from the two powered-down tanks. He had no idea what sort of schedule these men would keep, but he decided it didn't matter. He tossed the roll of bills to the Sergeant.

"That's triple what they told us it would cost for me and my young Lieutenant here. We don't have much time to get this done before my CO starts wondering where we went. And Simon needs to be... *sworn in*."

Again, I just can't imagine those words coming from Rufus, but they did, because they had to. Because he couldn't start shooting until he saw for certain what was going on in there.

It was still possible that Azure Horizon was a gambling house, or something else that was technically unauthorized, but not as horrible as we were all expecting.

The Sergeant caught the bills out of the air, and then looked from Rufus to Keynes. He remained suspicious, but a handful of hard currency made him more flexible. After a moment of contemplation, his eyes settled on the Lieutenant.

"Kid don't look like he'll last too long. Twenty minutes."

Rufus shook his head, "He may not, but I'm not spending that sort of cash on less than an hour. We can lock up behind ourselves if you like."

"Fucking unlikely. Forty-five minutes," the Sergeant haggled back.

"Done," Rufus said.

"Leave the guns," the Sergeant then pointed at the MAG-90 dangling from Rufus' vest, and our Major grinned and shook his head.

"And have to explain to my CO when it goes walkabout? No. But I promise I won't kill anyone."

The Sergeant started to protest, but there was something unnerving about Rufus' stare — perhaps it was his mismatched blue and brown eyes. Better not to argue with Special Branchers who'd already paid.

"Suit yourself. The girls get twitchy around guns though."

The Sergeant grinned when he said that. It's impressive that Rufus didn't take some punitive action at that moment, because the temptation right then must have been great.

Our team went forward after that, the Sergeant waving them through. Together, they entered the lobby of the Azure Horizon community center — the place that had once been the ridiculous headquarters of the Guild's provisional government. Now it stunk of something entirely different.

At least there were no screams. The place was closed; there was no reason for screaming.

A clerk was sitting at a desk just inside the lobby, and to Rufus the young man appeared quite farcical; a typical rear-echelon type with a desk full of pads with lists on them. He scowled up at the two Branchers, not caring about which service they were from, "I take it you bribed your way in after hours? Typical. Well it's self-serve. I'm not parading them down here for you, so go pick for yourselves. Girls in the old day care at the top of the stairs, boys down the hall in the utility room."

As he said that, he reached into a drawer under his desk and pulled out two key cards. "Rooms are upstairs to the left. Go there first and drop your equipment. Might want to keep mags with you, since I don't have any guards. And be careful, some of them bite. If you kill one, just leave the corpse in the room and we clean up for you. It's covered in your door fee."

Yes, this clerk said that.

No, I don't know what comment I can possibly provide that adequately sums up my reaction to his words. The sound of an old-style gunshot, maybe.

Door fee?

"If you want more than one, or anything freaky, that's fine, but you better keep control of the situation. If more than two people end up dead, you get barred for a month. Though I doubt you boys will be here that long."

Nice of him to explain the fine print. I really don't know what I can add here.

I wonder what sound a flamethrower makes...

Clearly, it was good that Rufus was there instead of me. He stayed focused on the job at hand: scout the situation, then secure and wait.

That in mind, our Major looked at Keynes, and together they passed the desk and climbed the stairs to the second floor. The air was warmer up there, and the smell much worse. They went to the left, as they'd been told, and located the rooms they'd rented for forty-five minutes. Keying each one open, they found them to be converted offices with cots in them.

Next, they swept the rest of the rooms in that wing, quietly breaking the locks to make sure none of the converted offices were occupied. Once they were satisfied that they were alone, they headed back past the stairs, down the corridor to the right.

This was where Karen, Charlie and I had gone when we'd visited this place — the Guild Elders had met in a room at the end of the hall. But Rufus and Keynes didn't have to go that far. The daycare that had been full of children in *The Independent Squadron* was now stripped of furniture.

Instead, it was full of people. Women and girls, to be more particular.

I'm not going to provide any more description than that... how about you think of the worst possible way to keep people confined. Got that mental image in your head? Good. Be glad that's as bad as you can imagine, because there's a good chance what Rufus and Simon Keynes saw was worse.

They stared for a whole minute, shocked at the sight.

After that moment Rufus turned sideways, and pointed to the Defense Command patch on his sleeve, hoping that would communicate something to the captives. Only a couple seemed to react. But they'd realize soon enough that change was coming.

It was difficult for Rufus and Keynes to move past that room, but they did. As they reached the next set of windows, they were able to look down on what had once been a modest but well-cared-for football pitch. It was now basically a pad of dirt, and there were dark splashes of blood all across it. On one end were tall stakes with chains on them — undoubtedly used for binding bayonet targets to, Rufus surmised. The rest of the place was just a killing field.

For target practice and bayonet practice on live prisoners.

It's the sort of place you just stare at, with disbelief, disgust and horror... a bunch of words unequal to the task of truly conveying the feeling it produces.

After looking at that place, our elite pair finally got to the utility room, and found the boys there in much the same situation as the females in the daycare. After they stepped back away from the window in the utility room's door, Keynes looked at Rufus. The Lieutenant, being a Brancher, had better composure after seeing these things than I do now, having just described them in print.

"Can we release them, or do we have to sit on this place until Colonel Ronald gets help to us?" he asked quietly.

Rufus was thinking about the same question. They had approximately forty minutes, maybe a bit less, before the checkpoint guards came looking for them. There was no way this group of people could be moved in that time. They had to hold here... quietly get rid of the guards and the clerk, and then wait until the battalion could come down and secure this building.

Drawing his comm, Rufus tapped over to Colonel Garth Ronald's frequency, and with a verbal shorthand they'd developed during the long mission to Mercury, he started to get orders.

The basic gist of them: hold tight and wait for the cavalry. Ronald would try to have help there within the hour.

So that's what they did.

Forty minutes passed all too quickly. Keeping their eyes on the clock, Rufus and Keynes watched the time go by. They couldn't start releasing people, in case someone in a fit of deserved insanity betrayed the Special Branch plan. They couldn't even take down the clerk, because the Sergeant they'd dealt with when they arrived came in to chat for a while, and if any noise was made, their hostile intentions might be betrayed before help arrived.

And to answer my editors' questions, help was needed — not because a couple of powered-down tanks and a handful of blockheads would be trouble for Rufus and Keynes, but because the Imps might try to 'get rid of the evidence' if a fight broke out. All those people, restrained in two rooms with only a pair of Branchers to protect them... it could be a bloody slaughter if shooting began, so best not to take any chances until it was absolutely necessary.

Patience was needed. Brutal patience.

"If Ronald can't get us help by the time they come up here looking for us, we'll need to take out that squad and commandeer one of the tanks," Rufus explained his plans to Keynes as the forty-five minute mark passed. "Then we hold here until the cavalry arrives."

The young Lieutenant nodded, then checked his MAG-90. As ever, the weapon was good to go... but making certain was never a bad idea. There was a good chance it'd be used soon.

Rufus looked at his watch. By now, the Defense Command battalion had to be filtering into the Capital Dome, following the calls of our advance teams to trouble spots, and disarming the blockheads... perhaps destroying them.

Sure, the brigade on this rock had tanks, but they were a lazy garrison force accustomed to terrorizing civilians. Garth Ronald had Mercury veterans with him, along with skiffs and heavy weapons. Azuma's brigade of blockheads would be easily outmatched.

So help would come soon... though not *quite* soon enough.

Watching from the top of the stairs, both Keynes and Rufus saw the army Sergeant finally look at his watch and groan, "Bet the kid was too nervous to do it. I'll go pull the fuckers out."

The clerk's answer was inaudible — that rear echelon bastard was too busy calculating his profits, or some other damned thing, to really care. But the blockhead NCO started up the stairs, swinging his energy rifle causally as he climbed.

It was time to switch back to Special Branch hand gestures; Rufus directed Keynes to go back down the corridor and to find the nearest emergency exit, then to work his way around the outside of the building so he could come at the checkpoint from the outside.

Meanwhile, our Major would deal with things indoors.

Sounds to me like a lot to convey by hand gestures, but they're Special Branchers… it just works that way.

Keynes set off, and Rufus let his MAG-90 drop and dangle from its harness, then unbuckled a couple of the bindings on his vest. Acting time. He backed up a few paces, then started advancing towards the stairs, working on those straps and buckles as if he was getting dressed.

As planned, he almost ran into the Sergeant just as the man reached the top of the stairs.

"Was coming to get you," the blockhead said gruffly, and Rufus finished doing up his gear.

"Got my money's worth," our Major replied, again demonstrating his excellent deceptive powers.

Apparently, the Sergeant saw those words as an opportunity for bonding, and he grinned. They weren't far from the daycare, so he moved that way, to look over the captives.

"You like girls, right Major?" the man asked, showing Rufus his back as he walked towards the glass-walled enclosure. Silence apparently counted as a confirmation, because he then continued speaking, "Ramona is my favorite. She's been here for six months and she's still tight as a—"

They make the glass of daycare windows out of a transparent, laminated material that's supposed to be shatterproof. I point this out because, when the Sergeant's head went through it, there was no shattering sound, just a thud as section of the paneling gave way. And some gasps from the people inside.

The impact caused a skull fracture and some brain damage for the blockhead, but he was lucky to be alive after what he'd been saying. Rufus' moral compass could be awfully clear, and awfully unforgiving.

As the bastard crumpled, Rufus held a finger up to his lips, asking the captives inside the daycare to be quiet. Then he turned and quickly descended the stairs, his MAG-90 still dangling from its harness. By the time he reached the clerk's desk, the man was standing with folded arms and tapping his foot impatiently.

"Where's the Sergeant? He better not be fucking Ramona again, he hasn't paid…"

Another son of a bitch who's very lucky Rufus didn't simply decide to kill him. With all due speed, the Chinese Major broke both the man's legs, and slammed his forehead onto his desk with force enough to compel a loss of consciousness.

Then he tapped his comm, "Ready to go, Simon. I'll shoot, then you come in."

There was no verbal reply — Lieutenant Keynes was lying in wait, and didn't want to betray his location. Rightly so.

When Rufus went out the front door with his MAG-90 up, there was no contest, and there was no mercy. It was textbook. It was clean. It was brutal.

After everything we've gone through during this series, you know how good Special Branchers really are. And the Imperial Army just *isn't* — especially their scum-sucking garrison troops on Egesta. So it wasn't difficult to pile up comatose blockheads in the lobby — the hardest part was carrying their bodies inside.

By that time, a hovercar escorted by a skiff was pulling up in the Azure Horizon parking lot — as Ronald had promised, reinforcements.

While they secured the building, Rufus and Keynes went back upstairs and finally started unchaining the captives. A few spat on the Special Branchers, and a few punched at them. Some offered, or demanded, hugs, and some just didn't want to be touched or seen.

I should do a better job of painting this scene for you. Help you picture it. Help you understand what it looked like, felt like, and smelled like for Rufus when these people were unbound, and had to face their 'rescuers'.

But I won't. Because you're better off without those explicit pictures in your head. If you really want them, go to the archives and look up Rufus' report. Or just imagine… imagine what it was like for someone like 'Ramona' (not actually her name), who'd been confined and abused for six months, to suddenly be free and safe.

Imagine the skepticism, too. The fear that, really, all we were doing was taking over the facility for our own needs, and that we might treat them a bit nicer, but demand the same things. Also imagine the anger among those who still desperately wanted to lash out at someone for the harm that had been done.

There was nothing stereotypical, or heroic, or grand about this rescue. It made no one feel good, in that classic movie sense.

But after reflecting on it for a long time, Rufus told me that it was one of the best things he'd ever done in his career. It was fundamentally the right thing to do, and he and Simon Keynes had pulled it off.

Unfortunately, across the domes of Egesta, there were many other, similar sorts of rescues that needed to be carried out. And some very unlikely people were taking part in them.

CHAPTER FIVE

WHAT SHELBY, ADRIENNE AND EUGENE SAW

Typically, you don't send your Helm and Navigation Officer to ground during a mission like this one, but remember, the reason we got Shelby McLaws on *Wolf* was because Andrea knew her from the old days aboard *Friendly*.

And it was during those old days — almost at the end of them, in fact — that *Friendly* had been at Egesta.

In other words, Shelby had been here before. And while she'd been aboard ship for some of that time, she'd still seen things… experienced things… that made her determined to come back and help fix this situation.

None of us were going to tell her no.

When we started to form teams down in the landing warehouse, she found herself with Adrienne Thompson and Eugene Sengooba — another rather stacked team, considering all three of them were department heads aboard *Wolf*. More risk that we arguably shouldn't have been taking, more leaders who might have been better utilized if we spread them out across a series of small units…

But on the flip side, more elite teams of the very best officers in the service, meaning they were that much better equipped to cope with this extraordinary place.

Instead of taking a car out of the lot, this trio of *Wolf* officers decided to start their tour of the dome on foot, moving out from the warehouse and heading towards the center of town. This was Shelby's suggestion, because it was apparently a route she was familiar with — she'd covered it on a foot many times during her last visit, and the 'before and after' comparison would probably be quite informative.

Adrienne, who'd seen horrible things in the space outside the domes last time, wanted to get a sense of what it really was like inside the place, so this walking tour with Shelby would be a perfect opportunity. Eugene simply decided to tag along, in case they needed some help.

I think it's fair to say he was a bit protective of them both, under the circumstances. Remember, he'd recently been promoted to the almost-defunct rank of Master-At-Arms, and was essentially our chief of security. Knowing that Rufus had attached four Special Branch officers to Karen and me, and with Andrea and Wes hurrying off on their own, Adrienne and Shelby were the two highest-priority persons left for him to look after. So that's what he'd do.

Just as well: he knew this dome, and had seen his share of crimes committed here last time. It would have been foolish for anyone to reject his presence, and the thought never crossed Shelby's or Adrienne's minds.

So off they walked, through the districts that separated the warehouse from the center of town. There were mixed buildings in this area — some denser housing for workers, some light industrial plants, and some basic convenience stores, all of which were operating because it was the middle of the day. Sparse sounds of life occasionally emanated from these places... but it all was too quiet, like it had been muted.

Just go ahead and guess by what.

And there were no people in the streets. On a work day on Egesta, you got from home to work as quick as you could, because lingering on the street might get you noticed by a blockhead patrol, and taken in for questioning.

Despite being alive, then, the city almost seemed empty. And as they started down the sidewalks, the first thing that struck Shelby was how haunted it all seemed.

"Not too... unpleasant... yet..." Adrienne Thompson was apprehensive, which is slightly remarkable. I've flown with her, and know the steely quality of her nerves.

But Shelby had shared with her some of the more private stories of horror from Egesta, and she'd seen her own evidence. She knew there was a dark shadow over this rock, and now she was waiting for it to become obvious again.

"Seems the blockheads forced them to keep things out of the street," Shelby agreed.

Both women were walking with mags in hand, but hanging down at their sides. Eugene's sidearm remained in its holster — he knew he could retrieve it quickly if it was needed.

"I wasn't in this part of the city very much," our Master-At-Arms observed as they moved past some fast food places, and turned down a street which took them between a number of ore processing facilities.

Shelby's eyes roamed from side to side, a little wider than usual, and as unblinking as was reasonably possible. She didn't look back at Eugene's comment, but she responded, "When we secured the docking chutes, the Guild started to leave this area alone. It was too easy for us to get in the way of their fun..."

She was referring to things that *Friendly's* crew had accomplished (with barely more than 100 volunteers) before we'd arrived to help them.

"But in the beginning, they were bold. People tried to hide in this warehouse up here... I think it was a food warehouse, so they must have wanted to lock themselves in with the supplies..." Shelby waved her hand in the direction of a relatively nondescript building that was on the left side of the street ahead.

Then she didn't finish the story, which drew a glance from Adrienne Thompson.

The memory of what a team of four *Friendly* volunteers had found in that warehouse after the Guild gang had come and gone had shaken Shelby's normally-poised posture, and her typically cool expression.

It was better that she didn't describe what they'd found.

Eugene, for his part, was never one to pressure someone to speak of things about which they were uncomfortable — excepting, of course, matters of military necessity. But this wasn't such a matter, so he simply stared at the building as the trio of department heads passed it by. They moved on towards the center of town.

It took an hour for things to become visibly messier. Moving out of that area with the ore processing facilities and the warehouses, the three *Wolf* veterans entered a section of town that featured denser housing for workers. Low-rent apartment blocks, mainly, with some strip malls and diners to support them.

Workers evidently still occupied some of these places, but the word that could best describe the condition of the area was 'slum'. Perhaps 'ghetto'.

Some buildings featured unrepaired damage from what looked to be tank energy cannon shots, as well as the scorch marks and punctures synonymous with the liberal use of energy guns. Some places were boarded up, and others had tattered-looking people sitting on their porches, staring angrily at the uniformed passers-by.

Didn't seem like a good neighborhood... more like the Belt Widow side of some of the Belt colonies' seedier domes.

And three of our senior people were wandering through, on foot without backup.

Well, could have been worse. At least no one was shooting. Some sort of life *was* happening...

"Up there... that barber shop..." Shelby raised her hand and waved at a burnt-out store in one of the strip malls ahead. "That's where they used to use curling irons for... things they shouldn't be used for."

She'd told that story to Adrienne when our venerable wing commander had asked Shelby why she'd stopped curling her hair. As long as I'd known our southern belle Helm and Navigation Officer, she hadn't curled it, but apparently Adrienne had seen pictures from the old days.

The answer had been that, after seeing curling irons put to incorrect uses on Egesta, she'd never wanted to touch one again.

Fair enough.

Not knowing that story, Eugene simply nodded, but the Master-At-Arms was getting a gut feeling about something entirely unrelated to the barber shop. They were passing a low apartment block — a stubby concrete structure that was both practical and depressing, with three floors and tiny windows.

Nothing around this building was alive. None of the people they'd seen on the streets were going near it. All the blinds were closed, and the windows had been barred from the outside.

Looking up the stairs to its front door, Eugene also saw that a short wall had been erected there... almost like a small guard post, but with no sentry occupying it.

A lot of clues, then, that this was a place to check out — that it was a facility not unlike the one Rufus and Simon Keynes were at the very same moment entering in Dome Five.

"Lieutenant, Lieutenant Commander..." Eugene still didn't feel right referring to either Shelby or Adrienne by their first names, as they were commissioned officers while he was a warrant. Neither would have minded at all, but that was irrelevant...

As they both stopped and turned back to him, he nodded towards the apartment, "We might want to investigate that. See if it's a target for Colonel Ronald."

Shelby actually felt the color drain from her face, and Adrienne remembers one of the few flashes of genuine angst that she'd felt in years. Both agreed, though, and so with Eugene leading the way, they backtracked to the path that led up to the building's front door, and started to reinforce their mental fortitude. Whatever was coming next, they knew, was going to be bad.

I suppose they were right. But not entirely.

Eugene was about ten meters from the front door when he heard the first shot from an energy gun. He assumed, naturally, that someone was shooting at him, so he dropped to one knee and pulled his mag from its holster. Of course, our Master-At-Arms wasn't a Special Brancher, but I think it'd be quite naïve to suggest that he, or any of our regular SF, were not able to handle themselves in most situations.

Shelby and Adrienne got low behind him, and the fighter pilot asked the question first: "Shots?"

Nodding, Eugene listened and waited. It was quite quickly clear that no fire was coming at them... and then something else occurred to our African Master-At-Arms: someone inside might be destroying the evidence of their crimes.

The thought was so grim it made him wince, but as soon as it came to him he knew instinctively that it was almost certainly correct. He looked back to his officer comrades, "They might be trying to kill witnesses. Are you willing to follow me in?"

As if to punctuate the intensity of that request, a man screamed from inside the building, and Shelby and Adrienne found their breath shortening. Nevertheless, they both nodded. Neither woman would be counted among *Wolf's* typical shooters — they were almost the opposite — but this was Egesta, and the demands of the situation were more than enough motivation for them to adapt.

With a nod of his own, Eugene looked back to the front door. He took three breaths, and in the time needed to fill and empty his lungs, he reviewed as many possibilities as he could think of. How many blockheads? How would they be armed? How ready would they be for a Defense Command intrusion? How would they react?

Going blind into a situation like this is inevitably much more terrifying than it ever appears to be in the movies. It's not so easy to just run in with your mag drawn, assuming that it'll be okay because you're one of the protagonists. There can be bad guys sitting right beside the door, ready to blow you away as soon as you run through...

But some days, that's the risk you have to take. Your adrenaline pumps, your heart rate soars, and away you go... probably trying not to think about the consequences if you're in over your head.

This is exactly what Eugene did, and what Shelby and Adrienne did behind him. They launched themselves forward at a dead run, and as they climbed the few stairs up to the front door, they were greeted by the first unexpected and grizzly sight: a blockhead with the top of his skull shot off. The man had probably been at the makeshift guard post Eugene had noticed earlier... and someone had managed, through luck or skill, to cut off the top of his head.

They didn't pause to study him, though, as another scream came from inside. Because of the way the sound echoed inside the building, they couldn't tell if it was from the first floor or the second. What they did realize as soon as they entered the dim, dank and stinking facility was that it was more of a boarding house than an apartment.

Single bedroom flats densely packed on all the floors, and communal bathrooms. All of the doors were off their hinges, too, to make the rooms easier to access, and to make sure the captives chained to the cots in each one were easy to see from the hallway.

I'll avoid the details again. My tolerance, probably like yours, can only take so much of this. The fact that Egesta had more than one facility like this and Azure Horizon really is… *monstrous* isn't too strong a word, I don't think.

This place had some differences from what Rufus was discovering in Dome Five, though. Most notably, there was a dead blockhead (not wearing any clothes below the waist) lying on the stairs, with a rather gruesome wound where a certain element of his anatomy should have been.

There was also another Imperial soldier down in the corridor to the left, looking like he'd been shot in the face, based on the location of the blood pool. Interestingly, if that word can be forgiven in such a brutal scene, both men had energy guns in their hands — someone had downed them while they were armed.

Certainly, one was pantless, but he'd probably been ready to shoot. And someone had out-shot him…

Another scream, this one clearly from the second floor. A man was wailing for mercy, and with three dead Imps now in sight, it seemed a fair guess that the call was indeed coming from a blockhead.

Rescue was a tough sell in that moment, considering what Eugene, Shelby and Adrienne were seeing through the doors to the rooms. Even the few that were visible from their position just inside the entrance were enough. A team of medics was needed here, with whatever equipment was required to detox the people chained up. It appeared they'd been drugged to inspire cooperation…

Eugene blinked against those sights for now. Something was happening upstairs, and no more could be done for these captives until the building was completely secure. There could be more blockheads, or someone else…

Pointing up the stairs, the Master-At-Arms led his two companions carefully around the fallen blockhead, and silently edged his way to the second floor landing. As he scanned the hallways around him over the barrel of his mag, he saw no sign of someone in need of mercy; two more Imperial soldiers, one with a gun, were down on the floor.

Gesturing to the left, Eugene sent Shelby and Adrienne that way, then he went to the right. In one of the rooms, the torture must be happening…

Shelby was doing a good job of keeping her shock in check. She might vomit later — no shame in that — but as she led Adrienne to the left, she kept her mag ready, just as her father had taught her, and she kept her eyes to the doorways on the right side of the hall. Coming up behind her, Adrienne covered the doorways to the left.

Each one contained a little travesty, things far more deliberate than what Shelby had seen during her previous experience on Egesta. The Guild had never bothered with trying to keep its victims alive — they'd just go out and get more. But the blockheads were conserving their resources with military efficiency…

Maybe that vomit was going to come up sooner than Shelby had planned…

Before it got a chance, someone put a boot into her back with so much force, she went almost head first into he corridor wall. Her arm got up to protect her face just in time.

Adrienne whirled on the attacker, who'd come out of nowhere, but hands were already on our wing commander's body, and her mag was wrenched from her grasp. She found herself on the floor, her stomach radiating pain which had appeared with no warning.

Hearing the commotion, Eugene turned back in their direction, and hurried up the hallway. He was the only one who got a clear look at the attacker: a woman in her forties wearing business-casual attire, with a cold look in her eyes.

Seeing there was one more Defense Command officer in the corridor, that woman came forward with Adrienne's mag in her hand. Eugene stopped instantly with his own sidearm leveled, and as the attacker approached, he read her body language.

He'd been in the field with Special Branchers before, and though this woman didn't quite have their assurance, he could recognize that she'd had training. Eugene never had bothered with the advanced hand-to-hand courses; he'd always believed that his skill with a mag would be enough for his job.

Now this woman came at him fast, seemingly not interested in using the mag she'd taken from Adrienne. Eugene instantly recognized her goal: get into grappling range, dodge his panicked first shot, and then immobilize him before he could manage a second.

A prideful SF would have tried to out-punch her in close... and that, he expected, was what she was counting on him to do.

Instead, he was practical: he backed away quickly, keeping the distance between them open, and managing to keep his torso and shoulders level on target. His sight picture, to use marksmanship terminology, didn't change.

So it was really quite easy for him to drill her with a mid-power mag shot that put her on her back.

As she went down, Eugene recognized that she rolled her shoulder to absorb some of the impact. That was training — something only experienced military personnel would normally know to do when being hit by a mag bolt. Filing that away, he kept her covered until he was convinced she was out, then stepped over her, retrieved Adrienne's mag, and hurried back to his two colleagues.

Shelby was a bit woozy after her almost-head-first date with the wall, while Adrienne was up on her hands and knees, perched over our Helm and Navigation Officer with a concerned expression, "Shelby... Shelby?"

They were both fine, ultimately, so Eugene handed Adrienne back her mag, then advanced to the doorway from which the attacker must have emerged. Inside, chained to the bed, was a blockhead. The man was in a state of distress. That's the best way for me to explain it. The girl whose place he'd taken on that bed was sitting in a chair opposite the bed, wrapped up in a disgusting blanket. She hid her eyes with her hand as soon as Eugene stepped in.

"Please help me! *Please!*" the blockhead whined from the bed.

Eugene stared at him for a second, then decided to ignore him. A surgical team would be needed to remove those things that had been introduced into the soldier's physiology. If Eugene tried to do anything, he expected he'd leave intestines on the floor.

I might have been tempted to give it a shot, but Eugene Sengooba is a genuinely good man, so instead of doing anything for or about the blockhead, he approached the girl. Holstering his mag, he crouched down beside her chair, and steadfastly ignored the pungent odor coming from the blanket she was wrapped in.

"Hello there," he said gently, using a rich tone that had often calmed his daughters after their nightmares. "My name is Eugene, and I'm here to help you go home."

I suppose what follows might come across as altogether cliché. The girl spread the fingers on her hand just enough to see between them, and to look at Eugene's face. He smiled brightly, trying to look a bit like a teddy bear. He expected that, after being in a place like this one, the girl would have a difficult time not finding anyone in a uniform threatening, and he was right.

But, nevertheless, he tried.

"Where's… mom…?"

The question was essentially whispered, and it immediately explained the identity of the fierce woman who'd been shot in the corridor. Made Eugene glad he'd kept his mag setting low.

"She's unconscious, but she will be alright," he said honestly.

Not the most comforting answer imaginable, but the girl seemed to accept it. Probably had no choice.

"How about you come sit outside with two friends of mine, Shelby and Adrienne. I'm going to call some of my colleagues to come help you, and everyone here."

The girl stared at him through her fingers, but said nothing. Eugene was reluctant to reach out to help her up without an invitation, but as the blockhead on the bed start screaming, it seemed important she be gotten out of the room.

She seemed resigned when Eugene's arms closed around her filthy blanket, and lifted her upwards. Her legs basically fell off the chair, and they seemed unable, or unwilling, to do any of the work of holding her up. Her toes dragged along the carpet as he carried her out of the room.

Shelby was sitting up against the wall when Eugene got there, Adrienne still crouched over her, checking her responses. The arrival of the girl prompted them both to direct their attention to more pressing matters, and as our Master-At-Arms set down his charge beside Shelby, both officers quickly put their hands out to steady her.

Drawing his comm, Eugene moved down the corridor and called immediately for help. They didn't need a security team here — maybe an extra guard, but not a proper team — but they did need doctors. Lots of them. And the sooner the better. The request was made.

Shelby's mind seemed to clear instantly at the sight of the girl beside her on the floor. It looked as though her legs were twisted uncomfortably, so Adrienne straightened them. Her ankles were chaffed and bleeding, and her leg muscles appeared to be quite weak. Her toes did wiggle a bit, so it seemed that she wasn't paralyzed at least…

After making that assessment, Shelby tried to make eye contact with the girl. It didn't work. Absurdly, the best comparison our southern belle could come up with was that trying to catch her eyes was like trying to pick up a slippery fish — every time you tried to grab it, it jumped away.

So even as she leaned back and forth, and tried to follow the girl's ashen gaze, she found their eyes never connected.

I don't think I need to explain why.

After a moment of trying, Shelby looked up at Adrienne, and those two shared dark stares. Not only was the magnitude of this place terrible — all these rooms, used for this horrible purpose — the depth of the destruction was nigh incomprehensible. I'll talk more about the damage done to people who suffered the blockheads' recreation later, when we join Jim Hannigan at the ICC… but here was a textbook case of exactly the sort of carnage we expected to find in these facilities on Egesta.

This girl turned out to be seventeen.

When Captain Angela Kerr awoke from her mag shot, she was on a stretcher in the hall of the boarding house she'd raided. Eugene's mag had been set to moderate, so the effect of his shot had worn off after only a couple of hours.

There were other reasons the shot hadn't put her out for the expected day, but I can't explain them. Suffice it to say, her training had taught her some tricks to resist mag fire that we don't want to publicize, because if a group like the Belt Widows find out about them, it could spell trouble.

No one was monitoring her, so she sat up and immediately got to her feet. There were Defense Command uniforms in the hallways around her — all medics, it seemed, and none of them paying her any attention. They were helping the countless victims of Summergrove House (the name of this establishment) out of the building, and into waiting hovercars to go to the hospital.

That was good, but Kerr honestly couldn't afford to care about any of these other young people. Other parents could worry about their sons and daughters… her child was her concern. Valerie Kerr had been safe… Angela had pulled the blockhead off her, and then chained the fucker up and started to get angry…

She closed her eyes for a second, frowning as she tried to remember exactly what had happened after she'd rammed the rebar into him. Someone had interrupted…

Opening her eyes again, she started to remember, but mental processes stopped when she realized a mag was pointed at her, from across the hall. *Just* out of reach, where she couldn't grab it without stepping forward.

The black man holding it was the same one who'd known how to take her down. A wily Defense Command SF guard… actually, Angela didn't recognize the rank insignia he was wearing.

"You obviously have had training. And considering you're here, I'd say you were a Boscawen Mercenary?" Eugene asked that casually, even though he was training his mag on the woman he thought would have been down for a day.

She replied with a nod, "Retired six years ago. Captain Angela Kerr. I stayed here with my husband and my daughter."

"Blockheads knew better than to take her, until recently?" our Master-At-Arms had surmised a bit more about the situation in the hours since he'd pulled Valerie (who'd finally whispered her name) out of her room.

Nodding again, Angela took a deep breath, "They kept trying to get her. She was finally taken. So I came to find her. Where is she now?"

"Surrounded by a security team, on the way to the hospital, which we're taking over. I'll take you to her immediately, if you promise not to try to kill me," Eugene was being relatively frank, and really quite accommodating. He had daughters, he'd have done no differently.

Well, perhaps not the rebar. But that was just a personal preference.

Angela Kerr studied him for a moment, "You're… who?"

"Eugene Sengooba, Master-At-Arms, *DCNS Wolf.* We just learned what the Imperial

Army has been doing here, and we're going to liquidate them."

Not putting too fine a point on it.

After another moment, Angela Kerr nodded, "Alright then. My word. Do you need to put me in cuffs?"

Eugene's mag was abruptly back in its holster, and he shook his head, "There are still plenty of blockheads around. Grab one of the guns we took off the dead troopers here, in case someone tries to jump us."

I know, that might seem like an unreasonable leap of faith for Eugene, considering how Angela had tried to take him down. But he was counting on her wanting to see her daughter again, and he was right.

They left the horrible place.

The hospital's cleanliness was actually the trigger that made Shelby vomit. It was so clean, so pristine. Clearly, there were people in this dome, and across Egesta, who needed to be helped in this facility, but the place was largely abandoned.

That was too wrong, and it left her running to one of the empty waste bins at the nurses' station, and emptying the few contents of her stomach in a painful series of heaves. By the time she recovered herself, and found a mouth-cleansing foamer tablet, she realized she'd lost sight of Adrienne and the girl they'd escorted in — Valerie.

She searched around for a few minutes, watching as more people were led into the facility. The nurses and doctors on staff were being herded out by some of Garth Ronald's SF — no one knew if they could be trusted with these patients, so they'd be sent home and screened later…

Finally, she passed the right door, and stepped in. Adrienne stood with folded arms in the corner of the room, while Rufus' new medic, Selma Koestecki, worked on Valerie as gently as she could.

A doctor would have to follow up this exam, of course, but Selma's initial attentions would help. An injection to cure HIV and Hepatitis were administered first, and then the test for SIGD came back negative — no need for gene therapy, which was good. After that, her fractured right forearm was wrapped, and she was put on an IV to try to counter the drugs in her system and to fight her obvious malnourishment.

There was no time to clean her up at all — that could be done later, once the more serious problems were dealt with.

Through it all, no eye contact to be found. It was somewhat disconcerting, really, but no matter; the important thing was that she got better.

Selma was actually packing up her kit and leaving when Shelby arrived, and that left Valerie alone in a bright white room with two of *Wolf's* department heads, neither of them sure what to say.

It was uncomfortable for Shelby and for Adrienne, but that was fine. They could handle uncomfortable. What was most important was that Valerie, and everyone else who'd survived the ordeal of that place, were coming to the hospital for treatment.

When Angela arrived with Eugene about fifteen minutes later, she rushed straight to her daughter's bedside, and that was the first time anyone seemed to make eye contact with the seventeen-year-old girl.

Eugene moved to stand beside Shelby as the reunion took place, but he quickly found it somewhat improper. These two deserved privacy, not an audience, and Shelby and Adrienne both concurred. They stepped out of the room, to wait beside the door for Angela to emerge.

Out there, they discussed what they'd seen, all of them feeling a bit of shock, and none of the pride that I suppose they would have been allowed to feel after getting help to these people. Down the corridor, in the waiting room, the first of the captives from Azure Horizon were beginning to come in, and that sight was enough to darken any moods that threatened to improve. So the trio simply stood, and decided what to do next.

Shelby ultimately chose to take the blame. As did Adrienne. As did Eugene. Ironically, these three — the heads of *Wolf's* Helm and Navigation department, Wolfstar Squadron and our fighter group, and our security staff couldn't agree on who would be responsible for what came next.

They all later came to me, individually, and accepted full responsibility.

It was Eugene, though, who delivered the news.

Leaving Shelby and Adrienne outside, the Master-At-Arms quietly re-entered the room, and found that mother and daughter were still somewhat composed, Angela whispering reassuring things to Valerie from a chair pulled right up to the side of the bed.

Of course, the former Boscawen Merc heard the heels of Eugene's boots as he entered, so she knew what was coming next. She considered reaching down to the energy gun tucked into her belt — the gun Eugene had told her to pick up — but that wouldn't have been right. Defense Command was now seeing to her daughter's care, and resisting arrest would only jeopardize that... though the Merc rightly expected that, even if she did force Eugene to put her down, we'd have continued to care for her daughter.

No matter. She'd been given the opportunity to get her daughter to safety, and now she'd pay the price. That was fair enough.

"Mommy has to go," she whispered, feeling a stab of tears — rare for her — as she came to her feet.

Valerie didn't like that at all, but was too darkened to protest.

Turning to Eugene, then, Captain Kerr took a deep breath, blinked against the tears that were trying to well up, and nodded, "Thank you for letting me see her."

Our Master-At-Arms nodded, "Of course. We're going to head back to our duties. If you need anything else, ask someone to contact me directly on your behalf."

Angela didn't catch on immediately, "I think I'll represent myself at the trial."

Eugene stared at her. Then he said: "Stay here as long as you like. We're not going to enforce visiting hours... though you may want to consider going home to get some rest. I wouldn't leave my daughter's bedside either, but you should understand that you're free to go home, and come back, and go home, as much as you'd like to. And that won't change."

He was getting less subtle with his message. He wasn't actually going to explicitly say 'there will be no trial'. Saying so might have implied that there was a reason for one to take place.

But there was no evidence of wrongdoing, and no witnesses except for a gravely wounded blockhead who would later be hung as a war criminal. Once the bottom third of his torso was sufficiently reconstructed for him to stand trial.

Angela Kerr blinked. And blinked again.

She understood what Eugene was saying. She could have asked explicitly for clarification, but she didn't need to. Better not to even utter such a question out loud.

There would be no trial. Her place now was looking after her daughter.

And that's what she'd do.

"Thank you, Master-At-Arms Sengooba," she extended her hand, and a tear did make its way down her cheek.

"Look after your daughter. She'll be strong, if you help her," he said, and took her hand.

They parted ways. Eugene returned to Shelby and Adrienne, and then the three of them — a bit worse for wear — went back out on patrol. Because they felt there might be more to do.

Angela Kerr sat down beside her daughter and spent the next week in the hospital at her side. No one ever bothered her. Today, Angela, her husband, and Valerie are all Imperial citizens. They chose to move to Earth — to Africa, in fact — a few years after this incident. They live in Uganda, coincidentally in the town where Eugene and his family still live to this day.

To answer my editors' questions, no, I haven't just outed Angela Kerr as a murderer. Granted, those dead blockheads in the boarding house might be attributed to her — a couple of their families tried that a few years ago — but there's no evidence and no witnesses to her actually killing anyone. We decided not to charge her for assaulting Adrienne or Shelby.

And even if someone did have evidence of her killing those soldiers, the extenuating circumstances and the need to save the lives of every captive in Summergrove House would be sufficient justification for her actions. Under Imperial law, no crown attorney would prosecute the case. Angela has that assurance in writing from the Attorney General of the Empire, thanks to a call someone made to Craig B. Macdonald.

She deserves all the peace in the world, as does her daughter.

As do so many other Egesta survivors…

But unfortunately, it's not time to focus on the aftermath yet. Because we still hadn't finished dealing with the blockheads. There are a couple of other stories to tell from this bad day.

CHAPTER SIX

WHAT MATT SAW

With so many Defense Command officers going out into the Egesta Capital Dome and doing what a certain British Commander might call (to our faces) 'stupid stuff', it was quite clear that we needed to leave the warehouse and its connections up to *Wolf, Nova Scotia, Friendly* and *Artemis Agrotera* in the hands of someone we could trust.

This person, perhaps unsurprisingly, would be none other than Matt Baxter.

It wasn't necessarily a job he wanted — obviously, having been with us during *The Independent Squadron*, then as *Wolf's* XO, he had a history with this rock, and he wanted to help deal with the new problems...

But after our quick huddle, he'd watched Wes and Andrea, Adrienne and Shelby and Eugene, Rufus and Simon Keynes, and Karen and me all disappear. That left him as the only senior officer in the warehouse, and considering this was the most important tactical position on the rock, he realized he'd have to stay, and keep it well controlled.

Once Garth Ronald's battalion was on the ground, and the Capital Dome was secured, Matt could turn this job over to someone less senior... but in case trouble arose before we were able to exact submission from the blockheads, he'd remain.

It's hard to say whether that was better or worse for him, but then, Matt's never been one to delude himself. He knows that a lot of what he might have seen in those hours he was watching the warehouse could have been difficult to cope with.

It didn't matter, anyway; his job was to make sure we didn't somehow lose our control of the docking chutes. Things would only get worse if the blockheads realized we were moving in to take over, and managed to cut our connection to orbit before Colonel Ronald was able to land.

So Matt held out patiently, pacing around the warehouse, occasionally stepping outside to look around for any signs of fighting, and generally waiting for things to progress. Compared to what you've already read, this might seem a dull job. Perhaps, by some empirical standard of interestingness (shut up, it's a word), it was dull.

But it was punctuated in the middle by a conversation that I think needs to be included here, because it really does explain a great deal about what was going on, and why.

Matt had just come back in after looking around outside for a few minutes. When he'd seen no billowing clouds of smoke, he'd been satisfied that none of us had started blowing stuff up yet, which was good. He knew Colonel Ronald's troops were soon to arrive, and once they did, his anxiety would lessen a little.

Thinking about these things, he strode through the long, narrow corridors formed by the boxes and crates that filled the warehouse. It would be fair to say that, when you got out of the main cargo-moving lanes, the facility did feel rather like a labyrinth. Matt wasn't sure who had organized it, how or why, but it was easy to get lost in, particularly if you happened to be preoccupied.

This is why Matt stumbled upon the 'pen' where two of his SF from *Friendly* were standing guard over the dozen blockheads who had been guarding this facility, and who had surrendered immediately upon our arrival.

Now, because I've written this book without the usual narrative process, I don't know how clear I've been about what happened when we reached the warehouse. A dozen Imperial soldiers were watching this place, led by Major Wang-Roth. The Major had immediately surrendered, and provided what limited information he could about the disposition of his unit.

You see, Wang-Roth told us he had resisted the orders of Brigadier Azuma... that he hadn't wanted to participate in the war crimes. As a result, he and any similar-thinking members of the brigade were ostracized, and basically confined to out-of-the-way posts like the warehouse, and other backwater jobs across Egesta's domes.

This wasn't complete fiction: the Egesta Inquiry would investigate these claims of non-involvement, and many of the men like Wang-Roth would indeed be acquitted of wrongdoing. They would also often supply testimony to the prosecution for the cases against big fish like Azuma.

So the blockheads that Matt ran into in the labyrinth were, in fact, the 'good' ones. And you realize how difficult it is for me to use the word 'good' in relation to the Imperial Army.

However, Matt knew none of this when he stopped before them, and even if he'd been aware, being 'good' didn't absolve them of some hatred by association. The two SF who were watching them weren't exactly being friendly to the blockheads, and Matt found himself without any sympathy for them either. These men may have stayed personally out of trouble, but their comrades had done just the opposite.

Hard to ignore that fact. Hard not to ask: 'How could you let your friends *do* this?'

That all being the case, when Matt arrived, he stopped for a moment, and stared at the sullen band of men in uniform. A couple were clearly hoping to suck up... they looked up at him eagerly, and he could sense they were considering what they could say, to absolve themselves of any responsibility for what had gone on.

Our British Commander's stare seemed to be enough dissuasion, though, and they remained silent. All except one, who stood slowly, and turned to present himself to Matt. It was Major Wang-Roth.

"Commander, may I speak with you privately?"

The question didn't sound at all insubordinate to Matt — nor was it pleading, or self-serving. It didn't sound like the question of a person looking for special treatment... but that was just reading tone. Matt was well prepared for the Major to start begging as soon as they got away from this group...

One way to find out.

"Major," he nodded, and then pointed back the way he'd come. Best to speak in the privacy of the crate maze.

Wang-Roth stepped out of the pen — which, I should explain, was basically an area surrounded on three sides by twelve-foot stacks of ore crates — and led Matt away. Our Commander wasn't going to show this man his back. No sir.

It took them a couple of moments to turn a corner, and get far enough away from both the other prisoners and the receiving area where Defense Command personnel were milling around. Wang-Roth waited until he knew they were both well out of earshot, then stopped, turned to Matt, and took a deep breath.

A lot was riding on the Imperial officer's opening statement. Not everything — Matt wouldn't decide this man's fate, there would be trial. But whatever impression Matt formed of the Major would influence my thoughts of him, and might in turn affect the way he was characterized to the special prosecutors when the Inquiry got into full swing.

Who was Major Wang-Roth? What could he possibly say?

"Commander, I find myself in a very difficult situation," was the opener, and I think we can agree he was pretty much stating the obvious.

Folding his arms, Matt scowled, "Major, I think that might be the most political way to put it."

Wang-Roth paled somewhat, and apparently looked rather ill. He took a deep breath, then moved over to the nearest line of crates and found one that was jutting out enough for him to perch on.

"I'm an officer, Commander. So technically, what happened here could come back to me. But you have to understand, I wanted nothing to do with any of it. And my men the same — these here, they weren't all my men originally. But we were all brought together by our common refusal to be a part of the atrocities."

Matt's reaction to this explanation was lukewarm. He was willing to listen, which is a sign of his open-mindedness, but at the same time, this argument could very easily turn into whining and pleading. And none of that would be stomached from any blockhead on this rock.

"If you didn't want to participate in their crimes, why didn't they send you to Mercury?" *Friendly's* Commander asked that pointed question, drawing on the interrogation skills he'd developed over many years as our security chief.

Wang-Roth looked up at Matt, eyes slightly wide, then hung his head, "They wouldn't let us go. They feared that we'd report them."

At first blush that seemed pretty flimsy, considering the ease with which the rumors of the atrocities had spread in the Venus hospitals. But it was conceivable that those who resisted were perceived to be a greater threat — more likely to actively seek out the Military Police or the Shore Patrol and report the incidents.

And, of course, the fact that it had taken our very best — Charlie — so long to piece together the real story about Egesta also suggested that the army leadership might have been right in assuming word wouldn't spread easily, even with rampant rumor...

Nevertheless, the validity of the excuse wasn't Matt's to decide. He knew, as we all did, that some sort of trial or inquiry would hear the evidence.

Wang-Roth still wanted to talk, though, and he continued: "Listen, Commander... I don't know how it is in your service. But there's a culture. You must understand that. There's an expectation in our army that you are one of the team. That you do everything together. You are comrades, and you stick up for each other. You watch each others' backs, you don't go against the current..."

It sounded to Matt like an avalanche of clichés was about to come, so he cleared his throat. That noise stopped Wang-Roth, and looking up at Matt's disinterested glare, the Major decided the Commander got the point.

"It took a lot for each of us to step out of line. Many of us had our lives threatened for doing it. We're not involved with the people who committed the crimes. We're *not*."

It sounded self-serving now, and Matt didn't appreciate that. Though he did understand, at least in intellectual terms, what Wang-Roth was trying to get across. The notion of turning against your comrades was no more popular in Defense Command than it was in the army... we just had (and have) *very* different expectations for behavior.

Matt considered swelling up with some DC pride, and giving the army Major a lecture in what the culture of an armed force was *supposed* to be, but he decided this wasn't the time. Not yet. First he needed to give the blockhead a bit more rope — see whether he'd hang himself.

That meant demanding more information.

"You wear uniforms, and you carry weapons. You could have protected the people here."

A massive oversimplification — Matt knew it couldn't have been so easy — but one being used judiciously. Again, Matt had tricked many pirate prisoners into giving up information back in the pre-war days, and though his skills were a bit dusty, they were still sharp enough.

Wang-Roth shook his head in a rush, his expression revealing both frustration and anxiety, "No... I mean. What could we do? Could we try to overthrow our own chain of command? These orders came from the Brigadier! If we tried to defend anyone, to stop someone looting or bayoneting... or raping... we'd have been traitors. They wouldn't have just confined us, they'd have killed us, and blamed the Guild. We'd be risking our lives!"

As you can see, Matt's prompting and Wang-Roth's undisciplined answer had opened up some threads that could be used. Our British interrogator went with the last one first.

"Isn't your job to risk your lives?"

Wang-Roth's eyes shot wider, "For citizens of the *Empire!* And for the *Emperor!*"

Matt had him exactly where he wanted him — it was like pulling puppet strings, "So you don't have a conscience. You couldn't take the initiative and see what was right. Just the letter of your duty... they're not citizens, so you stand by and do nothing?"

Again, he was purposefully oversimplifying. There were, in fact, cases where Defense Command would have to sit by and not help non-citizens too. It didn't happen often... and honestly, I can't think of an example right now... but it's conceivable. But in this context, the implication was all that Matt needed.

"*What could we have done?*" Wang-Roth almost yelled, but it came across as pleading instead of angry. "My job is to keep my men alive. They refused to rape and murder, and so my job is to make sure they get home to their families, so they aren't punished for doing the right thing!"

That's what Matt had been waiting for. That was the argument — the *only* argument — that really would have any traction with him. Because this was a good point: as an officer, your responsibility is to the people you lead, as much as it is to the mission. As we talked about a lot back in *The Forge Fires*, sometimes those responsibilities clash — sometimes you have to sacrifice your people to complete the mission.

But never can you forget the gravity of that sacrifice.

Now, in the midst of a terror like Egesta, it's still a pretty inadequate argument (at least by my reckoning) to say that you didn't try to save lives because it would have put your own people at risk. They should have been willing to take the risk, and to right the wrongs that their comrades were undertaking.

However, there is a kernel of legitimacy in the argument. The dilemma is one I can recognize, and that Matt could afford *some* respect. It was a purer motive for inaction than, say, simple fear for one's life. Or worse, fear of getting caught.

If Wang-Roth had said, 'We had to stay out of it… we knew you'd be coming back, and we knew there'd be consequences', that pretty much would have ended the conversation.

Now, the talk could go on.

"You were in a difficult position, I'll grant you," Matt changed tacks to let Wang-Roth cool. Now was time to give a little understanding — a little more rope — and to test to see what the Major did with it. If he started feeling like he'd gotten through to our Commander, and if he even so much as joked about behaving in this way to dodge the consequences, the show would end.

"Major, our military culture in Defense Command is similar. It's true that you should never be put into a situation where you have to clash with the women and men you've trained with… who you've fought a war with."

That was the slack, and Wang-Roth let out a sigh of relief, nodding, "Exactly. It's impossible. My men didn't know what to do. I didn't know. Making an example out of some of the hardest troublemakers, right at the beginning… I could be talked into that. They were setting off bombs, they were still trying to continue the fight. We had to show them there'd be no mercy…"

He trailed off there, hoping Matt would say something helpful. Our Commander remained silent — this was one of those times to leave an uncomfortable void, and to let the nervous prisoner fill it.

"…but it got out of control so quickly. Reinforcements arrived… men had needs and there were no garrison towns around where they could satisfy them. They should have just handled it. But they didn't, and nothing I said resonated with my officers. Eventually I made a nuisance of myself. We all did. We were ostracized. We weren't *men*, so we were sent here."

Some interesting admissions, and nothing that contradicted Wang-Roth's statement that the well-being of his men was his priority. Matt started to get the sense that the Major was indeed genuine in that statement. He was clearly misguided… but he was also caught in a difficult situation, as a result of the military hierarchy of which he was a part.

Because, as the Inquiry would ultimately find, a lot of the blame here did belong right at the top, with those who decided that the blockheads should not only be 'granted these privileges', but that they should be expected to take full advantage of them, to improve their abilities as fighting men.

After all, there's nothing like rape and murder to hone your skills as a solider.

Good luck explaining to me, or to any civilized person, how that works. I'm sorry, but knowing how easy it is to bayonet a guy you handcuffed to a post wasn't going to help anyone disarm a hidden bomb, or out-shoot a Martian marine who was running to cover and returning fire.

So yes, the rot in the army started right at the top, which made it impossible for those who disliked the orders lower down to do anything substantial about it.

But there would have been ways for those who were innovative, and who had courage enough to try. Hiding people, even befriending people. Making a pact with your unit to stay away from some folks… doing something distasteful, like claiming some people who needed your protection as your 'personal' victims. There could be no fair solution. There could be no protection of the group. But trying to save *someone*, by any means, would have been better than sulking about your inability to save anyone.

Or so I would have thought. Come to think of it, that would have just been a smaller scale version of what we'd done in *The Independent Squadron*, and what Andrea had done before we arrived.

Save *someone*.

But that was the difference between our military cultures. I've talked a lot about this over the past books, I think, but it's worth really driving home now. Different armed forces have different expectations, and different ways of training and encouraging their people. As two sets of parents might raise their kids differently, Defense Command and the Imperial Army were vastly divergent.

And we were much, much superior to the blockheads.

Yes, there's some professional pride — even hubris — in that statement… but after Egesta, could you really argue?

Matt couldn't. Instead, he'd finally heard enough to allow him to deliver the lecture that he'd wanted to give earlier.

"Disobeying an unjust order from the top is never simple," the Briton said dryly. "But the difference between your service and mine is that our Admirals would never *order* us to commit a crime like has been done here. Because they *know* we would not comply. Defense Command's 'culture', as you put it, is one of protection, Major Wang-Roth. We fight wars and we kill pirates, but our purpose is always quite clear. We are here to serve the Empire, and to protect its citizens and its resources. And it is only right that we extend the same courtesy to neutral powers when the opportunity arises. Only enemies need feel our wrath, and even then, we give them respect."

Wang-Roth's head hung a bit as he listened, and Matt wasn't done.

"We kill. We make mistakes, Major. But we never set out to do prejudicial harm to those who cannot defend themselves. And if somehow we found ourselves in a situation like this one, it would not have been so difficult for our junior officers, and our spacers, to stand up to those in command, and to make it clear these actions would not be carried out. So we'd be luckier than you were. I'm sure a tribunal will take that into account when they judge you. But for now, you must live with your conscience, Major. We cleaned up this mess once, when it was created by criminals who wore our uniforms. As you know, we hung those bastards. Now we will clean up the mess that your army has made. And you'll simply have to wait to see if you and your men swing along with Brigadier Azuma."

Not to put too fine a point on it.

Commander Matt Baxter was finished with this conversation. He'd been a little bit generous to Defense Command, but not too much. Because, as he said, we ultimately existed to *defend*. It's right there in the name, and though we can't always follow that doctrine, we take it very, very seriously.

Wang-Roth returned to his men, and Matt continued to wait for Colonel Ronald.

When the battalion landed in force, the process of taking the Capital Dome really didn't end up being very complicated. That was no surprise to Matt, or to any of us, considering the amount of experience the fighting men and women of Ronald's unit possessed.

A bunch of garrison blockheads simply didn't compare to the desperation and, honestly, the skill of some of the Martian marines they'd faced on Mercury.

The mechanics of overwhelming the dome could fill a book by themselves, I suppose. How to direct force, how to intimidate an enemy without firing a shot… lots to commend Colonel Ronald for, and really, I think I'm doing him a disservice by simply telling you that he did a great job, instead of taking the time to show you how it worked.

Apologies, Garth.

But the point I want to get at for the moment is what Matt did after Ronald's forces took control of the Capital Dome — namely, he went looking for a place to do some good. Dome Three, according to one of Wang-Roth's men, was home to a pretty extensive 'comfort center', so that was the Briton's destination.

Taking a team of eleven SF and volunteers from *Friendly*, all of whom had been waiting patiently at the warehouse with him, he headed for the crossing between domes, and got set to break some heads, and assist some people in need.

Things didn't turn out quite as he expected.

The entrance to Dome Three's tunnel was abandoned by the time Matt and his unit got there (all piled into a large hovervan… one of the ones you can rent if you're moving houses, with that cube storage box on the back). A tank lay on the ground, deactivated and alone, and it looked as though the soldiers who'd been guarding the place had high-tailed it, possibly looking for shelter from the Defense Command storm that was clearly starting to brew, or maybe seeking to destroy evidence…

Didn't matter. Matt looked over the checkpoint carefully, contemplated command-eering the tank (and elected against it, because logistically, it'd be difficult, and tactically it might be unwise in case the DC skiffs in the air didn't realize who was running it), then pressed on into the tunnel.

So far, so good.

As the van passed through the dimly-lit tunnel, Matt checked his mag, making sure the power cell was in and charged, that the relays were clear… everything was good to go in case there was shooting. He didn't spend this time pondering — he had seen plenty during his last visit here, and he knew better than to wonder about what to expect at their destination.

The tunnel was a long one. I recall the trip to Dome Five back in *The Independent Squadron* felt interminably long, and this one was no better. In fact, Dome Three was actually the furthest away from the Capital Dome, and since the cube van they'd commandeered wasn't fast, it really was taking a while.

Finally, though, the light did appear at the end of the tunnel, and when it did, Matt nodded to his driver — one of *Friendly's* SF — to cut speed.

"There might be a checkpoint at this end," he said, looking back over his shoulder and through the window into the cube, where the rest of his people were sitting. "If they have a tank… they could blast this thing. We better stop here and most of us proceed on foot."

Prudent thinking from Matt — a reflection of his many years of experience in these matters. Nodding to the driver (who smiled nervously at the prospect of getting blown away by a tank), Matt opened his door.

"You lead, we'll keep to the tunnel walls and follow you," his orders were clear, and confident.

The driver nodded, and then Matt hopped out, hurried around back, and opened the cargo door so his other nine people could get onto their feet. It only took a couple of moments to get in order, then five shooters moved up the tunnel wall to the right of the van, the other five mirrored them on the left.

At walking pace, the van advanced again, and moved towards the light… sorry, the clichés are impossible to avoid.

Matt was leading the team on the right, and as usual, *Friendly's* skipper was right at the front. As they drew near the end of the tunnel, and began making out the shapes of what looked like a checkpoint silhouetted against the simulated daylight of Dome Three, expectations for the mission quickly changed.

Energy guns make a distinctive sound, and Matt knew it very well. People screaming also make a distinctive sound, and he was equally familiar with that too.

In the confined space of the tunnel, the sound waves had nowhere to go, so they all piled right down to Matt and his team, and gave warning of trouble ahead.

No time to waste, and not enough time to be cautious. Matt held up his hand, waved forward, and then started to jog, his mag in hand as he went. His team followed, then the team on the opposite wall, and finally the van switching on its high-beam headlights to show the way.

They moved fast, in no small part because the gravity plating in the tunnel (not Felix-Wolfe manufacture) was a bit dodgy, and the grav quotient in there was about two thirds Earth normal. As the team hurried along, though, they got heavier, as the better plating of Dome Three was set to around ninety-four percent Earth standard.

Didn't matter, they got to the end of the tunnel quickly.

But not quickly enough for some.

We still honestly don't know what the blockheads were thinking. I mean, executing your victims so they can't testify makes a certain sort of perverse sense, but why had they brought so many to the checkpoint to do it?

Matt realized as he emerged into the simulated daylight and squinted, there were nearly 100 civilians in various states of distress, penned together just beyond the tunnel mouth, and a dozen blockheads were separating them into groups… some of which had already been gunned down.

At first we thought they were people from the Capital Dome, sent through quickly so Ronald's troops didn't find them, but after interviewing the survivors, we learned they were indeed from Dome Three… that they'd been brought to the tunnel entrance from points all across the dome, to be disposed of…

Makes no sense. Didn't matter. Matt was now on the scene.

"You will cease your executions at once, or you will be summarily put to death!"

It's fair to say that those words, bellowed in Matt's sharp British accent, were a little over the top. Putting someone to death... it's a very old-school threat, and it's debatable as to whether it was within his legal means under those circumstances.

But if you want to get the attention of a bunch of blockheads who are whipping themselves into a bloodlust, showing up with a bit of Shakespearian menace is not a bad thing.

Backing it up with a team of hardened SF shooters carrying sidearms and MAG-90s doesn't hurt either.

Matt's force was strung out into a line across the mouth of the tunnel. Including him, there were only ten people — the driver was still in the cube van, in case it was needed for something. The blockheads had a tank, and at least a dozen soldiers were in sight.

Moreover, the Imps were carrying energy guns. As I think I mentioned back in *The Almost Coup*, in our standoff at the Geraldine Coilier Show, those guns don't have a 'low' setting. If you get hit with one, it's like getting shot with a metal projectile. And none of Matt's officers had so much as a protective vest on.

But each and every one of them wore an icy expression. They'd been here before, or they'd been to Pion Rock, or some even to Mercury... they'd fought a war, and now they were angry (to put it mildly) and ready to take their chances.

The blockheads, on the other hand, were desperate — trying to destroy evidence, if you'll permit me to explain mass murder in such clinical terms.

I would have expected them to believe they had nothing to lose now — to believe that they might as well go out with a blaze of glory, killing as many Defcoms as they could.

And maybe some among them would have... but others didn't have the stomach. They were cowards. They were bastardly, murdering cowards.

When the first soldier let out an inexplicable yelp, dropped his rifle and thrust his hands into the air, it started a chain reaction. A half dozen soldiers did the same, and then those who continued to hold their weapons found themselves outnumbered. A few more thus laid their rifles down, and raised their hands, forcing the last among them to do the same.

Tactically, they'd had the advantage. But Shakespearian threats and some very professional SF convinced them not to try their luck.

And, let's be fair: the blockheads clearly knew we'd landed a battalion — otherwise, they wouldn't have started killing people. They expected we'd take over, and they may not have realized that Matt's team was on its own out here... that there weren't 100 other SF and Special Branchers and a couple of skiffs sitting just far enough back in the tunnel to be unseen.

It wasn't worth the risk for them. They'd preserve their lives — at least until the Inquiry.

There were a few cries of relief from the people who'd been corralled for execution, and plenty more wails of sorrow — some survivors could count their friends and family among those already killed by the blockheads. Thirty-one lay in that grim state on the ground, and Matt regrets to this day that he hadn't arrived sooner, to be able to save those individuals.

I feel like I'm not saying quite enough about them — that I'm failing to convey how many layers of tragedy those people experienced. Not only were they victims of the blockheads, they were executed just *moments* before rescue arrived. Cruel. Bitterly cruel.

And imagine how sympathetic Matt was to the executioners.

"Get these bastards into the van," he ordered, and then drew his comm. He alerted Colonel Ronald to the situation and requested reinforcements — it seemed entirely likely that more blockheads were in the dome, though their desire to fight would be questionable. Nevertheless, better not to be caught flat-footed, particularly with so many civilians out in the open and no immediate means of escape.

After signaling for that support, Matt ordered two of his SF guards to try to get the crowd into the mouth of the tunnel — at least there they wouldn't be so exposed. The rest of his team was herding the blockheads into the cube of the van. A few of the bastards were puffing up and resisting a little (though not enough to warrant punitive response — they were clearly doing it for show), while others just sullenly trudged to the place of their imprisonment.

It seemed that all of them realized they were facing some pretty severe consequences.

Matt watched the procession for a few moments, then found his attention being drawn by a teenage boy who was wailing quite loudly as he cradled the limp and deceased forms of his two parents. That sight drew a wince from the British Commander, and he sighed deeply. The boy was kneeling in the midst of the thirty-one dead, and it seemed he was now alone in the world.

Because the blockheads had been destroying the evidence of their crimes.

One of Matt's migraines started to appear as he watched. He'd need to dose up with some powerful painkillers to try to prevent it ballooning out of control... but that obviously wasn't his current priority.

People were dead... others needed to be saved...

"Please, sir! Please! We were ordered! We had no choice!"

That plea erupted from behind Matt, surprising him. His eyes jumped from the grieving boy, and he turned around, seeing a blockhead who wasn't much more than a boy himself, struggling against one of *Friendly's* SF as she dragged him to the van.

Matt found himself advancing on this boy with even strides, his glare drilling into the young Imp's eyes.

"We were *ordered!*" the soldier pleaded again. He sounded genuinely stricken, and his desperate expression seemed to invoke a strange sort of pity. After his earlier conversation with Wang-Roth, Matt did understand the argument that was being made — that a soldier, trained to obey orders, could not be held responsible for following orders.

And he honestly didn't know whether this blockhead boy would be held responsible for the dead bodies in the street...

"Please, sir... I'm sorry. I can't be blamed for this... I *can't*... it'd kill my mother..."

Remember what I mentioned earlier about Matt giving Wang-Roth enough rope for a self-hanging? That particular comment would qualify as sticking one's own head in the noose and leaping from the gallows.

"Your mother?" Matt didn't lose his temper often. But when he did...

Advancing on the blockhead, he got hold of the Imp's collar and wrenched him free of the grip of his SF guard. The kid panicked, presuming this would be the moment when the maniac DC officer dragged him into the street and shot him in the head.

But Matt wasn't me, so instead he dragged the sniveling little bastard towards the fallen civilians, and the wailing boy.

"You see that boy? Do you know what killed his mother?"

The blockhead lost it. Whined and bawled like the cowardly little shit he was. He blubbered so much that Matt didn't even have to answer the question aloud — didn't have to remind the bastard that his energy gun had done that work.

Instead, *Friendly's* British commander released his prisoner, letting him fall to the ground in an inconsolable state, "Your mother will just have to learn to cope when she watches you swing."

He turned and left that blockhead behind him, knowing his anger had bubbled up too much, but not really regretting that fact. His SF collected the sobbing soldier, and threw him in the back of the van, while the rest of the civilians were sheltered in the tunnel.

A couple of vehicles carrying SF and Special Branchers arrived about forty-five minutes later to assist with securing Dome Three.

Matt didn't enjoy the experience. I suppose that's a grand statement of the obvious, but it's nevertheless true. After his interactions with the blockheads, he found himself asking tough questions — what *would* he have done at that age, if put in this situation… if all the loyalty and the devotion to duty that had been seeded deep within him throughout his career had demanded that he commit war crimes?

It's easy — very easy — to sit in an armchair and talk about how your moral compass should always guide you. But it's also well known that peer pressure can lead to abnormal behavior, that a mob mentality can be destructive, and that the coercive abilities of a hierarchical structure like the military can have a profound influence on one's life.

What if I ordered Matt to shoot some civilians? Would he do it?

He had to wonder. He had to question. Because he'd spent his career as dedicated to all of us in the Belt Squadron as we were dedicated to him. And it was hard to say that he would turn away from us, even under those circumstances.

This, you see, is how some of the greatest crimes can be committed. Because people allow outside factors, and sometimes internal biases, to alter or suspend their sense of morality.

The blockheads had believed that, because they were outside the Empire, they were ruled by no law. As the special prosecutors pointed out, they were in fact subject to the martial law they themselves imposed, so the codes of that military act were used to prosecute them. Had they not declared martial law (under the authority of the Empire) our courts might not have had jurisdiction…

But they had. So they'd pay.

And what about Matt's question? If I'd ordered him to kill thirty-one non-combatants, would he have done it? Maybe. But here's the thing: that's not an order he'd ever be given. And indeed, the last bastard who wore our uniform and showed such disregard for human life was named Sean Cook. He triggered this mess on Egesta, and he'd swung for it.

CHAPTER SEVEN

WHAT KAREN AND I SAW

Well, we've seen a lot of the damage that was done by the blockheads on Egesta. We've seen more than enough of their recreation centers, of their war crimes and atrocities, of their excuses and their defenses, and we've even seen a bit of how the people of Egesta coped. Some of them.

Now, though, we need to take a look at the leadership of the Imperial Army — at Howard Pedro Azuma, the man whose hand I'd shaken when he and his tanks arrived back during *The Independent Squadron*, and who, by many measures, was truly responsible for this situation.

Had he come to Egesta and led his forces in a professional manner, making peace and creating the stability necessary to build a new bureaucracy, it was entirely possible that instead of stopping civilians being executed, we'd have been returning to Egesta in 2234 to witness the first elections of a new government.

That's a bit ambitious, I'll admit — from chaos to a new order in three years is tough under the best of circumstances. But the rock could have been on that path. Instead, it had turned into what you've been reading about: a giant garrison town where the blockheads could take what they wanted, and would leave nothing behind when they left.

Nothing but death and horror.

Azuma was the target both Karen and I were after when we got down to the warehouse. Everyone else could go and do the things I've already talked about, but Azuma was ours, no matter where he was or what troops he had in front of him.

Realizing we were somewhat dedicated to this objective, Rufus wisely decided that we could use the services of his Special Branchers — that's why Captain Clarissa Hutchinson stuck with us, along with Lieutenants Maggie Joyce, Bobby Franek, and Selma Koestecki. We didn't add any SF to the group; we wanted to fit in one vehicle, and with four Branchers, we were already a potent force.

Honestly, a lot of what was said down in the warehouse is a blur. I remember watching Wes and Andrea go off together, seeing Shelby and Adrienne leave with Eugene, accepting Rufus' detachment before he left, and noticing that Matt was staying put... but along with Karen, I mostly focused on Major Wang-Roth. I didn't care about the story he gave to Matt later, all I wanted from him was the location of the Brigadier General.

He gave it to me, to the best of his knowledge at least.

As Karen and I clustered with Clarissa and the Branchers, a grim mood settled over us.

"Back to headquarters," Karen's tone was quiet as she checked her mag.

"I wonder if they redecorated after we left," I muttered, and though in some tones the reply might have come across as an attempt at lightening the mood, this time it certainly wasn't.

"Should we acquire a vehicle, sir?" Clarissa Hutchinson asked after that, and Karen glanced up at the Special Branch Captain with a nod.

"Something roomy, if you can find it."

Again, it had the potential to be a light comment, but it didn't come out that way. With a nod, Clarissa hurried off to check the parking lot for a hovercar to suit our needs, waving for her team to follow. Karen and I lagged behind, neither of us with much to say, but deciding we'd best hang together.

Emerging from the warehouse into the Capital Dome was yet another uneasy transition. The sights, sounds and smells of the city this time weren't as pronounced, but there was no question of where we were.

Cars were beginning to disappear from the parking lot beyond the warehouse as we followed the Special Branchers — Andrea and Wes had one, Rufus another. I noticed Shelby, Adrienne and Eugene setting off on foot. Dozens of other teams were similarly finding ways to get out into the city...

And there was no sign that we'd been noticed yet. Surely the Brigadier must have been warned about the Defense Command ships coming to dock. One would expect him to pay attention to such developments, and to take steps to respond — to at least try to control our access through formalities and niceties that could keep us tied up for hours.

But there appeared to be no organization. And, as you've already read, it was pretty clear that there was no central control. The blockheads weren't coordinated, weren't responding with any sort of military sense. That was good for us.

Still, that's me getting ahead of myself, sort of. As Karen and I stood outside the warehouse and waited for Clarissa to boost our ride, we didn't know what to expect.

"Quiet today," Karen said, looking up at the dome that was simulating daylight for us.

I nodded, "As if nothing's going on."

Perhaps nothing *was* going on. Perhaps Charlie had it wrong, and we all had it wrong too. I actually let that hope stick with me for a couple of seconds... but it didn't last. There wasn't really any way it could.

After a few minutes, a limo pulled up in front of us. A genuine, stretched out, tinted-windows limo. The passenger window rolled down, and Clarissa leaned over from the driver's side so we could see her.

"I was hoping for a truck of some kind, but this might do it, sir, ma'am."

We should have found a way to smile, because there was something positively ridiculous about this. But we didn't. Instead, I nodded, "Might confuse them further. Well done, Captain."

Leading the way, I headed to the back door of the limo and opened it, allowing the Special Branchers who'd been waiting to enter first, and Karen too. Then I slid into the low-slung vehicle, and shut the door behind me.

It smelled too clean — like it had been recently scrubbed out and refinished. Perhaps that was for the best... I didn't really want to think about what limos might have been used for on Egesta.

"You know the way to the HQ, Clarissa?" Karen had slid up to the seats that were closest to the driver's cockpit, and the partition that would usually keep the wealthy debauchery separate from the driver was down, so we could see the Captain.

"Yes ma'am," Clarissa replied immediately. "I studied the maps pretty carefully...

figured that might be useful."

It certainly was. Without Charlie here... or Ben Belete, or Raza Weiss or Terry Schroeder, or any of the other veterans of last time... any familiarity our current Branchers could have with this place would be helpful. And Clarissa Hutchinson, I think, was determined to prove that despite not having been here before, and despite not being as experienced as someone like Rufus, she was still an elite officer in our special forces.

She didn't really need to prove that... we didn't doubt her credentials at all. But aside from the ridiculous situation on Mars, we hadn't been into many scrapes with Clarissa and the rest of the new team, so I think they were determined to make sure we knew that they weren't just a bunch of replacements. They were elite, as Special Branchers always are, and they brought a lot of skill and wisdom to the table.

We wouldn't underestimate them — no one would.

Our limo floated away from the warehouse, and along the main drag we'd had to march down last time. I spent a lot of the time looking out the windows, seeing how relatively orderly everything appeared. The crimes being committed here clearly weren't so haphazard as before... which was no comfort at all, because it meant people were being methodically abused. Out of sight, away from public view, the blockhead comfort centers and training fields were doing all the damage.

But it wasn't spilling over into the streets, because Azuma liked his city to appear as clean as possible...

There were unrepaired weapons strikes as we floated past a residential area — fighting had gone on here — but there were no bodies in the streets, and no smell of death permeating everything. Still, it felt to me like there was desperation in the air. Perhaps I was just expecting that atmosphere, and thus my subconscious tricked me into feeling it... but my subconscious and I have a generally honest relationship. I think the desperation was there, and genuine.

We continued on at an even pace, Clarissa not inclined to speed because doing so would have drawn more attention to us, and being a stretch limo, we were already getting our share of notice. The few people who were outside stared as we went past, perhaps knowing who the previous owner of our vehicle was, and reacting to that perceived presence.

Perhaps fearing that they'd been caught on their way between work and home, and that they'd be grabbed to become a night's entertainment.

They wouldn't be. We were going to headquarters, and then to get a hold of the Brigadier. He would be our entertainment.

After a few minutes of floating, our stretch limo pulled up at the base of the steps leading into the government building. This place was still the military HQ for Egesta — still the nerve center, from which all the operations (and presumably all the crimes) were orchestrated.

As I opened the door, Lieutenant Maggie Joyce insisted that she lead the way out, and I didn't argue. As her boots hit the curb, she covered a couple of different directions at once with her MAG-90. Bobby Franek followed, with Selma Koestecki in third position. Then Karen and I slid out, and we all found ourselves on the stairs leading up to that familiar place.

The guard post was abandoned — the one we'd left at the entrance was gone, but the blockheads had installed another one… which wasn't being used. As the limo touched down and Clarissa joined us in front of it, we all shared uncomfortable glances, and then I took a deep breath and started leading the way.

What would we find?

An easy answer would be: 'Not much.'

That would be a largely accurate answer, too, because when we stepped through the familiar front entrance, the place seemed haunted instead of crewed. We looked left, then right. Bobby Franek and Maggie Joyce took the stairs up to the second floor to have a look around, and Karen and I joined Selma and Clarissa in pacing very slowly and silently through the bottom level.

It was pretty obvious that the staff here had cleared out quickly. A couple of half-eaten lunches were on the table in the communications room, and half-empty cups of coffee could be seen on numerous desks, most of them still warm.

By the time we emerged onto the terrace at the back of the government building, and looked over the giant park where Mark Gunney had accidentally killed the woman who'd started shooting at Guild fighters, we had a pretty good idea of what must have happened.

"They figured out we were landing, and they ran for it. They're probably trying to get rid of evidence right now," Karen said almost under her breath, folding her arms as she stared out at the park.

I nodded, then turned and looked back at the building, "Seems likely. I'm surprised… I'd have expected them to try to control our access, if they had warning."

She nodded but had nothing to add, so we stood silently for a moment, her facing one way, me facing the other. We didn't know where Brigadier Azuma might have hurried off to, and we didn't know what his staff would be doing… somehow, we had to locate that man.

"See if we can find a location for him?" Karen asked quietly.

I nodded, "Let's check his desk."

By the time we got upstairs to what had once been the Governor's office… and which subsequently had become Andrea's office, ours, and then Azuma's… Bobby Franek was already giving the Brigadier's pads and papers a thorough look. We all knew we needed evidence of the goings-on here — something that would stand up in a trial.

But there didn't seem to be anything incriminating. Running a brigade in the Imperial Army is, in some respects, a lot like running a squadron in Defense Command: there's plenty of paperwork. And that's all we found.

Legitimate reports about security, personnel, supply… none containing any hints that war crimes were being carried out. I suppose I would have been surprised if they had left a paper trail — even they had to realize how damning their actions were, right?

Surely.

"There's nothing, sir," Franek looked up at Karen and me with a frustrated sigh as he delivered that report. "I could have missed something… but… no sir. I don't see *anything*. And no addresses or notes that suggest where the Brigadier might have run to."

That wasn't good at all. If he was out there, and he had some sort of reserve command post, it was entirely possible he could begin to organize his men, either to directly resist us, or at least to eliminate all evidence of their crimes.

And we all knew what 'eliminating evidence' was a euphemism for. Matt saw it first hand, not long after this.

"Dammit," I didn't completely contain my own frustration, and I moved over to the window of the office to get a look outside. It wasn't as though I'd be able to see where Azuma had fled — it'd be too stupid even for him to set up his hideout, or wherever he'd gone, within viewing distance of the headquarters. He'd have to know we'd take this building first.

Planting my hands on the ledge of the window, I took a couple of deep breaths, and then let my head sag. My eyes fell from the buildings on the horizon to the narrow car park that was just below, and I shook my head. They'd all left here so quickly, it looked like they'd abandoned a half-dozen luxury hovercars in the lot.

Bastards had probably been using those as personal transports — less conspicuous than floating around in a tank, or a military truck. I could just picture Azuma, in all his hubris, turning up at a mansion that was filled with depravity, hopping out of one of those cars and sauntering up the walk to do some raping or killing.

Trying to show the whole damned solar system how important he was. How much of a man he was. With his fancy stolen cars.

Fancy stolen cars. Each of which would have a guidance computer.

I straightened up immediately. It's rare that I actually think I have good ideas. The last one that I really credit myself with was the moment I figured out that the *Idaho* trap was set using Phosgene gas. Now I had another — two in four years. A personal best.

Turning sharply, I found that Karen had approached me from behind, and the look on my face must have been brighter (a morose version of 'eureka', perhaps) so she frowned.

"There's a lot full of luxury cars out there. Think their computers might have a list of destinations visited on this rock?"

Karen blinked, and then we all stampeded our way out of Government House to start breaking car windows.

Within about five minutes, we'd discovered all those fancy cars had repeatedly shared one destination, and it wasn't in the Capital Dome. We punched it into our limo's computer and headed for the tunnel to Dome Two.

"The checkpoint will probably be alerted," Karen was checking her mag's power cells again, even though she hadn't used it since the last time she'd done so. "We may not get through."

That was true. This was still before Ronald's troops had been deployed into the dome, though we'd made the call to Zail Patel to start inserting them immediately. We were fairly confident we knew where Azuma was, and we wanted Ronald to be able to take this dome before the blockheads seized any kind of initiative.

"Clarissa… if it looks like they're going to blow up the limo, please don't let them," I offered that rather profound comment to the Special Branch Captain, and she managed a laugh.

"If you insist, sir."

Good sense of humor, Clarissa Hutchinson demonstrated there. Despite the circumstances.

We knew we were on an unlikely mission, and we had the sense that ours wasn't the only unlikely one going on in that moment. But we were after Azuma, and we weren't turning back.

It took a few minutes of driving to get to the tunnel entrance, and as we slowed down, all eyes were turned towards the windows. We wanted to see what sort of checkpoint we'd have to run... whether they'd be ready for us... whether they'd have fled their posts.

"There's a tank and about six guys," Clarissa reported, having the best view through her windshield. "And they really don't look too alert."

I frowned at that, as did Karen, and we both awkwardly half-climbed over the partition to the driver's compartment to take a look for ourselves. Sure enough, there was a tank sitting on the ground, its hoverpad off, and a handful of soldiers who appeared to be playing cards.

"They trying to lure us in?" Karen voiced that question thoughtfully, and we both sat back.

"There's no way... they haven't been warned?" I was no more certain that she was.

But they sure didn't look worried. Perhaps... maybe... some sort of communications breakdown? How could Azuma have gotten through there without warning them?

It didn't make sense... but not making sense wasn't enough to keep us from trying *something*.

We were in a limo. Maybe... if they weren't ready... we could bluff them. At least long enough to get explosives on the tank.

"Could one of you get a shaped charge on that armor without being seen... if we roll up and cause a distraction?" I directed that question to our new Special Branchers, and their reaction was, honestly, pretty funny. Not a lot of things could be funny on Egesta, but I swear, the three Lieutenants in the back of the limo all perked up like eager puppies being asked if they wanted to go for a walk.

Now, I love dogs, so that's no insult to these officers. I believe I even compared Karen to a puppy back in *The Fleet Clash*, so that's proof that it cannot possibly be an insult.

But they all surely wanted to do this.

"Maggie's the best at exploding things," Clarissa pitched in helpfully from the driver's seat, and Lieutenant Joyce confirmed that assessment with a very enthusiastic nod. She didn't actually start saying 'Pick me, pick me, please pick me!' but it was implied.

And we wouldn't say no.

"Alright. We bluffed our way through Guild roadblocks last time. We'll try it again. Clarissa, you're our driver. We've been invited by Brigadier Azuma to come to his location, to enjoy his hospitality. If need be, I'll roll down the window to confirm. It'll confuse them, hopefully get us through."

Karen was staring at me as I said that, and an unfamiliar observer might have thought she was surprised, or disapproving. Instead, she demonstrated yet again that we were in sync, continuing my orders almost as if she could read my mind: "If they don't buy it, Maggie blasts the tank and we all shoot down the soldiers. If they do buy it, we'll wait for

Maggie just inside the mouth of the tunnel."

Simple.

Popping the door, Maggie Joyce jumped out with her pack, and then Karen nodded to Clarissa. We started to move ahead.

Once again, on Egesta, we'd talk our way through a roadblock.

The blockheads at the checkpoint were surprised to see a limo pull up, but their reaction wasn't as militant as we feared it might be. Fancy hovercars were, after all, regular sights at this location.

Clarissa raised the partition to the rear compartment as she slowed our approach to the barricade, wanting to be sure she conveyed the impression that she was a lowly driver with VIPs in the back. The fact that she was a Brancher would probably raise some eyebrows, but we remained optimistic.

"Get ready for trouble..." I narrated needlessly, and in the back of the limo we all tensed.

We waited uneasily, watching as a shadow moved up alongside the vehicle, then listening to the muffled sounds of voices through the partition glass as Clarissa gave her story to the sentry.

You've probably seen moments like this in the movies — the moment before everything goes pear-shaped, and the actors have to start shooting their way through, risking discovery by the guards on the far side of the tunnel and jeopardizing the mission's success...

Then the hoverpad hummed louder, and we started floating ahead at a slow and steady rate — not at all like we were racing away from tank fire. Karen and I looked at each other, both thinking the same thing: no way we just got through without having to empty the limo for inspection.

After a moment we slowed down again, just as the shadows of the tunnel swept over us. Then the door opened, and Maggie Joyce climbed back in, looking a little disappointed as she did. Once she shut her door, the partition began to lower, and we floated forward at higher speed.

All eyes turned to Clarissa, and she spotted our stares in the rearview, then shrugged, "They just waved us through."

Perhaps it shouldn't be a surprise that the unprofessional fools who would let a situation like Egesta happen in the first place could also have some lax checkpoint personnel... but it was a surprise (I know, another one). A limo and a plausible excuse and you could just breeze through?

Well, it would be stupid for me to complain too much, considering the alternative could have been a messy shootout in which we all could have been tank-blasted... but it still makes me shake my head. Anyway, we were on our way to Dome Two.

The Administrators' Club is what the building was called. Those words were engraved in fancy script on a sign outside the carefully-manicured hedge that surrounded the building and its grounds. Even looking at it from across that hedge, it was obvious the place stunk of pretension.

You probably know the sort of club this was — it's the place where the high and mighty go to sit around in expensive old chairs and talk about how frustrating it is to be smarter than everyone else. As I think I've stated before in this series, I tend to have a tough time relating to those who choose to perceive themselves as naturally superior. I'm fine with someone who has talent and skill and is proud of that fact… just not someone who's arrogant about it, and treats others poorly as a result.

Hedging yourself off from the people around you? There are very few circumstances under which that wouldn't strike me as arrogant, and this place wasn't one of them.

In fact, it was the opposite, because as we pulled up to the gate and peered out the windows at the pompous place, we all knew what was going on here.

There was a two-storey manor house, undoubtedly full of victims of one sort or another, and perhaps some willing servers who were surviving the blockhead occupation by 'paying dues' to its leadership.

You know what I mean.

When we stopped at the gate, a blockhead in a dress uniform hurried up to Clarissa's window, and she rolled it down without raising the partition this time — didn't seem necessary.

"Guests were requested by Brigadier Azuma. Rear Admiral Barron and Commodore McMaster."

The guard was very well turned out, as you'd expect at a facility like this one, and he seemed eager to please.

"Of course," he answered helpfully. "If your officers would like immediate service, I can call ahead and have rooms and entertainment prepared."

There was absolutely no sign that he'd been informed by headquarters that trouble was coming… and if the guard at the front gate didn't know, it seemed increasingly unlikely that Azuma and whoever else was inside would know either.

It was very much looking like the HQ staff had bolted to cover their own tracks, and hadn't bothered to warn their Brigadier. Loyal people, these blockheads…

I put that thought aside as Clarissa looked back at me — she wasn't sure what sort of answer to give the keen guard about our entertainment. Since the partition was down, I decided to weigh in on the question.

Leaning forward, I smiled at the man, "We'll choose our own entertainment when we get in. Thanks."

He seemed almost pleased that I'd spoken to him — like it was an honor. Talk about upside down perspectives…

"Of course," he stepped back and waved us forward. "Please park wherever is convenient."

Then he was gone, and Clarissa raised her window again, "Think he'll call ahead and warn them we're coming?"

I sat back and looked across at Karen, who shrugged, "Don't think it matters now. They can't have enough guns in that building to stop us."

Matter-of-fact, but also menacing… she was obviously ready for a little bit of goddess-worthy wrath. I wondered as I saw that look in her eye whether the building would remain standing when she and I were done with it.

And that wasn't hyperbole. I was literally wondering if it would be standing, or if we'd knock the thing down, as we had once been known for doing.

"Check weapons everyone," Clarissa called back to her officers, and Bobby Franek, Selma Koestecki, and Maggie Joyce all started their final, frankly unnecessary checks of their MAG-90s.

Karen and I gave our sidearms another once-over, then returned them to their holsters.

"We'll talk our way in," I said evenly as we floated up to the building. "Don't get belligerent unless they do, or unless Karen and I do. Whichever comes first."

"Safe bet it'll be us first," Karen added helpfully.

Had Charlie and his old squad been with us now, these instructions would have been redundant, but we figured it was better not to leave anything to chance with the new people. We didn't have anything to worry about, though.

As the limo landed, and the pad stopped humming, Clarissa turned back to look at us, "Alright, ready?"

I nodded, then glanced at Karen. She nodded.

Then we all nodded one more time, which probably sounds absurd, but that was our final confirmation. Bobby Franek opened the door and we started piling out, Clarissa joining us from the driver's compartment.

We took a moment to look around at the landscaped grounds, all carefully maintained so that the officers who spent time here would have a lovely Earthgreen environment in which to commit their atrocities.

The building itself was very old-Earth style, with simulated stonework and traditional windows that looked like they were emulating a mansion from New England... or perhaps old England. I'm not too good identifying specific architectural idioms. Suffice it to say that such a building style on an asteroid came across, as I say, a bit pretentious.

It was made even more ridiculous by the guard who was at the door, unarmed but in dress uniform, looking like a footman for a Lord.

I nodded in his direction, and our party of armed officers strode quickly that way. He didn't even turn his head to look at us as we approached — like a palace guard, he just stood pat. Which, come to think of it, probably makes sense, since the Imperial Army was responsible for guarding the Emperor's palaces on Earth. They'd be accustomed to standing still and doing nothing.

Karen and I glanced at each other as we approached this guard, and our hands stayed near our mags even though we knew the Branchers behind us could shoot this fellow long before our sidearms got out of their holsters.

Still, it was a matter of principle: hands close to mags, just in case.

But again, confusingly... perhaps almost humorously... the caution seemed to be unnecessary. We stopped in front of the door of this mansion, and the sentry simply came to attention. Six armed Defense Command officers were arriving, and all this guard did was stand to.

Good for us, not so good for the people he was supposed to be guarding... but again, it would be stupid to complain.

After watching his inactivity for a moment, Karen and I shared another glance — we were doing that a lot, since speaking under the circumstances didn't quite seem covert enough. Then I turned back halfway and shrugged at Clarissa.

If we didn't have to start shooting until later, that'd be fine… we wouldn't give anyone inside enough warning so they could start disposing of witnesses.

Casually, I moved over to the door and opened it, then held it as Karen and the Branchers entered the Administrators' Club. When I followed them inside, I found we were all in a lobby that was paneled in simulated dark wood (this place pulled out all the stops to make it look like a cigar club on Earth).

Sounds of laughter were coming from rooms on the ground floor. There were other sounds, too — pleas and screams — that were clearly audible from upstairs, and from out back, but the laughter was the loudest.

The juxtaposition of noises was… striking. We were all thinking what you're probably thinking: what sort of person can laugh in the presence of such suffering?

You know the kind. You're about to meet them.

Stepping forward, I came up alongside Karen, and after yet another knowing look, she turned back to our escort, "Selma, Maggie, can you go upstairs and turn down the volume?"

There was no hesitation from these two; they had MAG-90s and other people-punishing tools, and they were going to get to make good use of them.

"Clarissa, Bobby, join us?" I gave the other instruction. Together, we walked towards the sounds of the laughter.

The room amounted to a cigar lounge. It contained a half dozen expensive imported leather armchairs, and the décor was a pathetic and expensive mashup of old Earth paraphernalia meant to inflate the egos of the members. This, I have to say, was a decorating choice made by the original owners of the club, intended to make the wealthy members of Egesta's upper crust feel more Earthy.

That the leaders of the Imperial Army were basking in such a gaudy, stupid environment was telling, though. They were as pretentious as its originators…

"The disco ball doesn't really go with the nineteenth century wood paneling, or the twenty-first century fireplace," I observed as we entered the room.

As opening lines go, it probably wasn't the most dramatic I could have managed, but it was hard not to comment on the painful mix of styles (and clichés). Of course, because I didn't lead with something menacing — 'you're all going to hang' — the four haughty blockhead officers occupying chairs in the room laughed in a sporting fashion. They thought I was a friend making idle banter.

"Quite so, I said the same," one billowed. Not bellowed… he sounded like a sail billowing in the wind. Yes, it sounds like something… something very puffed up.

"Damn your eyes, Ping, I think it's stylish."

That was, in fact, the first thing I heard Brigadier General Howard Pedro Azuma say when we went back to Egesta. Not a good line for melodrama.

"Gentlemen," Karen sweetly added her voice to the room, and by now the four blockhead officers had decided to turn around and see who had joined their fun. "By the time I leave here, you'll all be under arrest. Conscious or not."

They thought that was a joke too. Until they saw us.

I could pretty much read their minds when they finally turned in our direction.

There was an immediate rush of terror, mixed with confusion. How exactly had we gotten here — both to their club, and perhaps more largely, to Egesta — without them being informed?

I suppose I need to introduce those present: Brigadier Azuma, of course, as well as Colonel Ping Mullcahey, Colonel Dimitry Callahan, and Lieutenant Colonel Poul Bux — the head of the brigade, his Chief of Staff, and his two regimental commanders. Sitting in a room together laughing about skewering civilians with bayonets while people were being murdered on the back lawn, raped on the top floor, and while Defense Command was landing.

Azuma struggled to his feet, and I could see him trying to decide exactly what to do — to call for a guard, or to try to conceal what he was doing. I could see the color flooding his cheeks… could imagine the feeling of blood rushing to his head as he tried to figure out what to do…

"Say something," I needled him abruptly, which is not what I'd planned to do. I stepped forward, and as I approached I slid my mag from its holster. The other blockhead officers stayed in their chairs, perhaps glad that I wasn't fixating on them.

When I stopped right in front of Azuma, he opened his mouth to say something. He wasn't afraid — he was too arrogant for that — and he was going to try some sort of retort. I took away his opportunity by doing something else I hadn't planned.

With my left hand, I grabbed Azuma by the throat. He tried one of the often-taught maneuvers that's supposed to get you out of a throttling grip, but I'd done this enough times during the pirate-hunting days to counter him without difficulty.

I then looked to the right, out a large old-style picture window to the back lawn, where a dozen posts stood, bodies of recent bayonet targets still dangling from the chains attached to two of them.

I dragged Azuma in that direction, considered trying to throw him through the window, but instead decided to take him out through the door. I'm sure he was struggling through this, but Clarissa Hutchinson later informed me that he wasn't having any success with his attempt.

Once we were out on the lawn together, I deposited (Clarissa says 'threw') Azuma onto the grass in front of one of the posts, then stepped back, "You should probably stand up. A lot of blood in that grass."

Azuma sat up, then looked down at the grass before turning his eyes back up to me, "You think blood fazes me, Barron?"

I shrugged, then smiled, "I wouldn't presume to assume."

We were close to one of the posts that had a body dangling from it, so I moved over for a closer look. The corpse was that of a middle-aged man, a bit overweight and balding — probably a worker who'd walked too slowly on the way home from the factory. It looked as though all his blood had run out, down his clothes and pooled on the ground.

That's the most clinical way to describe the gore.

I studied this man for a second, frowning thoughtfully as I considered the causes of death. Clearly he'd been a teaching tool — his last moments of terror and pleading for mercy had been useful in helping some of the soldiers of the Imperial Army get mildly better at bayonet drill.

Drill that clearly they'd need, considering all the harsh combat operations they had ahead of them, now that the war was over. And which would have been very helpful for them dealing with improvised bombs on Mercury.

If my sarcasm starts pooling too much, watch your step so you don't slip.

"Under the arm?" I asked as I studied the various puncture marks that had let the dead man's blood escape him.

Azuma didn't answer, so I glanced back at him, "Howard, bayonet goes under the arm?"

The Brigadier stared at me, and as his surprise at what was happening started to clear, I could see his anger beginning to build, "Yes. Under the arm."

Of course, that wasn't the only wound on the dead man. One went straight through the heart, more had slashed open his stomach, a few were in the legs and the shoulders…

"How many uses do you get out of one living target?" I asked, trying to count the wounds.

Azuma again failed to answer, so I glanced back again, "Howard, you clearly have to use the same target more than once. How many?"

"As many as we can," he said darkly.

"Efficient," I nodded.

Azuma's anger was starting to turn into confusion again, because I wasn't lecturing him. I wasn't screaming, or threatening, or menacing. If anything, it probably appeared that I was *enjoying* his work. And that didn't make sense to the good Brigadier.

"You… what are you doing here, Barron?" he finally managed to ask a coherent question, and I glanced at him.

"If your brigade had a scrap of discipline, you might have found out sooner. When we got to your headquarters, it was empty. I suppose your staff officers are all off trying to cover their own tracks."

That wasn't really an answer to his question, but the implication — that we were coming for evidence — made the man's face sour.

"We keep *order* here, and you should respect that order!" he snarled. I think he was probably trying to get a rise out of me.

Bad luck for him, we were past the point where I'd take the bait.

"Perhaps we should, Howard," I looked back at the dead man dangling from the post, and then tilted my head. "But you and I both know I won't do that. So tell me, Howard, what do you think I'm going to do to you?"

Azuma fell silent, and as I looked at him again, I was blasted with a glare of indignance.

"Aren't you going to take a guess?" I asked easily, and his lips twisted into a snarl.

"You wouldn't dare!"

Why do they always actually say 'you wouldn't dare', even when the answer doesn't quite fit the question asked? Couldn't they try different wording, at least — something that hasn't been used over and over by movie villains and cliché bad guys for hundreds of years? In this case, a 'you'll do nothing' would have worked. But he wasn't that creative.

"You'd be surprised how daring I can be," I prodded him again.

This time he didn't bother answering — too prideful, and probably still too confused.

"Stand up," I broke his silence. Grudgingly, the Brigadier complied, wiping his hands on his trousers as he did so.

I approached him, my mag still in hand, hanging down at my side.

"You wouldn't dare," he actually repeated it. Said it again, even though he had no idea what I might actually do to him.

"Wouldn't dare do what, Howard?" I asked, my cool smile remaining as I reached out with my free hand and patted his shoulder. "I'd never dream of putting a mark on you."

He was very confused, so I moved my hand from his shoulder down to his lapel and brushed it off — made sure it looked fit for a court martial, "No, I've got something different in store for you. You're coming with me back to Earth, in chains, and when we get there, I'm going to put you on trial for all of this. And the people of the Empire will see what you've done here, and they'll convict you to swing from the gallows, same as Sean Cook did. And when you swing, it'll discredit the army, and your Emperor, and we'll use that to unravel the parochial imposition your kind have been making on the Empire for the past century."

He stared at me, and confusion now had turned into disbelief.

"You put this to the people, they'll side with me," he eventually answered deviantly.

Whoops, sorry, that was supposed to say 'defiantly'.

Just after he said that, he felt a hot breath on his neck, and he turned his head slightly to discover that Karen had appeared behind him, and was now leaning in, her face coming close to the side of his head as she studied him.

"I doubt that," she whispered. "But if they do, imagine what *I'll* do to you."

Howard Pedro Azuma's ego was a powerful force indeed, and he snarled and stomped away from Karen, then glared at me, "Threaten me all you like. Defense Command cowards wouldn't have the balls to do what you say. We train *men* to have the balls to do what it takes. You sit in fucking ships and watch on monitors while the war goes by. If you want to torture me, then I challenge you to a straight fight. We'll see who wins."

Boy had we ever rattled him. And we hadn't even threatened him, strictly speaking. Not yet. But it seemed about time.

"Well, that may be so, Howard," I stopped almost nose to nose with him. "We could fight it out right here. See how many uses we get out of your body target before you bleed out like the poor fellow chained to that post did. I think we can beat a dozen, don't you, Karen?"

"Fingers and toes get us to twenty automatically," she replied. She was always better at math.

I think Azuma realized that the pitch in both of our voices was not wavering at all. I think it got through to him right then that maybe, just maybe, we were serious. Because he shut up and glared at me.

"I don't think Howard's going to test us," I said, and my smile widened with the words. "I think Howard's going to come back to Earth with us, and stand trial for his crimes, and then die like a common criminal."

Karen's face appeared right next to Azuma's one more time, and she smiled at me as she spoke in soft, almost seductive tones, "A pity. But I suppose it's for the greater good."

The fight drained out of Azuma, at least for now. His arrogance was a powerful force, and it obviously returned by the time we got him to *Wolf* (if you'll recall the first chapter), but at this moment he fell silent. It was in that state that we left him, just as Bobby Franek arrived with bindings for the Brigadier's hands. We'd be taking him to a cell, and there he'd rot.

As Bobby dragged Azuma away, I holstered my mag and turned back towards the dead man dangling from the post. It was a grim sight, and I couldn't help but wonder when he'd been killed. If we'd been a few hours earlier, could this fellow have survived? It's the sort of question that can drive you mad, wondering if you'd just been a little bit faster, not waited those extra few moments…

"We'll have to get an operation together to start identifying remains," Karen holstered her mag with a sigh.

Pulling her ponytail up onto her left shoulder, she fell silent and stared at the victim for a moment. Then, as she pulled her hair tight across the side of her neck, she took a breath, "Been a while since you've been that mean to somebody."

I glanced at her fleetingly, then returned my gaze to the victim, "Has it?"

She nodded, then said: "I guess the fiery mutilator of doom and extraordinary agony wouldn't be threatening enough to a guy who knows they don't exist."

I smiled again, "That's extraordinary *pain*, not agony."

"Right," she agreed. "You were very convincing."

As she said that, her hand closed around mine, and she squeezed once, very firmly, before letting go. I looked at her again, for longer this time, and nodded.

"Thanks. So you were you."

She met my gaze, paused, then nodded.

"And we were both… just being convincing."

I shrugged, "You weren't planning to pin his head to the ground with a bayonet, were you?"

It was a little bit on the nose, and she winced, but then shook her head.

I smiled, "So he walked away, into custody, and we're here ready to get on with things. I think that's a sign that we're both completely in control."

Karen stared at me, and started to nod, but then stopped and bit her bottom lip, "I'm never worried that you're not *in control*. I'm worried about what parameters you set for acceptable behavior while you're being controlled."

It was the first time she'd frankly made that point to me in years, and my eyebrows went up.

"I…" my first attempt at an answer stalled, and recognizing that, she gave me a few seconds to collect some thoughts.

Turning towards her, I stepped in close and found my eyes drawn to the side of her neck hidden by her ponytail, "Those parameters don't change very easily. Even this place wouldn't move them far enough for you to need to worry."

That was the truth. Karen took a deep breath, then nodded, "Right."

Right indeed.

With that settled, Karen and I went to help search the grounds for other captives — people who would have been victims of the bayonet, or the bedpost, had we not arrived in time. There were forty-seven on the grounds.

CHAPTER EIGHT
WHAT JIM HANNIGAN SAW

We needed Bunny Fox to take some pictures. I hope you remember Bunny, because I know I've done a poor job in mentioning her presence aboard *Wolf* during all these books. After 2232, when she'd survived the *Idaho* trap that had killed Jocko, Summer and Destiny, she'd stayed with us.

She was the only camera operator trusted by everyone aboard *Wolf*. She'd been to hell with us, almost literally, and we wouldn't allow anyone else aboard to try to document our war. So all the old footage you've seen of me, or Karen, or Rufus, or Jim Hannigan came from Bunny.

And I should point out that she'd stayed with us despite all the shooting we'd been mixed up in. There were two reasons for that: she felt connected to us after the Jupiter mission, and more importantly, she and Jim were very close to getting engaged. So close, in fact, that some of the junior officers had a pool going about when our elite XO would pop the question.

Such good-feeling pools obviously had nothing to do with what we needed from Bunny now, though. We knew that whatever evidence we collected against the blockheads would be questioned profusely by the Emperor — he'd claim we had faked it in an effort to discredit him.

Bunny, however, was still an accredited member of the press, and though her close relationship with us wasn't much of a secret, her producers at the major Imperial network I can't name would back her credibility to the hilt.

If she collected footage of atrocities, it wouldn't be considered gospel truth, but it would be a lot harder to argue with than something I recorded.

Rightly so.

So we needed Bunny to take some pictures. This process could only begin after we'd secured Egesta — after Ronald's troops had absolute control of the domes, and the Imps were taken into custody. Theoretically, that might mean there'd be less horror to see, as our first-responders dealt with the worst of it… but it wouldn't be a good job.

Jim, being understandably wary of what she might see, resisted us making the request of her… but finally agreed, provided he could follow her around. He knew how bad it would be, and to quote him: "I didn't look forward to the nightmares. Mine or hers."

That was fair enough.

The day after Garth Ronald declared Egesta secured, Jim and Bunny went down to have a look around, accompanied by Clarissa Hutchinson and Selma Koestecki.

Despite being a day after the very worst, they were able to record a lot of evidence — many damning things that were used to great effect in the Inquiry. But for all they saw, and for all the vid they provided to the tribunals, there was one moment that defined the entire mission for Jim and for Bunny. Kindly, they've both permitted me to share it.

They were in the Capital Dome, and after hours of closely examining crime scenes, captive 'bunkhouses', and human remains, they ended up at the Immediate Care Centre.

Can't remember if I've already explained this, but the ICC was our name for the hospital, which was now being completely staffed by the doctors that had landed with Garth Ronald's battalion, and headed up by Conrad Rhee. If that name sounds familiar, remember he was *Artemis Agrotera's* chief physician... he'd been with us out at Jupiter, had saved Kris Jacobs' life, and had tried desperately to come up with a treatment for Phosgene poisoning during the *Idaho* incident.

He was one of the best surgeons in the Navy, and it has to be said, the people of Egesta were lucky that he'd stayed aboard *Artemis Agrotera*, and was now with us on this mission. They were doubly lucky, too, because Alicia Morgan was down there with him — *Wolf's* very fine physician was helping run the place.

On this second day of our landing, the ICC was still getting set up. Decisions were being made about where to treat people, how to treat them, and what to do with them once their physical problems were solved. It was not pleasant work, but then we were on Egesta, so that's pretty much stating the obvious.

When Bunny and Jim arrived to get pictures of the facility, they didn't know what to expect. After they'd spent hours viewing sites where carnage had been wrought, they thought it was entirely possible that the Capital Dome hospital would be a scene straight from hell. There probably wouldn't have been time to clean up the evidence left behind by blockhead doctors honing their surgical skills on people who didn't need surgery, or performing experiments to advance their understanding of horrifying things.

On the other hand, they thought it was possible that the hospital had only ever been used to treat the blockheads themselves, and that all those people who'd been brutalized and butchered — and who could truly have used the help of the facility — never saw the inside.

Of course, we know the second possibility proved to be the correct one. Had the hospital been turned into a shop of horrors by the Imperial Army, Alicia Morgan and Conrad Rhee would never have let ICC be housed there. Too much psychological trauma to people who'd already been through too much. But the blockheads had mostly kept the hospital to themselves, and as such, it remained clean and free of the grimmest associations of Egesta.

As Jim led the way into the facility, which was fairly modern and very clean, he found the relative quiet to be uncomfortable. Hundreds of people had been brought in over the past thirty-six hours, dozens of them in the waiting room as he stepped in.

Because things were still being set up, there weren't enough doctors or medics to see them all. The blockheads had 'fired' most of the original hospital staff, and it would take us days to screen the doctors we'd thrown out when we arrived. In the meantime, there would be a long waiting list, as the initial rush of patients were triaged and situated. Battered people with hollow eyes, some incredible-seeming wounds, and tattered clothes or survival blankets, sat around in the waiting room. All of them were silent. None of them complained, or cried, or did anything that might seem natural based on their plight.

When Bunny arrived beside Jim, she swept over the waiting room once with her camera, and then lowered it.

"I can't shoot this," she said softly. "It's too horrible."

Considering some of the things they'd seen that day, her statement might have seemed remarkable. But death and murder sites were one kind of brutal… this was different. This was a room full of people who seemed to have been stripped of their humanity. That seeming absence of humanity in the room deeply disturbed Jim — he looked from face to face, occasionally meeting the empty eyes of a man, woman or child who'd lived through things that no one should ever experience.

It was not a good feeling, and he decided not to linger. He nodded towards the corridor past the nurses' desk (now being run by two SFs, there to control what we'd expected might have been a desperate rush of people seeking treatment… which we obviously weren't seeing, probably because word hadn't spread that we'd taken the place over). They nodded as Jim went by them, and Bunny followed, looking back at the waiting room as she did.

"They're just… sitting there…" she said, sounding somewhat confused as she was led away.

Jim figured he understood, at least intellectually, what was motivating those people. Or, perhaps, what *wasn't* motivating them.

"They've been through enough to cause them to shut down," he commented, slowing as open hospital room doors started appearing ahead. They were entering a wing of the ICC that was presumably full of victims who'd already been processed — possibly some of the worst-suffering people on Egesta.

Realizing what had grabbed Jim's attention, Bunny slowed down too, and they both took deep breaths, wondering what exactly they would find as they proceeded further into this facility.

Fortunately, a helpful interruption prevented them from imagining too much on that front.

"Jim…" it was Alicia Morgan, coming around a corner they'd just passed. "Bunny… here to see our arrangements?"

Obviously these two knew *Wolf's* doctor extremely well — Alicia had been responsible for Bunny's treatment during *The Dark Cruise*, and had supervised the many weeks of recovery that had followed.

As the couple turned towards the doctor, Bunny held up her camera, "I should record this. Show that you're providing proper care for these people…"

Alicia hesitated for a moment — the idea of sticking a camera in the face of these patients seemed quite wrong — but she knew that Bunny, perhaps more than anyone else, understood the sensitivity with which these people should to be treated. She'd lived through her own traumatic medical crisis, after all.

"Come with me," our doctor decided aloud, and then began the guided tour of ICC.

Uncomfortable is a word Jim uses a lot when he recalls the time he spent following Alicia through the hospital. Neither he nor I think that word fully encompasses the breadth and depth of the feelings he and Bunny were sharing, but it's the only term that doesn't feel overdramatic. And that's something he insisted I try to get across when I wrote about this event.

There's a temptation, he explained, to make an experience like this about 'me' — to focus too much on how traumatizing it was to see people in hospital beds. But such an emphasis would be profoundly unfair to the people who were actually suffering. They had real reasons to talk about trauma.

Witnessing the after-effects of war crimes isn't traumatic enough to warrant sympathy, or drama, at least as far as Jim's concerned. So for him, it was just uncomfortable. Very, very uncomfortable.

The ICC was five floors, and though Alicia didn't take Jim and Bunny around to every room, they got to see a lot, and have the main parts explained to them. There were special wings set aside for the treatment of people who'd suffered certain kinds of war crimes… obviously those who'd been bayoneted and survived were getting different physical treatments than rape victims.

At this stage, though, even Alicia wasn't sure what sort of psychological care would have to come next — that wasn't her field, and there was still too much unknown about the victims.

All she could say for certain was that the road ahead would be very long.

And that message, ultimately, was the one she left with Bunny and Jim. As they stood in the cafeteria on the top floor of the hospital, Alicia shoved her hands deep into the pockets of her lab coat, then looked around.

"We're only scratching the surface now," she said with a sigh, which Bunny caught with her camera. "We… there's a lot we have to figure out. But we're getting started. We've stopped the bleeding."

She was speaking metaphorically, not medically, because some people were still bleeding… but her point was quite right. The first small steps towards helping the people of Egesta were being taken, and that was something.

"I need to get back down there to admittance. We still have a backlog…" she continued, and then with a nod to Jim and to Bunny, she blinked and added: "Thanks for the excuse to get away for a while."

Bunny caught that part on camera too, but funnily, it never made it to air. She figured too many people would interpret it as Alicia not wanting to do her job. Clearly, that's not what our doctor was thinking… she just needed beathing space, a little time away so that she could reset and go back to more countless hours of helping people through terrible things.

Anyway, she left Jim and Bunny in that cafeteria, which was empty. Even the sandwich counter was shuttered. Once she was out of earshot, and Jim was confident they were alone, he turned to Bunny, and what she calls his 'white knightliness' kicked in.

"Are *you* okay?" he asked earnestly.

No denying, she'd shed some tears when she'd gone through this place. One look through the glass at the pediatric ward had her sobbing, in fact. I'm amazed the medics in there could remain composed.

Jim, then, felt the need to reassure her, and he did so with a hug, "It's alright… we should go…"

Bunny nodded against his shoulder. To use her words, she was feeling out of her depth. She was a good camera operator. She'd actually been the sound technician on

Jocko's old crew... but all of her career, beginning when she'd done communications at university because she'd thought it was an easy degree to do while spending many long nights out with the football team, she'd always considered herself to be 'just a girl'.

She didn't see herself as cut out to be in Defense Command, and as such Jim's protectiveness was appreciated — his chivalrous streak fit her well.

After a moment, their hug ended, and with an arm around Bunny's shoulder, Jim led them towards the stairs. As they went, Bunny's eyes stayed to the side, and she looked through every open hospital room door as she passed it. Quiet patients in each, all of them seemingly in a similar state to those in the waiting room.

The first few she passed without much reaction. The fourth one tugged at her emotions a bit. Then the fifth one made her stop.

Surprised, Jim stopped too. He wasn't sure what Bunny was doing, even when he followed her gaze into a room with a single occupied bed. A young woman — a girl, honestly — was lying there, blankets pulled right up around her pale face as she stared vacantly out the door. It wasn't clear if she was looking at them, or just staring into the space that they happened to be occupying, but Jim got the sense that Bunny was feeling a connection.

And that, he knew, couldn't end well. She was holding things together, but that was easier to do at a distance. Getting up close and personal with a destroyed individual just wasn't wise...

"We should... probably..." he began to speak, but it was too late, and Bunny slipped out from under his arm and moved silently into the room.

The eyes of the gaunt patient followed Bunny as she made a wordless approach. She detoured to lay her camera down on a table against the wall of the room, then moved over towards the bed. As she did this, Jim slipped into the room behind her, but stopped and leaned against the wall beside the door. He didn't want to get too close to the bed until he was needed... some of the female patients he'd seen in the ICC had clearly been agitated by the nearby presence of a male. They had every right to be wary, under the circumstances.

But Bunny was obviously not male. And she obviously wasn't quite grasping the gravity of the damage done to some of these people. She was witnessing incredible suffering, and at last, she wanted to get close to it, to try to help a little.

Jim didn't harbor any optimism, this being Egesta. Still, Bunny wanted to try.

"Hi there," the camera girl said softly as she came up to the side of the bed, and then leaned over the bundled-up patient.

Hollow eyes stared back. No response whatsoever, of course — why would this young woman try to answer after all she'd been through? What Jim knew, and Bunny didn't know, was that under circumstances like these, you really do have to acknowledge reality. Sometimes it's better to leave a person in peace, particularly after he or she has suffered so much. Trying to make them better will only end up damaging you — it's not very logical to try to rescue someone, only to yourself become yet another person in need of rescuing.

That's a simple lesson of combat, and as a veteran Defense Command officer, Jim Hannigan knew it.

But he wouldn't preach. He'd let Bunny come to the conclusion on her own, because he never believed in telling her — or anyone — what to think… and in a situation like this, he doubted his warning would be well-received anyway.

"My name's Bunny. You don't have to say anything," our camera operator pulled a chair over to the side of the bed and sat down. The girl under the covers stared at her, eyes following her all the way. "You remind me of my sister. Her name is Joy. She has hair like yours."

Aside from the stare, there continued to be no response from the girl in the bed, and Jim took a deep breath. Bunny wouldn't give up easily, he just hoped she wouldn't be too distraught when the patient's damage proved impossible to break through.

"I think you have very pretty hair," she continued, and Jim winced.

Perhaps the blockheads would have said something similar to this poor person, while they were committing their crimes. The compliment was thus not one Jim would have offered — he wouldn't have said anything that could even possibly have brought up memories of what had happened, or why this particular individual may have been singled out for the treatment she'd received. Pretty hair… not worth mentioning right now.

But Bunny was from a different tradition. And there was a lesson to come.

It began when she reached out and very gently pressed a hand against the patient's cheek. Jim nearly leapt across the room to stop her, but he wouldn't have gotten there in time, and sudden movement probably would have startled the nameless girl as much as physical contact. Instead, then, he looked on apprehensively — no telling what associations that sort of touch might bring.

"Do you think you could use a new friend?" Bunny asked gently as her hand touched the cold cheek. "I think you may have to be here for a while, but when you're out, I could use a new friend. I lost my two best friends in the war."

Another thing officers like Jim and I wouldn't do is try to make an emotional connection with someone who had no reason to want to connect with us. I mean, as Jim said, what would give him, or any of us, the right to try to make friends with people who'd suffered because of our poor judgment?

All we could do was come in, help, apologize, and try to get them back on their feet… then they could hate us forever, perhaps rightly so, for bringing in the Imps. We wouldn't be so naïve as to try to become peoples' friends. Just wasn't realistic, or perhaps even right.

Knowing all of this very well, Jim thus wondered how acute this patient's reaction would be to Bunny's slightly clumsy but well-intentioned appeal.

And what happened next didn't surprise Jim one bit.

Or, wait, sorry, I got that backwards. It surprised him a whole lot.

If he'd been sitting down, he'd have fallen off his goddamned chair.

From under the cocoon of blankets, a pale hand emerged, and seeing it, Bunny reached down and took it.

"I'm Kini," the girl in the bed said in a surprisingly clear tone.

"Your hand's really cold… need more blankets?" Bunny asked quite easily, and Kini shook her head.

"No, I'll warm up."

Jim apparently didn't do a good job of not looking surprised. Bunny still needles him about his dropped jaw from time to time.

At first he wondered if he'd misjudged the condition of this patient — perhaps she'd been injured, but surely she hadn't spent seventeen days in a blockhead recreation centre, where she was raped more than seventy times.

Nope, that's exactly where she'd been.

So according to the established wisdom among Defense Command officers like Jim, me or even Karen, Kini Powell had no business being in any way conversational, or strong, or anything else. No person — male, female, old or young — could be expected to have borne such abuse well.

We all knew this to be true. We'd seen much suffering during the war, and therefore assumed that we knew a lot about what we were witnessing.

But Bunny was smarter than all of us.

Jim thought — as we all would have — that she was just being naïve, and that the people in the ICC were disinterested in life, beyond healing, beyond human. We perceived them to be victimized people in need of Defense Command's protection, who in time might reclaim some of their lives, but who would forever be scarred.

Factually speaking, I don't think we were entirely *wrong* about that. But we were very ignorant of the many different ways people cope with tragedy. They don't all do it the way we do, with the sort of quiet and earnest resolve that is embedded in Defense Command's military culture.

Kini Powell, for instance, is now a citizen of the Empire. She runs a bakery on Earth, and she remains good friends with them both (Bunny in particular). She'll tell you that the scars of Egesta have never left her — she's incredibly candid about the nightmares, the flashbacks, and the trauma.

So, she is certainly facing all those things that we knew she'd have to face, but she's handling them differently than we thought possible. She wasn't 'beyond help'.

Bunny's success with Kini didn't mean we'd have to all start following her example for every person who came into the ICC. Not every patient needed this sort of personal connection. But with this simple interaction, Bunny opened Jim's eyes (and subsequently, all our eyes) to the fact that we needed to get over our brooding pessimism, and open our minds to trying to do different things to help.

Trying to make friends in a situation like this one was often futile, naïve, and stupid.

But it was also probably better than *not* trying.

It took a strong person to realize that, in the midst of the horror of Egesta — a strong person who wasn't prejudiced by her expectations about duty, and who was less poisoned by the war.

Bunny Fox. Who knew?

Well, Jim knew, and now he knew even better.

After an hour of chatting that was both somehow meaningful and yet blissfully light — talking about clothes, and family, and hair, and things that I'm really not equipped to get into — Bunny said that she and Jim had to go. She promised to return, and Kini said she looked forward to it. That's the truth, too, because while all the doctors and medics were going out of their way to be gentle with her, Kini needed someone who could see past her recent ordeal, and talk to her as a friend.

Good work, Bunny.

Now, Jim's going to possibly shoot me for including this next part of the story, but I want to put it in anyway, because I'm a soppy fool, and I think it was brilliant.

As soon as they stepped out of the room — Bunny feeling awfully good about her chat with Kini, and Jim honestly still having a hard time believing it had happened — he stopped. Confused, she stopped too, and then he put his hands on her shoulders.

"You really shouldn't have done that," he said, though he admits he wasn't sure what he was referring to.

"But…" she started to wonder if she'd done something wrong, because Jim *never* disagreed with her actions in such a direct, firm fashion.

Then, in confusion, *Wolf's* XO pushed *Wolf's* camera person back against the wall of the hallway. This is something he also never did.

And then he kissed her. Full on. I know, makes *absolutely* no sense, and it certainly doesn't fit the mood of the ICC, but he did it anyway.

As he said to me later, after making me promise (on pain of a duel) that I wouldn't repeat his words in print: "I was overcome by the moment, but I certainly don't regret it. You find someone who can stay strong and see something good in a place like Egesta… that's an attractive quality. You add that to the fact that she's really beautiful, and you're already in love with her… well, that's the recipe for a significant kiss."

Good old Jim, trying to hide his embarrassment by sounding matter-of-fact and analytical… Now, before you start worrying that Jim's going to shoot me, I *did* get permission from the other participant in this reputation-shattering kiss.

Bunny's words: "You HAVE to put it in. It was REALLY GOOD."

Sorry, Jim.

Anyway, I should now point out that these two were officially engaged very soon after this visit to the ICC, and Lieutenant Connie Lev (who at this time was still with *Wolf's* bridge Sensors and Communications section) won the marriage pool. Bought herself a new cello with her winnings.

There hasn't been much of anything to smile about in this book, but I think this is one moment when we all can. Thanks to Bunny Fox.

CHAPTER NINE

THE RECOVERY

Dramatic kiss excepted, Egesta left us all numb. A couple of days of exposure to the horror and we couldn't really feel anything anymore, which was to be expected, I think. No matter how horrible and destructive the sights, you can only remain outraged for so long. Eventually you just become numb to everything.

It's what happened to many of us by the end of *The Independent Squadron*, and this time was essentially the same. However, being a bit more familiar with these numb feelings, and with their possible long-term consequences, we decided we'd take steps to try to mitigate their impact. It was as much as we could do.

The first step was to limit shifts on the ground for people who seemed to be taking it worse than the rest, and to institute regular breaks for everyone else. Just because you looked like you were handling it alright didn't mean you were, so all of our volunteers, SF and Special Branch were expected to spend at least eight hours a day aboard one of the ships docked to the rock.

Time aboard a ship probably doesn't sound like much of a respite, and in reality, it likely wasn't. But being in a place where you could go around a corner without worrying that you might stumble onto something pretty dastardly... that was a mental break, at least for me. Our ships were familiar places, operating by a set of rules that we all knew and accepted. The structure, if nothing else, was calming.

During these break periods, people would do any number of things. Often, the officers would check in on their departments, and make sure that all the systems (that were mostly stood down because we were at dock) and the skeleton crews serving them were still running fine.

But beyond those brief work-related tasks, there was a lot of time off.

The rec deck on *Wolf* was quite full. People were in the gym, working out. There was a lineup for the punching bags, go figure. The target ranges were also very, very busy, usually with groups waiting their turn to go in. Many of our crew seemed to go shooting in small teams — a collective catharsis, with people telling each other what they'd seen, while they all fired mag bolts through human-shaped targets they could imagine were blockheads.

The movies that were run in the theatre saw good attendance. Only comedies and musicals were shown — light fare that didn't evoke thoughts of what was going on down on the rock. The swimming pool was busy, because some people found submerging themselves in water to be soothing. And, of course, the Officers' Club and the Enlisted Club did brisk business... according to Jim, we nearly ran out of booze.

Shelby McLaws and Adrienne Thompson were two of the patrons who helped run down our supply of liquor. Of course they didn't get drunk and disorderly in the Officers' Club — that wouldn't have befitted either of them, as senior members of the command staff — but they did amass a collection of empty glasses on their table.

The second time on Egesta, Shelby told me later, had been tougher for her than the first. That surprised her, because the first time through she'd seen most of what Andrea had seen, but as is always the case with these sort of events, it had influenced her differently. Part of that, she supposes, was because the first time she'd been a relatively junior officer. She hadn't felt *as* responsible for the chaos as Andrea did, our Irish skipper having been the senior DC officer on the ground at the time.

That's just Shelby's guess, though. Andrea hasn't commented one way or the other.

Anyway, given this setup, I suppose now I should begin the narrative with Shelby and Adrienne speaking of dark things as they sit at a table in the Officers' Club, staring at the empty glasses on their table.

But I can't actually do that, because neither of them said much of anything. They sat next to each other on the bench that made up one side of the table, and drank their liquor and stared.

They, remember, were numb. There were few things they could do to find any real relief.

Matt Baxter lay in the dark in his cabin aboard *Friendly*, cursing his head. The migraine that had begun on Egesta had now ballooned, and as was sometimes the case with such epic headaches, this one had developed an immunity to the numerous powerful drugs that usually broke it.

So Matt simply lay in the dark, and endured the pain.

He thinks now that the fiery throb actually kept some of the sights he'd seen on Egesta from clouding his mind as he lay in the blackness. Nothing that he'd encountered had really been beyond what he'd been prepared for, but still, he'd expected to see grim visions at night.

The pain kept them at bay. Perhaps that was by design — perhaps his subconscious had decided to use head pain to protect him from a different kind of agony. A more insidious kind.

Matt didn't know, and didn't care. He lay back on his bunk, a cold pack on his head, eyes closed.

Jim Hannigan sat with Bunny as they rolled through the footage she'd shot on the rock. It wasn't easy viewing, so she only tended to go through it when he was with her. Obviously she could have done it on her own, but she preferred it this way, and so did he.

I don't think I ever give Jim enough credit, but he really was handling this better than many of us. As usual, he was quietly and confidently going about his business, doing his job and making sure no one had to worry about the things he was responsible for. That's the most valuable kind of professionalism I can imagine, and we were very lucky to have him.

Bunny was lucky to have him too — and he was obviously lucky to have her.

Now they watched scenes of horror together.

I tried to read reports from Mars. We were keeping in regular contact with Belt Two, so the latest developments from the Mars Convention were flowing at a regular pace.

We hadn't returned any news about what we'd found — we didn't want to risk it getting picked up before we had our evidence collected — but we could call in for the latest updates.

And though John and the Prime Minister and Craig B. Macdonald were hammering out the peace treaty that would end the biggest war in the history of the solar system, a war which had killed some of my friends, hurt many of my friends, and which had caused me to do a lot of killing… I couldn't care less.

As I've said, numb.

I stared at a pad talking about the limits that were to be put on the size of the Martian Navy. It said things I should have wanted to know. It talked about how the Union of Solar Asteroids — that still-mysterious band of rocks that was finally starting to get our attention — had in fact built the *Tharsis*-class Battleships for the Martian fleet. Bort McWebsbert had told me some of that, but there were more details now. Who signed the contracts, why the Union had been selected over Martian yards…

Under normal circumstances, I would have found all of this properly fascinating. And down the line, a few books from now, I'd need to know all of it.

But for now: numb.

Instead of reading, I kept looking up, and watching Karen. She'd fallen asleep, and as her head shifted uneasily on my pillows, I wondered what she was dreaming about. After three days here, she hadn't threatened to pin anyone's head to the ground with a spike, which was definitely a good thing. She'd seemed a bit concerned now and then that she might get the urge to go off the handle, but nothing came of it.

She was under control. The slip in *The Mars Convention* had just been bad luck — a consequence of stress and a tiny bit of carelessness.

Now she actually seemed a bit concerned about me, which was obviously unnecessary. I wasn't going to go off the deep end. It would serve no purpose — becoming some sort of nasty vigilante would only help the Emperor. And besides, I'd never do that sort of thing with Karen around. If she was in trouble, then *maybe*. I'd lost my cool a bit when I'd thought her lost during the Fleet Clash.

So she didn't have to worry. I remember distinctly thinking that to myself twice as I stared at her, and neither time did it feel to me like I was trying to convince myself it was true. It just was.

As Karen shifted again, I saw that her ponytail was up on her left shoulder, and as it fell across her neck she took hold of it, pulling it down against the skin on the side of her neck. So I did know what she was dreaming about, and it wasn't Egesta.

"God. Get a ponytail," I repeated to myself quietly, and smiled.

So long ago.

Karen slept and I pretended to read.

Wes Pellew was angry with himself. After years of progress, he'd suddenly and almost inexplicably regressed into the brash young officer who challenged people to duels because he was indulging his own pain. He still didn't know what had possessed him to bring his flight gloves down to Egesta in the first place — he'd only kept the damned things as a reminder of what mistakes he could never afford to repeat.

But now, as he sat at his desk in his cabin, he was grappling with the fact that he'd very nearly done it all over again. Thank God Andrea had stopped him.

You must understand, Wes wasn't pitying himself as he sat there. Quite the opposite, he was angry at himself. He was thinking about what his *outburst* would have meant for his crews. The Independent Squadron would need to be reassembled when peace was restored, and if Wes turned back into some bastard who went around serving his own grief and trying to shoot anyone he perceived to be a criminal, he'd never be fit to lead them again.

His job was to look after his ships and his crews. Simple.

Getting carried away and letting old emotions run roughshod over his common sense couldn't be allowed. That was, in fact, the very sort of behavior he'd been trying to counsel Andrea against. And now she'd actually saved him from it.

Ironic.

And telling.

Wes thought about Andrea — thought about what her intervention said about her progress. She was, he knew, a truly remarkable person. He hadn't spoken to her since he'd stormed off that street, as she'd been down on Egesta, administering things. Alone among our senior officers, she was acting normally — normally for the old days — so she was doing a lot of the heavily lifting at Government House.

There would be trouble again when she left Egesta, Wes was fairly certain of that. But given the progress she'd made, he remained confident she could weather whatever troubles came. And he would help her in whatever way he could. He owed her that much... and for all the darkness that usually clouded their interactions, he liked spending time with her.

So Andrea's progress was a consolation to Commodore Pellew. But, of course, before he could try to continue helping her, he did need to settle this personal issue. He had to hammer it into his head that he was past trying to avenge Sara.

To accomplish that, he'd need to see the prisoners he'd tried to shoot — look the bastards in the eyes and then turn away. Then he could be satisfied that he was back under control.

Activating his desk terminal, Wes began to search the prisoner lists. Colonel Ronald's SF and Special Branchers had been meticulous in keeping records of everyone captured, so it shouldn't be too tough to find the man... what was his name? Willie. Willie... Hay?

He started scrolling through the lists of prisoners, sorting alphabetically. But there was no Willie Hay.

For five minutes, he sifted the list, certain he must just be reading past the name. He was tired, and he knew fatigue could make him miss things.

But the man's name wasn't on the list.

That fact left plenty of reasons to be concerned, but Wes chose to jump to no conclusions. Instead he activated his comm, and sent a realtime signal over to *Wolf*, because we were keeping the searchable master database of all Imperial Army personnel taken on Egesta.

Eugene Sengooba appeared in a window on Wes' screen with a nod, "Good evening, Commodore."

"Morning, Eugene," Wes answered absently. Then blinked, "Sorry. Evening."

Our Master-At-Arms smiled and shook his head, "What can I do for you, sir?"

"Searching for four prisoners Captain Kiley and I took while we were down there. I can't find them on the list…"

Frowning, Eugene looked away from the viewfinder for a second. He was in the security office on *Wolf*, so he was calling up the prisoner lists on another screen.

"Have a name, sir?"

"Willie Hay…" Wes said slowly, trying to remember if that was right.

Eugene punched the name in, and then *Wolf's* computer started searching. Because Defense Command OS XX is so smart, it checked for alternate spellings of 'Hay', and looked up all the different names that 'Willie' could be a nickname for.

But it came up blank.

"Nothing here… possible that you might have mixed up the first or last name?" Eugene asked gently. He figured, quite rightly, that memories from the past few days could become slightly unclear.

Wes frowned, then nodded, "Possible. Run similars?"

Eugene nodded, and asked *Wolf's* AI to look for similar-sounding names.

Willie Ney popped out.

"How about Willie Ney?" our Master-At-Arms asked, and Wes thought for a second and then nodded.

"That must be him," the Commodore said with a tired smile. "Sorry, brain cramp."

Shaking his head, Eugene slowly began to frown, "You said 'prisoner'?"

Wes stopped smiling, "Yes I did."

There was a pause as Eugene opened a report on the other screen, his frown deepening as he quickly read it, "You were there when they were turned over to SF?"

For a second, Wes wasn't able to process the words. He felt a lot of blood rushing to his head, and then his mind began to race. What was going on…?

"I… what's the problem, Master-At-Arms?" he sounded more severe with that question than he'd intended to.

Eugene blinked, then looked back at the screen, "Sir. They're in the morgue. Mister Ney and his three comrades were killed by a mob of Egesta civilians before SF could intervene."

A mob? There'd been no mob.

There'd only been…

He'd left them with Andrea.

Dear God, he'd left prisoners with Andrea.

A sudden, eerie calmness settled over Wes as those thoughts crossed his mind — the same sort of calmness he got in combat, when things looked grim but he still needed to be able to think and act.

"The cause of death confirmed by a medical examination, Eugene?" he asked carefully.

Our Master-At-Arms doubled-checked, then nodded, "Doctor Rhee signed off on it at the ICC."

A mob?

There were a lot of thoughts crowding around those two words, but Wes refused to focus on any of them — to risk letting himself draw conclusions. Not yet.

"Thank you, Master-At-Arms," he said slowly, with an air of dread.

Eugene's natural security instincts by now were telling him something was wrong, but looking at the report on his screen, and seeing that it had been filed by Captain Andrea Kiley, he decided he was going to refrain from pursuing further inquiries for the moment. He had a feeling — a correct feeling — that Wes, who was senior to the report's signatory, would find out more.

"Last I heard, Captain Kiley was in Government House, sir," our Master-At-Arms offered quietly, and Wes blinked, realizing Eugene understood the implications.

Nodding, the Commodore of the Independent Squadron took a breath, "Thank you, Eugene."

He didn't say anything more. He didn't want to promise to get to the bottom of this, because even if he did discover something, he didn't know what he'd do with it. And Eugene was similarly uncomfortable — investigating one's own Captain was not a job any security officer could ever want... let alone our Master-At-Arms...

Better to leave a lot unsaid.

The link cut, and Wes grabbed his tunic and sidearm and headed for the chute that connected *Nova Scotia* to Egesta.

CHAPTER TEN
GONE

When Wes arrived on the steps of Government House, it was with a profound sense of foreboding. Considering this was Egesta, I suppose a sense of foreboding could hardly be unexpected… but this was a different kind of dread than one usually found on the rock.

You know why. I don't need to reiterate it.

Andrea Kiley…

Pausing at the bottom of the steps, the Commodore of the Independent Squadron took a breath and collected his thoughts. He didn't know what to expect from Andrea — flat denial, angry acknowledgment, or something in between.

He hoped she'd have an innocent explanation for the death of the four prisoners. He couldn't imagine what would qualify as an innocent explanation under the circumstances, but he hoped she'd have one.

Otherwise… it was going to be quite a problem.

Honestly, he didn't know what he'd do, so he tried not to dwell on it too much.

Wait and see what she had to say for herself.

With another deep breath, he started to climb the stairs, nodding absently to the SF who were posted as sentries on the door. There'd been no violence to speak of — the blockheads had decided against trying to shoot it out, and the people of Egesta were too broken and weary to express their rightful outrage in a physical way.

Nevertheless, sentries seemed like a good idea, so they nodded to Wes as he passed them.

For a moment, Wes could imagine exactly what it would look like if he had to call those guards to come and drag Andrea away on murder charges.

He didn't like that mental picture one bit.

Inside, Government House was largely silent. Not too many officers were staying on Egesta, as I mentioned before, so only Andrea and a few rotating staff were in the building. Wes had no idea where any of them could be found, so he checked the likeliest places on the ground floor before he decided to try upstairs.

When he got to the second floor, he found silence — whoever was working here was doing so without much chatter. He passed one open office door and saw two young officers frowning over various blockhead pads, doubtless looking for documentary evidence of crimes committed here. He didn't disturb them, just moved on to the old Governor's office.

Coming to a stop outside that door, he looked in uneasily, and saw Andrea was indeed seated at the Governor's desk, frowning as she read through pads of her own. She didn't notice him as he stepped across the threshold into the room, but when he pushed the door shut behind him, the click of the latch drew her eyes up.

When she saw him, her frown melted away and she smiled, "Good evening,

Commodore Pellew."

Again I needn't drive home the point that Andrea was acting and sounding like her old self. She lowered her pad as she started to read Wes' expression, and her smile faded back to a more neutral look, "Something the matter?"

Wes folded his arms and took a few steps towards her desk, studying her as he moved, "I need honesty from you right now, Andrea. I'm going to ask you questions, and I need the truth."

There was no doubting the severity of those words, and as Andrea realized this wasn't any sort of casual visit, she pushed her chair back and stood.

"You have any reason to think I'd lie?" she asked.

Wes stared at her, studied her face for a moment, then shook his head gently, "I don't know what to expect from you right now."

He wasn't sure if it was a good sign that Andrea hadn't immediately realized what he had come in here to discuss — if she'd been concerned about the fate of those prisoners, wouldn't she naturally have assumed that he was here to confront her about them?

Or perhaps she was just playing it cool, and not revealing she had anything to do with it. Guilt probably wasn't going to factor into the way she handled this…

Not wanting to actually have to say the words, and ask the question, Wes tried to read more of Andrea's thoughts through her eyes. Unfortunately, his telepathy wasn't on that day. No matter how much he stared, he couldn't figure out what she was really thinking.

He couldn't even figure out what he *hoped* she was thinking.

"Wes?"

Andrea's question shook him out of musing — he'd just been staring at her. The fact that he was so out of sorts about this was a telling sign.

"Four prisoners who I nearly shot in a duel," he said sharply. "Where are they?"

As the question reached her, Andrea's expression twitched slightly, but not in the way Wes half-expected. She didn't suddenly look nervous, or guilty, or desperate. She didn't look like someone who'd just been caught.

Instead her brow creased, and she appeared a little confused, "Last I checked, the ICC morgue. You need to see them?"

Wes just stared at her again, but he caught himself before letting it go too long this time, "How did they end up dead, Andrea? When I left, they were alive."

He didn't prompt her about the mob — better not to reveal how much he knew of the story, to see if she offered him a different explanation than she'd put in the report. This was an old-school interrogation tactic we used on pirates, and cops have used on criminals forever, so it didn't seem likely that Andrea would fall for it. But it was worth a try.

Now she tilted her head, "After you walked off, all those people who'd been watching from their front porches came out into the street. Wanted to know why we weren't finishing them off."

Consistent story. But Wes didn't remember the sounds of any mob as he was leaving… not that he'd been in a clear state of mind…

"I… don't recall signs of that."

Andrea's tone remained balanced, and she seemed not at all frustrated with the questions, even though they were rather serious.

"They did come out," she said reassuringly. "I tried to intervene, but by the time the backup arrived there were almost 100 people in the street. I couldn't stop them all."

Backup. Wes frowned slightly, then tilted his head, "The backup you called witnessed the mob?"

She nodded, and then rounded her desk and approached him, "Yes they did. By the time they arrived, the four men were dead in the street, and the mob was breaking up."

The closer she got to him, the more Wes wanted to believe her. This, I suppose, must sound corny, or perhaps melodramatic. But Wes admits it openly: he wanted Andrea to be innocent, and as she stepped nearer, it just seemed to increase the reassurance that came with her words.

Surely, after all the difficulties of the war, and after the lessons she'd learned on the mission to Io, over Pion Rock, and in the last battles against the Martians, she wouldn't have let herself go in a moment's lust for revenge.

He wanted to believe her.

But he wanted that so badly that he was suspicious of his own conviction. Wanting to believe her didn't make her right.

"We haven't heard of mobs cropping up to deliver justice anywhere else," he said a little darkly, and Andrea stopped.

"Shelby, Adrienne and Eugene had the vigilante mother," she pointed out, referring to Captain Angela Kerr.

Wes hesitated, then nodded, "Yes, but she wasn't a mob. A Boscawen Merc's different than getting people out of their houses into the street to stomp four blockheads."

Andrea's eyes narrowed slightly, but she nodded, "Okay. So our street was unique."

She almost added 'but you saw how the Imps killed that woman,' but realized it might sound like she was trying to shame Wes with his own moment of indiscretion — remind him that he had lost control.

Wes continued to meet her gaze as she fell silent, and finally he asked, "Did you?"

"Did I what?"

"Kill them? Or incite the mob?"

That was it. That was the question. Was Captain Andrea Kiley responsible for the death of four Imperial Army soldiers who'd been taken prisoner by Defense Command?

There seemed to be an eternity of silence after Wes asked the question. I know people say that a lot — that something seemed to take *forever* — but this time it really did feel like time had ceased movement. Because the answer to the question would undoubtedly change everything. Even if it only took a second or two for Andrea to reply (even now, Wes really can't remember how long it actually was) it was still an endless delay.

I know that feeling, I think. Time just stops, and there you are, your mind overclocking as it tries to come to grips with what's about to happen, even before it arrives.

Goddamned miserable feeling.

"The mob killed them," Andrea said with some finality. "And they certainly didn't need me to give them any motivation."

It was almost an answer. If confirmed, at least, that Andrea hadn't shot them. But she hadn't actually said that she didn't incite the mob. Wes immediately recognized that seeming evasion, and then realized he had to decide what to do with it.

He could just let it be. Not ask the question to which he didn't want to know the answer, and try to get on with things. Or he could make her be up front with him. He could force her to put the truth on the table, and then if she was responsible...

What would he do if she admitted to murder?

As much as he wanted to believe that he could look the other way for Andrea, that wasn't in his character. If she'd killed them, she would have to face proper trial. Perhaps an inquiry would clear her... but it wasn't Wes' decision to make.

If prisoners died because of her actions, she needed to be held to account.

He hated that, but he needed to know.

"They didn't need you to incite them?" he struck back uncomfortably, and then hit her with the question: "But did you incite them anyway?"

So there it was. Again, the wait seemed endless. Andrea stared at him, and behind her eyes he imagined he could see her thinking, calculating, plotting what to say. He imagined she was spinning a story that she thought would satisfy him.

He imagined now she would lie, and he would have to take the necessary steps... but she didn't look uneasy. She was totally in control.

"No."

It was a flat word, hard to argue with, and when she said it, Wes almost didn't realize she'd answered him. She then took a step back, and he met the move with a deep frown.

"You didn't."

It was both a statement and an implied question, and Andrea's brow seemed to twitch as she heard it.

"No," she answered again.

And this time she sounded frustrated.

Wes didn't believe her. He actually didn't believe her, and it was almost a shock to him when he realized it. It was even more of a shock to her.

She started to get angry — not a reaction she'd have expected from herself. She tried to check her frustration, but it didn't work.

And Wes got angry too, because he didn't believe Andrea. That anger was both for himself and for her — he didn't trust her, which to him felt like a betrayal of his personal values... and at the same time, she was giving him a reason not to trust her, which made the betrayal her fault, at least in part.

Dammit.

God dammit.

He strode forward suddenly, closing the distance with Andrea in a flash, "I shouldn't have left you there."

"Because now you don't believe me. Can't trust me after all, right?" she shot back, sounding somewhat wounded.

Perhaps rightly so.

It was an awkward moment for both of them.

"Tell me *what happened*," Wes insisted now — and knowing Wes, I can say honestly that such a forceful demand is not one you'll often hear from the Independent Squadron's Commodore. He's rarely angered, rarely demanding.

"You left me there, and they were killed by a mob," Andrea didn't stop herself in time.

She mentioned Wes leaving, which she knew instantly was going to sound as though she was blaming him.

Wes didn't miss the shot, "My fault, then?"

Cold, cold words from Commodore Pellew, and being on the defense and not willing to give ground, Andrea hit back hard, "You were ready to start avenging Sara all over again. You were about to lose everything you've gained for some irrelevant quest for revenge of a dead woman. I made sure you didn't. I made sure that if anyone did something stupid and lost all the progress they'd made, it'd be me. Because I'm still broken."

Stepping back, Wes felt as though he'd received a body shot. Bringing up his dead wife in an argument with him was unwise. It was deathly unwise. Even if the rest of the argument was about how he was better… and even if she may have had some sort of valid point… you just don't bring up Sara.

Andrea might have thought she understood the importance of this principle, but she didn't really have a grasp of what was about to hit her. Wes had been too kind for too long for anyone to suspect he could be so vicious.

There are few things Wes really regrets. Aside from letting Sara die (which wasn't his fault, but he still regrets it because he can't *not* regret it), and killing Belt Widows at the risk of his own life and the lives of others, the following words are at the top of his list.

"When you lose someone you actually *love*, you can talk about Sara. When you fail as a combat officer, and let children get spaced, you don't have the right to criticize. I've been understanding for as long as I can. Your self-pity is disgusting, and I'll tolerate no more of it. Find your own way, or shoot yourself. Make a choice. But if you ever come at me with Sara again, I'll make the choice for you."

Between the time she'd left Egesta back in 2231 and now, it's fair to say few things had ever truly rattled Andrea, save for her own skewed perspective. But Wes' words did the trick.

I'd heard their kind before. Prompting them is how I got Wes to challenge me to a duel one day years before. And believe me, I count myself lucky that I never heard them again after that. The man loved his wife, and rightly so. And unless you've loved someone and had them torn away by a bastard like Grant Merger, and you know how that feels, you'll never understand exactly the sort of rage it can produce.

I know it a bit more than I'd like.

And, sorry, it was the Belt Widows who killed Sara. Grant and his Syndicate of pirates weren't in on that particular murder.

The pure hate that seemed to spill from Wes' words pushed Andrea backward, until she found herself sitting on the edge of her desk. Watching her back up, the Independent Squadron's Commodore said nothing more. For a moment, his hot glare burned her skin, and then he swallowed.

It took him a second to remember what had brought him here… dead blockheads who he'd have shot given the chance. And then he recalled Andrea's answer, and the report Eugene had read to him, and realized that even if she was lying, there would be no evidence.

And he still didn't know if she was lying. She could have committed a crime, sacrificing all the progress she'd made towards normality. He'd spent so many months trying to help her find her way back, in fits and starts whenever she needed the help.

Now she could figure it out by her goddamned self.

Was it a rational reaction? Certainly not. Was it morally right? Doubtful. Was it fair to Andrea, or to Wes? Couldn't tell you.

But their connection was cut, as far as Wes was concerned. And as he turned and left the office, Andrea watched the door shut behind him in utter shock. She wasn't ready for someone to tell her off. As she said to me later, we'd all been awfully kind and understanding with her, trying to let her get back to normal at her own pace.

Now — *finally*, she thinks in retrospect — somebody had told her she *had* failed on Egesta the last time. Someone had told her what she'd always believed. And it was actually a relief.

Then, she realized with a hollow feeling, she couldn't talk to Wes about how it felt, and that made everything much worse again.

The misery of Egesta.

CHAPTER ELEVEN
JARRING SIDEBAR

We're actually going to leave Egesta now, at least for a little while. My editors and I have wrestled with this quite a bit — we know it's jarring to suddenly move away from that rock, since we've been talking about it since the very beginning, but in order for everything else that happens in 2234 to make sense, we have to.

We did try mixing what follows into chapters throughout the book, to stagger the interruptions and give you a little break from the horror, but it never fit together properly, partly because what you're about to read happened after Wes stormed out of that office. So apologies for the sharp turn, but it's necessary.

And hey, it gets us away from Egesta, though admittedly not for anything enjoyable.

We're going back to Belt Two where we're going to say hello for the first time this year to two dear friends of ours — Belt Squadron elites from before the war, who spent their time during hostilities making sure the Empire's trade flowed.

Well, strictly speaking, one of them worked on the flow of convoys; the other was a crucial intelligence asset.

Of course I'm referring to Marshal and Mel Samuels.

It's been too long since we've heard from either of them, honestly. Because of the direction the story has taken us over the past number of books, there's been precious little opportunity to show what they've been up to, and to explain again how critical their work was to us winning the war.

Some think that because Marshal left *Alberta* and wasn't at Mercury or the Fleet Clash, his contribution was somehow less than ours. These people better keep their voices down, because I don't agree, and I don't have much of a conscience when it comes to duels.

What you need to understand is that the main reason we had such a powerful fleet by 2233 is because the Earth and Lunar shipyards never ran out of supplies. There were never *any* appreciable shortages of critical war materiel. And as you undoubtedly know, most of the ore and a lot of the simpler manufactured parts that go into warships start out in the Belt colonies.

That's why we'd settled them in the first place: they are literally rocks full of minerals that we can mine and use to build stuff.

Had the Martians been able to cut the supply lines between Earth and the Belt, we wouldn't have had the new *Asia*- and *Australia*-class ships, or the *Hokkaido*-class battleships. John and Greg wouldn't have been able to pull enough battleships out of Earth space for the Mercury assault. Sela Kinder wouldn't have been able to take over *Guangxi* and fight that ship to great effect. Bruce Arama wouldn't have used *Adelaide* to save Karen's life.

We'd *needed* those ships. And we had them, thanks to the incredible efforts of our space docks and their workers... thanks to the brave crews of our merchant fleet... and, no doubt, thanks to Commodore Marshal Samuels, who had gone back into history, found the convoy system used in wars at sea, and adapted it to suit our needs.

Oh, and just to add to the mix, he'd also administered that system with a huge amount of skill.

I know, I'm talking up Marshal's role a great deal, but with good reason. We take a lot of the Empire's economic might for granted, and we shouldn't. A whole other series of books could be written on what Marshal had to deal with, but I'll leave that to others.

For now, we'll join him as he sat in his office in Belt Two. The convoys were no longer necessary, now that hostilities were over, but he was still operating them until peace was officially signed. Very few merchants were opting to stay in the system now that the fighting had halted, which basically made running convoys a formality, but Marshal was still diligently making sure they were available.

He was enjoying a relatively easy afternoon, sitting back at his desk and reviewing a list of ships, when his comm binged. He glanced up at the screen in his office, leaned forward and tapped the console to activate the display, and found Captain Fiona Kellerman was on the line.

Last time we saw Fiona, she was a Lieutenant Commander denying me and the entire crew of *Wolf* access to pudding. Now, apparently, she'd earned her way up to Captain of Belt Two. Monster.

"Sir… I've got a real strange request here for you."

Marshal frowned and lowered his pad, "How strange, Fiona?"

"You know Peter McKnight?"

Strange indeed. Laying the pad down on his desk, Marshal narrowed his eyes and turned his chair slightly, "He's on Earth."

Fiona shook her head, "No, he just came in on *Geiser*."

Frowning, Marshal took a few seconds to put thoughts together in his head. *Geiser* was one of the liners that had just made the trip from Earth outside of convoy protection. And Peter McKnight was Chief of Staff to one of Belt Two's most senior Members of Parliament, Leslie Cavanaugh. The House of Commons was sitting, so why was he of all people on a transport to Belt Two?

This was all very strange, at least to Marshal. During his time working the convoy system, the fact that he remained basically at home in the Belt colonies meant he'd built a fairly good rapport with the local politicos — both the rock governors, and the MPs and Senators who represented the colonies in Parliament.

Most of them trusted him, which is no mean feat considering they were a pack of politicians. But that's what happens when you do your job the way Marshal had… yes, I'll stop praising his work now. Maybe. My editors say I'm beating a dead horse, but hey, you know how much I like glue.

Sorry, that's an old joke about how they used to make glue a long time ago… and I'm seriously not going on a tangent about adhesives.

Anyway, the fact that McKnight was on Belt Two was interesting indeed. Why was Fiona Kellerman bringing it to his attention?

Leaning a little further forward, Marshal looked at his Captain, "Is he asking to speak with me, Fiona?"

She nodded, "Called the special number and asked if you could meet him at a coffee shop down on… Fifth, I think."

Marshal frowned at that, and then glanced at his clock. He was due to meet Melissa for dinner in a couple of hours… he could make the detour, find out what was going on.

"Alright… no idea why he doesn't just come here, but I'll meet him. Can you tell him I'll be there at 1600?"

"Yep, I'll let him know."

With that, Fiona Kellermen cut the feed, and Marshal Samuels sat back and pondered. Very strange.

Melissa Samuels sat at her desk off the main training gym. She was, of course, our Defense Command Intelligence Station Chief for Belt Two, but being a superagent (even a retired one) she still wanted to keep up a cover. It was useful, particularly considering it had been she, before marrying Marshal, who had infiltrated Grant Merger's Syndicate, and had brought the bastard down.

So now, aside from being a super spy, she was also the head coach of Belt Two's best competitive gymnastics team, getting ready for the Imperial games of 2236. Her team was out practicing with one of her assistant coaches, which is fortunate because I know nothing about gymnastics, and thus would not have been able to provide any plausible scene descriptions if she'd been out there with them.

I mean, 'A young person tumbled'? Tumbled into what? My editors already hate me enough as it is.

But that's irrelevant, because she was at her desk, going over some gymnastics-related paperwork, when someone darkened her door. Mel hadn't actually heard this person approach, which she took to be a sign of one of two things: either she was losing her edge, or the visitor was well-trained.

And she knew she wasn't losing her edge.

She had a mag within easy reach, so now she innocuously moved her right hand towards what looked like a mail tray, before looking up to see who it was.

As soon as she recognized the person, she moved her hand away again, "It can't be a good sign that you're here."

Camila Barrai was another of DCI's superagents, a proud Argentinean who was known to be one of the best infiltrators around. Her heyday had been around Mel's time with the Syndicate, and like Marshal's wife, she too was now a 'retired' station chief.

But her posting was on Earth, last Mel had heard. So her appearance in the doorway of Belt Two's premier gymnastics training centre suggested something was amiss.

"I just came in for a visit," Barrai said gently. "And I realized Peter McKnight was on my transport."

That sounded plausible to anyone who might be listening in — Mel immediately recognized it as one of those coded ways of explaining the situation when you're afraid you're being bugged.

But this was her office… it was possible it was being monitored, but highly unlikely…

So whatever was going on had to be serious… very serious, if Camila Barrai had followed a senior MP's Chief of Staff out to Belt Two.

"Let's take a walk," Melissa came to her feet, and Barrai nodded.
"Of course."

Peter McKnight was his usual gray-haired, mustached self. Marshal picked him out as soon as he arrived at the Turnbull Coffee House — one of the spots he knew politicos in Belt Two tended to use for their out-of-office meetings. It was quiet, and discreet.

Standing as Marshal arrived, McKnight extended his hand to the Commodore, "Hey Marshal."

"Peter," was the easy reply, and then they sat without going to the counter to order anything. "I suppose Leslie knows you're gone?"

Chuckling, McKnight sat back in his chair, "She sent me. Hopefully I won't have to stay long."

I should pause here to tell you that McKnight was one of the political types that Daragh Ryan actually wouldn't hate. Believe it or not, he actually used to be a firefighter on Belt Two, and only had gotten into government work when Leslie Cavanaugh was elected and he'd been looking to retire. Good fellow, so Marshal trusted him.

"Is there a message, or something like that?" Marshal cut straight to the point, and McKnight began to shake his head — not to say no, but in mild disbelief.

"It's crazy," he said. "The Emperor's about to make a play to bring down the government."

That was crazy. And now I'm going to have to take some time to explain it, so hold on for a section of dry but essential exposition. We've known for a long time that his eminence the bastard Luther Gregory III was going to make the play to defeat Prime Minister Gabriel Pope... at last the plan, or part of it, was being brought to light.

Remember that Pope and his government were from the Empire Party — the party whose platform is, in the end, one of Imperial unity. Other parties claim to be for the unity of the Empire, but forgive my bias, they're mostly lying. Pope's party held a majority in both the House of Commons and the Senate, meaning it could pass whatever legislation was laid down by the Prime Minister and his cabinet. It also meant that, realistically, Pope was much more powerful than the Emperor.

But, as you know, the Emperor was an egotistical bastard who looked back on the decades — indeed *centuries* — of political evolution within the Empire, and hated it. You see, since the beginning, Parliament had gradually been clawing power away from the Emperor. Bit by bit, he was becoming a powerless figurehead, and Luther Gregory wanted to be a despot.

So now he was using some of the privileges he had left to try to break Pope, and seize control. This process had started through Dave Caldecott just before the war, but had been suspended by the Martians.

Now, it was starting again.

But the natural question: how could the Emperor defeat Pope when the Empire Party had control of both houses? The simple answer: by breaking the Empire Party.

Because, like all big political parties in human history, the Empire Party had different factions. During the last race for leadership, Pope, supported by Craig B. Macdonald, had taken over, but Olivia Bennington, now his deputy Prime Minister, had represented at least a third, and perhaps closer to half of the party. She'd made a deal with Pope that after he retired, she'd become party leader (and then presumably PM), but she wasn't particularly patient.

So now, with Pope and Macdonald both away at Mars, she was planning to let the government fall. The process would be simple: Luther Gregory's acolytes in the Earth Party — the official opposition — would introduce a non-confidence motion, one that could bring the government down. Bennington would then order her faction of the party to abstain from the vote, and the government would fall.

The Governor General — Luther Gregory's henchman at this point in time — would then appoint the Earth Party leader as the Prime Minister, a result that would humiliate Pope and force him to step down. Then Bennington would rise to fill his place as Empire Party leader, and defeat the Earth Party when their shaky government collapsed.

Simple. Elegant. And you'd better believe that in return for this chance to humiliate her old foe and eventually become Prime Minister, Bennington would give the Emperor whatever he asked for. Well, perhaps not everything, but a lot of things… little things that seemed unimportant, but which he'd use to unravel our system of government.

All of this, you see, is what Peter McKnight said to Marshal Samuels in very low tones. It sounded bad to our elite Commodore, but he was also confused: unless Leslie Cavanaugh was planning a coup to overthrow Bennington, why did she need to tell the senior Defense Command officer at Belt Two? And beyond that, why send her Chief of Staff in person, instead of a coded message?

But McKnight wasn't done explaining the situation. And in a park across town, neither was Camila Barrai.

"We think Dave Caldecott's people are still controlling DCC," Barrai said to Mel as they strolled down a path past a playground (just as a reminder, DCC is Defense Command Communications). "Daragh and John dumped them all there to keep them from endangering warships with their incompetence, but we think they're now reporting to the Emperor's cronies. We cannot send even coded signals without some concern that, if they pass through a communications ship, they will be stolen."

That was an ominous prospect, and Mel frowned as she heard it. I should say that Barrai had just given all the same exposition to Melissa that McKnight had given to Marshal, so they were on the same page in terms of learning about this plot.

"So you had to come here directly," Mel finally responded aloud, then shook her head. "But why does Leslie want to get word to Marshal? She can't be planning a military intervention in government affairs… he'd never do it."

Barrai came to a stop and looked around them, watching for any sign of surveillance. It seemed unlikely that the Emperor would have ears on Belt Two — and particularly, ears that these two superagents couldn't instantly spot — but extra prudence seemed worthwhile.

Finally, she answered, "Bennington needs the Belt caucus to join her betrayal, or she won't have enough votes to bring down the government. One of the arguments she's using with her faction is that Defense Command has turned into a bunch of out-of-control cowboys, running roughshod over Imperial principles. But there are sixty-four Belt MPs in the Empire Party who should know better..."

"And twenty-six Belt Party MPs who should also be wise to the fact," Mel added.

More exposition to explain this further: Bennington was counting on a group of sixty-four MPs who represented the Belt colonies to remain loyal to her block when the opposition attempted to bring down the government. Twenty-six other MPs were from the tiny Belt Party, which was focused only on the Belt and its best interests.

If those 100 didn't abstain during a confidence vote, Bennington wouldn't be able to bring down her own government in the Commons.

And Marshal Samuels had, at the very least, met with each of those 100 over his recent years at Belt Two. He knew more than half of them on a genuine first-name basis, and had gone out of his way during the war to make sure all of their constituent rocks were as well looked after as possible.

So, if Bennington was trying to turn the Belt caucus against Pope and Defense Command, who better to change their minds back than the one DC officer they all knew they could count on?

Peter McKnight had come to bring Marshal Samuels to Earth.

"So Leslie's still the head of the Belt caucus?" Marshal checked that fact after Peter McKnight finished explaining the situation to him, and the Chief of Staff nodded.

"She's getting ignored by quite a few of the members, but she's still the leader of the group. Which is surprising, because Bennington knows we're on Defense Command's side," McKnight said. "But I suppose she thinks there's nothing we can do."

Marshal took a deep breath and nodded. He was a strong supporter of the Empire Party, but he also believed that the military had no business interfering in the operations of government. That said, meeting with MPs and talking to them about the choice they were about to make... speaking to them as a respected friend and colleague, and without coercion... that would be acceptable.

Perhaps even crucial.

He knew what damage the Emperor could do if he was able to claw back some of his powers. If Marshal could find a way to stop this move, he would.

"You have a ship booked for the flight back?" the Commodore asked after a moment's pause, and McKnight shook his head.

"There wasn't time."

Nodding, Marshal sat back in his seat, "I'm going to talk to Mel at dinner. We'll try to leave tonight, and you can come with us if you like."

Smiling with genuine relief, Peter McKnight nodded, "I'm ready to go. I'll be at the Barrett until then."

That was it: Marshal Samuels was going to Earth. The government had to be saved from itself.

Plans for a nice dinner that evening in the Samuels household didn't work out. Marshal was leaning against the counter in the kitchen, sipping a cup of coffee when Melissa came through the door.

After the usual clatter of shoes coming off and keys being dropped, she called from the porch down to the kitchen, "You get passage booked to Earth?"

Marshal's first reaction was one of understandable surprise — how had she known? But then, of course, his wife was one of DCI's elite, so it was only natural that she knew. She might even have more information than he did, but they could talk about that on the way.

"We go aboard *Hikawa Maru* at 2100. Straight run to Earth at high speed, should be there in about six days."

"Think that'll be fast enough?" Mel started opening the hall closet to check to make sure that her coats and boots — not well-used in Belt Two's controlled climate, but necessary for a trip to Capital Island — were ready to be packed.

"Hope so," Marshal called back.

Wasn't much more he could do than hope — it would take time for a confidence motion to be prepared, and presumably Leslie Cavanaugh wouldn't have sent her warning too late for it to do any good...

"I'm going to go pack. Can you get supper started?" Mel called down the hall again, and Marshal smiled.

"Already on," he said, and then to confirm, the quick-cooker binged behind him. "Ready now, actually."

"Good timing!" Mel replied, and came to the kitchen so they could wolf down supper.

Then it was packing, and preparing to take an inconspicuous and unannounced vacation to Earth.

Captain Fiona Kellerman was shopping when she got the call.

This, for some reason, strikes me as comical — of all the places we might think of where a Captain could be when she's interrupted with important business, a shopping trip isn't among the most common.

But that's where she was — in the shoe section at a major Belt Two department store, looking at the latest arrivals. Quite a few new shoes had come in lately, owing to the end of hostilities, so now she was catching up on styles and deciding which ones she preferred.

In the middle of sliding her foot into a new brown thing (sorry, I'm as much of a shoe expert as I am a gymnastics expert) her comm beeped on her hip. Pausing with a frown, she tugged it out of its holster and keyed it on, "Kellerman."

There was a pause, then Marshal's voice: "Sorry to bother you after hours, Fiona, but Mel and I are heading to Earth... leaving tonight at 2100."

That certainly wasn't what she'd expected to hear, so she frowned, "Um... alright, sir. This to do with that cup of coffee you had earlier?"

Being a sharp officer, Fiona wasn't about to mention McKnight's name in public.

"Yes it is," Marshal answered. "I'll send orders transferring command of the Belt Station to you until I return... or someone else returns in my place. Sorry to leave it all on your shoulders."

Fiona's frown deepened, and she sat back on the shoe-fitting bench, "Not to worry, sir... you *will* be coming back, right?"

Another pause, and then Marshal chuckled, "Depending on how this vacation goes, I may not be in the service much longer."

Nothing like ending on an ominous note — well done Marshal. Fiona lowered her comm slightly, then raised it again, "I see. Good luck, sir."

"Thanks, Fiona."

The line cut, and Fiona sat there for a couple of moments, not really sure what she should think. Eventually, she returned her comm to its holster and attempted to turn her attention back to the shoes she was trying on, but that didn't work. Her thought processes had been derailed… she was suddenly the senior officer on Belt Two, and the commander of the Belt Station.

That was all a very big deal… but it somehow seemed irrelevant. Whatever Marshal Samuels was returning to Earth for sounded serious indeed.

Obviously, it was.

Peter McKnight was waiting with his attaché case in the boarding lounge for *Hikawa Maru* when Mel and Marshal arrived, each with a small suitcase.

Raising his hand in a wave, the Chief of Staff approached the pair, "Glad you could book the passage so quickly."

Marshal nodded, "I know the master of *Hikawa* pretty well… he was happy to have us."

McKnight smiled, then turned to Mel with an extended hand, "Nice to see you as well, Melissa."

They'd met at some social functions on Belt Two over the past couple of years, so McKnight was familiar with Melissa Samuels. He didn't know, of course, that she was with DCI — as much as I casually throw that fact around now, back then it was highly top secret.

Playing her part, Mel smiled and shook McKnight's hand, "Yes… I still don't know why we're going. But Marshal says it's important."

She sold that very well — but then, she always had the ability to make a lie come across as truth. That's why she was so good at her job.

"We better get aboard," Marshal preempted any further conversation along these lines, and gestured in the direction of the chute up to *Hikawa Maru*. McKnight nodded, then stepped aside and waved that way.

"Ladies first," he said.

Proper gentleman was this Chief of Staff, and with a smile and a funny little half-nod, half-curtsy, Mel led the way. She alone of the trio noticed Camila Barrai boarding the ship ahead of them. There'd been no time to officially inform Barrai of this departure, but being another wily DCI veteran, the Argentinean had naturally figured it out on her own.

So four people were bound for Earth aboard the liner *Hikawa Maru*.

When Fiona Kellerman got to her apartment and logged into her mailbox, she found the orders Marshal had promised: she was officially in command in his absence. Had she been a shallower sort of person, she would have delighted at what this meant for her career — she'd already scaled the rank ladder to Captain much faster than many other officers in the fleet, owing to Marshal's need for an effective officer of her caliber assisting at the higher levels of the convoy system.

Now she was commanding Belt Two base, and the Belt Station, at the ripe age of twenty-seven. That, needless to say, was a feat.

Of course, no matter how good an officer she happened to be, I'd always remember her as the one who denied us pudding. At this moment, I'm having difficulty recalling exactly when she did that… *The Gallant Few*, probably… but I hold a pudding grudge.

She knows it. I know it.

And you don't care, so I'll move on…

After checking her orders, she returned to her inbox, and there she found two encoded messages. She frowned at them, and then saw that they'd been forwarded to her by Marshal. One was addressed to Rear Admiral Ken Barron (hey, that's me!) and the other to First Lord John Fiora. Both were to be uploaded to *Wolf* when we did our next comm check-in.

They were *not* to be sent by any other means.

Frowning at those very specific sending instructions, Fiona wondered what Marshal's concern was. She'd gotten quite good at predicting his intentions over the past couple of years — that's one of the reasons they made a good command team — but this didn't seem logical.

The message to *Wolf*, sure, should wait — it was easier for us to call Belt Two than it was for them to try to align a signal laser to hit Egesta, a rock they didn't have regular communication with.

But the message to John, who was only at Mars, could be easily sent — just fire the laser to the appropriate relaying DCC ship, and it would be passed along through pre-established coordinates to *Bonaventure*, which was even now sitting over the red planet.

Without knowing about the concerns of Caldecott's loyalists in DCC possibly handing signal traffic to the Emperor, the orders seemed inefficient. But Fiona trusted that Marshal hadn't lost his mind, so she did as she was told; she moved the two messages from her inbox into a priority encrypted file in the waiting cue for *Wolf's* next check in.

Word would be spread, just the way Marshal prescribed.

Dropping her bag on the bed of the VIP stateroom in *Hikawa Maru's* forward section, Melissa Marshal put on a relaxed smile, then turned and nodded to the ship's master.

Stanley Liebovitz was a relatively young skipper, and he ran *Hikawa* very well. He and Marshal had interacted a number of times, and now he was only too happy to help the Commodore get to Earth in a speedy fashion.

"I hope nothing too serious is calling you back," Liebovitz said with a smile as Marshal shook his hand.

"Just some business," our Commodore Samuels confirmed, not exactly lying. He trusted Liebovitz, of course, but there was no point openly airing the political problems of the Empire just yet. There was still a good chance Bennington's whole plan would never be attempted. "Just get us there as fast as you can."

Grinning, Liebovitz released Marshal's hand, "That's what we do. I'll leave you two to get settled in. If you need anything, just call the Steward. He hasn't had many VIPs aboard in the past two years, so he'll be happy to have someone to dote on. Join me for dinner?"

Marshal glanced back at Melissa, then returned his gaze to Liebovitz, "We're both tired tonight. Dinner tomorrow?"

"Of course," the master nodded. "Good evening to you both!"

With that, the skipper left his esteemed guests, and as the door closed Mel instantly pulled out a hand scanner, something that I still can't completely describe for good old [square brackets security reasons], but which quickly told her that they probably weren't being bugged in this cabin.

It wasn't a guarantee, but considering the last-minute booking and the fact that none of the usual surveillance technologies could be detected in the room, they felt relatively free to speak.

"He's very nice," Mel observed about Liebovitz, and Marshal replied with a nod.

"We were lucky we could make his flight. We'll get to Earth fast…"

Nodding, Melissa sat on the end of the bed, then reached into her shirt pocket and produced a disk. Marshal was turned away from her, arms folded as he paced and thought about this mission.

"I just hope I can get through to the caucus. I know a number of them pretty well, but that might not be enough to convince them not to back Bennington. She's got a lot of influence… and now that the war's over, I'm sort of yesterday's man. They don't need me to keep their convoys safe anymore. And politicians can have short memories…"

His voice trailed off, and he shook his head. There was no guarantee that he could truly get through to any of the MPs Leslie Cavanaugh believed he could sway…

But, obviously, he was going to try.

As his eyes returned to his wife, he frowned, "What disk is that?"

Mel was staring at it as she turned it around in her fingers, and then she looked up at her husband, "Remember, back during Glorious February, Haley Briand came to see me, just before going out to the Solar Asteroid Union and vanishing?"

Marshal approached his wife with a frown, "I think so."

"This is what she left with me. In case the Emperor ever tried to make a play against Defense Command."

Sitting beside his wife, Marshal examined the innocuous-seeming disk with a frown, "She thought it would help?"

Nodding, Mel lowered it, "She did. I haven't looked at it. But we might need it."

"We'll have to remember it for later," Marshal agreed.

Appropriately, because it's that disk that I kept telling you to remember for later. From before Haley Briand went off and did other things that you'll have to remember even later than now.

Marshal Samuels and Melissa Samuels were on their way to Earth, ready to try to stop a political disaster that could eventually hand the Empire back to the Emperor.

Having established all that, we can now go back to Egesta, which I'm sure we're all excited to do, to see how the news hit us after our next comm check with Belt Two.

CHAPTER TWELVE

SERVING A PURPOSE

Apparently, I had fallen asleep in my chair. This was a bit of a turnabout — Karen was often the one who nodded off, or at least that's how I remember it. But now I woke with her nudging me gently.

"Bridge calling," she explained as I snapped awake, and I frowned and tried to shake my mind into coherence before looking at the chrono.

It was 0041 — just after midnight — so it probably wasn't much of a surprise that I'd drifted off. It was much more of a surprise, though, that I was getting a call from the bridge at this hour. Something serious had to be happening...

Reaching down to the floor beside my chair, I picked up the remote, fumbled with it for a moment, then opened the call. Jim Hannigan had the watch on this particular night, so he appeared. He was standing in Andrea's day cabin for the call — I suppose he didn't want to show my cabin off on a bridge screen.

"Just did our nightly comm check-in with Belt Two," he began immediately, knowing that even half-dazed, enough of my brain would be functioning to allow me to process his words.

I digested them for a second, and then my frown deepened. When floating around Egesta, one didn't expect to be awakened in the middle of the night with a call from Belt Two. What could possibly be happening there that was serious enough to warrant a special warning...

"Are the peace talks breaking down?" Karen managed to come to that question before I did, and I stiffened at the prospect.

If the war started up again... I just... none of us would respond well to that turn of events. We were done with the war. We were done with the Martians. They had better not be trying...

"Worse."

Jim's reply left me even more confused. I was tired, and still waking up, so cut me some slack on that one. What could be worse than the Martians flaring up again?

"Marshal Samuels and his wife are on their way to Earth, and he left a message for you," Jim continued. "I haven't read it, obviously, but the fact that he's on his way back..."

Earth?

Something was happening on Earth?

The Emperor.

Of course. The man who we hoped would be discredited for the horror of Egesta must be trying something.

"Alright Jim... can you wake up Matt and Wes, and get Andrea up here too. We should probably all find out what's going on immediately."

Nodding, *Wolf's* XO reached off-screen to deactivate the feed, "I'll get them into the briefing room immediately."

"Thanks."

With that, the line cut, and I huffed. I was tired, I was orbiting Egesta, and now the Emperor was probably up to something.

Glancing at Karen, I found her playing with the end of her ponytail, studying the hairs there with undue intensity.

This was delightful — the Emperor was probably forcing our timeline...

It's not often you could get a group of Belt Squadron veterans together into a room and call them all disreputable-looking, but tonight our elite group... even Karen... appeared rather out of sorts.

Matt Baxter was suffering with his damned migraine — it still hadn't broken — while Wes was clearly perturbed about something (we didn't know about his confrontation with Andrea), and Andrea was back to seeming isolated and cold. I can only assume I looked like a guy who'd just been woken up after falling asleep in his chair.

None of us were actually complaining about being awake and present, but we were all far less positive than was our norm.

Once we settled in, I didn't wait around: I loaded up Marshal's message on the briefing room's main screen, then hit play.

I'll only transcribe a segment here: "Hi Ken. Just had a visit from Peter McKnight, who is Chief of Staff for Leslie Cavanaugh. Apparently the Emperor has struck a deal with Bennington to bring down the government. She's going to have her faction of the Empire Party sit on their hands for a confidence vote, while Pope and Macdonald are still away. Cavanaugh has asked me to come back to try to talk the Belt caucus out of this... I might be able to, but if there's anything you have that can help us discredit the Emperor, we need it at Earth as soon as possible...

"Oh, and you can't trust any DCC comm ships. I haven't been able to alert First Lord Fiora at Mars because we can't get a direct signal to him. It seems DCI and the MPs are convinced that Dave Caldecott's people are controlling the communications side. Apparently a lot of cronies were dumped there to keep them out of the way during the war. Now, there's a chance anything we send through regular channels will end up in the Emperor's hands. So if you can get a direct message to *Bonaventure*, they need to be warned."

He went on to fill in more of the context, all of which I explained to you in the last chapter. I can say honestly that the report did nothing to improve the moods of the people in the room.

When Marshal's warnings finished, and he wished us good luck, we all sat silent in the room for a few minutes, digesting everything that had been said. We needed to figure out what our role in the coming attempted coup would be.

"That bitch Bennington," Karen surprised me with her forthright spite for the Deputy PM. "Didn't trust her when she was running for leadership... guess I was right."

She certainly was.

"We'll need to get the evidence about the army's actions here back to Earth immediately," Wes' tone was dark, and he leaned forward, lacing his fingers together on the desk in front of him. "The evidence… the prisoners… if we can get there and have enough to start a trial as soon as we arrive…"

I began to nod; the Emperor would have a tough time arguing that Defense Command was being too cavalier when people saw some of the vids we'd collected, both from Bunny Fox's footage and from some of the trophy recordings the blockheads had made of their crimes.

Not to mention the prisoners.

"Will they be able to call the vote while the PM is still out at Mars… and the Emperor, for that matter?" Andrea asked cooly.

I was rusty on Parliamentary procedure, but apparently Matt wasn't, "They can call it. It's up to the Government House Leader to set the date of the vote… and that'll be Hector Ling, one of Bennington's people. So yes, they can have the vote while the PM is away. And the Emperor doesn't need to preside over it. The Governor General can do that."

"Could the House be prorogued… if they shut down the session…" Karen began thinking out loud, but Matt continued to impress — and disappoint — with his knowledge.

"Governor General has to approve any prorogation. And Bennington would have to ask. Safe bet neither will happen."

By now I was rubbing my head. I hated politics. Still do. Don't get me wrong, I think government is a true calling — leading people is an important responsibility. But politics, the games that are played as people vie for leadership, I hate desperately. I expect many of you do too.

Such useless bullshit… Pope was a good PM, and Macdonald was a good Foreign Minister. We had been fortunate when Bennington and her faction of narcissists had been defeated by him in the race for leadership of the Empire Party… but now, because both men had decided to do what was right, and had gone to Mars to make sure the Emperor didn't ruin the peace… now their government was vulnerable.

For years, their strong personalities had held the great Empire Party together, despite the deep rifts within it. While they were both on Capital Island, they could browbeat and intimidate some softer MPs into toeing the line… but when they were away, it was much easier for Bennington to bring those weak-kneed traitors around to her side.

"So we have to get back there, and use our evidence to discredit the faction that Bennington is trying to align with," Karen concluded, flopping back in her chair and dancing her fingers across the tabletop before her.

"Make it political suicide for anyone to side with Emperor," I agreed.

"We also need to make sure John knows, and the PM," Wes added. "And we can't leave Egesta to its own devices either."

He had that right. Just because our government was trying to eat itself didn't mean we could pull up sticks and run from the mess we'd been dealing with for this entire book. The Empire could survive a political crisis without blood running through the streets (we hoped) but any hint of chaos on Egesta would likely just restart the cycle of death and chaos.

We weren't going to let that happen again.

"We can leave Zail and Colonel Ronald to maintain the situation here…" I began thinking aloud about our predicament, my tired mind trying to turn tactical again. It took more effort than it should have. "We need to get a ship into direct line of sight with Mars to get a call to *Bonaventure*… maybe even bring some evidence directly to John and the PM…"

A few prisoners for the First Lord and the PM to interrogate might prove useful…

"And then obviously we need to get word and evidence home to Earth," I concluded the summary on that point, and as I fell silent, everyone at the table brooded.

I spent that moment thinking about who to send where. It was unlikely that our return to Earth would be contested this time; unlike the situation we found in *The Almost Coup*, Defense Command wasn't full of Caldecott cronies anymore. Or, at least, the fleet wasn't. The disadvantage was that they were all on DCC ships now, monitoring our messages… but from there, they couldn't try to shoot us if we entered orbital space, the way the Light Squadron under George Parks-Dawes previously attempted.

So did we send one ship home, one to Mars, and leave one with *Artemis Agrotera*, to continue monitoring Egesta? Or should we take a larger force home, in case additional support was needed?

"I can take evidence to Mars."

I was surprised to hear that suggestion from Wes, but it certainly wasn't unwelcome. Looking across the table at my friend and counterpart, I think I frowned, "You sure?"

"The Emperor's behind this, so I should be in position to help John with him. You get the prisoners and the evidence home. I was never any good at storming the Geraldine Coilier Show anyway," he explained, and with those wry last words I managed a grim chuckle.

I doubted strongly that we'd have the chance to use that particular platform for our evidence a second time… as soon as we arrived in Earth orbit, blockheads would probably shut down the studio.

"I can stay here, or come with you," Matt now took his turn, his words still quite uncomfortable — his migraine was really slaying him.

Leaving him and *Friendly* at Egesta would provide an extra layer of protection to Colonel Ronald and his mission, but would it be better to have his help on Earth? Half-hopeful expectations aside, I had no real idea of what to expect when we got home… but by process of elimination, it was inevitably Karen and I who'd be going, and that probably made the most sense anyway…

For Matt Baxter, then: stay or go?

"I think it's important we keep a presence here," Karen came to her conclusion first, and as ever, it was a good one. "I don't think we can afford to take any more chances with the wellbeing of these people… Plus, the fact that we're keeping two ships and a battalion here will be a clear signal that it's a serious situation, and that we're treating it as such."

There was, indeed, a political dimension to keeping our forces at Egesta. If we all packed up and went back to Earth with our 'gotcha' evidence, but didn't care about those we'd left in turmoil, that wouldn't exactly seem right, would it?

No, it wouldn't, seeing as it'd be *wrong*.

So there were a couple of good reasons to leave Matt here, and even though the place gave him migraines, the elite Commander Baxter knew his presence would be essential.

That in mind, he nodded, "Very well then."

With that, I needed only look to Andrea, then Karen, and both women nodded. Andrea then spoke darkly — the way she'd been speaking before our return to this hellish rock, "We'll head for Earth?"

I nodded, "Get Andy to start warming the reactors. As soon as we get everyone and everything we need aboard, we'll boost hard."

Andrea came to her feet as I said that, "I'll wake him now and begin the preparations."

Then she nodded to Matt, and left the room.

At that point, I didn't notice that she and Wes had made no eye contact. It didn't seem relevant… and to be fair, in the grand scheme of things, it really *wasn't* relevant. Turning my chair back to Matt and Wes, I sighed.

"So, are we in the frying pan or the fire now?" I asked with grim humor.

Wes cocked an eyebrow, "We're in a place so bad it defies metaphors."

He wasn't wrong.

"In that case…" I rose from my chair, and everyone else in the room did the same, "… good luck Wes, Matt."

I stuck out my hand to my friend Commodore Pellew, and he took it. Then Matt did as well. We all knew what had to be done — one of us to stay at Egesta, one to warn the Prime Minister and see what could be done about the Emperor, and one to go home, and fight against a Parliamentary takeover…

Karen then shook Matt's hand, and Wes' hand, and without pause, our exhausted comrades headed out of the briefing room.

As the door shut behind them, Karen sat down on the edge of the table, folded her arms and looked at me, "Think we'll be able to get there in time?"

It was the question none of us had wanted to ask, because we didn't have any idea about the answer. How far along was Bennington's plan? We were six-and-a-half days away from Earth at maximum cruising speed… would we reach Capital Island after everything had gone to pieces?

"Well, if we're not in time, I expect we'll be arrested on arrival. Or something like that," I said distantly, and stared at a patch of wall for a moment in exhausted thought before glancing back at Karen.

I thought I saw some of the old anger in her eyes, and then she confirmed my observations with hard words, "They'd start a civil war if they tried to arrest us. They have to know they'd lose it."

We'd been much more sporting during *The Almost Coup* at the start of the war… back then, it had been a battle between the Fiora Ring and the Caldecott Circle.

Now… now it was a self-righteous Emperor trying to discredit and destroy the officers and spacers who had just protected the Empire through the biggest war in the history of the solar system.

So we had a lot less tolerance in 2234 than we did in 2231.

What that would mean for the Earth… we'd just have to wait and see.

After a few more minutes, Karen and I headed to the bridge, and began sending more orders that would allow us to boost.

Chapter Thirteen
Something To Remember For Next Year

As we get closer to 2235, I can be somewhat less ominous with these chapters detailing things that will be important 'later'. Here's another one, and while it may again be a bit jarring to leave the central narrative of the book, I think it's important to touch on this.

Because, as we were deciding who was going to go where, someone else was deciding who else to send where.

Sorry, I think that sentence failed. But suffice to say, someone with a whole other plan involving the Empire was giving marching orders, and those orders were going to prove significant in 2235.

This person was on Etat Valcour, one of the rock-states of the Solar Asteroid Union… and the reason we know he was making moves is simple: Haley Briand had infiltrated his office. I suppose I should be more coy about that, but let's be honest, most people figured it out after I dropped her name back in *The Forge Fires*.

Remember, there was a young and awfully superagent-like girl going by Julie Pichot, who was reportedly a refugee from the Forge, and who was looking for a new life of opportunity in the Union? She visited the office of Miss Sonia Hart on *Venus Three*… Hart, who apparently worked for the Governor of Etat Valcour?

Well, thanks to all of that ominous hinting, we had eyes in the Governor's Office on Valcour — including bugs so advanced that the bastard's anti-surveillance sweeps couldn't detect them. These bugs weren't perfect, and as a result of some things I'll get into next year, we only have fragments of what they recorded… but we got enough.

Enough to recount the scene that makes up this chapter.

Young Julie Pichot had been taken under Sonia Hart's wing. This is a skill superagents have — they can endear themselves to others, and also take opportunities to get close to power, all while seeming naïve and wide-eyed. As an assistant to an assistant, Julie got to see a few things that were sensitive now and then, but she was careful never to go out of her way to see important documents. Showing such an interest was a sure way to arouse suspicion.

So, in the many months since the fall of the Forge, Julie had become Hart's reliable helper, and that was a very good place to be… because Hart had returned to Etat Valcour, and was now working in the Governor's Office. Actually, strictly speaking, she was working in the office next door, but that doesn't matter.

It was from her desk outside Hart's office that Julie heard of the situation that was building in the Empire, because through connections I'll explain next year, the Governor of Etat Valcour was also able to get the latest news from our comm grid… and now he was making careful plans for all contingencies.

Plans that required Sonia Hart to put things into motion… and when Hart needed to put things into motion, Julie was the worker who tended to push the buttons and make the calls.

"We need to get a hold of these four people..." Hart perched on the end of Julie's desk, delivering those orders as she laid a pad in front of her assistant.

Frowning, Julie reviewed the names and faces displayed on the pad, "I don't recognize any of them."

Hart chuckled, "That's good. They're fixers, you're not supposed to recognize them. They'll be based on Etat Concord."

Julie knew about Etat Concord; that was the Union member asteroid with the massive shipyards — the one where the *Tharsis*-class battleships had been constructed. It was the only rock in the Union that had somewhat regular contact with outside governments, so that made it a likely base for 'fixers'. They would have anonymity and protection from the Union of Solar Asteroids, as well as the ability to hop a ship to the Empire or the Imperium.

Julie suspected that such fixers had already been out at least once — back in 2232 — and she later wrote that hunch down in a confidential place... but she still had no proof. Now wasn't the time to probe, either: Miss Hart was telling her to get in touch with these fixers, and that's just what she'd do.

"Should I tell them anything in particular when I get a hold of them?" Julie asked the correct question, and Hart shook her head.

"Just tell them to come here. The Empire won the war, but it appears that our hopes are coming true anyway... the Emperor might be trying to seize control of Parliament."

Because Julie's fictional backstory (the spy term is apparently 'legend') held that she'd been an Imperial citizen living on the Forge, she could allow herself to look shocked at the implication. Obviously, it was no surprise to her — just as it wasn't a surprise to Hart. In their own way, each of these women had been given reason to expect a play from Luther Gregory III.

"So, we need them... to observe that?" Making sure to sound a tad confused, Julie pushed a little bit farther for information.

The question drew a smile from Miss Sonia Hart, and with a shaking head, she stood up and started to move away from the desk, "No, we'll need them for a different purpose."

It was cryptic and menacing, but there was nothing more our young superagent could ask to get clarification. Instead, she studied the four faces of the people she was to contact — the two men and two women displayed on the pad.

The first was named Angelo Connaught, and he looked like a perfectly ordinary bearded man, with kind eyes. Probably meant he was some sort of killer.

Next to him was Sylvia Connaught, who didn't look anything like him, so was likely his wife. She had dark hair but bright blue eyes... probably another killer.

Ludwig Grenfell was the third person, and he was quite young — perhaps only in his mid-twenties, presuming the picture was current. He also had that approachable look that made her imagine him as a bringer of death.

The last person was definitely a killer too: Dejana Soeur, who had a look of competent menace that Julie Pichot recognized — it was a look she saw at the office holiday parties back at DCI. People like Melissa Samuels had it.

What did the Governor of Etat Valcour want with these four? And what work had he given them before? There was no way to know, but Julie had a feeling that sometime in the not-too-distant future (or, say, in the next year), they'd turn up and trigger something significant.

For now, there was nothing she could do, so she started the process of sending confidential messages to Etat Concord, to get these people to come to Valcour.

Returning to her own desk, Sonia Hart thought about the four names she'd provided to her young assistant. Unlike Julie, Sonia knew exactly what those four had been up to in recent years — as Julie was doing now, she'd helped orchestrate some of those past operations.

That the Governor was certain he could send them into the Empire and get the outcome he wanted was... ambitious. But then, the complex plans of the man with whom Sonia Hart now spent her nights had carried him from darkest defeat to the leadership of one of the Union of Solar Asteroid's most powerful colonies.

There was no question he was bound to become President soon, and these four fixers would help. Because even though the Martians had failed — in spite of the *Tharsis*-class battleships that the Union had helped build — the Empire could still play its part...

It was so complicated, it hurt Sonia Hart's head. She wondered again what she'd gotten herself into — what she'd been thinking when, after Egesta, she'd decided to make this trip into the unknown reaches of the solar system. What she'd been thinking when she'd decided to get so close to a man whose name she'd heard before, and who she knew could only be dangerous to be around. He'd been terribly wounded by a woman once — a woman who'd always been just out of his reach, right up until the moment she'd betrayed him and destroyed him.

Sonia knew the Governor's stare was always on her — he was always suspicious. But hopefully by now he realized that she could be trusted... that she wasn't going to try to sabotage his plan.

Why would she? If it worked, it would bring everything to him that he deserved, and that was coincidentally what she wanted. Whether it would turn out to his advantage... that was for them to discover together.

But it would be dangerous. Very very dangerous. Because if it all worked, she expected that what remained of the Empire would be quite angry, and willing to go to great lengths to get revenge.

Great risk, great reward...

As those thoughts ran through Sonia Hart's head, she leaned back in her desk chair and gazed towards the ceiling. A bunch of undetectable surveillance bugs stared back at her, capturing her expression as she pondered the future.

We won't have much longer to wait to find out how right, or wrong, her predictions would be.

CHAPTER FOURTEEN

SCATTERING

"Don't shoot the Emperor when you see him," I suppose I said that as a joke, but both Wes Pellew and I were in the sorts of moods that meant it was good general advice.

I was sitting on the end of my bed in my cabin, and Wes was in the same spot in his quarters aboard *Nova Scotia*. Both his ship and *Wolf* were about to leave Egesta, and before we headed to our respective bridges to oversee the departure, we wanted to talk about what was ahead one last time.

"I'll keep a wrench handy," Wes answered dryly, then shook his head. "If things get bad on Earth, you're going to have to send warning through a comm ship. We'll need some code words in that case."

That was a very good thought — one that hadn't occurred to me. Usually I resist things like 'code words' because, under most circumstances, they're campy, daft and only serve to confuse things further.

Now, however, they could prove highly significant.

"If Bennington's plan is going ahead and there's no way within the political process to stop it, I'll say... I'll mention the time you were served intercooler fluid instead of coffee in the pub on Belt Nine," I recalled that story — which I think I mentioned back in *The Forge Fires*, when Wes, Mik and I were in that bar — as a good option for our code.

Wes chuckled, "Yeah, okay. And if you find that the Emperor is doing something outside of the political process that means we can legally depose him, mention the fish in your orange juice."

"Good. Fish means you can catch the bastard... I suppose that makes a certain kind of sense. And if everything's taken care of, then I suppose we can just speak openly, because it won't matter if Caldecott's minions hear it," I concluded, and Wes replied with another nod.

We sat silent for a moment after that, both wondering what exactly we'd find when we got to our respective destinations. Because of transit times, Karen and I would reach Earth first, so undoubtedly we'd be the first to experience the joys if Bennington's plan succeeded. In that case, Wes would find himself in a very difficult situation when he arrived at Mars...

If Bennington's plan was thwarted, though, things would be reversed, and instead of facing the chaos of an Emperor in a self-righteous mood, the Independent Squadron's Commodore would be in place to help put the bastard in irons...

Or whatever would happen to Luther Gregory III. Actual chains weren't likely, I knew, but it was still satisfying to imagine.

"Well, nothing like getting mixed up in another power struggle," I finally broke the silence with those words, and Wes shrugged.

"I was doing just fine without having to deal with those. Hopefully there aren't too many more."

"Peace would be nice," I agreed.

There wasn't much more time before our departure, so we both decided to conclude our conversation simultaneously, "Good luck with the Emperor, my friend."

"Good luck with Parliament," he replied.

It was as much as we needed to say; Wes cut the link, and after a moment's pause, I took a deep breath and headed for the bridge.

By the time I stepped through the bridge hatch, preparations for departure were almost complete.

"Ready to break away from the chute," Shelby McLaws was back at her post, and as ever, our Helm and Navigation Officer projected a genteel air of confidence as she reported *Wolf's* status. I suppose I noticed that confidence more at this point because it was a refreshing change from recent days on Egesta — she was making a particular effort to put the harder things out of her mind.

"All hands ready to cruise," Jim Hannigan added his report from Operations, and again, his tone was crisp and even.

Our veteran men and women had not been left unmarked by Egesta. But they weren't going to fall down now that the Emperor was making his move. They all knew what was going on — rumors spread fast — but now, as I moved up to the front of the deck and took my place beside Karen and Andrea, I decided to officially fill everyone in.

"Felicia, shipwide intercom please," I nodded to our Sensors and Communications Officer, and she passed the command on to the appropriate technician. The Battlelink viewfinder at the front of the bridge centered on me, so my words could be passed along to all hands aboard *Wolf*.

"I know most of you will already know exactly where we're going, and why. Some of you probably even know more than I do about our mission. If you're one of those people, please stop by to tell me what the hell the Emperor thinks he's doing... but just to make it official: we're going to Earth, with all possible speed. The Emperor is playing political games to try to bring down the government, and our old friend Marshal Samuels has gone ahead to try to talk some Parliamentarians out of falling for his trick. Our job is to get there, and to make sure the whole world... the whole *Empire*... knows what Luther Gregory's loyal infantry did on Egesta. I think folks will have a hard time buying any of the Emperor's arguments after they see what his personal troops get up to. So batten down everything. We're going fast and hard, and when we get to Earth, we don't know what we'll find. That's all for now."

Felicia cut the intercom link with that conclusion, and I took a breath and folded my arms.

My editors pointed out to me that this address was pretty unusual — that I didn't often speak directly to the entire crew. I told these editors they were wrong, of course, but then discovered they weren't. This is, as far as I can tell, the first time I'd gone on shipwide with my crew, since the start of this series.

I used to do it much more often as a Captain, but I'd decided that as Commodore and then Rear Admiral, it wasn't my place — Karen and then Andrea were supposed to make these announcements to *Wolf's* women and men.

But this time I forgot my place... and neither Andrea nor Karen blamed me for jumping the gun. We were about to cruise into a possible coup, so it was probably for the best that the Rear Admiral (who was most likely to end up on the gallows if everything went totally wrong) was the one who explained the mission.

"Nice speech," Karen smiled and nudged me with her elbow. It was good to see that smile — even though we were both tired, and we were just off Egesta, and we were heading towards a political crisis, she could still smile.

Insert your own goddess comparison here.

Standing on Karen's other side, I could see the darker mood that had resumed control over Andrea's expression wasn't just because of the late-night meeting. That is to say, she was looking dire again, the way she had before our return to Egesta. Leaving the place was actually difficult for her, but she wasn't complaining. Of *course* she wasn't complaining.

"Good luck out there, don't do anything too stupid."

I hadn't been ready for Matt Baxter's farewell, but as he gave it I looked up and saw that he was on realtime comm, projected into screen three.

Smiling, I glanced at Karen and then back up to him, "You better start worrying now. Don't think we'll have any other choice."

"God, my head hurts enough as it is," he grumbled, and then sobered. "If it goes badly, don't let them arrest you. Come back here, and we'll sort it out."

That was the first comment I'd heard since Marshal's warning that truly drove home the potential gravity of this situation. Because Matt was right: if this all went poorly, and Parliament was turned over to the Emperor's faction, many Defense Command officers — many supposed heroes — could find themselves under arrest, and going before drumhead trials.

Due process probably wouldn't matter, either — the Emperor and the Governor General would likely push for rapid convictions under whatever bogus legislation they passed with their new government.

It really could get that bad. It didn't seem likely, but it *could*. And if it did, Matt was pointing out that we could make our escape, rally with our loyal ships, and take severe action.

As that understanding settled in, my good humor dimmed, "Hopefully it won't come to that. But thanks, Matt."

He nodded, and then he cut the link from *Friendly*.

Moments later, with a nod to Shelby McLaws, Andrea ordered *Wolf* away from Egesta. As soon as we were clear of the docking chute, we turned and burned for Earth, making 198 kps.

CHAPTER FIFTEEN

SO, BACK TO CHAPTER ONE

We began this book with me sitting across the table from Brigadier General Howard Pedro Azuma, the monster of Egesta. It was the day after we left the rock that Karen and I decided to interrogate this man, to see if anything he said could be used in a quick and expedient fashion against the Emperor. We had plenty of damning evidence, but we figured it could only help if we found more.

Now, you know how our meeting with the good Brigadier ended, but not how it began — not why Karen stormed out. So here you go, the rest of that scene.

As Karen and I arrived in the observation chamber outside the interrogation room, Eugene Sengooba greeted us with a neutral expression, "Ready to speak to him, sir, ma'am?"

Eugene was being painfully polite with that question. Wes had never followed up with him about those prisoners who'd ended up in the morgue, and without Commodore Pellew's information, he wasn't going to bring it up with Andrea... but now he was concerned with what might happen if any of his officers got a bit too angry with prisoners around.

It was, of course, a fair sensitivity to have considering the circumstances.

At the time, I didn't read that deeply into Eugene's question, though, and I simply nodded, "We are. You don't need to stay for this, Eugene. We won't need any backup."

Having talked to him about Andrea's situation since, I now better understand why he looked a bit uncomfortable with my suggestion.

"It'll be fine, Gene," Karen added with a reserved smile, and after a moment of reflection, our Master-At-Arms decided to trust us. After all, we weren't in quite the same situation as Andrea Kiley had been.

Karen and I waited as Eugene left the observation chamber, and then we both peered through the glass at Azuma. He was, of course, confined to his chair... a polite way of saying he was chained to the desk and floor. And he looked as haughty and defiant as before.

"He still doesn't believe he did anything wrong," Karen observed darkly.

"Probably not," I agreed. "Let's explain it to him."

We should have talked explicitly about how we'd handle it if either of us lost our cool with this bastard, but we didn't. A little overconfidence, perhaps... no. Honestly, I think we were both just afraid that if we spoke about what to do if things got out of hand, we'd realize how easy it would be for us to lose our grip, and thus decide not to go in at all.

We were going in. We were going to talk to this bastard.

As we went through the door into the interrogation room, Azuma greeted us with a sneer, "Here they are, the hypocritical Defcoms."

Karen gestured for me to take the chair opposite Azuma, while she folded her arms and remained standing. She never liked to sit down when interrogating people.

"Hypocrites. He starts by calling us hypocrites," I began my counterstrokes immediately, glancing at Karen as I did.

She nodded, "Yes he does. And now he's going to explain his reasoning to us, and sneer the whole time because he's convinced he's going to make us realize how irrelevant or self-deceiving we are. He's got it all worked out."

We weren't exactly pulling our punches, and Azuma did seem to be thrown by our forthright approach. That's why we took it.

But he recovered, sustained by his arrogance, and leaned forward, "You want me to burn, and you want to bring down the Emperor. And the only evidence you have is how we treated some people *not* protected by the laws of the Empire."

"You declared Martial Law, which means they *were* protected under our statutes," Karen shot back.

"We'll see if that bullshit holds in court," Azuma grinned.

I didn't like to see him grin.

"Now," the bastard continued, "I've figured out what really stings you about what we did. About my orders."

Here it came. Both Karen and I knew he was going to try to get 'philosophical' on us — and I put 'philosophical' in single quotes because it's the sort of philosophy that you only ever get from petulant, self-important, dense monsters who are too stupid to live.

Sorry, that was a bit over the top.

"You're either envious, or you're afraid to admit that deep down, you both would do the same. Or something worse. Just look at the two of you, standing so proud and self-righteous. You follow the rules of Defense Command because you're afraid of what you'd become if you didn't. You're the real monsters... you can't even control yourselves, I bet. Unless you cling to your rules. I did something you *wish* you could do... I helped my men see past the rules... and that scares you, so you want me to burn."

Well. What do you say to that?

My glare was fixed on Azuma's face, and I knew I shouldn't let anything he said get to me. I knew that, and I struggled to make sure I acted in accordance with what I knew.

I should have looked at Karen, but for once I didn't notice that she was looking at me. She was trying to gauge my reaction — to see how I was holding.

I guess I didn't look like I was doing too well, because she decided to intervene, "You really think that's some sort of revelation, do you?"

I was surprised by her words, and I blinked free of my pondering as she stepped towards Azuma, arms still folded as she glared down at him.

"You think you're going to surprise us with the fact that sometimes we want to do things that the rules don't allow?" her words were hard. "You think you'd want to be in this room with us if we *didn't* abide by the standards we've created for ourselves in Defense Command? If we simply went by what was allowed in the Articles of Empire?"

Azuma was too arrogant, and arguably too 'tough', to be easily menaced, and the lack of concern on his face only served to increase Karen's growing anger, "How long do you think I could keep you alive, Howard? How long do you think you could last with a knife working inside you?"

That was the sound of a line being crossed, and I cleared my throat.

Karen stopped as she heard that subtle interruption, and then she turned and stared at me for a moment before moving back to the side of my chair.

"You just prove my point. You're monsters. You just want to kill for the fun of it, for no good reason…"

As if we didn't have a good reason.

"I don't think you'll get an argument from either of us, Brigadier," my answer came out softly, coldly. "I think you're probably right. Maybe we wish we could murder you and every one of your troops right now. But long ago, we made a decision to abide by a certain set of personal principles. And one of those principles is that we stop people like us who don't choose to abide by them. Because we know how bad they can be."

I could actually feel the anger radiating off Karen as I spoke, and Azuma sneered again, "Isn't the Empire lucky to have a couple of sociopaths appoint themselves as the protectors of all that's good."

"We're not sociopaths," I replied. "We're healthy, well-balanced individuals."

Karen then tilted her head, "Well, with selective consciences."

"Don't see how that's any different," Azuma looked up at her. "Listen to you, trying to rationalize who you are. I can see through your shit. You're cowardly little pussies who want to kill, but are too weak to do what needs to be done."

I'm biased, but I think by now, any sense of logic had flown right out of his argument. Didn't matter, though, because what came next put an end to our tag-team 'interrogation'.

Azuma looked right at Karen, "Since you're a woman, I get that you don't have the balls to act…"

I think he finished the sentence with an indictment of my manhood, but I wasn't listening, because I recognized the smile that immediately came to Karen's face. She needed to leave the room quickly, or we'd have a real mess — both literal and in terms of paperwork — to clean up.

"Karen," I only needed to say her name to get that message through to her. She really wanted to express her rage, and her buttons were being well-mashed. It was intolerable, standing there and listening to a man who'd been directly responsible for the rape of literally thousands, perhaps *tens* of thousands of women, say such a thing.

And being a goddess, with righteous anger and the ability to transfer that fury to a target through numerous physical means… well. She needed to leave the room.

She turned and stormed out, and as she did, I realized that my calm needed to remain, now more than before. Karen tended to get to a boil before I did, but when I went over the top, I tended to do so in a more clinically destructive fashion than she did.

Things we'd long ago left behind, coming back to haunt us thanks to Egesta…

I continued on with Howard Pedro Azuma for a while, and if you don't recall what was said, you just need to flip back to the start of this book. He wanted a trial by a jury of his peers. He wanted the Empire to vindicate his twisted, brutal, and wrong actions.

And he wanted Karen and me to realize we were no better than him.

We chose to prove him wrong.

Chapter Sixteen
The Corner

When Karen got stressed, she danced. Usually. Sometimes she'd find less benign ways of venting, but mostly she danced. I didn't really have a comparable solution, so after I got away from the interrogation, I went back to my cabin and got in the shower. As Karen had discovered earlier, hot water pounding down on a head was enough to dislodge grim mental pictures. Also, after being in the room with Azuma, knowing he'd at least get to trial, I felt filthy.

My editors are beginning to get nervous. Our exchange with Azuma — and Karen's whole 'selective conscience' thing — isn't making sense to them. After all the stories we've been through in this series, they're not seeing much evidence of either Karen or me being secretly evil monster people.

That's good, because speaking for myself, I'm not a secret monster person. Karen neither.

But part of the problem with starting a series of books in the middle of our careers — at the start of the Martian War instead of back in the Academy days — is that you don't get to see how we both got to be where we were by 2234. I think we all probably know at least one person in our lives whose past surprises us — who, for instance, could have ended up in a much less pleasant life, had they met different people, or made different choices.

We all probably have at least one childhood friend who turned out for the worst, made the wrong decisions, and ended up menacing the entire Empire with his evil plots and his Syndicate of Pirates... Er.

Anyway, how Karen and I came to be where we were now, as generally positive, cavalier, professional fleet officers wasn't a completely direct trip. There were some meanders near the beginning, and some stops along the way, when circumstance demanded. Some of it would probably surprise you, considering where we ended up, and that's fine.

The bottom line is that we'd gotten to a good place. The after-effects of the war... by which I mean, the people we'd lost, and the suffering we'd seen... had left us a bit sensitive and inclined towards repeating some of the meanders, but by and large, we'd chosen who we were going to be, and we were being those people.

Karen, for instance, regretted spiking Josie through the head on Pion Rock, not because it didn't need to be done — you know as well as I do there wasn't much choice — but because she'd delighted in it for just a moment. She also regretted threatening to pin that man's head to the floor in *The Mars Convention*. She'd had much less justification for violence there... but she *hadn't* done it. She'd chosen to keep to the set of values that she now cherished, and I think it's fair to say that's all any of us can do in life.

Having someone tell you that adhering to such values was a sign of weakness was frustrating — hence the hot water that I was using against my head — but it wasn't going to change anything.

I don't know if that explanation helps. My editors are still trying to fit things together, which I find sort of funny, because not only have they been reading these books for a long time, they've also been working with me for years now. I hope it makes sense to you, though, as the reader.

After about twenty minutes under the shower, I finally turned the thing off, and then stood in the dryer for a moment before grabbing my robe off the back of the bathroom door and heading out into my cabin.

Karen was lying sideways across my bed when I emerged, her feet dangling over the side and her hands up, palms covering her eyes. She heard me step into the room and let out a sigh, "Can we talk about something that isn't supposedly philosophical right now? I think if we start trying to talk about how much we've changed and how Azuma's wrong… but how we just have to overcome the stress of the war and we'll be alright again… I'm going to scream and run head first into a wall until I fall down and hurt my knee."

Well. That wasn't what I was expecting.

I stopped and stared at her with pretty much complete surprise, and she seemed to sense my reaction before she pulled her hands away from her eyes, "Seriously. All I can think about right now is my state of mind. Obsessing over how I nearly pinned that guy's head to the floor on Mars, or how I nearly went off on Azuma. And I know you'll say something reassuring like 'yes, but you didn't do either of those things, so there's nothing to worry about, you're just going to have to get used to making those choices again'. And I know you'll be right when you say it. So can we just not talk about it?"

I opened my mouth, but I really didn't know where I could go with any sort of commentary. Didn't matter, I didn't get the chance.

"And after everything we just saw on Egesta. I mean, I know in some ways it's very disrespectful to the thousands of victims there to try to get back into good spirits, but if we do nothing but brood the whole way home, we won't be honoring their memory, we'll just be damaging our effectiveness when we get there. It's more important that we make sure the people of the Empire know what's happened to them than that we feel morose on their behalf. What good does self-pity do for us, anyway? So shouldn't we just get past it for now, find some quiet and enjoy ourselves a little?"

By this time, I was actually starting to get entertained, so I feigned like I might have something to say, which seemed to set her off once more.

"I mean, I don't feel like dancing, or working out, or even going for a swim. But a good meal and I'm sure I'll figure something out. We just need to get back to our old tempo. Not obsess over trying to get back to our old selves in spite of everything. We just have to shut up and return to the routine, and that'll make the difference. Don't you think so? I think so. I think that's what we need to do, and we're going to need to be at our best and most cavalier if the Emperor's plan is going to be thwarted. So I think that's what we should do. If you do. I mean, I might be crazy here. I'm just so tired of thinking about so much heavy stuff. It's exhausting to always wonder if you're on the right track, or if you've given up on the things you believe just because you got angry."

When she trailed off that time, I knew exactly what to say — or, more precisely, what to ask: "Are you on drugs?"

Karen blinked, and looked at me, "No. I mean, I don't think so."

I nodded, then folded my arms, "I see."

She stared for a second, then sat up, propping her elbows on the bed behind her to hold herself halfway off the bed, "What's that mean? Do I seem completely crazy?"

"Well," I shrugged. "I'm standing here in a bath robe, and you're going on and on about how you want things to get back to normal, and to stop obsessing over all this 'deep stuff' that's been dominating our thoughts of late. So you're either on drugs, this is a dream, or we seriously need to get you some recreation, before you burst."

She bit her bottom lip and frowned, which — and I'm sorry I have to say this — was adorable. I've dangerously compared Karen to a cute puppy before in these books, and I have to do it again now. Because she looked like a cute puppy trying to decide something entirely too serious, and looking ADORABLE as a result.

I know, it's inappropriate to dwell on something like that, but this entire exchange was just so surreal.

"So…" she finally began to speak slowly. "I'm not wrong to want to try to get into new headspace."

"Nope."

"But I sound crazy."

"Like your brain is overloading a bit."

"I need to take my mind off it all."

"Pretty much."

She nodded again, still looking adorable.

Then she said: "I need some recreation."

I agreed: "Seems like a good place to start."

Thoughtful frown remaining, she let her back drop down to the mattress again, then folded her arms and started kicking her feet back and forth as they dangled over the side of the bed.

"Any recommendations?" she asked.

Thrusting my hands into the pockets of my bathrobe, I shrugged, "You could try knitting. I hear knitting's good."

"Hmm," she answered. "Knitting…"

After a few moments of pondering, Karen decided knitting wasn't the best option, so she chose something else, that was more obvious and convenient.

Wolf raced on towards Earth at maximum speed, and once both our heads cleared, we started to grapple with what we'd do when we confronted the Emperor's plot against the government. With some difficulty, we left the demons of Egesta behind us… or as far behind as we could. For now.

We had to win the peace. The Emperor had to fall.

Once we got to Earth.

AFTERWORD

So there we are, through our final visit to Egesta. I apologize again for not having quite the stomach to stay with the story on the rock long enough to properly recount all the details. I don't know if you'd have wanted any more, and if you do, it's all in the Archives. Fill your boots.

My editors have asked me to comment on the eventual scope of the horror — the numbers. You might know there's been much debate about the figures, and a lot of good people who helped run the Inquiry on Egesta have struggled with them. The problem, quite simply, is we don't know whether the last census data we pulled out of Egesta's central government computer is accurate, or if someone started erasing names in it to cover their tracks.

So the numbers vary. Some, like 5,000 victims, seem ridiculously low. Others, like 2.8 million, seem impossibly high. The number I tend to settle on is around 300,000. I'm not saying it's right, but between the Guild and the blockheads, between the rapes and murders, I think that's probably in the vicinity.

I wish it was less. I wish it was none.

Anyway, take that number only as my opinion. I'm not going to wade into any arguments about the quantification of horror. It's not something worth arguing over, just know that it happened. Know it and make sure it doesn't happen again.

This nightmare was, in a way, behind us now. It would play a crucial role in the book ahead, and for years afterwards we'd continue to revisit it, as the Inquiry went to work figuring out what had gone wrong, who was responsible, and why so many had died as a result.

I don't want to get into any of that now, though — obviously, the Inquiry's final report is publicly available if you want to know more.

For us, the next fight was with the Emperor. After *The Almost Coup*, I think it's fair to say this battle was almost inevitable — he wanted power for himself, we wanted power for the elected Parliament. He wanted the authority and influence of Defense Command broken, we wanted him deposed.

And we all had to work towards these ends within the framework of the Empire's parliamentary system.

Or if we didn't, whoever broke the law first needed to have a damned good excuse, and confidence that he or she would win the ensuing fight once the line was crossed. Otherwise, the Empire could collapse, just after winning the biggest war in human history.

So there's a lot still to come as we enter *The Pax Terra* and *The Articles of Empire*. By the end of it all, though, I think it's fair to say we'll find a little peace… before we go on to 2235. Because while we could somehow avoid the 'deep stuff' after Egesta, there'd be no getting away from it next year. Anyway, enough cryptic foreshadowing. Keep well until next time!

THE
PAX
TERRA

THE AUTOBIOGRAPHICAL REMINISCENCES OF
ADMIRAL THE LORD KEN BARRON FOR 2234

THE MARTIAN WAR - 15

KENNETH TAM

FROM THE AUTHOR

One of my personal frustrations about our democratic system of government is that, sometimes, it can be reduced to little more than a team sport. A person backs a certain political faction because he or she agrees with its platform, or part of its platform, or because that's the faction preferred by everyone he or she knows, or because it's popular, or stylish...

And then sometimes that person starts to disregard the opinions of anyone who doesn't share his or her loyalty. Those who disagree somehow lose their right to have differing views.

What happens when we stop listening to everyone who supports the other side of the debate? What happens when we automatically declare them to be ignorant, or dangerous, or treasonous, or naive... and simply try to dismiss their ideas?

Bad things happen. A lot of polarization, a lot of self-sustaining and self-righteous indignation. Nothing that helps fulfill the actual responsibility of government.

What we're about to watch within the Empire is very much a case of that team sport mentality. One side will win, one side will lose, but I think the question deserves to be asked: is either side truly right or wrong? And if so, why?

The answer won't be given in this book... and indeed, the debate will rage long into 2235. For now I just suggest you take a look at both sides with a suitably critical eye... and of course, cheer on the Fiora Ring and the elected civilian government, because they're inevitably on the side of justice!

Ahem.

Once again I have thanks to offer. Many real-world friends of mine have been serving for years as characters in this series, and two more have joined the cast in this book. I extend my gratitude to all of them — they make for brilliant company.

Peter Caron, my very good friend, continues to be a tireless and fundamental contributor to this series, and I thank him very much yet again. By the same token, my friend Wes Prewer never fails to come up with new levels of excellence. Witness the new trailer for 2234-2235, which you can find online at our website. Thank you, Wes.

And finally, as ever, my parents Jacqui and Peter continue to excel as the guiding partners in Iceberg Publishing, and the best family I could ever ask for.

Atlas too.

– Kenneth Tam

PREFACE

And so we come to the savage world of politics. I know we've dipped our toe in already — we started this whole Martian War adventure with an almost coup after all — but now we're going to see something a good deal more dangerous.

I think a lot of people are surprised when they learn that the closest the Empire came to falling during the war years was in 2234, and that it wasn't because of enemy action, but due to the Emperor's battle with his civilian government. I don't know if I was surprised… I'd known more about what happened before the Battle Over Earth than many people, so I probably wasn't a fair person to ask.

But surprised or not, and ready or not, the threat was coming.

Now, I fully expect that some people are going to come to this book — number fifteen in a very long series — without having read the rest, because they're looking for my take on what happened in the clash for governmental supremacy.

I also know that, depending on when loyal readers last put down *The Egesta Crisis*, the details of the situation might be fuzzy. All that in mind, I'm going to preempt my publisher's demands for more context, and give you a quick reminder of where everything was.

The point to make is pretty simple: in this battle for control of Earth between Emperor Luther Gregory III and Prime Minister Gabriel Pope, both the top people were aboard *Ark Royal* — in Mars orbit. Negotiations with the Martians were almost complete by this time, but until a treaty was signed we were technically still at war. Whether that was a problem for the coup plans, or actually a good alibi, was up for interpretation. For better or worse, though, it meant that both the Emperor and the PM were both away, so proxies were going to do most of the heavy lifting.

You know the proxies pretty well on the PM's side. For instance, Second Lord of the Admiralty Daragh Ryan was going to have some influence — the crazy Irishman (who we actually haven't spent much time talking about since 2233) was going to have absolute control of Defense Command forces around Earth, since John Fiora was with the Emperor at Mars.

Along with him were a variety of Defense Command veterans… Marshal Samuels and his superspy-wife Melissa were coming in on a transport from Belt Two, ready to try to sway the Belt caucus against bringing down their own government.

At the same time, obviously, Karen and I were coming in as fast as we could from Egesta, with tons of evidence demonstrating how the Emperor's Imperial Army had spent years committing atrocities against the men and women of an unaligned asteroid.

The military cast wasn't the only one involved, though; the Prime Minister had a number of his key personnel with him at Mars, most were still around Capital Island, as were friendly MPs like Leslie Cavanaugh — though how much they'd be able to do was an open question.

On the ground, the Emperor had a different set of supporters. Obviously he had more than 100,000 troops from his Imperial Army, the single largest coherent ground combat force available on the planet at the time (DC had far more personnel, but none organized into a single ground combat formation). Beyond them, the main avatar for the throne would be the Governor General, James Hodson — his appointed ribbon-cutter.

Politically, he was also using Olivia Bennington, the Deputy Prime Minister (who desperately wanted to be PM). She was going to bring down her own government on a confidence motion — or, more precisely, she was going to make sure her loyalists in the Empire Party didn't vote to save their own government when the Emperor's lackeys in opposition put forward the confidence motion.

Either way, she was the opportunist... one of those politicos Daragh Ryan truly hated, and I'd say he had some justification.

Oh, and one other thing the Emperor had going for him: complete penetration of Defense Command Communications. Because during the war, John and Daragh had shuffled all the DC personnel who'd been loyal to former-Second Lord (and Emperor-lackey) Dave Caldecott out of combat positions, from which they could have cost us the war, and into DCC.

That worked great — we won the war, obviously — but now we couldn't send messages back and forth without worrying about interception.

Bastards.

So that's basically the landscape. Marshal, Melissa, Karen and I were all racing home to intervene in the impending political coup attempts. Simultaneously, Wes Pellew was bound for Mars with more evidence of the Imperial Army's crimes, so he'd be in position to help deal with the Emperor, if circumstances allowed.

It was a giant mess in the making. And now, we must see how it all turned out.

Well, no, you know exactly how it turned out. We just have to see what happened.

Well, I suppose we don't *have* to see...

Stop asking questions about my transition. Go to Chapter One.

CHAPTER ONE

CALM

Political storms often seem to come out of nowhere. This isn't because they're particularly different than other storms... it really just comes down to the fact that a lot of the factors that trigger them are insular — arguments in back rooms, confidential memos, secret quests for power... all those lovely things.

Most people in the Empire couldn't have been bothered with the Emperor's ambitions, or ours, because they were celebrating the end of the war. Our spat wouldn't be news until it blew up into something that everyone noticed.

I raise this point because, for the people who we're about to join for the first time in years, thoughts of political explosivity (just pretend it's a word) were hardly front of mind. They were more concerned with getting their feet under them again — and about time too.

Captain Kris Jacobs had fallen in love with a nurse. I know, I know, painfully cliché, but she went ahead and did it anyway. If you'll recall, Kris had gone from being my XO in *Wolf* to skippering *Lion*... then she'd been irradiated while saving her ship, and we'd just managed to keep her alive thanks to the self-sacrifice of her shipboard medical staff, and the excellent work of Doctor Conrad Rhee from *Artemis Agrotera*.

She'd come home after that hellish affair, and been in gene therapy pretty much daily through 2233. Incredibly painful, exhausting, harrowing... pick your word, none of them really capture how bad the experience was.

But the upside, at least, was that at Fengate Military Hospital, the facility in Sydney where she'd received treatment, the staff had assigned her a rather handsome nurse.

His name was Steve, and he'd basically been with her every day of the treatment — from when her radiation poisoning left her looking (to use her words) 'decidedly ugly', to when she was back to her usual, not-at-all-ugly self.

Anyway, Kris will be delighted that my re-introduction of her into this series has basically been a story of her love life, but she and Steve just renewed their vows at a lovely ceremony in Melbourne, and I was fortunate enough to be there, so I figured I'd open with the positive.

No, I'm not biased at all.

Kris was not with Steve on the day we're going to be talking about, though. She'd spent the previous week with him on a romantic vacation, which marked the end of her time in treatment, and now she was ready to return to duty... meaning she'd turned up at Admiralty House and was set to meet with Daragh Ryan about her new assignment.

But as she sat in the waiting lounge, thinking how much she'd enjoyed running through the surf in slow motion with her handsome nurse, Kris was quickly getting a vibe that the job she was returning to was going to be as interesting, or more interesting, than she'd been ready for.

See, as far as she knew, having just come out of treatment and from vacation, the solar system was settling down again. The Martians would sign peace any day, and then it would probably be back to pirate hunting... or, she was thinking, maybe a shore posting in Australia so she could spend more time... well, you know.

The electricity in the air at Admiralty House suggested a whole lot more was happening, though, and that certainty of trouble jumpstarted parts of Kris' mind that had been blissfully dormant for all this time.

Trouble.

By the time she was summoned into Daragh's office, she was ready for anything... good thing too.

Kris had never met the Second Lord of the Admiralty. She obviously knew his reputation, but meeting Daragh is inevitably a whole lot different than reading about him, or seeing him on screen.

The insane Irishman was pacing behind his desk when our intrepid Aussie Captain arrived, and he pointed to the door when she stepped through, "Shut that."

Wordlessly, Kris did as she was instructed, and then Daragh started, "I know I don't know you, but you're one of Barron's folks so I figure I can talk to you... holy shit, this is a mess."

That's actually what he said, and all Kris could do was blink a few times and fold her arms. Then, and we all love her for this, she answered, "You're going to swear in the presence of a lady?"

Daragh had his head of steam up, and was getting ready to spew a bunch of exposition dialogue about the Emperor (which would have been awfully convenient for me as I write this), but he stopped, frowned in confusion, then looked at her.

"What?"

Kris smiled, "Nothing, sir. I believe you were going to explode with rage?"

Daragh stared at her for a second, shotgun leaned back against his shoulder and face slightly red. Then he burst out laughing, which was somewhat unexpected, but Kris would take it.

"You're going to do alright, I think," Daragh grinned. "Don't suppose you fancy fat old Irish Lords, because I'm currently between girlfriends."

Kris shrugged, "Sorry, sir. Hot nurse just beat you to it."

"Damned nurses," Daragh muttered, then pointed to a chair opposite his desk. "Well now that you've disarmed me, sit down."

He sat too, which was pretty remarkable, and then laid down his shotgun and leaned back, "So you probably don't know this, but there's a huge political fight about to happen. The government's going to fall, the Emperor's probably going to take over, and then I'm likely to be arrested."

Kris Jacobs had lived through many surprises, and she was mostly prepared for this one, thanks to the atmosphere of Admiralty House. That being the case, she chose her reply carefully, "I see. Shit."

"Exactly!" Daragh slapped his desk with an open palm. "And all with the PM and John off at Mars with the fuckers."

I think that last word was supposed to be 'Martians', but it's Daragh.

"So, aside from being a sympathetic ear, does that mean there's a job for me?" Kris gently nudged the conversation in the direction of being on topic, and that just made Daragh grin.

Our elite Australian skipper was back to her old punchy self, and that meant the Irishman was on a level playing field — something he wasn't accustomed to, and something he certainly didn't mind.

"Most of the fleet we have in orbit right now is wartime-built and crewed," the Second Lord explained. "And God love 'em, they beat the Martians. I trust them all... but if the Emperor gets up to something criminal, it's going to take a certain sort of experience to be ready to stop him."

Kris frowned slightly now — she had missed that last year of hostilities, after all, so it was impossible for her to comment on the character of the crews who'd assaulted Mercury, or been part of the Fleet Clash.

The point Daragh was making was a reasonably subtle one — that officers like Bruce Arama, while unquestionably exceptional, hadn't been in the service proper when Caldecott's Inquiry had happened, so there was no way for us to be certain of where they'd come down if things got crazy again.

We'd need people who had a good sense of what the Emperor was really like, and new officers just might not have the experience.

I should point out that I'm not labeling Bruce one way or the other on this question — I've never asked him what he thought of Luther Gregory III — but the general concern stood. Daragh was more worried about it than I was, but then he'd been sitting on Capital Island for the whole war, getting hemmed in by politicos. All he could see were plans within plans, where those of us who'd done the shooting had a camaraderie that he fully understood (from his days at the Forge), but which realistically didn't exist for him.

So all of that is a long way of saying that Daragh wasn't sure who he could trust, and how much he could trust them...

But he knew he could trust Kris Jacobs, because she was classic Belt Squadron, and moreover, she was smart and witty enough to go toe-to-toe with him.

At this point in the conversation, though, she wasn't saying anything — she was waiting for him to pass along the details of her assignment. And he wasn't doing it, because he'd spun off into musing about how complicated the politics of his situation were.

After about five minutes of silence, she cleared her throat.

Daragh blinked, "Oh, sorry lassie."

"I was afraid I was going to have to kiss you to wake you up," she smiled with savage subtlety as she needled him, and the old Second Lord laughed and flopped back in his chair.

"You're bad for my fuckin' blood pressure!" he grinned. "There's a frigate in orbit, just out of the repair yards. You're taking her over and crewing her as you see fit, out of the pool of shipless officers and spacers we've got sitting around here waiting for something to do."

Kris' own smile started to fade at that — not because she didn't like the sounds of it, but because she was curious about what hull was to be hers. She'd read much about the 'new' Asia-class frigates, but she really had no love for them.

She wanted one particular ship, and as that thought was reflected by the expression on her face, she leaned forward and stared at Daragh across the desk.

"Don't tease me, Second Lord."

The Irishman shrugged a little, "I saved her for you. I know we're not supposed to call them 'her' any more, but I saved her for you. Knew you'd be back to get her."

Kris literally slid forward to the edge of her seat, "What ship?"

Leaning forward to match Kris' eager pose, Daragh let her have it: "*Lion.*"

That's right. Daragh was embellishing slightly when he said he'd held Karen's former ship exclusively for Kris — towards the end of the frigate's refit, he had done that. But the fact that the ship hadn't been restored and sent out for the Mercury assault, or even for the defense of Earth while the attack fleet was away, was mainly due to the problems they had decontaminating it.

Basically, when we towed *Lion* back from Io, they handed the repair job to a civilian yard. The folks there were well-meaning, but didn't really know how to handle the level of irradiation they were facing. Took them two tries to clean up the decks, then the ship was sent to Naval repair yards to have its damage taken care of… but there it was discovered that parts of the hull were radioactive. Long story short, *Lion* missed out on the end of the war because it was that badly wounded.

But now, it was back. And so was its skipper.

Kris Jacobs had nothing to say to Daragh about her posting. She simply stood up, and as she did, Daragh planted his elbows on his desk and looked at her.

Smile reforming, she leaned down and forward, then kissed him on the cheek, "Thank you, sir."

Now, fair to say that's not protocol. But freshly healed, and elated about getting her ship back, Kris was willing to go out on a limb, and Daragh was more than happy to be there with her.

"You're lovely, girl," the Second Lord said in an almost paternal tone. "Get up there and get fitted for whatever comes. Also see if there's anyone else you know you can really trust. I'll be in touch… God only knows what mess we're in for."

Kris nodded, and then stepped back to offer a much more formal salute.

Daragh waved her away, "Aw get out of here!"

With a last smile, Kris Jacobs did exactly that. She had *Lion* back, which was just right. It meant *we* had *Lion* back too — the family was reassembling.

More were soon to join.

CHAPTER TWO

SPY AND COMMODORE

Commodore Marshal Samuels was a master of strategy and organization. We finally — finally! — got to spend some time with him and his exceptional wife Melissa last book, and as I pointed out then, our former squadron-mate and wartime commander of the Belt Station had basically been responsible for the development of the convoy system that protected our trade during the war.

Without Marshal's excellent planning, we might actually have lost the war. And he never gets enough credit for that, as far as I'm concerned.

One of the benefits of all his work during the war was that he had a reputation with the politicians of the Belt — the Belt caucus, as they were known on Capital Island — and that meant he might be able to persuade some of them to avoid a catastrophic mistake, like letting the government fall and therefore giving the Emperor effective control of Parliament.

However, and I'm sure he'll love me pointing this out, one of the disadvantages of all that work during the war was that his hand-to-hand combat skills had gotten rusty. Very rusty.

Let's be honest, Marshal wasn't a big one for going into firefights back in the day — unlike Karen and me, he had the good sense to send his Special Branch and SF on operations, without accompanying them. So while I'd still feel just fine having him back me up in a bar fight, he wasn't ready for some of the situations that might come up if the Emperor attempted any form of coup while he was on the ground.

Fortunately, Melissa Samuels was *very* well versed in numerous ways to defend herself. To use one of her favorite expressions, she had the skills of the ninja (not *a* ninja, *the* ninja). And in that way spies do, she'd somehow kept up those lethal skills, even though she hadn't killed anyone in weeks.

"When do you practice this stuff?" Marshal's question was a good one.

It was said between deep breaths, as he recovered from a one-sided but sporting bit of grappling. Melissa smiled and shrugged, "It's like riding a bike."

"It's *nothing* like riding a bike," the Commodore from Belt Two protested.

And strictly speaking, he was completely correct. If you tried riding a bike the way Mel was delivering blows, something would end up dead. Seriously. Spies are as bad as Special Branchers. They can kill you with

No, that wasn't a typo. I stopped that last sentence with no word and no punctuation because they can kill you with EMPTY SPACE. I think it's a special quantum physics hyper attack or something…

And I just learned that I can massively frustrate my editors with an incomplete sentence. Duly noted for future use, because you know how much I

Sorry. I'll stop.

Anyway, obviously I've tangented into pointless nattering, so back we go to the narrative…

Mel and Marshal were in their cabin aboard *Hikawa Maru*, the liner that was was just two days from Earth orbit, and the spy had finally convinced the Commodore that, while she'd be following him around for most of his visit (supposedly sight-seeing, since her history as a spy was still top secret at this point), he might end up in a scrape when he was without a sidearm.

So they'd pushed the furniture to the edge of the room, and she was running him through the more accessible hand-to-hand techniques.

"I still don't think this is necessary," Marshal said after a few more deep breaths, then headed over to a side table where his glass of water stood. Taking a gulp, he shook his head, "The Emperor isn't going to be fool enough to supersede Defense Command authority and try to arrest me."

Melissa raised her eyebrows, "I don't think you should say that man is *not* any sort of fool. Because he is one. He's like the definition of one."

Marshal shrugged slightly and waved his glass, "Well okay, bad choice of words. But you know what I mean. To try to arrest me he'd have to have SF on his side, and with Daragh Ryan controlling Admiralty House, that just won't happen."

"He could send army troops. Blockheads will do whatever they're told," Melissa went for her own glass of water, though she hadn't even broken a sweat. Of course. Spies…

"Then I'd have SF looking out for me."

"But what if a blockhead came after you *before* an SF guard got to you. And remember, Special Branch is awfully depleted because of Mercury. It won't be like last time when Carrie Walsh was there to get Greg and John out of trouble. She's going to have a tough enough time learning to talk again… there are only twenty-two Special Branchers assigned to Admiralty House now," Mel had good points, and of course, ridiculous levels of detail.

Taking another gulp of his water, Marshal shrugged, "Well, alright. I see what you're saying."

"You can't *see* what anyone is saying," Melissa was needling him a bit now, because she was having fun.

"I'm glad you're coming along to protect me," he countered, and she grinned.

"Me too."

They weren't that far from Earth, and there were certainly colorful times in their near future. For now, though, let's leave them — before any more bruises were traded.

CHAPTER THREE
POLITICAL WONDERKID

Since the departure of Gabriel Pope, one of the greatest frustrations Daragh Ryan had been facing was communication with the Prime Minister's Office. There were a number of reasons for that difficulty, not least the fact that the media had caught Pope's Chief of Staff, Murt Sergeant, marrying a seventeen-year-old Mexican girl. And had uncovered the fact that she was the sixty-four-year-old's fourth wife. Concurrently.

That means four at once.

Now, strictly speaking, there are no limits to the number of spouses a person can have — it's not the government's place to tell you how many anniversaries you're going to forget — but since the war news was winding down, this little scandal was basically undermining the man's ability to do his job.

Not that Murt had been great at it. I don't even know how Pope ended up with that guy at his right hand, and perhaps I don't want to know... but he had, and now he was causing great complications.

Because while Marshal and Mel were practicing ways to kill people with the

Ha, did it again!

And while Kris was getting back aboard *Lion* and beginning to figure out her crew, the folks at PMO were keeping tabs on their counterparts in Olivia Bennington's office... and they'd discovered a crucial piece of information about the Deputy PM's plans (and by extension, the plans of the Emperor).

But that news was sitting on Murt's desk while he tried to avoid questions about the sordid messages he and his new bride had swapped from her school computer (not going anywhere near the details of that particular story).

The good news, if you can call it that, was that just before he'd left for Mars, Pope had appointed a new Deputy Chief of Staff for Earth Affairs, and that fellow was a bit of a political wonderkid. Two degrees, lots of experience on campaigns, and more enthusiasm than could be contained by a modest black hole.

And this kid, realizing that his boss was preoccupied with offers to appear on the Geraldine Coilier show, took the file and walked it over to Admiralty House himself.

It was the first time he'd been there, and he made an impression. You can see it on the security camera feeds, actually — he walks into the lobby wearing his black-on-black suit, strides up to the reception counter that has eternally been operated by Gerald and Betty, hands over his Parliamentary ID and asks to see Daragh Ryan immediately.

And Gerald and Betty both look at him, and his ID, and assume it has to be fake.

Because you have to appreciate that the wonderkid was only twenty-one, and he only looked sixteen. But they scanned his pass, checked the security files, realized that the precocious fellow was who he said he was, and then called the Second Lord.

That is how the first meeting occurred between batshit insane Second Lord of the

Admiralty Daragh Ryan, and completely unhinged Deputy Chief of Staff Schwartz T. Babcock.

Yes, *the* Schwartz T. Babcock. You really think more than one set of parents would have punished their child with such a name? Not since Victorian times, at least...

Daragh's mood had been in freefall since Kris had gone into orbit — our Aussie skipper had done her best, but the realities of an impending coup tended to bring everyone's morale down. As such, the Irishman was in no way ready for the effervescent attack that Schwartz was about to unleash.

Sitting behind his desk with his shotgun in his lap, the Second Lord wore a deep scowl as he watched the young staffer come in.

"You're a politico."

"And you hate political people," Schwartz said with a big smile. "I look forward to changing your mind, Second Lord. My name is Schwartz T. Babcock, and I represent the Prime Minister's Office."

Daragh's glare could probably have shattered glass, but Schwartz didn't so much as blink.

"This better be something important," the Second Lord said eventually, and Schwartz nodded as he held up the file he'd brought with him.

"It is. Let's go on a journey, you and I..."

Uninvited, he took the seat opposite Daragh and opened the file, then turned it in the Irishman's direction.

"We know when Bennington's going to call the confidence vote. She's making the next ways and means confidence, and it's going before the House and the Senate at 5:00 and 5:30 on Friday evening."

That actually was useful news, and as much as Daragh might have trouble with Schwartz's manner, he wasn't going to be petty.

"Shit, I was hoping you were actually going to justify me grabbing you by your stupid collar and throwing you out of here," he muttered, leaning forward to take a look at the report.

Of course, we should at this point turn to a discussion of the significance of a Friday confidence vote, since it was now late on Tuesday, and Marshal was due to arrive on Thursday, but instead Schwartz seized upon the banter. And I can't not go with it.

"You're the second person to criticize my choice of clothing," he said, and Daragh frowned and looked up.

"I... what?"

"Murt Sergeant criticizes it too. He thinks it suits me because I'm an 'obnoxious fucktard'. Tells everyone who'll listen that I am."

Not kidding. Daragh just stared, at this point entirely confused by the conversation.

"He calls his Deputy Chief of Staff that? Publicly?" the Irishman had to ask.

"Every day," Schwartz nodded, still wearing a political smile. "I die a little bit inside every time I hear it."

Daragh stared for another few seconds, then just shook his head and looked down at the file, "Well don't mind him, he's just worried someone's in his office who's going to take his job."

"And maybe his wife. Seventeen isn't too young for me, and from some of the things I've overheard she's very exuberant."

Daragh stopped reading for a minute, looked up, then looked down again, "I can already tell you're going to hell when you die."

Schwartz nodded, not missing a beat, "I'm glad we're laying the foundations for a great friendship now, since we're going to spend so much time together there."

As you can see, Schwartz was pretty much the same in these early days as he is now. He's either a talented performer, a sociopath, a politician... or maybe all three.

Daragh couldn't help but laugh, and then he shook his head, "You are obnoxious. But you're too fucking smart. Now please stop chattering and tell me what else. Friday vote?"

Switching back to the topic at hand, Schwartz leaned forward and glanced at the file as well, "They could have picked any day for that vote, but they chose Friday. And that's a bad sign."

"They know Marshal is on his way?" the Second Lord asked, and Schwartz nodded.

"We're pretty certain someone in Cavanaugh's office leaked that fact — and that he'll be here Thursday. So they know we're playing our biggest card on Thursday, and they still set the vote for Friday," the Deputy Chief of Staff confirmed.

Now we can go ahead and explain some things. When MP Leslie Cavanaugh had decided to send her Chief of Staff to collect Marshal Samuels and bring him back, the mission was supposed to be secret... but of course she'd told the Prime Minister's Office, and the PM's staff had told Daragh.

No one else was supposed to know, but it was Capital Island: word was inevitably going to slip out.

Now it had, and that meant that Olivia Bennington was aware of the threat to her plans to bring down the government... but she wasn't doing anything to preempt the threat. She could have called a snap confidence vote whenever she wanted to — the House Leader was one of her acolytes — but she hadn't.

She knew Marshal was coming, and she was going to let him have a crack at her Belt caucus, without whom she was stuffed.

Thinking about this interesting turn of events, Daragh immediately came up with two possible reasons for the confusing decision.

"Either Olivia is getting cold feet, and doesn't plan to take us down at all... or she has some other method for keeping Commodore Samuels away from the Belt caucus." Of course Schwartz had come to the same conclusion, and as the Deputy Chief of Staff voiced the possibilities, Daragh's frown got even deeper.

"Option one means we don't have to worry. Option two means she might try to stop him getting to ground. And that would take some sort of intervention that might qualify as unconstitutional..." the Irishman began thinking aloud.

He was implying that she'd have some sort of force attempt to keep Marshal from reaching Capital Island... and indeed, that was a big concern.

Schwartz nodded, "If she tries anything, it would give us latitude to do a bunch of different things. But in the short term, could be dangerous... if she catches us by surprise, stops him *and* no one notices until after a confidence vote, things could become very complicated. We'd be in the right but public perception could be very skewed."

He was, of course, completely correct. Imagine for a moment that Marshal and Mel tried to take a shuttle down to Capital Island, but their craft was diverted to Halifax by an unknown signal, and when they landed they found themselves surrounded by Imperial blockheads who in turn took them quietly into custody until after the vote.

Now, that would be illegal, and the logical thing would be for the Imps to kill them to hide the evidence, but Marshal's profile was too high. So what if they released him just after the vote, when a new PM was installed by the Governor General, and a new inquiry into Defense Command was mounted.

Then anything Marshal did to object — even if he had proof — would be cast into at least some doubt. A case could be made that he was inventing an illegal act to try to discredit the body that was mounting an inquiry into his (and all of our) activities. Public perception would be tangled up, and the legitimacy of the government unclear.

See? Messy.

Now, obviously, if blockheads tried to capture Marshal and Mel, they'd all be killed when Mel used her special quantum attack. And recall that both of them were being trailed by another superspy, Camila Barrai, so it would be 100 blockheads against two spies. Those Imps wouldn't just be dead, somehow they never would have been born… okay, I know, I'm over-doing it. But yes, it wouldn't be so easy for Marshal to be captured… but nobody knew that, because Mel was still under cover.

There were other complications too, which I'll get into later, but for now suffice to say that the possibility of a threat to the Belt Two team seemed quite real.

And Daragh was going to have to figure out what to do about it.

Fortunately, there was a frigate in orbit with a very trustworthy skipper aboard.

"Schwartz, I think I have an answer," the Second Lord declared as he thought of Kris.

"Daragh, I'm very proud of you. Would you like to share your idea, or would you like me to tell you that Captain Jacobs aboard *Lion* would be a valuable resource under the present circumstances?"

I'm really surprised Daragh didn't shoot the Prime Minister's Deputy Chief of Staff, but hey, that's Schwartz for you. He's never going to hell, because the day the grim reaper shows up, he'll talk the guy not only into voting for him, but into putting a 'Vote Schwartz' button on his robe. And maybe making a small donation to the next campaign.

I can just imagine that conversation…

By the way, to answer the question of one of my editors, neither Schwartz nor Daragh thought the reason for Bennington's inattention was ignorance or arrogance — both assumed that she would realize how much influence the Commodore commanding the Belt Station, who had kept all of those colonies safe for the whole war, would have with the politicos from that part of the Empire. How could they say no to the man who'd kept their constituents — their votes — safe and well-fed during the largest war in the history of human space settlement?

More on that assumption later.

CHAPTER FOUR
AND THEN US

With the vote now scheduled for Friday, it was hard to say whether Karen and I were going to arrive in time. While Daragh and Schwartz were having their sparring match, we were aboard *Wolf*, and just to change things up a little, we were in Karen's cabin instead of mine.

Of course, she was still on the bed, and I was still in the chair, but we were in *her* cabin. How daring. Scandalous, really...

Wolf was running at 197 kps for Earth — not our fastest combat speed, but certainly a little bit faster than we should have been going on a lengthy cruise. Andy Jenson was working some minor miracles to get us home as quickly as possible, because he (and everyone aboard, obviously) knew exactly what the stakes were.

We had the evidence, perhaps the only evidence, that could foil the Emperor's plan. Because no matter what lines that bastard had to feed the public — no matter what lies he could try to tell about us, or how he'd twist the truth, the fact was that any move he made to take control of the government would put Imperial troops into a very powerful position on Earth.

Imagine how people would feel about that, when they had visual evidence and prisoner testimony revealing exactly what the blockheads had done for recreation on Egesta.

You might think it's a low blow. Maybe it is. Maybe it isn't fair to tar all blockheads with the brush of Egesta... but no, I think it is fair. It wasn't just the few we located and arrested who had committed crimes, remember. The way we found out about the mess in the first place was because of gloating troops on Mercury.

Gloating troops.

Haha, I'm so awesome because I did something so horrific it's a war crime. Look at me. Can you see me over the sound of how awesome I am?

Any armed force with that sort of professional culture was incredibly dangerous, and we were damned if we weren't going to reveal that fact to the public at large. Especially because the Emperor's attacks on Defense Command, and on John Fiora's group of officers in particular, seemed centered on our attitudes and conduct.

We're cavalier cowboys, see. Think we run the place.

I won't bother arguing that — there's probably something to the cavalier part. Ahem. But I'd rather be cavalier and a gentleman than stoic and a rapist. Call me old-fashioned.

Anyway, sorry, none of that is part of the narrative. Karen and me in a cabin. Guess what we were doing.

Obviously, we were talking, and come to think of it, we weren't being terribly interesting. Again, this was travel, and no matter how much you might try to dress it up, traveling is dull — I've been hitting you over the head with that fact for the entire war.

"This is boring."

Karen's words, as ever, matched my internal monologue, and she added a yawn for good measure. She was lying on her front, as usual, but after she'd spoken she did the unthinkable, and rolled onto her back.

Sitting in the chair, I didn't notice at first, "I know. But... well, I don't think Geraldine Coilier is the way to go this time. We should land right on Capital Island, in case the blockheads try to block airspace once we're down. We don't want to have any real shooting break out, so if our first stop is Capital Island itself, we hopefully won't have any blockades to run."

"And there's no way orbital defenses are going to try to stop us this time," Karen agreed, still sounding bored. She didn't bother elaborating, but I know what she meant — with Daragh as Second Lord (instead of Dave Caldecott) we were likely to have a lot more support for our landing this time than we did in 2231.

We'd talked about this all before, you see. It was literally a matter of repeatedly re-hashing everything, hoping a slightly different angle would present itself.

"So all we need to do is pick a place to land..." I said, staring at the floor in front of my feet. "Not the main spaceport, but not too far from Terra Nova either. No interest in a hike through the woods while the fate of the Empire hangs in the balance..."

Hiking on Capital Island was not easy, anyway. The place was covered in bogs, moss, rocks... a good day out if that's what you were looking for, but you'd need to be as sure-footed as a wolf to get through. Even though wolves weren't native to the island... weird comparison.

"Your parents' place has a big lawn," Karen suggested, and I nodded.

"Yes, but I don't want the blockheads to flatten their house trying to stop us. So I'd rather somewhere that doesn't have houses and kids playing in the street..."

"We can just play it by ear," Karen suggested, not for the first time. "Until we see how they're deployed down there, there's no point trying to figure out where we land. We'll pick a quiet spot, and then make our way to the Parliament buildings, or one of the news studios, or somewhere with cameras."

She was definitely bored, perhaps even a little frustrated, and I looked at her with a frown, preparing to lecture her earnestly on how serious this was, and why it was not the time to be distracted by our own foibles.

Sounds like something I'd say, doesn't it?

Of course it didn't happen, because she was lying on her back.

"What are you doing?"

I asked that far too urgently, and Karen looked sideways at me, "Hm?"

"You're lying on your back," I sounded confused, and Karen shrugged.

"Well, I figured after all these years, I'd earned the right to turn over. It's my cabin, after all."

I stared at her for a second, watching her pick absently at the palms of her hands. Then I shook my head and looked back at the floor, "Well then."

Karen glanced at me, thought to say something, then stopped herself. For a moment we were both silent, and then finally I looked at her, "So you want to stop talking about this and just deal with it when we get there — cavalier style, like the old days? But not the bad old days, the good old days?"

"Exactly," she agreed, twisting slightly to look at me again.

I did a good job not paying attention. I deserved a gold star.

"So, we just have a couple of days to kill. Like in the old days," Karen said. "Well, except we're on the same ship now. Any ideas?"

Now, of course, my editors want me to elaborate on whether I had any ideas. However, I'll take this moment to repeat one thing Karen had just mentioned which I think is easily forgotten this far along in the series: she and I had been apart, on different ships, for most of the good old days.

As soon as we'd ended up together, the war had started.

You might go so far as to say that the war had even colored the time we did have together — that, once the Emperor was out of the way, we'd for the first time be able to enjoy the fact that we were on the same ship, doing our jobs, and seeing a solar system mostly at peace.

I was certainly looking forward to that reality.

I believe the literature types who aren't afraid to tell me I'm a hack would point to this page and say, 'Aha, the peasant is using dramatic irony.'

For now, though, Karen and I were still together. We'd enjoy it while it lasted…

Chapter Five

Lion Restored

It's safe to say the war had been a very different experience for Kris Jacobs. Her recent romance excepted, the whole affair had been hell. She'd started very well indeed, joining us on that first mission back in *The Rogue Commodore*, when we'd managed to uncover the Martian plot to team up with pirates in a bid to beat us at the Belt… feels like years ago. Actually, it was years ago.

Then she'd pitched in against Sean Cook when Wes had gone toe-to-toe with the bastard after the first Egesta situation. Following that, though, it had been a straight run to Io, where she'd encountered Benjamin Conflans' squadron, and *Lion* had taken the savage hit from *Promethei Planum* that had caused its reactors to overcook, and had irradiated the whole ship.

While we finished off Bort McWebsbert's friend at Sinope, and then came home to deal with the Pions and Canaries, the Mercury assault and the Fleet Clash, she'd been in Fengate Hospital, suffering through treatments that, as I've already mentioned, are incredibly painful.

I reiterate this point because (and forgive the word choice here) I find it so very fascinating. In many ways, Kris had a worse war than most of the survivors of the Belt Squadron — though obviously not worse than the people we'd lost. But being confined to what could unkindly be called *torture* in a hospital, unable to take part in events that you feel you're supposed to be involved in… I don't know what I'd have done in her place.

Remember how intolerable I was watching Glorious February from Belt Two in *The Gallant Few*? I would not have been a gracious patient, I expect. Especially because fetching nurses wouldn't have had much appeal…

So when Kris stepped back onto the bridge of *Lion*, it wasn't just professional pride that she felt… it was like coming home. More, it was like being reunited with a way of life that she felt was a part of her. Sorry if that sounds a bit too poetic to be real, but even today she says that behind the birth of her children and her wedding, the day she got back to *Lion* was probably the happiest of her life.

Happier, mind, than the day she received command of that ship.

Of course, when she stepped onto the bridge, it wasn't quite like she'd hoped in her imaginings in the hospital — the ship wasn't just as she'd remembered, with a fine fighting crew, well-honed and covering every post. Only two people were on the bridge, and one of them was part of the maintenance staff.

He wasn't even trying to fix something important; one of the chairs in the Helm and Navigation Section kept reclining when it wasn't supposed to, so he was fiddling with it.

Kris nodded to him and then spotted the other person — the one she'd asked to join her aboard. The woman was standing at the front, looking at the bridge screens, all of which were showing *Lion*Net graphics, since none of the main systems were in use.

Sorry, I should have pointed out earlier that the frigate was still hitched to the repair dock — no need for anyone to be on watch, or any of the systems to be active. That would soon change…

For now, Kris strode to the front of the bridge and came to a stop beside her fellow Belt Squadron veteran.

"How's the side?"

"They filled it in and grafted skin over. Messy scar, but I'll be alright. How's the radiation?"

"Didn't kill me in the end," Kris answered. "You're my new XO, if you'll have the job."

Kate Levec had been promoted to Commander on my recommendation after she'd been shot right in front of me at Io, and now she nodded slowly, "I was hoping you'd say something like that, Captain."

"Kris. You meant to say Kris, but it came out sounding like Captain," our Aussie skipper quipped back.

"Whoops, how embarrassing," Kate allowed herself to smile at that point.

Alright, now I'll throw the brakes on the narrative for a minute and explain. Kate Levec had just finished her own recovery, because the reconstructive surgery needed to fill in that hole a Martian Commando had blown in her abdomen was no casual business either. She and Kris had been in different hospitals for the past couple of years, but they were both Belt Squadron veterans. That's a bond that means a lot, even today, so when Kris had started trying to figure out how to rapidly re-crew her ship (with the original crew scattered from Mercury to the Belt and back) she'd started by looking for senior officers from our old unit.

Kate was in perfect position, and while she'd gone out of action as a Sensors and Communications Officer, Kris figured (correctly) that she had the experience to take over the XO job.

So the first position was filled — and it was an important one.

Kris folded her arms as Kate absorbed the news of her new posting, and then let out a sigh, "So, the Second Lord wants us operational as soon as possible. And word is the ship is ready… how fast do you think we can get a skeleton crew aboard?"

The maintenance man was still working on the chair, and neither Kris nor Kate recognized him, so the XO decided to be careful with her answer, "We expecting a… quick assignment?"

Kris shrugged slightly, "Well I don't think Daragh was hitting on me when he said he was glad to have a trusty, veteran ship available for special operations. Not *just* hitting on me, anyway."

Kate's eyebrows went up, "I didn't realize he was single."

"I'll send you to the next meeting, if you like," Kris managed a smile, but there was no time for foolish chatter. "But we need at least 100 people, I think — enough to run the mains in a pinch. And just to make life difficult, we need them in the next day or so."

Now, if that sounds like a tall order, it is. Like a giraffe on stilts, standing on top of a hovercar which is passing over the Rocky Mountains. That's right, it's such a tall order it requires four separate elements of hyperbole.

First, keep in mind that DC Personnel was still being run by Caldecott's folks — the people, for instance, who were delaying Charlie Peters' promotion, and the promotions of other people like Eugene Sengooba (remember, we had to make him Master-At-Arms to get around them?). So getting people officially assigned to the ship in a day was virtually impossible, especially if the desk jockeys who missed the old Second Lord suspected that *Lion* was actually going to be available to do something unthinkable, like stop a coup.

But beyond the considerable bureaucratic mess involved, there was a very real problem in sourcing the right people. There were thousands of men and women milling around various DC facilities in Earth orbit and on the ground, waiting for ship postings — people who had also been wounded, or had lost their ships at Mercury or during the Clash. But they were all over the place, and under anything approaching normal circumstances, they'd have to be sorted, interviewed, assessed and then appointed.

Not something one could do in a day.

"Let's pull the files on anyone who isn't assigned right now, who served with the Belt Squadron… and maybe Wes' Independent Squadron… and then let's get them up here. I doubt there are that many in Earth space right now. We'll sort them out after they've arrived," Kris said finally, and Kate glanced sideways at her.

"How do we get them up here without them going AWOL? Can we get the Second Lord to unilaterally assign them?"

Kris had no idea, so she shrugged, "Why don't you call him and ask?"

She contained her smile at that, and Kate Levec nodded, "I think I might."

"I'll start searching the files," *Lion's* skipper confirmed, and then she turned and headed for her day cabin.

Leaving Kate behind, Kris went through the hatch into that small compartment, and then stopped and looked down at the floor with a sad smile. The yards had restored everything, but they hadn't got the carpet right. It was burgundy — the color from Karen's time. Kris was a teal sort of woman… you might remember that from *The Rogue Commodore*.

But that was alright, she'd fix it when she had a crew again.

She went to her desk, sat in her chair, spent a moment basking in the fact that she was back, and then began searching.

CHAPTER SIX

MANY IRONS

Daragh Ryan didn't have the power to unilaterally assign anyone to *Lion*, but after his conversation with Kate Levec, who he found to be positively charming (seems to be a theme so far this book and I don't know why — it's just how it happened), he did find a way to get the people up to the frigate.

Basically, he gave all the selected officers immediate personal leave — something that he *could* do — with the understanding that they'd use it to go aboard *Lion*. I suppose if Kris and Kate had been picking just anyone, that might have been a problem... people taking the leave and heading out on vacation... but Belt Squadron vets weren't going to turn down an invitation from one of their own skippers, to go aboard one of their own ships.

Anyway, more on that later, because Daragh's day was going from strength to strength... or, to use his words, from fuck-up to complete fuck-up.

"They're saying it's exercises?"

He was in Admiralty House C&C when he asked that question rather loudly, and the man who'd brought the news, Captain Ronald Davis (who was still in charge of Earth Sensors and Communications) simply nodded.

"Two divisions, claiming they're doing survival training on the Burin Peninsula."

Daragh was about as pleased as you'd expect, and I'll now explain why. The Burin Peninsula was on the southern shore of Capital Island, barely 200 kilometers from Terra Nova, the home of Admiralty House, Parliament, and everything else. Two divisions of blockheads — about 20,000 men officially, though Daragh suspected they'd be over-stuffed formations, with lots of extra troops along to 'observe' — would thus be an hour from the most prized target in the Empire. And there wasn't much of anything he could do about it.

Many sets of eyes focused on the Second Lord as he processed the news. The evening shift was on at C&C, but because of the tension most of the section chiefs had stuck around, skipping dinner with their families in case something exactly like this happened.

Now there was a simple question: how did Defense Command respond? Could we? It was a decision that John Fiora would undoubtedly have been able to provide some perspective on, but there was no way to ask him. It was all down to Daragh.

And the Irishman knew his first reaction (air strikes) was probably too strong.

Taking a breath, he looked to Ronald Davis, "Let's start some impromptu exercises of our own. Don't want our crews to get lax just because we're nearly at peace. Cancel all leave, have orbital defense Starlight squadrons start working on their atmospheric skills."

That was it: Defense Command was joining the unofficial arms race — the escalation of tensions between Earth's two governing factions, while both pretended everything was fine.

Ronald turned to head back to his consoles, but Daragh remembered something and stopped the man, "Actually, don't cancel *all* leave. Anyone with personal leave passes from me gets to keep them…"

Davis frowned but nodded, "Aye sir."

Too many irons in the fire… Daragh was really looking forward to retiring in peace soon. Back to the ponies that he didn't actually have.

Haha, the literary folks are pointing at the page and saying 'dramatic irony' again.

Schwartz T. Babcock was sitting at his desk, trying not to pay too much attention to the yelling that was coming from the office across the hall. Murt Sergeant had somehow been nabbed by a reporter over the comm, and now he was loudly defending the fact that he'd had to have the birds and bees conversation with his fourth wife.

As Schwartz points out, at least the Chief of Staff and his bride had that conversation before the wedding. Always spinning positive, that political wonderkid…

Anyway, the argument over morality was getting quite loud, and it was distracting just about everyone, so Schwartz was considering closing his door. His assistant Donna came in before he had the chance, and as he turned to her with his usual smile, her severe expression sobered him.

"News?"

"The army is moving troops to Burin for exercises, and Defense Command just canceled all leave and started exercises for their atmospheric defense forces," she answered, holding a message pad out to him.

He took the pad and read the particulars of the two messages, then sighed and sat back in his chair. This was, of course, a hell of a bad sign.

"Call Admiralty House for me. And let T.J. know that she might get questions during the morning press briefing. We'll have TPs for her."

Note from my editors: 'TPs' are political speak for talking points. Knowing that, Donna nodded and then left, kindly closing the office door behind as she went. That, at least, put the traumatizing love life of the Chief of Staff out of Schwartz's mind.

Small comforts.

Daragh got back to his office just in time to take the call from PMO, and given the stellar mood he was in, he wasn't looking forward to the conversation with the wonderkid.

"Schwartz, if you're about to fucking complain, they moved first," the Irishman declared as the screen activated.

The Deputy Chief of Staff wasn't expecting that sort of greeting, but he held his own, "I heard that. And I wasn't going to complain. Our communications people are working on it over here. My guess is the message we'll send out to the public is that the exercises were unofficially coordinated. Eyebrows hopefully won't go up if it looks like we're just making sure all our planetary protection forces are shipshape, and haven't lost their edge since the shooting stopped."

See, that's why Schwartz T. Babcock was on the Prime Minister's senior staff — he knew his stuff, including how to make an arms race look like a good thing. Not a prelude to a possible coup.

The fact that there was no criticism of Defense Command's move was an honest surprise to Daragh, and the Second Lord relaxed slightly as he sat down on the edge of his desk, "We'll stick to that story if we're asked."

"Hopefully no one's really paying attention," Schwartz said. "But never count on that. My question for you is what we do next. There's no way you can be seen to take the first action. If the Imperial troops come this way, they're actually going to have to do something criminal before you start strafing with Starlights."

Daragh let out a sigh and nodded, "And I figure they have the same orders. It's going to be the weirdest fucking race not to actually *do* anything. But if Samuels gets in safe tomorrow and does his bit, then they'll have to act."

Schwartz nodded slowly. Looking back on this whole incident, the wonderkid tells me he regrets missing the obvious flaw in that plan, but it's one I'll get into later. For the moment he was more focused on the immediate question: "Things are clear for him to arrive?"

Daragh nodded, "The fleet up there is active now. Lynn Bokai has the Heavy Squadron, and I don't have any reason *not* to trust her… but more importantly, *Lion* is getting crewed in a hurry. If there's an important job, I'll give it to them."

Even though Daragh didn't really know Kris or Kate that well, their reputations and allegiances carried a lot of weight… which has to be pretty obvious by now, so I probably didn't need to say it again. No matter…

Schwartz took a breath, then nodded, "Okay. Well, it's going to be an interesting journey we take over the next couple of days…"

Daragh scowled, "You keep saying *journey*. Doesn't make any sense."

Chuckling, the Deputy Chief of Staff shrugged, "Suffice to say it's one of my endearing idioms."

"You said suffice wrong," Daragh shot back — Schwartz is one of those people who say 'suffiss' instead of 'suff-ice'.

Weirdo.

"Wait until I start singing. I took theatre in high school. If I fail at this job, I think I have a future on the stage."

Again this was supposed to be witty banter, but Daragh had the antidote for it: "Kid, you fail at this right now, we both might have a future on the gallows. Let's stop the chit-chat."

Schwartz sobered — visibly stopped smiling — for the first time the Second Lord could remember, and then he nodded, "I'm with you, Second Lord. Whatever happens, and whatever Murt is dealing with across the hall from me, believe that the Prime Minister's Office is not going to leave Admiralty House out in the cold on this one. The Emperor won't beat us both."

Daragh told me later that this felt particularly strange — suddenly finding oneself being genuinely reassured by a twenty-one-year-old… actually respecting someone as outwardly ridiculous as Schwartz T. Babcock could be… even having a serious conversation with a guy with that name.

But that's why the wonderkid was on Douglas Pope's staff. He was the real deal, as we all know today. Of course, Schwartz will tell you that this conversation was the beginning of a beautiful relationship. Daragh once told John that it was the day he willingly tied an anvil to his ankles. I think they meant the same thing.

For now we can go back to *Lion*...

CHAPTER SEVEN

INSTANT CREW – JUST ADD WATER

The fact that Kris' first day back on the job ended with a virtual all-nighter might have been considered a bad sign by some, but she was more than sufficiently rested for the gig. She did end up passing out on the couch in her day cabin for a couple of hours once all the necessary orders were issued, but basically she was on the job all night.

It was exciting, really. A sense of urgency, a serious situation to deal with... it was the way she'd secretly hoped to return, and frankly, I'm glad it was her doing it. Not many officers would be quite so gung-ho to dive straight into a crisis like this one.

As she woke up from her quick overnight nap, yawned and stretched, she went back to her desk and checked on the status of her orders. It's probably of no interest to you, but the way something this chaotic works is relatively simple: if you're one of the chosen crew, you get a call to your personal comm, and whenever you check it you reply with a quick acknowledgment message.

If the Bureau of Personnel issued the orders in a standard package, you'd be sent a hard copy message in a folder (because we're still traditional like that) and be provided with travel instructions... but again, Kris had none of that at her disposal.

Her message said 'reply to me, then contact Kate Levec to confirm your leave pass, then find a way up here.' So basically, each woman and man from *Lion's* new crew had to find his or her own way, which wasn't terribly easy (they were coming from all over the world, at all hours of day and night), but these were Belt Squadron vets.

I know, I'm probably beating that point to death, but nevertheless, it was relevant to Kris as she was making her decisions.

When Kris woke up and checked her messages, she found that seventy-four people were already on their way to the Naval yards where *Lion* was docked, and that some of them had even reached the orbital facility. She wasn't sure if those people would have come aboard yet, but either way, seventy-four was a very good start.

Another forty-three were departing soon too... enough of a crew to get *Lion* working, at least in the short term.

Deciding she'd need to be fit to receive these people, Kris headed out of her day cabin and went to find the travel bag she'd dropped off in her quarters. She'd need to clean her teeth and see if there was any food aboard...

It's a testament to how deserving of praise the old Belt Squadron folks were that, as they arrived aboard *Lion* and found the ship largely abandoned, they simply chose quarters for themselves and started to get settled.

I suppose that may not sound too impressive, so once again I'll set a little context. Imagine you show up at a new job working with a bunch of old friends, and when you arrive you find the building is mostly abandoned. You don't know what your actual job is going to be, but you know what you're good at and the area where you're probably going to end up, so instead of waiting around or looking for someone to answer your questions, you decide to go choose a spot for yourself, and start unpacking as much as you'll need to get started.

That's what the veterans did when they began to trickle aboard while Kris and Kate — the ship's only two officers — were getting ready for another long day.

I don't know, maybe it's not that significant, but I notice it. It's the little things that separate the great from the good, and the Belt Squadron from the great...

After Kris and Kate were both freshened up and feeling slightly more human (I don't know if I've mentioned, but all-nighters aren't my favorite thing ever), they met on the bridge, and then activated the shipwide intercom.

"Good morning everyone aboard, this is Kris Jacobs," the Aussie skipper began. "I'd like to speak with all of you as soon as possible... let's meet on the Rec Deck, in the enlisted club. Should be big enough for all of us, and if one of you has any kitchen savvy, we might be able to start the day with some food. Meet there by 0600... and if someone is going past the lock, tell the yard sentry to send people our way please."

That was the morning message — can't imagine anything less formal, but it worked. No fewer than eleven people told the sentry at the end of *Lion's* airlock chute (a short chute because they were in a yard) where to direct new arrivals, and when Kris and Kate reached the enlisted club on the Rec Deck, the place smelled of simbacon and eggs.

Nearly fifty people were present too, collected into groups based on the ships aboard which they'd previously served together.

There was a *Lady Grace* group centered around Lieutenant Allison Ting, who'd taken over as Helm and Navigation Officer of Karen's old corvette not long before the Fleet Clash. From *Cheetah* there was a larger contingent, headed up by Lieutenant Commander Roy Canter, who had been Mark Gunney's Chief Engineer. Most of the people in both of those groups had been with their old ships until the Fleet Clash, but had not been reassigned since. They were getting stir crazy.

No wonder they'd been so eager to get up to *Lion*...

A third senior officer was present as well: Lieutenant Alek Nosov, who'd been Katya Romanov's Helm and Navigation Officer aboard *Sackville*, but who'd had to take compassionate leave when his wife was in a very nasty accident in Sochi. He'd been put ashore to look after her and their two sons during the treatment period, and she had fortunately recovered, but his ship had moved on without him.

Around him were junior officers and crew in a similar situation — people who hadn't lost a ship, but for reasons of circumstance, injury or illness, had been left behind at one point or another during the war. Now they had a Belt Squadron ship to return to.

All of these folks were sitting around when Kris and Kate turned up, and they noticed immediately when their new skipper arrived. The greeting at that point did not involve everyone coming to attention and offering salutes, because that would have been a little too formal under the circumstances... they instead started up a loud and lengthy round of applause. They were congratulating Kris for her recovery, and for the actions that she'd taken back at Io to save the ship they were all now aboard.

That was a good moment, and Kris tells me she wishes she could have enjoyed it more. Knowing her, I think she was actually hugely embarrassed by it — and probably a little bit more moved than she wants to admit — but that's not relevant.

Kate waited by the door while Kris moved up to the bar at the front of the club, pulled a chair from a nearby table and climbed up on it to address everyone.

"Thanks for getting here so quickly," she said. "We have a lot of sorting out to do, but basically we need to be ready to cruise within hours. We're not going anywhere... at least not yet. But we need to be ready."

At this point she had a decision to make: did she confide in her crew the details of the situation they were now confronted with — the chance that there could be a coup, and that as a trusted ship, *Lion* could be plunged into a complicated situation? It was the first time she'd met a lot of these people in person, would that be too much?

You know the two words I'd bring up in answer to that particular question. One starts with a B, the other an S.

Wait, no I don't mean bullshit. I was going to say Belt Squadron. But now I'm slightly perturbed by the fact that the initials are the same. But I suppose bullshit is one word, not two. Still, weird...

"I don't know how closely you've been following the situation on Capital Island, but I spoke to the Second Lord yesterday. There are complicated days ahead, and I expect we could be faced with some difficult choices. And while there are plenty of ships in orbit, I think the message for us is that, even though we've been a crew for all of twenty minutes, and for a lot of you this might be your first time aboard *Lion*, we're going to be one of the trusted players. Because our history together with the Belt Squadron counts for a lot. They know where our loyalties lie, and that's to the Empire first and always."

It was good rousing stuff that Kris was saying, and she saw a lot of approval in the faces of the people she was addressing. The approval increased, though, when the first plates of simbacon and eggs came out of the galley and were laid on the bar behind her. Like Kris and Kate, most of the people in this room hadn't slept much while they'd been figuring out how to get to *Lion* as quickly as possible.

Now fuel had arrived, and no good skipper would try to stand in the way of it.

"I see that I just got overshadowed," Kris grinned. "Come on, eat. Enough speeches, we'll figure out who does what while we're chewing."

With that, the new crew of *Lion* gallantly started chowing down.

Chapter Eight

The Morning Begins

Hikawa Maru reached Earth's security zone early Thursday morning — not terribly long after Kris and her new crew started eating. That still put them a few hours from orbit, and from sending shuttles down to the planet with passengers... but they were close.

Neither Marshal nor Mel had slept well the night prior, owing to the gravity of the day ahead, but now they showed no signs of fatigue as they packed up their kits, and again reviewed their plans for the day.

"So the shuttle takes us down to the civilian landing field across from Parliament," Mel repeated the landing point again, and Marshal nodded. She continued, "Then Peter takes us across to Cavanaugh's office. They pull together the Belt caucus for a mid-morning meeting, and you go in with them."

"Yep," Marshal agreed. He was only half-listening, because he had the entirely separate concern of what to say to those people. All of the complications of getting there, and getting out again, required serious thought... but if he didn't convince the caucus to switch sides, it was all pointless anyway.

"I'll stick with you... there'll probably be some SF around who'll help if there's a problem, but listen, if things go wrong and you have to get out without me, go straight to Admiralty House, and get a call through to DCI HQ. If Thea Fostopolos gives you any grief, tell her she'll answer to me."

Marshal began to nod absently at that assertion, but then the menace of the last comment led him to look at his wife, "I will..."

He didn't ask why the Vice Admiral in charge of Defense Command Intelligence would be answering to a quasi-retired superagent, but then the way the spooks worked was a bit different than the way the fleet did. Mel Samuels, formerly Mel Fox, was well known as a lethal woman... that probably counted for a lot to the head of the service, who had gotten to her job by a less dangerous route — Thea had never been a field operative.

Anyway, hopefully there would be no circumstances under which Marshal had to flee from the Parliament buildings... despite what everyone seemed to think, he doubted this was going to blow up into any sort of militant action, especially after the events of *The Almost Coup*. Hadn't everyone learned something from that experience?

"I'll be fine," he said after a moment's thought, and then he returned to packing his kit.

Mel looked at him for a moment, then quietly pulled a box out of her bag — an old box she'd had for years. Opening it, she found her compact little MAG-2, a relatively rare weapon that was small, very concealable, and none too sympathetic. It had gone out of service with Defense Command right around when the old EP-5 had been adopted, because it was considered 'too powerful'.

See, when you set the thing on non-lethal, it didn't kill... but it did have a tendency to leave behind third degree burns, or chew off the odd limb, depending on where you hit someone. They were popular sidearms for spies, who usually had to source them from the oddest places.

Mel had never given hers up, and while she and every other superagent, present or past, was adept with any mag you care to name, this was her personal favorite for complicated days.

You better believe she'd be carrying it today.

Hikawa Maru got closer to Earth.

There was a complication as *Lion's* bridge crew started to sort itself out: there were two Helm and Navigation Officers (Allison Ting and Alek Nosov), and three times as many Helm and Navigation personnel as were needed at the moment. That would be great if *Lion* was asked to take an impromptu cruise through a comet trail — there'd be no shortage of flight expertise — but it left the bridge with an awful imbalance.

Because the Sensors and Communications section had exactly one person in it: Able Spacer Justine Alto.

Now, as you might be able to tell, Sensors and Communications required more than one person, so this made for a fun meeting when the bridge crew got together after breakfast.

"So," Kris was standing at the front of the bridge with her back to the screens, arms folded. The Helm and Navigation people were standing comically to one side of the bridge, while Able Spacer Alto stood on the other. "I know this is going to be somewhat difficult, but we need six volunteers to move over and work Sensors and Communications. Any of you have any cross-training over there?"

Two hands went up, and then without her saying anything, the spacer and the junior officer who had some experience working either sensors or communications shuffled out of their crowd, and moved over to Alto's side.

"Any of you decent at either sensors or communications at the Academy?"

Three hands this time, and again, Kris didn't have to say anything to get the volunteers to move.

"Alright. And last but not least, anybody feeling particularly lucky this morning?"

No hands went up, but finally one more person shuffled across to the Sensors and Communications side.

That was six, and Kris smiled, "Excellent, thanks. Alek, Allison, join me and Kate up here will you? Stations for the rest of you."

There weren't enough chairs for all the Helm and Navigation staff, so they decided amongst themselves who would be sent below to assist Roy Canter's engineers in getting things running — there tended to be a closer relationship between the helm people and the engineers, since they all depended on engines.

While that happened, Alek and Allison joined Kate and Kris... sorry, let me stop here and say it's very odd how many people seemed to have first names starting with the same letter on *Lion*. Obviously it wasn't planed, but the alliteration is getting a bit noticeable, even to me. Anyway, sorry, they all met up at the front of the bridge, and Kris looked at her two new officers.

"I need one of you to take over as security officer, and find a team of at least five...

preferably ten or twelve... who are good with mags, and who we can deploy in a pinch. If the day gets complicated."

Again, she wasn't going to *tell* either Lieutenant to do the job, because she didn't know them well enough.

Alek looked a bit stern at the suggestion, but glancing to Allison, Kris found a thoughtfully interested expression, "I will take that job, if Alek agrees."

"Yours, certainly," he replied with a nod.

That was it — the senior staff was essentially filled. And yes, it really was done in a rather casual fashion, as there was no time for anything else. But it worked, because these people were... well, you can say it to yourself.

As Alek returned to his consoles, and Allison headed to the operations section at the rear of the bridge to start considering who to press into her security staff, Kris and Kate turned back to the screens at the front of the bridge.

"Need me running Sensors and Communications?" the XO asked softly, and Kris nodded.

"I'll look after Operations while you do," the Aussie skipper confirmed.

They'd both be pulling double duty, but that was fine. The ship would be ready.

Daragh was standing in his office with arms folded as he watched *Hikawa Maru* reach orbit. Like everyone else in this chapter, the Second Lord had not slept particularly well, and now he had the look of a mild madman as he stared at the arriving liner's icon.

Still no attempt to interfere with its approach, though honestly it would have been a surprise if anyone had tried to intervene at such an early stage. People like Fifth Lord of the Admiralty Lynn Bokai were not in John's inner circle, but they were still good Defense Command officers — and they controlled Earth's defense zone from Battleships like *Hokkaido*.

No, the real danger would begin when Marshal's shuttle came down to land. The ground really was the realm of the army, and of Bennington's people too. If Marshal's shuttle was waved off without reason, Daragh would have to jump in with special authorization for the craft to touch down at Admiralty House's field... and then the real fun could start.

He could just picture blockheads arriving and insisting that the craft could not land, for some trumped up reason, and things could only go more badly from there...

Just as Daragh was thinking these things, there was a knock at his door. It was an unexpected interruption, so he shut off his screen before letting whoever it was in, "Come."

The door opened and revealed a young Special Branch Major with whom Daragh was only loosely acquainted — he was now the senior Brancher on Capital Island, since Carrie Walsh had been downed at Mercury.

"Morning Isko," the Irishman greeted the Filipino, and Isko Caacbay nodded in return.

"Second Lord. You'll be happy to hear I was able to call in a favor, and have an extra squad of Branchers join us today for joint training. We now have forty-eight officers on Capital Island, all here in Terra Nova."

Well, that was good news... though 'good' wasn't exactly the word that went through

Daragh's head when he heard it.

"The two divisions the blockheads moved into Burin overnight number around 33,000, including a shitload of armor," the Second Lord replied.

Caacbay tilted his head slightly, "I'd heard. I won't indulge in too much bravado and say that they should have brought more with them, sir. But you and I both know they should have."

Isko Caacbay had done a tour on Mercury, and he was pretty confident in himself and his other Branchers. That was fair — they were Branchers, after all — but the odds against them were something close to 700 to one.

"Just stay ready," Daragh said quietly, and Caacbay nodded, then departed.

Turning on his screen again after the door closed behind the young Major, the Second Lord sighed and folded his arms. He had no idea what to expect from this day... it just needed to happen.

And since we aren't as confined by the strictures of linear time as he was, let's skip ahead so we can see how it goes down.

CHAPTER NINE

FIRST STEPS

If any of *Hikawa Maru's* other passengers had a question about why Marshal, Mel, and Peter McKnight got a shuttle all to themselves, the Belt Station's Commodore never heard it. Not that he would have been listening.

It was around 0900 Earth Standard Time when the shuttle slipped away from the liner's hull and dove straight for Capital Island. Marshal was sitting in a window seat in the comfortable cabin, and as he watched Earth grow to fill his window he took a series of deep breaths to keep his nerves in check.

Mel was sitting at a window seat on the other side of the narrow aisle, going through her own calming rituals — ones that she hadn't really had to make use of since her days as a supposed Syndicate Captain, back when she'd helped us track and defeat Grant Merger.

As reintroductions to the active spy life went, this was a real doozy…

From his window, Marshal was the first to see a squadron of F-194 Starlights running through the upper atmosphere. Frowning, he watched them crisscrossing in what appeared to be atmospheric combat maneuvers… Daragh probably had them on 'exercises', he figured.

Of course he was correct.

Mel saw the same streaks, but she didn't pay them too much attention. If something was coming to shoot them down, she'd have no control over it now, so she just kept her focus.

Their shuttle dropped through the atmosphere.

"Message coming in from Admiralty House," Kate Levec saw the notice on the communications console before the helm officer who was gamely trying to crew it realized what the flashing icon meant.

Kris was behind the operations consoles at the back of the bridge, but she looked up at the report, "Realtime? Let's have it on the main screen."

Stepping out and around the consoles, Kris moved to her old spot at the front of the bridge as a *Lion*Net loading screen appeared, buffering the message. It didn't take long, and when Daragh appeared he looked pretty disheveled.

"Can you break dock soon, Kris?"

The Aussie skipper nodded, "Whenever you need us to."

"Do it. The delegation we've been waiting for just entered the atmosphere, so if there's to be any creativity, it'll be sooner rather than later."

Kris didn't need to be told twice, "Understood. We'll go into orbit over Capital Island, so we won't be far away if you need a pickup, or a drop off."

It was as much as either of them were going to say over the comm — this was realtime, not secured Battlelink (which, in retrospect, might have been unwise, but they got away with it). The Second Lord nodded for one more second, then vanished from the screen.

Looking first to Kate, then to Alek Nosov, Kris gave the order: "Prepare to break dock."

Schwartz T. Babcock was waiting in his office, much as Daragh was, but his assistant Donna was sitting across the desk from him as they watched the progress of Marshal's shuttle on his screen.

Donna was just over thirty, but she had absolutely no problem with the youngster she was working for — Schwartz had earned her appreciation from his very first day at PMO. By now she was ready to take a mag bolt for the wonderkid, and as he watched the icon of the shuttle spiraling down towards Capital Island, Schwartz couldn't help but glance at her and wonder if today might be the day when she'd need to.

What *was* going to happen today? If it was a coup, then shots at the Prime Minister's staff really weren't out of the question. He hoped it didn't go that way, but if it did he'd have to make sure a lot of people in the office, Donna particularly, got home safe.

They were his responsibility, as far as he was concerned — Murt Sergeant be damned.

"So, if one of Bennington's people tries to deny them permission to land, they go to the Admiralty field, not to ours?" Donna asked, glancing across the table at Schwartz.

Nodding, the Deputy Chief of Staff took a breath, "If they get denied, it'll mean there's trouble coming. Daragh figures it's safer if that trouble goes to a military facility, instead of the Prime Minister's Office."

He was right, it would be better not to have tanks rolling up PMO's lawn... though again, the day was young. Who knew how it would end.

"I hope they just let him land," Donna said.

"Me too," Schwartz agreed.

The North Atlantic was under the shuttle's hull when Marshal blinked himself free of his mental preparations. He watched the waves go by under the morning sun as he settled back into his seat with a bit more comfort, and then he looked across at his wife. She was smiling at him.

"Got everything set in your head?" she asked, knowing the answer.

He nodded, "I think we'll have a very good talk. I haven't seen these folks in a while, but I think they'll be interested in what I have to say."

"They certainly will."

The shuttle was rocking a very little in the turbulence as it coasted along, and then suddenly they were over the Capital Island coastline. They weren't making the approach straight over Terra Nova; they'd come over land a little bit to the north, and as they made a turn over Gander and redirected towards the capital city, Mel and Marshal watched trees and ponds blur past beneath them.

Not long now.

Daragh activated a realtime orbital view of the shuttle's approach just as it began to cruise over land. A camera from the orbiting battleship *Honshu* had the small craft in its sights, and followed it along as it coasted over the trees and finally came into sight of the capital.

To all but a few people on the entire planet, the shuttle couldn't have seemed anything but innocuous — the wealthiest passengers aboard a liner who had paid to be delivered specially to the capital, first thing in the morning so they'd have more time for sightseeing. Happened all the time.

But Daragh's heart rate was up to a point that probably wasn't healthy for his years, and time was running awfully slow.

Tapping into the comms chatter between Terra Nova approach control and the shuttle, he was able to hear everything that was said between the craft and the tower... and the closer they got, the more he expected to hear an override. Something ominous — 'Shuttle HM-0401, wave off as you are not cleared for landing.'

Or maybe something more melodramatic: 'Traitors cannot land here.'

But the shuttle came over Terra Nova and slowed right down, then moved into position to touch down in its slot at the civilian field across from Parliament. It had to hover for a moment, waiting for a tourist sub-orbital bus hopper from South America to get out of the way, but then it put down its landing feet and came down gently to ground.

Just that simple.

Daragh switched to a local surveillance cam to watch the next part, his heart pounding really hard now. They had made it... unless the shuttle exploded.

Or what about the South American bus? What if there were assassins or kidnappers aboard...

So many things that could happen. He had to wait to see...

Marshal got to his feet, fairly confident that there would be no further complications. They'd gotten safely to ground, and they were a two-minute walk from the Parliament buildings. Peter McKnight, Leslie Cavanaugh's Chief of Staff, came up the aisle behind Marshal and Mel — he'd been sitting in the back — and nodded to them both before leading the way to the front of the cabin, then down the ramp.

Following closely, the Belt Station Commodore took a refreshing breath of perfect Capital Island air, squinted against the sun, then turned towards the Parliament buildings. Mel was right behind him, donning her sunglasses as soon as she reached the top of the ramp.

She did love the air on Capital Island, and though real sun was always harsher on her eyes than the simulated daylight in an Earthgreen dome, nothing compared to the warmth. She descended the ramp behind her husband, looking like a proper Commodore's wife while still keeping her hand near the MAG-2, which was concealed neatly in a dampening holster against the small of her back.

Together, the three of them started walking, with Mel trailing far enough behind to keep an eye on every person who was on foot or in a vehicle nearby. There were plenty.

She was the only one who noticed the shuttle's fourth passenger slip from the craft — of course, yet again, Camila Barrai had found a way to stay close. It would be good to have her around if trouble started...

◆◆◆

"That's good, they got down safely," Donna looked at Schwartz, and the Deputy Chief of Staff frowned.

"It is good…" but he didn't sound convinced.

There was another shoe waiting to drop, and he didn't know what it was. Folding his arms, he watched the security camera feeds that showed Marshal, Mel, and Peter McKnight approaching the front steps of the Parliament buildings. They were barely 400 meters away from the spot where Schwartz sat, and he was half tempted to go out there to meet them.

But that would be the wrong message. He had to sit tight and just watch.

Something would happen soon.

Entering the Parliament buildings is never a particularly casual affair. It was Thursday morning, and there were a dozen SF on duty as McKnight led Marshal and Mel inside. He had his pass, so they waved him to the staff line, scanned him quickly, and he was through.

Most visitors had a much more complicated time, though if you're a recognized Defense Command officer like Marshal Samuels, the guards are inevitably less suspicious.

The Ensign commanding the detail spotted Marshal immediately, and since he was in uniform, waved him straight to the staff line as well, "Commodore, welcome to Parliament."

Nodding, Marshal glanced back at Mel — who was quite calmly lined up with some of the tourists waiting to get in through the regular gate. He considered asking to have her come through with him, but decided against it… nothing to show that he had reason to think she needed special treatment.

He then remembered she was armed.

As Marshal joined McKnight on the other side of the checkpoint, the Ensign remained close by, "Is there anyone you need me to contact for you, sir?"

"No," Marshal shook his head quickly, trying not to look over the Ensign's shoulder too furtively as Mel reached the front of the check line. "We're having a meeting… we're expected."

The Ensign nodded, and behind him, Mel smiled sweetly at the SF at the checkpoint, then stepped through. Anybody trying to take a weapon into Parliament is destined to have a serious disagreement with the SF at the gate. The only ones who get away with it are brass — if they're high enough up on the chain to tell off the guards — and Special Branch.

Spies never get a pass.

But as Marshal watched anxiously, he remembered that his wife, and many superagents of her kind, had a tendency to make their own passes. The holster for her MAG-2 was made of special magic stuff that I can't really explain here, and the sensors missed the weapon altogether.

Obviously I won't get into details of why and how — if you're curious, maybe you should call SF and ask them how you can smuggle a weapon through security at Parliament. See how that conversation ends. And no, I won't pay to replace your front door after they've knocked it off its hinges.

Anyway, Mel came up behind the Ensign with a lovely big smile, "My, there's so much security here. Does it take many of you to protect the government?"

The question surprised the young officer, and realizing what his wife was doing, Marshal introduced her, "Ensign, this is my wife Melissa."

"Oh, I'm sorry ma'am, we'd have taken you through special as well," the young officer said as he stood aside and turned to her. "And it's no small job here, ma'am. There's at least seventy of us on duty at all times."

That was good to know — seventy SF in the building on the current shift. It was down from the 124 that were supposed to be on the job, but then everything had been reduced since Mercury. The people we lost on that assault, and the people who were still there as part of Greg's occupation force, were sorely needed back home...

Something we'd get to grips with later. For now, they had places to be.

"If you'll excuse us, Ensign, we have to get to that meeting," Peter McKnight cut in politely, and the young officer nodded.

"Of course."

With that, they headed down one of the corridors towards Leslie Cavanaugh's office. They had made it through the cordon safely... what else could get in their way?

Behind them, Camila Barrai breezed through security just as Mel had, and she joined the South American tourist group until such time as she was needed. She had a feeling she would be.

CHAPTER TEN
THE MEETING

Daragh Ryan was more than a little confused, and when Marshal made it safely inside Parliament, the Irishman got Schwartz T. Babcock on the line. As the Deputy Chief of Staff appeared, the Second Lord shook his head.

"You think they really are arrogant enough not to worry?"

Schwartz took a deep breath and then shook his head, "I don't know. But I'm not letting down my guard just yet."

"Me neither. *Lion's* going into orbit right over our heads, by the way."

Though Schwartz wasn't sure what precisely a frigate could do if tanks started hovering into town, he nodded all the same.

"We'll have to see how the meeting goes, I suppose."

That's all they could do.

Marshal met Leslie Cavanaugh in her office and they chatted for about twenty minutes. It was a private conversation — Peter McKnight went to his office to start summoning the rest of the Belt caucus to a quick meeting, while Mel stood in the waiting area of the small Parliamentary office and read the posters on the walls.

"Become a page for the House of Commons," she read one, then looked to another. "Wash your hands."

The décor was eclectic, if nothing else. She was feeling confident enough to pay attention to what was on the walls now — they were inside, and it seemed that Olivia Bennington's agents, whoever they were, had yet to set any real traps for them.

Of course, there was still plenty of opportunity for trouble, so she wasn't going to let her guard down entirely...

After their twenty minutes of chatting, Leslie and Marshal emerged from her office, and Peter McKnight joined them. Leslie greeted Mel in standard political fashion, remembering at least one relevant personal question for the Commodore's wife (to demonstrate that she cared and was deserving of a vote) and then together the four of them headed down the corridor to one of the caucus meeting rooms.

When they arrived, Leslie entered first, followed by Peter. Mel and Marshal waited in the hallway to give Leslie a chance to announce them. Listening at the door, the Belt Station Commodore heard his introduction: "I know we've heard a lot from the Deputy PM's office about the dangers of letting Defense Command have the run of the place. I know it's hard to remember now how desperate we all were back in the early days of the war. But I think it's important we listen to what they have to say, and remember that just before this mess started, the political enemies of Defense Command were the ones doing a lot to handcuff the Navy's ability to protect our colonies. We have a chance to stop the same from happening again. I know a lot of you think I'm wrong about that... but I have one person you need to listen to."

She nodded to Peter McKnight, who opened the door for Marshal. As our elite Commodore entered, Mel followed as far as the inside of the door, then stopped and put her hand on the small of her back, scanning the crowd.

There were more than fifty people present, and she recognized every one of them… all politicians. She let her hand fall from the small of her back… though not too far. Just in case.

Marshal wasn't thinking about security as he strode to the front of the room and thanked Leslie. He was entirely centered as he turned to the Belt caucus, and he noticed that most of the members seemed awfully surprised to see him.

"Ladies and Gentlemen, I got here this morning, just in time to have a conversation with you about what I think is happening. I want to start by stressing a simple point: whatever you do tomorrow when you vote on that confidence motion is up to you. This is a democratic body, an Empire built on the representation of the people by elected persons such as yourself. Defense Command is a tool of the government, and we will not interfere except to stop someone from coercing you. But I don't think any of you have been coerced."

He paused and found that his statement — meant to allay any concerns in the room — seemed to bring no reaction.

So he continued: "You all know me. We went through a lot together during the war, and when you all left your colonies to come back here for the current Parliamentary session, most of you were either escorted by my Belt Squadron ships in a convoy, or were taken aboard one of my ships directly. You saw the Navy's value during the war, and I hope that gives me the credibility to speak to you about the wellbeing of the Empire.

"I wouldn't presume to tell you your business as legislators. You're the right people for your jobs, and you know the requirements of your service as well as I know the requirements of mine. But I will tell you that, if we were back at the Belt and one of you told me there was a chance you were going to bring down your own government, while the Prime Minister was at Mars finalizing a peace treaty, I'd have problems with the idea.

"Does change need to happen? Maybe. However, what does it say about the people pushing for change if they're trying to do it when the opposing voices are all away? And not just away on some sort of careless holiday, but out there securing peace for the Empire? I know you've heard things… heard that Defense Command has been trying to influence government, or has been making its own policy during the war. But you all have worked with us closely… you've seen what we do. We're not all perfect, but we're also not the sort to run from a discussion.

"So this is my advice: if you believe what Bennington has been saying about the need to disentangle the government from Defense Command's influence, then let's start having some real conversations about the issue. But let's have the conversations with everyone together in one place, at one time. Let's not try to rewrite policy while the heads of government and the Emperor aren't even on the planet."

There was a knock on Schwartz T. Babcock's door, and as it opened he and Donna turned to see T.J. Gregg, the Prime Minister's Press Secretary, leaning in with a scowl.

"The Governor General and the Deputy PM just called the Parliamentary press corps to the steps outside Center Block. They've got guards with them."

Schwartz blinked. Press corps?

And then it all fell into place.

"Get Tony and Cam to the meeting room, I'll be right there," Schwartz said quickly. "I have to make a call."

"One more point I want to make," Marshal was nearing the end of his remarks. "If you're worried about the military being involved in politics, I think that's fair. I just want to remind you… maybe warn you… that the Imperial Army is not neutral. That it is a tool of the Emperor, and his Governor General, and that if anyone in Parliament is cooperating closely with the heads of state, Imperial troops might be involved. I won't make any accusations, I have no evidence. But all I will say, one more time, is that you and I have worked together. You know how Defense Command operates… you know that we stand by our word, and if you take drastic action when the confidence vote comes tomorrow, the consequences could be greater than you think."

"What is it?" Daragh asked urgently, as soon as Schwartz appeared on his screen.

"I'm sorry, Second Lord. We should have realized what was happening… do nothing. Don't say anything right now. Let us do the talking."

The young Deputy Chief of Staff's words inspired no confidence, and added no clarity to the Irish Lord's understanding of the situation, "What's going on?"

Schwartz shook his head, "The Parliamentary press corps is on the steps of Center Block. Turn on the news, and get your Special Branchers ready just in case."

There was no applause in the caucus room as Marshal finished and departed, but Mel gave him a quick hug of congratulation as they stepped out into the corridor, followed by Peter McKnight. Leslie Cavanaugh remained with her fellow politicos, to drive the message further home.

"Thanks for doing that, Marshal. I think it'll make a big difference," Peter said easily as they headed for the office, so they could collect their things and then be on their way.

"We'll head over to Admiralty House and wait to hear from you about how things are looking," Marshal replied with a nod.

He hoped he'd done enough.

CHAPTER ELEVEN

THE MISTAKE

The press conference was on every news channel in the world, because it was a Thursday morning and there wasn't much else happening (Murt Sergeant's marital problems aside). Daragh watched it live, as did Schwartz T. Babcock and the remains of the Prime Minister's senior staff.

Now, I'm going to explain the choreography of this little show very carefully, even though you've probably already seen it — obviously, the footage isn't tough to come by, since it was a press conference.

Olivia Bennington and Governor General James Hodson arrived at the front of the Center Block of Parliament not by coming through the building, but by walking around the outside from behind. And when they came, a full platoon of Imperial soldiers in dress uniforms followed.

Those soldiers weren't the ones from Burin — they were the GG's personal guard, or at least part of it. He had 250 men in town to ensure his safety… because clearly, a lone political appointee requires that much heavily-armed protection while he's living in the capital of the Earth Empire.

A single podium was set up for Bennington and Hodson to share, and it was well-covered by the cameras and parabolic microphones of the press corps by the time those two were descending the steps. Everyone was interested to see what was coming, though on a dull Thursday morning the most they could hope for was early news about the peace with Mars.

The fact that blockheads followed the pair was interesting though — particularly to those reporters who had been on Capital Island in 2231. They didn't think anything like that might be happening again — surely the fools wouldn't want to repeat such a daft almost coup — but it was an ominous memory all the same.

When they arrived at the podium, both Bennington and Hodson looked suitably grave, and the Deputy Prime Minister began immediately, "Ladies and Gentlemen, thank you for joining us on such short notice. Today we have been informed of serious allegations of corruption within our government, and it is my unhappy duty to report them to you."

Corruption. Just wait for it.

"Tomorrow, the government was to present a ways and means motion to both houses of Parliament," Bennington continued. "Because of the declining threat of military action due to the ceasefire, this motion would take the first steps towards reducing our Empire's military expenditures, and reducing the size of the Defense Command Fleet. This is a necessary step, as we need to preserve fiscal responsibility in our Empire."

Daragh, by now, was staring at the screen in his office. Staring so hard you'd swear it would shatter. In PMO, Schwartz was already shaking his head — the motion was supposed to include nothing about defense spending, but he assumed that Bennington's people had changed it without bothering to inform the Prime Minister's Office.

"This morning, without any warning, Commodore Marshal Samuels, commander of the Belt Station, arrived here at Parliament, and went into a secret meeting with certain elected officials from our government. His aim was not just to lobby against this bill, but indeed to threaten the government with dire consequences if the bill was passed. We believe Samuels' efforts have the full and total approval of Admiralty House, as well as some members of the Prime Minister's personal staff."

I'll get to the things that were wrong with that statement in a minute: it was at this moment that Daragh and Schwartz both began to wonder if there was any sort of evidence out there that would connect either of them to Marshal's arrival. Because obviously our elite Commodore wasn't on Earth for the purpose Bennington said he was, but she was trying to make it look nefarious. Was there anything either the Second Lord or the Deputy Chief of Staff had done to make her job easier?

"This morning, Admiralty House canceled all leave for Naval personnel in Earth space, and even now, atmospheric attack squadrons are conducting exercises over our heads. The threat is clear, and so I have been forced to ask the Governor General to dissolve our government, and to provide security for Capital Island until this situation is resolved. As my last act as the acting head of Earth government, I now order all Defense Command forces to take *no action* against this effort. If you do, you will merely prove your intention to seize power. Democracy must rule in the Empire, or all you have just fought to win in the war was for naught."

I cannot describe the rage her last words instilled in officers across the Earth security zone. First, her move was probably the most effective public relations attack she had at her disposal — she was framing the situation so that if we lifted a finger to prove that she was, in fact, taking part in the Emperor's plot to steal control of the government, we would appear to be the ones guilty of attempting a coup.

And then to try to tell us why we'd fought the war, just for her positioning purposes... well, we didn't take that too nicely.

Hodson picked up now: "As Governor General, I have dissolved the government, and I echo Miss Bennington's demands for cooperation. I have contacted the Emperor about this situation, and his orders to me have been clear: Imperial Army troops will take over security of Capital Island, and will also be picketed to protect key locations across Earth against Defense Command treachery. If Defense Command has nothing to hide, as they claim, then they will cooperate. The evidence will tell the story. For now, I am ordering the arrest of Commodore Samuels, and the detention of Second Lord Daragh Ryan. Admiralty House will be shut down immediately!"

That bastard clearly thought he was in a very strong position, which he sort of was. I'll get into the analysis of all of this shortly, but as you probably know, the press conference didn't end on that note.

"Stop this charade immediately!"

Schwartz T. Babcock was a young and enthusiastic Deputy Chief of Staff. Had he been older or more reserved, there's no way he'd have sprinted from PMO to the steps outside Center Block, and yelled so loudly to get his own word in before the press conference ended.

But he did, and probably a good thing too.

"The Deputy Prime Minister and the Emperor, through his Governor General, have been colluding in an attempt to defeat the Prime Minister," he called, and the microphones turned in time to catch his charge. "That they are willing to go to such extremes, including ordering illegal arrests and issuing illegal orders to our Defense Command, is a sign that they are attempting to stage a coup without being obvious about it!"

"Another conspirator arrives to attempt to save his skin!" Hodson bellowed, drawing the reporters and microphones back to him. "This proves the inclusion of the Prime Minister in this plot. Pope too must be arrested!"

As you might guess, this is where the reporters really started to wonder about what they were hearing.

But there was more, because as Schwartz got closer to the podium, the GG waved a squad of blockheads to intercept the young politico. That raised even more eyebrows.

And that still wasn't the end, because completely oblivious to the press conference going on outside, Marshal, Mel and Peter McKnight emerged from Center Block's doors at the top of the stairs, and took the first few steps down before realizing there was a circus twenty meters away.

"There he is! The conspirator! Arrest him at once!" Hodson was probably the weakest link in this whole attempt, because his self-important sense of melodrama was seriously jeopardizing his credibility.

A dozen Imps turned and leveled their energy guns at Marshal and Mel, then started clomping up the stairs. This drew cries of shock from some of the members of the South American tourist group, who were emerging just behind our elite pair.

As the troops came on, McKnight turned and hurried back into the building where he yelled a single word: "Coup!"

Marshal stood defiantly on the stairs, not sure what had been said in his absence, but certainly not cowed by a bunch of blockheads, "You can't overthrow the government with your ploys, so you send in the troops? You're going to swing for your treachery."

That got picked up on a bunch of parabolic microphones, so it added to the confusing mess of stories and counter-stories that the media now had to chew on.

"Resist and you will die!" one of the Imps barked — also picked up by the media.

Marshal had no intention of resisting. But Mel wasn't about to let her husband get black-bagged.

If you're going to come out of superspy-retirement, there are few more dramatic ways to do it than the one she picked. It's funny to watch the news footage, because you have to run it in slow motion to actually see everything she did in the next thirty seconds. The results were clear enough, though; a bunch of blockheads rolling down the stairs, a few leaving trails of blood behind them.

None died, of course — because she's that good and knew it would be a headache if she actually killed one of them — but they weren't going to take anyone prisoner. Then she was suddenly in front of Marshal with her MAG-2 in hand, and then out of nowhere, Camila Barrai was behind our elite Commodore with a MAG-3 — her own weapon of choice, apparently.

Seconds later, twenty-two guards of the Parliamentary SF detail were hurrying down the steps from the front door with tac vests and MAG-90s.

"What's going on, sir?" the Ensign in charge asked Marshal, and the Belt Station Commodore shook his head.

"They just tried to arrest me, we don't know why."

"Not happening," the Ensign said sharply.

As the SF fanned out on the steps, the blockheads lined up behind the GG turned on them with energy guns leveled, creating a good old-fashioned standoff, with Defense Command outnumbered and Marshal and Mel in the middle.

Schwartz T. Babcock then drew attention back to himself — he was in a staring contest with the blockheads who'd been sent to take him, but who had stopped just short when the fighting started.

"The charges the Governor General and the Deputy Prime Minister have leveled are serious ones, and you media are smart enough to see how perfectly they've been positioned. If we take any action to stop the illegal takeover of this government, they can claim that we are the criminals. I know you're smarter than to fall for it!"

It was a good, quick assessment of the situation, and the reporters in the Parliamentary press corps had been around the block more than enough times to know bullshit when they heard it. But there were two very different stories going back and forth as they listened — the less likely tale that there was a DC-PMO conspiracy against democracy, and a much more likely story that the Deputy PM and the Emperor were making some sort of play for power.

The problem was, our side was unprepared for this sort of attack... we were focused on the vote, and as Schwartz had realized too late, we'd failed to grasp the fact that all the Emperor's people needed to launch their takeover was some implication, no matter how flimsy, that we were trying to interfere with democracy.

We'd played right into the bastard's hands — we'd been so paranoid about what he'd done last time that we'd set up circumstances that would look good for him and his cronies. We were too cavalier, we'd been reckless, and that let him put us in this bind.

Around the time that Daragh was having this revelation — watching from his office — more troops entered the shot. Another company of blockheads was coming around the building, using the same route the GG and Deputy PM had taken. As they came into sight, Marshal made a quick decision.

"We're leaving, right now. Let's get to Admiralty House."

He nodded to the Ensign as he spoke, and the Parliamentary detail followed as Marshal, Mel, and Camila started moving. Seeing the situation, Schwartz backed away from the blockheads who had been coming for him, then followed. Wisely, the Imps didn't give chase.

"There is your evidence, ladies and gentlemen. They will not stand and face the charges!" Hodson declared, and you really could tell he was getting carried away. The glorified ribbon cutter had a taste of supposed power, and he was working it real hard.

"All media will now be offered special protection, to avoid your being targeted by Defense Command!" he declared. "Thank you!"

Nice note to end on. And as he did, blockheads moved to envelop the press corps.

This was perhaps the biggest mistake the stupid bastards made, but I'll explain that in a minute.

Watching the end of the feed, Daragh turned to his desk and keyed the comm, "Alert the fleet to stand by for orders, have Major Caacbay prepare to defend Admiralty House."

There was a pause on the other end of the line, and then the lights in the buildings shut off, "Sir, we've been cut off from all orbital communication. They just switched off our connection to the main power grid too. Backups will be online soon... but we're being jammed."

Of course they were. Because as stupid as the bastards were, the Emperor's folks had learned last time that leaving Admiralty House in operation during their attempt to take over was a bad idea.

Alright, time to do some analysis.

Chapter Twelve

Analysis

I'll always remember Charlie Peters' first reaction to all of this when I told him about it later. His exact words: "Well, we certainly walked into this one, didn't we?"

He's completely right. Because when you take a step back and look at that press conference/showdown, as the media had to, you see a situation where right and wrong, legal and illegal can be difficult to distinguish. We were all running close to the edge, but some went over… and that *some* wasn't us.

If you go back to the original situation we thought we were walking into, we were facing the possibility of Bennington bringing down her own government and then giving the Emperor effective control of both houses. After that, we figured there would be a slew of drumhead trials, trying to neuter Defense Command before a new election could restore the status quo.

To prevent this, we were taking completely legal and I think correct steps: we had Marshal going in to remind the Belt caucus of what they were preparing to throw away, and Karen and I were coming back to provide evidence of what the Emperor's troops — and Defense Command's would-be replacements — could do when they let their power go to their heads.

See how well drumhead trials worked in the face of some widespread public outcry.

But the Emperor had predicted, quite correctly, that we'd get involved, and though he figured we wouldn't actually overstep ourselves, it wouldn't take much to make it look like we had.

So using Marshal's visit as an excuse, he'd had Bennington trump up a charge of corruption which allowed her to make a perfectly legal request to have the government dissolved. But here's an important point: when you dissolve a government, another one is meant to replace it. You can have an election, or under rare circumstances the leader of the opposition can be asked to form one.

The Governor General did neither, and this is where it all went wrong, at least from my point of view. With no mandated government in place, he started giving unilateral orders for arrests, which the Imperial Army would conduct even though they had no legal authority. He was basically trying to seize control of the Empire on behalf of the Emperor.

As I mentioned before, they were clever about this — Bennington basically painted a picture that implied the corruption ran too deep, and that the government could not be trusted, so it had to be this way… but that was more than a stretch. Basically, we had an appointee of the Emperor trying to dictate government, at least in the short term, until all the evil conspirators could be taken into custody.

Now, if you could cut through the bullshit and see that story as it was happening during the press conference, then things would be clear enough: this was an attempted coup, dressed up in some neat excuses.

But the problem was that nothing was crystal clear in the moment. They were good at clouding their story in enough uncertainty to get away with it, so while the reporters standing there were scratching their heads, thinking something was rotten about the whole thing, there was enough of a possibility it was true that they couldn't jump one way or the other. After all, going public with such a massive lie, backed by troops, would be a career ender at the best... a hanging offense at the worst... so surely neither Bennington nor the GG would be so daft as to do it unless there was some truth behind their accusations.

There's a saying, I think, that if you make the lie big enough...

So the media was on the fence, and that could have been all the latitude these coup-throwing bastards would have needed, at least for a while. But fortunately for us, they over-played their hand.

Perhaps realistically, the GG, the Emperor, and Bennington realized it wouldn't take much time at all for reporters to start digging into the story, and then the whole fiction could unravel with relative ease. So instead of letting them do that, the Parliamentary press corps was taken into custody for its own safety.

I don't know if anyone believes it anymore when they're told they're being taken anywhere 'for their own safety'. The jaded veterans of many Parliamentary scrums certainly weren't fooled... but that didn't matter either, because thanks to Dave Caldecott's old loyalists, the Emperor's side had control of Defense Command Communications, including the Capital Island comms grid.

So a switch got flipped and every system went dark, then started hyperventilating. That last word is my own, because I can't remember the actual technical term, but it basically means that the various massive comm grids on the island were switched into 'make loud screaming noise' mode, jamming every comm signal in or out.

And then, for final good measure, the blockheads around the world started moving against their targets. Remember Hodson said they'd protect certain key locations? Turns out all those locations were news transmitters above a certain broadcast power. The entire might of the Imperial Army left on Earth was spread out around the world to 132 transmitter sites — including the studio for the Geraldine Coilier show — to make sure the only information that got out from the government or military was under the Governor General's personal control.

Misdirection, confusion, and then silence. It was a mess, and of course, it was just getting started.

CHAPTER THIRTEEN

AMBIGUITY

Kris Jacobs had been expecting trouble, but like everyone else, she'd assumed there were limits. Nope.

As the feed from Capital Island winked out, and then all communications from Admiralty House shut down, Kate Levec looked up from the Sensors and Communications panels she was supervising.

"The blockheads are starting to move from Burin over to Terra Nova. They'll be in the city within an hour."

Of course they would be. That made perfect sense.

Kris just stood at the front of the bridge, arms folded, and wondered what the hell they could do about the situation. Strangely, the Deputy PM's order that Defense Command do nothing didn't hold much sway.

Like testing to see if a woman is a witch by tying her to an anvil and throwing her in a deep lake... if she finds a way to float, she must be a witch, and therefore should be burned. Only by doing nothing (and dying) does she prove her innocence. Fair deal.

Fortunately for us, Kris was a witch — sure as Marlene Stoll was one. And it's never a good idea to cross a witch.

"Signal coming from *Hokkaido*... to all ships," Able Spacer Alto reported, interrupting that internal monologue about sorcery.

"Screen two," Kris nodded, and then the Fifth Lord of the Admiralty, Lynn Bokai, appeared.

As I think I explained a long time ago, Fifth Lord is a parking position — a place you put Admirals when you don't have anything better for them to do. It doesn't include any key administrative responsibilities, though obviously John and Daragh had decided that they could put Lynn in charge of Earth's local defense forces.

That was a fine decision for the war itself — made sure there was a steady hand in orbit in case something elsewhere went terribly wrong — but keep in mind the fact that, when we attacked Mercury, it was Greg Noyce who commanded the mission, along with Marlene Stoll.

I don't mean to be unkind, but Lynn Bokai was an officer of a different cloth, and her message was in keeping with that composition: "Fifth Lord to all Defense Command ships and personnel in Earth Space. Clearly, the allegations leveled by the Deputy Prime Minister are not correct. However, given the ambiguity of this situation, we must be careful in how we respond. Our actions will be scrutinized, so I will contact the First Lord for direction, and we will act according to decisions he makes in consultation with the Prime Minister. In the meantime, all exercises are canceled, and all personnel are expected to avoid involvement with this situation until further orders are received."

The signal cut, and Kris was left standing on *Lion's* bridge with eyebrows raised.

"I can see why Daragh needed us," Kate observed, and our Aussie skipper nodded.

Sure, this was going to get complicated, but it went against the grain to sit there and do nothing... so Kris wouldn't.

"Looked like Marshal was heading to Admiralty House, along with a bunch of other key people," Kris began thinking aloud. "We have any Starlight pilots aboard? And a shuttle?"

Daragh Ryan had never told anyone, but he had some real — not *blank* — shells for his shotgun. You probably won't know what this means, but he had fifty 12-gauge slugs, and 100 rounds of 00-buck sitting in his desk. Of course, they were sealed and clearly marked so he never accidentally loaded them into the firearm — safety was, despite what you might think, a huge priority for him.

Well, a large priority. Perhaps not *huge*.

Anyway, the six-round tube magazine of this 12-gauge was loaded with 00-buck when he stood at Admiralty House's front door, waving Marshal, Mel, Camila, and Schwartz inside. The Parliamentary guards who had joined the escape linked up with Major Caacbay, to assist with the defense.

They'd be needed.

As they got inside, Daragh wasted no time getting them into the C&C. Down there was safe — if the place was overrun, it was even possible to cut it off from the upper floors, and it was deep enough into Capital Island's rock, and sufficiently reinforced, that you'd probably need *Bonnie's* lasers to even get close to hitting it.

Though Daragh didn't really want to find out how secure it could be... it seriously went against the grain to hide at a time like this.

Still, it was a safe place to talk, so as they reached a meeting room off the main C&C chamber, the Second Lord shook his head, "Fucking fucker fuck fucks."

Because Daragh said it, I think it was a sentence.

Marshal didn't seem to pay any attention, "We'll be secure here for a little while... but I think we need to get our story out there as quickly as we can."

"Can't do that from here," Mel checked her MAG-2. "Are there any small craft we could commandeer? It's been a while since I've flown, but I hear it's like riding a bike..."

Daragh turned his eyes on Mel Samuels, then gave her a critical eye, "You're a spy, aren't you?"

"The one who delivered Grant Merger's Syndicate to us," Marshal cut in with the answer. "We met when I 'captured' her ship. Best interrogation of a pirate skipper I ever did."

Daragh looked from Mel to Marshal and back again, "Well, sorry you had to blow your cover. Answer to your question is 'fuck if I know'. That shuttle you came down in might be at the civilian field still, but damned if we can get there. We've got very few Branchers and SF..."

"Escape to the woods then," Mel said. "We can hike some-where, get a ride to the mainland. I have a disk from an agent... she brought it to me a long time ago, but told me it'd be helpful if the Emperor made a play again. Seems like the time to use it."

"Hiking will get you nowhere, trust me," Daragh disagreed, and then he narrowed his eyes. "That agent... Haley Briand, she called herself?"

Mel was actually surprised — that was her name, of course, and the fact that Daragh knew it was interesting.

"I think I have a copy of the same disk upstairs in my safe. You looked at it yet?"

Mel shook her head, "She asked me to give it to Greg Noyce, and I did... but I copied it in case. Never viewed it."

Daragh nodded, "Same. I'm supposed to look after John with it, and I bet it's something that discredits everything that bastard Emperor is pulling right now. Good thing we have two copies of it here in a building with no access to the outside world."

For the first time, Schwartz weighed in, "Defense Command is always in the right place at the right time. Let's get a look at the disk, so we know what we wish we could do with it."

"Kris, I'm getting an urgent message from *Hokkaido*... they want you to turn back."

That was Kate Levec's voice, coming through the comm speakers in the cockpit of the shuttle that Kris Jacobs was herself helping pilot down to Capital Island. It had been a very long time since she'd flown a small craft, but with one of her extra Helm and Navigation spacers in the second seat, it was manageable enough.

Along with two Starlights — both being piloted by officers who hadn't been in fighters for years — and another shuttle piloted by Allison Ting, Kris' craft was dropping straight down towards Terra Nova. There was no way this mission was turning back — not with all those tanks so close.

Once 33,000 Imperial troops took control of the city, it would be impossible to do anything without starting a fight, so the only way to get Daragh and Marshal out was to act immediately, while blockheads were still thin on the ground.

It was a logical conclusion, and whatever Bokai was worried about, Kris wasn't going to give her a chance to intervene.

Asking forgiveness was easier and so forth.

"Don't accept any signals until we're on our way back up, Kate. Hopefully I'll have the Second Lord to run interference by then," Kris replied to her XO.

"Right. Take care down there, skipper."

The signal ended, and as it did Kris' little group leveled out in the sky above Capital Island. They were close to Terra Nova, and there was no time at all to waste.

"They've got 150 men out there, no heavy weapons yet," Major Caacbay had come down to the C&C to report on the situation. For the moment, it was quite manageable — he had forty-eight Branchers and close to seventy SF (thanks to the arrival of the contingent from Parliament). That put the odds at close to one-to-one, and Daragh could tell the confident young Major was eager to start putting the blockheads in their place.

But there were 33,000 troops in Burin, and they had to be coming fast. First priority was to get somewhere with access to the planetary communications system...

"Think we could fight our way to the civilian landing field, see if we can get a shuttle and reach orbit?" the Second Lord put the question to his Special Brancher flatly, and the man replied with an immediate nod.

"Of course, sir."

It seemed a little too confident, but at this point Daragh didn't have the luxury of questioning. He looked to Marshal, Mel, Camila, and Schwartz, and then sighed.

"We have to assume that they've basically got Parliament in hand. And there are more SF in Terra Nova, but we can't coordinate with them because of the jamming. So basically… we run the fuck away."

Aside from the addition of the unnecessary expletive, it was a fairly concise assessment of the situation.

Schwartz nodded, "I'd love to get back to PMO, but the bottom line is while we're here, they have the power. Anywhere else, we do."

Mel had been certain of the need to get away from the minute she'd found Admiralty House was cut off, so now she nodded a little more emphatically, "Every minute we spend talking is another minute for the tanks to get closer."

She was back in action, and clearly she'd been missing the thrill. Now her prodding words were the deciding ones: the Admiralty House security detail would help them fight their way to the landing field…

"Sir, shuttle spotted coming in!"

That call came across the C&C, not from a sensor operator but from an SF guard who'd bounded down the stairs to report on the visual observation.

And in case you're wondering, there are no stairs leading to C&C. As before, I'm just not going to tell you how to get down there, since it's still top secret.

"Or maybe we have a ride…" Schwartz frowned quizzically, and Daragh actually smiled.

"That beautiful Australian lady… by God, I knew she'd be good for us."

Marshal frowned, not having been looped in on Kris' return to *Lion*, and certainly not accustomed to anyone — particularly an Admiralty Lord — calling her 'beautiful'. But Daragh was feeling flamboyant. How unusual.

"Starlights, see if you can blow the blockheads away with your landing thrusters," Kris was watching out the window as a long, open-order line of Imps tried to close in on Admiralty House.

One of the pilots replied to her words: "I'll try not to kill them, ma'am."

The shuttle was obviously atmosphere-proof, so she couldn't hear the roar of the F-194's landing thrusters as it swept low, but the blockheads looked like they were suddenly in a gale, and in due course they ran away like a bunch of thug sissies.

I think their term is 'withdrew in order', but Kris says 'sissies', and I'm not in a position to disagree.

As the way was cleared, the Aussie skipper flipped the switch that lowered her shuttle's landing feet, then let her copilot touch down while she rose and headed to the hatch. Feet touched ground, the door swung open, the ramp dropped, and then Kris hurried down to Admiralty House's front lawn, where a surprised SF Ensign came to meet her.

They tried to talk, but the engines of the Starlights hovering overhead, and noise of Ting's shuttle landing behind them, were too much. Following the Ensign inside, then, Kris came face to face with Daragh and everybody else as they hurried up to their escape.

"Two shuttles… it'll be tight to evacuate everyone, sir, but I think we can do it," was Kris' introduction.

"Well that's the first good news of the day," the Irishman replied, and then turned back to see who was near. Major Caacbay seemed a good choice, so Daragh addressed him, "Evacuate everyone right now. Fast as we can."

The Special Brancher nodded, then left at a run.

"Let's get to *Lion*, Captain," Daragh said, and that's what they did.

Quick aside: A fair question about this whole mess was what the hell did John Fiora, Douglas Pope, the Emperor, and everyone else at Mars think of it? They were almost done working on the final draft of the peace treaty — the document meant to usher in the Pax Terra (the title of this book) — so wouldn't they now suddenly have a fistfight or a constitutional crisis or something?

Probably, had they known. But aside from a coded signal to the Emperor saying "Things just got started here" there was nothing. Lynn Bokai's message to *Bonaventure* certainly didn't make it through.

This probably doesn't come as a shock to you — the Emperor faction's plan depended on cutting off communications, and they'd succeeded. Daragh and Marshal and Mel and Kris and Schwartz were on their own.

Sort of.

CHAPTER FOURTEEN
OVERRULED

Lynn Bokai was fuming by the time she finally appeared on *Lion's* main screen, and I suppose I can sympathize with her situation. One of her Captains — who wasn't even really 'hers', so to speak, since *Lion* was being crewed by a bunch of people on leave and was barely even quasi-official at this point — had blatantly defied her, potentially jeopardizing Defense Command's reputation in the coming political battle.

"What the hell did you do, Captain Jacobs? Who do you think you are to defy my explicit orders?"

Not the warmest of introductions, but Kris was completely unfazed.

"I was thinking action was a good option, ma'am. Particularly since two divisions of Imperial Troops were about to make it impossible to pull anyone out of Capital Island without firing shots." Tempted though she was to be insolent, our Aussie skipper decided to keep her tone down to simply 'insubordinate'. Good of her.

"That is for *me* to decide, Captain. I am relieving you of command immediately, and sending my Flag Captain to take over *Lion*. You will be arrested and confined to your brig until this situation is resolved."

That was all by the book, but of course Daragh wasn't a by-the-book type. Had he not loaded his shotgun with actual projectiles, this would have been the moment he fired off a shot. But instead of putting a hole in *Lion's* newly-restored ceiling, the Irishman just barged into the Battlelink viewfinder's range and started roaring.

"I'll fucking come over there and relieve you, Lynn. You watch it. Your ships are now under my command, so you bring everyone to standby action stations, and wait for my orders."

All in all, it was one of his milder outbursts I think. Lynn probably disagreed.

"You were named as being under suspicion, Daragh," she countered immediately. "Anything you do now will cast suspicion on yourself, and all of us."

See, this is why Daragh had been so determined to have Kris in orbit. What the Fifth Lord was saying was by no means incorrect, but the fact that having suspicion cast on her seemed reason enough for her to do nothing... well, sorry, it was wrong.

"You spineless fool, listen close. What if I'd said the GG was guilty of plotting to stage a coup? What if I'd said it before he falsely accused me? Would that change things?"

Scowling, Bokai puffed up, "I don't like your tone—"

"Fuck my tone, would it have changed things?"

She stammered for a second, then half-nodded, "Well, probably..."

"That's your fucking problem right there. Because whatever people say in the media, your job is to follow orders from your direct superior, and only if the civilian government declares me unfit and I'm relieved of my post can you disregard me. And I just heard this funny fucking story where the Emperor's crony dissolved the civilian government at the request of someone who had dubious authority to ask for that. Either way you look at it, there's no civilian government to overrule, so I'm fucking overruling you. Now by God don't make me come over there and fucking shoot you!"

These are the sorts of exchanges between superior officers that subordinates aren't ever really supposed to see, but the circumstances of this particular coup left Daragh with no option but to give both barrels on reasonably open comms.

And let's be honest, he enjoyed doing it. The day had been frustrating, and Lynn just happened to be the first person the Second Lord could really unload on.

After a long and uncomfortable silence, Fifth Lord Bokai replied with the insolence that Kris had avoided earlier, "At your command, *sir*."

She then cut the link.

Letting out a long breath, Daragh turned away from the main screen and found everyone on the bridge staring at him. Realizing it had been a bit of a show, he cleared his throat awkwardly, then looked at Kris, "Looks like they did a good job shining up *Lion* for you."

Nice subject change, and Kris kept up, "Yes... ship looks good indeed. Sorry to change the subject, but should we get together in the conference room with Marshal and the PMO person, and figure out how to save the Empire?"

Daragh grinned, "What an idea. Lead on."

There were innumerable advantages to being in orbit during a crisis like this one, not least the ability it provided to see where all the Imps were, across the entire planet. Though *Lion* remained directly over Capital Island, the frigate was patched into the sensor grid for the entire home defense fleet, and despite Bokai's attitude, the ships of that force had turned all of their eyes towards the planet, and were happy to share what they saw.

Unsurprisingly, it was complicated.

"They're more clever than I was hoping they'd be," Schwartz T. Babcock had recovered from any ill effects of the standoff — not that there would have been many — but now he was only barely containing his concern for the people he'd inadvertently left behind at PMO.

Would a blockhead be putting a gun in Donna's face?

The fate of the Empire was a grander concern, of course, but defying many peoples' assumptions that he was a cut-throat wonderkid who would sacrifice anyone or anything to get ahead, he actually was concerned for his people.

Another reason Pope had him on the senior staff at such a young age.

Anyway, the observation the young Deputy Chief of Staff had made was perfectly correct. Studying the Imp deployments from orbit, Daragh and his compatriots aboard *Lion* discovered one simple thing: the soldiers of the Emperor had been scattered across the globe in such a way as to give them total control of planetary communication.

Every broadcast and relay site was occupied, and while the occupation forces were often pretty modest — small enough that the SF and Special Branchers of the Heavy Squadron of the Home Fleet could overwhelm them — the fact remained that to even get access to planetary communications, Defense Command would have to initiate combat.

Which would put us in the wrong, or at least give the Emperor's people more evidence to use when they tried to make us look wrong. Was the population on side with their story at this point? Daragh doubted it… but doubts weren't enough. So far all the excesses had been committed by the blockheads, and it had to stay that way.

If only there was some way they could broadcast Haley Briand's recording… but even if every ship in the fleet beamed it down to the planet, the Imps could block it.

A mess. A real mess.

"So what do we do?" Kris finally asked, exchanging glances with Marshal, Schwartz, and Mel before looking to Daragh.

The Irishman sighed, then looked at the clock. The day had actually disappeared — it was 2000 hours Earth Standard Time. The sun would soon set over Capital Island, and while the notion of some sort of night operation seemed appealing, he had no idea what it might be. He had the whole force of the Heavy Squadron at his disposal, but it did him no good just now.

He didn't know if time was actually on his side… but maybe he could make it so.

"Let's give it a couple of hours," he said. "Let's see if they do something that helps us."

It was not the sort of active idea he or Kris had been hoping for, but it was a sensible one.

Doubly sensible because of something they didn't even know about.

CHAPTER FIFTEEN

HOMECOMING

"My compliments, Andy. You're a miracle-worker."

I paid *Wolf's* Chief Engineer that compliment over open ship's comms, because he deserved it. It was late Thursday night, Earth Standard Time, and our fair frigate had just blazed into Earth's security zone — one of the fastest passages from Belt Two to the planet in a comparable orbital season.

Standing on the bridge with Karen and Andrea, I was slightly relieved to see that our home planet was still there... though it was not a terribly grand comfort. We needed to know what exactly was happening on Capital Island before I'd feel better or worse — were we in time?

Obviously not. I think this is another dramatic irony moment, but I'll defer to the literary specialists.

"We're two hours from Earth orbit," Shelby McLaws announced from behind her bank of consoles.

"The fleet is in position, as one would expect, sir," Felicia Khalid added from Sensors and Communications.

At the back of the bridge, from behind the Operations consoles, Jim Hannigan pitched in an opinion instead of a report: "I have a bad feeling though."

Glancing back over my shoulder, I frowned, "You really had to say that?"

"Well I do," he answered, and then Andrea Kiley chimed in too.

"Fucking bad feeling indeed."

It's been a while since the end of *The Egesta Crisis*, so let me just remind you of the *epic* falling out Andrea had with Wes on that asteroid. Remember, she'd invoked the name of Wes' dead wife during an argument about her mental health... didn't go well.

By the same token, Jim and Shelby were still in the process of burying their own less-than-pleasant experiences into the back of their subconsciouses, where the memories could do no harm (in the short term). So aside from Karen and I, who seemed to have reacquired our stride with a bit more ease, everyone was a little bit off. Just a little, but still.

"Alright, let's get there," I said eventually, deciding not to indulge in speculation. Then I glanced at Karen, and she had a gentle, thoughtful frown creasing the top of her brow.

"I think this is going to be interesting," she said.

"Is that a statement of the obvious?" I asked.

"Uh. Yeah," she answered, and then smiled.

"Ship passed the outer markers about forty minutes ago, but we've been directing everything at the surface," Ronald Davis had been a Captain for longer than Kris, but that didn't matter under the current circumstances; *Lion* was short-crewed, and the Admiralty House C&C staff were pitching in wherever they could.

The master of Earth Sensors and Communications was thus filling in for Kate Levec as temporary SCO, and as he took over the job he noticed the arrival of a new vessel on his screens.

"We have a read on its transponder?" Kris approached the Sensors and Communications consoles, and Ronald looked up with a nod.

"DCNS *Wolf*."

Apparently you could have heard a pin drop at that particular moment on *Lion's* bridge, and then a lot of people started smiling. I don't want to sound like I'm blowing my own horn, but I suppose if you were in a tough situation and you wanted help, this would be good news.

So good that Kris nodded to Ronald, "Give me shipwide."

Daragh, Marshal and Mel were sitting in *Lion's* briefing room, again going over the recordings that Haley Briand had left for them, when the comm cut in.

"Do you hear there, this is your Captain speaking. Just wanted to let you know that a new ship has entered our defense zone… *Wolf* will be in orbit in about an hour. Get rest while you can, I expect there's going to be some cavalier stupid stuff happening soon."

As good news went, that was pretty decent, and Marshal looked up, "He was at Egesta."

Daragh frowned — there'd been no official word of *Wolf's* deployment to Egesta, remember, because we'd tried to keep it quiet when we headed out that way. And we certainly hadn't broadcast what we'd found, especially after Marshal's warning about the comms being compromised.

Now, the Second Lord was in the completely wrong state of mind to imagine that being at Egesta could have been much help under the current circumstances.

"Well at least he's here now. Fresh eyes might make this mess more manageable."

That was true too, because if anyone could come up with a plan to get control of the planetary comm grid without firing too many shots — a plan that Daragh, Marshal and Mel couldn't come up with themselves — it was Karen.

I would also attend, but mainly my function would be to nod, and point at things.

We'd soon see what schemes we could arrange.

"I suppose *Hokkaido* is flag out of this group," I said, looking at the icons of the Heavy Squadron on *Wolf's* main screen. "Any ships we know out there?"

Felicia was sifting through the large formations that we were seeing, but none seemed to stick out as being particularly friendly. The best survivors of the war had gone with us to Mars, after all, so what remained at Earth were the ones who had been best suited for home defense…

"Holy damn."

Karen surprised me with those words — they weren't the sort of thing she'd usually say. I frowned at her, then looked up at the screen again, just in time to see the marker that one of Felicia's techs placed beside a frigate icon on the screen.

"Give me enhanced cam," Andrea noticed it too, and gave that order before either Karen or I could think to.

The main screen flipped to live pictures, while the sensor display bumped to screen two.

No question, that was a *Predator*-class frigate, and a fine looking one too.

"They polished it up real good, didn't they?" I smiled, then looked at Karen again.

Lion had been her ship, of course, and it had done her no good at all to see it battered at Io. As I recall, she and I even had to dance (much to Mik's chagrin) in order to put the thought of its torn hull out of her head.

Her ship, her crew.

Now *Wolf*'s sister ship stood tall and proud in orbit, gleaming as its running lights flashed against the darkness of space. There are few sights that could have been more welcome upon our arrival, and then to punctuate the moment, Felicia interrupted.

"Signal coming from *Lion*, it's Captain Jacobs."

"Damn me," I blurted, because Kris had been with me and Matt Baxter on *Friendly*, and then on *Wolf*, and it had been nothing but misery to see her shot up at Jupiter.

She was back, and she had *Lion* back. I knew that was thanks to John and particularly to Daragh, and I was grateful. For all the people we'd lost — and there were many — at least this restoration was complete. At least we had *Wolf* and *Lion* back together.

If there was some minor problem with Imperial politics, it was no great mischief; these two ships together could do anything...

Such positive thoughts were flooding my mind as I nodded to Felicia, and then screen three brightened with a loading graphic. The buffering didn't take too long, and then there was Kris, standing jauntily on her shiny bridge, arms folded and a grin on her face.

"If two ships could hug in space this would be the moment," the Aussie skipper greeted us. "And I'll probably hug each one of you soon too."

"I think that's fair," I answered brightly, and completely forgetting the circumstances of this trip, I was about to plunge into personal questions... but then Daragh interrupted to wreck the mood.

Barging into the side of the picture, looking like he'd just come off a bit of a bender, the Irishman waved, "Hey Barron, so the Imps have control of Capital Island and we have no way of breaking into the planetary comm grid without starting a civil war. Can you hug later, and help now?"

I stared at Daragh for a minute, and as I did I heard Andrea ordering Shelby McLaws to put us alongside *Lion*, in orbit directly over Capital Island.

After that pause, I glanced at Karen, and then looked back to the Second Lord with a profound and inspirational reply, "Maybe?"

Hey, I was honest.

CHAPTER SIXTEEN

BOLD PLANNING

Wolf got to be host for the meetings that followed — as much as Karen would have liked to go aboard her old, now-restored *Lion* for a visit, too much of the evidence we had about Egesta was stacked up aboard our ship... not least Howard Pedro Azuma III, who was still chained up in our brig, pouting in his self-deluded way.

Obviously there was a lot of catching up to be done, so it was 0230 in the morning before Daragh had us mostly up to speed, and we'd shown him, Kris, Marshal, Mel and Schwartz T. Babcock what we'd found on Egesta. In turn, they showed us what Haley Briand had left for them... and all told, we knew we had everything we needed to put an end to the chaos on Earth.

There was no way the Emperor or his Governor General would be able to assume control of the Empire when those things came out. It was arguable whether the throne itself would even exist after the scandal... that would be for someone else to worry about.

For now, we needed to come up with a plan about how to get everything in front of the public at large, and that was going to be tricky.

"We'll have willing partners in the media, I suspect," Andrea Kiley joined us for our brainstorming session, leaving the watch to Jim Hannigan.

Her Irish brogue was matched by Daragh's: "Once they get a look at this stuff especially."

The Second Lord's point was a good one — if you step back again and look at the entire situation from the media's point of view, what story do you see? How about an Emperor and an Imperial Army concerned that their crimes on Egesta were about to be revealed, and trying to take preemptive action to discredit those coming with the evidence.

Well, that's one way you *could* see it, but after all those reporters had been taken into custody by the blockheads it was difficult to imagine that they'd be sympathetic to the Emperor's side of the story.

"If we can position it so it looks like this has all been to cover their tracks, it'll be a disaster for their side," Schwartz T. Babcock voiced the thought, steepling his fingers as he sat across from me at the briefing table.

I was still having trouble with the wonderkid's name, but I'd noticed the way Daragh seemed to respect him, and that struck me as a sign that he wasn't just an oxygen thief. Maybe he was cut from the same cloth as Craig B. Macdonald... I'd certainly give him a chance to prove himself.

"Should we stoop to that level, though? There's no way they could have known we were at Egesta... we covered our tracks," Karen seemed to slip into Charlie Peters' normal role of the moral conscience rather easily... which given her past seemed almost funny.

I looked at her, and she noticed, then shrugged, "Well. Why twist the truth when we don't have to?"

"Maybe we just don't comment one way or the other," I suggested, looking from her to the rest of the people around the table. "If the media wants to invent a connection, or finds one that we overlooked, more power to them. We just show up and report the facts as we saw them, and still see them."

Everyone nodded, so that was that. We knew what we had to tell the world — we simply had to show two sets of video footage, with a little narration, and then we'd let the dominoes of the Emperor's influence fall.

Easy. Right?

Yeah no.

I was pretty confident that the footage would have the desired effect, as long as we were actually able to spread it far and wide… but the other side knew we were dangerous when we got in front of cameras. That's what the whole denial-of-media scheme was all about.

"The question is who we go after down there," Marshal Samuels leaned forward and tapped the controls in front of him, calling a planetary map up onto the briefing room screen. Little red flashing dots marked every place where the blockheads had moved in to roost… and the bastards had been thorough.

"I can talk to Jim about finding a way to hack into the grid from a remote site…" Andrea suggested, but Kris shook her head.

"I was talking to Kate about the same before you guys turned up. They've got all the hubs, the control points. Best we might be able to do around their block is show our footage to a local area. That might get us something, but not enough to be worth tipping our hand…"

She was right, and didn't need to elaborate further… though I will here. If we broadcast our damning information, and only a few people saw it, but one of them happened to be a blockhead who reported back to Capital Island, we'd give the GG and Bennington time to come up with some counter.

No, we needed total access, and then we needed to dump the footage everywhere across the globe. Same as we had in *The Almost Coup*.

"The evidence is pretty damning," Mel spoke up for the first time in the meeting. "If we have to fire some shots to get it out there, I think that'll be forgiven. I mean, people are going to see what we're saving them from."

That was a very good point too — this wasn't just a matter of political infighting now, there was a question being asked about the danger the army might pose to the civilians it infiltrated. In defense of the people, we could probably get away with some blasting…

But what if there was a camera? The blockheads certainly expected us to try, so they'd have to have cameras, maybe even reporters, ready to pounce as soon as we did anything aggressive. We'd have to find a way to shut those cameras off from the grid, or the whole planet could end up watching a live feed of us attacking Imperial troops…

The whole planet could end up watching.

I blinked at that notion — a rare good one for me — and then glanced at Karen. She was staring thoughtfully at her hands (undoubtedly seconds away from the same revelation) so I looked up at everyone around the table again.

"If we do anything, they're going to have to broadcast it — they want to send their 'evidence' about us to everyone, as sure as we want to air our recordings of them," I said.

For a moment there was silence, and then true to form, Karen swept in to back me up, "So to get them to open the grid for us… we just attack."

I nodded.

Great, so all we had to do was give the Imps the evidence they needed, and then they'd stop jamming for long enough to tell everyone…

"If we got into their system before the attack… put in a hijack without them realizing, and then as soon as they open the taps we start broadcasting our package instead of theirs…" I continued, realizing I had no idea how complicated what I was suggesting might be.

"They'd have to see their own footage when they watched it back, or they'd shut us down," Karen reminded me, and I nodded.

We were basically talking about doing a variation of that gag you see people do with surveillance cameras in old movies — have the screen in the office show one thing, while something else is really going on. But this would be pretty complicated… they'd see the live feeds their cameras were showing, while we'd be broadcasting a recording…

Like I said, I had no idea about the technical viability of the notion, but we had some of the best Sensors and Communications people in the fleet with us, so I had to hope.

Of course, there was another problem, and the Second Lord of the Admiralty quickly identified it for us: "So you're talking about landing a secret team to hack the grid somewhere, then attacking in force so that we'll give them something to show off, and then when they open the taps to show it, we take over in secret?"

I nodded, and Karen did too.

"Why the hell would they want to broadcast live, unedited footage of a firefight between us and them?"

Aha. Yes, that was a good question — there was a chance they'd broadcast battle footage live, as it happened… but an equal chance that they'd wait, edit it, and then broadcast the most favorable version after the fight was over. How could we work out the timing?

"The only reason they'd probably go straight to air is if it looked like we were about to flatten them… full attack from orbit, giving them no time to broadcast it later," Marshal put in, leaning forward. "And that's more collateral damage than I think we should do."

"Definitely too much," Schwartz agreed with a nod. "But getting people to broadcast things when you want them to is possible. You just have to be good at manipulating them."

He said that with some certainty, and all eyes turned to the political wonderkid. He smiled again, and shrugged, "Not saying I'd know how…"

Of course he knew how… but then, so did we.

"What if… what if we got in the GG's face?" Karen frowned slightly and looked at me. "If we were in the room with him and Bennington, we might get one of them to panic, open the switches."

That was true — we *might* — but then we might not. And that was if we were in the room with them.

I met Karen's gaze and thought about it. We'd done alright with Azuma… maybe we could find a way…

"I could do it," Schwartz said with some finality. "I know Bennington, I know how to work her. She's not that complex… otherwise the Emperor wouldn't have her so enthralled."

Eyes shifted from Schwartz to us and then everyone looked back to Daragh. The Second Lord was sitting back in his chair, arms folded and scowl deep, "Team goes in first… you three are with it. You escort some comms team to a point where they can hack in silently, and wait. Then you get yourselves captured and taken to their leaders, then we attack and you convince them to air it live."

Taking a breath, I nodded. That was quite a few moving parts — a bold and complex plan, more elaborate than most of the things we'd tried in the old days.

"Sounds like something Grant would come up with," Mel put in quietly from her end of the table, then paused before adding, "That's why they wouldn't expect it."

A very fair point, because the plan was intricate. Though it was also cavalier in its way — it insisted that we use our abilities to make it all work.

"I don't like it at all," Daragh said after a time. "So make it work fast."

That was it; the crazy Second Lord of the Admiralty, whose famous tactics of the past included wiggling his ship, was sending in a high-risk strike to stop a coup.

"If it doesn't work, we're truly fucked," the Irishman added sharply. "Because I don't know if I can actually order us to wipe out the army…"

"You can," Schwartz interrupted. "Remember, the Governor General just dissolved the government without appointing a new one. He then relieved the lawful police and military of the Empire, on no authority recognized in the Articles of Empire. This is unconstitutional. Don't forget that. It's Defense Command's duty to restore a lawful government elected by the people."

We all stared at Schwartz, honestly appreciating the sense of clarity his words provided. When you're talking about invading your own capital, and possibly doing a lot of shooting, it's easy to lose your perspective. But, of course, there was another problem.

"So what if the GG catches on and asks the Leader of the Opposition to form a new government, and as Prime Minister, that idiot orders us to stand down?" Karen asked quietly.

Schwartz sat back and shook his head, "Then things are a lot more complicated."

Great. Just great.

"Alright," Daragh said eventually, deciding there was no point dwelling on how close to the line we really were. "Set it up, take whoever you need."

I nodded, and Karen nodded, and then the meeting broke. We needed to move fast; the stealth team would have to land under cover of night.

Chapter Seventeen

Bad Déja Vu

When you're landing to do something this tricky under the noses of more than 30,000 blockheads, it goes without saying that the first person you call is your Special Branch Major. Rufus and his five officers were ready to go again — well, they were never *not* ready — and I think they particularly liked the sounds of the plan as we explained it to them.

Considering the danger, that might seem weird, but remember that already this year they'd dealt with deadly mobs in a capital city, and blockheads who deserved painful justice. This brought everything together for them in a neat little package with a bow.

Rufus started prepping the Special Branch assault shuttle for us about twenty minutes after our planning meeting broke, and you better believe he loaded it with things he could use to cause explosions.

Tanks to him were just big targets...

We sent Schwartz with Rufus, since the Deputy Chief of Staff was going to be our civilian cargo for the mission, and then Daragh went off to record narrative segments for our damning video. Jim Hannigan would help edit those words together with our various recordings, so the resulting vid would appear as one large package when broadcast.

With all of that happening, Karen and I had just one more job: we had to find a Sensors and Communications Officer who could go down aboard the shuttle, locate the appropriate hack-in point, and run our feed at the exactly the right moment. This search didn't take particularly long, and I didn't really like the result either.

"You're sure you can spare her?" Karen had picked up on my discomfort about Kris' suggested officer as soon as I'd heard the name. We were headed to the lock that connected *Wolf* to *Lion* when the suggestion was made.

"My skeleton crew's been augmented by the entire staff from Admiralty House. Ron Davis can run my Sensors and Communications while she's gone... even though he's actually senior to me..." our Aussie skipper replied evenly.

She hadn't really picked up on *why* her suggestion that we take Kate Levec down with us wasn't going over well with me. I suppose most of her memories of Io are focused on an event that was far more deadly than the careless landing attempt we made with Charlie's team — the one where Kate had stepped out of the hatch first, and lost a chunk of her midriff as a result.

And then you'll probably remember how I went on autopilot and lost control of what I was doing... or as Karen preferred to say, lost perspective, because I was in control — making sensible decisions — I just wasn't making them for good reasons.

Anyway, all that drama was left behind in *The Jupiter Patrol*, and I didn't want to revisit it now... but Kate was the right person for this. Felicia Khalid — who had taken over from Kate after that day — was damned good at her job, but realistically, we needed to have at least one of our two frigates fully staffed by its normal, experienced crew.

Lion was improvising, so it was much less damaging to take away that ship's XO and defacto Sensors and Communications Officer.

We finally reached the lock connecting *Wolf* to *Lion*, and we found Kate was there waiting for us — evidently, Kris had called ahead and told her to meet us. It was the first time I'd seen her in years, and the moment threatened to be about as awkward as you might expect.

But there was no time for awkward — or for humor to defuse the awkwardness. Just straight down to work.

"We're going to get them to open the feed... but when we do, we need someone to hack in, overwrite what they're sending with our package, and keep them from realizing what we've done," Karen explained without even pausing to say hello.

Kate had been our Sensors and Communications Officer on *Wolf* for a few months, and she slipped right back into that tempo.

"I'm going with you, then," she said firmly — a little too firmly, because as she looked at me I could see the faint lines etched around her young eyes quiver slightly. She was remembering what it felt like to have a hole the size of a softball in her side.

I could have said something — tried to lighten the mood, or reassure her, but I didn't. Instead I stuck with business, as was appropriate, "We'll need you to figure out where to hack in, and then Rufus Chang will get you there and make sure you stay safe. Karen and I will be taking Schwartz Babcock to Parliament, to get ourselves captured and brought to the GG."

Kate's eyebrows went up, "That wise, sir?"

I stared at her for a second, then replied, "I don't really care."

That was an honest answer, I think... perhaps a revival of the cavalier feeling from the old days. Wise or not, dangerous or not, Karen and I were damned well going to do it.

"If you can get them to drop their jamming control, I could probably do what we need from Admiralty House," Kate began assessing the situation aloud as I mused. "All the equipment we could possibly need will be there, we could bring some portable power to get it online. As long as they haven't physically cut the connections to the grid, we can make it work. I'll talk to Captain Davis to confirm."

"Good, we're departing in an hour or less, so hurry," Karen concurred with a nod, and then Kate took a breath and turned for the chute.

Kris watched her go, frowning as she tried to comprehend all the undercurrents of anxiety she was sensing. She actually didn't put together the reasons we were all tense until she read *The Jupiter Patrol*, and then she was apparently a bit embarrassed she'd forgotten.

I don't think any of us can blame her, considering the radiation dose that scrambled her brain so soon after the incident.

Anyway, with quick nods to each of us, Kris followed her XO, and Karen and I watched them go for a moment before turning and heading for our cabins. We'd need to put on our flightsuits — we'd escort Rufus' shuttle down in our Starlights, and have those planes with us just in case we needed them...

As we walked, Karen pulled her pony tail up onto her left shoulder, "You think this is going to be trouble?"

"I'm hoping they don't decide to hang us on the spot," I replied.

"We need a good landing point outside their defense grid," Rufus Chang was planning with great speed as he and his team loaded up the shuttle. He had a pad with a realtime orbital scan of Capital Island in one hand, a crate of grenades in the other, and he was talking while he lifted.

"What sort of outer perimeter do they have?" Captain Clarissa Hutchinson asked, hauling a crate of night vision gear up the ramp into the craft.

Pausing, Rufus took a look at the visual again to reconfirm: "Not much of one. They're stacked up all over the priority targets, including Admiralty House. We'll have to get in through the [access point in the woods]."

Sorry, but there's no way in hell I'm telling you how they were actually getting into Admiralty House. The blockheads didn't know the route existed then, and aside from certain key Defense Command personnel, no one knows about it now.

How did Rufus know? Daragh had told him, but I've skipped that entire scene because the whole thing would basically be in [square brackets], and I'd have to fill it with complete fiction. I don't think I'd have any skill as a fiction writer, so you get a cop out. Sorry again.

"That's good for us, though, right boss?" Simon Keynes put in. "Easier for us to find a spot to land?"

That was true — the fact that the blockheads were expecting an attack from space had led them to neglect setting up a perimeter around Terra Nova… and that makes a fair amount of sense, I have to admit. Why have units standing at the edge of town, staring into the woods, when we could land at any location in the city? Better to keep your troops at the places they'll end up protecting.

Fortunately for us, that meant we could land somewhere out of town (but close) and get in quietly.

Moreover, I should add that the blockheads had no access to orbital surveillance — we had slaved all defense satellites to our fleet, and if any one of them started sending telemetry to the planet, the board of every Sensors and Communications monitoring station in the Heavy Squadron (and *Wolf* and *Lion*) would have lit up, and allowed override.

So all the blockheads had was ground-based detection; active and passive scans that could be partially blinded by terrain, and fooled by stealth systems.

We could go anywhere, as long as we were out of sight… it was just a matter of picking a place. And guess who had an idea.

"You may not like this," Schwartz T. Babcock said, catching Rufus' mismatched eyes, "but I know a guy. He was…"

Another square brackets conversation followed, which Rufus didn't like completely, and which is going to make the next couple of chapters complicated. But it would get us to ground, and where we needed to go.

So let's get there…

+++

Before we end the chapter, one of my editors asked why we didn't just take Captain Ronald Davis with us for this mission — being Earth's Sensors and Communications Officer, he'd know Admiralty House's systems better than anyone.

Without being unkind, let's just say that assault landings are for officers of a certain demographic, and Ronald had left that particular composition behind in his younger years. His vintage never negatively impacted his duties at Admiralty House, of course, but asking him to roll with Special Branch into the middle of an island covered with 30,000 troops?

Better to send a spry young Commander, who'd just spent a year working herself into peak physical condition as she recovered from her wounds.

And one more point: Kate Levec was Belt Squadron. As much as she didn't want to have a repeat of the Io incident, she wasn't about to be left behind on a job she could do. She had something to prove to herself, I think... or no, a better way to put it: she had some demons to exorcise.

Maybe I did too, but believe me, that wasn't going to be top priority. We had an Empire to save, and that was rather more important.

CHAPTER EIGHTEEN

SQUARE BRACKETS

It was a familiar feeling, diving after Rufus' assault shuttle as it ran down into the atmosphere, leveled out over Cape Breton, and then started skimming the cliffs and the waves on the way across the Cabot Strait.

Karen was leading the way, I was bringing up there rear, and though she and I were both rusty, we'd flown in this part of Earth's atmosphere often enough to know exactly how to handle the low altitude. We had to pay close attention, of course, but it was quite manageable.

As we got over Capital Island itself, we kept to the treetops, and stayed quiet on the comms. The blockheads were still jamming pretty loudly, but our short-range communications were powerful enough to cut through the interference. Unfortunately, using them that way would have gotten us noticed.

We were bound for a strip mall that sat about twenty kilometers outside Terra Nova, in the middle of the forest. The place had been built in anticipation of new subdivisions, but thanks to the war, those subdivisions hadn't shown up yet. Still, the four stores in the complex were occupied, and one of them was owned by Schwartz's friend.

Now, this friend — let's call him Keith Pine, which may or may not be his real name — had worked at the Ministry of Agriculture when Schwartz interned there a few years before. On the side, Keith was a big fan of historical reenacting, role-playing games, and other things that I'm honestly not familiar with. While working as an employee of the government, he'd run a side business selling wares related to those interests — evenings and weekends, you understand — and after a few years, that business had taken off. He'd quit government and made *Wired and Woven* his full-time work.

That's obviously not a cover story. No one could make something like that up.

So why did Schwartz think we needed to go see Keith Pine under these circumstances?

Well, as the Deputy Chief of Staff said, Keith was a Renaissance man who knew his way around town very well.

I'll leave it at that.

The strip mall wasn't tough to find; as we closed on Terra Nova, Karen spotted it coming up fast and immediately dropped her speed — and her engine noise — to its lowest possible level. Behind her, Chet Srisai, the faithful assault shuttle pilot who was the lone survivor of *Wolf's* original Special Branch complement, instantly matched speed. I managed to do the same.

Within seconds we were hovering over the compact parking lot in front of the stores. There were only two cars there, but it was tight and the shuttle was big, so it took Chet a few seconds to turn and find a place to set down safely. As soon as he did, Karen followed, picking an unoccupied corner and elegantly lowering her Starlight into the gap. Then it was my turn.

In my defense, the parking lot really wasn't very big.

The massive crunching sound, followed by the rocking and the sharp drop to the ground, meant that I'd landed on one of the cars. Yes, you can say 'again', because I did the same during *The Almost Coup*. Call it symmetry, I suppose — not a reason to suspend my flight license...

Ahem.

As soon as my landing feet were on solid ground, I shut down the mains and popped the canopy. Emerging into the dark, cool night, I hurried towards the shuttle as the hatch swung open and the ramp came down. Karen met me at the bottom, and she was looking past my shoulder at the wreckage of my landing.

It had been a nice sporty blue car, with fins and everything. You could just tell that someone thought the world of it, and now it bore the footprint of an F-194 Starlight. Plus the scraping drag marks from when my plane slid off.

"Didn't you do that to Geraldine Coilier's car last time?" Karen asked.

"It brought us good luck then," I shrugged.

"Good point."

We said nothing further; Rufus led his team down from the shuttle, and then Chet joined the six officers, carrying his own MAG-90. Right behind him was Kate Levec, and that was quite a reminder — it had been Chet, as I recall, who had helped cover us when I'd been desperately trying to fix Kate's wound.

Schwartz was last out, and as we watched him come down the ramp we followed his eyes to the front of the *Wired and Woven* store, which was dim. Inside only soft nightlights seemed to give any hint of what we should expect, so with a glance at Rufus we started that way.

Of course Rufus led our group, not just because we were covering relatively open ground that could be dangerous if blockheads appeared out of nowhere... but because Schwartz had given him the whole story about Keith.

The story you aren't getting.

Reaching the store's front door, Rufus found it was locked. He easily convinced it not to be locked anymore, then led the way inside, followed by Maggie Joyce and Selma Koestecki. I went in next, then Schwartz, Kate and Karen, Chet, Bobby Franek, Simon Keynes and Clarissa Hutchinson.

Not sure if that order matters, but that's the way we were lined up.

And as soon as we got in, we were confronted by a tall, gloomy guardian: a medieval suit of armor, with a big old broadsword in hand. In the darkness of the store, it really was pretty ominous, and we all eyed it a little too warily. None of us were panicky, you understand — it's just one of those instant reactions you have when you see something creepy like that in the dark.

And then it started to raise its sword.

You better believe seven Branchers (including Chet) hosed the thing with so much mag fire it started to melt. Probably not the best way to introduce ourselves to Keith, because as soon as everyone fired we realized that he was probably inside. And dead.

"Dammit," Rufus was the first to lower his rifle and hurry over to the molten wreck. "Selma..."

As the team medic, Selma started to move, but then was interrupted.

"Don't shoot me when I say this, but you break it, you bought it."

That voice came from the left — behind the cash counter, and everyone turned just as the house lights flipped on. Keith was standing there, complete with his long hair in a ponytail and his goatee... and no kidding or exaggeration, he had a double-headed broadaxe in one hand, and a MAG-2 in the other.

"Was there someone inside?" Rufus asked, his MAG-90 trained instinctively on the man.

"Animatronic. Like most of my stuff, it's supposed to add realism," Keith answered easily.

Obviously the animatronics had done their job...

"It got it killed," Karen observed.

"I'll bill the Navy," Keith replied with a shrug, then looked from her to me and back. He knew who we were — knew very well, in fact.

"Frankly, I'll consider myself lucky," he added. "When the two of you show up at a store, it quadruples the chance that the building will collapse. We calculated the odds."

Karen blinked, as did I, and then she responded first, "We're trying not to do that anymore."

I pressed straight on to a different question: "You obviously recognize us, then?"

Keith nodded. He didn't seem surprised to see us at all, really — looked almost as though he'd been waiting for us.

But how, you ask, could he have known? Square brackets, that's how.

"You too, Major Chang. And your entire team. Big fan. Hi Schwartz, glad you're not dead," the store owner continued casually, sliding both weapons back into his belt.

"I'm glad you were working late," the Deputy Chief of Staff replied with a wry smile, because he knew something about Keith's living arrangements that I can't really get into.

The axe-carrying former agricultural systems designer shrugged, coming out from around his counter. As he moved, I got my first chance to look at the properly-lit store; it was full of... everything. Chainmail armor, puppets (which moved like the armor had, following you with their eyes)... even person-sized statues of humanoid wolves, cats and bears in Naval-looking uniforms. They were all staring at us too... very disconcerting, especially the white tiger.

"What's this?" I frowned, approaching the statue of Felix and reading the tag. "I see." *Got the cadence wrong.*

Keith came to a stop next to me as I turned my gaze to the gray wolf statue, but he didn't even notice the Earthers. Instead, he was looking out the front window of his store, at the landing job we'd done.

"Did you land in the parking lot?" he asked.

"I sorta landed on a car. Kinda," I turned away from Caine and replied a bit sheepishly as I followed his gaze out the window.

"Red car?" the question sounded tentative but was still menacing because Keith had both a MAG-2 and an axe in his belt. He seemed nice enough, and his store was very eclectic, but that didn't mean he'd take the destruction of his beloved car well.

"Blue," Karen answered for me.

We all held our breath.

"Oh that's the building owner's car. He's a bastard. Anyone hungry? I expect you're going to fight the coup, and that'll work up an appetite."

Phew; I nodded, and Keith turned and led us all back towards the checkout, and to the curtain behind it. As we filed after him, every puppet in the store watched us go. Damned animatronics.

"You all know I'm Keith, right?" he asked, looking back over his shoulder as he led us into the store's storage space. We nodded, and then he continued, "Well, it's great to have you all here. I'm a big fan, of course. We've developed an entire role-playing card game based on your exploits in the Belt."

That's true, actually. Not everything in this chapter is completely accurate (only the most insane parts are perfectly true), but apparently, as part of his career change, Keith had decided to use his skills and experiences to create role-playing games, which he quite enjoyed.

Even if, when he said it, it sounded rather surreal.

"Sounds... like fun?" I replied, and Keith chuckled.

"I'll offer to teach you the rules once the Emperor's plot is defeated."

"Guy has his priorities right," Karen approved of his sentiment.

Rufus then grumbled something which reflected a rivalry of some sort, but that I won't repeat because it would need to be square bracketed.

We found a long table at the back of the storage area, and Keith gestured for each of us to take a seat. A screen was set in the wall over the table, but all it was showing was static.

"They've been jamming everything since the press conference. I figured you guys would have a response coming, but I didn't guess you'd think of me, Schwartz," he said.

That was a lie, he'd been expecting us. I suppose he didn't want to sound immodest.

As we sat down, he switched off the screen and then took the chair at the head of the table. Two piles of playing cards were in front of him on the table, and I noticed that one pile had a Defense Command black sun on the back, the other had... a Syndicate emblem. Like Grant Merger's old Syndicate.

"That's the game?" Karen nodded to the stacks, and Keith looked down.

"Based on when the Belt Squadron fought the pirates before the war. That's how I know you walking in here quadruples the chances the building will collapse — when we were writing the rules, we did a calculation based on media reports of what happens when you arrive at a place of business."

I blinked, and looked at Karen. She blinked, and looked at me.

There were lots of things I think we could have said, but eloquent as ever, Karen got back to Keith first, "It's really only four times?"

"We rounded down," he shrugged.

"So there's a coup and we need to stop it," Rufus interrupted grumpily, leaning forward and planting his elbows on the table. "We need to commandeer a vehicle to go to [some place on Capital Island that would perhaps grant us access to Admiralty House]."

"And we need you to help us — me, Karen and Schwartz — get caught and brought to the Governor General's location," I added. Look at that, didn't need square brackets for anything I said.

Keith glanced from Rufus to Schwartz and then back to me, "Sounds like it's going to be interesting. I've got a van out back that we use when moving stuff out for festivals... Major Chang, you can use that to get your team to [the place you are going to which may or may not grant you access to Admiralty House]. I can take everyone else in my car."

Well, that was easy.

Rufus was still a bit unhappy, though. It's a good thing Mel had stayed aboard *Wolf*, or God only knows how tetchy he'd have been. Wait, is that a clue... nah, surely not. Because then it would be in square brackets.

Anyway, we had transport, so the next phase of insanity could begin.

CHAPTER NINETEEN

SNEAKING

Loading up for our respective missions was not terribly interesting; Rufus and his team checked out Keith's van, found it was well-serviced and had some after-market features that would help it get to all sorts of places, then loaded up all the kit they'd brought with them for the day — explosives, power cells, some diagnostic equipment that Kate needed, and so forth.

Then they loaded Kate up too — put her in the back with five officers, while Chet hopped in the driver's seat. He was a hell of a pilot with an assault shuttle, and perhaps unsurprisingly he was cross-trained with just about any sort of vehicle he might need to operate.

Rufus would be riding shotgun with Chet, but before they took off, he wanted to check out Keith's car — the transport Karen, Schwartz and I would be taking to our capture. Keith said it was good, but you know how it is between Special Branchers and retired Ministry of Agriculture types. Always suspicious of each other...

"Looks... fine," Rufus said finally after circling the vehicle a few times.

Karen and I were standing back from the car as Rufus inspected it, while Schwartz and Keith were still in the store choosing the best route into Terra Nova. My parents lived not far from the capital, and I'd spent a lot of time in the town, but I didn't know my way around it the way those two did.

So while we Naval decoys waited, Rufus turned on us with a scowl and approached grimly, hitting us with his unsettling stare, "I don't like you riding off on such a foolish mission with someone like Keith."

He sounded like Matt Baxter and Charlie Peters all at once, and both Karen and I immediately felt a flash of the old days — Matt insisting that we not do 'stupid stuff', and Charlie just shaking his head and keeping us from dying.

And while this plan of ours was in some ways more sensible than, say, flattening a building... it was capitally dangerous.

"If you get yourselves killed, I'll kill you," our Chinese Major said flatly, and we both smiled — at least he was willing to lighten the mood.

But at the sight of our smiles, he stepped forward, and his glare got glarier. More glare-ish. You know what I mean.

"You don't get it," he said with no shortage of menace. "If you die, I will find my way to the gates of the afterlife. I will kill the guard, I will find you, and I will kill you there. Do not get yourselves killed, or you'll regret it."

To this day I don't know if that was supposed to be a joke, but I can pretty much bet that, up in heaven, God put down his newspaper, said 'uh-oh', and asked Jesus to triple the guard on the gate.

Haha, yeah, we all know that didn't happen. God knew he'd never see us, but I think the devil probably got a bit worried.

Anyway, Rufus decided those inspirational words were enough, and left us behind. Heading back to the store, he glared at Keith, growled something to him about his damnable former profession, and how he'd incinerate his immortal soul if anything happened to us because of him, then headed for the van.

Chet powered the craft as soon as Rufus arrived, and they left without ceremony — there was no reason for them to wait.

That left Karen and me standing in the parking lot, staring at Keith's red car.

"He's meaner than Charlie," she said quietly after a long silence, nodding her head backwards to indicate Rufus. "Charlie never actually elaborated on how he'd kill us after we were dead."

It was true. But Charlie is my best friend, so I had to defend his honor, "You know that Charlie would do it, though. He really cares that much."

He does. He cares enough to break into heaven to kill us for being stupid...

Oh look, here came Keith and Schwartz to save us from exploring that rather questionable line of discussion. I'm saved from Charlie's wrath...

"We're thinking we can drive straight to the PMO," Schwartz announced as they emerged from the store. Keith was still wearing civilian clothes, and his axe and his MAG-2 remained tucked in his belt.

"Schwartz left people behind," the shop owner said, nodding to his young friend. "Should be enough of an excuse for you to go back there. Make it look like you two were just being cavalier, trying to do everything on your own to stop this coup. John Fiora and Greg Noyce did the same last time."

That was a good point — if anyone wondered what two high-ranking, high-risk people like Karen and I were doing in Terra Nova, we could say we were just following in the footsteps of our elite First Lord in *The Almost Coup*.

It was flimsy, but it might get us into the room with the GG...

"Alright," I nodded as those thoughts rolled comfortably through my head, then I reached into my pocket and pulled out an orbital flare.

Now I should have been a good writer and explained the orbital flares earlier, but you know better than to expect that of me. Remember that the blockheads were jamming every comm channel in and out of Capital Island? Well, we needed a way to alert Daragh that we were ready for him to send every Special Brancher he had down from orbit, to attack Terra Nova. That in mind, we had orbital flares.

Nothing fancy, these — they were about the size of a drink coaster, and had powercells that would last about ten minutes... but in that ten minutes, once activated, they'd fire a conical laser into orbit. Anything looking straight down at the city — like, say, *Wolf* — would see the flare, and be able to track it back to its source.

My flare, and the duplicate Karen carried, were green. Rufus' team had several blue ones. Our job was to put them somewhere with clear sky above as soon as we were ready... in Karen's case and mine, meaning when we were about to be captured.

That in mind, I reached out and handed my flare to Keith, "You should take this. I don't want you coming in with us... the blockheads will get up in your grill and mess up your store if you're identified. But when you see us get nabbed, set that off, then go get your wife out of town."

Keith had a wife? Maybe. Or maybe I'm making that up.

Yes, I'm being annoyingly coy.

Looking at the flare, Keith frowned, then nodded, "Okay. I can come in and break you out if things go bad and no Special Branchers arrive."

That was a very kind offer, but Karen shook her head, "Your time with the Ministry of Agriculture gave you many skills, but direct infiltration wasn't among them. We'll look after ourselves, you take care of you and yours."

It seemed that Keith was eager to shoot some blockheads, but he also had plenty of life ahead of him — a store to run, a family… all the good things that normal people have, and that folks like us pine for in a fashion that might almost seem ridiculous…

He was willing to keep what he had now.

"Okay. I'll get you right in close, then I'll stay out of sight and send up the signal," he agreed, then gestured to the car. "Let's go."

Hard to argue with that, so we piled into the red vehicle and headed for town.

Rufus stared out the windows as the van hurried towards the entrance to Admiralty House. I can tell you literally nothing of what he did or didn't see out his window. For all you know, he could have been headed to Addis Ababa to go through a temporal distortion field that would take him back to 2023, from whence his team would fly to Terra Nova, dig themselves into the ground beneath the eventual site of Admiralty House, put themselves into stasis pods with timers to wake up on exactly this day, and then cut their way up through the floor of the C&C and start work.

Or maybe they flew in on the backs of dragons.

What I can tell you is when they did get into Admiralty House (I can't even tell you where they arrived within the building), they knew that the place was surrounded by close to 8,000 Imperial Army troops, with about eighty tanks in the immediate vicinity.

Of course, none of those guards had any idea that Rufus' people had arrived, and even the troops who were posted inside — and there weren't many, because the blockheads didn't know there was any way into the building — hadn't gotten down to C&C, because there were no obvious stairs or elevators.

Still, silence was essential as the Special Branch team led Kate into Admiralty House's nerve center. The place was completely dark, so night vision was required in order to get in without running into any of the consoles, or kicking over a bucket or any other thing that might be lying around to create undue noise.

Once the Sensors and Communications section was found, a few portable lights were set up, then Kate took a chair and began wiring in her power sources. There was a lot of work for her to do — the first step being to get the consoles online — but things were certainly starting off on a better note than the last time she'd tried to hack into a Defense Command comm grid…

There was no secret about where Karen, Schwartz and I were headed. Keith was a very good driver — you'd swear he'd driven fast little hover cars around tight corners on Belt Six, while chasing Syndicate pirates, or something like that. Of course he hadn't, but let this be a lesson to you: never underestimate anyone who works for the Ministry of Agriculture.

And more to the point, never cross someone whose hobbies (and store) include items made of chainmail, or who carry axes around on a casual basis.

We were all silent as we made our way over the trees to Terra Nova proper, and that didn't change as we dropped from the treetops down to the street on the city's edge. As I mentioned earlier, there were no checkpoints for us to avoid, though Keith was quite rightly concerned that there might be roving squads of blockheads keeping an eye on the approaches to the city. That in mind, he elected to take a circular back route into town.

Driving through the suburbs was very interesting. It was nothing like Egesta, thank God, because there were still plenty of lights on, plenty of families visible. Most people had left work early because of the day's events, but only some had chosen to exit the city… most of the drama was in the government district, and these families figured any action wouldn't spill out into the residential areas.

That said, there were plenty of neighbors meeting on porches and street corners, and every one of them was armed either with a pistol or rifle of some make or model. Some were clearly older surplus weapons — tired EPKs that we'd sold off for low prices as part of civil defense programs — while others were hunting or sporting weapons, and some were the very latest MAG-90 models that had been made available for civilian purchase.

"Anyone want to take a bet on who they'll side with if things get ugly?" Karen asked as she watched some of these people through the tinted windows of Keith's car.

I was riding shotgun next to Keith, so I looked back at her with a smile, "You, obviously."

Sure I was being a bit lame, but I believed what I said. Trust me, if you saw Karen in a firefight, you'd side with her. You totally would, don't deny it.

And though I was clearly quite biased, I had to believe the people here — specifically here in Terra Nova — would largely side with the civilian government that employed so many of them. That's just a fact of electoral history… capital cities often tend to reflect the party in power at a given time, because that party hires like-minded people to fill the bureaucratic and administrative posts in town.

A lot of Empire Party supporters here, then… and hopefully even if they'd once supported Olivia Bennington, they'd hate the blockheads more than they disliked Prime Minister Pope…

Not that we ever wanted them to have to back their preferences with action. Because while an armed population can theoretically defend itself against occupation (good luck to the Martians if they ever tried to land and stay), in Terra Nova right now there was a blockhead for every three civilians. Given their arms and armor, that would give the Emperor's troops too much of an advantage if a no-holds-barred street fight broke out.

No, we had to convince the Imps that their cause was completely lost — that billions of people across the planet would lynch them if they so much as tried to assert policing authority.

Then there'd be no shooting… then there'd be no civil war.

Hovering from the residential outskirts of town into a light commercial sector, Keith slowed right down. There were some cars floating up and down Quinn Avenue, one of the main drags, so he kept us to the side roads and skirted around the most obvious approaches.

We kept quiet as we drove down Smallwood Road, then turned onto Williams Avenue.

"This will take us right to the Prime Minister's Office," Keith said quietly as we hurried up the street.

That was our warning to start getting ready, so both Karen and I pulled out our mags and checked their power cells. We didn't anticipate doing much shooting — preferably none, since that might encourage a return of fire that could be rather unpleasant — but we had to be ready all the same.

Schwartz sat beside Karen, who was staring at her hands as she readied her weapon, and then he looked up at her, "So, I don't want to seem selfish, but you're going to keep me from dying, right?"

Glancing at him, she shrugged, "You don't seem selfish."

And that was all she said. See, we're here to inspire confidence — it's what we do.

The government district was on us pretty quickly, and as soon as we nosed up to the intersection that would take us over to the PMO, a blockade of tanks and Imps appeared ahead. All the glass on Keith's car was tinted, so we weren't visually obvious inside, but the pickets certainly saw that a vehicle was getting close to their lines.

A few tanks turned their main guns towards us, just in case we didn't notice them noticing us.

"Guess we'll park somewhere close and let you make the trip on foot," Keith said, and then turned at the intersection, heading away from the government buildings. No one followed — there was still enough innocent civilian traffic around to make it seem unnecessary.

If a real attack was coming, there were 12,000 blockheads with armor support here... one car with infiltrators was not a big enough threat to warrant pursuit.

Turning again, Keith took us down a side street, then into a parking lot where he landed us quietly. He climbed out first, then checked the area carefully to make sure there were no immediate observers. We were clear, so out we all climbed and nodded to him. He nodded back, climbed into his car, and shut the door. He'd find a vantage point from which to observe us... we'd proceed through the darkness until we got caught.

As his car floated away, Karen and I drew our mags and stood on either side of Schwartz. That was it for Keith — nothing glamorous, he'd just gotten us to where we needed to go in a decidedly unnoticed fashion. As if he'd done this sort of thing before.

Nah.

"So, any idea of how we get ourselves captured?" the young politico asked.

"I have a couple of ideas," Karen replied.

"Me too," I said.

We headed towards the Prime Minister's Office.

Chapter Twenty

Witnesses

As you've probably seen in the various historical records of this whole mess, some of the orbital cameras being pointed at Capital Island by the Heavy Squadron had excellent resolution. That being the case, Daragh was able to stand on *Wolf's* bridge next to his fellow Irish officer, Andrea Kiley, and see some very close-up birds-eye views of the situation below.

It made for interesting viewing.

Of course they tracked Rufus until his team reached Addis Ababa, or wherever they went, and then popped the flare on Admiralty House's roof — completely unnoticed by the huge blockhead blockade force that was surrounding them.

And they watched our red car as we made our way from the strip mall all the way into town, and were dropped off a couple of blocks from the government buildings.

"Looks like it's all going to plan," the Second Lord said quietly as Keith's car left us behind.

"Did you just say that out loud?" Andrea asked, looking up at him with a scowl.

He opened his mouth to reply, then frowned, looked a bit sheepish, and glanced down at her, "I… sorry, lassie."

"Sharp as a beach ball, aren't you?" she muttered, shaking her head and folding her arms.

There aren't many officers in the fleet who could get away with saying that to the Second Lord, and Daragh didn't know all that much about Andrea… but she had that unforgiving-raven-haired-angry-Irishwoman thing that Irishmen know better than to test. Instead of attempting to pull his massively superior rank, then, our Second Lord conceded the point and looked back to the screens.

"I have been known to bounce if asked nicely."

I don't know if that's an Irish joke, or just something he made up, but Andrea actually smiled when he said it. Certainly wouldn't have expected that… but hey, they're Irish. They're crazy. Almost as crazy as flag officers born on Capital Island…

Rufus approached the bank of consoles where Kate was working and stopped to watch her progress. He didn't say anything — he figured it would be counter-productive to interrupt *Lion's* XO while she was trying to get this rather vital patch working.

Eventually, though, the fact that he was watching drew her attention, and she glanced up from the consoles while she kept her hands moving.

"We have power, I'm just tying everything together so we can do what we need to do."

Rufus had never really worked with Kate — she'd been on *Wolf* while he'd been on *Lion* on the way out to Jupiter, so even though they were both Belt Squadron, they didn't share any particular shorthand.

"Think it'll work?" the Major decided to ask, and Kate shrugged.

"We have the most advanced communications gear on the planet in this room, so I'd like to think so. But thinking doesn't count for much."

It was hard to argue with that assessment, so as Rufus overlapped his hands on the butt of his MAG-90 — which was hanging in its familiar fashion from the harness on his vest — he nodded.

"Worth a try."

Aboard *Lion*, Kris Jacobs was watching the bridge screens as various ships from the Heavy Squadron reported their landing forces were ready to launch. There were a few hundred Special Branchers in orbit — a very small number compared to what there would have been without Mercury, but still enough (we hoped) to create the distraction we needed.

Assault shuttles were warming up on flight decks, black-clad elite officers were checking their kit, and a cargo shuttle with some skiffs aboard it was even being prepared. The bad news — or at least one piece of it — was that we didn't have any proper assault ships handy. There were a dozen landing craft on Luna, but it was on the other side of the planet and they weren't prepped for any sort of operations.

So this was going to be highly improvised, and entirely risky.

The only advantage we did have was air power — and let's be fair, that was a major plus. Unlike in a dome, where getting Starlights into action is next to impossible, over Earth our atmospace Starlights were fully capable.

Indeed, the whole reason we had planes with wings and atmospheric control surfaces (obviously unnecessary for space combat) was so we could project force into the skies over Earth. One of the good ideas that bastard Ian Hawke had put forward was that our fleet should have such an ability — that maintaining separate air and space fighter corps was stupid and redundant.

Now Kris watched as the markers for every flight in the Heavy Squadron, aboard *Wolf* and the orbital stations, went from red to white to green on *Lion's* monitors. That was over 10,000 fighters, most of them F-194s. Many of the pilots were reservists, and there were real concerns that if they went into action over Capital Island they'd get over enthusiastic and do more damage than they were supposed to... but they were there.

And Kris knew they were being prepared with no missile armaments — only their mags were armed for strafing. Because trust me, detonating an X9 Shipkiller missile on a planet is not something you want to do, unless you're planning on redrawing a map. Their warheads might be next to useless in a vacuum against ships with variable-grav compressed armor, but in an atmosphere around unarmored buildings... well, you get it.

That all said, we weren't going to just throw 10,000 planes at Capital Island along with the landing — that would have been a disaster in its own right.

Adrienne Thompson would take Wolf and Wolfstar Squadrons down with the first wave, and then call for reinforcements as needed. The most experienced pilots would get into action first, and then the rest would follow as required. Hopefully, our broadcast would get out quickly, so most of the fighters never touched atmosphere...

Hopefully.

Folding her arms as she watched the preparations on her screens, Kris knew that this could easily be the first day of a horrific civil war, and she didn't like the feeling.

But we'd make it work.

Our Grant Merger-style plan would succeed.

Soon...

CHAPTER TWENTY-ONE
HALF-HEARTED

Honestly, I don't know how hard we tried to make it look like we were sneaking towards the Prime Minister's Office. We crouched a little, and darted from cover to cover, but we were in the middle of a street, and though it was night there were thousands of blockheads keeping an eye on the approaches.

When the first spotlight was turned on us, followed by four more, and then lots of guns as well, we stopped in the middle of the street with our hands up, and then did what we needed to do to avoid getting shot.

"I'm Ken Barron, and this is Karen McMaster," I called, making sure as many people heard as was realistically possible.

"We're trying to sneak into the Prime Minister's Office," Karen added, and that was a little on the nose. "If you won't tell, we won't."

Like I said, this was a bit of a half-hearted sell job.

It did earn us fine treatment, though. As the spotlights imprisoned us in their ring of light, we couldn't see too much of the Imp line — we were looking into quite a glare. It was very dramatic, then, when a full General (the wonderfully-named Martindale Lackner) appeared right in front of us, hands on his hips as he sneered.

"So it's the head of the snake, right into my lap," he snarled, and Karen immediately dismissed his macho manhood.

"You like other peoples' snakes in your lap, General? There are a lot of ways I could take that, and all of them make me think less of you as a man."

Now don't get your hackles up, she wasn't trying to insult anyone but him — because she recognized dear Martindale from various news reports, and knew that he was famous for aggressive *womanizing*. That's two womanizers in one book — Murt Sergeant and General Martindale Lackner. Interesting.

Anyway, Lackner bristled at Karen's implication, and he actually raised his hand as if to strike her.

"Oh calm down, General," she said sweetly. "There's virtually nothing you could do that wouldn't make me think less of you as a man."

He hit her. Full on punch, with everything he had in his bulky frame. Right across the jaw. Now Karen is tough, but physics is physics, so she was knocked down to one knee by the blow.

Holding the back of her hand up to her lip, with blood trickling from the corner of her mouth, she looked up at me, "You just going to stand there while he beats me?"

I shrugged, "You asked for it."

At this point, Schwartz — who had been standing back and trying to keep from getting shot, looked at me with quite the frown. Before he could say anything, Lackner snorted a laugh.

"Didn't realize you actually had balls, Barron."

I think he meant it affectionately.

As Karen got back to her feet and shifted her weight a little unsteadily, the General came closer. His eyes moved to Schwartz, "So I'm guessing I know why you're here. And I'm surprised you thought you could get through our lines."

I shrugged, "You think we're really that stupid? Maybe we saw the writing on the wall, and decided the only way for us to get a good bargaining chip out of protective custody in orbit was to promise we'd try to smuggle him somewhere."

Lackner's eyes turned to me and narrowed, "Say that again."

I stepped in closer, lowering my voice, "Schwartz is our bargaining chip. And I want to be the next First Lord. Take us to see the GG."

As I said it, the General looked back at young Mister Babcock — the kid's eyes were wider than any of us had ever seen them. He started moving his mouth, trying to say something, but no sound came out.

Then my hand settled on his back, and I smiled, "Don't worry, Schwartz, I don't intend to let them kill you."

"Intend?" he croaked the question.

Lackner looked from me to him and back, then turned and saw Karen still nursing her mouth with the back of her hand. She'd taken punches before, she was fine. Though she did seem irritable, which was stupid of her. I mean, she's not supposed to talk to a guy like that, when he's got thousands of guns pointed at her, and not get a little correction.

She was lucky he didn't shoot her in the gut, but from the glare she gave him, it was clear she still didn't appreciate her good fortune.

I did appreciate it, though — when Lackner looked at me, that approval was written on my face. He studied me carefully, then finally made his observation, "I don't believe you, Barron. But... maybe you're not as full of shit as you seem."

"That sounds to me like the beginnings of an uneasy minor truce that'll probably end up with you shooting me," I smiled. "But I'll take it."

Lackner laughed again, then raised his hand. Suddenly we were surrounded by a dozen blockheads, "Follow me."

Follow we did, and I could feel Karen's glare boring a hole in the back of my head the whole way. Our first fight in a long time, I guess...

Watching from the top of a building a few blocks away, Keith pulled out the flare and activated it. The signal was sent.

Standing on *Wolf's* bridge, Daragh actually spotted the green flash on the live camera feed before Felicia Khalid was able to call attention to it.

"There!" he pointed at the screen, then did a quick calculation in his head based on where the flare had been triggered, and the other details the cameras were showing. It would probably take ten minutes for us to get to the Governor General's chamber, so he'd just have to delay a little. "Send the signal: all shuttles launch in five minutes."

Orders raced out from *Wolf*, and the assault was prepared.

✦✦✦

The government buildings were basically covered in blockheads, and just about all of them stared at us as we walked. No civilians — politicians or reporters — were in sight, which I took to be a largely negative sign.

I don't think Karen was visibly noticing anything.

We passed the Prime Minister's Office, then the Parliament buildings themselves, and made our way to the Governor General's office and residence at Hibernia Hall. I suppose it made sense that Hodson and Bennington both would be holing up on that familiar turf during the scuffle that they were trying to cause — and the place was very well protected by arms and armor.

As we entered the lobby of the ornate building, I had to admit the decoration wasn't actually that obnoxious — especially not when compared to what we'd seen recently on Mars and Egesta. Evil though the Emperor's faction was, its members weren't so tasteless as our enemies.

I didn't get to enjoy the spectacle for very long, though — instead of being led to any of the normal places guests might be received in Hibernia Hall, we were taken to a set of stairs concealed somewhere where I can't say (and which probably weren't stairs either), and eventually found ourselves in the Governor General's personal bunker.

Like C&C at Admiralty House, the Governor General's bunker was dug deep into the Capital Island rock, and was well-shielded from orbital attack. It was a relatively modest complex, but then it was meant only for the GG, his staff and family. As we entered we proceeded down a corridor that was overdramatic in its lighting, passed some rooms with closed doors, and then went through large double doors at the end.

Lying behind those doors was a hybrid between a warship's bridge and a throne room. Actually, it reminds me of the war room on Belt Two, where Marshal, Wes, Charlie, Karen and I had watched Glorious February. The GG had a pedestal chair at one end of the room, and it was turnable. All around him were screens, and there were a couple of consoles, with a few blockheads running the vid and sensor feeds.

There were also a half-dozen energy guns in the room, I should add — one on the hip of General Lackner, three with the guards who'd escorted us down here, and two with the sentries on the door.

Not as many as I was expecting, frankly.

As we entered, and the heavy double doors closed behind us, Governor General Hodson turned his chair in our direction. Bennington wasn't here with him, which was reason for some confusion — perhaps even concern — but we'd work with what we had.

"So you come down here and supposedly turn yourselves in?" the GG asked with his overdramatic flare. "Seems like a weak ploy, Admiral Barron."

I shrugged, "It would be. But there's only so many times you can save the Empire before you start wondering whether there's room for vertical movement."

Hodson smiled, then chuckled, "I look forward to your attempts to convince me. But whether this is a ploy or a true change of heart, and do keep in mind that I doubt the latter seriously, I am indebted to you for bringing Mister Babcock here. He will be most entertaining for us as things progress."

He sounded like a man in control, and that was fine: if he felt in control and confident, he'd be more likely to get arrogant and throw open the comms when the time came.

"And Commodore McMaster, you really are more beautiful in person... though you seem to have a swollen lip. I hope General Lackner wasn't too harsh when bringing you in," the GG enjoyed saying that, and Karen didn't enjoy hearing it.

"We had a disagreement," she said sharply.

I glanced back at her, and then jerked my head almost invisibly to tell her to shut up. She glared at me, and the GG turned from her to Lackner, "A disagreement you seem to have had the last word on, Martindale."

The General smiled, "You once asked me why I wear my War College ring, now you know."

Laughing gently, Hodson nodded, and I took a step forward, "This is all very entertaining, I know. But let's not waste time. I have some propositions that you won't believe at first, but I think we can come to an understanding."

The Governor General narrowed his eyes at me, then steepled his fingers in front of him. He was curious, though not completely gullible. I'd have some work to do, even if Karen was only going to stand behind me and fume.

CHAPTER TWENTY-TWO

THE ATTACK

Adrienne Thompson was settled into the familiar world of her cockpit when the order came to launch. Our veteran flight commander was ready for this mission — very ready indeed. There were many reasons for her preparedness, not least the fresh memories of what she and Shelby McLaws had seen on Egesta. The blockheads on the ground — her possible targets, if things turned out a certain way — would feel her wrath for everything she'd seen, as well as everything they were responsible for now.

Assault shuttles started boosting from all the ships of the Heavy Squadron as she and the pilots of Wolf and Wolfstar Squadrons hurtled down into the atmosphere at maximum safe velocity. It was a scene she imagined would be quite dramatic on the screen of any skywatch operator in the capital.

Even the Imperial Army's limited ground-based detection units would be able to see the cloud of descending craft, so hopefully the bastards would turn on their cameras...

"Alright, the minute they flip the switch to start broadcasting, I'll be able to jack their feed and send it back to them."

Kate Levec was smiling with deserved pride as she sat, arms folded, behind Admiralty House's Sensors and Communications consoles. Rufus was still standing by and watching her, so it was to him her report was addressed.

With a nod the Major drew in a breath, "Is there any way for us to know when that time will come?"

"You mean see when the attack is coming down from orbit?" Kate asked, and Rufus nodded.

"Afraid not," she answered. "There's no way for me to power up any kind of sensors without them noticing, and even if I tried, Captain Davis told me they'd cut off access to the external grid anyway. We'd only be able to see what the sensors on top of this building can pick up..."

"And we'd give away our position," Rufus finished the thought, bringing a nod from *Lion's* new XO.

"Well then," Rufus said quietly. "I guess we just wait."

Imagine how much fun that was.

It didn't take long for Keith to get to the condo (or house) that he and his wife (or maybe he didn't have a wife) lived in, and to get her to a place of safety. After that, he found himself at a playground in the middle of one of the subdivisions on the outskirts of town, looking up into the night sky.

The sun would be rising soon — the sky to the east was already beginning to lighten, which meant the attack which would begin under the cover of darkness would finish with the sun shining over the capital.

That probably would make no difference at all, though — both sides had equipment suited to night fighting and day fighting. If anything, that in-between twilight time would be a little more complicated (night vision in growing light isn't always the greatest) but he expected both sides would figure it out.

How messy would the fight get?

Looking up at the darkened sky, Keith was able to see what looked like a whole lot of shooting stars spiraling downwards from orbit. At least two squadrons of Starlights, leading down a force of assault shuttles... probably enough to represent every Special Brancher from the Heavy Squadron in orbit.

Those men and women would be mostly inexperienced, Keith knew — Branchers who had just come through selection, and who hadn't been to Mercury. Not like Rufus Chang, a Brancher who even Keith wouldn't mess with, or Charlie Peters, a Brancher who Keith *really* wouldn't mess with. When Charlie got into a fight in the Belt, he increased the chances of all the pirates in the room being killed or taken into custody by forty-nine times. He also doubled their chances of finding religion, and mending their ways out of fear.

Proven facts.

Unfortunately the officers coming down from the Heavy Squadron weren't that good, at least not in the estimation of one of the Ministry of Agriculture's best former system developers. Now, I would tell you that they were good — they had to be, to pass selection — but Keith is much less... er... in awe of Special Branch than I am.

He would say that the kids coming down in those shuttles were a little too cocky, and while they were an order of magnitude better than the blockheads, their over-enthusiasm could lead to considerable complications when the fighting began.

Because there were still people in the city — Terra Nova was by no means a clean slate ready for destruction. This was a very delicate operation, and Keith just hoped the Branchers coming down understood as much.

Adrienne, for all her anger, knew exactly what she had to do. As her squadron dropped to treetop level and raced towards Terra Nova — coming in from the east, over the waves, instead of overland from the west as we had during our covert landing — she could see powerful shafts of light start to reach up into the sky over the city.

And then, because the blockheads had actually prepared for her, those shafts of light started pointing her way.

This was a surprise — none of us had been too privy to the anti-air tools the Imps deployed, and even if we were, I doubt we'd have considered fast-tracking spotlights to be particularly worrying. We lived in an age of planetary sensors grids, after all — who cares if you have a spotlight elevated off the back of a truck that can spin in virtually every direction, and keep track of a craft as it roars past at any speed?

Nobody, of course... except when that light isn't the only thing on the mount tracking the target. Add an energy gun to the fast-tracking turret, for instance, and you suddenly have something a bit more dangerous... especially when you're sitting in the cockpit of one of the marked planes, coming over the waves at Mach 4 and wondering what else the bastards might have up their sleeves.

"Wolfstar leader to group, break and overfly. Watch your spacing and keep those lights moving."

The audio quality of Adrienne's orders was reduced by the signal jamming the blockheads were still beaming over the comms, so they arrived in the ears of her pilots with a very noticeable hiss, but got through. Unfortunately, anything with enough power to get from plane to plane through the jamming could also be detected on the ground. The blockheads couldn't quickly break the encryption of our comms, but they could track the transmissions, and use them to figure out exactly how many planes were coming in, how fast and where.

Combined with the other ground-based search tools they had, this gave them a pretty good ability to target Adrienne's wing...

The question was, who'd fire first.

Keith watched the skies over Terra Nova from the playground he'd selected as a viewing area. It was a good location, unsurprisingly — on top of a hill, with a clear lookout over the city. He followed the Starlights as they were lit up, and then he watched them break in a seemingly chaotic fashion.

Did they ever dance.

With shafts of light remaining locked on them, the planes split from a solid group of twenty-four into twelve pairs, then started weaving at supersonic speeds.

I suppose I should say that, when he viewed this, Keith wasn't able to follow much — planes dancing back and forth in the air at such velocities were hardly easy to keep track of, and only the lights that seemed glued to them gave any hint of the dance they were performing...

It was enough to give him quite a headache. The spotlights crossed back and forth, wove and dove, climbed and fell... it is not, in fact, an urban legend that one person watching the display from his porch discovered he was epileptic because the light show brought on a seizure.

But while the supersonic Starlights were impossible for the lights of the army to miss, the stealthy Special Branch assault shuttles were much less obvious. In the midst of all the sky chaos, the army computers remained coolly familiar with the twenty-four fighters that were overhead, but the shuttles were running low and slow, and were only intermittently appearing on sensor screens...

Keith spotted one of them when a shaft of light clipped it... but his visual identification wasn't duplicated by any of the scanning teams the army had in position to watch the approach. Covered by the fighters, then, Special Branch arrived over Terra Nova.

Major Isko Caacbay was the senior Brancher available to lead the landing on Terra Nova, and I suppose that speaks to Keith's observations: Isko had been a Captain for one tour on Mercury, had come home with a promotion, and had taken over the Capital Island defense detail. He was by no means unqualified, and I wouldn't even say he was inexperienced, but he was young and eager and of a different character than someone like Carrie Walsh, his predecessor.

That said, Carrie hadn't done a tour on Mercury when she'd been appointed to the job Caacbay now held — she had pirate-fighting experience, but no warfighting, so perhaps Isko was more qualified, even at his younger age.

But if he didn't fall into the inexperienced category Keith had in mind, many of the other officers coming down with him certainly did… and that made what came next very tense indeed.

As the feet of his shuttle came down in a mall parking lot, two blocks away from the government buildings (on the opposite side from the way we'd gone in), Isko was already on his feet, and rapidly descending the ramp from his craft.

His team was behind him — the original detail he'd taken with him for his new posting at Admiralty House, all of them ready and willing to do harm. The shuttles from the rest of the Heavy Squadron came down in the same parking lot, including the cargo hauler containing the seven skiffs. Those were unloaded and crewed very quickly, though if you'll recall from *The Mercury Assault*, the light, fast, airlock-friendly craft weren't really cut out for fighting hundreds of tanks…

Still, it was a powerful force that got to ground unopposed — close to 300 Branchers, plus skiffs. Certainly enough to do some damage, even when the blockheads numbered 33,000.

But Isko wasn't going to leap to the offensive just yet. The game of chicken had to continue a while longer.

Keith didn't know why the shuttles hadn't landed on the Parliament buildings. His thought process on this was pretty straightforward: if Special Branchers had begun to land right in the blockheads' lines, the Imperial troops would almost certainly have had to open fire — and given the number of tanks they had, they could have brought down many of the shuttles short of landing.

That, I think you'll agree, would have been a very clear sign that they were the bad guys…

But while Daragh understood that killing all the Branchers of the landing force would have been a clear public relations win, he wasn't about to order it. And Keith didn't disagree, he just… well. He had a bigger view of the situation, and were it him coming down in one of the shuttles, he'd probably have risked diving straight into the blockhead lines.

Of course, landing our force in the middle of the blockheads could have backfired rather easily. With such an advantage in numbers, the Imps could have surrounded and overrun the landing shuttles without firing shots… and as a result, isolate and cut off our only concentrated response force in short order.

So there were plenty of arguments, and Isko had ultimately picked the mall as a rally point for his force so that he could choose an approach that would give his officers the best chance of surviving what was to come.

Keith figured that out from his vantage point on the playground, but before he could manage any further analysis, a few dozen people from nearby neighborhoods — all of them carrying weapons of one sort or another — started appearing around him.

None were paying any particular attention to Keith — the spectacle of a landing on

Terra Nova was more than sufficient to keep them distracted.

But then one woman came to a stop beside him, "You seen the whole thing so far?"

Pausing, Keith nodded, "It's pretty crazy."

"Will we win?" she asked.

Keith blinked, then looked at this woman. She was cradling an EPK in the crook of her arm, but aside from that, he had no way to guess what side she associated herself with. Then he realized that all the people in the playground around him were armed, and that if even a few of them represented opposing sides, it could all get messy.

Whatever my hopes, there was no way to tell for sure how many people sided with who. The Emperor had to have *some* support...

"I think we should get back to our homes... if one of those Starlights gets shot down it could drop anywhere, so our families need to be in the basements at least..." he suggested forcefully, hoping the words would compel action from the assembled onlookers.

It didn't — they kept watching.

Keith considered his options, then determined his first responsibility was to his wife (if he had one). That being the case, he silently drifted away from the playground, and made for a secondary viewing point.

If trouble broke out in a civilian crowd, he wouldn't be part of it.

Adrienne — and all of the pilots from *Wolf's* two squadrons — found the constant maneuvering to be quite exhausting. Flying in atmosphere was in many ways the catalyst that had created space travel as we know it, but compared to the sort of maneuvering one could do in space, it was positively inhibitive.

And there was no way to lose the lights. The damned things — one of the innovations of the Imperial Army that probably had no use except for this exact situation — had Adrienne's Starlight, and every other one of *Wolf's* planes, well and truly locked.

If shooting started, and there were lasers or mags or even energy cannon hitched to those tracking mounts, it would be lights out for the entire squadron. A steep price to pay to get the blockheads to fire first, but Adrienne knew it was possible that was the way things would have to go.

"Wolfstar leader to all wolves, let's quit the acrobatics. Standard overflights by squadron, opposing vectors on rotation. They have us locked, but we're not going to pull the trigger until we have to."

Without delay, the Starlights from Adrienne's two squadrons reformed and began carrying out her orders. Below, Major Caacbay's Branchers got organized and prepared to march on the Imperial Army... and all the while, the blockheads sat by waiting.

They were going to make us fire first.

And we would.

CHAPTER TWENTY-THREE

FAILED GAMBIT

Two forces were very obviously moving towards a clash with each other, and that meant all the preconditions we'd required were now in place. There was enough reason for the Governor General to soon open the comm grid, to broadcast the fight, but only if we convinced him.

How many people would die before he flipped the switch for us? It was a question that we didn't really want to think about... one we knew was probably going to have an answer other than 'none', unless we came up with something pretty remarkable.

And we weren't remarkable.

As I stood before the Governor General's elevated chair, he looked down at me with an arrogant smile. On the screens around us, video and ground-based skywatch scans of the landings swirled around. He looked from me to those displays every little while, seeming quite interested.

"So the timing works out that, just as you get here, your troops arrive too," Hodson said eventually. "Shall we move past the niceties, Admiral Barron? Get to the part where you threaten me with your massive armed forces."

I was watching Hodson closely, trying to figure out exactly what he thought our intentions were. He clearly believed we had an ulterior motive in getting captured — the notion that we were here to turn in Schwartz for personal favor was weak.

But did he realize we wanted him to open the comm channels?

"What will it take for you to believe what I'm saying?" I folded my arms and offered a slim smile.

The Governor General steepled his fingers before him, then leaned back in his chair to think about the answer.

"I suppose it'll be a matter of what you do, as much as what you say. Because if I were in your shoes, Barron, my first aim would be to do something, anything, to convince me to give the orders for our troops to open fire on your assault forces."

Maybe that was it — maybe that's what he thought Karen and I were playing for. If so, it was fortunate for us... he thought the last thing we wanted was to be the first ones to fire under the circumstances?

Well, consider that he didn't know we had a broadcast of massively damning information ready at our disposal. If the way we acted in trying to take back Capital Island was the only evidence we had to show people, then we'd damn ourselves if we fired first.

"Do you even have operational control of your army?" Karen spat that question with some venom, and I looked back at her and winced at the on-the-nose question.

She didn't seem to appreciate my questioning look, because she glared at me, but I ignored that and looked back to the Governor General, who was laughing.

"Really, she's not actually thinking that she can bait me into ordering the attack?"

Hodson's retort was sharp.

I raised an eyebrow, then shrugged, "I wouldn't think anyone would underestimate you quite so much."

The Governor General's eyes narrowed and he turned his gaze to me again, "You think you can either flatter or enrage me to the point that I order my Generals to pull the trigger first..."

He let that implication — perhaps accusation — dangle for a moment, then tilted his head, "But you don't seem too concerned about it. So either you have another plan to try to get a win out of this situation..."

"Or maybe, just maybe, there's something I can get out of this," I answered. Then thought to add: "For both her and me."

I didn't get a look at Karen's expression, but when Hodson did, it made him smile, "Seems all she wants is to do harm to me, Admiral. Not sure I should let her have anything she wants."

"She'll remember where she fits when she calms down," I assured, then turned in the other direction and waved my hand at Schwartz.

The Deputy Chief of Staff was trying to be as small as possible — and he wasn't too big an individual, so small was quite doable for him. Realizing that he had my attention, the political wonderkid's eyes widened and then he looked from me to the Governor General and back.

"I can't tell if you're actually being serious now, Admiral," the wonderkid said in a hiss, and I shrugged.

"I'm pretty sure you can tell. If you couldn't you wouldn't be on Pope's staff. You'd agree, wouldn't you Governor General? He's sharp."

"He is," Hodson replied, sounding as though his compliment bore great importance. "But he serves the wrong master. As do you."

"Oh get over it," I turned back to Hodson. "I know this isn't going to be an easy sell, so I'll offer something of value. First, I'll let the DC forces out there fire the first shots. Then, at your discretion, I will record a statement that implicates John Fiora, Daragh Ryan and Douglas Pope in a conspiracy to control the next election. I'll say I just found out about it, and that's why I made a hasty return to Earth."

Any good humor drained from the Governor General's face, and I could see the wheels turning in his mind. He knew such a statement would go a long way towards legitimizing everything — having Fiora Ring officers side with the Emperor would be a clear indicator that, however clumsy the attempt had been, the blockheads had in fact been on the side of good the whole time.

It was not an offer he could ignore offhand, even if he was fairly convinced there had to be a catch. And, because I knew he was waiting for the other shoe to drop, I decided to give it to him.

"There are conditions, of course." Turning, I pointed my finger at Schwartz, "I know you don't like him, but I want him spared any punishment. The rest of the PMO staff can be hung for all I care, but I think this kid has potential. You can throw him out of government, but maybe in a few years he'll see the error of his ways and come back in to help us."

Hodson frowned at that unexpected demand, then looked over at Schwartz. Unsurprisingly, the Deputy Chief of Staff's jaw was dropped with shock.

"I don't want your *charity*," he sounded genuinely disgusted at the thought.

"Shut up, kid, you'll thank me when you get your first girlfriend," I shot back, and the words earned me a delighted laugh from the Governor General.

"Ah, Barron, I want you to know that I'm actually hoping you're not full of shit. I think you'd be entertaining to have around," the GG said, and I shrugged.

"You don't get to be a media darling without some redeeming qualities. Condition two: you're going to protect Craig B. Macdonald, the Foreign Minister."

That removed Hodson's humor again, and he began shaking his head immediately. I took that as a good sign — he was starting to react to my conditions as if he thought the conversation was a serious one.

"Not possible," the Governor General's tone was flat, but I narrowed my eyes and hit him with a glare. He asked: "Why do you care about the Scotsman?"

I took a couple of steps towards the elevated chair, but not enough to worry any of the guards in the room, "He was with us on Mars, and he's actually a good guy to have around. I know the PM is going to have to go to trial for your plot here to work, but I don't see why you *need* the Minister of Foreign Affairs in the mix too. Just let him retire."

"He's too high up. I can try for prison time, but he's going to trial," the Governor General said evenly, and then I narrowed my eyes further.

"Seems to me like we're actually bargaining here," was my answer, and that's when the GG paused, then sat back in his chair.

Silently, he seemed to review the situation in his mind. He knew the Emperor had it in for the entire Fiora Ring, and Karen and I were high up on the list of offenders who needed to be liquidated in the most expedient, arguably legal way available.

But securing a new government under dubious circumstances like these would take endorsements, and though having Bennington on side meant there was some political cover, Defense Command remained the biggest challenge to the new order.

Because, then as now, we were everywhere. Every police station, every comm ship, every dome in the Empire. No truly senior officers were closely aligned to the Emperor's cause... he had some hope of getting Mik Mikaelsen aboard, but that was a work in progress.

What if a few concessions could get the famous Ken Barron?

It was sufficiently tempting, so the Governor General stood up from his chair, linked his hands behind his back, and stepped down from his elevated seating platform. He didn't come any closer, though — obviously he still didn't trust me. No, the calculation was more about what he had to lose...

"I might bargain with you, Barron... but not until after your forces fire first. Not until after I know you've let them commit that suicide."

I frowned at Hodson's words, "We can talk after one of my old colleagues pulls a trigger? Shouldn't you wait to see how the battle goes, make sure I'm not here planting a bomb to cripple you in mid-fight?"

The Governor General continued to consider me carefully, then moved his hands around in front of him, and folded his arms.

"Yes," he said. "But of course I can listen to the rest of your terms now. Might as well not wait for the action to begin."

I wasn't sure if that prompt had another motive behind it, but I decided to push ahead anyway. Folding my arms to match his, I shifted my weight from foot to foot and bladed my body slightly, so I was looking at him a little sideways. No idea why I did that, I just did.

"I'm the new First Lord. No questions asked. My officers — the ones I led during the war — stay out of trouble. We can negotiate about Wes Pellew, Mik Mikaelsen and Marshal Samuels."

"I'll need at least two of those on drumheads," the Governor General said immediately.

I shook my head, "You get one. Only one."

Hodson stared at me. I got the distinct feeling I was being tested.

"What about your lady there," he then asked directly. "I presume I don't get her."

I shook my head, "Obviously not. Once I've got Admiralty House, I'll make sure she has a good posting that suits her talents."

"Very kind of you," Hodson replied. "Guess she's earned that much."

He was implying that Karen had earned her favorable treatment through more than just her capabilities as an officer, and her intelligence. I smirked slightly at the implication, and shrugged, "You think you're on to something no one else figured out?"

"Oh I'm sure many have figured it out," Hodson countered, then moved back to the terms under negotiation. "So we get Fiora, Ryan, Noyce and Stoll. All of the Admirals above you are fair game, and you'll endorse whatever story we need to put out."

I nodded, and the Governor General took a breath. He then looked over my shoulder at General Lackner, "You swept him for cameras and bugs. He's not recording this so he can discredit us later?"

"Checked him for everything," the blockhead officer replied evenly. He too seemed tickled about my apparent change of heart, though he was more accepting of it that Hodson was. The reaction of a simple soldier, as opposed to a wily political appointee bent on domination.

The Governor General nodded slowly, then looked from me to Karen and back before making it official, "If your troops fire first, you have a deal. Though if you try to cross us, you know you're dead, and your woman too."

I smiled, and then nodded, "Deal. We should talk about broadcasting my stateme—"

Of course neither Lackner nor his guards saw Karen move — none of them realized what was happening until she'd already managed to pull the daft General's sidearm from his hip, and had launched her attack.

I didn't see it either, I just felt the effects. Being pistol-whipped across the temple by Karen is not pleasant, trust me on this. Particularly when she's in a bad mood.

"Shut *up*," she really snarled that order at me, and I had no choice but to obey as I toppled sideways to the ground.

So much for her self-control — it was obvious to everyone else in the room that she was displeased. Livid, in fact.

And this is where the plan, which had seemed so controlled and well-in hand, departed stage left, to be replaced by fury.

Hodson held up his hand to the blockhead guards as he watched Karen point her captured gun at my head.

"Really?" the GG was smiling again, "you think I'll fall for the 'he's a traitor' ploy? Give me the gun, Commodore McMaster… and beware that those slow guards behind you are still good enough to shoot you in the back."

"Fuck you," Karen looked from me — now writhing a little on the floor as I braced my palm against my throbbing temple — to the Emperor's appointee. "Of course he was playing you. He has no intention of keeping his word."

Well, that pretty much threw away long minutes of carefully-crafted dialogue.

Hodson found the answer interesting, and though he stepped back a couple of paces — not a bad precaution, considering who he was talking to, and her unstable state — he decided to let the drama ride, "Go on."

"He thinks he can walk in anywhere and get what he wants. But if you're willing to do that deal, you won't do it with him. Do it with me. And I don't have conditions. No one else to save, no mess. I just want the top job, and that's it."

Hodson's smile was a skeptical one — this was, as far as he was concerned, one bluff too many. From all he'd heard of Karen and me, it was conceivable that the two of us together might turn on some of the people above us, and even abandon some of our comrades… but her turning on me was completely unrealistic.

Maybe that's why Schwartz's expression had gone from carefully-controlled shock to confusion.

"Karen… what are you doing?" he asked.

But that question in itself was too rich, and Hodson chuckled, shaking his head, "No. No you had some credibility until you tried this. But you two would never split…"

At that point he looked down on me, but even though my head was just clearing from the first bout of pain that came with the blow, my expression reflected genuine surprise, faintly restrained by my brain trying to figure out what the hell Karen was doing.

The fact that I wasn't quipping something, wasn't yelling 'Karen, stop!' or anything else bad dialogue writers from movies would have me do in a situation like this… that made the Governor General pause.

He was a political operator, well accustomed to reading people in the Emperor's court. That meant he could read expressions better than many, and mine was too ambiguous. People trying to sell a lie tend to have more coherent reactions than people truly reacting to a surprise.

But maybe I was just a good liar.

"Why don't you kick him a few times, Commodore McMaster? Prove that this isn't a trick?"

Karen's eyes turned on Hodson fast, "I'm not here to fucking prove something to you. You want me to kick him? You want me to shoot him? I'm not going to do that. I can't."

She sounded… desperate. Certainly not controlled, and the Governor General frowned. She was saying she couldn't do anything to prove her position, but then if she'd been lying and trying to prove herself, wouldn't she have done something — kicked me, or shot me in the leg, or something like they do in the movies, to prove when good people go bad?

And then she turned on me suddenly, and unleashed something far more excruciating than her powerful fists, or the gun in her hand, "Aren't you going to *say* anything? Always letting me take the hits… I get stabbed by Josie, I get the phosgene on *Idaho*, I get my ships shot out from under me every time. All the time. And you're the Admiral? Because you got lucky when Erica Martin put you alongside that ship at Deep Black?"

Her voice was so raw it was hoarse. She jabbed her finger at me as she bellowed, and I tried — really tried — to melt into the floor under her withering words.

"You know why I'm the Commodore and he's the Admiral? Because he got lucky," Karen turned back to Hodson. "Of course you know. And ever since then, it's been a pat on the head. All the time. Oh he says he knows it was just luck, but I know when I'm being soothed." She turned on me again, striding over and bending at the waist so she could yell down, almost directly into my ear, "You think I don't know?"

I cringed. It's impossible to fake the reaction I was having. It's impossible to pretend to have a soul-chilling, strickening moment.

"I'm not just arm candy. I'm not just some pretty companion here to answer his questions and remind him that he's better than everyone else," she turned back to Hodson, and by this time she'd worked herself to the point of tears. "I'm tired of that. He's trying to save everything right now, but I'm tired of that. I don't want that. I've done my bit. I've done all I can. I don't want him dead, I don't want that. But I can't stand being his foil anymore."

Hodson stared at Karen. Everyone did. Her energy gun was dangling from her fingertips, she was sniffling against tears, and realizing she was in a state she would never have allowed herself to be in — had she not been out of her mind with whatever the hell you call this — she started to wipe her eyes with her sleeve.

No Imp in the room could doubt that the shock on Schwartz T. Babcock's face was genuine. He was a young man, and even were he older, I doubt he could ever have seen anything quite this… thing.

I don't know a better descriptor.

Realizing I really did need to say something, though, I pushed myself up off my side, and once in a seated position I shook my head, "This wasn't a good idea…"

I wasn't referring to Karen — or at least I didn't mean to be — but she was very obviously keyed up, and she heard it the way she wanted, or more properly, *needed* to hear it at that moment.

Turning on me with red eyes, she suddenly sounded very cold, "I could count your good ideas on one hand."

I just stared at her.

"Was it a good idea that got Kris irradiated? Was it a good idea that got Erica killed? Or maybe it was a good idea," she paused just to make it hurt more, "to put Lia in the line of fire, so she could get cut up the way you let her get cut up?"

Could have heard a pin drop. I think it was clear from my expression that I'd have liked to hear one — perhaps the pin from a grenade, so we could put an end to this.

But none did. Chest heaving slightly with every labored breath, Karen stared at me, her eyes bored right down into me.

And I let myself reply in a way that I probably shouldn't have.

"I shouldn't have taken a chance on you that night."

No one else in the room had any idea what I meant — no one other than Karen. I'm sure they all thought different things, but they were all wrong. No one else knew what it had been like, the night she and I first met.

All she knew is how lucky she'd been that it had been me. And it was the apparent resentment that she held for me that was fueling this whole goddamned outburst.

It was also the one moment in our history together about which she couldn't argue, or reimagine to suit a bruised ego, or a furious rage. Because she knew how I'd first seen her, and she knew how she'd seen herself.

Finally I got a punch in that connected, and though she didn't do anything dramatic — didn't stumble, didn't fall — I could see her shoulders slump, and her composure go. She let the energy gun drop to the floor beside her feet, and shook her head once.

We were all silent for a few moments — the calm after the storm, really, and then Hodson moved up behind Karen, trying, confusingly, to offer a reassuring pat on the back.

"Don't touch me," she stopped him short with cold words. "The deal."

The Governor General looked at her — he was seeing her in profile from the side, and she looked... well, undignified is the polite word. Then he looked at me, and as I sat on the floor and stared down at my boots, it was pretty clear that the fight he'd just witnessed had robbed me of any interest in the civil war that was brewing.

"If your side fires first, and you testify, we'll make you First Lord," he said quietly.

She nodded, and then turned away from me and him. As she did, her gaze reached one of the screens showing vid from the world above, and she let her head loll sideways and pointed dejectedly to it.

"Looks like you missed the start of your civil war."

Blinking, Hodson turned to the screen, and sure enough, skiffs were making a strafing run on the blockheads guarding Defense Command Communications Center.

"We started it. You've got your proof," Karen sounded tired now, the way anyone does after pouring so much emotion into words.

The Governor General looked from the screen to her and then back to the blockheads at the consoles, "Rewind the picture. Let me see for certain who shot first."

They did as they were told, and by the time the picture was queued, I was looking as well. It was indeed a skiff that fired first, and as I saw it, I let out a single breath. Hodson looked back at me with a smile, "Gallant effort, Barron."

Then he looked at Karen, "I don't think that was... anything other than a mistreated woman being honest. If you are good to your word, we will be good to ours. Please tell me I didn't misread you."

"Don't try to sooth me, Hodson," Karen's voice regained some of its edge. "Put me on camera. Hell, do it right now. I'll tell the world we shot first, while you run the pictures."

She turned to Hodson, and the Governor General looked at her with more than a little surprise. Scowling, she wiped her eyes and nose, "What, not pretty enough?"

"We'll get a mirror and some water in here, so you can splash it on your face," the GG said, pointing to one of the guards, who rapidly departed to collect the items. "We need a story..."

"Let's just keep it simple. I've just discovered that the charges of corruption are true..."

she paused, and then looked over her shoulder enough to see me out of the corner of her eye. "We were both down here to investigate the charges, but I was the lucky one to get to you with news in time. So I'll be the lucky one made First Lord this time. I can't elaborate on the case yet, but the evidence is clear: that's why Defense Command is launching an unprovoked attack on the defenses."

It sounded like she was getting her composure back, and as the soldier returned with mirror and water, she fixed herself up. I just watched in silence, and Hodson watched me watch. I think he actually felt sorry for me, so he finally caught my eye and said, "We'll honor her wishes about you."

"I wish you wouldn't," my reply was patently bitter.

"All the more reason to do it," Hodson smiled. "Death is easier than living in someone's shadow, wouldn't you say?"

Ironic for the Governor General — an appointee whose authority was borrowed from the Emperor — to say in quite that way. I didn't have the energy left to point that out, though. Schwartz moved over to me and crouched, his face gaunt.

"She's really…"

I nodded, "I know."

Karen didn't look back at me when Hodson led her over to the space in front of his chair, so the viewfinder could catch them both for their broadcast. It was pretty obvious to everyone that she couldn't *stand* to look.

I watched her back, then my eyes darted over to one of the screens. One skiff was on the ground, burning fiercely. The rest had withdrawn. Special Branch was good, but there was only so much you could do against dozens of tanks.

"Ready to broadcast live," one of the blockheads at the consoles reported, and Hodson nodded.

"Let's tell our story," the Governor General said.

So they did.

CHAPTER TWENTY-FOUR

BUT NO ONE LISTENED

Kate Levec had been staring at the communications consoles, almost lulled into a daze by their inactivity. And then suddenly, her board went from red to green. She sat up straighter in her seat, and her hands began to fly — feeding back the broadcast to the sending console, and then hitting play on our pre-recorded vid, just as planned.

I know you've probably seen it (or an edited version of it) but I'm going to take you through it again. As bombshells go, this was a powerful one...

Daragh Ryan appeared on the screen, looking severe.

"Ladies and gentlemen, you know me. You probably don't like me much, and I'll be just as happy as you to get back to the quiet solitude that I enjoyed before this damned war. But right now I have a job, and that job is to protect the integrity of our system of government. What the Governor General and Deputy Prime Minister are doing right now is not constitutional. They've unilaterally dissolved a working government and not asked any other elected Members of the House of Commons to form a replacement. Instead, they're trying to govern on their own, in between the law, using the excuse that Defense Command is corrupt. That's their excuse for having troops occupy Capital Island and broadcast centers the world over."

Pausing for a moment, Daragh suddenly looked his age, and a whole lot older.

"This is a lie. You know Defense Command, you see us every day. Some of you probably hate us. You may have gotten speeding tickets from our Constabulary. You may have lost someone to pirates when we weren't there in time to stop them. You may just think we're cocky and arrogant and that we need to be taken down a notch. Or maybe you see us the opposite way. Maybe you see us the way we try to be — the people who do our very best to protect you, and this Empire. But however you see us, good or bad, I hope you know, deep down, that we're not here to try to take government away from you."

He paused again, looking grave.

"I've been in this uniform on and off for forty years. I've lost good people. I gave up the chance to have a life. They made me a Lord, even when I asked them not to. And I have never tried, and I will never try, to subvert this government."

One more pause. "The same cannot be said of my counterparts in the Imperial Army."

At this point, footage from Egesta began to run. And it wasn't vid that was suitable for family viewing. There's no question that, working with Jim and Bunny, Daragh had gone for shock value — for shots from inside the bunkhouse where Angela Kerr had rescued her daughter, and rebarred a blockhead.

"While this war has been going on, soldiers of the Imperial Army have been occupying, and indeed training, on Egesta. Remember Egesta. Remember that place. This is what the Emperor's soldiers were doing there while Defense Command was fighting Martians."

The images just kept coming. Dead people tied to posts, used for bayonet practice. Victims of repeated rape, drugged and tied to beds. The survivors of places like Azure Horizon. If this broadcast had come under any other circumstances, the complaints would have been epic — showing this stuff to a general audience, tuned in because there was nothing else on the air and they knew a civil war might be starting — was seriously inappropriate.

But we had to.

And after about three minutes of footage, we turned to surveillance records from *Wolf*, of General Howard Pedro Azuma.

I was sitting at the other end of the table from him, and he was snarling at me, "They needed to be informed of who was boss here. We had to dominate them. So we made their pretty ones our sport. And hotheads who were causing trouble or resisting became bayonet fodder. After two months, we had complete control of the situation. No one would dare challenge the new government. They're not Imperial citizens. They're scum. They don't deserve any better."

That was all from the soliloquy he delivered to me in the first chapter of *The Egesta Crisis*.

Daragh appeared again, "He says they apparently had control of Egesta after two months. But they didn't stop, the Imperial soldiers. For close to three years. But maybe they wouldn't behave that way here. Because you're all Imperial citizens. Maybe they'd stop after a few months."

It was a low blow, but the Imps had earned it. Earned it by murder and death on Egesta, and treachery and treason on Earth.

"I wouldn't like to give them a chance to gain complete control here. The whole point of our government is to balance elected and appointed… that's the way this Empire was built in the beginning. No one has total control."

Again Daragh paused, and then he sighed, "But that's not how the Emperor sees things. Those were his troops on Egesta. I don't know if he knew what they were doing there, but I do know that he wants to take control of this Empire in a way that is beyond the Articles of Empire. I know it not because I'm a biased Defense Command officer, though I figure I probably am that too. I know it, you see, because of something he said a few years ago, when he was asked if Dave Caldecott might have been working for the Martians."

And then Hayley Briand's disk played. The one she'd made sure John, Daragh, Greg and Mel had copies of. The one with the footage taken by her button camera the day she, John and Greg had stormed the Emperor's mansion back in *The Almost Coup*. Footage everyone had forgotten about.

Luther Gregory had looked directly at her, and because the button was at a certain level on the front of her tunic, he was looking right at it (while he leered at her). Then he said the words that ended his reign: "He said there might be some risks to the Empire, but risks are just risks. And frankly, to get rid of you all, and your idiotic methods, I'd *risk* the Empire. But maybe you're right. Maybe Caldecott was working for the Martians. God knows how that'd be sorted out, but yeah, he knew I hate you showboating idiots… he might well have tried to use that to hurt me."

Daragh flashed back onto the screen, his face tired, his head shaking, "He was worried the Battle Over Earth was going to hurt his position. Not us, mind. Him. Not the Empire, but his throne."

Then footage of Egesta began to play again, and the Emperor flashed up in a small window in the corner (just so we could show that what he said next was a real quote, not an edited-together one): "You better hope the Martians come, John, or you and your Admiral and your pretty little girl here are going to get executed. And hell, you might get executed even if they do. Borrowed time now, John. Borrowed time."

The screen went black then, before fading into Daragh again, "I've never cared for the Emperor. I don't think that's much of a secret. But it's not the job of any one man or woman to decide government. That's why the Lords pick the Emperor, and you elect your governments. It's not my job now to tell you what to do about this man, Luther Gregory. It's not the job of any one of you to decide. We have many hard choices ahead... but for now, there's a simple one. A very simple one. Do we want the Imperial Army to replace Defense Command on the streets of Earth this day?"

He stopped, and remained silent for a full ten seconds, staring at the camera the whole time. Then he answered, "If you want things back the way they were, get in the streets in those cities where there are Imperial soldiers. Rally with Defense Command forces there, and march through the streets. And look up when you do, because the Heavy Squadron of the Home Fleet, and every fighter we have, will cover you. It won't take long."

Last pause, and then the words that I personally think ended Daragh's life, at least as he knew it: "I've believed in this Empire for as long as I've lived. Never has it tried to take away the rights of anyone, never has it given up on the belief that we have the right to be free. That does not stop today. No bastard and his toy soldiers can take it away from us. I'm Second Lord of the Admiralty Daragh Ryan, in orbit aboard DCNS *Wolf*. I'll see you when this is through."

That was the end.

The end of a lot of things.

Chapter Twenty-Five

One Ending

I can't remember what Karen said. There's a recording of it somewhere, but I couldn't really bring myself to watch it... and it really didn't matter. All I know is that she kept to the story that they'd discussed, and that after she and Hodson spoke, footage of the battle between Defense Command and the Imperial Army was rolled live.

Which was great, because when we ended our broadcast, and the Imp feed took over again, all it showed was Special Branchers — drastically outnumbered — firing on tanks... and Starlights swooping in and strafing away.

It probably sounds a lot grander than it looked, because to keep collateral damage low, the fighting was taking place at Defense Command Communications Center — a building right on the coast, with open space around it — and the firing was sparse.

Still, it was enough to show people around the world that we weren't about to let the blockheads have their illegal government... or their way. Take that last word in whatever sense you like.

As the footage came up, Hodson let out a breath, and then a laugh, "At last!"

Again his overdramatic flare from the press conference resurfaced — though at least this time it wasn't on camera. Karen stepped away from him, looking battered as she moved back in our direction. She wouldn't make eye contact with me.

Schwartz remained crouched beside me, and he was managing to keep the quizzical look off his face. We were both wondering, though: had it worked? Forgive me saying, but it fucking better have. Jesus.

As we were wondering, the double doors at the back of the chamber opened in as much of a hurry as their heavy bulk would allow. An officer of the army rushed in, "Sir, why did you broadcast the Second Lord's message?"

Hodson didn't seem to hear the question at first, but as the officer rushed over to the consoles and had one of the soldiers there key up a recording of Daragh's message, the Governor General turned with a frown. Before he could ask what was going on, the vid started rolling.

It was Hodson's turn to wish someone would drop a pin — do anything to break the hold the vid suddenly held on the room.

At one point he cried out over Daragh's voice, "Who saw this? Did everyone see this?"

The officer who had come in nodded vigorously, "Reports from all over the world... we thought the only way anyone could show something that widely was if it originated here..."

I wish I could have seen Hodson's face in that moment, but his back was to me. Instead, I scurried sideways across the floor and grabbed the energy gun that Karen had dropped for me during her tirade, got to my feet, and shot General Lackner in the knee.

Behind me, Karen disarmed one of the guards, then shot the others. I didn't see her do it — didn't have to — but it was cold, fast and efficient. They all lived, which they should feel awfully lucky about.

Then Karen closed the double doors, locked them, and we both turned on the Governor General, the officer who had come in, and the unarmed soldiers who'd been crewing the consoles.

By the time Hodson turned to us he was pale, and his mouth was hanging open.

"I'd kill you where you stand," I said flatly, leveling the pistol at his head. "But no. You're going to order the restoration of the government as it stood yesterday. You're then going to prorogue Parliament. You're going to order all Imperial troops back to their bases, and you're going to lock yourself in here and hope we have the good grace to guard this place against the mob that's going to come to cut off your head."

He looked from me, to Karen, to Schwartz, and then back.

"I…"

"Yes," Karen said. "Yes you did. Give the orders, quickly, because I'm in a very bad state of mind right now."

She started to walk towards him as she spoke, and he backed away quickly, hands up before him as hopeless shields.

"Open communications… planetwide!" he yelled that in a panic, and the blockhead running the appropriate console obliged.

Staggering back to the place on the floor from where just minutes prior he had delivered his supposedly triumphant orders, he spoke like quite a different man, "All Imperial Army units stand down and return to your bases. I have been informed that I have been deceived. The orders of yesterday are countermanded… the government is not dissolved, it is prorogued. I intend to cooperate in the investigation of these heinous crimes. I apologize for the terrible misunderstanding."

Oh, well he apologized for the terrible misunderstanding. The men and women of Defense Command who had been killed or injured in our attack — nine of them, against thirty-three blockhead casualties — would take immense comfort in that.

I considered shooting him. Really did. But he lived.

As the feed cut, he turned to us and started to plead for his life. I can't remember the words, just the disgust as I waved towards him with my energy gun, "I changed my mind, don't stay here or I might cut off your head myself. Go back to base with these blockheads, and we'll come find you later."

I think he said something, or some things, but I didn't care. He hurried for the door, and the Imperial Army soldiers present did the same, taking their wounded with them. They knew they'd been outplayed. They knew that, even if they managed to kill us in this room, they'd never survive if the whole of Defense Command, backed by the people of Earth, came down on them.

They feared for their lives, and rightly so.

The result of this, of course, was that Karen, Schwartz and I were left alone in Hodson's war room. Schwartz was wearing a broad smile of relief, and under just about any other circumstances, he might have taken the chance to highlight some of his acting achievements of the past few minutes… his shocked and confused looks had been splendidly genuine.

But looking at Karen and me, he knew better. Because as he would say later, his performance was mightily bolstered by Karen's in particular, which struck him as more real than imagined.

More real than he could know.

Karen didn't really make eye contact with me. She instead walked to the front of the room — around the raised platform on which Hodson's chair sat, and stood there. Staring at the screens on that side of the room.

I forgot Schwartz even existed and followed her, tucking my energy gun into my belt as I did. Had to keep the thing with me, just in case some bastard came back looking for last blood... but I needed my hands.

Karen put her gun down on the platform and stared at her hands. She then reached up and pulled her ponytail onto her left shoulder, and pulled it hard against the side of her neck. When I got around the platform and closer to her, her eyes were locked on the floor. Her face was gaunt, her posture uncommonly poor.

She looked exhausted, in so many ways.

I reached her without making a sound, and reached up silently and put my right hand on her left cheek, softly feeling the tender flesh where Lackner's fist had connected. She winced at the touch, but her eyes stayed fixed on a point well away from mine.

Then she seemed to remember herself, and her eyes climbed to my shoulder. She craned her neck around and looked at the side of my head, where the butt of her energy gun had made sharp contact. A lump was starting to grow, and it was tender too, so I flinched when her fingers delicately prodded it.

I looked at her as best I could while she checked me — but she didn't look back. She was silent, stony-faced and gaunt. When I reached up and pulled her hand away from my temple, and then looked at her, she looked away... and then she decided there was no point anymore.

So she looked at me, right in the eyes, and a little quake of emotion shook her. She pulled on her ponytail, as though she were trying to stretch it the whole way around her neck. I reached up and slid my hand under hers, then pushed the ponytail away and frowned at her neck.

"There isn't a scar," I reaffirmed, and she looked away.

"There is, and you know it."

Of course I did.

Karen's composure, you know by now, was really quite impenetrable. She could be moved to great anger by injustice, but never to tears. In point of fact, there was only one person who she hated so much that she'd have an emotional reaction when they crossed paths — one person in the whole of creation, and that person had been here today.

If you're wondering, she had no apologies to make, nor did I. We'd known coming into this place that Hodson would be a tough audience, and that we'd have to play a gambit so raw that he couldn't help but believe it. Nothing she'd said had hurt me, and nothing I'd said had hurt her. We spoke so openly and honestly to each other all the time... there was nothing unsaid, no feelings of guilt we hadn't already admitted to each other.

And indeed, the attacks we'd leveled were not ones we'd ever launched on each other, but ones we'd launched against ourselves in each others' presence.

That was the point, I think.

She and I shared one great thing in common: deep down the people we hated the most were ourselves. Or, particularly, the people we'd once been.

Maybe that helps explain why we were so obsessed with self-control, and not swearing, and stopping injustices like Egesta. Maybe all those things reminded us of the sort of people we once thought we'd become.

The nightmares we could have lived, all by ourselves.

Karen had come so close to hers today — had lived it. She'd dragged out a hated irrationality she'd long ago silenced, and put it on display for all to see. The angry, bitter young woman who I'd met one night under the most dubious of circumstances... the person she was most ashamed of, and had vowed never to be again.

The only chance she had of making Hodson believe her was to unleash the raw, wounded rage of that young Karen... to remember what it had been like in a time before she had a partner who challenged her to be what she wanted to be, and asked her to make a similar challenge in return.

Biting her lip, Karen let out a breath, "You took a big chance that night."

After words like that, there was literally no reaction I could have other than putting my arms all the way around her and pulling her very close. I defy you to try to do differently in similar circumstances.

So her face buried into my shoulder, and I pressed my cheek into the side of her head. "So did you."

It was absolutely true.

We stood there, seemingly welded together, breathing in time with each other and completely oblivious to the entire world. Standing at the back of the chamber, Schwartz T. Babcock knew it would be entirely inappropriate for him to say even a single word, so he backed from the room in silence, and closed the door.

Contrary to some rumors, he states categorically that he never witnessed Karen and I share an emotional kiss, as though we were the most intimate of lovers and had been for years. In fact, he states the very opposite — that he only saw us hug... as though we might have been the most intimate of lovers for years.

Believe whatever you like. When the doors closed behind Schwartz, neither of us even noticed.

CHAPTER TWENTY-SIX
BABCOCK ARRIVES

When Schwartz T. Babcock emerged from Hibernia Hall, the scene of panic was pretty interesting. There were hundreds of blockheads still running around, but they were paying him — and everything else — no attention at all. It was like they were clearing out of a house party after the cops had been called... they were running for transports and tanks and then getting the hell away from the place they'd been so staunchly defending moments prior.

One of my editors asked me why that was so 'easy' — why they didn't hang on to try to bargain for terms. It was the shock of the footage, as far as I can tell... not the shock to them (they're from the same military culture that permitted the Egesta crimes in the first place) but the realization that the people in cities and towns around the world had seen it, and probably wouldn't care much for it.

The Imperial Army had 33,000 troops in Terra Nova. There were nearly a million people on Capital Island, and as we saw earlier, most were armed. Throw in orbital strikes from Defense Command (and Starlights picking off tanks — the only real safe haven against mobs of attacking civilians) and you see how bad things could be.

Were mobs in the streets likely? Well, they didn't stick around long enough to find out. I think there would have been. Not to unduly compare the people of Earth to the people of Mars, but recall what happened when Germaine Blovuspaco and his ridiculous fellows led the uprising there... they thought we'd come to rape and pillage, and they weren't going to let it happen.

This time, we had uncompromising visual proof of the danger, and I think the only real difference between the very human reaction of the Martians, and the very human reaction of the citizens of Earth, would have been in effectiveness.

Because our people were armed, not denied the ability to defend themselves by a government that was seeking to oppress them.

I suppose that's a point I never made during *The Mercury Assault* or *The Fleet Clash*: our invasion of Mercury would have gone a hell of a lot worse if the Martians had permitted their civilians to privately own weapons. All those insurgents who had to collect weapons from the dead could have been armed from the start... but weren't allowed to be, because if they had mags (or whatever the Martians call them) there as a chance the Martian oligarchy could be overthrown.

Anyway, that's a tangent I'll leave behind for now: suffice to say that it was you, the people who live in our Empire and raise families and pay taxes, who the blockheads were most afraid of. They could thump their chests and talk all day long about how they were going to crush Defense Command... but in the end, you had them outnumbered millions-to-one.

They ran, which was the smart thing.

I suppose I should also admit that the fact that these folks ran is an indicator that not everyone in the army leadership — and indeed, the Governor General himself — shared Howard Pedro Azuma's complete disregard for humanity as a whole. Unlike him, these people realized that the citizens of Earth might have some objection to the treatment of the people of Egesta… what a shocking notion.

But don't worry, I'm not giving them too much credit. The blockheads knew enough to cut and run, but they'd been stupid enough to start this mess in the first place, so they could go to hell.

Anyway, wandering back to the narrative, Schwartz descended the steps from Hibernia Hall, then crossed the government complex at a jog. Overhead, two Starlights were hovering back and forth, watching the departure of the Imps, and when they saw the suited young Deputy Chief of Staff, they altered their course so they could stay over his head.

He didn't think they could have recognized him from two hundred meters up, but *Wolf's* pilots are the best, and they did.

The visual was thus pretty startling when, from Center Block, people started to emerge from the offices where they'd been confined. A huge crowd was forming on the steps outside the building — steps that the day before had been the site of the press conference.

Some were MPs, others were Senators, and the entire Parliamentary press corps was with them too — released from the conference room where they'd spent the night under guard, and filming fast while they interviewed politicians to get reactions on everything that had happened.

They'd all seen Daragh's broadcast, by the way — the blockheads had piped the attack feed everywhere, particularly to the reporters, because they were a key audience.

When Schwartz tried to get past this huge crowd, he didn't have much success, not least because of the two planes that seemed to be following him like bodyguards.

"Schwartz! Schwartz can I have a comment?"

"Mister Babcock, does this mean that Bennington is still in her position as Deputy Prime Minister?"

"Were you involved in the broadcasting of that feed from the Second Lord?"

The scrum started to form around the young Deputy Chief of Staff in a hurry, but he held up his hands and then managed to make himself heard over all of the people surrounding him, "A statement will be issued shortly. For the moment I have to check on my staff, to make sure the Imperial troops did no harm."

With that, he rather brusquely forced his way out of the scrum, and continued his jog, flanked by Starlights. Special Branch officers arrived on the Center Block steps as he departed, checking to make sure everyone was healthy after their confinement.

It didn't take too long for Schwartz to get to the Prime Minister's Office. He found the guard posts that had been set up there by Lackner's troops were as abandoned as the positions everywhere else around the government buildings, so he entered unchallenged. Hurrying up the stairs, he went into the lobby and found no guards present, then hopped over one of the security barriers to get past the scanners.

He took the back stairs two at a time, then finally reached the floor that held the

Prime Minister's personal office, and the offices of all the senior staff. Going door-to-door, he found each one empty. Every vacant office made him hurry a little faster — it wouldn't have made any sense for the bastards to do anything to the Prime Minister's staff at the end... but what if they'd been quietly liquidated right after capture?

Schwartz thought of his people and didn't like that prospect at all, so he kept moving and looking until he confirmed that the entire floor was abandoned. Hurrying back down the stairs, he started to check the lower-level offices until he decided that the blockheads must have — *had to have* — grouped everyone together under guard. The cafeteria was probably the likeliest place...

Hurrying to that door, Schwartz burst through in dramatic style, and staggered to a stop before a crowd of his colleagues. They all remained seated as they saw him come in, and he stopped in surprise at the sight.

"What are you all..."

Donna got to her feet and came over to him, "We'd hoped you'd gotten away."

Schwartz blinked, then looked around the room. There was no screen.

"Didn't you hear the blockheads leaving?" Schwartz asked, directing the question both to Donna and the room. "They're pulling out, we've won."

People looked up at the Deputy Chief of Staff with some frowns and a bit of disbelief, and then Chief of Staff Murt Sergeant got to his feet, "You think you're funny, fucktard?"

Schwartz turned to the old bastard, then approached him with a smile. The Prime Minister's Chief of Staff was looking bitter as ever, and though he wasn't by nature a physically violent person, the political wonderkid felt a strong urge to grab a lunch tray off one of the nearby tables, and hit him across the face with it.

Instead, Schwartz stopped right in front of his boss, tilted his head, and stabbed him with words: "Murt, I'm pretty sure you know this, but I don't respect you. I did once. I used to think you were good at your job, and that excused a lot. But you're not good at your job. You should have been the one working with Ken Barron and Karen McMaster to play the Governor General. You should have been the one working with Lord Ryan to get off the planet in the first place. Instead, you were talking about fornicating with a seventeen-year-old girl. If you ever work in government again after this, I'll be very surprised. If your four wives stay with you when you're a bitter commentator on political affairs for some third-rate local news channel, I'll be even more surprised. And if you call me an obnoxious fucktard again, I can promise you misery for the rest of your days."

Sergeant stared at Schwartz, and as he did the pieces of information that the Deputy Chief of Staff had carefully seeded in his declaration — the mention of me, Karen, and Daragh — started to help people really realize that there had been a change outside.

The old Chief of Staff didn't quite know what to say — not that he was at a loss for words in the classic sense, but he was trying to figure out if there was a chance that Schwartz wasn't lying. Because if the wonderkid now had friends in Defense Command's Fiora Ring... and had worked with them to stop a coup... it would be very, very necessary to stay on his good side.

Silence was the best solution to Sergeant's problem, so he said nothing, and Schwartz took that as victory enough. Turning back to Donna, he nodded towards the door, "We can get back to our offices. The press is out there looking for a statement, so Tony, T.J.,

Cam, we need to get into a room, I need to tell you what happened, and we need to figure out our messaging. We've got half an hour or less."

That was it; back to work at the Prime Minister's Office. All these people had slept in a cafeteria, had eaten nothing but junk from vending machines (the cook hadn't been taken prisoner with everyone else), and hadn't changed clothes... but that didn't matter. When you're on the top rung of staff for the elected leader of the Empire, you end up living a life that doesn't include the sorts of comforts that normal people enjoy.

Not a life for everyone, but young Schwartz T. Babcock figured he had a future in it.

Haha, that irony thing again.

CHAPTER TWENTY-SEVEN
LORD RYAN RETURNS

Shuttles were landing outside Admiralty House with some regularity by the time one of *Wolf's* made its way down to the building. Kris had sent back all the people she'd evacuated from the command center of the Navy, so people like Betty and Gerald were back at their reception desk, and Ronald Davis was back down in C&C, uncrossing some of the wires Kate Levec had been forced to cross to get the plan to work.

Rufus Chang was on the lawn with his team and Kate when that *Wolf* shuttle arrived — they were planning to hitch a ride back to Keith's store, to pick up their own shuttle and then head back to the ship.

When the feet of the craft touched down, and the ramp dropped, the first one off was none other than the Second Lord, and as his feet reached ground again, the nearby officers and spacers who were getting back to their posts let out a cheer.

Rufus and Kate and our folks didn't cheer, though that's not because they didn't like Daragh... just didn't seem like it'd be the right reaction.

As the Second Lord stopped at the bottom of the ramp, he waved a bit uneasily to those people, then spotted *Wolf's* Special Branch Major and approached him. He took a second to shake Kate's hand and congratulate her on a job well done, nodded to each of Rufus' team, then finally directed his attention to our Chinese Brancher.

Now, I think I mentioned this before, but after Rufus had been singled out for punishment back in the Dave Caldecott days — for reasons he's never actually shared with me, but which you know must be related to him being too competent for Caldecott's liking — Daragh had taken notice of the Major. Any man who the squeaky old Second Lord thought deserved exile to Luna was someone Daragh was going to pay attention to, so while they didn't really know each other, there was some connection between the two.

"Fine work, Major. How much of a mess in there?"

Rufus shrugged, "They never attacked, so I didn't get to blow anything up."

That brought a smile to Daragh's face, and he shook his head, "What fucking sort of coup doesn't let you blow up at least one thing?"

Rufus didn't smile, though he answered in kind: "Are you volunteering your office, sir?"

The Second Lord laughed, "Be my guest, I hate the fucking place."

With that, he patted Rufus on the shoulder and stepped past him, heading for the front door.

The last of the people who'd come down from *Wolf* — mainly Admiralty House staffers who hadn't fit on Kris' first shuttles — disembarked, then Rufus waved his team up into the craft and they headed for Keith's store.

Keith wasn't there.

+++

Daragh was in some ways disappointed to discover that Admiralty House really hadn't been damaged in any way. That probably sounds odd... it was just that, after such a dramatic set of events, it felt like he should be coming back to an office that showed some signs of distress. There were none.

Not even muddy boot prints on the carpet, or files strewn around as if the blockheads had been searching for something. As people started filtering back into their offices and logged back into their computers, they found things pretty much as they'd been when the power went out. It was a letdown.

As he paced through the halls, though, Daragh realized with some trepidation that his shotgun was not with him — and he couldn't remember when he'd last had it. Maybe aboard *Lion*? It was a great prop, but as much as he worked to make people think he depended on the thing, it really wasn't vital. He hadn't even thought of it while he was dealing with the fate of the Empire.

Probably a good thing.

It was interesting for the Irish Lord, though — he'd spent the war mostly watching from the back benches, making sure that everything we needed for the fight was ready in a timely fashion. Now he'd just had a brush with the front lines again, and it reminded him of the exhilaration of the old days at the Forge, when that base really had been in the thick of it.

I don't know if you've read much about Daragh's early days, or seen the few good movies about them, but suffice to say he really had paved the way for people like Greg, Marlene, Karen and me to do our jobs the way we wanted to. It had been his madness that had put the fear of God into the solar pirates, and had established the tradition that results mattered most. If you wanted to be insane or cavalier or anything else within the strictures of decency, it didn't matter as long as the results were delivered.

I suppose this crisis was a little like that — peace for Earth, the Pax Terra, through whatever unorthodox means got the job done. There were numerous complications to sort through... figuring out the actual state of the government now would be a task that brought no shortage of headaches, and after that, the Emperor himself would have to come back from Mars to face the music... but the job was done.

Shotgun or no, that thought satisfied Daragh as he finally reached his office and stepped inside. As he rounded his desk and lowered himself into his chair, he took a breath and prepared to start working... then he stopped.

Leaning against the wall in the corner, arms folded as he looked out the window, was Keith.

Daragh managed to stop himself jumping out of his chair in surprise, and then he frowned at the man, "An axe? And ponytail?"

Keith looked from the window to the Second Lord with a shrug, "I like it."

"You would," the Irishman said. "What the hell are you doing here? I thought you retired to Venus."

Shaking his head, Keith turned slightly against the wall, so he was more properly facing Daragh's desk, "Not at all, I had a long and productive career with the Ministry of Agriculture, then opened up a store of my own. Happened that Schwartz T. Babcock knew me, and knew I was familiar with this town, so he brought Barron and McMaster down to my store for a quiet insertion."

Daragh blinked, "Well I'll be damned. Here all this time and you never even popped round to say hello."

Keith shrugged, "Figured you were busy. Second Lord now and everything."

"Bah," the Irishman shook his head. "I was enjoying my retirement. I'll be enjoying it again soon."

Tilting his head, Keith considered the Second Lord, "You really think so?"

"Well unless you're here to kill me for my bad jokes and my cursing, I think so," he shrugged.

Chuckling, Keith shook his head, "Who have you ever met from the Ministry of Agriculture who'd ever kill anyone?"

"Did you really work over there?" Daragh shot back, and Keith nodded.

"I certainly did. Spent a few years on a number of valuable projects. Made a difference and enjoyed it. Different pace of life."

"I'll bet," the Second Lord said. "So now you're going back to the store, you said? Missing the excitement at all?"

"Of the Ministry?" Keith smiled.

"Sure, that."

Keith paused for a moment, then looked out the window at the various Defense Command personnel coming and going. The scene would have been in many ways reminiscent of the Forge, had the Renaissance man ever been there during Daragh's time.

"It was interesting seeing the new generation at work. Read a lot about them... researched them. It's different now than it used to be, but not in any of the ways that really matter. They're young, though..."

"Some of them are bloody older than you," Daragh shot back.

Keith shrugged yet again, "True."

"As I recall, when they put me out to pasture, you weren't all that much older than Schwartz T. Babcock," Daragh added.

Keith smiled, "You know how it is over at the Ministry of Agriculture. They start you young, and they retire you a little less young."

It was true, and Daragh nodded, but said nothing. For a moment both men were silent, and then Keith sighed and stepped away from the wall, "You realize what they're going to do to you yet?"

Frowning, Daragh leaned forward in his chair and planted his elbows on his desk, "Who?"

Keith studied the Irishman for a moment, seeming the slightest bit somber, "You'll see soon enough. When it happens... if you need a hand... call me."

Stepping forward, Keith dropped his *Wired and Woven* business card on the Second Lord's desk.

"I'm going to go see my wife," the axe-carrying man said, and Daragh looked up.

"Well done. I'm sure if I have any questions about raising crops on my pony farm, I'll call you."

Keith was already at the door when those words reached him, but he stopped, looked back, and nodded, "Something like that."

Then he left, and if you check the feeds from the cameras covering Admiralty House's corridors, none of them seem able to see him when he leaves. Those crazy Ministry of Agriculture types...

Sitting back in his chair, Daragh Ryan folded his arms and frowned thoughtfully. He had no idea what Keith was thinking, but he'd know soon enough. Because while the Second Lord of the Admiralty thought his troubles were at an end, he'd learn his fate before the end of this year. And it would not be a good one.

CHAPTER TWENTY-EIGHT

THE GREAT REVEAL

By the time *Nova Scotia* arrived over Mars, a whole lot had happened. To begin with, the peace treaty was ready for signing, and that was a very big deal — the war would officially, well and truly, totally and completely, be over. Peace in our solar system. The Emperor's Pax Terra.

But there was more — much more.

I don't think the timing could honestly have worked out much better. Wes Pellew was on his bridge as *Nova Scotia* reached realtime range with *Bonaventure*, and when he signaled to the flagship, Captain Lennox Williams answered immediately.

"Commodore Pellew, good to see you back with the fleet."

Wes was not, I must say, in a particularly positive mood for this trip. Recall that his departure from Egesta had followed a rather nasty spat with Andrea Kiley, and there'd been little do other than stew about that as he came back to Mars.

Nevertheless, he wouldn't turn down a polite greeting, "Len, how have the talks been?"

Bonnie's Trinidadian Captain shrugged and smiled, "They are almost over, if that is answer enough for you. And when they end, a lot will be ending at the same time. I presume you have not heard anything from Earth lately?"

Wes shook his head, "I haven't, though I know what Ken was bringing there. I've got more of the same to share, in case it's needed."

"In time, more will absolutely be needed," Williams said. "For now, what Admiral Barron showed up with was more than enough. Stopped the coup just in time."

That was good news, though a little bit of a letdown — Wes had, I think quite understandably, been hoping to be the bearer of the Empire-changing news.

"But here's the best part," Williams continued. "They're getting ready to sign the treaty, so *Ark Royal* has been isolated from all but priority communications traffic. Mik shut down the whole receiver array."

Wes blinked, "Does he know?"

"He most certainly knows. But no one else on his ship does, except for the First Lord, the PM and Foreign Minister. They were afraid the Emperor would demand terms on threat of tearing up the treaty, so we're waiting until it's signed."

That was, well, awesome.

"When do we do the reveal?" Wes' mood began to shift, and Lennox Williams looked away from the viewfinder momentarily, checking the clock. "In about two hours."

Like I said, the timing couldn't have worked out any better.

John Fiora had learned more about diplomacy than he ever wanted to know. To be fair, he'd be the first to tell you that the lessons learned aboard *Ark Royal* over Mars were of a certain kind of diplomacy — a 'we're the winners and your demands can burn in hell' kind — but it was diplomacy nevertheless.

And it was slow.

Douglas Pope and Craig B. Macdonald had done everything possible to expedite matters during the negotiations, but both the Martians and the Emperor seemed determined to take their time... the latter bastard was undoubtedly trying to drag things out so his coup could work back on Earth.

But now it was time to sign, so John sat on one side of the long table in *Ark Royal's* Emperor's quarters — a massive hall that was completely impractical aboard a Naval ship, but which had served as the central hub for many of the negotiations that had taken place.

John kept thinking how great a cargo bay it'd make...

"We are, now at last, ready to sign the peaceful agreement to end this most unfortunate conflict that has so harmed the familial relations between our two great states."

That was Heinrich Dewar, the man who (you might recall from *The Mars Convention*) believed himself to be the job that he was. That man was sitting at the right hand of President-for-Life Godwin, the 'true ruler' of Mars, who seemed unremarkable to John — a large, pale-faced man who spoke little, and sniffed disdainfully just about any time an Imperial representative talked.

I have no respect for the man, nor any interest in trying to find out if he really was a living stereotype, or if there was more nuance behind his attitude. Maybe he really was a nice guy, but I don't care in the slightest. He deserved to be dead, probably, and I'm sure as hell not going to spill ink trying to make you realize that, if it was even the case.

"We look forward to this momentous occasion," our dear Emperor, soon to be out on his ass, replied with equal pomp.

Pope and Macdonald were sitting on the left hand of the Emperor, and they both nodded — neither indulged in the bullshit ceremonies that had been part of the convention, and John was of a similar mindset.

They all prepared to sign the document to make peace official, then the Martians would be sent off *Ark Royal* and the real fun would begin.

Christian 'Mik' Mikaelsen was waiting in the arrivals lounge while Wes' shuttle landed. Looking through the glass out to the repressurizing landing deck, *Ark Royal's* Commodore could just manage to pick out *Nova Scotia's* shuttle around the veritable horde of small craft that now resided there. Plenty of guests were aboard the carrier today, and while it had been explained to the Emperor's people as additional security for the signing ceremony, the fact was that every ship in the squadron had sent over Special Branchers and SF to help monitor 'the great reveal'.

Remember, the Emperor had 1,000 blockheads with him as his personal escort aboard the carrier, and though Mik did have plans in place to isolate many hundreds of them, and blast them into the void if necessary, he rather hoped it wouldn't come to that. Between Branchers and SF and volunteers, he had more than 1,000 shooters ready to contain and disarm the Imperial troops. He was hoping no shots would be fired in the process.

Once the bay beyond the glass repressurized, the hatch on Wes' shuttle opened, the ramp dropped, and the Independent Squadron's Commodore descended, followed by shooters of his own — *Nova Scotia's* veterans from Egesta. They crossed the bay and entered the lounge, and as Wes led them through, he spotted Mik and extended his hand.

"Glad we made it in time."

Nodding, Mik looked at the shooters from *Nova Scotia*, each of them armed and all of them looking a bit... humorless, "I hear things were as bad on Egesta as we feared."

"Worse," Wes didn't mind saying so, and his word was corroborated by the grim expressions of his detail. "So, talk to me about the plan. I presume we don't get to shoot the bastard?"

"The Emperor?" Mik frowned, and Wes nodded.

I don't think either of these two gentlemen will mind me pointing out that they were coming to this particular moment from different trajectories. Mik's frustrations had been great — between Luther Gregory's ham-handed attempts to charm him and the general complications of trying to run a ship with so many blockheads in its belly — but he hadn't been to Egesta, and he didn't have the sort of profound anger that was fueling Wes.

Because... well you probably read *The Egesta Crisis*. Wes was not in a good way after leaving that place, and in the end, the troops who had committed the crimes there belonged to Luther Gregory. Add to that the fact that this bastard was trying to take over the Empire for himself... well.

Wes was more ready to shoot the man than Mik was.

"We're going to have to wait until the Martian delegation gets off the ship, and then we're going to turn and burn for Earth immediately. We don't want to give him the chance to do something to sabotage the peace," Mik explained.

Nodding, Wes looked back to his people, "We'll sit tight."

"Once things get started, remember that there are 1,000 Imperial soldiers aboard this ship. I do *not* want corridor fighting as they try to save their Emperor and take over. If it comes to that, we'll abandon ship, disable from *Bonaventure*, and tow the whole lot of them home."

Mik sounded decidedly unimpressed by that option, and I don't think anyone could really blame him. Carrier or not, stuffed with blockheads or not, *Ark Royal* was his ship, and he wasn't inclined to give it over to the Imperial Army.

Wes nodded in understanding of that point, and then took a breath, "Okay, where do we wait?"

"Follow me," Mik turned towards the hatch, and the *Nova Scotia* crew followed as he led them deeper into the ship.

The Martian shuttle departed from the Emperor's main flightbay — one that had been decorated in a fashion sufficiently ornate to meet the discerning standards of the man who wanted to reign supreme. Watching it go from the similarly-ornate departure lounge, the Emperor, John, Pope and Craig B. Macdonald all remained silent. Obviously this was a grand occasion for the Empire, but none of them were thinking in quite those terms.

Quite a shame that the official end of the Martian War had to be so clouded in backstabbing politics... but such is the nature of the political beast, I suppose.

"Gentlemen, your service to the Empire has done credit to you," Luther Gregory declared after the space doors closed behind the Martian ship.

John just shut his mouth; he knew it would be better to let Pope and Macdonald do the talking, at least for now. Keeping such a massive secret — that the Emperor's plot had been tried and had failed — was not something our First Lord specialized in. I guess it's a good thing he never lied in an attempt to corrupt the government, it wouldn't have gone well.

"We should conference about the way to present the news to the people of the Empire," Douglas Pope was a good man, and a great Prime Minister, but he was also very talented at keeping the truth off his face when he needed to.

"Right now?" Craig B. Macdonald put in, playing the part of the tired and reluctant chorus. Didn't want to make the Emperor think there was a surprise in store for him, after all.

"The message to our citizens must be clear and coherent," the Emperor directed that lofty point to Macdonald, and the Foreign Minister rolled his eyes without any care for Luther Gregory's station.

"Oh well then, let's go fucking do it," the Scotsman turned for the door, and John fell in behind.

Luther Gregory didn't like the Foreign Minister... well, that's a statement of the obvious. But suffice to say that Macdonald knew exactly the sorts of things to do to push the Emperor's buttons, and this was one of them. Patent disrespect wasn't appreciated... ironic, since patent disrespect is exactly what Luther Gregory III showed to all of the institutions of government in the Empire.

Aha, you see what I did there. Yeah. Take that Emperor.

But my future published jabs weren't the ones that were going to get the bastard on this day. As Craig Macdonald led the powerful party of leaders back through *Ark Royal*, towards the meeting rooms where they'd spent so many weeks, the Emperor didn't seem to particularly notice the lack of Imperial troops lining the corridor along the route.

That was good. Special Branchers had done their bit in making the guards who stood post (needlessly, aboard a Defense Command ship) disappear in a silent fashion. None were harmed, of course, but they all ended up unconscious in the brig, without alerting their peers in the barracks that there was anything wrong.

By the time they reached the Emperor's personal section of the ship, there were a few guards, but as the group made its way past, those guards were quickly removed in a similar fashion. It would have been too conspicuous for them to be gone in advance of Luther Gregory's arrival, you see.

"I think the most important thing for the people to understand is that this was an effort of their whole government," the Emperor was saying as they passed through the outer chamber of his quarters, then the inner chamber.

Pope looked sideways at the Emperor after those words, "Whole government, as well as its Emperor?"

"I am the government as well, Prime Minister. You know that, you should abide by it."

The two black men were taking thinly-veiled shots at each other as they finally made their way through the last door into the Emperor's throne room.

"You might want to reconsider your position on that, sir. Because you're not going to *be* the government for much longer, even if you are now."

Wes Pellew was sitting on the throne, legs crossed in such a fashion so that his left ankle was sitting on his right knee, allowing him to pick at the sole of his boot. He didn't even look at the Emperor as he spoke, so he didn't get to see the reaction — which he regrets.

"What... how dare... you!"

It was funny to John, because the Emperor was as bewildered in this moment as he had been when, years prior, a certain party of Admirals, backed by a spy, had burst into his bathroom while he was shaving.

"I still don't think you should be sitting in his chair," Mik was leaning against the wall to the left of the throne, and stretching the drapery that hung over the metal bulkhead pretty badly — so badly that the pathetic material even started to tear.

Hearing the ripping sound, Mik looked up at the rods from which the fine woven fabric was suspended, "Whoops. Sorry, wouldn't want to rip your textiles and turn this space back into a usable compartment or anything."

Luther Gregory started to puff up — he was in his full Emperor's finery, in his own throne room, and he wouldn't tolerate this sort of behavior. Already he was suspecting some sort of subterfuge, but he knew that these fools would only play into his hands if they tried to take him into custody without cause. The Governor General would have a perfect excuse to overturn the government...

Still, he wasn't going to be captured without a fight: "Guards!"

Doors on either side of the throne room immediately flew open... and fully-kitted Special Branchers strode in.

"You traitors have silenced my guards. So be it," Luther Gregory snarled, folding his arms and literally turning up his nose.

"We've done a little bit more than that," Craig B. Macdonald said, approaching the throne and frowning at Wes. "Can I try the chair? Always been curious."

"Sure," the Independent Squadron's Commodore nodded, putting both boots back on the deck and getting up. Craig then settled into the throne and rocked it back slightly.

"I can see why he likes this chair," the Foreign Minister directed that comment at Pope, who ignored it as he moved to the Emperor's side.

"Your coup didn't work. They got control of Capital Island and the whole communications network, but you're not so bright as you think, Luther. We knew for weeks you were playing at something, and that you had compromised our communications."

The great baritone that helped Douglas Pope deliver such powerful speeches was reduced to a menacing growl now, and the Emperor turned on the Prime Minister as he heard the words, "Claim what you like. Nothing you could have done would stop what comes. Don't you understand, our very case is that you and Defense Command are co-conspirators. Any action you take against the throne, against *me*, is proof of your illegal aims."

He sounded awfully pleased with himself, and as he spoke, Wes and Mik exchanged glances. The man really believed what he was saying.

"I seem to recall you hating us for a different reason," John Fiora stepped forward for the first time. "I seem to remember you calling us 'showboating idiots', and disagreeing with our methods. That's fair enough. But you don't get to change our methods by unilaterally taking control of the government. That's a coup, Emperor. That's what you do when you can't win an election."

"Or what you do when you think you're more important than the real people who live and work in this solar system," Wes' words were sharp, and he came up behind the Emperor. Mik had to take a second look at the Commodore's hands to make sure he wasn't carrying a wrench — destroying Luther Gregory's face might have felt great, but it would have been tough to explain when they got back to Earth.

"The other thing you didn't count on was that we went to Egesta," a certain righteous menace filled Wes' voice, and the Emperor turned to face the Commodore.

"Egesta? Why should I care about some rock cursed to be outside the domain of our Empire?"

Wes tilted his head and wished for a wrench, "Because when your army commits heinous war crimes... rapes and murders thousands... and we get it on tape... it makes the people of the Empire awfully reluctant to let you and your troops replace us."

Luther Gregory's reaction was over-animated — his face twisted in surprise, and his jaw dropped as he gasped, "What do you mean, war crimes?"

"I don't think there's much point putting on a show," Pope cut in. "Whether you knew or you didn't know, those troops are yours. Defense Command belongs to the government — the elected government. Our team just won a war. Your team chained young boys and girls to beds and drugged them up to be raped for weeks before they were killed."

"You think your guys are going to win any public relations wars with their trousers around their ankles?" Macdonald added from the throne, and his tone was acid.

The words struck like a bolt of lightning, and a wide-eyed Luther Gregory actually stepped back, away from Wes. Maybe he hadn't known — there's never been any conclusive proof one way or another — but whether he did or didn't, the revelation was still a startling one for the big silk stocking full of shit.

That's right, I broke out the Talleyrand reference for this bastard.

"You're going to come back with us, and we're going to put you on some sort of trial in front of the whole Empire. Your army is going to be reduced to a bunch of sentries and boyscouts, God only knows what's going to happen to your throne..." Macdonald continued from the chair. "Everything you've ever stood for, worked for... it's all going to go away in a flash. And if you're lucky, you'll die at the end of it."

"But you probably won't be lucky," John came around Luther Gregory. "Borrowed time, you said to me once. Well I'm going to lend you all the time you need." Our First Lord got right in Luther Gregory's face, "You'll be exiled, like Napoleon, so that the memories of how great you once thought you were can tear away at you, for many years to come."

Staring at the First Lord's angry eyes, the Emperor for the first time seemed to realize that he'd lost. He grasped for hope, I'm sure — hoped that this was all a bluff, that the coup could still go ahead and pull him out of this mess...

But I think he knew. It wasn't the worst moment of his life — that came later — but it was really the beginning of the end. And in many ways, it's the beginnings of ends that are the hardest. They're moments where all the good feelings, all the hope, fall away.

Nothing about the road ahead was going to be good for the Emperor, and he knew it.

Silently, he staggered away from John, and everyone in the room watched as he moved towards the wall. His head hung as he went. When he came to the drapery that concealed the bulkhead he reached out, pushed it aside, and braced himself on the cold metal with one hand.

"You don't see it, do you? Don't realize what you're all doing? Defense Command, the civilian government… this Empire is too large to be ruled by many voices. Like Rome before, we must unite now, before the colonies start to wonder if they can take their leave of us. Before we face the possibility of dividing what is great, into many parts that are small."

Shaking his head, he paused, then spoke again to the wall, "Thousands of voices, too many ideas, all of them treated as equals because of the Articles of Empire. The rule of the mob, don't you see? Nothing will get done. There will be no vision, only the appetites of those with no understanding of how to rule. They watch the trash on the vids. They laud you fools for acting like apes in their defense. They love the spectacle, not the real decisions upon which their fates truly live or die. It is to these people you are turning over authority. It is upon their wisdom that you are basing the future of our Empire. And you will see us destroyed."

Can't get much more explicit than that. Everyone simply watched the Emperor's back as he swayed against the wall, his words growing more and more desperate. He truly believed that there was danger… that the Empire, the greatest expression of human civilization in the history of our species, was nearing its decline.

It was a different way he saw the world — a different understanding he had of what was valuable. Because in the end, what his point boiled down to was simple: his vision of what the Empire should be was more important than yours.

I want the Empire to be great. I think it can be a force for good. But the only reason it has that power is because I'm not the only one who believes as much. You have to believe it too… billions of you must. Only the shared belief, the shared work we all put in can make the Empire function as a great entity.

If some of you don't want to be in the Empire any more, forcing you to stay with the rest of us isn't going to make the whole any stronger. It's just going to weaken us from within. So I'll never tell someone they don't have the right to leave — voting with your feet is a time-honored tradition.

All I will tell you is to choose carefully, because while leaving and running out on your own might seem appealing, if you're only doing it to avoid the hard work of helping us build something great, then you'll probably find yourself cold and alone on the day when you need us most.

It's your choice, though. That's what I believe. The Emperor disagreed; you had no choice but to belong. That, to me, was wrong.

Mik Mikaelsen believed it was wrong too. For the first time, the Commodore who had taken the Emperor to Mars approached the man, and spoke to him softly, "You think we don't know that the road ahead is difficult?"

Luther Gregory's head lifted and he looked at Mik.

"We know. We know that every day, and every vote, is a danger. But to me, to many of us, what defines the quality of the place we live is not how easy it is… it's how well it serves its people. How well it harnesses their collective will to do great things. We'll take the risks, and we'll fight the battles. We will all have a say, and I think together, we'll prevent the disaster you foresee."

I think you might be getting a preview there of Christian Mikaelsen's future career. He was brilliant as a Naval officer, but he wasn't destined to stay long with the fleet…

For now, he was still with Defense Command, and as the commanding officer of the ship in which they all stood, it was his honor to put an end to this, after so many years.

"Lord Luther Gregory III, Emperor of the Black Sun, I arrest you on suspicion of treason. You have the right to remain silent. Anything you say may be used against you during your trial. Any information you do not volunteer now may be questioned if you later use it as part of your defense."

As Mik delivered the familiar words, one of the Special Branch officers who had come into the room stepped over to move the Emperor, but Mik stopped him with a hand, "We've done enough. Luther, you will be confined to these quarters. If you attempt to order any sort of attack on my crew, your soldiers will be neutralized by whatever means are necessary. You will be returned to Earth."

The Emperor — still officially the Emperor, I suppose — nodded slowly, and that was really the end of it.

The Defense Command personnel and the politicos left Luther Gregory trapped in his chambers, to be haunted by thoughts of what had been, what might have been, and what would never be. It took a few hours to secure the blockheads, but in the absence of any orders to resist from their Emperor, the troops did what was sensible: they surrendered their weapons and confined themselves to their quarters in the ship.

They were actually sealed in there, too… if they had tried anything, there would have been a single button to push, and then they'd all be committed to space. Ruthless maybe, but when that many troops were in the belly of your ship, ruthlessness had its place.

That's how it all finished — quietly, after so much drama, so much buildup. I'm sure something more explosive would be more fitting for the movies, but this was better by every other measure.

Once it was done, Pope, Macdonald, Wes and John went for some celebratory libations (coffee for Wes). Mik Mikaelsen returned to his bridge, reflecting quietly on what he'd heard, what he'd said, and what he imagined his future might be.

Ark Royal, led by *Bonaventure* and followed by the rest of the diplomatic mission, boosted for home.

The war was over. And so was the intrigue.

Peace at last.

CHAPTER TWENTY-NINE

REWARDS

The dust settled around Capital Island, and Earth, with surprising ease. Though the attempted coup had been a massive event in the history of our planet and Empire, it had gone unnoticed by many. It might surprise you to know that some forty-three percent of people polled after the event didn't have any details about what had taken place.

Twenty-one percent of those people thought the Governor General had succeeded in creating a new government.

How could people have missed it? The same way they miss everything in politics, because of apathy. Maybe that's one of the things Luther Gregory was fearful of — that people who don't study politics all the time don't know how to make an Empire great.

Maybe they don't, but here's the tough pill to swallow: the job of a government, of Defense Command, of anyone in power, is not to force a place to be great. It's to serve the people. If the people want the place to be great, then yes, it's the job of the elected and appointed leaders to satisfy that want.

If they want the place to simply keep things running while they engage in debauchery, then it's the responsibility of the government to follow those marching orders.

I think the key to keeping our Empire strong is pretty simple: we need to educate our people, young and old, on why 'greatness' (however you choose to define it) is vital — why this great experiment of civilization we've embarked upon deserves to continue. Call me an idealist, but I have faith that folks will continue to want greatness for the Black Sun.

And that's enough time on the soapbox for me.

Kris was nowhere close to a soapbox. She, instead, was in her day cabin aboard *Lion*, with piles and piles of personnel pads stacked up around her. Now that the crisis had passed she was back down to a skeleton crew of Belt Squadron veterans, and she had to do a lot of recruiting and reorganizing to make everything work.

She was determined to have *Lion* in decent fighting trim before the Emperor's convoy got home, not because she anticipated any trouble, but because she wanted to be ready for whatever came next. No Captain wants his or her ship to be only partially capable... a Belt Squadron Captain least of all.

Of course, the holes that needed filling were many, and as the door chime sounded, Kris knew the challenge would soon be even greater.

Looking up from the pad she was reading, Kris called out, "Come in."

Kate Levec opened the door, then closed it behind her as she approached the desk, "Holy pads."

Kris looked up, "I know, right?"

"Yeah," Kate sat down across the desk from her skipper, then let out a sigh. "So, where do we start? We need a Sensors and Communications Officer... I'm guessing you don't want Allison Ting to stay on for Security..."

Kris shook her head, "We need to start at the top and work our way down, I think. It's going to be hardest to find an XO."

Kate began nodding, but then looked up with the sort of frown you'd expect. Before she could ask any questions, Kris threw a folder at her. The startled Commander managed to catch it before it splayed open and vomited its printed contents over the floor... then she started to realize the implications.

"Go on then," Kris muttered, returning her gaze to her pads, and containing a smile.

Kate flipped open the folder and found the name 'Lady Grace' at the top of the page. If you'll recall, Karen's old corvette had been damaged during the Fleet Clash (I lost my head slightly when it happened), and Elise De Winter had died in the fight. Much of the crew was still with the ship as it was put back to rights over the first part of the year, but no new commanding officer had been appointed.

Until now.

Because, and I have to say this, Kate had been lucky. She'd never served any space duty as a Commander and Executive Officer, so posting her to command a ship — particularly one with the history of Lady Grace — was a bold move. But the officer who had been responsible for allowing our message to broadcast out instead of Hodson's was inevitably going to be rewarded, and though she'd have a lot of on-the-job learning to do, she'd have a solid crew backing her up.

So that was it, Kate Levec was going to Lady Grace, which was soon leaving Luna to join Wolf and Lion. Kris would remain in command aboard her old frigate, and she'd need a new XO. Finding one would be interesting indeed.

"Know anybody who I could steal?" Kris asked after Kate had processed the news sufficiently to look up again.

Shaking her head, Lady Grace's new skipper answered honestly, "I hadn't thought much about it."

She certainly hadn't, but that was fine. They had time — the war was over.

The thanks for Rufus was to be a promotion, but even after the coup's defeat, we couldn't get any promotions through the damned bureau of personnel. Instead, he got a letter from Daragh Ryan offering him any post in the Empire.

Reading that message, which was printed on paper and sent up to Wolf on a courier shuttle, the Chinese Major stopped for a moment to consider what posting he most desired. Then he turned to the screen in his cabin — where he was, sorry for not setting that up properly — and dialed Admiralty House.

He was one of the few people who could get a message straight through to Daragh, so after a few moments of waiting, the Irish Second Lord appeared, "Ah, Rufus, got my letter?"

"Yes sir," the Major with mismatched eyes replied.

"Excellent. What post should I put you down for?"

"For the moment, I don't see the point of moving anywhere. Can I use this later, when the time is right to move on from Wolf?"

Typically these sorts of post-crisis promotions come with 'limited time offer' written in fine print on them somewhere — so the natural answer for Daragh would be to say no.

But Rufus isn't the sort of guy who you say 'no' to under circumstances like these, so the Irishman smiled.

"I think I can remember to tell whoever ends up in charge here to take your call when it comes."

Rufus nodded, "Thank you."

We were keeping our Special Branch Major, which was good news indeed — I really wouldn't like to think about trying to get used to someone new in the year that followed. Though, well, I won't get into the many discussions related to that comment until they're pertinent.

Which means not now.

After the messages started flowing back and forth between *Bonaventure* and Earth again, Schwartz T. Babcock found himself named the youngest Chief of Staff in the history of the Earth Empire's PMO. That's no mean accomplishment, I think you'll agree, and Schwartz deserved the promotion.

Of course, you and I know he wasn't destined to stay long in the job, but that's not really relevant — when that message arrived from Douglas Pope, it was a great moment for the political wonderkid.

Not such a great moment for Murt Sergeant, of course. The fuming former-Chief of Staff stormed out of the PMO, screaming that Pope was a disgrace and didn't deserve to be Prime Minister anymore, and that he'd do everything in his power to make sure someone else won the next election.

Yes, great. Let me again wonder at how this guy had risen to such a high position on Pope's staff… sometimes they creep through the detection nets, I guess. No rhyme nor reason to it.

Of course, he didn't just leave to go home and have a stiff drink. Once he left, Murt Sergeant went to West Terra Nova High School, waited until the final bell, and then picked up his fourth wife. They left town, and I really don't want to think about how difficult a situation that must have been for her. In so many ways.

After that, Murt Sergeant dropped right off everyone's screens. I hear he's in Africa now, though I don't know what he's doing. The fucktard.

Schwartz decided not to move into Murt's old office, so he was still sitting behind his usual desk when Donna came in with some files. She was smiling down at her young boss, "I think being Chief of Staff makes you look taller."

Smiling at her, Schwartz shrugged, "Really? I thought that's what the platform boots were for, but if the job does it too, I'll be ready to play basketball any day!"

Schwartz T. Babcock is an impossible political opponent, then as today. But as much as you may want to hate him and his style, you have to understand that one of the reasons he's still doing the business on Capital Island is because he's genuinely likable, and dare I say, good.

That's why Douglas Pope took a chance on him. That's why Daragh listened to him when it mattered most. And that's partially why the Empire still has an elected government.

Well done, wonderkid.

CHAPTER THIRTY

TIME SQUARE

The last people to be offered rewards for their part in stopping the Governor General were Karen and me... and because it tends to be more difficult to promote Admirals and Commodores, we just got our thanks in person from Daragh.

"Anything you ever need, I'll owe you," the Second Lord said. At the time I didn't think I'd take him up on the promise, but I was wrong...

However, as normality slipped back into people's lives, Karen and I knew we needed to do something. One thing that frustrated us both was that the war had ended — signed on the dotted line, over! — but all anyone seemed to care about was the Emperor's defeat.

And not even everyone cared about that, because politics was boring, and there hadn't been enough shooting to turn the story into an action thriller. People's tolerances for shooting were high because of the war... so even when a coup basically happened, it was dull.

The end of the war was even more dull, though, because it meant no shooting at all. Mindful of the need to combat this apathy, Karen and I decided to reward ourselves (in a strange way) by calling a press conference. Everyone was invited, and because we'd been involved in the coup, lots of reporters showed up on lawn outside of Admiralty House when we made the request.

We put in a special call to Jessica Qing, of course, and made sure she and her camera had the best spot and forewarning of what we were going to say. Though it had been a couple of years since we'd seen her, we still had the bond we'd built at Jupiter, and that sort of mutual experience counts for a lot.

Bunny and Jim were engaged, for instance.

As we watched the crowd of media grow outside Admiralty House, Karen and I waited in John Fiora's empty office. We were both still a bit... tentative, I suppose. Getting through that battle with Hodson had really been quite exhausting, and however much a goddess you might be, it takes time to bounce back after turning yourself that far inside out.

But this conference would help, we figured. And it would call some attention to the end of the war.

"You sure you want to do this?" Karen asked with a frown, looking again at the black and white reference photo I'd printed for her.

I nodded, "Yeah, I think so. And we can make it pretty ambiguous too. I know Jessica is going to want clarification on what we mean, but either way, it's exactly the sort of thing people need right now, to remember where we're at."

"I think you're just using that as an excuse," a small smile tugged at the corners of Karen's lips. "You know it's the only way this happens."

"Mmhmm," I replied with a smile of my own, and she laughed gently, then leaned into me a little and pulled on her ponytail.

We waited until 1400, the time we'd told everyone to show up, and then headed out of John's office. No one in Admiralty House knew what was going on — they figured Daragh might have a press briefing or something — but even he poked his head out his door in confusion as we went past.

Heading through the lobby, Karen and I both took deep breaths before emerging into a relatively bright Capital Island afternoon. It was overcast, but the clouds were thin and there was no harsh sunlight beating down into our eyes. Better for the cameras, I guess.

Karen and I remained silent as we moved up to the podium that had been placed there for us, though we waved to a few reporters, and specifically to Jessica Qing. Taking the podium, Karen raised a pad that had been laid there for her, then brought up the remarks that we'd prepared on its screen.

"Good afternoon, ladies and gentlemen," she said, and her wooden delivery was actually a bit comical. As if Karen didn't know how to talk at a press conference... but she was doing it for effect. "My name is Karen McMaster, and I'm a Commodore with Defense Command. I would like to introduce Rear Admiral Ken Barron. Ken commanded the Belt Squadron before the recent war, and then took over a formation called the Jupiter Force during hostilities. He commanded that force in engagements at Io, during the assault on Mercury, and during the Fleet Clash. He also helped escort the Foreign Minister to Mars ahead of the recent Convention. I had the privilege of serving with Ken during all these missions, and a few others, so it is my immense pleasure to introduce him to you today, for a special statement."

I don't think we could have confused the media any further without speaking a language other than English. You see, that sort of introduction is the canned political diction that you usually get at bad press conferences and standard political ribbon cuttings. We had never — ever, *ever* — used it.

And everyone certainly knew who I was, and who Karen was, so introducing ourselves was, well, ridiculous.

We kept an eye on some of the reporters' faces as Karen read the lines, and a few seemed to think it was a joke — they smiled and nudged each other, wondering what dinner theatre we had in store for them at 1400 in the afternoon.

Those were smart reporters.

Karen stood aside, though not really far enough aside for me to get the podium to myself. I nodded to the reporters as I took my place, and suddenly found myself more anxious than I'd been in a while... odd, you might think, because of all those battles I was in, according to Karen's introduction.

But as a good officer, I pushed through the concerns. Duty first. Duty to the Empire.

So I took a breath, squared my shoulders, and began my statement.

"Ladies and gentlemen, the war against Mars is over."

With that, I turned to Karen, slid my arm around her lower back, and as though we'd done it before, we stepped into each other and kissed.

Ahem, to repeat for you speed readers who skip words: Kissed.

And in all-caps: KISSED.

You know we did. You've seen the footage. Everyone has seen the footage.

And it was quite a kiss, let me tell you. People commented that we looked like we'd been doing it for years. Like our bodies pressed against each other all the time. Like our hands were familiar with each others' shapes… okay enough of that.

Interesting observations. No comments coming from me, though.

Now, I was supposed to dip Karen, because we were trying to recapture the pose of a photo taken in Time Square, New York, at the end of the Second World War… but I kinda forgot to try to dip her. She didn't notice, and I certainly didn't. And neither of us particularly cared.

I kissed Karen in front of the Parliamentary press corps. She kissed me in front of everyone in Admiralty House who had a window. 'The kiss seen round the Empire', they called it. 'War is over', they called it. And trust me, if you want to get the end of the war to the top of the evening news, this is one way to do it.

As sacrifices made for the war effort go, this one was pretty manageable.

So the Empire had its answer — clearly Karen and I were together-together, not just close friends. Right?

Because we're evil, people most certainly did not have their answer.

After we finally finished kissing, we could hear a pin drop. The press corps seemed to be swelling — getting ready to burst with questions — but there was a pregnant pause first.

And then Karen, who is brilliant, returned to the podium and said, "Unfortunately Rear Admiral Barron does not have time to take any questions. Thank you for attending today."

We left the podium, and the questions roared behind us.

"Is that the first kiss?"

"Was it good?"

We didn't answer any, but we did invite Jessica Qing into a meeting room in Admiralty House, where we showed her the picture we'd used for reference, and explained on camera that we thought it was necessary to generate discussion around the end of the war, and this seemed an agreeable way.

"So," Jessica asked us both, as we sat side by side, "Does this mean you two have been together the whole time, or are getting together now? Or was this a stunt to publicize the end of the war? Because… most friends don't kiss like that."

Karen and I looked at each other, and then I answered, "Jessica, did you know that, when we walk into a commercial place of business, our presence increases the chances of that building collapsing by a multiple of four?"

"True fact," Karen used the redundancy on purpose, and then smiled.

Jessica could have gotten frustrated, but she'd come into this pretty certain that we wouldn't give her a straight answer… and we didn't. The speculators could keep speculating, though those people who thought Karen and I were just friends had a real hard time figuring how we'd managed to kiss for close to a minute without stopping to breathe.

That either required practice and experience… or we were very talented amateurs.

Take your pick — I'm not telling, because that would be no fun.

And as one of my editors assures me, I'm no fun at all.

AFTERWORD

So that's it, the war is over and you can throw these books away...

Or, I suppose, you can wait around and see how we sorted out the Emperor when he got home, and how everything else fell into place once the treaty was signed.

Next book is *The Articles of Empire*, and you can tell it'll be important because, for the first time in this entire series, the title has four words in it, instead of three. Whoa! It'll be our chance to check in with just about everyone from the war... see how Charlie and Lia are doing, and Marlene, Greg, and all the old Belt Squadron gang. I want to make sure we're all feeling pretty good before we get to 2235, because that year is going to be something different. It's important to see where we were coming from.

Until then, keep well, and do yourself a favor: go out into public and kiss someone. Preferably someone you know in advance, but if not, just make sure you ask first. Never know what can happen, but I assure you, it'll be fun.

Or you might end up in jail. If that happens, you're on your own.

What a weird note to end on. Til next time...

THE
ARTICLES
OF EMPIRE

THE AUTOBIOGRAPHICAL REMINISCENCES OF
ADMIRAL THE LORD KEN BARRON FOR 2234

WOLF

THE MARTIAN WAR - 16

KENNETH TAM

FROM THE AUTHOR

If you cast your mind all the way back to *The Hawke Mission*, you might recall that I discussed how the Earth Empire was built as a futuristic version of the 19th-century British Empire (minus the scientific racism and the suppression of indigenous peoples). That comparison seems pertinent again as we wander into the post-war period, and start figuring out what to do with the throne now that Luther Gregory's plot has been revealed.

You see, the British have a tradition of dealing with upheaval in a way I'm honestly partial to. Winston Churchill probably summed it up best with KBO – 'keep buggering on'. See, under the British model of government, you don't tear down a whole system just because it's flawed. You patch it up if you need to, and you keep muddling along.

That's one of the reasons the British don't have a unified constitution, just a tradition of Common Law that finds its origins in the Magna Carta... which was signed in 1215.

Contrast this with the French tradition, begun with the Revolution against the Ancien Régime in 1789. Not to over-simplify, but if the French don't like the way their government is working, they simply topple it and begin again. They've done it five times to date (six if you count the attempt of the Paris Commune in 1871), and though each of those revolutions had their own particular origins and implications, I think the broad comparison is worthwhile. After Cromwell, the British pretty much decided rebellions and revolutions were more trouble than they were worth, and decided to work within the system to make changes. I'd wager this approach saved a lot of lives.

Now the Earth Empire has to choose which path to follow. An Emperor has made a play to take over both halves of government through some nefarious means... some would certainly be forgiven for demanding his head, and the end of the throne.

But what happens if you open up the constitution and start performing major surgery? Can the Empire survive? That's the question the leaders have to grapple with in this book. Time to find out whether it's KBO, or down with the Articles of Empire...

Now as ever, many characters in this book owe their existence to the real-world friends upon who they are based. Thanks to all those fine people for adding to this cast of characters.

My good friend Peter Caron's advice has really helped shape much of what you're about to read — though he may not yet realize precisely how. Nevertheless, continued thanks to him, because he's awesome.

Similarly, I again thank my friend Wes Prewer, whose art and enthusiasm have continued to propel these books. Just wait for 2235...

Jacqui and Peter are my parents and partners in Iceberg Publishing, and they are the best. Just like Atlas.

– Kenneth Tam

PREFACE

So here's a question that no one in the Empire had ever answered before the events of this book: what do you do when you've caught an Emperor trying to mount a coup? It's not easy. See, the knee-jerk reaction might be to eliminate the throne — get rid of that branch of the government, and completely turn the running of the Empire over to the elected Parliament.

I probably wouldn't have minded that option, but a good forty percent of the population wouldn't have liked it so much — not that they were all fans of Luther Gregory, they just believed that the throne had a place in our state, so long as it was occupied by the right Emperor.

But if we had to keep the whole Emperor institution, what could we possibly do to diffuse the tensions that had led to *The Pax Terra*?

A whole bunch of things. There were too many possibilities for me to list here and now, so I'm just going to leave all those for the book itself. Instead, I'm going to explain how the next 60,000 words are laid out, because it's a bit unusual. We actually have to cover about five months in this book, owing to the fact that so much of the political decision-making took its sweet time.

So: the first third of *The Articles of Empire* is going to cover the choice made about what to do with Luther Gregory, and what poor fool had to replace him. The second part will be about the execution of the plan, and we'll finish on the high note of the Empire Day celebrations at the end of the year.

Then I'll end with an afterword that sounds suitably ominous and distraught, because this is the last book before 2235... and I've seriously been considering breaching my contract with these damned publishers and moving to Io before I have to write that damned year.

But no, I'll stay, and you'll get to read about everything.

For now, though, the good stuff. I know it's politics, and some of you hate that, but I promise it'll be worthwhile. Because there's nothing like dishing dirt about Emperors to keep you intrigued... especially if you've been under a rock and you don't know who succeeded Luther Gregory to the throne.

Ha!

Alright, that should be sufficient setup... let's get going...

CHAPTER ONE
TIME OFF

How do you spend your time off? Perhaps you like to take it easy at home — laze around a bit, watch some TV, spend time with the family, catch up on sleep? Maybe you travel to different parts of the Empire — there's a lot of it, and you'll find many interesting things in the various corners. Maybe you pamper yourself at a posh resort — there are plenty around and I hear they're nice. Maybe you take some classes, and do the self-improvement thing. That's a good one as well. Perhaps you don't believe in time off, and you'd rather keep on working. Hey, whatever you prefer.

Now take a guess at how Karen and I were killing time while *Wolf* sat in orbit of Earth, waiting for the Emperor's convoy to get back from Mars.

Beach? Nope.

Brothel? Nah.

Clubbing? Well, actually, sort of...

The warehouse was dark, but then most warehouses are in the middle of the night. That's why big-time criminals, or youngsters with delusions that they are big time criminals, like them so much — great place to hang about and do illegal things.

This particular warehouse was nestled in Toronto, the largest city in Canada (home to the Geraldine Coilier Show, if you'll recall), and as the night wore on, a great many miscreants filed into it. They were having a meeting.

There was much for these gang people to discuss, because one of the stories that doesn't get told often (or well), but which was very much part of the war on Earth, was the fact that organized crime spiked in 2233, largely due to the fact that SF was spread so thin supporting the invasion of Mercury.

A lot of people don't realize that the number of Constables in the various precincts across Earth dropped by twelve percent that year, some of them actually going to Mercury during the assault (or after the assault to help with policing), others called up to posts like the Belt colonies or Venus, to replace SF who had indeed made the assault.

Now, twelve percent might not sound like much of a loss, but it is. Trust me on this — there were holes in the crime-fighting net that wouldn't have been there had we been able to land marines on Mercury, instead of SF.

That's a discussion for another time, though.

Most important right now is that the organized criminal element had seized upon the opportunity to start increasing opportunistic operations, and was looking to meet (in Toronto, for whatever reason) to discuss ways to maintain its growing influence when those veterans of Mercury got home to refill the Constabulary ranks.

It was an ominous situation... but here's the thing you have to remember about Defense Command: all the branches, from fleet to intelligence to security forces, are part of a single big entity. Now that the war was over and we had all those ships sitting in orbit, full of crews who were frankly starting to get a little bored, reinforcements were at hand… reinforcements who happened to be very experienced in dealing with organized criminals — or pirates, which are the same thing, just with ships.

"I think we need to call this meeting to order," the senior boss of the represented organizations declared once all the required delegations arrived. They were all standing around a long table that had been placed in a clear area in the center of the warehouse — an artificial meeting room, not entirely unlike the holding pen where we'd kept the surrendered blockheads back on Egesta.

As the meeting was called to order, the heads of the eleven represented gangs moved to their seats, while their personal guards — two each — stood around the perimeter of the 'room'. Outside, watching various access points and the approaches to the warehouse, another thirty enforcers were on duty… so basically, there were approximately sixty hardened killers in this warehouse. For now.

"Thank you all for coming, ladies and gentlemen. Together, we have achieved a great deal in the past year, and that progress must be continued, no matter what Defense Command throws at us. Together, our ten organizations represent the beginning of a new era in crime on this planet…"

A bit of a predictable opening for the guy, let's be honest. This was Tanner Fosse, the head of the Knights… no idea why they were called Knights, because they weren't roaming around in armor with swords, but that was their name.

They sure weren't Belt Widows…

Anyway, by interjecting that piece of context, I've wrecked the tempo. See, as soon as Fosse said there were ten organizations represented at the table, everyone frowned — guess what, gangsters can count past ten!

Then one of them — a blonde woman with absurd lipstick, really big sunglasses and a huge poncho that looked like it fell off a Mexican stereotype truck — made it official, "There are actually eleven of us here."

She then looked back at her entourage — a Chinese guy who looked unimpressed and a slick cool fellow with an Afro, both wearing ponchos as ugly as hers — and confirmed, "I'm counting right, right?"

"Yes ma'am," Afro dude replied with a nod.

"See," she said, lacing her fingers together.

"Only ten were invited," Tanner Fosse scowled as he too counted the people around the table, then came to his feet.

Of course, in a room full of people who are used to shooting at each other, any one guy coming to his feet meant most of the others had to do the same, and then all the strong-headed guards got agitated.

There was some chest thumping, both literal and figurative, and everyone glared at everyone else.

"I bet someone here is a plant from the Defcoms!" the blonde announced, pulling the sunglasses down to the tip of her nose and looking over their rims at the people around the table.

"It must be a trap!" another gang boss, Turbo Funk Master Feldman IV (not kidding) declared with alacrity.

That made everyone even more agitated, so weapons started to emerge from their poorly-hidden carrying harnesses.

Tanner Fosse then punched the table a few times, demanding silence, "How is this possible? I only invited ten!"

"Don't you recognize the ones you invited?" Feldman-4 (he's a gangster Turbo Funk Master, he's not good enough for me to keep using Roman numerals) demanded, and the head criminal scowled even more deeply and then started looking at the people around the table more closely.

He went face to face, but for some reason couldn't pick out the odd one. Still puzzles me why he was that daft, but hey, gift horses and whatnot. I suppose if they were smart, these bastards would have left Earth and teamed up with Grant Merger's Syndicate...

They hadn't because they were small-time hoods. Far beneath us, I suppose, but still fun.

"I'm the baddest-ass-est killer at this table," the blonde with the poncho declared as the discomfort continued.

"Not as badass as me!" another woman, Martha Lu, countered, driving her first into the table. "Bitch."

"Let's not start fighting amongst ourselves, please!" Tanner Fosse protested, trying ironically to sound like some sort of statesman-diplomat. "The intruder must be among us."

"Anyone not recognize anyone else?" Feldman-4 asked then, and everyone looked around again. Most of these people didn't cross paths on a regular basis, but they were familiar enough with each other that a complete stranger should not have gone unnoticed.

That in mind, you really would have expected them to clue in at this point.

Taking off her sunglasses and throwing them to the table, the blonde gangster produced a mag from under her poncho, "I know who it is!"

Everyone turned to her, and around the perimeter all their guards got tense and ready to shoot.

No one did anything, though — they just waited for the blonde to announce the bad guy... or more properly, the good guy.

Instead she just stood there, rather surprised by the lack of uptake on her revelation.

"So who is it?" Feldman-4, the Turbo Funk Master, insisted, and the blonde frowned.

"Just a second and I'll show you," she said finally, beginning to sound frustrated.

Using her free hand, she pulled her poncho up and over her head, then dropped it on the table.

Still no one moved. They all stared at her, waiting for the news. Someone here was going to get *so* shot... if the blonde would just spill it.

For three minutes — I'm not kidding, three whole minutes, we have it on camera — the standoff continued.

Then, finally, I walked up to the table in disgust, throwing both my poncho and my Afro wig (which looked totally rad on me, by the way) on top of Karen's poncho and sunglasses.

"Have you never seen a flight suit before?" I demanded angrily, waving at Karen.

We were both wearing our usual flight gear — we'd come down from *Wolf* in our

Starlights after all.

"So what?" Martha Lu demanded. "Who's the…"

Oh sure, then they all got it.

"It must be the lipstick," Karen frowned, glancing at me.

"Holy shit, it's Barron and McMaster!" Feldman-4 actually sounded excited, and no one at the table reacted the way they were supposed to.

At a time like this, mags were supposed to be brandished, and we were supposed to be assured that we'd never take them alive, or that we'd never make it out of there alive — take your pick, we heard it all. Once, someone actually started yodeling. Trying to explain that in a report to Greg Noyce was awkward…

But this time, they all just stood and stared at us.

What we discovered later, when Constables interviewed some of these hoods, was that they were actually star-struck. I know that probably sounds self-congratulatory or otherwise bullshit, but seriously, some of these small-timers thought this meant they'd truly made it — they were as heavy and dangerous as the Belt Widows, or the Syndicate.

If you're going to get busted, apparently it's better to go down to celebrity fleet officers than to the hardworking Constables who are the real reason you're in the slammer.

Haha, 'slammer'. Listen to me use the lingo…

"If you're all finished staring, you're under arrest," I finally broke my silence, and as I did, Rufus' team appeared in the warehouse.

The rest of the guards on the perimeter of the building and at the entrances had not been much of an obstacle for the Special Branchers who had come with us — Rufus' team and two others from the Heavy Squadron — so now we had the crooks surrounded.

"Surrender, or we will shoot you all," Rufus moved towards the table, MAG-90 out from under the poncho as he gave firm orders.

And that was it, we figured.

Except that Tanner Fosse, the bastard, was probably a little less of a lightweight than the rest of the people at the table.

He broke into a run, and as he did his two goons started raising their mags to open fire. This led to them being shot into comas by the Branchers… but as soon as we started blasting, every other idiot with a mag in the room did too. Two of ours got clipped (no harm done, thanks to tac vests) but the Branchers were distracted by shooting thirty baddies, and Fosse got a head start.

Interestingly — inexplicably, if I'm honest — none of the gangsters put Karen or I in their crosshairs. Instead, they shot at the Branchers… well, maybe that's not inexplicable. The Branchers were a much bigger threat, after all. The point is that Karen and I were free to chase, and that's what we did.

Fosse was fleeing on foot, so we had to run. Flight boots aren't the greatest for such chases, but we had some experience in that area, so we took off — leaving behind an irritated Rufus, who was busy shooting gangsters and yelling that we better not leave. We managed to keep Fosse in sight, as he raced into a massive shipping crate… and then, of course, the bastard flew out the other side in a high-speed skiff.

Not an armed Special Branch skiff, of course — just a narrow and fast hover runner that rammed its way out the service entrance, past the SF blockade outside, and off towards downtown Toronto.

As we came to a stop next to the crate, and panted to catch our breath… well, it was just me panting… Rufus caught up, "Dammit. We'll put out a bulletin…"

"Nah, we'll get him," Karen said enthusiastically, and then I nodded.

"Yeah. You look after things here."

Rufus didn't like it when we said things like that — I swear he was channeling Matt Baxter, because his stare was steely. I was afraid for my immortal soul if I got myself killed, because Rufus would find it and blow it up…

We didn't stick around to indulge in that sort of conversation, though. Instead, Karen and I headed out the exit at a quick walk, dashed over to our planes — which we'd landed in the parking lot *without* crushing any cars, thanks very much — and got their engines going.

As I slid my helmet onto my head, I tapped my comm into *Wolf's* grid, "Felicia, did you catch that skiff burning out of the warehouse?"

There was the briefest pause before Felicia Khalid, *Wolf's* Sensors and Communications Officer, came back, "Yes sir, we have it fixed moving westward from your position, heading towards the waterfront."

"Patch the tracking into our flight computers," Karen was on comms now too, so she gave that order and our screens brightened with an orbital scan showing Fosse's attempted getaway.

Firing up our atmo drives, we closed our canopies, jumped our planes into the air and started after him. Now, I don't care how fast your skiff is — how many super-chargers or speed holes it has — no hover craft of any sort can run faster than a Starlight.

Not even close.

Of course we didn't want to open the taps fully, because we'd have shattered windows and possibly downed some of Toronto's older buildings with the shockwave, but we nudged up the throttle and were on top of the gangster in just a few dozen seconds.

Unfortunately, he was down between buildings, and despite what you see in the movies, it's rarely a good a good idea to fly a plane down that low in a built up area. Still, we were above him… he couldn't get far. But he could go down.

"Underground parking garage, right there!"

As Karen barked that warning, I banked enough to look straight down, and watched Fosse's skiff diving into one of Toronto's old underground lots. There were probably some wheeled vehicles down in that rat hole…

"Call in for a cordon, will you Felicia?"

"Aye sir," *Wolf's* Lieutenant replied immediately.

So there were Constables coming, and that meant we could undoubtedly wait, flying orbits around the block and trying to make sure Fosse didn't crawl away on foot.

But does sitting and watching sound like something Karen and I would do, now that the war was over and we were being cavalier (and irresponsibly dangerous) again?

Didn't think so, and with that basic thought in mind I switched into hover over the lot, and started dropping straight down into street below. Sure there was some traffic, but I took it slow so the vehicles had time to stop or move before I dropped my Starlight into the middle of Yonge Street.

Wasn't awkward at all, and I assure you, nobody honked any car horns at me. That would be rude, and it's not a good idea to be rude to a frontline combat atmospace fighter, even if it has a no-talent pilot at the controls.

Karen came down at the back of the building in a parking lot off Maitland Terrace, so I didn't get to see her land. I'm positive no one honked at her — too many reasons not to.

As my canopy went up I leapt out of my ship with some youthful vigor... which was a little too much for my not-quite-so-young body, and slightly tweaked my knee. Didn't matter, I hobble-jogged towards the entrance to the underground parking lot, pulled my mag, and went right in.

This wasn't as dangerous as you might expect; the whole underground lot was very well lit, with no deep shadows or concealing gloom. If anything, it felt a bit antiseptic... but while that doesn't make for good dramatic atmosphere, I certainly wasn't going to complain. As soon as I entered the mostly-full lot (which did indeed include some old wheeled vehicles) I spotted the skiff down in the middle of a lane, still running.

Hurrying up to the side of the craft, I checked to make sure Fosse wasn't inside, and also tried to keep an eye on all the cars around — he could have been waiting for me somewhere amongst the vehicles, as much as I didn't think it likely. The guy was running, and though lashing out at your pursuers might feel good, it's also a great way to get yourself caught.

He was nowhere in sight... but I did spot a door — the entrance, in fact, to a club.

Leaving the skiff behind, I approached the door at a hobble-jog, then slowed as I read the words on the neon sign above it.

The club was called *Underpants Pillow Fight*.

Yes. That's a perfectly sensible name for a club. Of course.

There was no bouncer on the door, which struck me as interesting — anyone could come in off the street and go down the ramp, arriving at the entrance here... so presumably there was a guard of some sort stationed to keep the riffraff (or those not stylish enough) out of the place...

But perhaps Fosse had come through.

One way to find out — and guess how much I was looking forward to that.

Coming to a stop, I put the flat of my free hand against the door and felt the black metal surface vibrating. Loud noise — I think you young people call it 'music', but you are sorely mistaken.

Ah well, criminals had to be brought to justice and such.

Reaching down to the handle, I pulled open the old-style hinged door and was immediately hit in the face by the latest Top 400 hits. It was loud, dark, and there were all sorts of lights swirling and flashing and strobing inside.

Groovy.

In I went, leading with my mag, and the first thing I found was the bouncer on the floor cradling a bloody nose. Fosse was obviously here... presuming there hadn't been a club-fight.

Ignoring the fallen heavyweight, I moved slowly down a corridor and past a coat check. There were lots of stylish youthful people suffering from a nonsensical lack of clothing milling about, seemingly oblivious as they went to washrooms and drug rooms and rooms meant for other things…

Classy joint.

Eventually I emerged into the club's main area — a huge room that was deafeningly loud and packed with people. There was a bar along the back wall to my left, and a stage on the front wall to my right.

On that stage, and on the floor below it, people were getting down with their terrible, obnoxious selves. I don't know who told any of them that their crap performances were impressive, or God forbid attractive (isn't dancing supposed to make you more appealing to people you're trying to mate with?), but they sure thought they were awesome.

And because there were hundreds of them, in a darkened room with the worst lightning imaginable, I couldn't see Fosse. I knew he had to be here… hopefully he'd make a mistake and get himself noticed.

Or perhaps…

I took a few steps towards the dance floor, mag still up in my hand. A couple of girls tried to say something to me about my flightsuit — apparently I was being avant garde fashion-forward? — but I ignored them as politely as I could manage.

There had to be a central soundboard up there somewhere… something I could shoot to bring some quiet to this chamber…

Then I spotted Fosse. Some huge bruiser in the middle of the dance floor, who looked like he was well and truly intoxicated, was pushing the criminal boss. There was no way I could hear what was being said, but if I had to guess, the bruiser was defending the perceived honor of his date.

Fosse had probably tried to push his way between them… and there he went, the criminal boss smashed the bruiser's nose, drawing some screams from very intoxicated witnesses. I could just make out those screams, and I started pushing my way forward as a small brawl began to break out in the middle of the floor.

Now, Tanner Fosse was by no means the most dangerous criminal I'd chased — he'd be broken in half by most of the pirates the Syndicate hired — but he was still a gritty bastard, and he'd obviously seen himself through some scrapes.

Approaching through the intermittent strobe light that was attached to the latest song, I could see flashes of him taking apart a gang of three or four guys — it was like one of those artsy movies where they show flashes of a fast-paced fight on screen, as if you were looking at a still-print comic or something.

He was good, so I just needed to go ahead and shoot him…

People were backing away from the fight, so a little ring formed to give the battlers room. Of course, the process of clearing this space forced people closer together, meaning the closer I got to it, the tougher it was to make progress. I literally had to squeeze between the sweaty and stained bodies of the Empire's youth… shudder.

"Excuse me!" I kept yelling, because it's important to be polite, but no one could hear me and who knows if they'd even have listened if they could.

I raised my mag as high as I could and tried to point it at Fosse, but it was risky — to open fire now, with so many people between me and him, could have ended rather badly.

But if I didn't, surely he'd finish off the thugs and get away…

Of course he wouldn't. As the last of the club bruisers hit the ground hard, Tanner

Fosse looked in my direction, spotted my mag, then turned for the opposite side of the ring.

Karen was standing there, arms folded and expression quite charming, "Took you long enough."

I couldn't hear her over the music, of course, but that's what she said. Fosse did a double take, then stepped back and set himself up in his super-tough-guy fighting stance. Karen tilted her head slightly and then unfolded her arms, in a flash revealing that she had a mag in one of her hands.

Stretching it out towards the criminal, she lined up a shot… and then he kicked the weapon away.

Right out of her hand. The nerve of the bastard.

As soon as Karen was disarmed, Fosse leapt at her, swinging his fists in a suitably formidable-seeming manner. You know how this sort of thing ends, but it wouldn't have been professional for me to just stop and watch — I kept trying to force my way between the Empire's party-going class, and they slowly gave way.

By the time I got to the edge of the ring, Fosse was in pretty bad shape, and Karen was dusting her hands off in gallant style.

Finally the club owners realized that something was going down on their dance floor, and as they did, the music was cut and the house lights came up. There were a considerable number of confused and disoriented patrons in *Underpants Pillow Fight* — and the best part was watching the couples or threesomes who had been hanging off each other, as they got a look at their dancing partners in the harsh light of day. Er. Harsh light of house lights.

Let's just say 'awkward'.

I also saw for the first time that, on the stage, the club was living up to its name: there were a bunch of models up there in underwear, holding pillows with which they had been ardently bashing each other… doing so, one must assume, for their own enjoyment, since no one could have possibly seen them up there without the house lights on.

"What took you so long?" Karen asked as I emerged fully into the ring.

Holstering my mag, I shrugged, "I was dancing."

Haha — that was funny because I don't dance. Because you needed to be reminded of that to get the joke.

At this point, our status as celebrity officers was confirmed. Someone recognized us, and then everybody recognized us, and there was yelling and screaming and Karen was offered a pillow and invited to join the models on stage. Interestingly, they didn't extend that invitation to me. Sexist bastards.

Anyway, by the time SF caught up to us, we'd enlisted a couple of the bouncers to drag Fosse to the front door, where we were stuck signing autographs (yes, *autographs*). Contrary to the rumors, I did not sign any part of anyone's body.

When the cameras arrived, we did a little press scrum, refused to kiss, and then went for burgers.

Sitting in the Gold Arch Burger overlooking Lake Ontario, Karen and I were both typically sweaty and disheveled, and it felt about right. As you can tell from the way this book starts, we were doing everything possible to get back to that place of cavalier glee we'd occupied during *The Rogue Commodore*.

But the reality was rather far removed from that place.

Because though we'd done a media scrum as we left *Underpants Pillow Fight*, and we knew there'd be coverage of us on the news, the screens in the burger joint weren't showing us, they were running file footage of Luther Gregory III.

Under the man's picture, the caption read: "What do we do under the Articles of Empire?"

Reading that, I glanced back at Karen, "Think people are bored of trying to figure out constitutional law yet?"

"I'm surprised they weren't bored to begin with," she answered before having another curly fry.

I nodded and went back to my burger, but the question weighed on my mind. You could catch as many petty criminals as you wanted... the biggest one was still on his way in, and neither Karen nor I had any authority to deal with him.

That's probably not a bad thing, considering how sympathetic we'd been to many of his loyal soldiers on Egesta, but still.

"What do you think happens? Figure it'll be complicated?" Karen asked the question between fries, looking up at me as she did.

I shrugged, "Depends on what the Lords do. If they dig their heels in, we'll be arguing constitutional law for the rest of the year. If they realize we've got their entire piece of the governmental system over a barrel, and throw Luther under the bus, we'll be done pretty quickly."

See, that's the thing: the Lords had all the power in this situation. They were the ones responsible for Luther Gregory — they'd elevated the bastard to the throne. What I didn't know, and frankly what no one knew, was whether they were angry he'd failed to seize control... or angry that he'd tried in the first place.

If it was the former, and they tried to do anything to restore him — or protect him, or justify him — things could get very complicated. The Articles of Empire, which governed (and still govern) everything about our civilization, were robust, but they weren't perfect. The committee that wrote them — Luther Gordon the Great, Amy Valens, Natalie Quinn to name a few — they were all good people, but they'd been working fast and under a lot of pressure. There were loopholes, and it was entirely possible that both sides in a fight over the throne could find plenty of precedent somewhere within them.

So we basically had to hope there was no fight, or else we might end up with another coup...

Karen kicked me under the table, and I blinked.

"You're drifting off on me," she said, and then stuck out her bottom lip in an absurd fashion. "I'm not as watchable as I was before the war?"

I stared at her for a second, and then I shook my head, "Nope."

She started to smile, then frowned, "Wait. *Nope* I'm not more watchable, or *nope* I am more watchable."

"I think the guy at the bar is checking you out," I deflected masterfully, and Karen's frown deepened.

"Not my type," she said flatly, but I shrugged.

"He thinks you're watchable."

"Yes, but did he ever see me before the war?" Karen countered, having another couple of fries.

"Why don't you make his day and ask?" I smiled, and she grumbled something.

I went back to my burger, and to my obsessing over questions of the fate of the Empire. It would probably be a downer to end this long chapter on those thoughts — we went from hijinks of the old style to constitutional law — but such were the preoccupations of these days.

Would the Articles of Empire weather this storm?

Well, the funny thing is that they would, and they'd do so far more easily than anyone expected. But that's something we can talk about in the next couple of chapters; for now we need to end on the high note.

Completely out of nowhere, Rufus Chang was suddenly standing beside our table. Seriously, he just seemed to appear.

"Whoa, did you teleport in here?" Karen asked as he glared down at us.

"How did you even know we were here?" I added.

Rufus planted his hands on the table and leaned down, "You parked your planes in the middle of the street outside. Now you're going to finish eating in the next five minutes, and then we're going back to the ship."

He meant it. Like, seriously. It was as though he'd caught the kids out past curfew, and since both Karen and I had that thought at the same time, we had to run with it.

"Aw dad," Karen pouted. "Charlie always let us stay out late."

"Matt too," I added.

We both looked up at Rufus with those words, and his mismatched eyes revealed no particular humor. He could have said something, but instead he just folded his arms and glared… which was warning enough. We ate quickly.

Just as we were leaving the burger joint, our interviews *finally* got on the air. Stupid constitutional crisis stealing our thunder… It was like the old days, but not really.

The Articles of Empire were to be tested.

CHAPTER TWO

THE EMPEROR QUESTION

So let's talk a bit about those Articles of Empire.

Even before Luther Gregory III and the convoy of warships carrying him home reached Earth, the questions about what was to become of his throne were circling. All the evidence we'd collected at Egesta had been dumped into public access archives (along with serious content warnings so the faint of heart didn't look at it), and there seemed little question that the current Emperor and most of his leadership team were destined to be removed.

But after that, what would we do?

The question was one for the Venusian Lords — at least at first. I don't know if I've ever explained it, but the process of appointing an Emperor is not unlike the system the Roman Catholic Church uses to select a pontiff... you get all the old guys and gals together, and they mutter amongst themselves before deciding who will best serve the Empire for the coming decade.

Yes, it is indeed just that simple. It surprises me how many people don't realize that the appointment of the Emperor is in the hands of such a small group of individuals — and that they have unilateral and completely unchecked authority to choose whichever Lord or Lady they want.

If they choose someone who goes on to disappoint them, they can pull the plug after five years (recall her or him halfway through her or his tenure). If the Emperor does something requiring more immediate action, they can use extraordinary measures and yank him or her altogether.

But it was all up to them. The only influence public opinion played in their decision came in the question of legitimacy — they had to choose an Emperor that the people would accept, because if the people turned against the throne they could elect an anti-Emperor government, or worse, begin calling for the end of the throne altogether.

Since Pope's government was already pretty much anti-Luther Gregory, guess what faction the Lords needed to be most concerned with in 2234.

But what would they do? The first and most obvious decision was tied to the fate of the current Emperor. I think we all figured Luther Gregory was done — no matter how disconnected the Lords were, they couldn't hope to keep the people of the Empire on side given his statements, and the crimes that happened on his watch.

After that, they would presumably name a new Emperor, in their delightfully unilateral manner... but who? There were many great houses among the Lords, most of them with designs on the throne, but would any of their candidates have the confidence of the people? It was tough... and if the wrong person was chosen, and the next Emperor did anything to try to vindicate Luther Gregory III, a lot could go wrong.

All of this in mind, there were many people wondering what the Lords were going to do, including the leaders of the real… sorry, meant to say 'elected'… government. Douglas Pope and Craig B. Macdonald were aboard *Ark Royal* with John Fiora, and as the convoy entered the last three-day leg of its cruise home, they met on a daily basis to talk about the options.

"We may need to go straight into an election when we get back," Pope pointed out as we join the scene at a convenient moment where he can continue my exposition, at least partially, through dialogue.

"We're only prorogued," Craig shook his head. "But, I suppose we could, just to prove we have the confidence of the people."

The Scotsman's point was a good one — there was probably no reason under the Articles of Empire for an election to be called when the convoy returned home, because after the failed coup the Governor General had rescinded his orders to dissolve the government.

That said, there was certainly an opportunity for gain — going to the polls now, with a peace treaty and a disgraced Emperor as part of the campaign story, could yield big results for the Empire Party. A huge majority… security for Pope and Macdonald for another five years at least — with people loyal to them, not a welded-together party that had obviously not been as monolithic as everyone believed.

Clearly, then, a smart politician would seize the moment, and charge to the ballot screen.

"If we don't have to, we won't," Pope said firmly.

But wait… what? Oh right, Pope and Macdonald are the sorts of politicians Daragh Ryan doesn't hate, because they actually believe in serving the people. What a concept.

"When the time comes, not sure I'll want to stick around anyway. My era's been coming to an end for a while," the Prime Minister added, sitting back in his chair.

And yet again, I've failed to set up the scene. Pope, Craig and John were all meeting in the Prime Minister's quarters, sitting in the most comfortable wingback-style chairs you'll find aboard a warship.

At those words, both Craig B. Macdonald and John Fiora turned on their elected leader with sharp stares, "You want to quit now?"

Pope looked very tired. It had been over a week since the squadron had left Mars, but that had hardly been enough time for him to begin to recover, and now the man let out a long breath and offered a barely-noticeable shrug.

"You'd make a good PM, Craig."

The Foreign Minister stared at his leader and long-time friend, then shook his head, "I'm a drunk and a fool. Stop talking like a madman."

"If you're going to hand over power, I'd suggest you wait until after the Emperor situation is sorted out," John Fiora inserted his own recommendation, and unsurprisingly, his words reflected a great deal of tactical sense. "If we end up with instability around the throne, we're not going to want any hint that the government is not rock-solid."

Pope knew that, and really hadn't been suggesting an abrupt departure, but it was useful to hear the words from someone other than himself.

"The question is who the Lords are going to choose," Craig leaned forward in his chair with the comment. "They have all the cards right now… we can't do anything to influence them or it'll look like a coup again. Think they'll realize how important it is for them to come up with a good replacement?"

Pope raised his eyebrows at the question, then let out a sigh. Luther Gregory seemed to have their tacit support... or at the very least, he'd been able to secure guarantees of their non-interference when he'd launched his plan. Now, though, would they abandon his ambitions of restoring the throne's power, or would they save themselves?

Honestly, he didn't know. Pope had never cultivated a close relationship with the Venusian Lords — he'd never even visited their odd little enclave domes on Venus. Thinking about them now, he couldn't seem to get a clear line on how they'd handle the situation. Every time he found himself predicting their behavior, he stopped and wondered whether he'd been too influenced by his months with the Martians — whether he was accidentally assigning Martian characteristics to the Lords of Venus.

It was really quite confusing — altogether too much for his fatigued mind.

"I don't know," the PM said at last, then turned his gaze to John Fiora — the only Lord in the room, though his title had not yet been perpetuated. To answer the editors, remember that tradition allowed an Admiralty Lord to keep the Peerage after leaving that position, if the Lords voted in favor of the notion.

John was ready for the question, though that didn't mean he was confident in his answer: "I think they're going to understand the need for a new direction. The evidence from Egesta, and the moves the GG made, are pretty difficult to misinterpret."

"But appointed legislatures throughout history have a pretty shit track-record of actually reforming themselves," Craig pointed out, and owing to the truth behind the statement, John nodded.

Sure, the Lords might realize that some sort of 'reform' was warranted, but would their definition of reform be the same as everyone else's? Think of it this way: if you see the whole world from a top-down perspective, and if your daily concerns include another function at Lady Bertha's house, where you'll have to put up with her insufferable nephew Guthrie, you're likely to see a reformer as someone who wears a slightly different color top hat than you do.

Sorry, that's a bit of a caricature — we all know that Lords wear only one make of top hat — but you get the point. Change now needed to be big, and visible, and maybe even a little bold. Were the Lords up to it?

"If I could send a message to the senior Lords, it'd be to find someone way out of the box," Douglas Pope said eventually. "But they don't listen to me, and I don't think it'd actually help if I tried to convince them of anything."

That's a good note for us to end on, because while these three men — arguably the most powerful trio in the Empire at that particular moment — were talking about the question of the Emperor, on Venus, another meeting was being conducted.

Now, I was certainly not a part of the meeting that I'm about to describe, nor have I ever interviewed anyone who was. Thank God. Nevertheless, it was the meeting at which the decision about the next Emperor was made... and you can draw whatever lessons you like from the fact that the Head of State for the greatest Empire in the history of the human race could be decided in a session like this one.

The Lords had a lot of power. Still do. And as you're about to see, they're real winners with it too.

What follows is an abridged account of the famous meeting, as published by Lord Tam in his personal papers.

This guy is an egomaniacal ass, so I apologize in advance…

I was at the table with Lord Cowan, Lady Macabee and Lord Feingold. We were meeting separately because of the gravity of the situation — obviously we could not have Prewer, Chiang, Christensen, or that bastard Caron anywhere close to these deliberations. I'm sure they were meeting on the same subject, of course, but their notions of sanity are entirely divorced from reality, so we had no interest in their conclusions. Their idyllic notions of a 'more ethical' selection process have no place in the Empire, and they would do well to recognize this.

In any case, it was I who first suggested the noted hero for the post of Emperor. It was a great temptation for each of us, as the senior Lords, to lobby for ourselves to take over the position, but we recognized that rehabilitating the throne was the first priority, and that could only be accomplished by a Lord who already had the complete and absolute trust of the common people who toiled in their lesser ways to service the Empire.

Once the reputation of the throne was suitably protected, we could again appoint truly worthy Peers to the position of Emperor… but at the soonest, that would be five years hence, perhaps even ten years hence.

This fact quite distressed Cowan, who would be too old a man by that time to be Emperor, but both Lady Macabee and I were hopeful that we might be considered for the post in 2245.

Now, a vital point: the selection of the hero was indeed my suggestion. Feingold has claimed it, but he does so only to attempt to elevate his own station. I am friends with Feingold, and I believe he is a mostly agreeable man, but he is simple and not capable of a brilliant suggestion such as mine own.

It takes one who is both humble and brilliant at once to come to such a conclusion as the one I reached, and as clearly I am the only possessor of these qualities in the group of senior Lords, I think the evidence is clear that it was my suggestion.

Let this be a lesson to all future Lords of high station: follow in the footsteps of betters like myself, and be certain that you are humble in all things. Only then will you be able to aspire to the sort of greatness achieved by the Tam House.

Hope you were taking notes, because that (apparently) is all it took to make what was arguably the most important choice for Emperor since Luther Gordon the Great back in the twenty-first century. It was Lord Tam's idea to name the 'hero' Emperor.

And though many, many, *many* people questioned the merits of this suggestion, it was ultimately the one followed.

You see, in the end, the Lords feared the same thing we did — that doing anything that would start a governmental fight rooted in the Articles of Empire would be about as productive as an argument rooted in a holy text. Every side could find some passage, some obscure regulation that theoretically validated its position, and there would be no clear winner or loser.

No, that's not true, there would be a clear loser: the entire system of government. If the people of Earth and the Empire saw so much legitimate division and discord between leading factions, the result could be more than a little disastrous.

Keeping a working government intact and accepted was thus the first priority. The Articles of Empire, the glue of our entire civilization, weren't going to be challenged. And that meant Luther Gregory was going right under the bus... an expression that meant a lot more in the twentieth century when it was coined, because buses ran on wheels back then.

So like I said, the Articles were going to survive this whole crisis better than anyone expected... because we were all too afraid to open the can of worms they could represent. Of course, in protecting a 200-year-old set of regulations, we were going to have to sacrifice some of our own people.

Speaking of our own, though, let's skip back to Earth and check in with some of them. Always good to know where people are, before you toss some of them into the deep end...

CHAPTER THREE

THE NEXT GENERATION

One of the instructors at the Academy was an old friend of Karen's, and since we were clearly bored out of our skulls while we waited for the Emperor to get back to Earth, that instructor got in touch with our elite goddess-Commodore and asked for a favor.

We were more than happy to oblige.

"So they're not going to touch anything," Andrea Kiley's statement was exactly that: a statement. There was no question that any of the cadets flying up to visit *Wolf* would be allowed to so much as look at any of our finely-tuned systems without her explicit say-so.

Andrea was still not in a particularly good mood (to put it mildly) and the notion of a bunch of wet-behind-the-ears kids messing up her ship, just after it had managed to escape the war largely unharmed, was a bit tough for her to handle.

Karen was standing next to our Irish skipper in the arrivals lounge of bay two, and she nodded, "Not to worry, I've known Megan for a long time. She'll only bring up the best sort."

Raising an eyebrow at the assurance, Andrea folded her arms, "They're not touching anything. We just painted"

"Understood."

We had painted, by the way — the now-famous green 'victory stripes' had been added to *Wolf's* outer hull for the first time (looking quite sharp, of course, which is why they remain to this day) and the ship was shined and serviced and ready for action. Not that there seemed to be any action in the offing… that's why we had time to welcome cadets.

The situation was this: Megan Dunne, who Karen did indeed know from the old Academy days, had asked if she could reward some of the Atlantic Academy's brightest first years (some of them underage and admitted by special permission) with a trip up to our famous ship, and a personal tour with none other than their beloved goddess.

It was a way for us to help encourage the next generation (while alleviating our boredom), and it provides me with a chance to bring you up to date on a bunch of *Wolf's* crew. See, I'm getting decent at figuring out how to make this narrative thing work. Probably would be better if I didn't call attention to it, though…

The Academy shuttle was coming through bay two's space doors as Andrea folded her arms, so Karen and her Flag Captain waited in silence until it touched down, the bay pressurized, and the half-dozen cadets led by Lieutenant Commander Dunne made their way onto the deck.

"Here we go," Karen nodded towards the hatch.

Andrea's face remained stern, but together they went out to the deck to greet the party.

"Megan," Karen approached the Lieutenant Commander with a smile and an outstretched hand.

Dunne took the hand and shook it, smiling back in a way that's rather difficult for me to describe without you knowing the history she shared with Karen. Megan had been at the Academy at the same time as Karen and I, and she'd been a proper overachiever... one of the people who was expected to be skippering her own ship one day.

Things hadn't worked out that way, which Megan considers a blessing — if she'd been on space duty instead of on Earth, she'd probably have missed the last year of her mother's life, and that's certainly nothing to ever discount.

Still, a lot of what had changed Megan's course could have gone differently. It's not my place to suggest she'd have been happier — considering her mother's struggle, I think it was necessary that she was home — but. Well. Like I said, it's tough to explain without you knowing the history. Maybe you will one day, but not right now.

"Thanks for having us aboard, Karen," Megan released Karen's grip, then stepped closer to stretch her hand to Andrea.

"This is Captain Andrea Kiley," Karen made the formal introduction, and Andrea nodded curtly.

"Of course, honored to meet you, ma'am."

"Likewise."

Andrea didn't really go out of her way to put any warmth into that word, but Megan seemed oblivious, and the six cadets — five girls and one guy — were all too busy staring wide-eyed at the flightdeck to notice.

But then their gazes started tracking to Andrea and Karen, and all their eyes got a bit wider.

"Next year all of these six will be posted to training ships. None of them has ever been aboard a working warship before," Megan announced brightly, turning back to the cadets (some of whom really did *not* look old enough for space duty training). "Introduce yourselves to Commodore McMaster."

The first to salute was the young man, "Officer Cadet Evan Connors, ma'am."

Karen smiled and returned the salute, "Welcome aboard, cadet."

Then came Officer Cadets Annabelle Pierce, Blair Jovanovic, Areum Kim, Miyu Takahashi, and finally the last one...

"Officer Cadet Peyton Gale," she presented herself with a salute, and there was a jauntiness about her — even then — that was impossible to miss.

"Welcome aboard," Karen replied, then paused for a moment, looking them over.

"I'm sure Megan would appreciate it if I delivered some motivational speech about how one day I was where you are now, and since then I've risen to my current place, and that was through hard work and study and duty... but I suspect for you to get the chance to come up here today, you'd have to know that already. So no speeches, and no lectures. You earned the chance to see a living, breathing, fighting ship so we're going to show you around... give you a preview of things to come."

The smiles on the faces of these six were blindingly bright, and I suppose that makes sense — famous ship, famous crew, famous squadron, famous Commodore... you know how it goes.

"And you're not going to touch anything," Andrea Kiley added sternly, just in time to make sure no one got too comfortable.

The severity was rather misplaced, but the positive circumstances drowned out the negativity.

"Follow us," Karen said, then nodded back towards the observation lounge. There'd be plenty for them to see.

Since they'd started on the flightdeck, the first person these cadets needed to meet was none other than our fighter commander, Adrienne Thompson. It was midday when they arrived at the pilots' ready room and found her there, preparing the day's patrol briefing.

Because *Wolf* was here at Earth, and because Adrienne rightly thought it'd be a good idea to keep her pilots active, we'd offered to integrate our planes into the Heavy Squadron's standard patrol rotation. There were numerous planes around Earth, obviously, so that integration didn't mean too many missions, but when one did come along it was at least a different sort of flying than our fighter drivers were used to — a mix of atmosphere and void, and lots of civilian traffic to keep an eye on.

Today's patrol would be a lunar run for Wolf Squadron, so Adrienne was prepping the main screen displays to show the routes, the civilian ships in the area, nearby Naval ships, and all the other information a pilot would need to run a patrol in one of the densest traffic zones in the solar system.

When Karen and the cadets arrived (with Andrea lingering at the back, just inside the door) Adrienne looked up, "Ah, these the cadets?"

Nodding, Karen stopped ahead of the tour group, then stepped aside and indicated our flight commander, "Lieutenant Commander Adrienne Thompson. I'm sure you've heard her name, she's the best fighter pilot in the Empire."

There were some nods again, and it was easy for Karen to pick out the flyers among the cadets. Many future ship commanders were by this time coming through the Academy with absolutely no qualifications on Starlights, because it was increasingly being seen as superfluous — single-seat planes were a dying breed.

"Any questions for me?" Adrienne offered, leaning against the console at the front of the briefing room and folding her arms with a smile.

"Yes ma'am," Peyton Gale fearlessly opened up. "You probably hear what we hear: that the age of the single-seat fighter is coming to an end… that defensive technologies make warships too hard to hurt for small craft to really factor into combat anymore. We hear lots of game theory back and forth about that, but what do you think?"

Smart question, though Karen wasn't surprised. She had a pretty good read on this group.

With a shrug, Adrienne answered honestly: "They're probably right. At this point our job is better tied to recon than it is to combat. They'll never get rid of fighters for atmospheric defense, I don't think, but at some point they may decide to stop carrying us on warships. Time will tell."

It's funny: the debate about the fate of single-seat combat craft is one of the most contentious in armchair strategy circles, but if you ask the pilots themselves, they'll tell you pretty honestly that the plane is in decline. Why are they so candid? Because they're the ones who have to deal with the consequences if they're sent out in glamorous fighters…

with no ability to hurt their targets. Eventually stuff like that gets you killed.

Peyton was satisfied with her answer, so Evan Connors took his turn, "Ma'am, they say it's tough to keep up a stable personal life as a fighter pilot. Too many transfers, a different life tempo than ship officers. You find that?"

Adrienne paused for a moment and her smile grew a little knowing. Then she shook her head, "Nah. If you're worried about relationships, cadet, just find someone on your ship. It'll be fine."

Hard to argue with that either.

There were a couple of other questions, but pilots started arriving for the briefing so they were soon cut off. Next stop: Sensors and Communications.

Felicia Khalid had one of the most inspirational stories the cadets were going to hear that day. She was running some maintenance on *Wolf's* sensor suite when the cadets arrived at the array (the place where Jim and Bunny had once gotten into a bit of trouble on the way out to Io).

"I was a junior officer within our Sensors and Communications department," Felicia said. "Just before our posting to Jupiter, Commander Hannigan was promoted to Executive Officer from Sensors and Communications Officer, so a new department head was appointed, Commander Levec. At that time I did not believe I had the skills to fill the position, but I continued to dedicate myself to learning and perfecting my abilities. When Commander Levec was wounded at Io, there was no choice, I had to take on my current role. It was a difficult transition, and I did have to learn a lot very quickly... but my dedication and efforts had prepared me, and I have enjoyed the transition."

Modestly stated, I think — but a very useful message. You probably remember everything that Felicia had just explained... how in *The Gallant Few*, when Karen and I were looking through all those files, we'd put her aside because she simply lacked the experience.

But sure enough, she'd been ready to step in when Kate went down at Io. Some of the fastest promotions in Defense Command happen under similar circumstances, so it's really quite necessary for cadets to understand the importance of constant learning, and getting better every day.

For for all any of us knew, young Peyton Gale could be skippering a corvette before she had any business being a command officer.

"Ma'am, all of us here want to be Belt Squadron," that cadet asked as Felicia finished speaking. "As a younger member of that unit... do you think that's realistic?"

Felicia's eyebrows rose at the question. It seemed that Peyton had zeroed in on the fact that our Sensors and Communications Officer, unlike many of our senior officers, didn't carry a brash, cavalier air. So the underlying question was whether she was here by luck, or if we actually liked officers who didn't collapse buildings in their free time.

"If you are bright, and you work hard, and you come to us willing to contribute, we will welcome you. Once you are part of this family, I can assure you, the opportunities to grow will be many," Felicia said. "There is no one way to be a Belt Squadron officer."

Well said indeed.

Off to engineering.

+++

Andy Jenson had somehow typically forgotten that there was a tour coming. When he emerged from one of the service chutes, he was covered in chemicals and hardly looked the part of a senior officer... though in itself, that made an excellent point about the way a great Chief Engineer needs to work.

"Listen, it doesn't much matter what you look like," he said. "You're probably going to meet Shelby McLaws soon, and you'll be hard pressed to find one hair out of place. And she's brilliant as Helm and Navigation Officer. So you can be a mess like me, or as pristine as she is, but bottom line is if you're on this ship, you do what it takes to get your job done — and done properly."

It was impossible to argue with such sage wisdom, and it came from one of *Wolf's* unsung heroes. I know I've mentioned Andy on and off throughout the books, but the simple fact is that we spent four years fighting and flying under the most stressful of conditions, and he and his engineering crews are the reason there were no hitches.

Granted, the *Predator*-class ship is pretty reliable in general, and Andy had a couple of years of experience before the war to work out any kinks... but you've never once heard me complaining that *Wolf* could *not* do something it was designed to do, and that's because of Andy.

"Commander Jenson, where do you see the future taking you?" Megan Dunne herself weighed in with that question. She was asking if his long-term ambitions included a command of his own, or a bigger ship with newer engines, or something similar.

But Andy's answer was telling: "I'll stay on whatever ship Admiral Barron is on. And if they put him ashore, I'll follow Commodore McMaster. I've only ever been a Chief Engineer on Ken's ships, and I'm the only Chief Engineer he's ever had. Not going anywhere else."

It's hard to say thank you quite resoundingly enough for loyalty like that, but here goes: Thanks Andy. Wouldn't have it any other way.

Alicia Morgan was doing an appendectomy when the cadets stopped by the medical bay, so unfortunately they didn't get to speak with *Wolf's* resident life-saver. That would have been a good conversation, I think — it's easy for line officers to overlook the importance of the ship's surgeon, as we get all tied up in the glory of chasing bad guys and shooting at things... but as much as Andy kept *Wolf* healthy, Alicia kept everyone aboard as well as could be.

A healthy ship is as important as a happy ship, which is why we were so fortunate to have a fine medical officer like Alicia in our midst.

Bypassing that stop on the tour, then, Karen took the cadets to the security office, where Eugene Sengooba was in the process of sorting out personnel acquisitions. We needed more SF aboard *Wolf*, and though he held no commission and some of the people coming aboard did, he would still be in command. We'd get him an officer's rank as soon as possible... for now, he remained Master-At-Arms.

"Because of some timing problems at the bureau of personnel, we had to make Eugene a warrant officer instead of a commissioned one," Karen explained as the cadets arrived. "But he'll be a Lieutenant as soon as we can figure out the paperwork. He's earned it the hard way, come right up from the ranks and proved his excellence at every step."

She came through the door saying those things, so Eugene heard half of them as he came to his feet to greet the guests.

"Good day," he said with a bright smile — the warm expression that Jessica Qing had first noticed on the way out to Jupiter, when she put him in her story.

"Master-At-Arms, these cadets are interested in the workings of our ship, and of all the senior staff you've probably got the broadest view," Karen turned to him, and Eugene held up his hands with a small shrug.

"I have been in both the enlisted and officers' clubs, and due respect, the drink in the enlisted club is a bit better," he said.

Karen grinned, then looked back to the cadets. There was a very specific lesson she wanted the young people to take away from this — some young officers, graduating as teenagers and teeming with recently-acquired knowledge, get to their posts in the fleet and figure they can lord it over the long-serving non-commissioned personnel who are assigned to them.

Typically we don't recruit those types into the Belt Squadron, but it certainly happens, and if any person was clear proof that such arrogance was baseless and ridiculous, it was Eugene. Because thanks to the old rulebook we used when promoting him, he was technically the lowest-ranked person in the room — the Officer Cadets were senior to him.

Not kidding. I think it's a daft regulation, but it's one of those loopholes that came along through the old system... one of the reasons, in fact, we were getting rid of the rank of Master-At-Arms as soon as possible.

Karen wasn't going to let the lesson go by undeclared, either: "All of us standing on this side of the desk are senior in terms of rank to Eugene. But if any one of us, including myself, did not follow his orders on a security matter, it would be a mistake. You need to understand that when you get to your ships, rank is important a lot of the time, but you should never let it get in the way of collecting the best knowledge, and applying it to make the best decisions. You won't lose face for listening to an expert, no matter that person's rank."

It may sound like a bit of a platitude, but Karen's point was so vital I can't help but reinforce it. In the end, we're all in the service to defend the Empire. Whatever lets us do that better must be considered.

"I think you'll find, ma'am, cadets, that the people you lead will respect you all the more for that collaboration," Eugene added, his rich tone serious. "As officers, you must be leaders... the enlisted personnel must have confidence in your character, your intelligence and your capabilities. You don't get that respect by pretending to know something you could not possibly know... you get it by asking, listening, and then applying the special skills officers possess. Do that, and your people will follow you with great loyalty. I follow Captain Kiley, Commodore McMaster, and Admiral Barron with that loyalty, even now. And the crew of this entire ship... the entire Belt Squadron... is the same."

Karen found it as impossible as I would have to respond to that, so she awkwardly made some small talk and let Eugene answer questions about shipboard security and the shortage of SF personnel before scuttling out of the security office and heading to the bridge.

+++

Jim Hannigan had the watch, and Shelby McLaws was on duty at Helm and Navigation when the tour arrived. The cadets noticed neither officer at first, because being on the living bridge of a *Predator*-class frigate was far too immersing.

The setting itself was familiar — the Academy has bridge simulators that allow the youngsters to game just about any scenario you can think of, and physically those simulators are the same as *Wolf's* command deck… but the atmosphere was so different.

We were just sitting in orbit, going about regular ship-keeping duties, but there was still electricity for these kids. This was where they wanted to be, and what they wanted to do — they were the best and the brightest, after all.

"Does it ever get old, being up on a bridge like this one?" Peyton Gale asked the question without really thinking about it, walking towards the forward screens as she spoke.

Leaning over the Helm and Navigation consoles, Shelby spotted the fine young cadet and smiled, "It certainly does. Becomes routine, sometimes even frustrating. The magic you're feeling wears off after a few months."

Not… the answer you'd expect?

Stepping out from behind the Helm and Navigation banks, Shelby approached the cadets with her perfectly-finished walk, and not a hair out of place. All of the youngsters knew who she was because you might recall our Southern Belle had done a little moonlighting as a recruiting commercial spokesperson.

And as Andy had warned, she really was as pitch-perfect as she seemed in the commercials.

Though again, her message probably wasn't the one the cadets were expecting to hear.

"You get bored of the job?" Evan Connors asked, and Shelby shook her head.

"It's possible. You kill time any way you can… make friends, find lovers, get a hobby… but you also know that when you're here, on this bridge, you can make a difference. If you were trying to make a difference every minute of every day, you wouldn't survive too long."

Hard to disagree with that too. Granted, the Belt Squadron saw more action before the war than many other formations, and obviously you know what the war was like for us, but there were all those periods in between 'making a difference' when we could try to recover from the wear and tear of the fight. Recovery wasn't always possible — Andrea was standing proof of that — but the time was there.

And as you know, some of that time was simply boring.

"The opportunities can be whatever you make of them," Jim Hannigan came up behind the cadets, adding his own perspective to Shelby's. "I was Sensors and Communications for years, now I'm operations and may end up commanding my own ship some day. It's about working hard, and taking advantage of the opportunities that arise to learn as much as you can. And not believing you have to do it the way everyone else did it, because that's just not the case."

I know this chapter is basically turning into a motivational coaching session, but let's stop for a minute and look at the two officers talking to the cadets on the bridge.

I'd known Shelby for far less time than Jim — she'd come aboard *Friendly* after I'd left, and she'd been Andrea's protégé there, excelling and then following her to *Wolf* when

Erica Martin had transferred to *Cheetah* as XO.

She'd been groomed from a very young age to be officer material — finishing schools with advanced teaching methods, physical training, piloting skills… she was born for this job.

Jim Hannigan was different. Perhaps one day I'll write about the *Friendly* years… about when Jim came aboard as the very stereotypical Sensors and Communications Officer, with what he called the 'nerd idiom'.

Now he was our XO, with the absolute respect of everyone from fighter jocks to Special Branchers to spooks and he was engaged to an extravagantly (almost absurdly) beautiful woman, who he was devoted to and who was devoted to him.

Could he have simply allowed himself to spend his life in the pigeon hole of the 'nerd idiom'? Sure he could have. But instead, he realized that the idiom was only a construct based on some other peoples' experiences. He could be a 'nerd' with his own idiom — a communications guy who was also a fighting man, a fine leader, and Bunny's beau.

He decided to be that guy, and because he had worked hard and earned the respect of everyone aboard *Friendly*, then *Wolf* and the entire Belt Squadron, we were only too happy to watch it happen — and to help where possible.

So if the motivational speeches we were giving the cadets seem a bit much, I have to shrug, because when you look at how we all got to where we were by the end of the war, a lot of it had to do with those annoying platitudes you hear all the time.

The rest of it had to do with bald-faced luck.

Speaking of which, there was one more stop.

I had not forgotten there was a tour, I just forgot what time it was happening.

Sitting in the briefing room, I was supposed to be doing some paperwork when Karen poked her head in, but instead I was sitting back in my chair with my feet up, staring at the ceiling. I wouldn't say I was dozing, more that I was daydreaming, but either way it probably didn't look too professional as the cadets filed into the room at the table's opposite end.

"Before you go, I just wanted you all to meet Rear Admiral Ken Barron…" Karen was saying as the group came in.

In that moment I had a choice — try to correct my posture in a flash and risk falling off my chair and looking like a complete fool… or just go with the boots on the table.

"Hey…" I went with it, waving and using my feet to pivot the chair slightly. "Megan, how are you?"

Lieutenant Commander Dunne smiled in the same way she'd smiled at Karen, then replied, "Good to see you again, Ken."

As I say, long story.

"Why don't you all sit down," I turned my eyes to the cadets, then gestured to the chairs around the table. "I don't feel like standing up."

It was true, and it was cavalier, so I suppose it was in keeping with my reputation. Karen seated herself at the opposite end of the long table, with Megan at her right hand and a dour-looking Andrea at her left.

The rest of the cadets took their time choosing seats — there were more chairs than people, so it was interesting to see who sat where. Peyton Gale came all the way up the table to sit in a chair one down from my left hand — the closest any of the cadets dared to get to me (or my boots). As she settled in, I slowly and casually dragged my legs down from the table, then shifted in my seat and leaned forward, putting my elbows on the table.

"Enjoying the tour?" I addressed the question to everyone, scanning faces as the people all stared at me. By now they'd gotten comfortable with Karen, but I guess I was still a novelty.

When no one replied, Megan pitched in for her kids, "They've really enjoyed it. Very informative to be aboard a ship this famous."

That was awfully nice of her to say, and I shrugged, "Suppose so. You kids are the best at the Academy right now, otherwise Megan wouldn't have you up here. You've earned the right to get your questions answered, so by all means ask. Or we can just sit here and stare at each other for a while… whatever you like."

That was a bit of a challenge, I suppose, and I was interested to see who would take it up. Not that I'd judge these kids based on how vocal they were — I'd never been inclined to ask questions for the sake of asking them, so if they were silent because they had nothing to say, I could hardly grudge them that.

It was just always interesting to see what sort of people you were talking to, particularly when they were members of the next generation. One day these kids would be running the fleet…

"Sir, both you and Commodore McMaster seem to know Lieutenant Commander Dunne very well," Evan Connors spoke up. "Any stories from the old days you want to share?"

The only male cadet with this group was sitting right next to his instructor, and she looked at him with surprise at the forward question. It was asked in an appreciative fashion — that is to say, I think he was trying to give Karen and me the chance to boost Megan a bit… add to the lore that surrounded her at the Academy.

Normally I'm all for the boosting, but it would have been complicated this time.

"I have to dodge your question, cadet…"

"Connors, sir," Evan shifted in his seat, a little pleased that I was answering honestly.

"Don't get me wrong, one of the reasons Karen and I both are here is because of your instructor. She's got a great eye for skill, and she chose to help Defense Command by using that talent where it matters most, at the Academy. We sure as hell missed her out at the Belt, but it was the right choice she made."

Without doubt that was a creative take on what happened, but it was sufficient to bring a smile to the faces of the cadets — all of whom clearly liked their mentor. Rightly so.

"Sir…" Peyton started the next question, but stopped as my gaze shifted to her.

"Cadet?"

"Peyton Gale, sir…"

My eyebrows rose, but I didn't comment — just struck me that she had one of those names that seemed a bit too perfect, as though it was chosen by her parents specifically so it would be memorable when she was a huge celebrity success.

If that was their plan, I suppose it worked, didn't it?

"Sir, I'd love to ask about the nature of your relationship with Commodore McMaster..."

Whoa brakes. The kid had a spine...

"...but I think that might not be the best way to start my career. So instead I want to know... you're one of the greatest fleet officers in the history of Defense Command. Did you do that alone?"

The precocious little monster was asking me a question she knew I'd want to answer. And she knew I knew she was doing it. She had a knowing smile on her face. How insufferable is that? I swear, she was vying for a job right then and there.

"You threw that first line in the water pretty smoothly, cadet," my eyebrow arched as I started my answer, and she sat back in her chair, shrugging with a nervous smile. She wasn't actually nervous, she was just... well, you know that excited sort of nervous feeling you get when you're doing something of great interest, you deliver your part properly, and you're waiting to see what it'll get you? It's not quite *anticipation*, it's just eager nervousness?

Er. Maybe you don't know. Anyway, that's the expression Peyton was wearing on her face.

"So now you can tell your friends you asked, and that I smiled, and looked at Karen, and there was a moment of knowing silence. But that I didn't answer you."

Biting her bottom lip with a smile, Peyton nodded, "Thank you, sir."

"Precocious troublemaker," I muttered back. "And as for the rest, you did very well asking me a question you probably knew I'd want to answer."

Her smile grew bigger. I suppose there are questions you can raise about whether it's wise to give a youngster of Peyton Gale's age and inexperience a momentary victory in conversation with one of her elders and superiors, but I've always thought it best to recognize and congratulate talent when you see it.

Then try like hell to recruit that talent. That's how John and Greg got Karen and me, after all... and one awesome recruit out of two ain't bad.

"I bet you know what my answer is, too," I turned my eyes from Peyton to the other cadets. "The media can tell you whatever it wants to. I'm no better than anyone else in this squadron, I just happen to be the luckiest. I've had some career moves dropped into my lap, and that's helped. But most important are the people. No single officer in history has been successful alone. The whole structure of the Navy precludes that..."

I paused, looking at Karen as I built up for the familiar soapbox speech. And yes, I'm going to make you hear it (again) too.

"You've met the senior officers from this crew. You've seen that they're all the best. When you're with people like this, they make it possible for you to succeed. As the Captain of a ship, your senior officers make it possible for you to excel, to do things that people think are insane. You have to do your part, you can't just coast... but you can't parse your abilities from theirs. A crew is a team, and just because you have the rank doesn't mean you have any sort of moral superiority."

It was a message Karen had been reinforcing the whole time, of course — now the kids got to hear it again, so maybe it would stick.

"I wish more of the Belt Squadron were in orbit right now, because it's the same for a Flag Officer: you're only able to be good at what you do because of the quality of the

Captains you get to work with. They're as good as their crews, you're as good as they are… so if I know anything about logic, which I don't, that means that the only way to be *great* at anything in this Navy is to make sure you do everything possible to have the best people throughout every ship. And if they don't come in as the best, you help them become the best. Not by your standards, but by their standards. You work with them, be proud of them, and make them proud of you. And then when you ask them to fly to Jupiter with you, they say okay."

The kids around the table stared at me as I explained myself, and then I moved on to the last leg. Not to worry, the platitudes are almost done.

"If not for my closest friends and comrades… people like Wes Pellew, Charlie Peters and Karen there… I don't know what I'd be. The war's been rough on that front… Charlie's off in the Hawke Protectorate now, and Wes has his own squadron… but Karen and me, we're a team. And we help each other be good. You can't do anything… you can't really be a *great* officer, without friends. Which is why Karen's great. And why I'm not completely, embarrassingly terrible."

I smiled at the end of that soliloquy, and the cadets seemed surprised. Only Peyton looked particularly interested, but none of them got to say anything before an unexpected voice entered the conversation — to scold me.

"Get over the self-depreciation, would you? What you just described is the reason you're great. The whole fucking Navy would follow you to the center of the sun because they see how good you actually are at making excellent decisions under hellish pressure… and that you never think well of yourself for it. It actually gets irritating. Just admit how good you are. But the fact that you think everyone else is the reason for it, and that you actually believe we're all good, that's the reason you're the best. And that's a lesson for all you cadets: you get respect when you give respect, and respect will take you far in this Navy. Throw in smarts and talent, and you'll take over the fucking Empire one day."

Andrea Kiley, holy.

She was sitting back in her chair, drumming her fingers disinterestedly on the tabletop as she called me out, and though the delivery of her compliment was very backward — like I said, a scolding — and included at least two expletives, I rather entirely appreciated it.

Not that what she said I was doing was in any way unique to me…

At this point, one of my editors wrote in the margin "Stop arguing about how great you aren't and get this chapter over with!"

Ouch. Yessir.

The rest of the briefing room conversation was a little awkward, because we all got the sense we'd overstayed our welcome — Andrea wanted the tour over, and though Karen and I outranked her, *Wolf* was her ship. And remember from the last book, as Daragh discovered, she had that 'don't mess with me' Irishwoman thing going on.

When I finally came to my feet, and everyone else in the room did the same, we took turns shaking hands.

"Good luck on your finals. Don't worry too much about the marks… no one cares what you actually score. Just get to your ship postings, and do very well. Then I'll hopefully see you all again."

I guess that counts as an inspirational note to end on. Though she was nearest, I shook Peyton's hand last, and yes, what she says is true. While shaking her hand I leaned in close and said, "I don't know you, but I think you might be as bad at this as I am."

Smiling, Peyton nodded, "I hope so, sir."

Precocious and self-destructive. Obviously she'd have a career in service of the Black Sun.

The party departed, led away by Andrea, who seemed most pleased to be taking them all to the flightdeck. Karen stayed behind for just a moment, smiling at me.

"Whatever's wrong with Andrea, she sure told you off."

I shrugged, "I don't need my Flag Captain to tell me I'm full of it."

"Is that what I'm for?" Karen asked, and I smiled.

Something like that.

Karen headed out to catch up with the cadets, and I stood in the briefing room with that smile remaining rather daftly on my face for a few minutes. Then I realized that the paperwork I was supposed to be doing when the youngsters arrived still needed to be completed.

"Stupid bloody work because of damned stupid rank…" I muttered as I seated myself again.

I definitely was crap at my job, but someone was about to get a posting that he would be even more crap at…

CHAPTER FOUR

YOU MUST BE KIDDING

Admiralty House sees its share of dignitaries, as you might expect. Prime Ministers, Emperors, planetary Presidents... all sorts have come through the doors of Defense Command's Naval Headquarters, and just about all of those people have been greeted at the front counter by Gerald and Betty.

Remember, Gerald and Betty have been running that reception desk since the beginning of time. When the first mammals flopped out of the oceans onto the dry shores of land, they struggled their way up the beach and found themselves looking up at Gerald and Betty, sitting behind their counter and working away.

Obviously that's a bit of an exaggeration, but not much of one — you ask *any* Naval officer who served since 2190 and they'll probably remember these two. To call them fixtures of Admiralty House would be insufficient... I sort of think Admiralty House existed because they willed it.

They were pretty powerful people, and that makes what happened the morning before the Emperor's convoy reached Earth all the more remarkable.

Betty was sitting in her chair behind the reception counter, and then a shadow filled the main entrance. She looked up to see who it was, looked down again, and then looked up, jaw dropping in surprise.

Gerald noticed the surprise and looked up as well, just in time to see the procession of demons walk into the lobby. Now calling them demons is also an exaggeration... apparently that's my theme for the start of this chapter... but seven men in floor-length black robes, with heads shrouded by long hoods, certainly had a demony air about them.

They were either sent by the devil to harvest souls, or by that guy with the tower-mounted burning eye, to collect a piece of costume jewelry with writing on it.

Watching their entrance on the security feeds from that day, you'd swear you can hear a choir of Gregorian monks warbling in the background, maybe with some drums. And a screaming cat.

It was so genuinely spooky that the SF guards watching the lobby moved their hands to the mags on their hips, though no one drew — not yet anyway.

And it didn't get any easier when the lead robe walked up to the counter, leaned over Betty, and then raspily said: "We must see the Second Lord, on a matter of the greatest urgency."

Betty stared up into the shadows that covered the man's face, then proved herself to be as commanding as the grim reapers: "Do you have an appointment?"

"We need no appointment."

Cocking her eyebrow, Betty turned to Gerald, and the man narrowed his eyes. Neither of them liked the vibe these robed folks were giving off. They were probably wearing gauntlets, carrying cursed broadswords and riding things that looked like dragons.

All purchased at *Wired and Woven*, the store owned by former Ministry of Agriculture employee Keith Pine.

Anyway, Betty finally looked back to the robed man, then leaned forward and activated the comm to Daragh's office, "Second Lord, there are seven men in black robes waiting in the lobby for you."

There was a pause, and then Daragh's voice came on the line, "Any of them carrying a sickle?"

Before Betty could answer, the looming man raised his hand in a sharp, overdramatic motion, then slammed a metal rod — more like a scepter, I suppose — down onto the counter.

Suddenly all the melodrama made sense, and Betty found herself urgently shaking her head, "No sir. The leader is carrying what appears to be a black rod."

As she spoke, she eyed the end of the scepter-thing. Sure enough, there was a black sun on its bulbous end.

That's right. Holy shit.

Daragh was carrying his shotgun as he arrived in the lobby, and it was full of blanks in case he needed to deal with grim reapers.

Of course, he had a feeling the robes that had arrived for him were more nefarious than reapers — they weren't going to kill him, they were just going to destroy his life, his soul, and the principles that he'd long held.

And he couldn't shoot a single one of them.

As soon as they realized that Daragh had arrived, six of the seven robes formed a line, standing with about a foot between each of their shoulders as they faced him across the lobby. The scepter-bearer then seemed to float across the floor past them, soundlessly approaching the Second Lord of the Admiralty with his black rod.

"You are summoned to the palace, Lord Ryan. You are summoned and you must attend."

Daragh's shotgun was leaning back against his shoulder, and as he heard the raspy words he let it fall forward until it pointed down at the ground. He hadn't racked a shell into its chamber, but no one knew that, so as the growing audience — officers from Admiralty House who had been passing and couldn't help but stop — watched him move, most of them expected a shot.

But none came. Even us pro-elected-government types had a hard time when it came to the Gentleman Usher of the Black Rod. And if you're not up on your obscure governmental appointments, suffice to say that this guy is sort of the Sheriff of the Lords. He's the only one with the traditional authority to arrest someone like the Emperor... essentially, he's the chief enforcer for the Peers.

Daragh was a Lord, and the fact that the Venusians had ordered the Black Rod to come to Admiralty House for him... well that was bad.

It meant he was in the worst kind of trouble, and as much as every officer watching hoped that he would just open fire, or call for Special Branch, or *something*, Daragh knew better. Because after all that had just happened, if he of all people was seen to be disrespecting the Black Rod, it would reduce the calm that had finally settled over the planet.

Instead, he waved to a nearby SF guard, handed that woman his shotgun, and approached the hooded man.

"Am I going to like how this ends?" the Irishman asked.

The Rod tipped his head, which meant his cloak bent in an unsettling manner. Then he leaned forward just enough for the bottom of his pale jaw to emerge from the shadow cast by his hood.

"You have made yourself a very public face of the disgrace of the Emperor," he rasped, and Daragh sighed.

"No good deed..."

With that, the cloaks escorted Daragh out of Admiralty House. What divisions of blockheads hadn't been able to do, seven melodramatic guys in medieval monk-wear managed without a single shot. The Second Lord had been taken... and it was only going to get worse.

There was an unmistakable sense of dread as Daragh was led deep into the Government Palace. This was the same place that John, Greg and Hayley Briand had stormed back in 2231 — and as he arrived at the main building and was taken inside, our Irish Second Lord seriously wondered whether he could find an excuse to have the place leveled.

Call in a bomb threat and then have a training accident lead to a flight of Starlights cratering the buildings? Worth considering...

But such cathartic thoughts were only entertaining — they certainly weren't going to help the Irishman deal with the Black Rod. He'd need some sort of goddess to shake off the Lords' sheriff, and Karen was busy.

Ha, see what I did there.

Anyway, the seven robes and the Defense Command Admiral marched through the relatively ornate corridors of the palace's main building, making their way to parts of the place that tours did not see, and with which Daragh was quite unfamiliar. Again, not a good sign that they were going to areas unknown — if the palace had a dungeon, you'd be forgiven for thinking they were on their way to it.

But again, it was worse. So much worse.

Finally coming to a stop in a receiving room outside the Emperor's ceremonial chamber, all the robes turned to Daragh in a single creepy movement. Their faces remained buried in shadow, and the more melodramatic they acted, the more the Irishman wanted to punch one of them — just to prove they did indeed have noses that could be bloodied.

Best behavior... had to be on best behavior...

The Black Rod left the line of robes, and using his scepter he rapped on the door that led into the chamber. He knocked four times, and then four more times, then stepped back. It took a few moments — whole minutes of just standing and waiting — but then the doors creaked open, and another robe appeared from inside the chamber.

"I am the Gentleman Usher of the Black Rod, and I have under my escort Admiral the Lord Ryan of Donegal."

The shadowy robe inside the door bowed slightly, then shuffled backward to grant access. The Black Rod led the way, marching in with slow, ceremonial steps. Daragh watched him go, and then the other six escorts strung out into a semi-circle behind the Irish Lord, and started advancing towards the entrance. Without much subtlety, he was to be herded inside.

Daragh could have tried to get past them, but there was no point. Music to be faced.

Turning, the Second Lord tugged on the tails of his tunic, let out a harrumph, and advanced at a much quicker pace through the door. He had no idea what to expect inside the chamber — no idea even what the place would look like. Turned out it was fairly typical of an Emperor's chamber of that time... a truly massive space with drapery on the walls, overly ornate furniture, and elegant carpets that looked too expensive to walk on.

More important than décor, though, were the people present.

Seventy-six Lords and Ladies — every Peer who resided on Earth — was in the room, and all of them turned to stare at Daragh as he advanced through the door. Their aristocratic glares possessed a great weight, and our Irishman felt rather like he was walking face-first into a hurricane as his eyes swept across them.

Lord Somerset was the highest ranking among these Peers, and as Daragh came to a stop before the mighty audience, his Lordship stepped away from his fellows. Clad in his usual black suit with tails, Somerset looked severe as he considered the Irishman, "Thank you for joining us, Lord Ryan."

Somerset, you probably know, was English — and of all the Lords who reside on Earth, he's the one I was most familiar with. He had spent time as an elected Senator for the Empire Party in his younger years, and he remained active in planetary government. Unlike some of the Venusian Lords, he was a man well acquainted with the realities of Earth, and the entire Empire.

The wide respect he enjoyed meant he was probably the best-positioned Peer in the room to sentence Daragh.

"When the Black Rod shows up at your office, you do what he says. So probably better not to thank me," the Irishman folded his arms and scowled. "If you want your title back, you can have it. But if you try anything further, you're not going to have much luck. I'm not doing time in prison."

Somerset approached Daragh slowly at those words, shaking his head, "You will accept the ruling of your fellow Lords, Lord Ryan. We have discussed this at great length. You were the spokesperson responsible for changing perceptions of the throne in these last weeks. Luther Gregory was, I think we all agree, excessive. Some of us thoroughly disagree with his actions, and we are all aware that public opinion has turned quite sharply against both him, and the throne."

Daragh was half-tempted to quip something snarky — 'you bet it has' — but even his brashness, which had once allowed him to come into Admiralty House shooting, was muted in this company.

The Lords have a fantastic ability to look incredibly disapproving. It gets to you.

"The Lords on Venus... Tam in particular... have decided that the only way we can hope to preserve the reputation of the sovereign is to make an example," Somerset continued, his words becoming somewhat clipped. It seemed as though he didn't exactly like what he was saying — and he certainly didn't like Tam. But then, how could anyone? Such a bastard.

"His notion about what to do with you… has been approved by vote among the Lords of Venus. The Lords here on Earth have also voted, and by simple majority, the decision has been made."

Again, Daragh could have made some crack about the irony of a vote by unelected Peers deciding his fate as a man who'd never wanted to be a Lord in the first place. Instead, he was a little less acerbic: "I vote against whatever Tam suggested."

Somerset tilted his head and narrowed his eyes, "Your position will be noted, Lord Ryan. But it is too little, and too late. As a result of the actions you took during the recent crisis, and the reputation you cultivated in the popular consciousness during the war, you have become a symbol of everything the Lords were not intended to be. Many have said you've abused the title, disrespected it with your lack of effort in the presentation of yourself. Your actions against the Emperor have proven that there is a rift within the Peerage, and have as much as proven to the common people that Luther Gregory is a criminal. You have, in short, jeopardized everything we have stood for since Luther Gordon the Great created our new nobility."

Feel free to applaud.

"Now you must undo that damage."

Stop applauding.

"By a majority vote, and under the power invested in the Peerage under the Articles of Empire, the Lords of the Black Sun do now name you Emperor of Earth, Venus, the Belt Colonies, and all possessions of Empire as constituted by the government of the Black Sun."

Fucking scream. Scream real loud.

That's what Daragh wanted to do.

You know how sometimes it can take a few moments for devastating news to sink in? Not this time. Those words hit Daragh immediately, and he nearly fell over and vomited on himself.

The entire world started to fall away beneath his feet, then spiraled off into the distance. His eyes were open and he was staring at Somerset, but he couldn't see anything. It was the worst sort of sentence he could imagine for his crimes… the last revenge of a bunch of bastards (his words) who he had saved one time too many during the old days at the Forge.

How in the Holy Jesus Hell (him again) could anyone think it was a good idea for the most negligent Lord to become Emperor?

It was madness.

"You can't… do that…" he tried to protest, even though he knew he was wrong. Like I've been saying, the Lords could choose any Emperor they wanted from among the ranks of the Peerage… and Daragh was a Lord…

"We can do it, and we have," Somerset said sharply.

Of course they had, because this was the only compromise that would protect the throne — the only way to really satisfy public opinion without cutting open the Articles of Empire.

In other words, it was good politics.

Listen, whatever you say about the Lords — and there's a lot to say about some of them — they understand politics. They may play the game at arms length, and with only a vague notion of the wants and wills of the 'common' people, but they are schooled in the art of manipulation and political strategy from young ages, both through classroom lessons and experience.

One of the reasons Somerset himself had been such an effective politician was simply because he came from a family that *knew* politics, and that had been involved in it even before the beginning of the Empire. Experience matters, and in this case, it was seriously guiding strategy.

The throne was in peril — Luther Gregory's failed coup was making a lot of people ask if the sovereign, and by extension the Lords, could be trusted. But most of those questions were being asked because of a broadcast made by a Lord — albeit a reluctant Naval one — and that meant the answer was simple.

Daragh was not well-liked by the Peers, and there was no question that a batshit insane Irishman could make for a terrible Emperor (his words again, though undoubtedly the Lords agreed). But better a maniac who was loved by the people, than some stuffy conservative they didn't like or trust.

Give the throne to the Irishman for at least five years, let him make whatever mess while restoring the people's confidence in the title 'Emperor', and then Tam or any of the others could have a crack at it. Somerset himself was too old, but his son was coming up soon, and shared his father's talent.

One other element factored into the decision: Defense Command had been largely responsible for the defeat of Luther Gregory. While you know that we wouldn't have taken any punitive action against any Emperor unless he was pulling shenanigans like the one he replaced, the Lords were less confident, so they figured picking Daragh would bring us on side.

They may have got that backwards, because I've always seen this move as bringing the throne over to Defense Command's side... and the government's side for that matter — Daragh was a choice that would make Pope and Craig B. Macdonald happy. Either way, the change would keep us all from dragging out the guillotine and ending the Lords' reign.

And then there was the question of timing. I wish Somerset could have explained this to Daragh so I could switch back to dialogue, but he and everyone else in the room had started bowing to their new Emperor — awfully inconvenient for our narrative.

So here's my take: why elevate Daragh to the throne the day before Luther Gregory arrived? There was no precedent in the history of the Empire for the problems the latter man had caused, and though it wasn't clear whether he'd face criminal prosecution, some sort of Parliamentary inquiry, or even a Lords' Tribunal, the notion of having the current Emperor subject to any such investigation was quite dangerous.

That in mind, they'd stripped him of the title before he could get in front of the cameras —he'd have to face the heat as Lord Gregory. And though it was less common, Lords were still prosecuted in a variety of ways... nothing revolutionary about that.

Daragh being the Emperor could even add to the legitimacy of whatever justice was handed out, thus beginning the rehabilitation of the throne's reputation.

So you see, it really was an elegant solution to many of the problems the Imperial throne faced in those dark days.

Of course there would be questions. Some people thought that Daragh actually orchestrated events to have Luther Gregory thrown out, and himself installed... but that's bullshit.

Because when Daragh finally yelled loud enough for the Lords to stop bowing, and then staggered out of the ceremonial chamber chased by a chorus of "Blessings Upon the Emperor", he found the nearest plant and vomited into its pot.

He then insisted that the Black Rod take him out of the palace, and find him a bottle of alcohol. There was no way he was doing this sober.

So much for his quiet retirement, and his hatred of politics. Emperor Daragh Ryan now led the Empire... and as much as I sympathize with him, I have to admit, I think we were vastly better off because of it.

Even though he was batshit insane.

CHAPTER FIVE
OTHER LORDS AT LAST

While the Empire was in the process of changing its head of state, another rather important leadership transition was just beginning on the home rock of our most important ally. After delays, distractions, and misdirections about the fate of Lord Ian Hawke, the time had come for the Protectorate to learn the truth about who was in charge, and for any fears or concerns about the new regime to be put to rest.

The timing in this wasn't just coincidental; the instability caused on Earth by Luther Gregory's coup attempt had hardly been missed in the press of the Hawke Protectorate, and while you might think it would make the people of those asteroids more concerned about a change in their own government, it actually provided a useful juxtaposition — a demonstration of how bad a transition *could* be.

After all the planning and risk that had been taken to make sure there would be confidence in the new leadership, there'd be no hint of such danger in the handover at Hawke. Hopefully the people, and particularly the Hawke nobles, would appreciate how fortunate they were.

And if they didn't, they'd have to contend with a leader who was returning to them in a different form than they'd ever seen before. No more playing at being a ditsy courtesan. No more sock puppets. No more anything easy, because as she arrived in the court chambers for the first time since her departure in 2233, Lady Lia Hawke was visibly covered in scars.

Of course it had been no secret that Lia had been badly wounded during the Fleet Clash, but the scars were something of a surprise to the Hawke Lords and Ladies — all of whom had assumed Lia would have paid whatever the doctors required to hide the marks of her injuries.

Not so. Instead, my 'kid sister' wore a sleeveless and backless court gown that, prior to her deployment, would probably have been considered scandalous for the amount of bare skin it showed. Now it was simply shocking for the marks it displayed.

None of Lia's scars were particularly deep or wide — indeed, they all look rather fine — but the effect of seeing literally dozens of them all over her arms and back was quieting.

And with the visible scars came a new air. As she marched through the assembled courtiers and courtesans in the Hawke One throne room, Lia's expression was purposefully grave. She had seen war, had been marked by it, and the new lines around the corners of her eyes seemed to add decades to her age. She was making no attempt to hide the signs of her brutal experience.

In fact, she was doing just about everything she could to make it as obvious as possible. The Lords and Ladies had to believe in her new hardness — even fear her a little — and the regular citizens had to believe she had the experience and seasoning necessary to take over from her father.

She'd always had that, but now there was proof. Lots of it.

So she marched through the court chamber, listening to the hushed words being whispered between the nobles, and finally arrived at the foot of the throne that her father had once occupied. It was hers now, and there was no point pretending otherwise. Climbing the stairs, she turned to face the Peers of the realm, then lowered herself into the seat.

There were more gasps, because the secret of her father's death had been maintained until this moment — for her to sit on that throne was either an immense breach of protocol, or a sign of grave news.

"I return from war a different woman," Lia announced in a sharp tone. "I return to you alive, but orphaned."

More gasps, followed by pin-drop silence.

"All of you knew my father was ill. He died last night, and I was fortunate to be with him when he passed. Out of his love for me, he held on despite his poor health until the moment I returned, and then all was lost."

She paused for a breath — just a few seconds — and then continued with as much confidence as she could pour into her words, "I am Lia Hawke, Lady Protector of Hawke. This is my throne now, and I will serve you, noble Lords and Ladies, and the people of our asteroids with alacrity, wisdom, determination, and unwavering strength."

There could be no hint of doubt in any of her words — no regret, no mourning. There were Lords and Ladies in the room who might, if they sensed any cracks in her certainty, petition for more influence. Wasn't going to happen; Lia had more than psyched herself up for this. Maybe even too much...

"I trust you will all, at this moment, acclaim your loyalty to this throne, to my late father, and to myself," her tone remained icy, her stare over the room like steel.

There was another pause before Lord Aune stepped forward.

"I pledge loyalty to the Hawke throne, my Lady, and to she who sits upon it."

Aune was one of the loyalists, so it was no surprise that he was the first to say the words. Once he did, every Peer in the room was obliged to follow the pattern — whether they might have sensed any opportunities for themselves or not, to fail to follow courtly procedure at this moment would have been unwise...

And considering Lia's mood, possibly even dangerous.

For almost twenty minutes, the Lords and Ladies of the Hawke court announced their support of Lia. This might seem too easy, but trust me, the first declarations were only a minor detail. So much work was ahead for her... egos to be contained, people who'd had influence with Ian put in their place, new advisors sought...

And, of course, they had to make the news of Ian Hawke's death public, and go through motions of putting him to final rest. I hated that man in a lot of ways, and deservedly so, but he'd done enough right to deserve a proper sendoff. Lia would make certain he had one.

Clearly there was much to do, but the first piece of business after the initial loyalty check was something entirely different.

Something I've been looking forward to, I must admit.

Charlie Peters was a Special Branch Major (soon to be Colonel), and he'd recently done some moonlighting as a detective. If not for him, we wouldn't have learned about Egesta, and the Empire might have been under different ownership. In every way you can measure, he was an exceptional Defense Command officer, and to this day he remains my best friend, even though we see each other only rarely.

At this moment, Charlie was standing in the back corner of the court chamber, wearing some court dress that had been tailored for him in such a way that it looked like a dress uniform. He'd slipped silently into the chamber, taking advantage of the distraction Lia caused when she arrived in her bare-armed, bare-backed finery, and he'd remained unnoticed as the nobles pledged themselves to the throne.

Observing from his vantage point, he'd noted at least six people he was fairly certain didn't like Lia, or the fact that she was now in charge, so he made a point to check on them more in the future. For now, he was on the hook for something else.

"As my first act as Protector of Hawke, I will name a new Lord to this court. This man is a hero of the Earth Empire, and a champion of virtue, wisdom and idealism. He will also serve as my consort, ruling alongside me as a favored Lord."

Charlie was by this time pretty numb to the whole notion that he was being made a Lord. He hadn't really liked the idea at first, but he understood it was necessary in order for he and Lia to formalize their relationship... so it was a price he was gladly willing to pay.

Still, a lot of the people he was now in the room with — another dozen of whom seemed not to like Lia's announcement — weren't exactly the sort he wanted to associate himself with. He'd get used to it, of course, and he looked forward to the chance to build a whole new set of people skills in dealing with them...

But the bottom line was he'd be with Lia, all the time and officially, and that was worth being stuck with a title.

"Major Charles Peters, please present yourself to the nobles of this court," Lia called for him, and he moved forward from his quiet corner with steady strides.

More gasps of surprise. Everyone had heard the rumors about Charlie and Lia being together at the hospital at Venus — that was the whole point of them starting the rumors, after all — but the thought that she'd just go ahead and make him a Lord because they'd convalesced together was too much for some.

Perhaps that skepticism is understandable, but I'll be the first to admit that I'm hugely prejudiced and think anyone who complained about Charlie being made a Lord should be serving burgers in hell.

Making his way to the foot of the throne, Charlie stopped and looked up at Lia. She was a master at controlling all outward signs of her mood, but that's not necessarily why she wasn't smiling, even on the inside. Certainly, she loved Charlie... but this was business, the business of government, and she was forcing herself to feel nothing as she went through the motions. Not necessarily a healthy approach, but a responsible one.

Perhaps because of that genuine emotional isolation, the chill in her words led many of the assembled nobles to wonder whether she actually cared for Charlie at all — or whether he was, in fact, a mere plant from the Earth Empire, being sent as a pathfinder who would lead the way to Imperial annexation.

Sure, that sounds like him all over...

Like I said, lots of things that would have to be sorted out in the months ahead.

For now, there was just some pageantry: "Major Peters, as the Protector of Hawke I exercise my right to elevate you to noble status. Join us as Lord Peters."

It was just that simple. Charlie's very lucky I wasn't there, because I would have started hooting and hollering at this point. Instead the only noise that greeted his being made a Hawke noble was some polite applause — and there wasn't much of that.

"Thank you, my Lady," was his answer, and then Lia stood and held out a hand towards him. Taking it, Charlie stepped up the stairs to the throne platform, then turned to face the crowd of nobles. "My history is known, I come here to serve. I look forward to the chance to work with you all."

That was very nice of him to say, though he knew it wouldn't soothe the nerves of any of the Lords and Ladies in the room who were irked by the whole situation. That wasn't all of them — not even half were displeased — but enough were looking at these rapid changes with surprise and discomfort that...

Well, if I say 'there was a lot of work ahead' one more time, I think the chapter will implode. You understand, I know.

What I always find interesting about Charlie's elevation to the Peerage is how simple it was. Lia had decided that if they were going to take command in Ian's absence, she really needed to just come in and make her mark — trying to be too diplomatic or cautious would, as I mentioned, make others think they had a chance to exert influence on her.

So they'd done everything in one icy fell swoop: Lia to the throne, and Charlie behind it. And because of Lia's new image, and Charlie's very well-established reputation (these Hawke nobles had no idea that he wasn't the sort to kill casually), there were natural deterrents to anyone trying to interrupt their plans.

If only it were so easy for Daragh... because being named was just the first step for the Irishman.

The first step of many...

CHAPTER SIX

ANNOUNCEMENT

The press conference was held on the Admiralty House lawn, which meant that everyone assumed it would involve Daragh explaining how we were going to start releasing reservist crews, since their wartime service was now over. That was newsworthy enough to get the majority of the Capital Island press corps to show up, but they didn't seem too excited when they arrived.

The Black Rod's visit to Admiralty House the day before had gone completely unreported… people whisper about the appearance of the robes, but they never seem to call reporters. I find that interesting…

Anyway, Daragh was obviously going to give the press something to talk about.

This was the morning after his appointment, and he was very hung over, though being Irish and a Forge-fought Naval officer, he was able to cover that discomfort pretty well. Standing in his office… his former office now… he watched the reporters assemble, slowly shaking his head the whole time. The Black Rod was standing behind him, intent on keeping him from making a run for it.

"I'm going to need a staff," the Irishman said eventually. "After this conference, I'm going to be on the fucking hook. I need a real fucking staff…"

The Rod was not accustomed to Lords who lacked refinement in quite the way that Daragh did, and now the man leaned forward enough for his chin to emerge from beneath the shadow cast by his hood.

"Tell us who, and we will summon them, Your Highness."

It sounded like the grim reaper was offering to harvest some souls for the Second Lord. Former Second Lord. And as Daragh turned and looked at the robed figure, the image pretty much backed up the sound. But then, as he thought of exactly what he was asking, the whole situation matched up equally well for the Irishman.

Daragh would need good people with him, or the whole 'being Emperor' thing would end in quite a mess. But he couldn't trust any of the people like Hodson, the coup-happy Governor General… no one who had been trained to serve the Emperor by the noble finishing schools could be relied upon.

He'd need good talent, and he'd need it from outside the system. And that meant sucking people who didn't deserve to be absorbed in the affairs of the throne right into the abyss along with him.

Distasteful.

Taking a breath, Daragh considered some names, then paused and looked back at the Black Rod, "You have to keep your hood up all the time?"

There was a long pause, and then the Black Rod answered uncomfortably, "Since the beginning of our Empire, the Black Rod has not shown his face in public, Your Eminence."

Daragh frowned, then tilted his head, "What if I told you to?"

"I..." the Black Rod stopped, then continued in a half-defeated tone. "I serve the throne, Your Highness."

Aha. Smiling, Daragh nodded, "Right, then down with the hood. And what's your actual name, Black Rod."

There was a very uncomfortable moment of silence, and then the Rod reached up and pulled the hood back. Daragh was hoping for something dramatic — the guy to look like a ghost, or a demon — but he was just a middle-aged fellow, with pale skin. Obviously he never got much sun.

He didn't say anything, so Daragh took a step towards him, "Right, Rod, what's your name. And if you tell me it's Rod Black, I'll have a problem with that."

"Obediah Metcalf Dundurn O'Shaughnessy, Your Eminence."

Holy name. Were it me, I'd have cracked a joke about this fellow's parents accidentally buying a Martian baby-naming book, but Daragh seized on something far, far more important.

"O'Shaughnessy? You're Irish?"

"In name, Your Highness. Though I do not know where my lineage lies..."

"You're Irish!" Daragh clapped his hands with a laugh. "Alright then. I'll work with that. Irish. Obee, you are a weird demon-like man, but we're going to work together. And the first thing you're going to do is find me two people who are going to hate me forever."

Karen and I had no idea why we'd been asked to come down from *Wolf* for the press conference — we'd had nothing to do with any Admiralty decisions of late, and if it was just a courtesy (or worse, an attempt to get more media attention), we weren't all that enthusiastic. But Ronald Davis called Felicia and asked, and she asked us, and we said yes...

And indeed, it really did happen that casually. Remember, all we were doing at this point was interfering with law enforcement and giving tours to cadets... a run down to Capital Island (followed by dinner with my parents — my dad was cooking) would be a fine change of pace.

As we landed on the Admiralty field and climbed down from our planes, neither Karen nor I had any idea of what was about to happen. We were behind Admiralty House, so there were no cameras around, and we were chattering about something or the other...

We both fell silent when a guy in a robe marched out the back door of the building... and then another robed guy followed him.

For a moment, we both stared at the pair. They moved across the path from the door like reapers, and then disappeared into the woods behind the building, clearly not wanting to be seen by anyone...

"Were they...?" Karen's question died midway, and she looked at me.

I was frowning, and then I shook my head slowly, "Couldn't be. Why would they be here?"

It was a good question. Another good question would be why anyone seeking to leave Admiralty House without being noticed would do so wearing big cryptic robes, but hey, I'm not here to judge.

Either way, both Karen and I really began to wonder why exactly we'd been called down, and we wasted no time hurrying to the back door and barging our way into Admiralty House. Hurrying up the corridor, Karen in the lead, we peeked in through any open office doors we passed, wondering if anything was amiss.

Everyone we saw seemed edgy, but there weren't any grim reapers wandering around either.

Reaching the lobby, we both slowed and then stopped beside the counter where Gerald and Betty were attending their normal daily duties.

"What's going on... thought we saw a couple of black robes hurrying out the back?" I leaned over the counter and whispered that question to Gerald.

Without looking up from his screen, the perennial administrative master of Admiralty House shook his head slightly, "Black Rod. We're thinking the Second Lord may have been made Emperor."

Good thing I wasn't trying to drink something when I heard that — I would have spit it all over Gerald's counter, like you see in the over-the-top comedy movies.

Karen was beside me immediately, leaning over the counter as well, "Are you serious?"

"Am I ever not serious?" Gerald's tone remained flat.

"There was that time in 2226," Betty reminded from her post.

Gerald still didn't move his eyes from his screen, "That wasn't by choice."

I just stared at him for a second, then looked at Karen. She was wide-eyed, as I think she had every right to be, and then before we could say anything her gaze drifted over my shoulder and she tugged my sleeve.

Turning, I watched Daragh coming down the hall from his office... a frustrated-looking guy in a black suit (but interestingly, no robe) following.

As the Irish Lord spotted Karen and me, he waved us over, "You two, good. Come watch me throw away my life."

"As long as you don't throw ours with it," Karen quipped back instantly, and a bitter laugh escaped our Second Lord. Former Second Lord.

"You're both bastards, but you've done nothing wrong enough for me to sentence you to such a fate."

That statement was more of a relief than I think I should admit. But, convinced that we weren't about to be somehow dragooned onto the Emperor's staff, Karen and I followed Daragh and his escort — the Black Rod without his ceremonial gear, we later discovered — out the front door.

Keith Pine was working on some chain mail in the back room at *Wired and Woven* when the door opened. One of his team, Seanna, was on the counter, so Keith thought nothing of the visitor. It was mid-morning on a weekday — not typically a high-traffic time for the store — but whatever the person wanted, Seanna would help find it...

Or not. Keith had the hearing skills one acquires when one works for the Ministry of Agriculture, and as a result he could detect some uncertainty in Seanna's voice as she asked the person what he was looking for.

He was looking for Keith. The words were garbled by the wall that separated the storage room from the rest of the store, but our shopkeeper was used to making out garbled words.

So someone was here looking for him, and that person was unsettling enough for Seanna — who was a formidable young woman — to be uneasy.

Laying the chain mail down on the table beside him, Keith reached to the back of his pants, confirming that his MAG-2 was tucked in the waistband. Since the coup, he'd been keeping the weapon with him, just in case.

He then turned to face the doorway that led from the back room to the front counter. Whoever was coming, the Ministry of Agriculture vet was going to get a good look before he decided what to do... or how many times to fire.

Listening carefully, he heard Seanna's footsteps approaching the entrance... hurried steps, but definitely hers — she wasn't being dragged in any way. Heavier, slower footsteps were following... the guy (or very heavily built gal) might have a gun on Seanna, but didn't have her in hand.

Waiting for another second, Keith laid his right hand on the grip of his mag, then timed his breaths...

Seanna came through the door, looking anxious, then stood aside — good move on her part, Keith would have a clear field of fire.

Then came the intruder, and as soon as Keith saw the black robe his hand came away from his mag, and he started shaking his head.

"Keith Pine," the robe said his name grimly... like a reaper, perhaps.

"Let me guess, Daragh Ryan is going to be Emperor, and he told you to come fetch me?" the shop owner replied.

If the robe had allowed his face to be seen, Keith was sure he'd look as surprised as Seanna did — neither of them knew anything about the time Keith had spent working for the Ministry of Agriculture at the Forge. It wasn't something he often talked about.

"I told Daragh this would happen. He didn't listen, but I warned him..." Keith shook his head, then let out a sigh. "Alright then. Take me to your... our... leader."

"Anyone know what this press conference is about?" Schwartz T. Babcock swept into the PMO meeting room with that question, but he was greeted only by headshakes and some looks of confusion.

"Ron Davis just called me and told me to get everyone watching," T.J. Gregg, the Press Secretary, replied as Schwartz arrived in front of the screen that was glowing with a live news feed from Admiralty House.

The Prime Minister's Chief of Staff found an empty chair and settled himself down into it, steepling his fingers as he did so. His day had been complicated enough already, so he hoped this was just something routine — and he had every reason to expect it would be. Daragh had enough sense not to do anything politically sensitive without first consulting the Prime Minister's Office... but in the political game, it was rarely wise to assume, even when friends were involved.

"We're still waiting for Lord Ryan..." the news network's announcer said from the screen, and Schwartz took the time to study the setup of the conference. Nothing particularly special, just the usual podium in the same old place in front of the building.

Not that the setup would be a likely indicator of what was to be announced... it just gave Schwartz something to contemplate while he waited.

If this was going to be some straightforward piece of news, why didn't Ronald Davis actually tell T.J. what was happening in advance? What could be so secret that PMO couldn't know about it, but could then be explained to the world at a standard press conference? Maybe a retirement?

Hard to say. It was weird, though — very weird.

"This better not be some redeployment announcement," Tony Kiebler grumbled from a chair further back in the room. "I have a speech to write."

Tony was writing the PM's speech about the success of the Mars Convention, and though it was going well, he was largely grumpy — it was just his nature.

Before anyone had the chance to echo his complaint, or to counter it, Daragh appeared in the shot, followed by some dour-looking guy in a black suit, carrying a black stick, and Ken Barron and Karen McMaster... er, me and Karen. Sorry, I'm writing from Schwartz's perspective, but that sounded odd.

Anyway, Schwartz leaned forward with a frown as he looked at the podium party... the DC personnel were no particular surprise, but the guy with the stick... who was that?

"If they're just going to kiss again, I'm going back to my office," Tony griped, but Schwartz held up his hand.

"Hang on. Who's that... the black suit and rod..."

His words trailed off as his powerfully precocious brain went to work on the question. An answer didn't take long, but before he could say anything, someone gasped.

"I come for Schwartz T. Babcock," the voice was that of a grim reaper, and the robe was too. I know, I'm probably pounding that point to death by now, but seriously, it says something about the throne — at least the throne as it was — that the guys going around to recruit for it did a great impression of DEATH.

Coming to his feet, Schwartz turned to the meeting room door and found the looming robe there, "You represent the Black Rod... who is there on screen with the Second Lord... who... no. No way."

The robe said nothing, so Schwartz turned back to the screen, just in time for Daragh to reach the podium.

Then, in contravention to just about any guide to press conference rules you might care to cite, he started talking before reporters could even open their notebooks.

"You might notice that the Gentleman Usher of the Black Rod is standing behind me," the Irishman said. "The Lords just elected me Emperor. I voted against it, but now I'm stuck. So everyone bow, I'm you're Emperor."

"Oh. My. God."

"What the..."

Schwartz tuned out the exclamations of his staff and turned back to the robe at the door, "You're here for me?"

The robe bowed slightly in a nod, and the Chief of Staff to the Prime Minister realized in that moment that he was about to resign from his job.

You can't say no to the Emperor, meaning the House of Commons was about to lose its political wonderkid... at least for a little while.

◆◆◆

Back on the lawn outside Admiralty House, Karen and I felt about as awkward as you can. It was even more awkward than when we'd kissed on the very same spot.

To break the tension, I was even considering doing it again. For the sake of the reporters and all.

But there wasn't really any need to, because after the shocked hush and the confused looks between reporters, Daragh unleashed hell: "I'll take your questions now… Jessica."

Jessica Qing got the first question, and she asked what I think everyone who was watching Daragh in this moment was thinking: "Is this a joke?"

Daragh stared at her for a second, laughed and shook his head, "Jessica, you have no idea how much I wish it was."

Hard to put it any better than that.

CHAPTER SEVEN
PROMETHEUS

No one in the Empire was really ready for the news of Daragh's ascent to the throne. This wasn't just because people wouldn't have expected the Lords to choose him — though if the bookmakers were offering odds, the quickest way to become a trillionaire would have been to put a dollar down beside his name — it was mostly because no one expected the Lords to act so quickly.

Again I get to plug the title of the book, and say rapid action was required to make sure the Articles of Empire stayed out of the crossfire. The holder of the throne would not be charged with anything, but would in fact be the one in position to charge Lord Luther Gregory with whatever offenses were needed... if it even came to that.

So it was practical, but it was still a surprise — for the returning politicians and officers as much as it had been for the people on Earth.

John Fiora had transferred back to *Bonaventure* and was on the bridge during the last comm check before the squadron reached Earth, and he watched as the feed from the press conference was piped up onto one of the flagship's massive screens by Sensors and Communications Officer Jorge Allende.

Captain Lennox Williams was standing beside our elite First Lord when Daragh made his brief statement — announcing that he was Emperor — and the two men looked at each other with jaws hanging slack.

Everyone on the bridge... and it's a big bridge... stared at the Irish Lord on the screen, and then finally John managed to say: "Well... That's more paperwork for me."

It certainly was.

Douglas Pope and Craig B. Macdonald were in a briefing room with a dozen staffers, trying to catch up on the details PMO had sent them about the status of government after the attempted coup. Hundreds of MPs would need to be loyalty-checked by the party whip, and bureaucrats from all over the government had to be examined as well.

Anyone who'd been considered a friend of the Empire Party, and who had sided with Olivia Bennington, was probably going to need to find a new career. The PM wasn't going to have these people executed or anything so drastic, he was just going to remove them from his government, since they'd clearly had no interest in serving anyone but themselves and their faction leader.

Alright, that probably sounds a bit biased, but what do you expect, it's me.

While working away on these problems, the politicos in the room had turned off their wallscreen to prevent any distractions. They were awfully surprised, then, when *Ark Royal's* bridge crew overrode the controls on the display and started piping the press conference right into the room.

Everyone stopped and stared, and again jaws went slack.

A new Emperor, just like that...

"I suppose this makes our lives simpler," Pope said quietly after a moment. "They didn't want to have a fight on their hands, so they appointed the one person we couldn't complain about."

"Whether he's right for it or not," Craig agreed, and his comment, perhaps criticism, was quite fair. Obviously it's nothing that Daragh didn't himself feel.

Unlike most of us, who just absorbed the news with shock and went slightly numb, the two Ministers in the room then listened to Daragh handling the press corps questions. He did badly by normal political standards — he didn't sound 'on message' at all — but that was probably a good thing. The people would undoubtedly welcome a leader who spoke plainly to them... and quite selfishly, Pope would prefer working with the Irishman.

A friend on the throne... what a concept.

Craig B. Macdonald was less optimistic: "There'll be no living with that Irish bastard now. I bet he'll actually get himself those ponies."

Pope didn't say anything. He didn't really have to.

Obviously there was much shock and concern after the press conference, but while a lot of people doubted whether Daragh was really the right man to be Emperor, and others felt terribly sorry for him being saddled with such a miserable job, most people had hope.

Whatever his faults, Daragh was a good man — and Somerset and Tam and the rest of the Lords had a point when they said he was the face of Luther Gregory's downfall. Remember the broadcast he'd pre-recorded... the one Karen and I had convinced Hodson to show the world.

Accompanying those shocking pictures had been Daragh's face and voice... he had been the one who so genuinely conveyed the shock, sadness and pain we all felt about Egesta, and about the coup. While we could doubt his credentials, few could question that his heart was in the right place. That made this a pleasant sort of shock.

But there was one person in particular for whom news of Daragh's ascent to the throne was anything but pleasant... you'd probably be fair in calling it a deep personal insult. And for that person, the news was only set to make an already-terrible day positively devastating.

Luther Gregory III was preparing for his return to Earth — for the spectacle he knew he would become. *Ark Royal* and the convoy were due to arrive in orbit that afternoon, so much of the morning was to have been spent in solitude, with the Emperor (he didn't know he was 'former' yet) preparing himself.

During this spell of isolation there was a knock at the door of his personal chamber, and he had to actually get up and get it himself (his blockhead guards were all confined to quarters).

When he opened the hatch, he found Christian Mikaelsen there... our elite Commodore had decided that he best deliver the news of Daragh's ascent to the throne in person. For all that Luther Gregory had done wrong, Mik still gave the former Emperor respect out of courtesy.

Mik's a real gentleman that way... not sure I'd have been so enlightened. Luther Gregory probably never realized how fortunate he was on that front.

"Sorry to interrupt, Lord Gregory, but there's news."

The fact that Mik called Luther 'Lord' was the first hint, though the man lacked enough context to realize the complete significance of that choice.

"When do we reach orbit of Earth, Commodore Mikaelsen?" the Lord asked grimly, turning away from the door and marching back into his personal sanctum.

Mik followed slowly, "About four hours. We just made our last comm check with Admiralty House before we arrive. Have some news about the throne."

As he said that, Mik came to a stop and clasped his hands together in front of him — the way he would if he was in a setting that required respectful mourning. That wasn't a conscious decision, but reflecting back on it he found his choice of posture interesting.

The mention of the throne forced Luther Gregory to turn, his head low but his eyes finding Mik's, "The Lords... they didn't choose to recall me without hearing my testimony...?"

The way he phrased that question pretty much demonstrated that he'd expected no less, but hoped against it. The man wanted the right to speak in his own defense, and I suppose I am a bit sympathetic. A bit. Sort of.

But he didn't have that chance, and as he read as much from Mik's stoic expression, he turned away with some dramatic flourish, "How could they defy centuries of tradition?"

Mik tilted his head and narrowed his eyes slightly, "They might have asked the same question about you."

Lord Gregory froze at those words, then looked back over his shoulder with as much menace as he could summon, "You cannot speak for the Lords, Commodore."

Even had he still been Emperor, Luther's words wouldn't have fazed Mik at all. His return salvo was, as far as I'm concerned, a brilliant and reasonable counter: "You're right, Lord Luther, I can't speak for your Peers. But I can see this situation rationally, and I think you can too. You made your attempt, and you failed. It doesn't matter whether someone thinks you were right to try or not... by doing what you did, and failing to complete what you set out to do, you've put the throne and the entire nobility at risk. They had no choice but to make you wear this."

Luther turned around completely and stared at Mik as the Commodore delivered those words, then replied with a question, "Do you think I had the right, Christian?"

Mik stared at Luther and said nothing.

"Do you?" the Lord took a few steps forward, but Mik stood unmoving.

As I've said before, the Belt-born Commodore was no anti-Emperor partisan, the way I clearly was. He didn't assume the man to be inherently evil, or our position to be intrinsically right, just because it was ours. Attempting to influence the government was not really outside the Emperor's purview either — it was politics, as distasteful as it might be. But if the attempted coup had happened as it had been reported, then Mik couldn't tolerate it.

Still, he'd wait to see the evidence, and talk to the participants, and then he'd decide. That's the sort of fellow he is... and that's one of the reasons he's so respected in the position he holds to this day.

"A new Emperor has ascended to the throne," *Ark Royal's* Commodore finally broke the silence, and though he'd clearly evaded the question, what he said was more than enough to derail Luther's train of thought.

The Lord stood there, silent again, and for a moment he seemingly couldn't bring himself to ask the next question.

Mik took pity and didn't make him open his mouth, "Emperor Daragh Ryan was announced this morning."

According to Mik, there's no real way to adequately describe the expression that came over Luther Gregory's face as he heard the name. I suppose after all those grim reaper jokes, I could say he looked as though someone had started to tear his soul out of him, but that comes off as too melodramatic.

Suffice to say he was highly, highly upset to hear the new Emperor was Daragh.

It's not hard to understand why — whether his attempted coup had just been a power grab for himself, or truly was the only way he thought he could save the Empire, the fact was that a member of the enemy faction was now taking over his throne.

A man with no breeding, no quality, no special education… some common folks who earned their noble titles did have the gifts necessary to be Peers, but not Daragh. Not the Irish madman who had eschewed every honor the Lords tried to bestow upon him…

How could such a man do anything productive with the throne? His ascent would represent the beginning of the end… Defense Command controlling both the government and the sovereign. The end of the Empire…

That's all that Luther Gregory saw, and as his shoulders sagged he shook his head, "All is truly lost then. He… why…"

"Rationally, again, they appointed an Emperor who the people will like. Whatever his qualifications," Mik offered his explanation coolly, and then fell silent.

It took Luther a few moments to collect himself after that — he was despairing and Mik just stood silently and watched. This was a broken man, who had reigned over an Empire for years, but now was to stand trial before it.

He probably wouldn't be executed — the Lords would do everything they could to prevent that, fearing the precedent — but there would be severe consequences. Bastard had earned that much.

"What will they do to me?" Luther asked eventually, and Mik wasn't sure whether the question was meant to be rhetorical.

He decided to answer anyway, with quiet words: "Every day, from now until you die, you're going to remember who you were, and what you nearly accomplished. And every day, those thoughts will torment you, and torture you. The thoughts of how great you might have been… how great you believe you would have been. They will erode you."

Luther's eyes slowly traveled back to Mik's, and the Commodore met them firmly as he continued: "When those long days come, just remember, you weren't as close as you think you were. And the greatness you imagine wasn't real, just a dream. There's no point lamenting a dream. When you realize that, feel fortunate that you have the chance to accomplish something different with the time you have left."

At another time, Luther Gregory might have been insulted and defiant — argued, attacked, quipped… something. Anything. This time he didn't.

Like Prometheus, he would be tortured every day for the rest of his life… as long as he continued to believe his own mythology. He would have been wise to listen to Mik —

most people would be — but to come to wisdom from such a place of arrogance would be difficult. Trust me on this.

Mik didn't wait around for more conversation; at long last, he and his ship would be home again, so he headed for his bridge to make preparations.

CHAPTER EIGHT

THRONE TO THRONE

The business of government is seldom easy, and for Lia and Charlie, this fact couldn't have been driven home any better than by their days of planning for their first tour as the rulers of Hawke... which also just happened to be the late Ian Hawke's final tour of the asteroids he'd spent so long protecting.

See, in order to bring closure to the first great chapter in the history of the Protectorate, the founder had to be taken from rock to rock, so mourners from each asteroid would have the chance to pay their respects.

At the same time, Lia and Charlie needed to make public appearances and visit local governments, to make certain that everyone — not just the Lords and Ladies they'd already connected with in court — would understand that the Protectorate was in good hands.

You know I didn't think all that much of Ian Hawke, but even I will tell you this seems to me to be a cruel and prolonged end to his life. First he's kept breathing for a couple of years so we could get to the other side of the war before breaking the news of his demise... then when he finally dies officially, he ends up packed up and paraded around the Protectorate? I know it was necessary, but I suspect the old bastard would much rather have just been blown up in a ship during some battle.

The one left to suffer through all this was Lia, because despite his flaws she had loved her father, and there was no way for her to get the closure that came with his death until this pageantry was over.

That being the case, she was uncharacteristically silent as she sat at a table in her private quarters, looking over the list of official guests planning to attend the memorial ceremony on Hawke Four. At least two of them — a local Lord, and a local politico — were going to be headaches... testing to see how solid her grip was on power, wondering if they could get a little more influence for themselves. That wasn't a problem — putting such people in their place was easily done — but it was tiring.

Everyone seemed to want a piece of her, and even though she'd known that was going to be the way of it, and she'd prepared herself, it was still frustrating. There were more important things to be done, but before action could be taken these decks first had to be cleared.

A cup of hot chocolate suddenly landed on the table beside her hand, and blinking, Lia looked up at her consort. It was funny calling Charlie that, I'll be the first to say, but until there was a wedding, that was his title. And there was no mental bandwidth anywhere to even begin thinking about planning a state wedding.

"You check your mail this morning?" Charlie settled into the chair next to Lia, and she shook her head as she wrapped her hands around the warm mug.

Sipping his own coffee, Charlie leaned forward over the table and grabbed the remote for the room's wall screen.

"They settled on a new Emperor," he said. "And... well. Not necessarily the best choice from a governing perspective."

Taking a sip of the hot chocolate, Lia replied a bit too coolly: "Finding the best wasn't their first priority... they need to restore people's faith in their throne, or Pope might be able to have the whole sovereign side of government dismissed..."

Lia's frustrated tone would probably have put off many, but Charlie was immune, "Certainly true. But I'll show you what I mean."

Turning away from her, he activated the screen in her wall, then opened the message on the top of her mailbox. Included in the note was a vid clip from a press conference on the lawn of Admiralty House.

Lia put her mug down on the table, and her jaw actually dropped. Daragh Ryan was Emperor?

"That's... I..." she couldn't manage a more coherent initial reaction, and then she looked at Charlie. "It's either brilliant or incredibly stupid."

Shrugging, Lord Peters leaned back in his chair and drank more of his coffee, "Might be both. Things could look very different before the Lords get him out of there..."

Lia shook her head and took up her mug again, "Certainly."

At this point Charlie had rather been hoping for Lia to volunteer some of her usual ironic commentary, but she was already turning back to the lists she'd been consulting before his arrival, a frown creasing her brow. For a second he considered letting her slip directly back into her work, but a question surfaced in his mind, and he decided to ask it.

"So, what's the protocol? Are we supposed to show up at the coronation, or whatever it's called?"

Lia didn't look away from her lists, and her answer sounded almost dismissive, "Perhaps it would be fitting, but obviously we can't. We need to do this tour first, so our priorities are clear."

Again she sounded cool, though Charlie didn't respond outwardly to that tone. Instead he sipped his coffee and then offered his own confirmation of her interpretation, "If we go there before finalizing things here, it might send the message that we're too connected to the Empire... that I'm having undue influence for Defense Command."

"Got it in one," Lia replied disinterestedly.

For a moment, nothing more was said... and then that moment dragged on longer. Charlie sat at the table, his entire focus on Lia, but in that Special Branch way that doesn't involve any staring whatsoever.

The woman he loved was hardly teeming with warmth just now, and while he didn't think that was unreasonable, he was somewhat concerned by the signs he was seeing. Since their return to Hawke space, the stress had been mounting steadily on Lia's shoulders, and as much as he tried to step in to lift some of it, he got the feeling his efforts weren't being... noticed.

That's not quite the right way to say it, but speaking to Charlie about this, it's the best either of us could come up with. Lia knew he was there, knew he was ready to help, and yet somehow he was ignored when it came to figuring out the solutions to the problems that lay ahead.

She'd managed to get him appointed as her consort, and that was the end of it — at least as far as she was concerned. Now she had to move on to other things, and he'd be a part of them... but not a contributor.

I guess another way to say it was that Charlie felt like a fifth wheel... which makes sense if you know that old wheeled cars and trucks typically had four wheels, and didn't need a fifth. He was pleasant to have around, and even necessary in an emergency, but not useful.

Now obviously calling Charlie 'not useful' is about as sensible as calling him a shed. It's factually not even close to correct. And I'm not saying Lia was consciously thinking of him as such, just that she hadn't yet opened her mind to the fact that he could do more than bring her a warm drink when she was feeling the strain.

Sitting there next to Lady Hawke, Charlie was having these sorts of thoughts — wondering when she'd be able to recognize a valuable contributor... it would take time, and he'd just have to be patient and helpful until her perspective changed.

A lot of work, and a different sort of job than the ones he was used to... but Charlie was certainly eager to learn new skills. As if being able to kill you with a...

Whoops, not supposed to make those jokes anymore. If I keep making them, Lord Peters will send his peasants to club me to death with shovels.

Aha, I sense a new direction for my jokes about Charlie...

Anyway, our elite Lord Major soon finished his coffee, and eventually he stood and left the table unnoticed, taking Lia's emptied mug with him to the kitchen as she muttered to herself about some Hawke Lord who was undoubtedly going to be a nuisance.

Charlie listened to the words (he could hear them from the kitchen, because he's a Special Brancher) and filed away the names and the commentary for future use. He cleared up the dishes, then turned back to living room where Lia sat. Leaning against the frame of the kitchen door, he stared at her back for a few moments, noting the tension she was carrying in her shoulders.

Perhaps something as simple as a neck rub would be useful just now.

Crossing the living room again in silence, Charlie placed his hands on Lia's shoulders and began kneading against the clenched iron-hard muscles. She didn't seem to notice at first, then her head turned and she looked halfway back over her shoulder at him.

"Not now, okay?"

She did say it as kindly as she could manage, but it was clearly a no-nonsense dismissal. Charlie paused briefly, withdrew his hands and nodded, "Just let me know when."

Lia obviously hadn't figured out how to fit Charlie into her new life yet, but he was a patient, wise Special Brancher, so he left her to her work, and went to do some research reading of his own. There was a lot for him to pick up, and he wasn't going to waste time in getting a handle on it.

CHAPTER NINE

REUNIONS

Over the next few weeks, not a whole lot actually happened. There were many press conferences, some public trials and a few ceremonies, but they were all in the service of the key decisions that had already been made — they were, I mean, designed to strip Luther Gordon of his pride and influence, and to put Daragh firmly into the public consciousness as Emperor.

I'm not going to spend too much time on all these pieces of pomp and ceremony, in part because they're well-covered in the historical record, in part because I couldn't really be bothered about them.

What I always remember from this period in 2234 is the waiting. *Wolf, Lion* and *Lady Grace* sat in orbit, alongside the Heavy Squadron, and watched as the political and governmental matters sorted themselves out. But we had nothing to do.

More familiar faces from the war days were coming home all the time, though, and those reunions did help take the edge off. That being the case, I'll focus more on the people we got to see again — some for the first time in quite a while.

The first batch of familiar faces were of course the ones who'd been with *Bonaventure* and *Ark Royal*. John Fiora was massively in demand upon his return, especially since his Second Lord — the chief administrator of the Navy, in many respects — had quit for some stupid job in the public sector.

We didn't get to see him for days after his return, but we did have Mik and Wes back. And because it was the three of us, we decided to celebrate by going to a bar.

Now, this wasn't a Belt colony bar, or a station bar for that matter... it was a nice spot down on Capital Island called the *John Guy* (named after an old explorer, I think, even though it reads like 'some John guy').

Arriving in this quiet place on a Wednesday night, we found all the screens in the establishment lit up with footage from that day's trial of the Governor General and Emperor... a complete circus as some rather overzealous Empire Party MPs and Senators let the two men have both barrels.

"They're really getting uncivil," Mik observed, watching one MP who I won't name basically frothing at the mouth as she decried the criminality of the Emperor's attempt.

You know I had no love for the Emperor or his plan, but I had to agree with Mik's assessment. Every faction has its share of overzealous people (to put it mildly) and I don't think it reflected well on anyone when those folks were shown on camera.

"He's earned it," Wes was far less sympathetic. "He should consider himself lucky that he's even getting a public trial."

After Egesta, it would be fair to say that Wes really had no sympathy for anything connected to the throne... though the new reality of Daragh's appointment was going to confuse things.

"Any idea what effect Lord Ryan's appointment will have?" Mik avoided further discussion of the inquiries by switching to that question. He was looking at me as he asked, obviously hoping that because I'd been at Earth longer, I'd have a better sense of where Daragh was going to fit in the whole new scheme of things.

Shrugging, I sat back as the waitress arrived to take our orders.

"Black Sun for me," Mik ordered, and then Wes frowned.

"Coffee. Black, and don't try to put any intercooler fluid in it."

The waitress raised an eyebrow at that warning, then made a note on her pad and underlined it. After that she turned to me, and I paused thoughtfully.

"Scotch. A double and neat. JW twelve-year blend if you have it."

That was a switch, and Wes and Mik both looked at me, the former Commodore surprised and the latter smiling, "Wow, this crisis turned you into a drinking man."

"Just remembering how awful it was last time we all sat down together," I shot back, and then the waitress departed.

I should add that, because this pub was on Capital Island, and was pretty close to the government buildings, the serving staff was accustomed to seeing well-known people. No one went starry-eyed or asked for Karen's autograph when they saw us... we were just a bunch of Naval officers who had been in the news a bit, and who were probably a whole lot less dashing in person than we were made out to be.

Anyway, back to Mik's question; I shrugged in answer, "Well, we won't have to worry about a division of loyalties in government anymore. Whether Daragh decides he's going to try to dismantle the throne, or gut its powers... that's up to him."

"Wouldn't be a bad thing to do a little reining in," Wes said dryly.

I nodded, though Mik seemed more thoughtful, "Whatever he does will have to be handled carefully. If it looks like we've taken control and we're just doing whatever we like, now that the checks and balances are gone, I don't think people will appreciate it."

Again, Mik clearly had a very strategic view of this situation — partly because he hadn't been in the Fiora Ring that had been in the crosshairs for so long, and partly because he's just that sort of guy. He understands government, and more and more he was thinking he might end up as part of the Belt caucus. Time would tell.

The waitress returned with drinks as we let Mik's observation settle in, and then we raised our glasses.

"Absent friends," Wes said, and Mik and I repeated it.

Sipping my scotch, I took a breath and then leaned back in my chair, "Whatever happens to the politics, I think we'll probably be getting back to regular duties sooner rather than later."

Wes laid his coffee down on the table, "I've been wondering who to talk to about that. The old gang going to be getting back together soon?"

I shrugged again, "Well Isoruku and Katya are with Greg at Mercury, so they'll be coming in when he does. Last I heard, they're sending Lynn Bokai out to Egesta with Hokkaido and Honshu, to show we're serious about getting it right this time... so Matt will be returning. Kris is back, obviously, and Kate Levec has Lady Grace. That leaves Cheetah, and word is it'll be back online early next year. Mark should be ready to take over by then, too. Don't know if we'll get Alberta back... but if we head back out to the Belt again we'll probably roll everyone together."

That was a whole lot of names, so let me pause for some reminders, top to bottom. You might recall that Isoruku Togo of *Generous* and Katya Romanov of *Sackville*, both veterans of the old Belt Squadron, had been with us at Mercury, and after some minor damage they'd stayed out there with Greg's formation. They'd be coming back when Greg led his invasion force — including the old Heavy Squadron of the Home Fleet — home to Earth.

Because Egesta was such a horror show, we were going to be sending the Fifth Lord of the Admiralty out there with two battleships, to demonstrate how serious we were about helping put that rock back to rights. Bokai's arrival would allow Matt Baxter to bring *Friendly* home. You know about Kris and Kate, so then we skip ahead to Mark Gunney, who you'll recall was recovering from considerable frostbite after *Cheetah* got opened up during the Fleet Clash.

Well, Wes' former ship was soon to be back with the squadron, and Mark was doing well with his recovery, so we'd make sure that as *Lion* had waited for Kris, *Cheetah* would wait for him. If we returned to Belt Two, we'd catch back up with *Alberta*, now being skippered by Kasia Hu, and that would be it — the old Belt Squadron would be put together again, minus Aaron Ashby and *Honesty*, lost in 2232 at Jupiter.

It would probably seem like old times again...

But things had changed. There were new members of the family, joined during the war, who'd be gone again — for instance, Nancy Whitehorse's *Trusty*, which had been blown up during the Clash, and Bruce Arama's *Adelaide*, which had come in late and made a big impression. And ships aside, there were many men and women who'd been lost to death or injury...

So it wouldn't really be 'old times', but there would be some continuity. Some...

"Don't think you'll be on the team anymore, though, Wes," I said that a bit more grimly than I'd meant to. "Marshal either, for that matter. You're off on your own now. Bastards."

Wes chuckled slightly at that, then sipped his coffee before asking, "So I'll be sticking with the Independent Squadron?"

I shrugged, "Don't see why not. Imagine how much more we'll be able to do with a Marshal running the Belt Station, a well-led Indy Squadron, a fully-stocked Belt Squadron, and the independent belt being looked after by Commodore Christian Mikaelsen."

It was a very inviting prospect — Defense Command's efforts in the Belt would be bolstered by such a lineup of personnel.

"Imagine if they let you keep *Ark Royal* for independent patrols," Wes latched onto the notion with a grin directed at Mik. "That'd keep the peace pretty loudly."

The good humor we shared didn't quite spread to the Belt-born Commodore. He stroked his goatee a couple of times and then sipped his beer before shrugging, "I'll see. I'm not sure if I want to head back out there now. Honestly, I don't know if I'm going to stay in the service much longer..."

That was a surprise to both Wes and me — a couple of lifers, we really weren't sure what would become of us if we tried to quit.

"Something else have your interest?" I asked, and he shrugged and drank again from his pint.

"Talked to the Emperor a lot, particularly on the way back. Makes you think... there are ways people like us could make a difference in theatres like that," he bobbed his head towards one of the screens on the wall. "I don't like the way it's being done right now. Maybe the best way to change it is to get involved and work from the inside."

That sounded like a very tall order — one I certainly would have lacked the patience to consider. I wanted to get back to the Belt, where Karen and I could behave badly in public and help the Empire at the same time. Meanwhile, Wes wanted to go out there, find some bad guys, and wield a wrench...

But Mik really wanted to change the Empire. And you know, even then I was pretty confident he could do it. Guess I'm not always wrong...

While we three fellows were in a bar, Karen McMaster was in orbit, visiting with another of the skippers who'd come in with the *Bonaventure* Squadron.

Adelaide was mostly standing down when Karen got aboard — the ship's reservist crew had been granted extended leave, a precursor to them ultimately being demobilized and sent back to their civilian lives.

As a newly-built and battle-tested corvette, *Adelaide* would of course continue on, but with a new crew of professionals. This was thus the end of a brilliant chapter in the little ship's history, and whoever took over would have a great deal to live up to.

But that still lay ahead; a skeleton crew remained aboard *Adelaide* as it orbited Earth, and one of the officers who stayed was of course Commander Purhi Arama. Bruce was on the realtime comm regularly to his wife and daughters in Auckland, but he believed — entirely correctly — that it was his job as CO to let his crew get home before he did. When *Adelaide* was handed over, he would have to be the last of the ship's old crew left aboard.

When Karen landed in *Adelaide's* bay, most of the flightdeck's systems were being run by the computer. She landed her plane on the mostly-empty deck, waited for the bay to repressurize and then hopped out.

A spacer was waiting for her in the observation lounge, and directed her straight to the bridge — Bruce had the watch, and because there was only a skeleton crew aboard he couldn't turn that over to anyone to come down and greet her. That was fine; Karen hadn't spent much time aboard the newly-built ships of the fleet, and she was interested to see what they looked like from the inside. A little self-guided tour was in order.

What she saw was very interesting — structurally, *Adelaide* was laid out almost identically to a ship like *Sackville*, and that made sense. Remember, long ago I mentioned how the new ships built during the war were of older, commercial-yard-friendly designs? Well that fact was clearly evident as Karen passed through *Adelaide's* corridors.

But the fit, finish and feel was different than she was expecting. The style of the corridor walls and deck plating was more modern than on the old *Canada*-class corvettes... the interfaces were completely up-to-date, and even the corridor lights were of the new design.

An interesting mix of old and new... and obviously a combination that worked very well. At the time, she quite approved.

Reaching the bridge, Karen found the compartment to be a wee bit smaller than the command deck on a *Noble*-class corvette like *Lady Grace*, but it still glowed with life, and the few spacers who were on the deck seemed to be doing their jobs with a sense of purpose... even though they were just monitoring a standard orbit, making sure no collisions took place.

Bruce was at the front of the bridge, arms folded as he looked up at a screen showing the same inquiry which Mik, Wes and I were seeing in the bar on Capital Island.

"It still a gong show, Bruce?" Karen asked, approaching the screens as she watched Luther Gordon's face twist in horror at some question.

Turning back in surprise, the Maori Commander saluted quickly, "It isn't particularly civil, I wouldn't say. And welcome aboard, ma'am."

Karen favored the reservist with a smile, "Thanks for letting me visit. Your ship is very fine, Bruce... very fine indeed. Going to miss it?"

There was nothing Bruce could do but smile, "I will miss it, yes ma'am. But I couldn't miss any ship as much as I miss my daughters."

Pretty much impossible to argue with that.

Karen chuckled as she came to a stop beside the Kiwi, "Was that a subtle warning for me not to try to recruit you to stay on?"

"I was hoping it was less than subtle, ma'am," Bruce turned back to the screens as he replied.

There's no question, if we could have kept a skipper like Bruce with the fleet, he'd have been straight into the Belt Squadron and probably would have had his own frigate within a few years. But he was one of those unusual people who could leave... who had a life waiting for him outside Defense Command.

It would hardly have been right for us to try to keep him from it.

"The only favor I'd ask is that you make sure *Adelaide* goes to the right crew, ma'am."

"Absolutely," Karen agreed immediately. "Though I'm sure we'll be able to do more than that to recognize the work you did, Bruce. I know that personally, I'll help with anything you need. You're a contractor, right?"

Nodding, the Kiwi Commander deflected, "I am, but ma'am, I don't deserve any special favors."

"You saved my ship and me, you're not getting special favors. You've earned friends."

Karen's tone was insistent, and coming from a house full of women, Bruce knew better than to push back, "Well I appreciate that, ma'am."

Of course, Karen didn't know exactly what help our friendship might provide for an elite Maori officer when he went back to civilian life, but he wouldn't be forgotten.

Neither would many others...

CHAPTER TEN

POMP AND OTHER STUFF

There's no real template for an inauguration. This might seem surprising since we see them fairly regularly — every five or ten years, a new Emperor comes along and we have to do something to make the appointment official… but what we do varies, usually based on the tastes of the incoming ruler.

For instance, Emperor Radha Kapur had come in with a fairly ornate and expansive two-day ceremony hosted at the New Delhi palace, while Emperor Benedict Sosa had gotten everything over with in three hours on a rainy afternoon in Buenos Aires.

Luther Gregory III had himself gone the more ornate route, choosing to hold his ceremonies in Freetown, Liberia, a place he claimed was close to his heart (because he was black) even though he and his family had been on Venus for six generations, and it was questionable whether any of his ancestors ever hailed from that part of the African continent.

Still, it was a good photo op, or something such, so that's where he did it.

All those precedents in mind, Daragh Ryan had an interesting choice as he sat with Schwartz T. Babcock and Keith Pine, and tried to figure out exactly where to go, and what to do, for his big day.

"I could do it aboard a ship," was the Irishman's suggestion as we join the meeting. They were all sitting together in one of the smaller rooms in the Government Palace, pads covering the table before them as they brainstormed.

Keith was frowning over a book as he heard the words, and his answer was immediate: "Nope."

The new Emperor glared at his Gamesmaster's dismissive tone, but said nothing. Now let me pause to explain what a *Gamesmaster* is: Keith was officially the member of the Emperor's staff who would be in charge of entertainments.

You know, if Daragh wanted a poker night, or some football, or to hunt the most dangerous game, he'd talk to Keith to have it arranged. But Daragh wanted no games or entertainments, so he figured the otherwise-superfluous title would be handy for a trusted former-Ministry of Agriculture employee. No one would think too much of it if Keith came and went from the Emperor's side on a regular basis… and he'd have royal authority without any stupid ceremonial responsibilities, freeing him up to solve whatever interesting problems arose for Daragh's throne.

Yes, I'm being very cryptic and avoiding some square brackets here.

Also, since Keith had been busy making that card game about pirate-fighting in the Belt, I suppose he had some sort of game qualifications — in case anyone actually checked.

"I suggest you do it here, on the steps of Parliament," Schwartz T. Babcock voiced his own suggestion about the coronation, dragging us all back to the narrative, and drawing Daragh's eyes.

The political wonderkid was no longer the Chief of Staff to the Prime Minister; he was now the Personal Secretary to the Sovereign, which is a much more important job than it might sound. Basically, Schwartz was the Emperor's Chief of Staff — the title 'Personal Secretary' was just a relic from past monarchies (these days we shorten it to EmpSec — Emperor's Secretary). If Daragh needed his political will expressed to the government, the message would go out with Schwartz, and the young fellow would make sure that anyone who heard it *listened*.

Now the EmpSec leaned forward and looked at Daragh, "If we want to make it clear that we've put the troubles behind us and that the new government and the new sovereign are all on the same page, we're going to need a symbolic gesture like that one."

Keith continued to look down at his book, but he nodded, "Schwartz is right."

Daragh's eyes moved back and forth between his two advisors — the only two on his rapidly-growing staff he knew he could trust — and then the Irishman leaned back in his chair and grumbled, "I suppose."

"We also can't make it too short," Schwartz continued. "We don't need to go over the top, but it's important that we give people something worth watching. They're going to be expecting a lot of you, and we're going to have to frame those expectations."

Schwartz's words were sensible, but he was making political points that were too subtle for Daragh's mood. He didn't care about how the damned thing looked, he just wanted it over and done with...

"If you want, you can always hijack the event and make it about something you actually care about," Keith suggested, still not looking up from his book (seriously).

Schwartz's gaze shifted to the former Ministry of Agriculture man, and Daragh finally did as well, "What are you reading?"

"*Garnan's History of Things That Could Have Been, and Were.*"

Daragh didn't recognize the title, as if that mattered: "We are planning a coronation here."

"No, Schwartz is trying to plan it, and you're grumbling. I'll start jumping in with ideas when you realize this is your chance to hold a real memorial for the war — one the entire Empire will have to watch."

"Fine," Daragh huffed out the dismissive comment, then went back to pondering.

Schwartz frowned thoughtfully, looked down at some of the notes he'd been taking, then started to nod. Of course that was quite an interesting idea... instead of stuffing the coronation ceremony with a bunch of fluff and invented pageantry, why not use it as an opportunity to close the book on the war we'd all just left behind?

The Emperor saluting the heroes of Defense Command... it would undoubtedly displease quite a few of the Lords, but it would be brilliant optics, and a sign to the people of Earth that the division between throne and government was being bridged.

He started jotting down ideas immediately, leaving Keith to his reading and Daragh to his pouting. The Irish Emperor remained deep in thought — stupid being Emperor in the damned idiot palace with the stupid face coronation shit dammit.

Admittedly, I don't know if those are the exact words he was thinking during that moment, but he did write them down amongst his notes for the day. As you can see, being Emperor was already changing him, because he didn't say 'fuck' anywhere. It's tragic what power does to people…

"I have an idea," the new Emperor said after a moment.

Keith lowered his book and looked at Daragh, "Wait for it."

Schwartz looked up too, though his pen kept moving because he was getting all sorts of ideas about how to set up the coronation, now that the central message — Heroes of Empire — was established.

"We can make this whole damned coronation into something that matters… a real memorial ceremony for the war. That'd be a bit of healing for everyone, I think…"

"There it is," Keith tapped the tabletop, and Daragh didn't seem to notice.

Schwartz frowned first at Keith, then at Daragh, and then innocently made a good point, "But… didn't we already just put that on the table?"

"We did, but Daragh came up with it," Keith replied, and again Daragh seemed not even to notice they were speaking.

"But… what?" Schwartz was frowning deeply now, and Keith shrugged.

"Trust me, during my time [in the Ministry of Agriculture serving nowhere near the Forge and not participating in any sort of counter-piracy intelligence operations under Daragh's command], I got pretty good at making sure the right people came up with the right ideas."

Alright, I admit those square brackets may have just gotten a bit out of hand, but let's not dwell.

"But… but you're admitting right in front of him that you came up with it first."

Keith nodded, "Yep."

"But… that doesn't make sense…" turning his eyes to the Emperor, the EmpSec watched for any sign of reaction. Daragh just seemed to be staring off into space — or in this case, at the crown molding. "Can he even hear us?"

The Irishman blinked and looked down at the political wonderkid, "Of course I can fucking hear you."

"Language," Keith cautioned sternly, and Daragh grunted.

Schwartz just looked confused, "But. So. It was your idea?"

"What was?"

Blinking a couple of times, Schwartz looked from Daragh to Keith, then got back to taking notes on his pad. As the newcomer — who hadn't been privy to the weird repartee the old Ministry of Agriculture operator and former Admiral at the Forge had always participated in — gave up on trying to understand the pair, both of them smiled.

Being Emperor was a cruel fate, but at least there were a couple of good people around who could be trusted to make it tolerable.

The pompous coronation, which would double as a much more humble and respectful memorial service, was planned.

CHAPTER ELEVEN
MORE FUTURES

"Mik in politics... interesting."

Marshal Samuels and I were catching up in a coffee shop in Terra Nova, and I'd just brought up the fact that Mik had mentioned thoughts of governing. Marshal and Mik knew each other from the Academy, though they hadn't had too much chance to work together since those old days.

"He'd probably go a long way representing the Belt in the Commons," I said, drinking some orange juice that didn't taste altogether like it was made of oranges.

Nodding, Marshal sipped his coffee, "Sounds like that would be his priority. He mention if he's considering the Empire Party or the Belt Party?"

I shook my head, though I suspected that Mik's interests might lie more with the latter than the former. Marshal, on the other hand, was clearly aligned with the former, and the political dimension of everything that had happened in recent months was foremost on our minds as we sat down to catch up.

That in mind, I changed the subject with a rather pointed question: "You're running for the Gordons?"

Marshal had already been looking at me when I asked it, and the fact that his expression didn't change was answer enough. He remained still for a moment, then smiled very slightly and took a sip of his coffee, "Well I wouldn't run for the Picks."

We were dropping into old — ancient, really — political terminology, to keep our conversation in this public coffee shop relatively covert. For the first 100 years of Empire, the Empire Party caucus had been colloquially known as the 'Gordons' — after Luther Gordon the Great, who had been the guiding hand behind the centrist party's creation.

The 'Picks' were the Belt Party members — another old term referring to the fact that in the old days, the first MPs and Senators from the Belt colonies had been miners. The fact that no miners in the asteroids had ever used picks (at least not seriously) was irrelevant — Picks sounded better than 'laser cutters'.

The Earth Party was the Whigs (which made no sense at all because the term once referred to Liberals in the British Parliament), and the Black Sun Party was the Tories... though that caucus and its eighteen members were basically defunct, most having done the honorable thing and followed Douglas Pope into the Empire Party fifteen years prior.

Anyway, that's a dose of political history you probably didn't need.

Marshal was getting ready to leave the Navy, and to take up the nomination for one of the seats in Belt Two... and he'd run for Douglas Pope's Empire Party.

This was no great surprise, and though he hadn't told anyone, Marshal wasn't shocked that I'd figured it out: "Was wondering how long it would take for someone to call me on it."

I shrugged, "After what you did to get us out of trouble here, it's the right time. And

Pope's going to need to revitalize his cabinet soon. You'd make a hell of a Secretary of War."

Sitting back in his chair, Marshal held up his hands, "I'm not going to start with big ambitions. But I'll be there when I'm needed."

That wasn't false political coyness — Marshal wasn't the sort to pretend that he had no interest in the highest office, if the opportunity presented itself — but he also knew better than to go into a political career declaring he was after any particular job. Amateur moves could lead to significant embarrassments.

"So who's not running again?" I asked, taking one more sip of my orange juice before giving up on the bitter liquid and pushing the glass slightly aside.

"Twinkle McDonough," he replied, and I nodded.

That memorably-named MP was the deputy leader of the Belt Party, and she'd won the seat for Belt Two Dome Two without fail for the last fourteen years. Whatever new candidate the Picks chose to succeed her would have his or her hands full if Marshal threw his hat into the ring — a war hero with his profile and track record...

"So we're going to need a new commander for the Belt Station," I said thoughtfully. Nodding, Marshal laid down his coffee cup.

"I think so. You and Karen are sticking with the fleet?" he asked, and I nodded.

"Seems the only place fit for a couple of maniacs like us. Navy or prison, take your pick."

Chuckling, Sam shook his head, "Navy it is."

The reason Marshal and I were meeting in a coffee shop that morning was because the future-MP's wife was at Defense Command Intelligence Headquarters, trying to figure out whether there was any point to keeping her cover.

Remember, when the blockheads had tried to take Marshal on the steps of Center Block, Melissa Samuels and her MAG-2 had been one of the deterrents... and that whole escapade had been broadcast to the entire planet.

The chances that she'd been noticed were pretty good. If Grant Merger still had it in for her — and it was a safe bet he did, since she'd been entirely responsible for us finding him at Deep Black, and blowing his fleet to tiny pieces — then he had ample evidence with which to identify her.

That being the case, there were questions about what she should do... and witness protection was not an option.

"I just put it on the table," Thea Fostopolos, the somewhat-embattled head of DCI was personally meeting with Mel about this issue, and as soon as the notion of changing identities and going into hiding was brought up, our elite superspy shot it down.

"Nope," Mel said pleasantly, arms folded. "It's bad enough that I'm going to have to give up coaching my team, I'm *not* giving up my husband."

Because Marshal was such a public figure — even now, before his political run — it would be impossible to move him to Venus to start up life as a hairdresser, or whatever it is the DCI witness hiding program does.

Thea was not in a position to argue with Mel — despite being a Vice Admiral, the administrator of spies lacked the sort of experience that Melissa Samuels brought with her, and knew better than to try to quote standard protocols.

"We don't even know where Grant is these days, do we?" Mel asked after a short pause, and Thea sat back, shaking her head.

"I think Haley Briand had something on him, but then she disappeared in that Solar Asteroid Union place — where the Martians built their superbattleships. No one I've sent out to find her has come up with anything... or has come back."

That report struck Mel as interesting, and she frowned, "I saw Haley before she left... she didn't mention anything about Grant Merger."

Thea's surprise was evident, and she shrugged, "Well she didn't tell me much."

Not, I think you'll agree, something you'd expect the head of Defense Command Intelligence to admit so candidly. I try not to be too unkind to Thea, but as we've discussed before, under her watch intelligence got very, very spotty. She was an appointment John Fiora made in his first few months on the job at Admiralty House, and she'd come with all the highest recommendations... but she wasn't the sort of spymaster we needed. To be entirely frank, she found herself intimidated by people like Mel and Haley — people who'd been in the field and done notable things.

Handling the impersonal parts of the job — coordinating signals intelligence, monitoring, passive detection — she could do that well enough. But she didn't have the same lethal ninja-instincts of the superagents who could kill you with

Whoops, did that typo gag again. My editors hate the 'kill you with empty space' joke...

Anyway, I don't want to give anything away, but it was a safe bet that Mel could very capably move into Thea's chair, should circumstances allow. If Marshal was spending most of his year in the House of Commons, it'd actually be a perfect job for her...

But that's getting ahead of things. There was something about Thea's mention of Grant Merger — and her failure to be able to explain much about the man — that tweaked Mel's interest. She wouldn't say it to the chief spy, because like Haley before her, Mel wasn't sure what to make of the woman... but it was in the back of her mind.

Maybe the bastard had something else up his sleeve. Maybe he was up to something out in the Solar Asteroid Union... and if he was there, maybe he'd done some work with the Martians. The new Syndicate — short-lived and ineffective though it had been — was part of the Martian strategy for the Belt, after all. And the Tharsis battleships...

Interesting.

"Well, I think I'll wait to see what post my husband takes next, and I'll move with him. You can find some job for me, wherever I end up, can't you, Thea?"

It was much more a demand than it was a question — Mel wasn't rude, but she was certainly going to use her seniority in a situation like this.

Fostopolos took a breath, "Of course... But do you want an agent on you... extra protection?"

"You're going to put two on me, no matter what I say," Mel replied pleasantly, and Thea blinked.

A good chief spy would have smiled to acknowledge the fact that, yes, a target as wanted as Mel would be watched at all times — not necessarily for protection, but for counter intelligence (so that anyone who came for her could be caught and tracked back to his or her high-value master, Grant Merger).

Instead, Thea looked uncomfortable, "Um. Yes of course."

Good thing Mel gave her the idea.

"Then I won't make you pretend," the elite spy replied, coming to her feet. "Thanks for the meeting, Thea. I'm going to go have coffee with my husband and Ken Barron. The shop just down the street from here, we'll be there at least half an hour."

With that she departed, and Thea Fostopolos scrambled to get some agents on her tail.

CHAPTER TWELVE

FEAST OF ADMIRALS

Daragh, Schwartz and Keith didn't let any grass grow under their proverbial feet: once the theme for the coronation was decided, the date was easily picked. On November 11, 2234, Daragh Ryan would officially be crowned.

That gave them only a month to get things aligned, which sounds like a lot of time but really isn't.

While they were rapidly making plans, Luther Gregory and his Governor General were finally found (more like proclaimed) guilty of crimes against the Empire. The news wasn't as big as you'd think — by the time the frothing-at-the-mouth inquisition got to the sentencing stage, most of the viewing public had become bored. Only the most invested paid attention, and if they were hoping for drastic action, they were disappointed. The Lords made it known very early on that any attempts to hang either the Emperor or the GG would be cause for some vocal complaints... the sorts of complaints that could lead to another constitutional crisis.

It would take them another four months to decide that the sentence would involve the stripping of Luther's title, and his exile from Earth... but by the time that was settled, no one (including me) was paying any attention. Because it was 2235.

It was a similar story for the Imperial Army and the Egesta Inquiry. The cases against the blockheads wouldn't be ready for formal trial until 2235 — we had some of the evidence and offenders with us at Earth, carried aboard *Wolf* and *Nova Scotia*, but not enough. Lynn Bokai would be sending back every scrap of information her teams could suck out of Egesta's databanks, and once the prosecutors had that, the fireworks would start.

In the midst of all this waiting, then, the level of boredom increased for us fleet officers sitting in Earth orbit. Indeed, the only thing of particular interest to me was another reunion. Matt Baxter wasn't going to make it back from Egesta before the coronation, but a few other people needed to be there, and when they arrived over Earth John decided there was only one thing to do: feast.

Well, that makes it sound like we set up a medieval table surrounded by people wearing horned hats. Really it was just a dinner party, hosted in the Admiralty dining room — one of Admiralty House's better kept secrets.

And who was there? You bet: Greg and Marlene were most certainly back.

Every ship Admiral in Earth space was invited to come (no Commodores, unfortunately, or it would have been a real party), and though I had never met some of the attendees, the fact that Greg and Marlene were attending was *awesome*.

Being me, I got to the dining room earlier than everyone else, so when John arrived next (having come from his office in the same building, as opposed to me coming down from orbit and still being early), we chatted for a bit.

"How's Daragh taking it?" I asked as we both fixed ourselves drinks from the bar in the corner. Yes, there's a bar in Admiralty House… more than one, actually.

Shrugging, John leaned against the bar and sipped some wine, "I haven't been able to talk to him in a week… seems pretty stressed out though. You know what he thinks of politicians."

I nodded, sipping my scotch, "Lucky him. God help you if they choose to perpetuate your title… you could be next."

John grinned, "Hopefully they've learned it's dangerous to let Navy officers be Lords."

"They don't seem to learn that quickly," I replied dryly. "How are things here without him?"

Grin fading, John shrugged, "It's busy. Daragh was insane but he held a lot of things together through sheer force of personality."

He didn't need to say any more than that; John was now back from commanding a fleet at war, and every administrative problem in the Navy was lying at his feet. There were the Third and Fourth Lords, of course, but neither could do much to help — Third Lord was responsible for orchestrating the Defense Command budget (including everything from Constabularies on Earth to Defense Command Communications), while the Fourth Lord was the ceremonial ribbon-cutter of the fleet.

Basically, John was holding things together on his own.

"So, who are you roping in?" I put the question to him plainly, and with a shrug, our elite First Lord waved his glass towards the door.

"I don't think the Belt Station is going to need Greg anymore, and I want him to take over my chair when I retire."

It was rather an obvious choice — and that is by no means to suggest it was the wrong one. There were only two Admirals I knew who I would absolutely recommend for positions in Admiralty House, with no hesitation or qualification, and Greg was one of them. Marlene was the other, but unlike the Belt — which now had more than enough flag officers attached to it (me, Karen, Wes, and until they left, Marshal and Mik), Venus had no one else to command its fleet. If we promoted Marlene away from the second planet, there'd be no natural successor.

So Greg it was… for now.

"We'll also see about giving Venus a second in command, to free up Marlene. I can see her and Greg taking over this place," John voiced thoughts similar to my own, and I nodded.

"Any idea who you want for out there?"

John paused, then glanced at me, "You'd kill me if I sent you?"

I nodded, "Kill you with fire."

"Well then I'll figure something out. Someone like Marshal Samuels, maybe?"

"Empire Party."

John frowned, "Really?"

I nodded again.

"Mik Mikaelsen?"

"Belt Party."

John's frown deepened, "I don't want to pull Wes Pellew away from a combat squadron. So… hm."

"We'll figure it out later," I said, noticing shadows moving outside the door.

Sure enough, more Admirals had arrived; none I knew particularly well, or who you'd recognize. Well, you might remember Rachel Butler, who had commanded battleships at Glorious February and then had gone on to command the Heavy Squadron before taking time off for the birth of her first daughter. She was actually still on mat leave, but her husband had taken on babysitting duty so she could come to our fancy dinner.

I shook her hand, and I believe we made small talk about something, but it was unfortunately overshadowed (at least in my memory) by the evening's next — very awkward — encounter.

Shauna Cass entered the room.

This was the first time I'd actually seen Shauna in years — after the liberation of the Forge, she'd spent her time assisting Greg on Mercury. I have to say, there wasn't anything in particular that Greg needed her for, but she was an able administrator and when she'd made it clear to him that she didn't want to return to Earth (to face whatever music was waiting for her) he'd made room for her on his staff.

Since her return, she'd basically been forgotten — no one cared about the loss of the Forge now that the war was over, and we'd won. Of the few who did remember, most focused on the fact that the attack on the Forge had been the coming out party for the *Tharsis*-class battleships, and Bort McWebsbert. Few blamed her for not being able to hold the base in the face of overwhelming odds like those.

But she knew, as did some of us who'd been well-informed about the action of *The Forge Fires*, that she probably could have done things differently. The outcome might not have been any different... but then, maybe it could have been. How would things have turned out if Bort had tangled with Greg, or Marlene, or Karen?

In that case, those dear friends of mine could very well be dead... Bort included. But I shouldn't bother with such questions; the whole point is Shauna felt quite uncomfortable coming to a dinner like this, and upon seeing her, I felt uneasy too.

Oh, one more point before I begin our awkward dialogue: the reason John had to find someone to send to Venus to back up Marlene, and ultimately replace her, was because Shauna had been the one in that important position.

She wasn't anymore.

"Admiral Barron," the Scotswoman nodded to me as we neared each other, and her voice was quite low. She was looking around the room with quick glances, and when her eyes finally came back to me, I answered.

"Good to see you, Shauna."

I chose to be less formal, and hoped my tone was warm enough... though there's probably nothing I could have said that would make her happy to see me. Remember, I'd been the one who'd sent the first message telling her to fight to the death. Throws a dampener on any relationship, that.

"You're well, I hope?" she replied with the form question, still sticking to a strict monotone.

"Yes, you too. Admiral McWebsbert sends his regards."

I can't remember if Bort actually asked me to pass along his regards, but he must have if I thought to say it right then. Either way, I don't think it was the most sensitive thing to say — she winced at mention of his name, and then took a sharp breath.

"Convey my regards to him next time you're speaking," she replied.

We both fell silent after that, and I could see Shauna's eyes reaching past my shoulder towards the bar. A stiff drink probably wouldn't go amiss…

Before she went for her liquid support, though, I stepped closer to my once-counterpart, the woman who'd been to Marlene what I'd been to Greg, "Listen, Shauna, Bort's that good. He really hit us hard at the Clash, and if not for the *Bonnies*…"

Shauna blinked and looked up at me. She said nothing for a moment, then her eyes narrowed and she replied, "But you did have the *Bonnies*. You won."

I stared briefly, and considered arguing with her — pointing out that it was luck or fortune or that losing was something that would have happened to any of us — but I didn't. I chose not to get into that argument, because if Shauna wanted pity she wasn't going to find it.

Sounds harsher than I mean it to… I just wasn't about to take part in that sort of debate. The war was over, peace was here, and she'd find a place for herself somewhere.

"Have a good dinner," I eventually answered, and with another sharp breath the Scottish Admiral stepped past me.

The timing worked out pretty well: Marlene and Greg arrived seconds later, and Shauna's departure left me well-positioned to pounce. I did so, and we all shook hands and laughed about how good it was to see each other — how long it had been since I'd seen them both, Greg especially, and how Marlene's intervention in the investigation at Venus had led us right to Egesta.

So much to talk about, and now that I recall it, nothing that you haven't already heard. Which is sort of a shame, because Greg and Marlene don't get nearly enough page time in these books as it is, and now I have no reason to stick with them.

Instead, let me just remind you: Marlene personally saved the Empire twice, first by holding off the Martian assault force in *The Almost Coup*, and then by making it possible to find out about Egesta. In between she was part of a massive war effort that saved the Empire countless times.

So basically, she's so awesome you don't even know how awesome she is.

And Greg? Don't even get me started. First raid on Mars in *The Gallant Few*? Oh right, remember that do you? Along with Mik no less. And then that whole little successful invasion of Mercury — along with Marlene. The largest space-to-ground military action in human history, all under his watch?

Woot woot.

Sorry, I don't know what those last two words actually mean, but I'm told by the young people that they denote awesomeness, so I've elected to use them — much to my editors' chagrin.

Either way, we were all sitting down to dinner, and the table was a powerful one. John Fiora, Greg Noyce and Marlene Stoll… without them, we'd all have stupid Martian names like… Fiornoytoll… right now. Don't you forget it.

CHAPTER THIRTEEN

CORONATION

A coronation is not small.

Even when it's for Daragh, and every effort is made to maximize austerity, there are still certain expectations of Empire that must be met, and that means the scale has to be pretty considerable.

Neither Karen nor I had much affinity for big ceremonial events, as I think you've probably figured out by now. Had this been any other Emperor, we might have tried to avoid attending the coronation — there'd have to be an excuse we could use… perhaps an invasion of alien creatures… that looked like humanoid wolves, cats and bears.

How crazy that would be.

But this wasn't some random Lord or Lady, it was Daragh Ryan, so we gathered our courage (more like our patience) and took a pinnace down to Capital Island on 11 November, 2234, to witness his installation as the number one top head guy of the Empire.

Couple of points. We took a pinnace because we couldn't fly our own Starlights down — cockpits wrinkle dress uniforms, and more importantly, airspace over Capital Island was beyond locked down for the event. We'd have been stuck orbiting for about an hour while we waited for approval to touch down.

Another thing: we weren't technically just watching this big do, we were part of it. Every flag officer from the Navy who was in Earth space was part of the occasion with a special viewing gallery (basically a set of risers) behind the Emperor's platform. That meant we'd be staring out over Daragh's shoulders at a crowd of more than 50,000 onlookers.

Now, you could draw a couple of conclusions from that.

For instance, you might observe that 50,000 is a pretty small crowd for a coronation. True, but because this was being done on the steps of Center Block (or more precisely, on a massive platform built over those steps) there wasn't much room for audience seating. The smaller crowd would make the security burden a bit more manageable, at least.

The other thing you might realize about the seating position Karen and I had been sentenced to: everyone would be able to see our faces throughout the whole damned ceremony.

We couldn't so much as stick out our tongues or roll our eyes.

Daragh, I think, was getting at least some revenge on us — after this day, we'd be able to continue on with our enjoyable lives, cruising around the Belt and shooting at things, while he'd be condemned to the throne. This last discomfort was the least he could do to make us suffer in return.

Irish bastard.

Anyway, I think that provides all the context you need. Weird that I'm being responsible and doing so much explanation before I start the narrative of the chapter... guess the editors are finally getting to me.

Karen and I were sitting on the risers behind the podium. There was a line of chairs in front of us for Daragh and the appropriate Lords who had to do the crowning, as well as the ceremonial types like the Black Rod, who were now in suits instead of robes (and were probably going to be frozen by the end of the day).

Around us in the risers were a variety of people — we had Wes, Mik and Marshal in our row, and Greg, Marlene and John were in the one right in front of us. Others like Rachel Butler and Shauna Cass were also present, as well as people like Brigadier Peri Oktar of Special Branch, and Hirobumi Tesso, the head of DCSF (who I don't think I've mentioned in a very long time).

On either flank of our risers were massive orchestras, and microphones for what we assumed would be singers of some sort. Music was usually part of any inaugural ceremony, and sometimes it was the best part... though sitting between the two orchestras might not be so good for our long-term hearing.

Guess we'd soon find out.

Looking out over the crowd that was filling the chairs in front of the stage, we saw many thick patches of green — Defense Command officers were liberally spread throughout the audience, all of them eager to see one of their own be condemned to the highest office.

Civilians obviously filled out the rest of the crowd — many of them locals from Capital Island, but some of them flown in. Many Irish showed up, obviously surprised to see one of their countrymen being put in a position of such overt power.

As one of them said to me later: "If they had to pick an Irishman for that bloody chair, figures as sure as fuck they'd pick one who don't need to drink to be fuckin' crazy."

Daragh was as crazy as he was vindictive, because he'd insisted that we all come down very early, and now we had *hours* to wait. The weather was typical of a Capital Island November — that is to say, cold. Fortunately we were wearing dress uniforms instead of court dress, so we had good insulation (North Atlantic cold is *cold*, but uniforms built to keep heat in during a decompression in space take the edge off).

Still, Karen and I had our hands stuffed in our pockets as we sat and waited.

"This is festive," she commented eventually, and looking at her, I nodded.

"I agree completely."

Unfortunately the warmth of our uniforms did nothing to make the metal benches that we were sitting on any softer. Call me a cushy desk Admiral, but if I'm going to sit for an extended period of time I want a good chair... otherwise I'd prefer to stand, as I do on a bridge.

But no, we were on cold metal benches — more of Daragh's revenge, I was sure.

We'd landed shortly after 0900, and had been sitting since 0930. The Coronation was supposed to begin at 1100, but by 1125 the people coming to watch were still finding their seats. We'd been wallowing in boredom for weeks — keep in mind how dull this book has been — so we were pretty numb to it by this time... but we were still very glad when Daragh's thing finally began at noon.

The impending arrival of the podium party was marked by the beginning of music from the dual orchestras. It wasn't as loud for us sitting between the two as I'd feared, but it was still quite overpowering. *The Emperor's Processional* was the first piece to be played, which made me smile — as it always does — because I think it's ridiculous that our Empire has adopted a piece of music that began its life as cue for a villain. Nobody watches 250-year-old movies, I guess.

Then the players switched to more modern, more uplifting pieces, each of which subtly integrated some sounds of Daragh's heritage — and my own — violins, tin whistles, accordions and pipes. As the warmer music began, the party of Emperor-related people, led by the Black Rod, finally emerged onto the steps of Center Block, and it was with a great sense of relief that we all came to our feet.

The podium party consisted of a relatively long line of individuals, though past coronations had seen much longer ones. Schwartz T. Babcock and Keith Pine were among the dignitaries, and Karen and I waved to them a bit impishly. Keith waved back with a smile, though Schwartz was far too serious. Bringing up the rear of this line was, of course, Daragh himself, making his entrance the most dramatic of the bunch... as if it wouldn't have been already.

Before the eyes of 50,000 people, and cameras beaming the feed all around the world, our mad Irish Lord made his first-ever appearance in his all-white Emperor's suit. At the time it seemed an odd look for him, appearing a little too fine for his boisterous personality. He was clean-shaven and his hair had been recently cut as well... appropriate to the occasion, of course, but as Karen and I glanced at each other with muted smiles, we were both thinking the same thing: *we might have uncomfortable seats, but he's stuck like that.*

There was not an inordinate amount of ceremony as Daragh and the podium party moved to stand in front of seats in that row of chairs before our risers. Both Schwartz and Keith chose chairs beside the Emperor's, and that seemed a clear sign of who Daragh felt he could trust.

The rest of the party was made up of people we barely recognized. Lord Somerset was about the only one I could name, and because he was the senior noble on Earth, he was to be the official crowning guy, and also the emcee. I think both of those jobs had fancier titles for this occasion, but I don't know what they were because I clearly didn't research any royal protocol for this book. I look forward to your letters.

Somerset went to the podium after everyone in the long procession found their appropriate positions in front of chairs. No one sat, of course — we all had to be told to do that.

"We gather today to recognize the ascent to the throne of Earth's next Emperor, Lord Daragh Ryan."

Interestingly, he didn't start with any 'hear ye, hear ye' type old-English speech, which was quite a break from past tradition. Daragh had personally reviewed every script for the day's events with a red pen and a shotgun, and the result was altogether much more plain-spoken than otherwise would have been the case.

"Lord Ryan, please step forward."

We were all still standing, watching as Daragh approached Somerset. As he did, Somerset bent down and pulled something out from a shelf under the podium...

The black sun crown of Empire.

It was a very casual movement, but let me stop here and put a little emphasis on it:

The crown of the Earth Empire.

Which you've seen under the strictest of security regimes on display at the Imperial Annex.

Which is insured for more than a billion-trillion dollars with Lloyds of Luna.

Which is considered by monarchists to be the beating heart of the Black Sun.

Had been sitting on a shelf in the podium.

All morning. In Capital Island weather.

Once Somerset had the crown in hand he backed up and turned in the direction of the approaching Irishman, "Lord Ryan, you are now the Emperor of the Black Sun. Earth, Venus, the Belt and all associated territories of this mighty Empire now look to you as their beacon. Lead them well."

Daragh nodded.

Then Somerset put the crown on Daragh's head.

Then they posed beside the podium for a photo op.

Then Somerset went to stand in front of his chair, and Daragh adjusted the crown on his head.

Just in case you're wondering, this really wasn't in keeping with the protocols of a coronation. What I just described — and what you've probably seen on vid — basically amounted to the scenario used for a cheque presentation made by a local MP to a business in his or her riding. Or a ribbon cutting at a local supermarket.

The crown, for instance, was supposed to come to the podium in the hands of one of the Black Rod's compatriots (the Red Cushion), and then the Emperor-to-be was supposed to kneel, and I think someone was supposed to tap him on the shoulder with a sword or something.

Somerset was also supposed to declare the lineage and credentials of the candidate for the throne, and lecture everyone watching about the very important duties the Emperor would be responsible for in the coming years.

Like I said, Daragh had a red pen and a shotgun. And he was the Emperor, so he got his way.

"Alright, sit down," he ordered as he returned to the podium alone.

Everyone stayed standing for a few seconds — none of us had, frankly, been ready for this. Then Keith Pine dropped into his chair and started to get comfortable, and Schwartz T. Babcock more formally did the same.

Slowly, people started following the lead of those two men... but it was too slow.

"I said *sit* down, would you do that already?" Daragh demanded impatiently from the podium, and then the crown slid a little on his head, so it sat at a jaunty angle.

As he tried to straighten the thing, more people began to follow his orders. Most of the Naval officers on the risers were the last to obey — our uncomfortable seats and years of pacing on bridges had made us more inclined to stand.

But eventually we sat too, which was good because Daragh looked over his shoulder and gave us a bit of a glare.

When he turned his gaze back to the throngs of people before him, he shifted his weight from foot to foot, then spoke: "I'll be the first to say I'm making a mockery of this whole ceremony. If that offends you, I'm sorry, but everyone here knows that I'm not cut from the same cloth as most of the people who wear the thing that's now on my head. And I won't do you or them the disrespect of pretending otherwise."

Those frank words led to a ripple of whispers in the crowd. My eyebrows rose, as did Karen's — it sounded like Daragh was quite serious about getting on with the job, and not getting caught up in the pageantry.

That he held such desires was no surprise... but his success in exercising his will was. Usually even the most ardent reformers can be forced, by the simple inertia of process, to adopt most ceremonial practices.

Not this mad Irishman. Not at all.

"I have to give you a speech, now. I think it's supposed to be called an address instead of a speech, but it's actually a speech," Daragh continued, tapping the screen on the podium to life and watching as the words he was meant to read appeared.

That was the last time he referred to those notes.

Here's what he said, uninterrupted:

When you offer a man a title like Emperor, he's supposed to want it. He's supposed to see for a moment a whole bright future unfolding before him... the power and the influence, the respect and the fame... all of that, right before his eyes. He's supposed to see that, and desire it, and want to be Emperor.

I stand before you, all of you citizens of our great Empire, as a defective man. I will say to you honestly that I did not want this, certainly never sought it. Never looked at the throne and wondered what it would be like.

I have long been a man on the opposite side... a man who has, if I'm truthful, doubted the throne. Wondered why the thing is still in our lives, wondered why we still salute it when a government we elected sits in the building behind me, and charts our course through posterity.

Today, I should tell you that I don't doubt the throne anymore. I should tell you that our time of uncertainty is over, and that the future is, at last, a brighter one.

But it isn't — or I should say, it isn't yet.

This job came to me because of circumstance... because after all that happened in the last few months, I was the one thought most trustworthy on the golden chair. Now it is an opportunity, because if this role, if the title of Emperor, doesn't mean something to me now, I can make it mean something to me before I leave.

I cannot promise you all some great change to the Articles of Empire. There's no point trying to unwrite something that guided our Empire to such greatness. Not now, at least. But I can work with our government, and work with all of you, and find a place where the throne can sit, where the Emperor can be of use, and I can nail my chair to the floor in that place.

Make it so that the Emperor is fixed in a state, where he or she cannot undo the will of the people, and the wellness of Empire, for aims that serve neither, and desires that serve only one.

I have a lot to learn. So many things are perfectly unclear just now, but I have friends close at hand, some of whom I even trust. And the Admiralty, and the House of Commons, are all here, are still ready.

The Black Sun is in all our hands, and I think the outcome will be a positive one. Given time. Given patience. Given a little ingenuity. And given your support.

Because the Lords picked me. They never actually asked you, just assumed you wouldn't mind having a mad Irishman as your sovereign. Love that, or hate me, all I ask is your support, and your vision.

A long road is ahead of us, and much healing too. But by the grace of God, whatever one you believe in, or the grace of civilization, if you're the sort without religion, I believe there is success ahead.

So that is the message I leave for you. Our Empire is strong, it is great, and I mean to make it so that the greatness is never again put at risk by men like me, on thrones of gold.

I had always wondered what it would be like to be sitting there, in person, when one of the great speeches of history was delivered. Now I knew: it was really quite incredible. Cold and uncomfortable, obviously, but also incredible.

Daragh had written that speech, and he had internalized it. Every word was genuine, and his message was the greatest point. Quote-stealers (like me) would pull a few fine ones from it, my personal favorite being the rather poetic turn: "Make it so that the Emperor is fixed in a state, where he or she cannot undo the will of the people, and the wellness of Empire, for aims that serve neither, and desires that serve only one."

Not bad, Irishman. Not bad.

But Daragh hadn't left the podium, and as people tried to figure out whether they were supposed to applaud, or be silent, or do something else entirely, the new Emperor turned again towards the risers where we sat.

As he looked at us, he reached up to his head, and I thought for a moment he was going to straighten the crown, which was again tilted. Instead he grasped the black metal thing, took it from his head, and put it back on the shelf in the podium.

Someone get the smelling salts for the monarchists who just fainted.

The de-crowning surprised... well, everyone. And I suppose I should say at this point that we stayed mostly surprised for the whole chapter. Just go ahead and assume that's our reaction to everything that happens, and I'll stop hitting you over the head with it.

Turning back to the crowd, our new Emperor planted his hands on either side of the podium, and leaned forward.

"Now. The reason we all should be here has nothing to do with me. We have lately reached the end of a war... the largest space war in the history of the human race. A war that killed more than 40,000 citizens of this Empire, and wounded 200,000 more — the greatest losses we have suffered since the rise of the Black Sun."

Silence endured, and from our vantage point it looked to us like Daragh was building up some gusto. He actually cared about what he had to say next — cared a whole lot more about it than he did about the crown he'd just removed from his head. Again, here's what he said:

I am an old Navy man. I've fought my battles, lost friends, ordered women and men to their deaths. You know my stories, know how mad I may have been.

But I did not fight this war. I sat in Admiralty House, I watched the reports.

Those who did fight, and who are here, will tell some of the stories of the fallen. Some stories will be lost, though, because no one came home to tell them. All these stories, no matter when or where or how they came, are important.

It's easy to be swept up by thoughts of glory, or the cheap thrills of victory. It's easy to forget. It's easy, too, to be overcome by grief — to overlook the importance of the fight, because of the price that came with it.

As Emperor now I say this: we must not forget all those we lost. Centuries ago, this day — 11 November — was one set aside for remembrance of those fallen during wars. We gave up that day with Empire, for we fought no wars, but now I declare its return.

On this day, every year from now until the end of Empire, we shall remember those who fell, and why they fell, so that their sacrifice may never be forgotten.

War costs too much, and lies too often, for us to allow it to escape to the pages of history.

Hard to argue with that. Impossible to argue, actually. Every officer in the viewing stand probably felt the same as Karen and I did at those words — a bit stunned, but we squared our shoulders a little too.

Because this was the sort of thing a good Emperor could do with just a few words. No debate, no opposition commentary and no press conferences; an Imperial day of Remembrance could be born by the simple breath that carried the words.

And Daragh was making a statement — a great and powerful statement — that the throne was making peace with its former enemies... perhaps even that it had been captured by them.

"Trumpets!"

I didn't actually hear Daragh bark that order, because apparently I got preoccupied thinking about the state of the new Imperial order. I did, however, notice a bunch of Irish-looking men in finery moving along either side of our risers, then stopping at the microphones that had been set up for them. Behind those men, the members of the orchestras began to prepare themselves, the trumpeters raising the tools of their trade.

Through habit and training, I and every other Defense Command officer on the viewing stand stood immediately. We all knew what was happening; we responded by simple reflex. In the crowd beyond, green-uniformed officers and spacers recognized the reflex, and rose too. Everyone came to their feet again, just in time.

All alone, those trumpets began.

I felt a chill as soon as I recognized the tune. Every time, since they'd buried my grandfather, the Last Post always sent a chill down my spine.

I can't write what it sounds like, but if you haven't heard the Last Post, you might want to look it up. There's nothing qualitatively remarkable about the music, or at least nothing that a non-musician like myself could put into words... but it means more than I can say.

It's the music that put my grandfather, himself a Defense Command engineer, in the ground, and that has said farewell to the fallen of Empire since before humans had harnessed the power of steam.

What's most tragic about it, I think, is how uplifting it sounds. You listen to it and think, if you didn't know what it meant, it would actually make you feel good. But it doesn't, because it means the ending of a day — a day for a friend or a loved one. Someone you knew.

We had been fortunate in the Belt Squadron to lose relatively few to death. Nevertheless, the Last Post was for those who hadn't come home, not just ours but everyone's. And no one in the viewing stand was particularly comfortable listening to the notes.

The Last Post is not long, though — we all struggled through it, shoulders square and blinking an awful lot, because that's about all you can do when you fear you might be tearing up, and you don't want to do something so foolish while standing on a viewing stand at an Imperial coronation.

Blink a lot and wait for it to end, and then sit down again and remember lost friends.

It should have been that easy, but of course it was not, because Daragh wasn't about to do this by half measures.

As the Post was coming to its end, one of the Irish singers opened his mouth, and of course he began to sing — because it's a song, not a poem, despite what Bort thinks.

"Of all the money that e're I had…"

He spent it in good company. And all the harm he'd ever done, alas he'd done to none but him. And all he'd done, for want of wit, to memory now he couldn't recall. So we'd fill to him the parting glass — good night, and joy be to us all.

The Parting Glass.

It's a song. It shouldn't matter, but for centuries it has. And it started in those Celtic lands where Daragh started as well. And as his countrymen sang it in perfect, sorrowful tune, bagpipes joined in.

Nothing will make you feel sorrow quite like bagpipes. I don't mean that as a joke — I know some people hate their tone — but I find they cut so deeply when they're meant to be sad.

"Of all the comrades that e're I had…"

They're sorry for his going away. And all the sweethearts that e're he'd had, they'd wished him one more day to stay. But since it fell into his lot, that he should rise and we should not, he'd gently rise, and softly call, good night and joy be to us all.

All you can do is stand there. At some point you insist to yourself that you must stop feeling foolish for becoming emotional over some music. Because to us — to all of us in that viewing stand, and all the uniformed men and women in the crowd, this was the ballad that truly recalled for us the dead, the fallen friends, those who had gone before.

For me, too, this was the song that recalled that conversation with Bort McWebsbert. I can't quite articulate what recalling that discussion really made me feel… I suppose I just asked myself, quietly and deep down, whether the people we'd lost had fallen while killing other people of similar quality.

It's not easy, you see, to be unemotional. Too much to think about, all that pain you thought you'd happily repressed, to haunt you in your dreams for decades to come, gets one last hurrah.

And as the Irish singers raised up their voices, the pipes rose with them. A crescendo, in the truest sense of the word. Terra Nova was overwhelmed, and so was I, and so was Karen.

It seemed the only one who wasn't losing control of his emotions was Daragh, who stood at his podium with his hands reaching into the air, as if to touch the souls of the dead. He was Emperor, and he was bidding them all goodbye.

To illustrate that thought, none other than our own Adrienne Thompson, along with three other pilots from Wolfstar Squadron — all of whom had been over this very spot months before, during the coup — were suddenly overhead. Making a high pass with drives on low output to be as quiet as possible, the four planes surged over Terra Nova, and as soon as they reached the air above the audience Adrienne pulled up hard, her Starlight shooting into the sky.

If you've never seen the missing man formation — as it's been known since the earliest days of air combat — then you might not appreciate it, but as symbolism goes, it was a last punch for all of us.

I looked up and watched Adrienne fly away. And in that moment, I missed people like Erica Martin, Kyle Stranks, Carly Henderson and all the others we'd lost along the way.

And I thanked God that more weren't missing… that Charlie was still out there, that people like Wes had come through okay.

Most importantly, that Karen was still standing right beside me.

What would I — could I — have become if that wasn't the case?

I was glad I'd never have to find out… and because I was in the midst of an emotional memorial ceremony, I didn't scold myself for tempting fate with such a question.

Memorials are no guard against fate, unfortunately.

Though it felt as though it took forever for the final verse of The Parting Glass to leave the mouths of the tenors — good night, and joy be to you all — it did finally come. Struggling Defense Command officers with squared shoulders breathed some sighs of relief at that… not that any of us were embarrassed, just… relieved.

None of us had the presence of mind to realize that most of the orchestras sitting on our flanks had gone unused until the drums began to snare against the brief silence, and then the Imperial anthem began.

At least this one truly was uplifting — I know it has its critics, but I happen to like Black Sun Ascendant, and as we sniffled and blinked ourselves back into some semblance of formality, we officers, and every citizen of the Empire in the audience began to sing the words.

As we sung, I glanced at Karen, who was no less a goddess than ever, and she blinked against red eyes and shrugged a little. What else could she do?

We kept playing along for the rest of the coronation, but the work was done; Daragh was the Emperor, and we were remembering absent friends.

It was a surprisingly good day.

Chapter Fourteen

Visitations

The routine from rock to rock was basically identical, and Lia Hawke found that both frustrating and helpful.

While we crowned our new Emperor, she and Charlie were busy taking Ian Hawke's body from port to port in the Protectorate, doing all those things I mentioned back in the last chapter where we visited with them.

Constant mourning… it was its own kind of torture. The way Charlie put it to me seems the most succinct way to explain it: the worst job in the solar system.

He's not exaggerating. The trip got well past the point of this being a memorial, or even a political exercise. Every day was about her father, and the political implications of his death. Imagine having to go through such utter bullshit at the death of someone you care about. If you weren't careful, it could completely destroy your positive memories of the person who'd departed… and considering Lia didn't enjoy that many positive memories to begin with, this process was threatening to wipe out all of her affection for the man.

As Lia moved into the private chamber behind the visitation room at Hawke Four for another break, she was trying not to dwell on that possibility. She was focusing on the details she was learning… that Lord Whitcomb was either a good actor or really wasn't quite the bastard her father had thought he was, and that Lady Astin was pursuing Charlie, because she thought she could conquer any man she laid eyes upon.

It'd be entertaining if she tried… but politically difficult as well. Bitch needed to recognize that Lia was not to be trifled with, because such ambitions were a clear sign that some — Astin among them — still had their doubts about Lia's grip on power.

That was the biggest concern my kid sister allowed herself at this point. She'd been to three rocks so far, and the reception at each had been largely supportive. Some complainers had wanted more influence for themselves now that Ian Hawke was gone, but mostly they realized that Lia's clean succession meant they were out of luck.

Others, though, smelled blood where there was none. Lia was not weak, and anyone who failed to realize as much would be put down fiercely if they attempted anything.

No quarter would be given — could be given — if threats to her authority appeared. She had to lock the Protectorate right down…

The door opened and then closed behind Lia as she sat in the quiet room and thought these things. She did hear it, though she didn't pay much attention because there seemed to be no other sounds of movement. She was no superspy, but she was pretty good at hearing people coming up behind her. If she couldn't hear anyone, there was only one person it could logically be.

Settling himself into a chair opposite Lia, Charlie Peters shook his head, "Sweet merciful crap."

Classic Charlie there for you — the fact that a guy with a 'Lord' title said it just makes it that much more awesome.

"You enjoying the life?" Lia turned her eyes on him with the question, and her tone was sharper than she realized.

"Beats being blown up," Charlie shrugged in reply, and Lia stared at him for a moment, wondering if he was trying to one-up her. He obviously wasn't, and it certainly says something about her stress and frustration levels that she even considered the possibility… but she let it go.

Instead of commenting, she looked back at the entirely impractical high-heel shoes that were dangling from her hand — she'd taken them off during her retreat to this room because they were decidedly uncomfortable, and she found the discomfort much more difficult to tolerate than she had before her time in hospital.

She was mostly healed, she figured, but some things would never be the same.

Oof, that came off as a bit of a metaphor for her life, didn't it? I actually feel a bit embarrassed. Almost sounded literary…

"The footage of Daragh's coronation here yet?" Charlie changed the subject with that question, and she shook her head.

"I haven't seen it. But then we've been out there all damned day, haven't we?"

Lots of mingling in the room with her father's open casket, as lines and lines of mourners came through. A break like the one they were taking now was perhaps not the best idea, with so many people coming to pay their respects… but it was necessary.

"Well, I think it'll probably be pretty interesting," Charlie continued. "I can't imagine Daragh would do things the way anyone else has before… might set some new standards that we can adopt, reduce some of the pageantry."

Lia frowned at the words, "The pageantry is part of the job. You get used to it."

Charlie sensed more tension in those words, and realized that he might have inadvertently started down the wrong path. He began to backpedal as deftly as he could manage: "Of course not. Just curious to see how a Defense Command officer will look in all-white with a crown…"

It was too late.

"This is the Hawke Protectorate," Lia snapped, and Charlie just managed to avoid wincing. "What the Earth Emperor does is his business, we march to our own drum."

"Certainly…" Charlie kept his tone suitably soft, but Lia was already leaning forward to put her shoes back on.

"Then don't bring it up," her tone wasn't equally soft, and I think we can all agree she was not being terribly fair to her consort.

As she got her shoes back on, Charlie rose and offered her a hand, but she didn't take it. Getting to her feet, she headed for the door, "You stay here, you need a break."

With that, she restored her public mourning face and left the room. Charlie watched the door shut behind her and took a breath, then sat down and took another one.

If you somehow haven't already figured it out through this series, Charlie doesn't know how to be anything but the 'good guy' — the gentleman, to employ an over-used term. This might be ironic, considering the number of ways he could kill you… er… I mean… have his peasants kill you… but it's true.

That being the case, he's not very good at fighting in the relationship sense of the word. He goes from 'be nice to everyone' to 'cleanse with fire', and there's not too many options in between. As such, he simply refuses to fight in a relationship.

But that, he realized, was not what Lia needed just now. With all the frustration that was piling on, it seemed evident she was going to need to unload her anger and frustration on someone — anyone. He was the only one she could trust enough to actually share that sort of honest, cathartic experience with… but he'd never provoke her.

So basically she was a bomb waiting to go off, but she had too much self control to go off in public, and he had too much niceness and self-control to ever trigger the blast in private.

I think this sort of situation leads to quantum singularities or something. Being much smarter than me, Charlie was *certain* it would lead to a quantum singularity, and possibly the collapsing of all realities into some sort of massive reality gumbo. And no one likes reality gumbo. Or gumbo, for that matter.

Wait, I think that last line is going to get me in trouble. Hopefully my editors take it out.

Okay so I don't like gumbo. Deal with it.

Sorry, that's a juvenile diversion. The bottom line was that Charlie was going to have to find a way to get Lia to vent her frustration. Perhaps once she did that, she'd be ready to accept his help in dealing with some of these great challenges, and with that hope in mind, our elite Special Branch Lord-Major started considering his options.

No ideas surfaced immediately, but he knew he'd find a solution. It was Charlie, after all. He could figure out the meaning of life, if he thought it would be useful.

Come to think of it, maybe he already had…

CHAPTER FIFTEEN
WEAR AND TEAR

Matt Baxter brought *Friendly* home at the end of November, and we were all very glad to see him. Things on Egesta hadn't been too bad after our departure months prior — the worst, you'll remember, was over, and the continued presence of both Matt and Colonel Garth Ronald's battalion had been more than enough to maintain calm.

Nevertheless, Matt and *Friendly's* crew had spent a serious amount of time continuing to help maintain order, dealing with the wounded (all the possible definitions of that word applied on Egesta) and collecting evidence for the future tribunals.

The arrival of *Hokkaido* and the Fifth Lord of the Admiralty provided relief, but the trip to Earth hadn't been particularly quick — the orbital season had moved on from when *Wolf* had come home before the coup, so Matt actually had to travel by way of Venus when *Friendly's* freedom arrived.

No matter, he was back now, and that meant the old Belt Squadron was mostly together again — just *Alberta* was left out, but Wes was keeping *Nova Scotia* close enough for the time being to sort of replace Marshal Samuel's former ship.

There would definitely be a celebration ahead — we'd be gathering the old gang together on *Wolf* or somewhere — but as *Friendly* arrived in orbit over Earth, the first visit would be a more personal one.

We didn't bother docking *Wolf* and *Friendly* upon the latter ship's arrival, so I took my Starlight across to my old ship once it stood down from cruising stations. After such a long time away, leave was top of mind for most of the corvette's personnel; when my plane reached the ship's deck many of the crew had already piled into pinnaces for hurried runs down to the surface. They'd be seeing loved ones, or finding ones to love... whatever the particular circumstances warranted.

Once the space doors closed behind the last of those eager shuttles, I climbed from my cockpit and dropped down onto the deck. A quick look around confirmed that my former ship was as shiny and well-cared-for as ever — Matt of course would accept no less, as Andrea hadn't when she'd skippered *Friendly* before him.

Handing my helmet to a passing deck technician, I turned for the door to the observation lounge, and as I did it opened to reveal Commander Baxter himself. He came my way, I went to meet him, and we shook hands as soon as we met in the middle of the flightdeck.

"Welcome home," I said firmly, and Matt managed the tightest of smiles in reply.

"Thank you."

He sounded weary, which was hardly unexpected.

"All's well I hope?" I asked, and with a shrug, he nodded towards the observation lounge.

"Talk in my day cabin?"

I agreed, and off we went.

As Karen had enjoyed visiting *Lady Grace* after it had returned to the squadron, it did me good now to see my old ship was well, and its crew was healthy. Those we passed — some of them very familiar faces — nodded to me as I went by, and I greeted each of them as best I could. Some names escaped me, of course, but I knew them all by their quality.

Friendly, now as before, was a brilliant little ship.

The bridge gleamed as much as the rest of the corvette — seemed that the long transit had given Matt and his crew ample opportunity to go to work with the polish, so every metal surface looked inspection-perfect. It was grand to see.

After I'd done enough sightseeing, and handshaking of Matt's bridge officers, we headed into his day cabin, which used to be Andrea's day cabin, which was once my day cabin. Matt dropped into the chair that used to be mine, while I took the seat across the table from him, and then I laced my fingers and dropped my hands into my lap.

"So," I asked. "How's it been?"

Matt stared at me for a moment, then leaned back, "What would you say if I offered to retire?"

There's a question I wasn't ready for. From sitting comfortably I leaned forward and looked across the table at my old shipmate... the one who'd adopted me all those years ago, when we'd both been aboard this very ship. Kept me from doing stupid stuff. Made sure I lived despite being a cavalier idiot. Now...

"What?"

I should have had a better answer than that, but I didn't. Matt didn't look up at me as I asked it — he knew me well enough to have expected my confusion, and now he simply kept his gaze low.

"If I chose to resign my commission before the end of this year," he said slowly. "Would you be supportive?"

It was like hearing a parent ask if you'd mind them giving you up for adoption. Seriously, I know that might sound ridiculous, but this was Matt Baxter.

And he was asking to quit it?

I was dumbfounded. I actually wondered if this question was some sort of bad joke, but finally Matt looked up at me, and I could abruptly see how very old he'd become. It wasn't all at once, you realize — not as though Egesta alone had worn him down. No, he was suffering from the post-war environment... from the fact that obligations that had kept him going for so long were now behind him.

With all the immediate jobs out of the way, he was suddenly able to process everything he'd been able to ignore during the war... fights he'd been in, people lost, atrocities found. All those things can pile up inside a person, and eventually come out.

How it comes out is unique to each individual, and is also quite beyond our control. Some seem fine, then burst into self-destruction. Others wear it all the time, much as Andrea Kiley had since 2231.

For Matt, it was manifesting as fatigue — deep and desperate fatigue. He and his crew had spent weeks polishing their fine ship, hoping in some secret, silly way that putting a gloss on their hull would make them feel fresher.

It hadn't worked. And now Matt — the rock for his crew, and for me — was ready to throw in the towel.

As I looked straight at my old friend, I considered trying to talk him out of what he was thinking. I could try some compelling argument about how the tempo would be different... I could talk about how Karen and I would probably need him now more than ever before... I could talk about his career prospects, which were beyond bright...

All of that was irrelevant.

When a man decides it's his time to stop fighting, after doing so much of it for so long, you'd have to be supremely arrogant to claim you know better than he does.

If anyone ever doubted what Matt Baxter had done for our squadron, our Empire, or me personally, that doubter would have to answer to me in a duel.

So it seemed to be Matt's time.

Leaning back in my chair, I took a deep breath and let my eyes fall for a second, "Well."

"Sorry to spring that on you. It's been something I've needed to ask for a few months, rather wish I could have saved it for another time," Matt's tone remained dry, even a little grim.

I shook my head, then shrugged, "I really don't think you need to apologize."

Matt fell silent, and I did too. For a moment we just sat there, eyes pointed at different places on the floor because it seemed better for us both to be lost in momentary introspection. After that pause I took a deep breath and then shook my head.

"I can't tell you if it's your time, Matt. I'd never try. You want to go, just tell me how I can help. We'll make sure you're set up, wherever you need to be," I said it directly, hoping it was the right thing to say.

"I don't have any particular designs yet," Matt replied quietly. "I just... I'll make it effective in January. Give you some time to find a new skipper."

That was it. We were losing Matt Baxter... and I'd need to put someone else on the bridge of *Friendly*. Another lost friend... the old Belt Squadron wasn't quite so whole as we'd thought.

Many of the hulls were the same, and a few faces too... but we'd soon have to be something new and different. Different didn't mean worse, necessarily, but it's natural to lament change. Particularly when change means a dear friend like Matt Baxter.

"It's been an honor serving with you, sir."

Of course the bastard — that's you Matt, I know you're reading — had to say that. I hate it when people say that, and I hate it worse when they mean it. Matt meant it. And like a sonofabitch he even said 'sir' at the end.

I couldn't believe he'd said it at first, but my eyes jumped up to him and then I leaned forward, for the first time feeling a stab of anger, "Honored?"

Matt was surprised by my tone, so he met my gaze with a frown.

"You understand you're the reason I'm still alive, right? You know what having you watch my back meant for all those years. You realize that there aren't many people I'd trust with this ship, or with this crew... or with Karen. You know that *honored* is not a good enough word, don't you?"

I think my tone was a sign that I wasn't taking the news well. It was starting to sink in very slowly: Charlie was gone, and so was Marshal and ultimately Wes. Mark Gunney was on the sick list, Erica Martin and Kyle Stranks were dead. And now Matt Baxter, the rock of Gibraltar as far as I'd been concerned, was leaving.

He was staring at me, too, and then he decided to one-up me with his British cleverness, "You know that the Empire's still here because of you, don't you? You know that Karen's alive because of you. It has been an honor, and it has changed my life. A lot of lives, in fact."

I glared at Matt, absurdly frustrated with him. He was leaving. And worse, he was being eloquent about it.

"Damn you for that," I muttered, then got to my feet and paced to the far wall of the day cabin. A picture of *Friendly* was mounted on the bulkhead, and as I came to a stop nose-to-nose with the ship, Matt remained seated.

Silence endured for a moment, my mind racing as I started really processing the implications, and Matt just waiting.

Finally he changed the subject, "You kissed Karen at a press conference?"

I wasn't really paying attention when I answered, "Of course I did."

Then I turned around, and found that Matt had pulled his boots up onto his desk.

"You don't need me anymore, Ken," he said. "Whatever you think, you two are very different from the angry kids you were back when you needed me. I wouldn't leave if that weren't true."

Matt Baxter knew. He'd seen us before, and while he wasn't quite as close to us as Charlie Peters was, he remained one of the very few who did understand what he was talking about.

I stared at him for a moment, then let out a breath.

"You think people think Karen and I have been together for years now?" I asked, managing a smile.

Matt raised his eyebrow, "Have you been?"

The question made me grin, and I took another breath, "Who should take over *Friendly*?"

"Jim Hannigan," Matt had no trouble coming up with that answer, and it was pretty much obvious too. If Kate Levec was getting *Lady Grace*, Jim deserved *Friendly*.

"I'll make it happen," I said. "And…"

"Let's not get maudlin," Matt held up his hand. "Talk to me about the new Emperor. Are we all going to die?"

It was a severe question, and with a chuckle, I shrugged, "I don't know if Daragh's given us permission for that."

From there we began to catch up, as if somehow it was all normal.

But it wasn't normal, and nothing could be when Matt Baxter was leaving the Belt Squadron behind.

Chapter Sixteen

The Gang

With so much change in the offing, it became quickly clear to Karen and me that we needed to get everyone together one last time — a last hurrah for the old Belt Squadron, including everyone who could possibly attend.

It would be senior officers mainly, all the people who'd been together before the war, fighting the Syndicate… and a few special guests who'd earned their way into the company of the Belt Squadron.

Because there was so little activity in Earth orbit, and because the reorganization of Admiralty House had John tied up, we knew we had at least until the end of the year to plan this thing, but neither Karen nor I wanted to wait — word was that Daragh was going to host a massive Empire Day gala at his Government Palace, and we were all going to be obliged to attend, so early December was the best choice…

As if scheduling is something you need to worry about.

Anyway, on the first evening that worked for everyone, we called for the Belt Squadron Party — a decidedly uncreative name, but an accurate one.

Hosted in the Officers' Club aboard *Wolf*, we got everyone together. Obviously Karen and I were there, along with Andrea Kiley and Jim Hannigan. *Wolf's* senior officers were also welcomed — Rufus, Shelby, Adrienne, Andy Jenson, Alicia Morgan and Eugene Sengooba.

Wes Pellew joined us, as did Mik Mikaelsen (by special invitation, even though he hadn't been with us before the war). Marshal and Mel Samuels both came aboard too, and now that Mel's identity was gradually becoming public, there were no concerns about justifying her presence.

She'd brought Grant Merger's Syndicate under our guns, after all.

Kris Jacobs obviously came, and so did Kate Levec. Matt Baxter's impending departure had been made public, but he still had every right to attend, and he did. Isoruku Togo and Katya Romanov rounded out our old skippers, as Mark Gunney's continued treatments down at the military hospital barred him from travelling. We missed having him, but it was quite vital he focus on his recovery — *Cheetah* would be waiting for him when he was able to stand again.

Our last guest was, of course, Greg Noyce. Many great Admirals had relationships with the Belt Squadron, but remember that at the start of the war we had all worked directly for Greg, and though he was now on the not-so-secret track to become Second Lord, and undoubtedly to succeed John as First Lord in a couple of years, Greg remained the quintessential Belt Squadron commanding officer.

By the time he turned up, the party was in full swing… not that there was a whole lot of debauchery happening — we were a relatively well-behaved bunch, at least when ship-to-ship weapons weren't involved. Still, I noticed Greg arriving through the windows at the front of the club, and stepped away from Karen and out through the door to catch him as he entered.

Smiling, he extended his hand, "Good party?"

I took his hand and shrugged, "Well you just arrived, so I think it's now in freefall."

Chuckling, Greg nodded, "Sure…"

He looked inside the club for a moment, then nodded back towards the corridor, "Talk for a moment, Ken?"

We slipped away from the festivities, only Karen noticing we were gone. As we reached a quieter spot in the corridor I could tell Greg had business on his mind, "Marshal has requested to finish up with the Belt Station in 2235. He'll return for a couple of months to tie up loose ends, then we need someone new to command out there. And someone new to command the Belt Squadron."

It was a relatively loaded explanation, and I figured I knew what he was getting at. I wasn't wrong.

"You'll be Vice Admiral effective the end of January, and Karen will be Rear Admiral at the same time. Command of the Belt Station and the Belt Squadron are yours, however you choose to divide them," Greg said.

Not really a surprise. That might sound conceited, but I don't mean it to — there just weren't enough flag officers staying around for anyone else to get the jobs.

"Thought that might happen," I replied quietly. "I'll let Karen take first pick, but my bet is she'll want the space command."

Nodding slowly, Greg went on, "Wes will continue to have the Belt Anti-Piracy Force, and Commodore Mikaelsen will return to the Independent Belt as our senior officer on station. Though I understand he might be leaving as well?"

"In time," I confirmed.

Greg had attacked Mars with Mik, and then we'd all been at Mercury together. The soon-to-be-Second Lord knew what he was losing in that man.

"We're going to miss a lot of these people," he said.

"If they're in government, we're going to benefit from them," I shrugged in reply, and I suppose it was a good point because Greg agreed.

"True. Very true…" he paused. "You know any good Captains we should promote out there?"

I thought about that for a moment, then one name came to mind, "Sela Kinder was able to keep her ship with us through the whole of 2233. She's rising fast… she'd probably make a good deputy for Mik, and she could take over when he departs."

Greg nodded, and though I know Sela would have been noticed for her quality no matter what I said, I was glad to give her the plug. She was one of those who'd really earned our respect.

"Rachel Butler is going to Venus to be Marlene's deputy," Greg drifted on to a different part of the Empire with those words. "Marlene's being promoted to full Admiral, too."

"About time," I said — blurted, actually — and that drew a smile from Greg.

"The landscape will look very different in a lot of places when everyone stops moving. We should be alright, but there will be gaps if we lose too many more people."

It was a sober assessment of the situation, and I couldn't disagree. The war itself had cost us good people, but now a nasty mix of fatigue and opportunity were robbing us of some of the very best. That's why it was good that Greg was moving into Admiralty House; he'd be able to identify talent and get it deployed to the right places, at the right times.

After all, the Belt Squadron officers in the club behind us were all people he'd selected. All were damned good, as I think you've figured out by now, and though I represent a blemish on his perfect record of picking great officers, I think we can safely say Greg was a master at organizing a good force.

My editors are telling me not to be so self-depreciating. I'm not smart enough to understand what that means, so I'm ignoring them.

"We'll be alright," I said finally, concluding the little conference between Admirals. "And hopefully we won't have any heavy fighting to do for a long, long time."

It might have sounded like wishful thinking, but Greg nodded nonetheless. We hoped for calm… but for now, it was time to socialize.

Andrea Kiley was sitting at a table with Shelby McLaws and Adrienne Thompson, the two junior women carrying on in their usual, familiar style while the Irish skipper remained largely disengaged. She was gradually emptying the glass of beer in front of her, but aside from occasional glances up, she was keeping her focus largely on the tabletop.

She didn't notice it, but both Shelby and Adrienne were sharing concerned glances, and pointing a few at her. Neither was inclined to say anything — the skipper was free to be as antisocial as she wanted to be, and by this time her behavior wasn't really a surprise to anyone…

But there was a slightly heavier undercurrent than usual.

They couldn't put their finger on it, and frankly no one else watching *Wolf's* Captain could have either… no one other than the Commodore of the Independent Squadron, that is. Wes busied himself talking to Mik about the prospects for the Belt in the years after the war, a topic of interest to both since Wes' formation would be patrolling it extensively.

Strangely, neither Mik nor Wes recall much of what they were saying during this conversation. Wes was watching Andrea out of the corner of his eye, and he was completely preoccupied with her. This preoccupation wasn't tied to any particular emotion — he felt no regret over the words they'd exchanged at Egesta, and no anger either… for some reason he just needed to keep her in sight, and watch for any sign she might be preoccupied with him.

For his part, Mik was really struggling with decisions about his future. He was pretty certain he'd be going into the Belt Party when he left the fleet, but the question was when that departure was going to take place. Marshal was making his move relatively soon, but the Belt-born Commodore with the goatee felt he had more options.

He'd wait and see.

That approach would probably work for politics, but it wasn't much help for Wes. Our elite Commodore simply kept away from Andrea, and she kept pretending not to even see him. They were both constantly aware of each other, though… it was just beyond either of them to do anything more.

Andrea had invoked Wes' dead wife in the context of an argument. Wes had called

Andrea out on being self-absorbed. They had not spoken much since, and it was a fair question whether they ever would again, outside the requirements of duty.

Kris Jacobs cornered Matt Baxter at the bar and bought him a drink. Kate Levec came over as well, and together they laughed a bit about timing — how the two ladies were just getting back in time to watch their charming black Briton leave the squadron.

Matt was never built to be overly charming, but in possession of a drink and with the certainty that he'd soon be a civilian, the former security man seemed to loosen up. His laughter was an unexpected and pleasant addition to the Officers' Club.

While those three laughed, Karen found herself in front of Marshal and Mel.

"So you're finally able to stop pretending you're a civilian?" Karen put the question to the retired superspy, and Melissa shrugged.

"Soon, at least. Before Marshal makes any move for the House of Commons, it'll be important to get who I am out into the open. I'm not naïve enough to think Grant won't be looking for me, and high visibility won't help, but we'll take on extra security…"

Marshal smiled at that, "I doubt extra security will be better at protecting you than you are."

It was a good point — it was hard to imagine anyone, except perhaps a Special Brancher, who could protect someone like Melissa Fox. I mean, if she needed someone with a vest to take a shot for her, guards might be helpful… but it was hard to believe that anyone could spot a threat better than she could.

Karen smiled at that implication, "Well it'll be good to see you get the recognition you deserve. And if Grant comes after you, we'll make him regret it."

There was no doubting the certainty in Karen's words, and I'm sure you could understand why. She and Grant had been friends, though not as Grant and I had been friends way back when. She did rather hate the fellow… which is not to say I didn't, just that hell hath no fury like a goddess who has it in for you.

Anyway, Karen moved off to catch up with Katya Romanov, and just as she did, Rufus closed in.

It was rather funny watching Rufus and Mel in close proximity to one another… they both did such a good job of seeming nonchalant, but you could tell they both had the capacity to generate countless metaphors based on their killing abilities.

Who'd win in a fight?

That's a trick question, because any fight faced with the prospect of involving these two would grow terrified and run away before it began.

Oh yes, I'm saying they're so deadly they could kill a fight.

Shut up, it does make sense.

After some time catching up one-on-one, Greg Noyce tapped some cutlery on his glass, and brought the room to silence. Our former CO seemed genuinely pleased to be back amongst us, and we were glad to have him.

He also had warm words, which we appreciated: "When this war started, I knew we would not all come through. I am deeply saddened by the losses we have suffered, both to death and injury. But I believe this war has proved, beyond any doubt, that when a team is built on the principles of fellowship, partnership and collaboration, it truly can become a force to be reckoned with."

There were some 'hear hears' at that, and Greg continued, "Now that we have the fighting behind us, we all face new paths. Some of you will return to your old posts, some to new ones, and some will leave Defense Command. All of you will remain charter members of this Belt Squadron, and I want to take this moment to thank you for your service. God bless, good luck."

With that he raised his glass, and everyone present raised their glasses as well.

"The Belt Squadron," Matt Baxter made the toast official, and we drank.

That wasn't the end of the speeches though. If you find them terribly boring, accept my apologies, but I must include them because, frankly, they mean a hell of a lot to me. There aren't many chances in life when you get to address so many people who matter so much to you... and this was one of them.

One of the last ones, in fact.

"Next year we're all going to be sitting in our cabins, wondering where we've ended up, and why," Karen said from the middle of the club, turning so she could look around at the faces of her officers.

She was so good at this... wonderful. She didn't address a group like this one very often, but when she did, they listened.

"When you wonder how you came by your path, remember that you crossed through here. Remember us... this family, all of us together like brothers and sisters. All of us together as the closest of friends, bonded against anything you care to name by the fact that, when the Martians came, and when the Syndicate came before them, we looked to each other, and stood fast, and won," she paused, turning in place one more time to see everyone. "I have never served with a better force, and I never will again. To you."

The softness of her words — tenderness, almost — masked for me the one comment I should have winced at... the one that, as I read it back now, represented a clear temptation of fate.

No one else paid it any attention either, and we all drank. Leaning against the frame of the entrance door, I just looked on as we went through the ritual, and then hoped things were over and done with... but they weren't.

They all looked at me, and because this was my force, I realized I had to say something. But I didn't know what I could add — not after Greg and Karen. These were my extended family, as Karen had so eloquently explained.

They kept looking at me, and it got a little awkward. Finally I shifted my position slightly, though I continued to lean against the door frame. Then I started talking without really thinking about what I said... the best way, I think you'll agree, to make a fool of yourself.

"You all are the reason I'm still alive. You're the reason you're alive. If we tried to count the times lives were saved... if we could even know the number... it would be too much. If I'm ever asked to tell the story of this war, the message I'm going to have is simple: this Belt Squadron is the best. We are different. What we have here doesn't happen much. Some people don't believe it happens at all. But here we are. Here, in front of the Empire and history, we have made a difference. And I damn anyone, anywhere, to find me a better group of men and women."

I stopped for a moment, deciding that if I was to end on something supposedly profound, it might as well make sense.

"One day, this Empire will end, and whoever comes next will look to our history, and see legends. They will believe some of what they read, they'll dismiss a lot of it as myth. But the stories will live on. And one day, when the ashes of the Black Sun are long lost, the story of this squadron will endure. Men and women who reached out and made their mark, who suffered, fought, lived and died. Those who come next will tell our stories to their children, they will think we couldn't have been real. But we were real. We are real. And from now until the day I die, I will be proud to say that when war came to the Empire, I fought with the Belt Squadron."

They liked that speech, I think. One of them even made a (surprising low quality) recording of it on her comm. And we all drank to it.

I... well, you know by now how highly I think of these people. How good they were, and are. I just hoped that came through, because of the few things that I could offer them after all they'd done, sincere thanks seemed the most important.

We stayed together late into the night — one last hurrah before we all went our separate ways. Old spacers, a war over, and bright futures ahead.

CHAPTER SEVENTEEN

A SWIM

So we get to the end of 2234 — pretty much literally — and that means I don't have any more time to hide from the events that were destined to dominate 2235. You better believe I'm going to make the absolute most of what remains in this book.

And that means I'm actually going to talk about swimming.

It was finally confirmed that Daragh was indeed going to host a mighty Empire Day celebration at the Government Palace on December 31 — a New Year's Eve and religious-holiday-of-choice celebration, with Defense Command veterans invited instead of Lords.

The Lords weren't particularly offended; they didn't care to spend their free time with the Irishman anyway — Emperor or no, he wasn't their kind.

Of course, anything hosted at a palace was going to be fancy… court dress fancy, to be precise. We'd managed to make it through most of the war without getting back into that painful attire, but now we were destined to wear it all again.

At least this time it would be on a planet, so the lack of decompression provisions in the tailoring wouldn't be so disconcerting.

Anyway, it's fair to say that, when so many invitations went out to Defense Command personnel in December, a bit of excitement started to creep into the fleet. Daragh's bash was going to be huge, and it seemed that everyone was invited… he was going to blow the 'luxuries fund' he'd been given on a party for the people who, as far as he was concerned, deserved it most.

There'd be something for everyone at this massive party, and even I — *me* — was actually thinking it was going to be fun.

Me!

People started going down to Earth to shop for clothes, shoes and other things that you wear when going to fancy Emperor's galas. Dates were secured, and all in all, it might as well have been a high school prom.

Yes, we Defense Command officers, so accustomed to being responsible combatants, were looking forward to the chance to revive our youths and have some fun.

Karen was not immune to any of this. She went down to Earth and did some shopping, though whenever I asked her about it, she refused to tell me what she'd found. I was thus left in some suspense about what to expect… but since it was Karen I knew it had to be spectacular.

For my part, I dug out my court dress again, and much to my relief found that it fit better than it had back at the Hawke Protectorate when last I'd worn it. Less time in the gym meant my shoulders had gotten a little bit less bulky… right. Ahem.

Anyway, with this event scheduled to begin at 1800 hours on 31 December, there was plenty of preparation required. Aboard every ship in orbit, people would spend long hours making themselves look fancified, and Naval business would be secondary.

Normally I would chide such a mixup of priorities, but after the whole of this series, I think everyone had earned a day of fun.

What we hadn't earned — or I hadn't earned, anyway — was a 0430 start to the day.

"Why do you think this is anything approaching a good idea?"

I sounded like a grumpy child, because it was 0430 in the morning and I was standing on the deck of *Wolf's* swimming pool, watching Karen pull her ponytail up into a bun against the back of her head and then put on her goggles.

Yes, she was wearing a bathing suit. Yes, if you're the sort of person who finds the female form attractive, then you'd pretty much keel over at the sight.

But it was 0430, and fatigue has a way of masking even the most fundamental appreciations of life.

"A bracing swim to start the day," Karen's answer was far too enthusiastic as she began to stretch out her arms in a wiggly fashion.

Yes wiggly. Look I was tired, it was the best I could do.

"Bracing?" I scowled at the word as I remained on the deck.

"Absolutely," she replied with a smile, turning and stepping towards the water's edge. "I've always wanted to try this."

Watching her approach the side of the pool, my tired brain made only half the connections it should have. First of all, we were in *Wolf's* pool chamber and the door was locked. Pulling rank, Karen had managed to get the place reserved for us... which is a good thing, because you know how busy it gets at 0430.

Right.

Second thing that warranted some notice was that, as you might be aware, Karen famously couldn't swim. She had the facility for it but every time she tried she sank like a stone, started breathing water, and ended up lying on the deck afterwards coughing and berating herself for even thinking she should try.

Third, we were standing at the deep end of the pool — which metaphorically sounds about right for us, but also represented a clear and present danger to Karen's immediate breathing ability.

"Wait a second," I started to wake up just before Karen hopped from the deck, and then down she went into the water.

Well dammit. There was nothing for me to do but follow her in, because I actually could swim — did it competitively for four years back in school. Turning towards the water I took two quick steps and dove in.

The water was cold.

Bracing indeed.

Surfacing quickly, I turned and looked back towards the wall I'd come off, wondering if Karen was on the surface. On this end, the pool was seven feet deep, so if she was standing on the bottom her head was obviously going to be submerged...

Her head bobbed up from under the blue water after a second, and she was smiling as she fought to float, "I'm making progress!"

Splashing her way towards me, she crossed the water in a slow, steady fashion, until she reached a spot on the sloping floor where her feet could touch bottom while her head stayed above the surface. From there she walked the last couple of meters to me, sinking down with every step on the inclining floor so only her head would be visible.

As she came to a stop and pulled the goggles away from her eyes, she was beaming, "I think I want to learn to swim on our next tour."

I was still grumpy, just more awake about it, "First lesson: how not to swim at ungodly hours."

With a shrug that splashed her shoulders to the surface, Karen played silly-innocent, "Sorry, I'm not very experienced. I wish you'd show me."

Yeah yeah double entendres etc. She was being evil. I was convinced then that she'd decided on this early swim specifically to make sure I was extra tired during the gala… or something. But for the moment we were in a swimming pool all by ourselves, and the door was locked.

What was I saying about high school kids and fantasies and whatnot? Maybe that was fueling her silliness.

Anyway, the point she was alluding to certainly wasn't wrong — this was a very clear opportunity to get up to mischief.

That being the case, I turned towards Karen, reached out to her, and put a hand on her shoulder. Taking her feet off the pool floor, she drifted towards me slightly, and then I did what I think any of us would do under these circumstances.

I dunked her and ran for the deep end.

By the time she came up, gasping and trying to clear her eyes, I was in deep water.

"In over your head, are you?" I was being a bit of a bastard, you'll agree, but she was used to that by now. So she mounted her attack, and it was a good one.

There's no way to really write about horsing around in a pool. If you haven't done it, I think you really should — it's quite enjoyable. In a lot of ways it's like being in zero gee, but it's very different too, because you're surrounded by something strong and soothing… it holds you up, it lets you pass through it with ease, it gives you something to hold onto.

For those of you thinking in a certain direction, I'll tell you what it does *not* do: it does not make for good romance. I'm sure many people think being alone in a pool is a great recipe for some particular activities, but I very much disagree. Unless you can hold your breath for a really long time, find cold plating against flesh to be appealing, and like it when your skin starts pruning.

No, when we tired of chasing each other around, splashing and basically acting like a couple of kids, Karen and I ended up in the shallow end, sitting on the bottom of the lowest point in the pool — a section specifically designed to allow people to sit and go through range-of-motion exercises on damaged joints. Zero-gee movement therapy is good, but when you need to start adding resistance, water is the next step…

Anyway, we sat there, Karen sort of using me as a chair, since there wasn't much lateral room for us to spread out.

She'd finally stopped coughing, had let down her ponytail, and was clearly pretty pleased with herself.

"I think that's a great way to start the day," she declared after she'd consumed enough oxygen to restore her ability to speak.

"I think we'll find a better time of day if you plan on making a habit of this," I grumbled, pretty much right into her ear because of the way she was sitting.

I did notice that the water on her skin actually brought out the faintest line on the left side of her neck — there was actually a scar there, but only if you looked hard and knew to expect it. I decided not to mention that to her, as it wasn't in keeping with the mood of the day.

"Well, when we get to Belt Two, I suppose it may not be much of a worry," she replied, a little less happily.

My eyes drifted up to the side of her face, and I could see the corners of her mouth were leveling out from their smile. She was thinking about the reality that was to come: we'd be on different ships again, or more precisely she'd be commanding the Belt Squadron from *Wolf* and I'd commanding the Belt Station from an office on Belt Two Base.

Sure we'd get to see each other a lot, and there wasn't a war on so the concerns about separation could be less acute… but we were coming to the end of this luxurious period of being together all the time, with no one to shoot at and no one shooting at us.

It was sad, but by no means tragic, and realizing that Karen started to turn the corners of her mouth up again.

"Think of how happy we'll be to see each other every time I come home from a cruise," she turned her head to look right at me, and I think I managed to smile too.

"Speak for yourself," I replied, and she chuckled, then tried to elbow me in the stomach.

Fortunately, the water slowed the progress of that elbow sufficiently, and instead of pursuing further aggression, she just settled back against me and we talked some more. Starting the day with a swim was indeed bracing, I suppose, but eventually we did have to leave so that others could partake in *Wolf's* modest little pool.

There was an overblown high school dance to prepare for, after all…

CHAPTER EIGHTEEN

RAGEFUL

If I'd been at all clairvoyant, I might have sent a message to my good friend Charlie Peters, letting him know that a pool was a fine tool for soothing conversation with someone who wasn't having the best of days... or months, I should say.

The storm cloud that had been growing over Lia's head during the memorial tour was pretty significant, and as Charlie watched the tension mount he continued to wonder about the best way to deal with it. For the short term he simply kept out from underfoot — there was no point trying to stir up trouble when Lia needed all her energy for the people she was seeing.

But the time was coming for him to act; they had just finished their visit to Hawke Six, and that meant that everyone had seen Ian's body and paid their respects. The jockeying for position was over, at least for the short term, and Lia and Charlie were returning to their capital to take up the reins of leadership.

That meant there was time to trigger a fight, or do whatever was necessary to get Lia to start venting her frustrations in a healthy manner.

I'm sure you're thinking they could have just talked about it... maybe she could have taken up a hobby like dancing or target shooting. Yes, those are options, but Charlie, knowing Lia as he did, believed she needed a more dramatic catharsis. She'd spent so much time bottling up angry rants that she was bursting at the seams...

And given all the fine scars that now covered her body, I don't really like the bursting at the seams metaphor for her.

As *Zephyr*, the frigate that was carrying her, Charlie and Ian Hawke's body away from Hawke Six worked up to speed, Lia made her way back to her cabin. She'd sent the final farewell from the bridge, as was her protocol, and now she was going to find a bit of peace and quiet. The whole thing was over, she was exhausted, and she hoped that maybe fatigue would lead to rest, and that somehow rest would lead to an easing of frustration.

As she strode through the corridors of this ship, which was identical to *Whirlwind* but hadn't been to war, she started opening the flap on her tunic. She was, of course, in uniform aboard ship, because court dress didn't make any sense when she was acting as a fleet officer.

Reaching her cabin just in time for the tunic to come off, she opened her hatch and tossed the garment to the chair as she entered. It landed on Charlie, who was sitting in the dark with a severe expression.

At first Lia didn't notice her consort, but as she switched on the light and started untucking her undershirt, she turned and saw him sitting there with her tunic in his lap.

"What?" her question was sharp, and not particularly friendly.

Charlie stared at her for a moment, and as he watched her fold her arms he considered calling off his plan. But he was concerned, as I would be, that soft-pedaling the next part would just mean they had to deal with it over and over again.

Lifting her tunic out of his lap, he decided to use it as a prop. And then with more reluctance than you can probably comprehend, he proceeded to cleanse with fire.

"If you're serious about wearing this uniform, you have to stop pandering to every stupid tradition your father built into this government."

That was it, all he needed to say. Every word had been carefully selected over the course of several on-pad drafts, and then the delivery had been practiced for hours. Adapting the line to reflect the prop was a last-minute bit of improvisation, but it worked perfectly because the message Charlie needed to deliver was so clear in his head.

By asking what he asked, he triggered Lia's ongoing insecurities about her military abilities, the frustrations that she shared with him about the impracticalities of the court life they were leading, her love for and hatred of her father, and the fact that she secretly feared that Charlie was going to get fed up with all of it and leave her and the Protectorate behind. He also implied that fear was stupid, which was one of the more fundamental things that Lia had a problem with, and most importantly, thanks to the lecturing tone, he actually sounded like he was talking down to her.

Like I said, every single piece of that opening statement was calculated to press Lia's 'explode' button, and you will perhaps not be surprised to learn that it worked.

"Serious about the uniform? If you're serious about being a Lord here maybe you should show a little respect. I know this system doesn't work, and you know it too, but we can't change everything overnight, or they're going to turn on us. And everything we've worked for, everything my father built here, could turn into a fucking mess. You think I should let any one of these rocks spin off into oblivion? You think I should let the local Lords and Ladies prance around and give orders without any concept of what's really at stake?"

She paused very briefly for breath.

"Everything can't be as simple as it is in the fleet, or in Special Branch. You can't just blow up the problems, you can't be so direct. And even if I wanted to right now, it would look like I was following Daragh, because of course he just had to go and be the renegade. Take that chance away from everyone else. If I want to be like him I have to find a way to justify it that doesn't include the words 'because they're doing it in the Empire'. It's bad enough that my consort is a DC war hero… people think I can't even do this job on my own. They just assume that I'm still daddy's little girl. I show them my fucking scars…"

She tugged her untucked shirt up enough to reveal the criss-cross pattern of scars on her midriff.

"…I show them that I now have the texture of canvas, and they tut-tut and think I should get that fixed because it's not courtly. And yet they don't realize that I'm more qualified for this job now than my dad ever was. When did he ever fight a war? When did he have to be pieced back together by doctors for months? When did he do that knowing that all he had to come back to was the legacy of work that his parents laid down for him? He never did. No one ever did, but no one gives me any credit for it. I was good in command of that squadron. I really was… I know I was… but no one really sees it. No one respects it, and I don't understand why."

She let her shirt go, so it fell back to her belt.

"And he wasn't even there to tell me good job when I finally got back. He had to die, quietly and without me so long ago, and because of his stupid fucking government I couldn't tell anyone, not until I proved I was tougher than him… and I did that… I helped conquer Mercury and fought the Fleet Clash… but still they don't listen. And I don't want to have to keep doing this. I want to change things so they're like you say. I really do. But I can't. Not until everyone is so sure I have absolute control that they don't try to stop me. Because once they're afraid of me… then we can make this right… but until then…"

She was starting to run out of steam. She really was tired, because Charlie had figured for sure she'd be able to keep going a few minutes longer.

"I just… stop trying to tell me that I have to do something I know I have to do. Or if you really can't stand this, then go home. I accept that you couldn't have known what this was going to be like. I hoped you would be able to predict and understand… but no one can. This isn't a life, so if you hate it that much, just leave. I won't blame you, and the Lords will probably be relieved to get rid of a Defense Command spy in their court. I know you love me, or you used to, so I set you free. Go on, get away from this toxic place and just let me burn here. One day I might make it a place fit for you to come and stay, but for now you should go back to a place with rules that make sense for you."

She began shaking her head, and as the emotions finally started punching themselves out, tears formed. Finally she started to buckle — physically. She gradually bent at the waist as though there was a great pain in her abdomen, and planting her hands on her knees she let her head hang.

A lot of things started bubbling out of her subconscious then — things that really hadn't come free since we'd seen her at Belt Two, back in *The Canary Wars*. She had a tough time keeping on her feet, and finally she let herself drop down to one knee as sobs started to rack her body.

I've said it before, and again it applies: paradise was burning.

And it had to. It was like the forest fire that clears the deadwood from the undergrowth, and allows renewal and new growth. Cleansed by fire… sometimes it's not as bad a thing as it sounds.

Charlie watched Lia sob alone and broken on the floor for a moment. He didn't like watching, believe me, but he had to be sure that she'd gotten all the things she needed to say out of her system before he stepped out of the guise he'd assumed to trigger her response.

Counting back from ten, he watched her put both knees on the floor, and then both hands on her knees, and when the sobs continued, he figured that was enough.

This is the part where all the gentlemen who like ladies should take note, and all the ladies who like gentlemen can swoon appropriately.

Because he's a Special Brancher, Charlie can cover short distances faster than light. Shut up, it *might* be hyperbole. Before Lia had any idea what was going on, she'd been scooped up and deposited on the bed, and as she opened her eyes and tried to clear them, she managed to catch sight of her consort disappearing through the door to the kitchen.

She then discovered there was a box of tissues on the bed next to her, so she plucked a few and wiped her eyes, then blew her nose. She didn't want me to say the last part, because she doesn't think it's right for people to think of nose-blowing, but come on, we all know what happens when you really cry a lot. No one will hold it against her.

As soon as she could see again, but long before she felt any better, Charlie appeared out of the kitchen door holding up a container in each hand, "Chocolate or vanilla."

Lia really had no clue what he meant until she managed to focus her eyes and realize the containers he was holding were tubs of ice cream. That was... unexpected. She was in no way fit to answer, so Charlie decided for her: vanilla, because chocolate is for crazies.

In pudding, it's butterscotch that's for crazies, but in ice cream it's chocolate. So you shouldn't ever eat chocolate ice cream, just leave it for me and I'll deal with it.

Approaching the bed, he dropped the tub of ice cream and a spoon, then returned to the kitchen to put the chocolate container away.

Lia was, by now, more than a little confused. There were a lot of different ways she figured this scenario could have played out, but things were now seeming a little too well prepared. Like a plan was being executed, and she was being made a victim of Special Branch guile...

Trying to sit up, she put her hands on the bed behind her and began to shift position... but her fingertips brushed up against the edge of a pad. Recognizing the metallic feel, she turned uncomfortably and pulled the thing out from under the flap of the comforter, then turned it on.

Of course it was the pad Charlie had used to draft his question, so on the screen she saw the words: "If you're serious about leadership, you have to stop pandering to every stupid tradition your father built into this government."

And in the header at the top, she saw the document's file name: "How to make Lia say what she's not willing to say unless I set her off... Hi Lia eat your ice cream."

Not sure why Charlie made that the file name instead of just putting the text on screen next to the statement itself. Because of Defense Command's superior OS XX programs, a file name that long worked fine, though, so I guess he just figured it was a good place to put the message.

Now, Charlie had planned all of this out pretty carefully, but the one thing he wasn't absolutely certain of was Lia's reaction when she realized he'd intentionally set her off. She could laugh it off and everything would be okay, or if she had fight left, she could really, *really* come after him for having the audacity to think he could manipulate her.

As he emerged from the kitchen door with an awkward smile, it quickly became evident that there wouldn't be any laughing. Lia's expression was not particularly bright, and as she looked up at him she dropped the pad, "You think you can play me like this? Mister Special Branch with your fancy plan to make me have a cathartic moment and then eat *ice cream?* What are we, in high school?"

No, Lia, Karen and I were in high school. Charlie was trying to be a Special Branch-quality consort.

Sorry, I have no idea why I'm responding to her accusatory question.

Charlie, for his part, said nothing, though he did let his smile fade.

Struggling to get off the bed, Lia knocked the pad and the tissue box onto the floor, and then forced herself to her feet. Emotions were still very heightened, you see, and she was reacting in a fashion which didn't necessarily reflect rationality.

If she'd thought it through as Charlie had, then she would have eaten her ice cream like a good girl. Instead she strode up to Charlie and pounded a finger into his chest, "Who do you think you are?"

At this point, Lia was pretty much right in Charlie's face, blocking his view of the bed. But he'd watched her come over, and he was reading her body language... wait a minute.

With Special Branch dexterity, he put his hands on her shoulders and pushed her back a step, "Go get the ice cream."

Lia's emotions were still surging, and she found the order inconsistent with anything that she expected to hear, "What?"

Charlie pointed to the ice cream tub that was sitting on the bed, "I'm going to put it away so it doesn't melt."

"But..." Lia looked at the bed, and then back at Charlie.

And then our Special Branch Lord-Major demonstrated why he'd be as deadly in court as he was everywhere else: he could read people really well.

"Look, your emotions are obviously at a high peak right now, so there's no question that when you accidentally knocked the pad and the tissue box off the bed, you were making room that you intend us to occupy in a minute. But you forgot the ice cream. If that melts and starts leaking out of the container, it'll make the sheets..." he didn't want to finish that sentence.

"A sticky mess?" Lia folded her arms, raising her eyebrows. "You seem awfully confident of yourself. Think you can just insult me and I'll take you to bed? Really?"

Charlie raised his eyebrow, "Well that wasn't my plan. I was thinking deep emotional catharsis and bonding. But clearly it's yours."

Lia opened her mouth, and then closed it. She started tapping her foot on the deck and looked away with some entertaining frustration, "Am I really that obvious?"

Shrugging, Charlie tried to be kind, "You have a couple of tells."

Lady Lia Hawke sighed profoundly, then turned and waved towards the bed, "Well can we just get to it already? Please?"

Charlie shrugged again, this time more apologetically, "Sorry..."

"Yeah yeah, come on," Lia approached him and grabbed his hand, leading him out of the kitchen doorway. Then, as they got closer to the bed, she stepped behind him and leaned in closer to his ear. "Just one thing. I didn't *forget* the ice cream."

And I'll stop the scene there. I can hear Charlie's peasants at my front door, ready to murder me on his behalf for including quite this much of the story, but I think we'll all agree it was worth it. Still, I should end on a dramatic line...

The Hawke Protectorate was *in good hands*.

I'm dead, I know. But I'm right, too.

Chapter Nineteen

Palace Gala

Keith Pine was the Emperor's Gamesmaster, and when the Empire Day gala was announced, the former Ministry of Agriculture man quickly learned that his position also included responsibility for putting on big parties.

Well, that wasn't in the job description, but considering he had a budget which could — and I mean this — build a new *Australia*-class corvette, he figured he could put on a big spectacle of an event, which would actually be fun for the Defense Command personnel, as well as the civilians.

Open bar (well, bars), a ballroom that was the size of *Ark Royal's* main flightdeck, live music, and good food... the formula wasn't terribly complicated, but the logistics of getting enough resources in place for a guest list of over 6,000 was considerable.

Keith did it, though, and whatever he might say about the shortfalls of his organizational effort, don't listen to him. He has nothing to censure himself about.

On the afternoon before the massive event, Schwartz T. Babcock found the bearded Gamesmaster on the main stage (where a huge band was set to play that night), looking out over the cavernous Government Palace ballroom.

"Everything coming together, Keith?" the EmpSec asked as he stopped beside the Gamesmaster.

With a shrug, Keith looked to his younger counterpart, "Well, I haven't killed anyone yet."

Schwartz did not miss a beat, because he never does, "I'm not going to lie, that disappoints me a little."

I think that disappoints us all a little, Schwartz... wait, I'm doing it again. I need to stop replying to people's dialogue.

Anyway, the pair of them — the only two people on Daragh's staff who the Emperor well and truly trusted this early into his reign — were responsible for making the arrangements for this massive event, and they did a great job.

Nothing more they could have done, really... and as they made their preparations, so did the rest of us.

Every ship in orbit was sending a delegation down to the ball, which was arguably a bit of a problem for planetary security... but none of us were worried. If anyone tried to attack Earth while we were kicking up our heels, the outer detection grid would give us two hours' notice, and we'd all race back to our ships wearing our fancy clothes.

Things like that have happened before. If you'll remember, Wellington found out that Napoleon was marching towards Quatre Bras (and ultimately Waterloo) while at a ball in Brussels. This was totally the same thing.

Shut up Napoleonic historians, no one wants to hear you explain how I'm wrong.

Anyway, on every ship you care to name, ladies and gentlemen were getting fancified in a variety of ways. Wes, who was obliged to attend as a Commodore, was putting on a light-color court dress suit, for instance — nothing too elaborate — while Kate Levec on *Lady Grace* was 'taping herself into' one of the latest ultra-chic fashions, right off the Cleveland runways.

We couldn't all be as fashion-forward as Kate, of course; Matt Baxter was attending in a black suit with tails that looked rather like it had come out of the twentieth century. It even had a top hat.

Me, I just put on my old court dress, which was the only particularly fancy garment I possessed aside from a dress uniform, and waited for Karen to climb into whatever secret gown she'd purchased for this occasion.

Now, I hope it won't destroy my credibility if I admit that I was a little bit excited to see what Karen was going to be wearing. Because I was. There's a weird, juvenile sense of anticipation under circumstances like these... an irrational magical quality that I think kids feel when they're going to things like prom, but we blustery old people lose, and rarely get back.

Picking up a girl and going to a big fancy dance? We all probably have warm memories of such events from our younger years... or if you're like me, you have warm ideas about what it would have been like if you hadn't been the antisocial kid who went to the dance alone, if at all. So for some of us, Daragh's big gala was an opportunity to recapture youthful energy, and for others amongst us, it was a chance to live it for the first time.

Hm, I think that probably did cost me some credibility. Oh well.

I finished getting ready before Karen did, which was somewhat unusual, but to preserve the anticipated excitement of the reveal of her dress, I decided to wait outside her cabin door instead of simply going in and helping.

As I leaned against the wall outside her quarters and looked down the corridor, I watched as other people destined for the gala emerged from their cabins and made their way to the flightdeck. Jim and Bunny were attending, so they both departed his cabin with time to spare. Andrea was also attending — whether that was a good idea or not is up for debate — and she emerged from her cabin shortly thereafter.

I always remember that Andrea's dress was gunmetal silver and shiny... made her look like a polished warship. Somehow that seemed appropriate to her state of mind...

They all left their cabins, and then there was silence for a while as I continued to wait on Karen. It felt like this took a long time, though realistically I think it was just a couple of minutes.

I was well rewarded for my patience.

I seem to recall having a problem describing women's clothes back in *The Hawke Mission*, all those years ago. Well, I'm in the same boat now... all I can say really is that when Karen opened her hatch and stepped out, she had no business looking the slightest bit nervous.

Alright, to answer the editors: color was black with white highlight things, or something like that. Yes it did have straps, but they went up around her neck and exposed her shoulders. The bottom 'dress' part was wide, but not too poofy. The waist was... well, perfect.

I was supposed to say something when Karen stopped outside her closed door — be a gentleman, compliment her choice of attire and the way she carried it off. I really didn't manage that, though, and all I could think was that raccoons really weren't the greatest threat facing the Empire, whatever Charlie Peters said.

Because remember, that's what he and I had been arguing about in *The Hawke Mission* when Lia and Karen were trying on dresses for court... yeah.

"Is speechlessness a good thing?" Karen prodded after a while of my ignorant non-talking, and with a blink or two I clued in.

"What?"

She got the message, so we headed to the flightdeck.

Defense Command shuttles are excellent multi-purpose vehicles, but when you start loading them up with big ball gowns, it gets tricky. And there were plenty of gowns — the ladies on this flight outnumbered the gentlemen.

Against Jim, Eugene Sengooba and I were Karen, Andrea, Bunny, Shelby, Adrienne, and Alicia Morgan. Rufus, Andy Jenson and Felicia Khalid were looking after *Wolf* while we took off to the ball — none of them had much interest in Daragh's big party.

So while the ladies ended up in the aisle seats, the chaps mostly stayed on their feet, and as the shuttle took off and headed for Terra Nova I moved up to the cockpit to watch our progress.

I'll remember that view for a long time, I think; the entire fleet was strewn across orbital space, the sun setting around the horizon, and small craft falling down from every ship. You get immune to scenes like that over time in the Navy, but probably because of the general youthful giddiness of the occasion, this image really stuck with me.

And then we dove down to the atmosphere, and took our position in the long line of small craft making their way towards the Government Palace. A flight that normally would have been fifteen or twenty minutes would take quite a lot longer, because so many of us were clogging up the approaches.

That was fine, we had all night. I wasn't even tired yet, and I'd been up twelve hours (thanks to Karen's swim plan).

The palace landing fields were a tightly-packed parking lot when we arrived, and as more and more shuttles were landing on a regular basis, Keith had thought to arrange transport for guests from their parking spots to the front gates of the palace. Fifteen hover-buses made regular runs back and forth the whole time, and once we landed and descended from our shuttle, we all spotted the nearest one and headed towards it.

Looking around, I really had to be surprised at the scale of this party — rows and rows of shuttles were stretching in every direction, and a swarm of finely-dressed people seemed to be making their way to the palace.

As we got to the bus route and started to board the hovering vehicle, I also spotted the SF guards standing around the perimeter of the field. There was an open bar at this event... the last thing anyone needed was an officer to have a little too much and then to decide she or he could fly while intoxicated.

Keith really had thought of everything.

"Sir, ma'am!"

I recognized the voice that drew my attention away from the organizational spectacle I was witnessing, but it took me the briefest of seconds to place it. Commander Bruce Arama was sitting at the back of the bus, and beside him was a woman who I correctly assumed to be his wife.

As Karen and I shuffled our way back past rows of bus seats towards the Kiwi reservist, he and his wife both came to their feet.

"Bruce, good to see you!" Karen's greeting left no doubt that, even a couple of months after their last meeting, she still warmly remembered her Maori savior from the Fleet Clash.

"Daragh made sure to invite you," I added, coming up behind Karen and watching my feet so as not to step on her dress.

"Yes sir he did," Bruce replied, and then he turned and quite eagerly presented his wife, "This is Talia, my bride and the mother of my daughters."

Talia seemed a little star-struck, which I immediately decided we'd have to correct by the end of the night. If anyone in the back of the bus was a star, it was her husband — the man who saved Karen and *Lady Grace*.

As we all shook hands, Karen made conversation with Talia Arama, and I ended up beside Bruce, "How's life? Getting back to normal, I hope?"

Nodding, *Adelaide's* former Commander managed to smile, "Business is good. I'm still getting accustomed to running such a small shop. If we can find the work, we might go bigger... I'm pretty confident that now I could handle the extra organizational headaches."

The bus started moving as I nodded, "The Navy prepares you for all sorts of careers."

Bruce smiled, then chuckled, "Did you just quote a recruiting vid, sir?"

I paused, then pointed at Shelby — whose back was to us as she sat beside Adrienne, "I was quoting Shelby McLaws. But she said it in a recruiting vid... so yes."

"Then I suppose you can believe some things you hear on the vids," the Kiwi reservist smiled, and I instantly shook my head.

"You probably just got lucky."

Or we did, in having him join the fleet. However you slice it, it was great that Bruce was here.

The approach to the main entrance of the palace was, of course, a red carpet one. The media were lined up behind ropes the whole way along, with SF keeping them polite as notables passed through their gauntlet of cameras and microphones.

I keep mentioning SF, by the way, because there's a point I'd like to make: the Imperial Army should, by rights, have been in charge of security for an event like this, but because of the impending Egesta tribunals, the entire service had been stood down, and Defense Command had taken over security for the Emperor.

Some people have suggested that this was proof that Daragh being made Emperor was actually a coup of a different sort — in one fell swoop, we'd removed the Imperial Army, and its theoretical check against the tyranny of Defense Command and the elected government it represented...

Realistically it just meant that Daragh had actual, qualified personnel available for the job. And so did the rest of us, though the only thing the SF at this ball were going to be doing was drunk-wrangling, as I mentioned before.

Anyway, we let Bruce and Talia move down the red carpet ahead of us, so they'd be relatively free of the circus that we expected to draw. Already on this trail was Wes Pellew, and as he saw us arrive he waited so that we could all go in together.

There were a bunch of questions for Karen and me, of course — were we here together as a couple and so on — and we brushed those off with our usual dexterity, then linked up with Wes.

"I still hate these things," was the greeting the Independent Squadron's Commodore met us with, and I chuckled as I shook his hand.

"We all do."

We posed for a few pictures together — 'heroes' from the Fleet Clash — and then made our way inside.

The massive scale that we'd seen outside was easily matched within, because immediately upon entering the palace we were directed to the Grand Ballroom — the one, as I mentioned before, that you could run flight operations for 100 Starlights out of. Big place, and it was filling up fast.

As we entered the cavernous chamber, we came up against a wall of registration tables — it must have been 200 meters long — and as we neared the front, we found them crewed by palace staff, who were all masterful at smiling politely and making you feel welcome... even if this wasn't necessarily the sort of event they were used to.

We weren't a bunch of Lords — the usual attendees of these balls.

Reaching the front of the line at one of these tables, I identified myself and was handed a badgelink, into which I quickly programmed my name. Keith really had thought of everything — in a room this big, with 6,000 people in it, finding friends could be a nearly impossible endeavor. The badgelinks were little computers, about half the size of standard-issue comms, that would allow you to search the name of someone you're looking for, and home in on his or her position.

Registered and tagged, I passed the table and waited for the rest of *Wolf*'s delegation to come through. Wes had gone to another table, so he was first to join me, and we waited together in silence. He wasn't feeling particularly festive, largely because he was watching Andrea register...

Well, you get it. There probably wasn't a whole lot of good that was going to come of those two being together at a massive social function, but I didn't know about their problem, so I could hardly advise either of them on the matter. And really, I don't think I'd even have the right to...

Mik found us before all the *Wolf* people had finished registering, and already the Belt Commodore had a glass of fine beer in his hand.

Nodding to us with a smile, he lifted the drink, "Open bar has everything. This Emperor knows how to host."

"An Irishman keeping a good bar?" I sounded incredulous.

Mik laughed, "I know, a shock!"

Karen arrived next, and behind her the *Wolf* crew started to fan out, looking for various sorts of trouble in all their finery.

"Alright,"she said as she watched them go."Let's party."
Even I couldn't really argue with that.

On the far side of the ballroom, Marshal and Mel were talking to Craig B. Macdonald, the Foreign Minister who was of course drinking water. Craig's wife Megan — who the Scotsman will pointedly tell you is far too good for him — was also present, and they were talking about art when the Prime Minister arrived.

Pope, like Macdonald, had been invited to this ball as a sign of the unity between throne and PMO, and though neither of the two senior political leaders of the Empire was particularly at home in the palace, they weren't actually having a bad time.

"I'm sorry to interrupt," Douglas Pope nodded in greeting as he arrived, and Megan charmingly welcomed him.

"Not to worry, Douglas, you're just saving Marshal and Melissa from having to listen to me talk about painters they've never heard of."

Marshal is a cultured man, but she wasn't wrong. Neither he nor Mel did anything but smile in response to the Foreign Minister's wife's comment, and then Craig jumped in to help.

"We're peasants, every one of us," he grinned. "But now, since Douglas is here, does that mean we're going to talk politics?"

"I certainly hope so," Megan interceded. "I was boring myself."

Everyone chuckled politely, and then Pope turned to Marshal, "I will appoint you the candidate, if you so wish it."

That comment sounded quite as though it had come out of the middle of a conversation, not the beginning of one, but Marshal nevertheless followed quite easily. Looking at Mel, he nodded, "I've already spoken with the Admiralty, and they'll be ready for me to leave in the middle of next year."

Looking from Marshal to Craig B. Macdonald and back, the Prime Minister smiled with approval, "Good. We'll need you... our cabinet restructuring will leave a lot of gaps, when people like Olivia retire."

He was saying that the faction of the party that had slipped right into Luther Gregory's pocket wasn't going to be employed for much longer, and that there'd be room for good people like Marshal.

"Don't suppose we could convince you to run as well, Melissa?" Craig turned that question to our superspy. He knew the full story about her credentials, as did Pope — they were two of the few who did know at this point, though many more probably had suspicions or ideas.

But Mel was not crazy, so she shook her head, "I'll stick to a job where I can do unpleasant things to the bad guys."

Well said, Melissa, well said.

The political talk continued for a while, as the party really started to get into gear.

A band came to the stage once the majority of the gala's guests had made it through registration. By that time, most of the Belt Squadron officers had found each other and clustered around a couple of tables near one of the six designated dance floors. Some of us were chatting with each other, while the more antisocial types — this means me, Wes and Matt Baxter — mainly gaped at the sheer size of this massive affair.

So many *people*.

As the music began there was a flood of people towards the dance floors, and watching them move was like watching a tide change. From our own table, Jim and Bunny were part of the first wave — Bunny, it turned out, had trained in ballroom dancing in her younger years, and in preparation for this night she and Jim had gone to school.

"Holy shit, look at *Jim*," Kate Levec was sitting at the table we antisocials were standing behind, and as she made the point we all watched.

The man looked very much like he knew what he was doing, and Bunny looked very much like she was happy about it. The soon-to-be-Commander of *Friendly* and his soon-to-be-bride, were really enjoying the chance to dance.

They were the only ones from our group who were so eager to take the floor, though. Andrea got up and left the table, and Wes watched her go in silence. Karen was chatting with Kris Jacobs, and seemed content to let me wait in anticipation for the moment I'd be dragged to that floor, and made to dance.

With such dread, I wait for that moment.

"I only come to these things for the dancing."

That comment came not from any of our usual suspects, but from an Irish voice that seemed altogether too casual. Turning, Wes, Matt and I found ourselves face to face with a white-clad Emperor, a grin on his face, "Here they are, the Belt Squadron vets. John Fiora said you'd probably be over this way!"

With all the people in this massive ballroom, I hadn't yet taken the time to find John's table — one with Greg and Marlene also at it — but I made a note to locate them later. We could compare notes about this spectacle...

But first, obviously, I had the Emperor in front of me. Even though it was only Daragh.

"You know, this is the first thing I've had to do as Emperor which I haven't completely dreaded. A room full of Defense Command... that's the style!" the Irish Lord continued, apparently talking to us, even though Matt, Wes and I were all largely unresponsive.

Noting our complete conversational failure, Daragh finally shook his head, "Alright then, I suppose I'm not great company."

That was enough for me to finally shake myself from the stupor I'd been in, "Lovely palace you have here, Your Royal Highness."

That earned me a laugh, "Place should be flattened and turned into a military base. I'm trying to get them to let me turn my house back home into an official residence, but they say it'll have to be renovated in order to fit with the standards required for any Emperor."

I frowned at that, recalling what I knew of the former Second Lord's residence in Ireland. Remember, the place John went to collect him in *The Gallant Few* — the fog-shrouded house protected by an imaginary mine field, and home to no ponies whatsoever?

"Sounds like that would require a contractor you could trust..." I started sounding thoughtful, and Daragh's good humor was slightly muted as he realized I wasn't just making small talk.

"Know a guy, do you?" the Emperor asked.

This was absurd, but I nodded, "One of us, too..."

With that, I put an arm around the Emperor and led him away from the tables, so we could talk quietly.

Andrea Kiley stopped at one of the many bars in the ballroom to get a drink, and as she did she was spotted by a young hot-shot MP named Rousseau. He recognized her, of course, and he noticed that she was alone and getting herself a drink, so being an enterprising young political star he decided to move in.

Turning to head back towards the Belt Squadron tables, where she could continue to pass the night silently, Andrea didn't notice the approach of the snappily-dressed man, but he caught up to her by the time they reached the edge of the dance floor.

"Is no gentleman here to collect a drink for you, Captain Kiley?" he asked.

It was hardly subtle, and as she heard the words, Andrea came to a stop at the edge of the dance floor, then turned to face the speaker. Her glare was withering, but as soon as she got a look at him — and read the rather transparent interest in his eyes — something softened in hers.

Instead of taking his head off, which is what I would have expected, she did things that she never does; she bit her bottom lip and started using her free hand to play suggestively with her necklace.

"I choose drink-carriers very carefully," she said in a positively seductive manner, and that was enough for Rousseau to start unleashing both barrels of charm.

And he had plenty of that.

He was French.

Because they were on the edge of the dance floor as they began their exchange, both Andrea and her suitor were in full sight of Commodore Wes Pellew as they flirted and laughed in a very animated fashion.

Already Wes was dealing with enough conflicting emotions to bend a gravitational field, but this was just a bit too much. He found himself contemplating going over there and intervening, but he had no idea why he'd want to.

That's not true, he wasn't an idiot: he understood why he might want to. But in the broader context, he didn't know why he'd still have that sort of instinctive feeling given everything that had happened.

The chasm between him and Andrea was now wide and deep, and he had no right nor reason to try to make sure she made the best decisions to fuel her recovery.

He had no right to care whether she recovered at all.

So he stood with folded arms, and tried to make small talk with Matt Baxter as he watched *Wolf's* Captain flirt with a politician.

Bruce Arama didn't know many people at this party, and that left him and his wife in a bit of an awkward spot. They'd found an otherwise-abandoned table in the middle of the socialization maelstrom, and were camping out there as they watched officers and politicians go by.

"He's taller than I thought he'd be," Talia said of Greg Noyce as he passed, and Bruce nodded in agreement.

"Many of them are. It's like the opposite of movie stars," he replied.

"How about me, am I taller than you thought?"

Again, the disembodied Irish voice cut into a conversation from behind. Bruce and Talia both turned, but by the time they looked Daragh was already rounding the table and pulling out the chair beside the Maori Commander's.

The Emperor then dropped his badgelink on the table, "You're Commander Bruce Arama and guest, right?"

Neither Bruce nor Talia were any better at dealing with the sudden arrival of the sovereign than Wes, Matt and I had been, so they managed only to nod slowly at first, before *Adelaide's* former-skipper was able to make speech: "May I present my wife Talia."

"You certainly may," Daragh replied warmly, and then took her hand and kissed it. Irish charmer bastard.

At this point I feel like I should make a comment about how 'party-host Daragh' really did seem altogether sane, and even a bit charming. Is it weird for you? It was weird for us. But I guess he was just one of those guys who loved a party, and knew how to work one, even without a shotgun.

Anyway, he wasn't just sitting down to be polite, "Bruce, now listen. I have a house in Ireland, and I hate palaces, so I'm wanting to live in that house in Ireland. But the people who stuck me in this place tell me I have to make my house into an official royal residence, and that means a lot of renovation work. Now, you were at the Forge, right?"

Bruce managed to nod.

"Good, that means I can trust you…"

Because, remember, Daragh had been at the Forge all those years ago.

"…and you're a contractor, right?"

Another nod, and the Irish Emperor clapped his hands together.

"Great. So they tell me the budget we have to work with on the conversion is a million-trillion. Is that a lot for that sort of job?"

I think a million-trillion is a lot for any job. But again, I shouldn't be responding to dialogue.

All Bruce could do was swallow hard.

"Excellent. So could I hire you and your company to take over the project? I mean, it might require you to hire on others, but basically I want the man on top to be someone I can trust. And according to an anonymous source named Ken Barron, you're one of the best line officers he's served with, and he figures you can't be a bad contractor and a good line officer at the same time."

Bastard dropped my name.

There was a long silence fueled by disbelief and a little excitement, but Daragh was uncommonly patient in waiting for Bruce to get some words back into his brain. And then the Kiwi Commander did himself all sorts of favors.

"Well, I don't just take on any client. Does Admiral Barron vouch for you?"

"Pardon me saying this with a lady present, but not fucking likely!" Daragh grinned, and then he laughed loud and long, actually drawing some glances from people nearby.

That, I suppose we can say, is how Arama Construction — now Arama Empire

Construction — went from being an Auckland contracting business to being the leader in Earth-based elite building projects.

At this point you could complain about it being a clear case of nepotism… who you know helping you get a job… but Bruce deserved a favor, or a thousand favors. Karen was still around because of him, and more than that, he'd been through the Forge and the Fleet Clash and everything since, proving his excellence every step of the way.

There are plenty of great contractors and builders in the Empire, but I dare you to find one that comes with those sorts of credentials — the sorts of credentials that a man like Daragh Ryan could trust without question.

Exactly. So Bruce got the job.

As the evening wore on, and more of our table fled to the dance floor, I was left standing beside Wes, trying to make conversation. It's impressive, I think, that I made this attempt for so long without realizing at any point that he wasn't paying attention — he was watching Andrea Kiley and Rousseau, who had moved from beside the dance floor to on it.

Honestly, I don't even remember what I was trying to say to him — this is the point in the night where my memory starts to get a little bit subject-specific. Karen was soon to drag me out to the dance floor, and every time I looked at her, I had difficulty focusing on anything else.

"Excuse me," Wes finally said, I believe cutting me off in mid-sentence, though I didn't really care. He headed to the dance floor, and in the midst of someone twirling I lost sight of him. I went to sit beside Karen.

Andrea Kiley was nothing like herself — not the person she'd become — and so when Wes got near enough to her to see her expression, he stopped in the middle of the dance floor and really considered what her eyes were saying.

She wanted something — something simple and uncomplicated — and she was in the process of taking it.

Rousseau was an entirely willing partner in this; he had much less reason to bear such a direct attitude, but he nevertheless had it, and wanted Andrea for the same reason she wanted him. And in case you're wondering, it certainly wasn't for witty conversation.

Wes was having a tough time dealing with that. To this day he's not sure if the best word for it is jealousy or protectiveness… neither one seems quite right. When it comes down to it, he just didn't want to see Andrea waltzing off for a casual night in some politico's Capital Island apartment, just because the endorphin rush might make her feel something.

It wasn't the right path for her… or at least that was his opinion. But he knew, as you might be thinking, that he had no right to tell her how to self-medicate.

So there, in the middle of the dancing, he just stood still and stared.

Andrea didn't see him at first, but eventually on one of her turns she looked over Rousseau's shoulder and caught sight of him — a lone, light-suited figured in the crowd of merriment.

I think you'll agree, if this was a movie that moment would have led to something

— to a moment of catharsis, or a revelation that she was wasting her time… anything.

Instead, she just locked eyes with Wes, her gaze revealing the heartless metal that lay deep within her, and then she looked away. That was all.

Wes stared only for a few more seconds, then turned away from her and made his way off the floor, angling not for our table but for the exits. He didn't want to watch this, so he wouldn't…

He literally bumped into Mik, who was on his way back from one of the bars with another superior beer choice, "Getting a drink, Wes?"

The Independent Squadron Commodore paused, then shook his head, "Going to leave, I think."

That wasn't a good answer, and Mik said so: "Now I know you're not going to give up this early. You leave, who'll chaperone the rest of us?"

It was not a compelling argument, but if Wes was going to escape now he'd need to reveal precisely why he wanted to, and that was a conversation he simply couldn't have… so he gave up on his attempt, and shrugged.

"I suppose I have to stay, then."

"We'll make sure you get your money's worth!" Mik grinned, and then together the two Belt Commodores started making their way back to familiar territory — the Belt Squadron tables.

So there's no more putting it off. Karen and I were sitting beside each other at the Belt Squadron tables, and Kris had just been invited to dance by her Australian beau, who'd turned up late because he'd been on a weird shift at Fengate Hospital.

Mik and Wes weren't back, so that just left Karen and me.

Looking sideways at Karen, I found her to be well and truly, absolutely and honestly, completely and utterly beautiful. I don't know if I've ever come out and said that in these books — I'm great at beating around the bush and using all sorts of sly doublespeak to get the point across, but really, there's no point pretending that when she'd done herself up for this gala, she'd left any of the stops in place.

I would have been a fool not to dance with this woman, I think you'll agree. And that being the case, I decided that I wasn't going to make her ask.

"Karen, I think we're due on the dance floor."

She looked at me and smiled, "Time for our close-up?"

"Well I suppose there are probably cameras somewhere. We should think this through, though: how much of a spectacle should we create?"

Karen shrugged, which in her current state of dress really accentuated her shoulders and her collar bones. I do notice these things. Believe me.

You know how I once said when Karen smiled, I worried I might get hit by a bus or something? At this point someone could land a plane on my head, and I don't think I'd notice.

No peripheral vision, no situational awareness. I was quite completely, almost creepily, fixated.

And yes, I'll take my time repeating that sentiment to you, so that we can drag this waiting period out a little longer.

"Let's play the spectacle by ear," she said finally, extending her hand to me with her palm up.

I smiled, "Sounds good to me."

Then I took her hand, and we got to our feet.

The dance floor was pretty full, but it was big enough that nobody was bumping into anyone else. We didn't go too far from our table — we could have tried to hide from people like Mik, but then given that particular officer's previous opinions on our dancing, I think we might have wanted to show off for him a little. He wasn't back yet, of course — neither was Wes.

Really, it was just Karen and me, and some music.

Slipping my right hand around her waist, I took her right hand in my left and then she pulled in close to me. I think people might have started noticing us at that point, but I didn't pay any attention to them.

Everything about that moment — that dance — remains in my memory. Everything was wonderfully perfect, like you hear in the songs, or see in the movies. It was intense.

Though you're probably supposed to leave space between you when you're dancing in an Emperor's ballroom, we didn't, and our steps were not artful or fleet-footed or quick.

Really, it was just about the two of us, and I'm sure that anyone watching in that moment, caught up in the atmosphere that we'd generated around ourselves, would be absolutely certain that we were going to kiss, in fine movie style, right there.

Right there on the dance floor.

"So, what kind of spectacle are you thinking?" Karen asked that question softly into my ear, and if you'd heard the way she'd asked it, you'd know it wasn't a question so much as a suggestion.

I defy any man to turn down such a recommendation. Though if you ever had the chance and you didn't turn it down, I would have to kill you in a duel. Think about that.

After asking her impossible question, Karen pulled back enough to look at me, and then we did exactly what people do in these situations: stared at each other. I think our eyes had a conversation all their own — truly. I just... well. I'm no good talking about it, but by now you've been through enough with the two of us to understand.

That moment was laden with the sort of violin-backed magic that gets all sorts of people into all sorts of trouble.

And then a waiter bumped into Karen.

Lots of room on the dance floor, but the waiter hit her, and then turned with an apology before hurrying away, passing Wes and Mik both as they returned to the table.

Karen smiled at the interruption first, but then the humor wore off.

The magic was forgotten.

Marshal and Melissa were still talking to the Prime Minister when a waiter came by offering drinks. None of the trio wanted anything, so the waiter moved off, and then as conversation continued a second waiter with a tray of drinks moved in, being a pest as servers at these things often can be.

Melissa turned as the young woman approached, shaking her head to decline any beverages, then turned back to the PM.

Then her instincts took over, because she'd seen that server's eyes. Cold eyes. The eyes of a killer. And Melissa was standing with the Prime Minister.

By the time Mel wheeled, an injector gun was already in the server's hand. No one else saw it, there just wasn't time. That was the point — that was why it was clear this server was a professional.

Mel stepped in and blocked the injector's first swing, starting a fight — a *fight* — in the middle of the Emperor's gala. Realizing what was happening, Marshal got a hand on Pope's chest and pushed him back, away from the battle.

"Security! Now!" the Commodore bellowed.

They wouldn't arrive in time. Melissa was up against someone who knew how to fight, but no common assassin was equal to a superspy. Another swing with the injector gun was stopped short, and then despite her fancy gala dress, Mel got a roundhouse kick away, shattering two of the attacker's ribs and dropping her to the ground.

The injector gun slid across the floor, where another waiter bent down and collected it. Mel realized this and rose quickly to try to get between him and the PM... but instead he came straight at her.

Because, she realized, that injection was meant for her.

For *her*.

Not wanting to waste time, Melissa went for the MAG-2 that was tucked under the corset of her dress — not easy to reach, which is why she hadn't been able to get at it immediately, but she had just enough time to spare.

She shot the second attacker once, then twice, and he went face forward onto the floor, landing on the gun as he did.

The sound of shots should have startled the room — well, I'm sure it did — but there was another distraction.

Karen had pulled away from me, and with a frown she looked at her left shoulder where the waiter had bumped her. *Hit* her.

It was starting to swell already. It was starting to swell. She blinked a few times. Then she staggered back a step. I reached out for her but she held up a hand to stop me.

"No wait..." she said.

Then her eyes widened a little, and when next her mouth opened, blood starting falling out. So much.

People had been watching us. Everyone saw. Some people screamed. Wes and Mik were suddenly racing over, and they didn't have far to travel but it took forever because time meant nothing and I was standing and watching and this was actually happening and I couldn't believe it was actually real but it was and...

Karen McMaster began to crumple to the floor, and I was down there with her, I think screaming for a medic, I think screaming for anything. God maybe. Everything was so slow. No one could get to us, no one could help in time... I couldn't think or understand...

And then she reached up and touched the side of my face, forcing me to look down at her eyes.

This was happening. It was actually happening.

She was so scared.

I was terrified.

And we were completely right to be.

Because after all of this — after this whole war — it was now that the axe fell. It was now that he made his move.

Plans too complicated to work, that always seemed to.

A friend we'd once had, and an enemy we thought we'd beaten.

He'd struck again, and this time, struck so deeply.

You know who it was — a man I'd soon be hunting.

Grant Merger.

But for now, Karen was bleeding out in my arms, while I begged for help.

Begged and prayed, on the longest day of my life.

AFTERWORD

Grant Merger.
See you in 2235.

About the Author

Born in 1984 in St. John's, Newfoundland, Kenneth Tam holds both a Bachelor's and Master's degree in history from Wilfrid Laurier University in Waterloo, Canada. His MA thesis examined the creation and operation of the Caribou Hut, a hostel for Allied servicemen in St. John's during the Second World War.

In 2006, Kenneth received a prestigious Canada Graduate Scholarship from the Social Sciences and Humanities Council of Canada. He was also awarded a Balsillie Fellowship at the Centre for International Governance Innovation during 2006-07. In that capacity, he worked for Mr. Paul Heinbecker, Canada's former ambassador and permanent representative to the United Nations. He has served as a Communications Consultant for Kitchener–Waterloo's federal Member of Parliament, Peter Braid, and is presently an Advisor with Sun Life Financial.

Since releasing his first novel in 2003, Tam has promoted his books across Canada, speaking with junior and high school students, delivering writing workshops, and doing book signings at bookstores and Iceberg-organized events. He frequently appears as a guest author at science fiction events across the country.

Kenneth is a partner in Iceberg Publishing, the company he and his family started in 2002. He has authored many of the company's existing titles, and is also responsible for graphic design, including the company logo, website, banners, advertisements, and other marketing materials. He acts as a primary contact with printers and suppliers, and is also key in new author development and recruitment.

He remains very lazy about writing his author bios. When they told him to make this one longer, he mostly copied and pasted it together from the Iceberg website, www.icebergpublishing.com.

www.ingramcontent.com/pod-product-compliance
Lightning Source LLC
Chambersburg PA
CBHW030746030726
47497CB00001B/150